Praise for the Tran...

RICHARD PEVEAR AND LARISSA VOLOKHONSKY

"The premier Russian-to-English translators of the era."
—David Remnick, *The New Yorker*

"The reinventors of the classic Russian novel for our times."
—PEN/Book-of-the-Month Club Translation Prize Citation

THE COMPLETE SHORT NOVELS

Anton Chekhov

"If the institution of Russian literature as a cultural force in the English-speaking world has survived and thrived against all odds in the culturally disparate twenty-first century, it is due mainly to the efforts of Richard Pevear and Larissa Volokhonsky." —*PopMatters*

"A welcome gathering of the great storywriter's atypical longer works. . . . Invaluable. . . . A heartening confirmation of the matchless skill and humanity of one of the true masters."
—*Kirkus Reviews*

THE BROTHERS KARAMAZOV

Fyodor Dostoevsky

"One finally gets the musical whole of Dostoevsky's original."
—*The New York Times Book Review*

CRIME AND PUNISHMENT

Fyodor Dostoevsky

"Reaches as close to Dostoevsky's Russian as is possible in English. . . . The original's force and frightening immediacy is captured."
—*Chicago Tribune*

DEMONS
Fyodor Dostoevsky

"The merit . . . resides in the technical virtuosity of the translators. . . . They capture the feverishly intense, personal explosions of activity and emotion that manifest themselves in Russian life."
—*The New York Times Book Review*

WAR AND PEACE
Leo Tolstoy

"An extraordinary achievement. . . . Wonderfully fresh and readable. . . . The English-speaking world is indebted to these two magnificent translators." —*The New York Review of Books*

"A major new translation . . . [which] brings us the palpability [of Tolstoy's characters] as perhaps never before. . . . Pevear and Volokhonsky's new translation gives us new access to the spirit and order of the book." —*The New Yorker*

"Shimmering. . . . [It] offers an opportunity to see this great classic afresh, to approach it not as a monument but rather as a deeply touching story about our contradictory human hearts."
—*The Washington Post*

"Tolstoy's *War and Peace* has often been put in a league with Homer's epic poems; it seems to me that the same might be said for Pevear and Volokhonsky's translation of his great novel. . . . Their efforts convey a much closer equivalent in English to the experience of reading the original." —*New England Review*

Anton Chekhov

FIFTY-TWO STORIES

Anton Chekhov was born in 1860 in southern Russia. The grandson of a serf, he became a physician, paying for his education by selling satirical and humorous sketches to the newspapers. He soon turned to serious short stories, winning the Pushkin Prize in 1888, and went on to write plays, including *Uncle Vanya*, *The Seagull*, *Three Sisters*, and *The Cherry Orchard*, and novellas, including *The Steppe* and *The Duel*. He died of tuberculosis in 1904.

Together, Richard Pevear and Larissa Volokhonsky have translated works by Chekhov, Dostoevsky, Tolstoy, Gogol, Bulgakov, Leskov, and Pasternak. They were twice awarded the PEN/Book-of-the-Month Club Translation Prize (for Dostoevsky's *The Brothers Karamazov* and Tolstoy's *Anna Karenina*). They are married and live in France.

ALSO TRANSLATED BY
RICHARD PEVEAR AND LARISSA VOLOKHONSKY

Mikhail Bulgakov
The Master and Margarita

Anton Chekhov
The Complete Short Novels of Anton Chekhov
Selected Stories

Fyodor Dostoevsky
The Adolescent
The Brothers Karamazov
Crime and Punishment
Demons
The Double and *The Gambler*
The Eternal Husband and Other Stories
The Idiot
Notes from a Dead House
Notes from Underground

Nikolai Gogol
The Collected Tales of Nikolai Gogol
Dead Souls

Nikolai Leskov
The Enchanted Wanderer and Other Stories

Boris Pasternak
Doctor Zhivago

Alexander Pushkin
Novels, Tales, Journeys

Leo Tolstoy
Anna Karenina
The Death of Ivan Ilyich and Other Stories
War and Peace

FIFTY-TWO STORIES

FIFTY-TWO STORIES

· 1883–1898 ·

ANTON CHEKHOV

A new translation by

RICHARD PEVEAR AND LARISSA VOLOKHONSKY

VINTAGE CLASSICS

VINTAGE BOOKS

A DIVISION OF PENGUIN RANDOM HOUSE LLC

NEW YORK

FIRST VINTAGE CLASSICS EDITION, JANUARY 2021

The Library of Congress has cataloged the Knopf edition as follows:
Names: Chekhov, Anton Pavlovich, 1860–1904, author. | Pevear, Richard, 1943– translator. |
Volokhonsky, Larissa, translator.
Title: Fifty-two stories (1883–1898) / Anton Chekhov ; a new translation by Richard Pevear and
Larissa Volokhonsky.
Description: New York : Alfred A. Knopf, 2020. | Translated from the Russian.
Identifiers: LCCN 2019022613 (print) | LCCN 2019022614 (ebook)
Subjects: LCSH: Chekhov, Anton Pavlovich, 1860–1904—Translations into English.
Classification: LCC PG3456.A13 P484 2020 (print) | LCC PG3456.A13 (ebook) | DDC 891.73/3—dc23
LC record available at https://lccn.loc.gov/2019022613

Vintage Classics Trade Paperback ISBN: 978-0-525-56238-2
eBook ISBN: 978-0-525-52082-5

Book design by Maggie Hinders

www.vintagebooks.com

Printed in the United States of America
6th Printing

CONTENTS

PREFACE

Our intention in making this collection has been to represent the extraordinary variety of Chekhov's stories, from earliest to latest, in terms of characters, events, social classes, settings, voicing, and formal inventiveness. By chance the selection came to fifty-two stories—a full deck! But, as Chekhov once wrote, "in art, as in life, there is nothing accidental."

When Chekhov began to write humorous stories and sketches, he thought he was doing it simply for money. And so he was. His father's grocery business, in their native Taganrog, on the Sea of Azov, had gone bankrupt in 1876, and to avoid debtor's prison the family had fled to Moscow, where Chekhov's two older brothers were already studying at the university. Chekhov, who was sixteen at the time, stayed behind to finish high school, supporting himself in various ways, one of them being the publication of humorous sketches in local papers, signed with various pseudonyms. In 1879 he graduated and moved to Moscow himself, where he entered medical school, and where his writing, still pseudonymous, became virtually the sole support of the family—mother, father, four brothers, and a sister.

Chekhov paid no attention to the artistic quality of his sketches; he simply tossed them off, sometimes several a day, and sent them to various daily or weekly humor sheets, whose editors gladly printed them. But his true artistic gift—innate, intuitive—showed itself even in the most exaggerated, absurd, and playful of these early jottings. They were mainly jokes, often satirical, but he also played with words in them, for instance in naming his characters. In "At the Post Office" (1883), the postmaster's name is Sweetpepper and the police chief's name is Swashbuckle. The French tutor in "In a Foreign Land" is Monsieur Shampooing, the French word for shampoo. Corporal Whompov is the heavy-handed officer in the story named for him. In "An Educated Blockhead" (1885), the name of the accused is Slopsov and the justice of the peace is Sixwingsky, suggestive of a seraph. In "Romance with a Double Bass" (1886), the main character, owner of the double bass, is named Bowsky, after the instrument's articulator; we also run into such men as Buzzkin, Flunkeyich, and Flaskov. And there are others. These names have almost always been simply transliterated in English, giving no hint of their literal meaning in Russian.

After 1886, Chekhov stopped using such overtly comical names, but in later stories we still find characters like Zhmukhin in "The Pecheneg" (1897), whose name, while credible enough, also suggests pushing, squeezing, oppression. Chekhov also persisted in his transcribing of noises. The dog in "The Teacher of Literature" (1894) does not simply bark; his "grrr . . . nya-nya-nya-nya" pervades the story. The night owl in "The Pecheneg" keeps calling "Sleep! Sleep!" The wind howls "Hoo! Hoo!" And in his descriptions of nature there is a pervasive anthropomorphism—trees that swoon, rivers that speak, the "malicious, but deeply unhappy" storm in "On the Road" (1886), the previous day's mist in "Fear" (1892), which "timidly pressed itself to the bushes and hummocks." In a letter of May 10, 1886, to his older brother Alexander, who was also trying to be a writer, he offers some advice:

> For instance, you will succeed in depicting a moonlit night if you write that on the mill dam a piece of glass from a broken bottle flashed like a bright star and the black shadow of a dog or wolf rolled along like a ball and so forth. Nature comes alive if you're not squeamish about comparing natural phenomena to human actions . . .*

* Translation by Cathy Popkin, in her edition of *Anton Chekhov's Collected Stories* (New York: W. W. Norton, 2014), p. 517.

Yet in a letter dated January 14, 1887, to an acquaintance, Maria Kiselyova, who complained to him that he kept digging in the "dung heap" of immorality, Chekhov asserts: "What makes literature *art* is precisely its depiction of life as it really is. Its charge is the unconditional and honest truth." And further on he says of the writer: "He's no different from the run-of-the-mill reporter."* It is true that Chekhov's stories are filled with details of everyday existence, often very dark and always very keenly observed. He had an unusually wide personal experience of Russian life on all levels, and portrays a great variety of people: landowners, peasants, the military, bureaucrats, farmers, townspeople, clergy high and low, provincial school teachers, intellectuals, university students, boys, mistresses, wives, hunters, shepherds. In one story the central character is a boy two years and eight months old; in another the central character is a dog. But the stories he tells about them are hardly run-of-the-mill reporting.

The formal variety of Chekhov's stories is also far from "slice-of-life" realism. Sometimes he chooses suspended moments—on a train, on the road, in a cart—that allow for unexpected revelations, or pseudo-revelations. Many are essentially monologues, which occasionally lead to surprise reversals. In "The Siren" (1887), after a court session, the court secretary entices his superiors, even the stern philosopher, with an inspired and minutely detailed five-page discourse on Russian eating and drinking, ending with honey-spice vodka, of which he says: "After the first glass, your whole soul is engulfed in a sort of fragrant mirage, and it seems that you are not at home in your armchair, but somewhere in Australia, on some sort of ultrasoft ostrich . . ." There are doublings, as in the early "Fat and Skinny" or the late "Big Volodya and Little Volodya." In his notes for the rather grim story "The Bet" (1889), he first refers to it as "a fairy tale." The formal qualities of storytelling, of parables, anecdotes, and morality tales, are present throughout his work. It is nurtured by tradition, though he puts that tradition to his own use.

Chekhov was well aware of the political movements of his time and their main spokesmen. His characters refer at various moments

* Popkin, p. 518.

to Sergei Aksakov and the Slavophiles, to the Nihilists, to the utilitarian Dmitri Pisarev, to the populist Nikolai Mikhailovsky, as well as to the French anarchist Pierre-Joseph Proudhon and the German philosopher Schopenhauer. He was friends with the conservative writer, journalist, and editor Alexei Suvorin, who published many of his stories in his journal *Novoye Vremya* ("New Times"), but he did not share the editor's increasingly reactionary views, and broke with him over the controversy of the Dreyfus affair. Chekhov never espoused any ideas as a writer; he had no program, no ideology; the critics of his time wondered what his work was "about." Tolstoy wrote of him in a letter to his son dated September 4, 1895: "he has not yet revealed a definite point of view."* Chekhov revealed his attitude to the peasantry by offering a large number of them free medical treatment while living on his small country estate in Melikhovo. He showed his concern for the environment, not like the old man in "The Shepherd's Pipe," who bemoans at great length the dying out of nature, but by planting trees, like Doctor Astrov in the play *Uncle Vanya*.

In his stories, Chekhov does what storytellers have always done: he satirizes human pretensions and absurdities, he plays out the comedy of human contradictions, and ultimately, even in the darkest of them, he celebrates natural and human existence in all its conditional variety.

Richard Pevear

---

* Popkin, p. 505.

FIFTY-TWO STORIES

JOY

I T WAS MIDNIGHT.

Mitya Kuldarov, agitated, disheveled, came flying into his parents' apartment and quickly passed through all the rooms. His parents had already turned in for the night. His sister was lying in bed, reading the last page of a novel. His schoolboy brothers were asleep.

"Where have you been?" his astonished parents asked. "What's the matter with you?"

"Oh, don't ask! I never expected it! No, I never expected it! It's . . . it's even incredible!"

Mitya laughed loudly and sat down in an armchair, unable to stay on his feet from happiness.

"It's incredible! You can't even imagine! Just look!"

His sister jumped out of bed and, covering herself with a blanket, went over to her brother. The schoolboys woke up.

"What's the matter? You don't look yourself!"

"It's from joy, Mama! I'm known all over Russia now! All over! Before only you knew that in this world there existed the Collegiate Registrar Dmitri Kuldarov,[1] but now all of Russia knows it! Mama! Oh, lord!"

Mitya jumped up, ran through all the rooms, and sat down again.

"But what's happened? Just tell us!"

"You live like wild animals, don't read newspapers, don't pay any attention to publicity, yet there are so many amazing things in the newspapers! When something happens, it gets known right away, nothing escapes them! I'm so happy! Oh, lord! Newspapers only write about famous people, and now they've written about me!"

"What's that? Where?"

The papa went pale. Mama glanced at the icon and crossed herself. The schoolboys leaped out of their beds and, just as they were, in their nightshirts, went up to their older brother.

"That's right! They've written about me! Now all of Russia knows me! Take this issue as a keepsake, mama! We'll reread it sometimes. Look here!"

Mitya took a newspaper from his pocket, gave it to his father, and poked his finger at a place circled in blue pencil.

"Read!"

His father put on his spectacles.

"Go on, read!"

Mama glanced at the icon and crossed herself. The papa cleared his throat and began to read:

"On December 29th, at eleven o'clock in the evening, the Collegiate Registrar Dmitri Kuldarov . . ."

"You see, you see? Go on!"

". . . the Collegiate Registrar Dmitri Kuldarov, leaving the ale-house on Malaya Bronnaya Street, at Kozikhin's, and being in a state of inebriation . . ."

"It was me and Semyon Petrovich . . . It's all described in minute detail! Keep reading! Go on! Listen!"

". . . and being in a state of inebriation, slipped and fell under the horse of the cabby Ivan Drotov, a peasant from the village of Durykino, Yukhnovsky District. The frightened horse, having stepped over Kuldarov and dragged the sleigh over him, with Stepan Lukov, a Moscow merchant of the second guild, sitting in it, rushed off down the street and was stopped by the sweepers. Kuldarov, at first being in a state of unconsciousness, was taken to the police precinct and examined by a doctor. The blow which he had received on the back of the head . . ."

"I was hit by the shaft, Papa. Go on! Go on reading!"

". . . which he had received on the back of the head, was classified as slight. The protocol of the incident was drawn up. The victim was given first aid . . ."

"They told me to put cold compresses on my head. So you've read it now? Eh? Really something! Now it'll spread all over Russia! Give it here!"

Mitya grabbed the newspaper, folded it, and put it in his pocket.

"I'll run to the Makarovs and show them . . . I've also got to show it to the Ivanitskys, Natalya Ivanovna, Anisim Vassilyich . . . I'm off! Goodbye!"

Mitya put on a peaked cap with a cockade and, triumphant, joyful, dashed out of the house.

1883

FAT AND SKINNY

TWO FRIENDS ran into each other at the Nikolaevsky train station:[1] one fat, the other skinny. The fat one had just had dinner in the station, and his butter-smeared lips glistened like ripe cherries. He smelled of sherry and fleur d'oranger. The skinny one had just gotten off a train and was loaded down with suitcases, bundles, and boxes. He smelled of ham and coffee grounds. From behind his back peeked a thin woman with a long chin—his wife—and a tall schoolboy with a screwed-up eye—his son.

"Porfiry!" exclaimed the fat one, seeing the skinny one. "Is it you? My dear fellow! Long time no see!"

"Good heavens!" the skinny one said in amazement. "Misha! My childhood friend! Where did you pop up from?"

The friends kissed three times and fixed their tear-filled eyes on each other. Both were pleasantly astonished.

"Dear friend!" the skinny one began after the kissing. "How unexpected! What a surprise! Let me have a good look at you! As handsome as ever! A dear soul and a dandy! Oh, Lord God! So, how are you? Rich? Married? I'm already married, as you can see . . . This is my wife, Louisa, born Wanzenbach . . . a Lutheran . . . And this is my son Nathaniel, a third-grader. Nathaniel, this is my childhood friend! We were in school together!"

Nathaniel pondered a little and took off his cap.

"In school together!" the skinny one went on. "Remember how

they nicknamed you? They called you Herostratus, because you burned a schoolbook with a cigarette, and me Ephialtes, because I liked snitching.[2] Ha-ha . . . We were kids! Don't be afraid, Nathaniel. Come closer to us . . . And this is my wife, born Wanzenbach . . . a Lutheran."

Nathaniel pondered a little and hid behind his father's back.

"So, how's life, my friend?" the fat one asked, gazing rapturously at his friend. "You're in government service somewhere? Worked your way up?"

"That I have, my dear! Been a collegiate assessor for two years now and got myself a Stanislas.[3] Poor salary . . . but never mind! My wife gives music lessons, I make wooden cigarette cases on the side. Excellent cigarette cases! I sell them for a rouble apiece. Anybody who takes ten or more gets a discount, you see. We manage somehow. I used to work in headquarters, you know, but now I've been transferred here as chief clerk in the same department . . . I'll be working here. Well, and what about you? Already a state councillor I'll bet? Eh?"

"No, my dear, aim higher," said the fat one. "I'm already a privy councillor . . . I've got two stars."[4]

The skinny one suddenly turned pale, froze, but his face quickly spread in all directions into the broadest smile; sparks seemed to fly from his face and eyes. He himself shriveled, shrank, subsided . . . His suitcases, bundles, and boxes shriveled, cringed . . . His wife's long chin grew longer; Nathaniel stood to attention and buttoned his school uniform . . .

"I, Your Excellency . . . Very pleased, sir! A friend, one might say, from childhood . . . suddenly turns out to be such a dignitary! Hee-hee, sir."

"Enough, now!" The fat one winced. "Why this tone? You and I are friends from childhood—no need to go bowing to rank!"

"For pity's sake . . . It's not that, sir . . ." The skinny one started to giggle, shriveling still more. "Your Excellency's gracious attention . . . like life-giving water . . . This, Your Excellency, is my son Nathaniel . . . my wife Louisa, a Lutheran, in some sense . . ."

The fat one was about to protest, but written on the skinny one's face was such veneration, sweetness, and respectful twinging that the privy councillor felt sick. He turned away from the skinny one and gave him his hand in farewell.

The skinny one squeezed three fingers, bowed with his whole body, and giggled like a Chinaman: "Hee-hee-hee." His wife smiled. Nathaniel bowed, scraped with his foot, and dropped his cap. All three were pleasantly astonished.

1883

AT THE POST OFFICE

A FEW DAYS AGO we buried the young wife of our old post-master Sweetpepper. Having interred the beauty, we, following the custom of our forebears, went to the post office to "commemorate."

As the blini[1] were served, the old widower wept bitterly and said:

"These blini are as glowing as my late wife's cheeks. Beauties just like her! Exactly!"

"Yes," the commemorators agreed, "you had yourself a real beauty . . . A top-notch woman!"

"Yes, sir . . . Everybody was astonished looking at her . . . But I didn't love her for her beauty, gentlemen, nor for her good nature. Those two qualities are inherent in all womankind and are quite often met with in the sublunary realm. I loved her for another quality of the soul. Namely, sirs: I loved my late wife—may she rest in peace—because, for all the pertness and playfulness of her character, she was faithful to her husband. She was faithful to me, though she was only twenty and I will soon hit sixty! She was faithful to me, old as I am!"

The deacon, sharing the communal meal with us, grunted and coughed eloquently to express his doubts.

"So you don't believe it?" The widower turned to him.

"It's not that I don't believe it"—the deacon became embarrassed—"it's just . . . young wives these days are much too . . . rendevous, sauce provençale . . ."

"You doubt it, but I'll prove it to you, sir! I kept her faithful by various means of a strategic sort, so to speak, something like fortifications. With my behavior and my cunning character, there was no way she could betray me. I used cunning to protect my marital bed. I know certain words, a sort of password. I say these same words and—basta, I can sleep peacefully as regards her faithfulness."

"What are those words?"

"Simple as could be. I spread a wicked rumor around town. This rumor is well known to you. I told everybody: 'My wife Alyona is cohabiting with our police chief, Ivan Alexeich Swashbuckle.' These words were enough. Not a single man dared to court Alyona, for fear of the police chief's wrath. It used to be they'd just run away at the sight of her, so that Swashbuckle wouldn't get any ideas. Heh, heh, heh. Once you got mixed up with that mustachioed idol, you'd really regret it, he could slap five fines on you over sanitary conditions. For instance, he'd see your cat on the street and slap a fine on you as if it was a stray cow."

"So that means your wife didn't live with Ivan Alexeich?" we all drawled in surprise.

"No, that was my cunning . . . Heh, heh . . . So I really hoodwinked you, eh, boys? Well, there you have it."

Three minutes passed in silence. We sat and said nothing, feeling offended and ashamed that this fat, red-nosed old man had led us on so cunningly.

"Well, God willing, you'll marry again!" the deacon muttered.

1883

READING

An Old Coot's Story

ONCE THE IMPRESARIO of our theater, Galamidov, was sitting in the office of our bureau chief, Ivan Petrovich Semipalatov, and talking with him about the art and the beauty of our actresses.

"But I don't agree with you," Ivan Petrovich was saying, signing some budget documents. "Sofya Yuryevna has a strong, original talent! She's so sweet, graceful . . . Such a delight . . ."

Ivan Petrovich wanted to go on, but rapture kept him from uttering a single word, and he smiled so broadly and sweetly that the impresario, looking at him, felt a sweet taste in his mouth.

"What I like in her . . . e-e-eh . . . is the agitation and the tremor of her young breast when she recites monologues . . . How she glows, how she glows! At such moments, tell her, I'm ready . . . for anything!"

"Your Excellency, kindly sign the reply to the letter from the Khersonese Police Department concerning . . ."

Semipalatov raised his smiling face and saw before him the clerk Merdyaev. Merdyaev stood before him, goggle-eyed, and held out to him the paper to be signed. Semipalatov winced: prose interrupted poetry at the most interesting place.

"This could have waited till later," he said. "You can see I'm talking! Terribly ill-mannered, indelicate people! See, Mr. Galamidov . . . You said we no longer have any Gogolian types . . . But here, you see!

Isn't he one? Scruffy, out at the elbows, cross-eyed . . . never combs his hair . . . And look how he writes! Devil knows what it is! Illiterate, meaningless . . . like a cobbler! Just look!"

"M-m-yes . . . ," mumbled Galamidov, having looked at the paper. "Indeed . . . You probably don't read much, Mr. Merdyaev."

"It's not done, my dear fellow!" the chief went on. "I'm ashamed for you! You might at least read books . . ."

"Reading means a lot!" Galamidov said and sighed for no reason. "A whole lot! Read and you'll see at once how sharply your horizons change. And you can get hold of books anywhere. From me, for instance . . . It will be my pleasure. I'll bring some tomorrow, if you like."

"Say thank you, my dear fellow!" said Semipalatov.

Merdyaev bowed awkwardly, moved his lips, and left.

The next day Galamidov came to our office and brought along a stack of books. With this moment the story began. Posterity will never forgive Semipalatov for his light-minded behavior! A young man might perhaps be forgiven, but an experienced actual state councillor—never![1] When the impresario came, Merdyaev was summoned to the office.

"Here, read this, my dear fellow!" said Semipalatov, handing him a book. "Read it attentively."

Merdyaev took the book with trembling hands and left the office. He was pale. His crossed eyes shifted anxiously and seemed to be looking for help from the objects around him. We took the book from him and cautiously began to examine it.

The book was *The Count of Monte Cristo*.[2]

"You can't go against his will!" our old accountant, Prokhor Semyonych Budylda, said with a sigh. "Give it a try, force yourself . . . Read a little, and then, God grant, he'll forget and you can drop it. Don't be afraid . . . And above all, don't get involved in it . . . Read but don't get involved in this clever stuff."

Merdyaev wrapped the book in paper and sat down to work. But this time he was unable to work. His hands trembled and his eyes crossed in different directions: one towards the ceiling, the other towards the inkstand. The next day he came to work in tears.

"Four times I began," he said, "but I couldn't make anything of it . . . Some sort of foreigners . . ."

Five days later Semipalatov, passing by the desks, stopped at Merdyaev's and asked:

"Well, so? Have you read the book?"

"Yes, Your Excellency."

"What is it about, my dear fellow? Go on, tell me!"

Merdyaev raised his head and moved his lips.

"I forget, Your Excellency . . . ," he said after a minute.

"Meaning you didn't read it, or . . . e-e-eh . . . you read it inattentively! Me-chaa-nically! That won't do! Read it over again! In general, gentlemen, I recommend that. Kindly read! Read, all of you! Take books from my windowsill over there and read. Paramonov, go, take a book for yourself! You step over, too, Podkhodtsev, my dear fellow! You, too, Smirnov! All of you, gentlemen! Please!"

They all went and took books for themselves. Only Budylda ventured to voice a protest. He spread his arms, shook his head, and said:

"No, excuse me, Your Excellency . . . I'd sooner take my retirement . . . I know what comes of these same critiques and writings. On account of them my older grandson calls his own mother a fool right to her face and gulps milk all through Lent.[3] Excuse me, sir!"

"You understand nothing," said Semipalatov, who usually forgave the old man all his rude words.

But Semipalatov was mistaken: the old man understood everything. A week later we already saw the fruits of this reading. Podkhodtsev, who was reading the second volume of *The Wandering Jew*,[4] called Budylda "a Jesuit"; Smirnov started coming to work in an inebriated state. But no one was so affected by the reading as Merdyaev. He lost weight, became pinched, began to drink.

"Prokhor Semyonych!" he begged Budylda. "I'll pray to God eternally for you! Ask his excellency to excuse me . . . I can't read. I read day and night, don't sleep, don't eat . . . My wife's worn out from reading aloud to me, but, God strike me dead, I understand nothing! Do me this great service!"

Budylda ventured several times to report to Semipalatov, but he only waved his hands and, strolling around the department with

Galamidov, reproached everybody for their ignorance. Two months went by like that, and this whole story ended in the most terrible way.

One day Merdyaev, arriving at work, instead of sitting at his desk, knelt in the midst of those present, burst into tears, and said:

"Forgive me, Orthodox Christians, for making counterfeit money!"

Then he went into the office, knelt before Semipalatov, and said:

"Forgive me, Your Excellency, I threw a baby down a well yesterday!"

He beat his head on the floor and sobbed . . .

"What's the meaning of this?!" Semipalatov asked in astonishment.

"It means, Your Excellency," said Budylda with tears in his eyes, stepping forward, "that he's lost his mind! His wits are addled! This is what your silly Galamidov achieved with these writings! God sees everything, Your Excellency. And if you don't like my words, then allow me to take my retirement. It's better to die of hunger than to see such things in my old age!"

Semipalatov turned pale and paced from corner to corner.

"Don't receive Galamidov!" he said in a hollow voice. "And you, gentlemen, calm yourselves. I see my mistake now. Thank you, old man!"

And since then nothing has gone on in our office. Merdyaev recovered, but not completely. And to this day he trembles and turns away at the sight of a book.

1884

The Cook Gets Married

GRISHA, a chubby seven-year-old, was standing by the kitchen door, eavesdropping and peeking through the keyhole. In the kitchen something was going on which, in his opinion, was extraordinary, never seen before. At the kitchen table, on which meat was usually cut and onions chopped, sat a big, burly peasant in a cabby's kaftan, red-headed, bearded, with a big drop of sweat on his nose. He was holding a saucer on the five fingers of his right hand and drinking tea from it, biting so noisily on a lump of sugar that it sent shivers down Grisha's spine. Across from him, on a dirty stool, sat the old nanny Aksinya Stepanovna, also drinking tea. The nanny's face was serious and at the same time shone with some sort of triumph. The cook Pelageya was pottering around by the stove and looked as if she was trying to hide her face somewhere far away. But on her face Grisha saw a whole play of lights: it glowed and shimmered with all colors, beginning with reddish purple and ending with a deathly pallor. Her trembling hands constantly clutched at knives, forks, stove wood, rags; she moved about, murmured, knocked, but in fact did nothing. Never once did she glance at the table where they were drinking tea, and to the questions the nanny put to her she replied curtly, sternly, without turning her face.

"Help yourself, Danilo Semyonych!" the nanny offered the cabby. "What's this tea all the time? Help yourself to some vodka!"

And the nanny moved a decanter and a glass towards the guest, her face acquiring a most sarcastic expression.

"I'm not in the habit, ma'am . . . No, ma'm . . . ," the cabby protested. "Don't make me, Aksinya Stepanovna."

"What sort of . . . A cabby, and he doesn't drink . . . An unmarried man can't possibly not drink. Help yourself!"

The cabby gave a sidelong glance at the vodka, then at the nanny's sarcastic face, and his own face acquired a no less sarcastic expression: No, you won't catch me, you old witch!

"Sorry, ma'am, I don't drink . . . Such a weakness doesn't suit our trade. A workman can drink, because he sits in one place, but our kind are always on view, in public. Right, ma'am? You go to a pot-house, and your horse walks away; you get drunk—it's even worse: you fall asleep or tumble off the box. So it goes."

"And how much do you make in a day, Danilo Semyonych?"

"Depends on the day. Some days you get as much as a greenback, and other times you go home without a kopeck. There's days and days, ma'am. Nowadays our business isn't worth much. There's no end of cabbies, you know it yourself, hay is expensive, and customers are piddling, they'd rather take a horse tram. But all the same, thank God, there's no complaints. Food enough, clothes enough, and . . . maybe even enough to make for somebody else's happiness" (the cabby cast a glance at Pelageya) ". . . if her heart's so inclined."

What else they talked about, Grisha did not hear. His mama came to the door and sent him to the children's room to study.

"Go and study. You've got no business listening here!"

Having come to the children's room, Grisha placed his primer before him, but he could not read. All that he had just seen and heard raised a host of questions in his head. "The cook's getting married . . . ," he thought. "Strange. I don't understand why people get married. Mama married Papa, cousin Verochka married Pavel Andreich. But anyhow Papa and Pavel Andreich were worth marrying: they've got gold watch chains, good clothes, their boots are always polished; but to marry that scary cabby with the red nose, in felt boots—phooey! And why does this nanny want poor Pelageya to get married?"

When the visitor left the kitchen, Pelageya went off to the rooms and started tidying up. The agitation still had not left her. Her face was red and as if frightened. She barely touched the floor with the broom and swept each corner five times. She lingered for a good while in the room where Mama was sitting. Obviously it was hard for her to be alone, and she wanted to speak, to share her impressions with somebody, to pour out her soul.

"He left!" she murmured, seeing that Mama did not start a conversation.

"He's obviously a good man," Mama said, not tearing her eyes from the embroidery. "So sober, steady."

"By God, ma'am, I won't marry him!" Pelageya suddenly shouted, flushing all over. "By God, I won't!"

"Don't be silly, you're not a little girl. It's a serious step, you must think it over very well, and not shout for no reason. Do you like him?"

"You're making it up, ma'am!" Pelageya became embarrassed. "To say such things . . . my God . . ."

("She should just say: I don't like him!" thought Grisha.)

"Aren't you a prissy one, though . . . Do you like him?"

"But he's old, ma'am! Wa-a-ah!"

"You're making it up, too!" the nanny snapped at Pelageya from another room. "He's not forty yet. And what do you need a young one for? A face isn't everything, you fool . . . Just marry him, that's all!"

"By God, I won't!" shrieked Pelageya.

"You and your whimsies! What the devil do you want? Another girl would fall at his feet, but you—'I won't marry him!' All you want is to trade winks with mailmen and repetutors! There's a repetutor who comes to Grishenka, ma'am, she just stared her stupid eyes out at him. Shameless creature!"

"Have you seen this Danilo before?" the lady asked Pelageya.

"Where could I have seen him? I saw him for the first time today, Aksinya found the cursed fiend somewhere and brought him here . . . And so he landed on my head!"

Over dinner, as Pelageya served the food, the diners all looked her in the face and teased her about the cabby. She blushed terribly and giggled unnaturally.

("It must be shameful to get married . . . ," thought Grisha. "Terribly shameful!")

The food was all oversalted, blood seeped from the underdone chickens, and to top it off, during the mealtime plates and knives spilled from Pelageya's hands as if from a crooked shelf, but nobody uttered a word of reproach, since they all understood her state of mind. Only once Papa flung his napkin down angrily and said to Mama:

"Why do you want to get everybody married? What business is it of yours? Let them get married as they like."

After dinner the neighboring cooks and maids flitted through the kitchen, and the whispering went on till evening. How they had sniffed out the matchmaking—God knows. Waking up at midnight, Grisha heard the nanny and the cook whispering behind the curtain in the children's room. The nanny was persuading, and the cook now sobbed, now giggled. Falling asleep after that, Grisha dreamed that Pelageya was being abducted by a Chernomor and a witch . . .[1]

The next day came a lull. Kitchen life continued on its course, as if there were no cabby. Only from time to time the nanny would put on a new shawl, assume a solemnly stern expression, and go off somewhere for an hour or two, evidently for negotiations . . . Pelageya and the cabby did not see each other, and, when reminded of him, she would flare up and shout:

"Curse him up and down! Why should I think about him! Tphoo!"

One evening in the kitchen, when the nanny and the cook were assiduously cutting out a pattern, Mama came in and said:

"You can marry him, of course, that's your business, but you must know, Pelageya, that he cannot live here . . . You know I don't like to have someone sitting in the kitchen. See that you remember . . . And I won't give you the nights off."

"God knows what you're thinking up, ma'am," shrieked the cook. "Why do you reproach me over him? Let him rot! Why should I be stuck with this . . ."

Peeking into the kitchen one Sunday morning, Grisha froze in amazement. The kitchen was packed full of people. There were cooks from all the households, a caretaker, two policemen, a corporal with his stripes, the boy Filka . . . This Filka usually loitered around the laundry room and played with the dogs, but he was neatly combed, washed, and holding an icon in a foil casing. In the middle of the kitchen stood Pelageya in a new calico dress and with a flower on her head. Beside her stood the cabby. The newlyweds were both red-faced, sweaty, and kept blinking their eyes.

"Well, now . . . seems it's time . . . ," the corporal began after a long pause.

Pelageya's whole face twitched and she burst into tears . . . The corporal took a big loaf of bread from the table, stood beside the nanny, and started to recite the blessing. The cabby went over to the corporal, plopped down before him, and gave him a smacking kiss on the hand. He did the same before Aksinya. Pelageya followed him mechanically and also plopped down. Finally, the outside door opened, white fog blew into the kitchen, and the public all moved noisily from the kitchen into the yard.

"Poor thing, poor thing!" thought Grisha, listening to the cook's sobs. "Where are they taking her? Why don't Papa and Mama stand up for her?"

After the church there was singing and concertina playing in the wash-house till evening. Mama was angry all the while that the nanny smelled of vodka and that on account of these weddings there was nobody to prepare the samovar. When Grisha went to bed, Pelageya had still not come back.

"Poor thing, now she's crying somewhere in the dark!" he thought. "And the cabby tells her: 'Shut up! Shut up!'"

The next morning the cook was already in the kitchen. The cabby stopped by for a minute. He thanked Mama and, looking sternly at Pelageya, said:

"Keep an eye on her, ma'am. Be her father and mother. And you, too, Aksinya Stepanna, don't let up, see that everything stays honorable . . . no mischief . . . And also, ma'am, allow me an advance of five little roubles on her salary. I've got to buy a new yoke."

Another puzzler for Grisha: Pelageya had lived freely, as she liked, not answering to anybody, and suddenly, out of the blue, appeared some stranger, who somehow got the right to her doings and her property! Grisha was upset. He wanted passionately, to the point of tears, to be nice to this victim, as he thought, of people's abuse. Choosing the biggest apple in the pantry, he snuck into the kitchen, put it in Pelageya's hand, and rushed back out again.

1885

In a Foreign Land

SUNDAY NOON. The landowner Kamyshev is sitting in his dining room at a sumptuously laid table, having a leisurely lunch.
His meal is being shared by a neat, clean-shaven little old
Frenchman, Monsieur Shampooing. This Shampooing was once the
Kamyshevs' family tutor, taught the children manners, proper pro-
nunciation, and dancing; then, when the Kamyshev children grew up
and became lieutenants, Shampooing stayed on as something like a
male governess. The duties of the former tutor are not complicated.
He has to dress decently, smell of perfume, listen to Kamyshev's idle
talk, eat, drink, sleep—and that, it seems, is all. In return he receives
room, board, and an unspecified salary.

Kamyshev is eating and, as usual, babbling away.

"Deadly!" he says, wiping the tears that rise up following a slice of
ham thickly smeared with mustard. "Oof! It hits you in the head and
all the joints. Your French mustard wouldn't do that, even if you ate
a whole jar."

"Some like French mustard, and some Russian . . . ," Shampooing
pronounces meekly.

"Nobody likes French mustard, except maybe the French. But a
Frenchman will eat anything you give him: frogs, rats, cockroaches—
brr! You, for instance, don't like this ham because it's Russian, but if
they give you fried glass and tell you it's French, you'll eat it and
smack your lips . . . In your opinion, everything Russian is bad."

"I'm not saying that."

"Everything Russian is bad, and everything French—oh, say tray jolee![1] In your opinion, there's no better country than France, but in mine . . . well, what is France, honestly speaking? A little scrap of land! Send our policeman there, and a month later he'll ask to be transferred: there's no room to turn around! You can travel all over your France in a day, but with us you step through the gate and—endless space! Drive on and on . . ."

"Yes, monsieur, Russia is an enormous country."

"There you have it! In your opinion, there's no better people than the French. Educated, intelligent folk! Civilized! I agree, the French are all educated, well-mannered . . . it's true . . . A Frenchman will never allow himself to be boorish: he'll promptly move a chair for a lady, won't eat crayfish with a fork, won't spit on the floor, but . . . it's not the right spirit! He doesn't have the right spirit! I can't explain it to you, but, how shall I put it, there's something lacking in Frenchmen, a certain" (the speaker twiddles his fingers) ". . . something . . . juridical. I remember reading somewhere that you all have an intelligence acquired from books, while ours is inborn. If a Russian learns all your subjects properly, no professor of yours will compare with him."

"Maybe so . . . ," Shampooing says as if reluctantly.

"No, not maybe—it's true! Don't wince, I'm telling the truth! Russian intelligence is inventive! Only, of course, it's not given scope enough, and it's no good at boasting . . . It will invent something and then break it or give it to children to play with, while your Frenchman invents some sort of rubbish and shouts for all the world to hear. The other day the coachman Jonah made a manikin out of wood: you pull a string on this manikin and he makes an indecent gesture. And yet Jonah doesn't boast. Generally . . . I don't like the French! I'm not talking about you, but generally . . . Immoral people! Outwardly they seem to resemble humans, but they live like dogs . . . Take marriage, for instance. With us, whoever marries cleaves to his wife and there's no more talking, but with you devil knows what goes on. The husband sits in a café all day, and his wife infests the house with Frenchmen and cancans away with them."

"That's not true!" Shampooing, unable to help himself, flares up. "In France the family principle is held very high!"

"We know all about that principle! And you should be ashamed to defend it. One must be impartial: pigs are pigs . . . Thanks to the Germans for beating them . . . By God, yes. God grant them good health . . ."

"In that case, monsieur, I don't understand," says the Frenchman, jumping up and his eyes flashing, "if you really hate the French, why do you keep me?"

"What else can I do with you?"

"Let me go, and I'll leave for France!"

"Wha-a-at? As if they'd let you back into France now! You're a traitor to your fatherland! One day Napoleon is your great man, then it's Gambetta . . . the devil himself can't figure you out!"

"Monsieur," Shampooing says in French, spluttering and crumpling the napkin in his hands, "even an enemy could not have come up with a worse insult to my feelings than you have just done! All is finished!!"

And, making a tragic gesture with his hand, the Frenchman affectedly throws the napkin on the table and walks out with dignity.

Some three hours later the table setting is changed and dinner is served. Kamyshev sits down to eat alone. After the first glass, he is overcome with a thirst for idle talk. He would like to chat, but there is no one to listen.

"What's Alphonse Ludvigovich doing?" he asks the servant.

"Packing his suitcase, sir."

"What a dunderhead, God forgive me! . . . ," says Kamyshev, and he goes to the Frenchman.

Shampooing is sitting on the floor in the middle of his room and with trembling hands is packing his linen, perfume bottles, prayer books, suspenders, neckties into a suitcase . . . His whole respectable figure, his suitcase, bed, and table exude refinement and effeminacy. From his big blue eyes large tears drop into the suitcase.

"Where are you off to?" asks Kamyshev, after standing there for a while.

The Frenchman is silent.

"You want to leave?" Kamyshev goes on. "Well, you know best . . . I wouldn't dare hold you back . . . Only here's the strange thing: how are you going to go without a passport? I'm surprised! You know, I lost your passport. I put it somewhere among the papers, and it got lost . . . And here they're very strict about passports. You won't go three miles before they nab you."

Shampooing raises his head and looks mistrustfully at Kamyshev.

"Yes . . . You'll find out! They'll see by your face that you've got no passport, and right away: 'Who are you? Alphonse Shampooing! We know these Alphonse Shampooings! Maybe you'd like to be shipped off to some not-so-nearby parts!'"

"Are you joking?"

"Why on earth would I be joking? As if I need that! Only watch out, I warn you: no whimpering and letter-writing afterwards. I won't lift a finger when they march you by in chains!"

Shampooing jumps up, pale, wide-eyed, and starts pacing the room.

"What are you doing to me?!" he says, clutching his head in despair. "My God! Oh, cursed be the hour when the pernicious thought came to my head of leaving my fatherland!"

"Now, now, now . . . I was joking!" says Kamyshev, lowering his tone. "What an odd fellow, he doesn't understand jokes! One dare not utter a word!"

"My dear!" shrieks Shampooing, calmed by Kamyshev's tone. "I swear to you, I'm attached to Russia, to you, to your children . . . To leave you is as hard for me as to die! But each word you say cuts me to the heart!"

"Ah, you odd fellow! Why on earth should you be offended if I denounce the French? We denounce all sorts of people—should they all be offended? An odd fellow, really! Take my tenant Lazar Isakich, for example . . . I call him this and that, Yid and kike, make a pig's ear out of my coattail, pull him by the whiskers . . . he doesn't get offended."

"But he's a slave! He's ready for any meanness to make a kopeck!"

"Now, now, now . . . enough! Let's go and eat. Peace and harmony!"

Shampooing powders his tear-stained face and goes with Kamyshev to the dining room. The first course is eaten in silence, after the second the same story begins, and so Shampooing's sufferings never end.

1885

CORPORAL WHOMPOV

C ORPORAL WHOMPOV! You are accused of insulting, on the third of September *instant*, by word and deed, the village constable Zhigin, the parish elder Alyapov, the local militiaman Efimov, the witnesses Ivanov and Gavrilov, and another six peasants—the first three being subjected to your insults while in performance of their duties. Do you acknowledge your guilt?"

Whompov, a wrinkled corporal with a prickly face, stands at attention and answers in a hoarse, stifled voice, rapping out each word as if giving a command:

"Your Honor, Mister Justice of the Peace! It transpires that, by all the articles of the law, there is the following reason for attesting to each circumstance in its reciprocity. The guilty party is not me, but all the others. This whole business occurred on account of a dead corpse—may he rest in peace. Two days ago I was walking with my wife Anfisa, quietly, honorably, I see—there's a heap of various folk standing on the riverbank. By what full right have these folk gathered here? I ask. How come? Does the law say folk come in herds? I shouted: 'Break it up!' I started pushing the folk so they'd go to their homes, ordered the militiaman to drive them away . . ."

"Excuse me, but you're not a policeman or a headman—what business have you got dispersing folk?"

"None! None!" Voices are heard from various corners of the courtroom. "There's no living with him, Y'ronor! Fifteen years we've suffered from him! Ever since he got back from the army, we've felt like fleeing the village. He torments everybody!"

"Exactly right, Y'ronor!" testifies the village headman. "We're all complaining. It's impossible to live with him! We're carrying icons, or there's a wedding, or, say, some other occasion, everywhere he's shouting, clamoring, demanding order all the time. He boxes the children's ears, keeps an eye on the women like a father-in-law, lest there be some mischief . . . The other day he went around the cottages, giving orders not to sing songs or burn candles. There's no law, he says, that allows you to sing songs."

"Wait, you'll have your chance to give evidence," says the justice of the peace. "Now let Whompov continue. Continue, Whompov!"

"Yes, sir," croaks the corporal. "You, Your Honor, are pleased to say I have no business dispersing folk . . . Very well, sir . . . But if there's disorder? Can folk be allowed to act outrageously? Is it written somewhere in the law that folk can do as they like? I can't allow it, sir. If I don't disperse them and punish them, who will? Nobody in the whole village knows about real order except me alone, you might say, Your Honor, I know how to deal with people of lower rank, and, Your Honor, I can understand it all. I'm not a peasant, I'm a corporal, a retired quartermaster, I served in Warsaw, at headquarters, sir, and after that, if you care to know, in civilian life, I became a fireman, sir, and after that, weakened by illness, I left the fire department and for two years worked in a boys' classical primary school as a porter . . . I know all about order, sir. But your peasant is a simple man, he understands nothing and has to obey me, because—it's for his own good. Take this case, for example . . . I disperse the folk, and there on the bank in the sand lies the drowned corpse of a dead man. On what possible grounds, I ask you, is he lying there? Is there any order in that? Where is the constable looking? 'Why is it, constable,' I say, 'that you don't inform the authorities? Maybe this drowned dead man drowned on his own, and maybe it has a whiff of Siberia. Maybe it's a criminal homicide . . .' But Constable Zhigin pays no attention, he just smokes his cigarette.

" 'Who have we got giving orders here?' he says. 'Where,' he says, 'did he come from? Don't we know,' he says, 'how to behave without him?' 'Meaning you don't know, fool that you are,' I say, 'since you're

standing here paying no attention.' 'I,' he says, 'already informed
the district superintendent yesterday.' 'Why the district superintendent?' I ask. 'By what article of the legal code? In such a case, when
there's a drowning or a hanging or the like—in such a case, what can
the superintendent do? Here,' I say, 'we have a criminal case, a civil
case . . . Here,' I say, 'you must quickly pass the torch to the honorable prosecutors and judges, sir. And first of all,' I say, 'you must
draw up a report and send it to the honorable justice of the peace.'
But he, the constable, listens to it all and laughs. And the peasants,
too. They all laughed, Your Honor. I'll testify to it under oath. This
one laughed, and that one laughed, and Zhigin laughed. 'Why bare
your teeth?' I say. And the constable says, 'The justice of the peace,'
he says, 'doesn't judge such cases.' At those words I even broke into
a sweat. Didn't you say that, Constable?" The corporal turned to
Constable Zhigin.

"I did."

"Everybody heard you say in front of all those simple folk: 'The
justice of the peace doesn't judge such cases.' Everybody heard you
say that . . . I broke out in a sweat, Your Honor, I even got all scared.
'Repeat,' I say, 'you this-and-that, repeat what you said!' Again he
says the same words . . . I say to him: 'How can you speak that way
about an honorable justice of the peace? You, a police officer, are
against the authorities? Eh? Do you know,' I say, 'that for such talk
the honorable justice of the peace, if he's of a mind to, can pack you
off to the provincial police department on account of your untrust-
worthy behavior? Do you know,' I say, 'where the honorable justice
of the peace can send you for such political talk?' And the elder says:
'The justice,' he says, 'can't stake out anything beyond his boundar-
ies. He only has jurisdiction over minor offenses.' That's what he said,
everybody heard it . . . 'How dare you,' I say, 'belittle the authorities? You, brother,' I say, 'don't start joking with me, or things will
go badly for you.' In Warsaw, or when I was a porter in the boys'
primary school, whenever I'd hear such inappropriate talk, I'd look
around for a policeman: 'Come here, officer,' I'd say—and report it
all to him. But here in the village, who can I tell? . . . I flew into a rage.
It upsets me that folk nowadays are sunk in willfulness and disobedi-
ence. I took a swing and . . . not hard, of course, but just right, lightly,

so that he wouldn't dare say such words about Your Honor . . . The constable stood up for the elder. So I gave it to the constable, too . . . And so it went . . . I lost my temper, Your Honor, but, well, it's really impossible without a beating. If a stupid man doesn't get a beating, the sin's on your soul. Especially if there's something up . . . some disorder . . ."

"I beg your pardon! There are people who look out for disorder. That's why we have the constable, the headman, the militiaman . . ."

"A constable can't look out for everything, and a constable doesn't understand what I understand . . ."

"But don't you see that it's none of your business?"

"What's that, sir? How is it not mine? Strange, sir . . . People behave outrageously and it's none of my business! Should I praise them, then, or what? So they complain to you that I forbid singing songs . . . What's the good of songs? Instead of taking up some kind of work, they sing songs . . . and they've also made it a fashion to sit in the evening with candles burning. They should go to bed, but they're talking and laughing. I've got it written down, sir!"

"What have you got written down?"

"Who sits with candles burning."

Whompov pulls a greasy scrap of paper from his pocket, puts on his spectacles, and reads:

"Peasants who sit with candles burning: Ivan Prokhorov, Savva Mikiforov, Pyotr Petrov. The soldier's widow Shrustrova lives in depraved lawlessness with Semyon Kislov. Ignat Sverchok is taken up with magic and his wife Mavra is a witch, who goes by night to milk other people's cows."

"Enough!" says the justice, and he starts to interrogate the witnesses.

Corporal Whompov raises his spectacles on his brow and looks in astonishment at the justice, who is obviously not on his side. His popping eyes flash, his nose turns bright red. He stares at the justice, at the witnesses, and simply cannot understand what makes this justice so flustered, and why whispering and restrained laughter are heard from all corners of the courtroom. He also cannot understand the sentence: a month in jail!

"What for?!" he says, spreading his arms in bewilderment. "By what law?"

And it is clear to him that the world has changed and that living in it is no longer possible. Gloomy, dismal thoughts come over him. But, leaving the courtroom and seeing the peasants crowding around and talking about something, he, by force of a habit he can no longer control, stands at attention and shouts in a hoarse, angry voice:

"Brea-a-ak it up! Don't cr-r-rowd around! Go home!"

1885

GRIEF

THE WOODTURNER Grigori Petrov, long known as an excellent craftsman and at the same time as the most good-for-nothing peasant in the whole Galchinsky district, is taking his sick old wife to the local hospital. He has to drive some twenty miles, and moreover the road is terrible, hard enough for a government postman to deal with, not to mention such a lazybones as the woodturner Grigori. A sharp, cold wind blows right in his face. In the air, wherever you look, big clouds of snowflakes whirl, so that it is hard to tell whether the snow is coming from the sky or from the earth. Neither the fields, nor the telegraph poles, nor the forest can be seen through the snowy mist, and when an especially strong gust of wind hits Grigori, he cannot even see the shaft bow. The decrepit, feeble little nag barely trudges along. All her energy is spent on pulling her legs out of the deep snow and tossing her head. The woodturner is in a hurry. He fidgets restlessly on the box and keeps whipping the horse's back.

"Don't you cry, Matryona . . . ," he mutters. "Hold out a little longer. God grant we'll get to the hospital, and in a flash you'll be, sort of . . . Pavel Ivanych will give you some little drops, or order a blood-letting, or maybe he'll be so kind as to rub you with some sort of spirits, and that will . . . ease your side. Pavel Ivanych will do his best. He'll scold, stamp his feet, but he'll do his best . . . He's a nice gentleman, well-mannered, God grant him good health . . .

"As soon as we get there, he'll come running out of his quarters and start calling up all the devils. 'What? How's this?' he'll shout. 'Why don't you come at the right time? Am I some sort of dog, to bother with you devils all day long? Why didn't you come in the morning? Out! So there's no trace of you left! Come tomorrow!' And I'll say: 'Doctor, sir! Pavel Ivanych! Your Honor!' Get a move on, devil take you! Hup!"

The woodturner whips his nag and, not looking at the old woman, goes on muttering under his breath:

"'Your Honor! Truly, as before God himself . . . I swear, I set out at daybreak. How could I make it here on time, if the Lord . . . the Mother of God . . . turned wrathful and sent such a storm? Kindly see for yourself . . . A nobler horse wouldn't even have made it, and mine, kindly see for yourself, isn't a horse, it's a disgrace!' Pavel Ivanych will frown and shout: 'We know your kind! You always find some excuse! Especially you, Grishka! I've known you a long time! No doubt you stopped off maybe five times at a pot-house!' And I say to him: 'Your Honor! What am I, some sort of villain or heathen? The old woman's rendering up her soul to God, she's dying, and I should go running around to the pot-houses? Mercy, how can you? Let them all perish, these pot-houses!' Then Pavel Ivanych will have you carried into the hospital. And I'll bow down to him . . . 'Pavel Ivanych! Your Honor! I humbly thank you! Forgive us, cursed fools that we are, don't take offense at us peasants! You should have kicked us out, but you kindly went to the trouble and got your feet covered with snow!' And Pavel Ivanych will glance at me as if he's about to hit me and say: 'Instead of bowing at my feet, you'd do better, you fool, to stop guzzling vodka and pity your old woman. You could use a good whipping!' 'Exactly so, Pavel Ivanych, a good whipping, God strike me dead, a good whipping! And how can I not bow at your feet, if you're our benefactor and dear father? Your Honor! I give you my word . . . as if before God . . . spit in my face if I'm lying: as soon as my Matryona here recovers and is her old self again, anything Your Grace cares to order from me, I'll be glad to make! A cigar box of Karelian birch, if you wish . . . croquet balls, I can turn bowling pins just like the foreign ones . . . I'll do it all for you! I won't take a kopeck for it! In Moscow a cigar box like that would cost you four roubles, but I won't take a kopeck.' The doctor will laugh and say: 'Well, all right, all right . . . I get it! Only it's too bad you're a drunkard . . .' I know, old girl, how to talk with gentlemen. There's no gentleman I couldn't talk with. Only God keep us from losing our way. What a blizzard! My eyes are all snowy."

And the woodturner mutters endlessly. He babbles away mechanically, so as to stifle his heavy feeling if only a little. He has many words on his tongue, but there are still more thoughts and questions in his head. Grief has come suddenly, unexpectedly, and taken the woodturner by surprise, and now he cannot recover, come to his senses, figure things out. Up to then he had lived serenely, as if in a drunken half-consciousness, knowing neither grief nor joy, and now he suddenly feels a terrible pain in his soul. The carefree lazybones and tippler finds himself all at once in the position of a busy man, preoccupied, hurrying, and even struggling with the elements.

The woodturner remembers that the grief began the previous evening. When he came home the previous evening, a bit drunk as usual, and from inveterate habit began cursing and shaking his fists, the old woman glanced at her ruffian as she had never done before. Usually the expression of her old-woman's eyes was martyred, meek, as with dogs that are much beaten and poorly fed, but now she looked at him sternly and fixedly, as saints on icons or dying people do. It was with those strange, unhappy eyes that the grief began. The dazed woodturner persuaded a neighbor to lend him a horse, and he was now taking his old wife to the hospital, hoping that Pavel Ivanych, with his powders and ointments, would restore the old woman's former gaze.

"And you, Matryona, well . . . ," he mutters. "If Pavel Ivanych asks you if I beat you or not, say: 'No, never!' And I won't beat you anymore. I swear to God. Do you think I beat you out of spite? I beat you just so, for nothing. I pity you. Another man wouldn't care much, but see, I'm driving . . . I'm trying hard. And the blizzard, what a blizzard! Lord, Thy will be done! Only grant we get there and don't lose our way . . . What, your side hurts? Matryona, why don't you say anything? I'm asking you: does your side hurt?"

It seems strange to him that the snow does not melt on the old woman's face, that the face itself has become somehow peculiarly long, acquired a pale-gray, dirty-wax color, and become stern, serious.

"What a fool!" mutters the woodturner. "I speak to you in all conscience, like to God . . . and you . . . What a fool! I just won't take you to Pavel Ivanych!"

The woodturner lets go of the reins and falls to thinking. He cannot bring himself to turn and look at the old woman: scary! To ask her something and not get an answer is also scary. Finally, to put an end to the uncertainty, without turning to look, he feels for the old woman's cold hand. The raised hand drops back limply.

"So she died! What a chore!"

And the woodturner weeps. Not so much from pity as from vexation. He thinks: how quickly it all gets done in this world! His grief had barely begun, and the ending was already there waiting. He had barely begun to live with his old wife, to talk with her, to pity her, when she up and died. He had lived with her for forty years, but those forty years had passed as if in a fog. With all the drinking, fighting, and poverty, life had not been felt. And, as if on purpose, the old woman died just at the very moment when he felt that he pitied her, could not live without her, was terribly guilty before her.

"And she went begging," he recalls. "I sent her out myself to ask people for bread—what a chore! She should have lived a dozen more years, the fool, but she probably thinks this is how I really am. Holy Mother of God, where the devil have I got to? It's not treatment she needs now, it's burial. Turn around!"

The woodturner turns around and whips up his nag with all his might. The road gets worse and worse every moment. Now he cannot see the shaft bow at all. Occasionally the sledge rides over a young fir tree, a dark object scratches his hands, flashes before his eyes, and the field of vision again becomes white, whirling.

"To live life over again . . . ," thinks the woodturner.

He remembers that forty years ago Matryona was young, beautiful, cheerful, from a rich family. They gave her to him in marriage because they were seduced by his craftsmanship. There were all the makings for a good life, but the trouble was that he got drunk after the wedding, dropped off, and it was as if he never woke up until now.

The wedding he remembers, but of what came after the wedding—for the life of him, he cannot remember anything, except maybe that he drank, slept, fought. So forty years vanished.

The white snowy clouds gradually begin to turn gray. Darkness falls.

"Where am I going?" The woodturner suddenly rouses himself. "I've got to bury her, not go to the hospital . . . I must be in a daze!"

He turns around again and again whips up the horse. The mare strains with all her might and, snorting, trots along. The woodturner whips her on the back again and again . . . He hears some sort of knocking behind him, and though he does not turn around, he knows that it is the deceased woman's head knocking against the sledge. And it grows darker and darker around him, the wind turns colder and sharper . . .

"To live it all over again," thinks the woodturner. "To get new tools, take orders . . . give the money to the old woman . . . yes!"

And here he drops the reins. He feels for them, wants to pick them up and cannot; his hands no longer obey him . . .

"Never mind . . . ," he thinks. "The horse will go by herself, she knows the way. I could do with some sleep now . . . till the funeral or the memorial service."

The woodturner closes his eyes and dozes off. A short while later he hears that the horse has stopped. He opens his eyes and sees something dark in front of him, like a hut or a haystack . . .

He ought to climb down from the sledge and find out what it is, but there is such laziness in his whole body that he would rather freeze to death than move from his place . . . And he falls peacefully asleep.

He wakes up in a big room with painted walls. Bright sunlight pours through the windows. The woodturner sees people around him and wants first of all to show that he is a man of dignity and understanding.

"What about a little Panikhida, brothers, for the old woman?" he says. "The priest should be told . . ."

"Well, enough, enough! Just lie there!" Someone's voice interrupts him.

"Good Lord! Pavel Ivanych!" The woodturner is surprised to see the doctor before him. "Y'ronor! My benefactor!"

He wants to jump up and throw himself at the feet of medicine, but feels that his arms and legs do not obey him.

"Your Honor! Where are my legs? My arms?"

"Say goodbye to your arms and legs . . . They got frozen. Now, now . . . what are you crying for? You've lived, thank God for that! You must have lived some sixty years—that will do you!"

"Grief! . . . Y'ronor, it's such grief! Kindly forgive me! Another five or six little years . . ."

"What for?"

"I borrowed the horse, I've got to return it . . . Bury the old woman . . . How quickly it all gets done in this world! Your Honor! Pavel Ivanych! A cigar box of the best Karelian birch! Croquet balls . . ."

The doctor waves his hand and walks out of the ward. Woodturner—amen!

1885

The Exclamation Point

A Christmas Story

O N   T H E   N I G H T   B E F O R E   C H R I S T M A S, Efim Fomich Perekladin, a collegiate secretary,[1] went to bed offended and even
insulted.

"Stop bothering me, you she-devil!" he barked angrily at his wife
when she asked why he was so gloomy.

The trouble was that he had just come back from a party where
many things had been said that he found unpleasant and offensive. At
first they talked about the benefits of education in general, then they
moved on imperceptibly to the educational requirements for civil servants, about the low level of which a great many laments, reproaches,
and even gibes were voiced. And here, as is customary in all Russian
gatherings, they moved on from the general to the personal.

"Take you, for instance, Efim Fomich." A young man turned to
Perekladin. "You occupy a respectable post . . . but what kind of education did you receive?"

"None, sir. For us no education's needed," Perekladin said meekly.
"Just write correctly . . ."

"And where did you learn to write correctly?"

"Habit, sir . . . After forty years of service you get the knack of it,
sir . . . Of course, it was hard at first, I made mistakes, but then I got
used to it, sir . . . no problem . . ."

"And punctuation?"

"Punctuation's no problem . . . Just put it in correctly."

"Hm! . . ." The young man became embarrassed. "But habit's not the same as education. It's not enough to put in punctuation correctly . . . not enough, sir! You should put it in consciously! When you put in a comma, you should know why you're putting it in . . . yes, sir! And this unconscious . . . reflex orthography of yours isn't worth a kopeck. It's mechanical production and nothing more."

Perekladin held his tongue and even smiled meekly (the young man was the son of a state councillor and had the right to the tenth rank), but now, on going to bed, he was all transformed into anger and indignation.

"I've served for forty years," he thought, "and no one has ever called me a fool, but now just look what critics have turned up! 'Unconscious . . . Lefrex! Mechanical production . . .' Ah, you, devil take you! Anyhow, maybe I understand more than you do, even if I didn't study in your universities."

Having mentally poured out all the abuse known to him at the critic's expense and getting warm under the blanket, Perekladin began to calm down.

"I know . . . I understand . . . ," he thought, falling asleep. "I wouldn't put a colon where a comma's called for, which means I'm aware, I understand. Yes . . . So there, young man . . . First you've got to live, serve, and only then judge your elders . . ."

In the closed eyes of the dozing Perekladin, through a crowd of dark, smiling clouds, a fiery comma flew like a meteor. It was followed by a second, a third, and soon the whole boundless dark background spread out before his imagination was covered with dense clusters of flying commas . . .

"Take just these commas . . . ," thought Perekladin, feeling his limbs turning sweetly numb from the onset of sleep. "I understand them perfectly . . . I can find a place for each one, if you like . . . and . . . and consciously, not by chance . . . Test me and you'll see . . . Commas are put in various places, where they go, and where they don't. The more confusing the document, the more commas are needed. They're put before 'which' and sometimes before 'that.' If there's a list of officials, each one should be separated by a comma . . . I know!"

The golden commas spun around and raced off to one side. They were replaced by fiery periods . . .

"And periods are put at the end of a document . . . Where a big pause and a glance at the listener is needed, there should also be a period. After every long passage a period is needed, so that the secretary's mouth doesn't go dry while he's reading. Periods are not put anywhere else . . ."

Again the commas come flying . . . They mix with the periods, whirl around—and Perekladin sees a whole multitude of colons and semicolons . . .

"And these I know . . . ," he thinks. "Where a comma is too little and a period is too much, there we need a semicolon. Before 'but' and 'therefore' I always put a semicolon . . . Well, and the colon? A colon is needed after the phrases 'it has been decreed' or 'decided' . . ."

The colons and semicolons fade away. It is the turn of the question marks. They leap down from the clouds dancing the cancan . . .

"As if we've never seen question marks! Even if there were a thousand of them, I'd find a place for them all. They're always used when there's a request to be made or, let's say, documents are being examined: 'Where is the remainder of the sums for such-and-such year?' or 'Will the police department find it possible for a certain Mrs. Ivanov . . . ?' and so on."

The question marks nodded their hooks in approval and instantly, as if on command, straightened themselves into exclamation points . . .

"Hm! . . . This punctuation mark is often used in letters. 'My dear sir!' or 'Your Excellency, father and benefactor! . . .' But when in documents?"

The exclamation points drew themselves up still taller and stood waiting . . .

"They're used in documents when . . . well . . . that's . . . how is it? Hm! . . . In fact, when are they used in documents? Wait . . . God help me remember . . . Hm! . . ."

Perekladin opened his eyes and turned on his other side. But before he could close them again, the exclamation points appeared once more against the dark background.

"Devil take them . . . When should they be used?" he thought, trying to drive the uninvited guests out of his imagination. "Can it be I've forgotten? Forgotten, or . . . just never used them . . ."

Perekladin began to recall the contents of all the documents he had written out in his forty years of service; but however much he thought, however much he furrowed his brow, in his past he did not find a single exclamation point.

"How odd! Writing for forty years and never once using an exclamation point . . . Hm! . . . But when does the long devil get used?"

From behind the row of fiery exclamation points appeared the sarcastically grinning mug of his young critic. The points also smiled and merged into one big exclamation point.

Perekladin shook his head and opened his eyes.

"Devil knows what . . . ," he thought. "Tomorrow morning I have to get up for matins, and I can't drive this fiendish thing out of my head . . . Pah! But . . . when do we use it then? There's habit for you! There's getting the knack for you! Not a single exclamation point in forty years! Eh?"

Perekladin crossed himself and closed his eyes, but immediately opened them again; the big point still stood there against the dark background . . .

"Pah! This way I won't sleep all night. Marfusha!" He turned to his wife, who often boasted of having finished boarding school. "Do you know, sweetheart, when to use an exclamation point in documents?"

"As if I don't! I didn't spend seven years in boarding school for nothing. I remember all of grammar by heart. It's used in appeals, exclamations, and expressions of delight, indignation, joy, anger, and other feelings."

"So-o-o . . . ," thought Perekladin. "Delight, indignation, joy, anger, and other feelings . . ."

The collegiate secretary fell to thinking . . . For forty years he had been writing out documents, he had written out thousands, tens of thousands of them, but he did not remember a single line that expressed delight, indignation, or anything of the sort . . .

"And other feelings . . . ," he thought. "But is there any need for feelings in documents? Even a man with no feelings can write them out . . ."

The young critic's mug peeked out again from behind the fiery point and smiled sarcastically. Perekladin got up and sat on the bed. He had a headache, cold sweat stood out on his brow . . . In the corner an icon lamp glimmered cozily, the furniture was clean and had a festive look, over everything spread the warmth and presence of a woman's hands, but the poor little clerk was cold, uncomfortable, as if he were sick with typhus. The exclamation point no longer stood in his closed eyes, but before him, in the room, by his wife's dressing table, and it winked mockingly at him . . .

"Machine! Writing machine!" whispered the ghost, wafting dry cold at the clerk. "Unfeeling block of wood!"

The clerk covered himself with the blanket, but he also saw the ghost under the blanket; he pressed his face to his wife's shoulder, but it stuck out from behind her shoulder as well . . . Poor Perekladin suffered all night, but in the daytime the ghost did not leave him. He saw it everywhere: in the boots he was putting on, in his cup of tea, in his Stanislas medal . . .[2]

"And other feelings . . . ," he thought. "It's true there haven't been any feelings . . . I'm going now to sign my superior's Christmas greeting . . . but is it done with any feelings? So, it's all nothing . . . A merry-christmas machine . . ."

When Perekladin went out and hailed a cab, it seemed to him that an exclamation point drove up instead of a cabby.

Coming to his superior's anteroom, instead of a porter he saw the same exclamation point . . . And it all spoke to him of delight, indignation, anger . . . The pen in its stand also looked like an exclamation point. Perekladin took it, dipped the pen in ink, and wrote:

"Collegiate Secretary Efim Perekladin!!!"

And in setting down these three exclamation points he felt delight, indignation, joy, and he seethed with anger.

"There, take that! Take that!" he muttered as he pressed down with the pen.

The fiery exclamation point was satisfied and vanished.

1885

An Educated Blockhead

A Sketch

ARKHIP ELISEICH SLOPSOV, a retired second lieutenant, put on his spectacles, frowned, and read out: "The justice of the peace of the . . . circuit, . . . district, invites you, etc., etc., in the capacity of the accused in a case of assault and battery of the peasant Grigory Vlasov . . . Justice of the Peace P. Sixwingsky."[1]

"Who is this from?" Slopsov raised his eyes to the messenger.

"From mister justice of the peace, sir, Pyotr Sergeich . . . Sixwingsky, sir . . ."

"Hmm . . . From Pyotr Sergeich? What is he inviting me for?"

"Must be for a trial . . . It's written there, sir."

Slopsov read the summons over again, looked at the messenger in surprise, and shrugged his shoulders . . .

"Pah . . . in the capacity of the accused . . . He's a funny one, this Pyotr Sergeich! Ah, well, tell him: all right! Only he should prepare a good lunch . . . Tell him I'll be there! My greetings to Natalya Egorovna and the little ones!"

Slopsov signed and went to the room where his brother-in-law, Lieutenant Nitkin, who had come on vacation, was staying.

"Take a look at what sort of missive Petka Sixwingsky has sent me," he said, handing Nitkin the summons. "He's inviting me for Thursday . . . Will you come with me?"

"But he's not asking you as a guest," said Nitkin, having read the summons. "He's summoning you to court as the accused . . . He's putting you on trial."

"Me, is it? Pss . . . The milk hasn't dried on his lips yet, who is he to put me on trial . . . Small fry . . . He's just doing it as a joke . . ."

"He's not joking at all! Don't you understand? It says here clearly: a case of assault and battery . . . You gave Grishka a beating, so now there's a trial."

"You're a funny one, by God! How can he put me on trial, if we're what you might call friends? How can he judge me, if we've played cards, and drunk, and done devil knows what else together? What kind of judge is he anyway? Ha-ha! Petka—a judge! Ha-ha!"

"Go on, laugh, but he may well put you behind bars, not out of friendship, but on legal grounds, which will be nothing to laugh at!"

"You're cuckoo, brother! What are the legal grounds here, if he's my Vanya's godfather? Come along with me on Thursday and you'll see what kind of grounds there are . . ."

"And I'd advise you not to go at all, or you'll put him and yourself in an awkward position . . . Let him decide in absentia . . ."

"No, why in absentia? I'll go and see how he's going to judge it . . . I'm curious to see what kind of judge Petka's become . . . Incidentally, I haven't visited him for a long time . . . it's embarrassing . . ."

On Thursday Slopsov and Nitkin went to see Sixwingsky. They found the justice of the peace at proceedings in the courtroom.

"Greetings, Petyukha!" said Slopsov, going up to the judge's bench and holding out his hand. "Doing a bit of judging? Pettifoggery? Go on, go on . . . I'll wait, I'll watch . . . Let me introduce my brother-in-law . . . Is your wife well?"

"Yes . . . she is . . . Go sit there . . . with the public . . ."

Having muttered that, the judge blushed. Generally, beginning judges always get embarrassed when they see acquaintances in the courtroom; when they happen to have an acquaintance on trial, they give the impression of people about to fall through the floor from embarrassment. Slopsov stepped away from the bench and sat down in the front row beside Nitkin.

"Such importance in the rogue!" he whispered in Nitkin's ear. "You wouldn't recognize him! And he won't smile! Wearing a gold chain! Phooey on you! As if it wasn't him who daubed my kitchen maid Agafya with ink while she slept. What a laugh! Can such people judge anything? I ask you: Can such people judge anything? Here you need a man of rank, substance . . . so that, you know, he instills fear, but they just perched some nobody up there—go on, judge! Heh-heh . . ."

"Grigory Vlasov!" the justice called out. "Mr. Slopsov!"

Slopsov smiled and went up to the bench. A fellow in a shabby frock coat with a high waist and striped britches tucked into short reddish boots emerged from the public and stood beside Slopsov.

"Mr. Slopsov," the justice began, looking down. "You are accu-u-used . . . of assault and battery of your serving man . . . Grigory Vlasov here. Do you plead guilty?"

"What else! When did you turn so serious? Heh-heh . . ."

"Not guilty?" the justice interrupted him, fidgeting in his chair from embarrassment. "Vlasov, tell us what happened!"

"Very simple, sir. This gentleman, kindly see, employed me as a lackey, or, it might be argued, as a valet . . . Of course, our duties are a sort of hard labor, Your Excellency . . . Himself gets up past eight, but you've got to be on your feet with the first light . . . God only knows, will himself put on boots, or shoeses, or maybe go around the whole day in slippers, but you polish up everything: boots, and shoeses, and ankle boots . . . Right, sir . . . So himself calls me one morning to dress him. Of course, I go . . . I put his shirt on him, his britches, his boots . . . all good and proper . . . I start putting on his waistcoat . . . Here's what himself says: 'Give me my comb, Grishka. It's in the side pocket of my frock coat,' he says. Right, sir . . . I rummage in this side pocket, but the devil must have gobbled it up—there's no comb. I dig and dig and say: 'There's no comb here, Arkhip Eliseich!' Himself frowns, goes over to the frock coat, and takes out the comb, only not from the side pocket, as he told me, but from the front one. 'And what's this? Not a comb?' he says, and shoves the comb at my nose. All the teeth went over my nose. The whole rest of the day my nose kept bleeding. Kindly see, it's all swollen . . . I've got witnesses. Everybody saw it."

"What can you say in your defense?" The justice raised his eyes to Slopsov.

Slopsov looked questioningly at the justice, then at Grishka, then again at the justice, and turned purple.

"How am I to take this?" he muttered. "As mockery?"

"There is no mockery of you here, sir," observed Grishka, "I say it with a clear conscience. You oughtn't to make so free with your hands."

"Shut up!" Slopsov struck the floor with his walking stick. "Fool! Trash!"

The justice quickly took off his chain, jumped up from the bench, and rushed to his office.

"A five-minute break in the proceedings," he called out on the way. Slopsov followed after him.

"Listen," the justice began, clasping his hands, "what do you want, to arrange a scandal for me? Or do you like hearing how your cooks and lackeys polish you up in their testimony, ass that you are? What did you come for? I can't settle the case without you, is that it?"

"So it's all my fault!" Slopsov spread his arms. "You arranged this comedy and now you're angry with me! Arrest this Grishka, and . . . and it's done!"

"Arrest Grishka! Pah! You're still the same fool you always were! And just how am I going to arrest Grishka?"

"Arrest him, that's all! You're not going to lock me up!"

"So it's still the good old days, is that it? You beat Grishka, and Grishka should be arrested! Amazing logic! Do you have any notion of today's legal procedures?"

"In all my born days I've never gone to court or been on trial, but as I see it, if this same Grishka came to me to complain about you, I'd have chucked him down the stairs, and forbidden even his grandchildren to complain, to say nothing of allowing him to make his boorish remarks. Say simply that you wanted to make fun of me, to show your mettle . . . that's all! My wife was surprised when she read through the summonses and saw that you had subpoenaed all the cooks and cowgirls to the trial. She didn't expect such a stunt from you. It's not right, Petya! Friends don't do such things."

"But understand my position!"

And Sixwingsky started explaining his position to Slopsov.

"You sit here," he concluded, "and I'll go and make a decision in absentia. For God's sake don't show your face! With your antediluvian notions, you'll blurt something out so that, for all I know, I'll have to draw up a protocol."

Sixwingsky returned to the courtroom and went on with the proceedings. Slopsov, sitting in the office at one of the desks and, having nothing better to do, reading through some of the recently completed executive orders, heard the justice persuading Grishka to make peace. Grishka bristled for a long time, but finally accepted, demanding ten roubles for the offense.

"Well, thank God!" said Sixwingsky, coming into the office after the sentence was read. "Thank God the case ended that way . . . A thousand pounds off my shoulders. Pay Grishka ten roubles and you can be at peace."

"Me . . . pay Grishka . . . ten roubles?!" Slopsov was stunned. "Are you crazy?"

"Well, all right, all right, I'll pay it for you," Sixwingsky waved his hand, wincing. "I'm ready to give a hundred roubles, only so as to avoid unpleasantness. And God save us from having acquaintances in court. I'll tell you, brother, instead of beating Grishkas, come each time and give me a thrashing! It's a thousand times easier. Let's go to Natasha and eat!"

Ten minutes later the friends were sitting in the justice's apartment and lunching on fried carp.

"Very well, then," Slopsov began, downing his third glass, "you fined me ten roubles, but for how many days are you going to keep Grishka in the lockup?"

"I'm not going to lock him up at all. Why should I?"

"Why should you?" Slopsov rolled his eyes. "So he'll stop lodging complaints! How did he dare lodge a complaint against me?"

The justice and Nitkin started explaining to Slopsov, but he did not understand and stood his ground.

"Say what you like, but Petka's unfit to be a judge!" he sighed, conversing with Nitkin on the way home. "He's a good man, educated, ever so obliging, but . . . unfit! He doesn't really know about judging . . . It's a pity, but we'll have to unelect him for the next three-year term! We'll have to! . . ."

1885

A Slip-up

I LYA SERGEICH PEPLOV AND HIS WIFE, Kleopatra Petrovna, were standing by the door and greedily eavesdropping. Behind the door, in a small parlor, a declaration of love seemed to be going on; a declaration beween their daughter Natashenka and the local schoolteacher Gropekin.

"He's nibbling," whispered Peplov, trembling with impatience and rubbing his hands. "Watch out, Petrovna. As soon as they start talking about their feelings, take the icon off the wall at once and we'll go in to bless them . . . We'll catch them . . . A blessing with an icon is sacred and inviolable . . . He won't wriggle out of it then, even if he takes it to court."

Behind the door the following conversation was going on:

"Leave your character out of it," Gropekin was saying, striking a match on his checkered trousers. "I never wrote you any letters."

"Oh, no? As if I don't know your handwriting!" The girl giggled with affected little shrieks, glancing at herself in the mirror now and then. "I recognized it at once! And what a strange one you are! You teach penmanship, and your handwriting's like chicken scratches! How can you teach anyone to write, if you write so badly yourself?"

"Humph! . . . That doesn't mean anything, miss. In penmanship the main thing isn't handwriting, the main thing is that the pupils shouldn't doze off. One gets it on the head with a ruler, another's made to stand in the corner . . . What's handwriting! A waste of time!

Nekrasov was a writer, but it's a shame to see how he wrote.[1] They give a sample of his handwriting in his collected works."

"Nekrasov's one thing, and you're . . ." (a sigh). "I'd gladly marry a writer. He'd never stop writing verses as mementos for me!"

"I can also write verses for you, if you wish."

"What can you write about?"

"About love . . . about feelings . . . about your eyes . . . You'd read them and go out of your mind . . . Get all teary! And if I wrote poetical verses for you, would you let me kiss your little hand?"

"Big deal! . . . You can kiss it even now!"

Gropekin jumped up and, goggle-eyed, bent over the plump little hand, which smelled of egg soap.

"Take the icon," Peplov said hurriedly to his wife, nudging her with his elbow, turning pale with excitement, and buttoning his jacket. "Come on! Let's go!"

And without a second's delay, Peplov threw the door open.

"Children . . . ," he started muttering, raising his hands and blinking tearfully. "The Lord will bless you, my children . . . Live . . . be fruitful . . . multiply . . ."[2]

"And . . . and I, too, bless you . . ." said the mama, weeping with happiness. "Be happy, my dears! Oh, you're taking from me my only treasure!" she said to Gropekin. "Love my daughter, be good to her . . ."

Gropekin stood gaping with amazement and fright. The parents' assault was so sudden and bold that he was unable to utter a single word.

"I'm caught! Hitched!" he thought, going numb with terror. "That's it for you, brother! You won't get out of it!"

And he obediently lowered his head, as if wishing to say: "Take me, I'm vanquished!"

"I ble . . . bless you . . . ," the papa went on and also wept. "Natashenka, my daughter . . . stand beside . . . Petrovna, give me the icon . . ."

But here the parent suddenly stopped weeping, and his face became distorted with wrath.

"Blockhead!" he said angrily to his wife. "Addlepate! Is this an icon?"

"Ah, saints alive!"

What had happened? The teacher of penmanship timorously raised his eyes and saw that he was saved: the mama in her hurry had taken the portrait of the writer Lazhechnikov[3] from the wall instead of the icon. Old man Peplov and his spouse, Kleopatra Petrovna, stood with the portrait in their hands, embarrassed, not knowing what to do or say. The teacher of penmanship took advantage of the confusion and fled.

1886

ANGUISH

To whom will I impart my sorrow?[1]

E VENING TWILIGHT. Large, wet snowflakes swirl lazily around the just-lit streetlamps and cover in a thin layer the roofs, the horses' backs, shoulders, hats. The cabby Iona Potapov is all white as a ghost. He is bent over as much as a living body can bend, and he sits on the box without stirring. If a whole snowdrift were to fall on him, even then it seems he would feel no need to shake the snow off . . . His little nag is also white and motionless. She is so motionless, so angular, her stick-like legs are so straight that even up close she looks like a penny gingerbread horse. Most likely she is sunk in thought. Someone who has been taken away from the plow, from accustomed gray pictures, and thrown here into this whirlpool, full of monstrous lights, of incessant clamor and running people, cannot help thinking . . .

Iona and his nag have not budged from their place for a long time now. They set out from the stable before lunch, and there were still no passengers. Now evening darkness is descending on the city. The paleness of the lamps' flames gives way to bright colors, and the street commotion becomes noisier.

"Cabby, to Vyborgskaya!" Iona hears. "Cabby!"

Iona gives a start and sees through his snow-crusted eyelashes an officer in a greatcoat with a hood.

"To Vyborgskaya!" the officer repeats. "Are you asleep, or what? To Vyborgskaya!"

As a sign of agreement Iona gives a tug at the reins, which makes layers of snow pour down from the horse's back and his own shoulders . . . The officer gets into the sledge. The cabby smacks his lips, stretches his neck like a swan, rises a little, and, more from habit than from need, brandishes his whip. The little nag also stretches her neck, bends her stick-like legs, and hesitantly sets off . . .

"Watch out, you spook!" Iona at once hears a shout from the dark swaying mass behind him. "Where the hell are you going? Keep r-r-right!"

"You don't know how to drive! Keep right!" the officer says angrily. A carriage driver curses; a passerby, who was crossing the street and bumped into the nag's muzzle with his shoulder, glares spitefully and brushes the snow from his sleeve. Iona fidgets on the box, as if on pins and needles, his elbows stick out in all directions, and he rolls his eyes crazily, as if he does not understand where he is or why.

"What scoundrels they all are!" the officer jokes. "They try so hard to bump into you or fall under the horse. It's a conspiracy."

Iona turns to look at his passenger and moves his lips . . . He apparently wants to say something, but nothing comes from his throat except some wheezing.

"What?" asks the officer.

Iona's mouth twists into a smile; he strains his throat and says hoarsely:

"You see, sir, it's . . . my son died this week."

"Hm! . . . What did he die of?"

Iona turns his whole body around to the passenger and says:

"Who knows? Must have been a fever . . . He lay in the hospital for three days and died . . . God's will."

"Turn, damn it!" comes out of the dark. "Are you cracked or something, you old dog? Keep your eyes open!"

"Drive on, drive on . . . ," says the passenger. "Like this it'll be tomorrow before we get there. Speed it up!"

Again the cabby stretches his neck, rises a little, and with heavy grace brandishes the whip. Several times later he turns to look at his passenger, but the man has closed his eyes and apparently is not in the mood to listen. After letting him off at Vyborgskaya, he stops by a tavern, bends over on the box, and again does not stir . . . Wet snow again paints him and his little nag white. An hour goes by, another . . .

Down the sidewalk, stomping their galoshes and arguing loudly, come three young men: two of them are tall and thin, the third is short and hunchbacked.

"Cabby, to the Police Bridge!" the hunchback shouts in a croaking voice. "Three of us . . . twenty kopecks!"

Iona gives a tug at the reins and clucks his tongue. Twenty kopecks is not a fair price, but he does not care about the price . . . A rouble, five kopecks—it is all the same to him now, as long as there are passengers . . . The young men, jostling and foul-mouthed, come up to the sledge and all three try to get in at once. A discussion begins on the question: Which two will sit while the third one stands? After much arguing, fussing, and reproaching, they come to the decision that the hunchback should stand, being the shortest of them.

"Well, get moving!" the hunchback croaks, taking his place and breathing down Iona's neck. "Whip her up! Some hat you've got there, brother! Couldn't find a worse one in all Petersburg . . ."

"Haw-haw . . . haw-haw . . ." Iona guffaws. "So it is . . ."

"Well, Mister 'So-it-is,' get moving! Are you going to drive like this all the way? Yes? How about getting it in the neck? . . ."

"My head's splitting . . ." one of the tall ones says. "Yesterday at the Dukmasovs' Vaska and me together drank four bottles of cognac."

"I don't get all this lying!" the other tall one says angrily. "He lies like a trooper."

"God punish me, it's true . . ."

"It's as true as a louse can cough."

"Haw-haw!" Iona grins. "Such mer-r-ry gentlemen!"

"Pah, devil take you! . . ." The hunchback is indignant. "Will you get moving, or not, you old cholera? Is this any way to drive? Beat her with the whip! Go on, damn it! Go on! Whip her up!"

Behind him Iona feels the fidgeting body and quavering voice of the hunchback. He hears the abuse aimed at him, sees people, and the feeling of solitude slowly begins to lift from his chest. The hunchback keeps pouring out abuse until he chokes on a whimsical six-story curse and goes off into a coughing fit. The tall ones start talking about some Nadezhda Petrovna. Iona turns to look at them. Seizing on a brief pause, he turns once again and mutters:

"This week . . . it's . . . my son died on me!"

"We'll all die . . . ," sighs the hunchback, wiping his mouth after the coughing. "Well, move it, move it! Gentlemen, I decidedly cannot ride like this! When will he get us there?"

"Urge him on a little . . . in the neck!"

"You hear, you old cholera? It's a real drubbing for you! . . . No ceremony with your kind, or it's better to go on foot! . . . Do you hear, you dragon? Or do you spit on what we say?"

And Iona hears, more than he feels, the sound of a slap.

"Haw-haw . . . ," he laughs. "Such merry gentlemen . . . God grant you good health!"

"Are you married, cabby?" asks a tall one.

"Me? Haw-haw . . . mer-r-ry gentlemen! Nowadays I've got one wife—the damp earth . . . Ha-ho-ho . . . The grave, that is! . . . My son's dead, but I'm alive . . . It's a wonder, death mixed up the doors . . . Instead of coming to me, she went to my son . . ."

And Iona turns to tell them how his son died, but here the hunchback gives a sigh of relief and announces that, thank God, they have finally arrived. Having received his twenty kopecks, Iona follows the revelers with his eyes for a long time, until they disappear into a dark entryway. Again he is alone, and again silence comes down on him . . . The anguish that had subsided in him for a short time appears again and swells his chest with still greater force. Iona's martyred eyes roam anxiously over the crowds flitting by on both sides of the street: might he find among these thousands of people just one who would hear him out? But the crowds rush by, noticing neither him nor his anguish . . . The anguish is enormous, it knows no bounds. If Iona's chest were to burst and his anguish to pour out, it would probably flood the whole world, and yet it cannot be seen. It has managed to fit itself into such an insignificant shell that it is invisible in broad daylight . . .

Iona sees a street sweeper with a sack and decides to strike up a conversation with him.

"What time is it now, my dear fellow?" he asks.

"Going on ten . . . What are you stopping here for? Drive on!"

Iona drives on a few steps, bends over, and gives himself up to his anguish . . . By now he considers it useless to reach out to people. But before five minutes go by, he straightens himself, shakes his head, as if feeling a sharp pain, and tugs at the reins . . . He cannot bear it.

"To the stable," he thinks. "To the stable!"

And the little nag, as if understanding his thought, sets off at a trot. An hour and a half later, Iona is already sitting by the big, dirty stove. On the stove,[2] on the floor, on the benches people are snoring. The air is "cooped up" and stuffy . . . Iona looks at the sleeping people, scratches himself, and is sorry that he has come home so early . . .

"Didn't even make enough to buy oats," he thinks. "That's where the anguish comes from. A man who knows his business . . . who has enough to eat himself and whose horse has enough to eat, is always at peace . . ."

In one corner a young cabby gets up, grunts sleepily, and reaches for the bucket of water.

"Thirsty?" asks Iona.

"Right enough!"

"So . . . Good health to you . . . You know, brother, my son died . . . Did you hear? This week, in the hospital . . . Some story!"

Iona looks for what effect his words will make, but he sees nothing. The young man has covered his head and is already asleep. The old man sighs and scratches himself . . . He wanted to talk, as much as the young man wanted to drink. Soon it will be a week since his son died, but he has not yet had a proper talk with anybody . . . He needs to have a sensible, detailed talk . . . He needs to tell how his son fell ill, how he suffered, what he said before dying, how he died . . . To describe the funeral, and going to the hospital to fetch the deceased man's clothes. He had left his daughter Anisya in the village . . . He needs to talk about her, too . . . Does he lack for anything to talk about now? The listener should gasp, sigh, murmur something . . . It is still better to talk with women. They may be fools, but they howl after a couple of words.

"I'll go have a look at the horse," thinks Iona. "There's always time enough to sleep . . . I'll sleep all right . . ."

He gets dressed and goes to the stable where his horse is standing. He thinks about oats, about hay, about the weather . . . When he is alone, he cannot think about his son . . . He could talk about him with somebody, but to think about him and picture his image to himself is unbearably frightening . . .

"Chewing away?" Iona asks his horse, seeing the gleam of her eyes. "Go on, chew . . . Since we haven't earned enough for oats, we'll eat hay . . . Yes . . . I'm too old to be driving . . . My son should be driving, not me . . . He was a real true cabby . . . It was for him to live . . ."

Iona falls silent for a while, then goes on:

"So it is, my little mare . . . Kuzma Ionych is no more . . . Gave up the ghost . . . Just died for nothing . . . Now, suppose you have a little colt, and you're that little colt's own mother . . . And suddenly suppose that same little colt gives up the ghost . . . It's sad, isn't it?"

The nag chews, listens, and breathes on her master's hands . . .

Iona gets carried away and tells her everything . . .

1886

A COMMOTION

AFTER A STROLL, Mashenka Pavletskaya, a girl who had just finished her courses at boarding school, came back to the Kushkins' house, where she lived as a governess, to find an extraordinary commotion. The porter Mikhailo, who opened the door for her, was agitated and red as a lobster.

Noise came from upstairs.

"The mistress is probably having a fit . . . ," thought Mashenka, "or she's quarreled with her husband . . ."

In the front hall and in the corridor she met housemaids. One of the maids was weeping. Then Mashenka saw the master himself, Nikolai Sergeich, a short man, not yet old, with a flabby face and a big bald spot, come running out of her room. He was red in the face. His body was twitching . . . He passed by the governess without noticing her, and, raising his arms, exclaimed:

"Oh, how terrible this is! How tactless! How stupid! Wild! Disgusting!"

Mashenka went into her room, and here for the first time in her life she experienced in all its keenness that feeling so familiar to dependent, uncomplaining people who live by the bread of the rich and well-born. In her room a search was going on. The mistress, Fedosya Vassilyevna, a buxom, broad-shouldered lady with bushy black eyebrows, bareheaded and angular, with a scarcely noticeable little moustache and red hands, in face and manners more resembling a simple kitchen maid, was standing by the governess's desk, putting balls of yarn, scraps of cloth and paper, back into her work bag . . . Obviously the governess's appearance was unexpected, because, turning and seeing her pale, astonished face, the mistress became slightly embarrassed and murmured:

"*Pardon*, I . . . I accidentally spilled . . . caught it on my sleeve . . ."

And saying something more, Madame Kushkin rustled her train and left. Mashenka cast an astonished glance around her room and, understanding nothing, having no idea what to think, hunched her shoulders and went cold with fear . . . What had Fedosya Vassilyevna been looking for in her bag? If indeed, as she said, she had caught it on her sleeve and spilled things, why then had Nikolai Sergeich come running out of the room so red-faced and agitated? Why was one of the desk drawers pulled slightly open? The piggy bank, in which the governess put small change and old stamps, had been unlocked. But whoever had unlocked it had not managed to lock it again and had only left scratches around the lock. The bookshelf, the desktop, the bed—everything bore fresh traces of a search. The linen basket, too. The linen was neatly folded, but not in the order Mashenka had left it in when she went out for her stroll. It meant the search had been a real one, quite real, but why, for what? What had happened? Mashenka recalled the porter's agitation, the commotion that was still going on, the weeping maid; did it all have to do with the just-performed search? Was she mixed up in something terrible? Mashenka turned pale and, cold all over, sank onto the linen basket.

A maid came into the room.

"Liza, do you know why they . . . searched me?" asked the governess.

"The lady's two-thousand-rouble brooch has disappeared . . . ," said Liza.

"Yes, but why search me?"

"Everybody got searched, miss. They searched me all over . . . They stripped us all naked and searched us . . . And me, miss, I swear to God . . . Never mind the lady's brooch, I never even went near her dressing table. I'll say the same to the police."

"But . . . why search me?" the governess went on in perplexity.

"I'm telling you, the brooch got stolen . . . The lady went through everything with her own hands. She even searched the porter Mikhailo. A real shame! Nikolai Sergeich just stares and clucks like a hen. And you're trembling for nothing, miss. She didn't find anything in your room. Since you didn't take the brooch, you've got nothing to be afraid of."

"But it's mean, Liza . . . it's insulting!" said Mashenka, choking with indignation. "It's vile, base! What right does she have to suspect me and rummage through my things?"

"You live among strangers, miss," sighed Liza. "You're from gentlefolk, but all the same . . . it's as if you're a servant . . . It's not like living with papa and mama . . ."

Mashenka collapsed on her bed and wept bitterly. Never before had she been so violated, never before had she been so deeply insulted as now . . . She, a well-brought-up, sensitive girl, a teacher's daughter, had been suspected of theft, had been searched like a streetwalker! It seemed impossible to think up a worse insult. And to this feeling of offense was added an oppressive fear: what now?! All sorts of absurdities filled her head. If it was possible to suspect her of theft, it meant she could now be arrested, stripped naked and searched, then led down the street under guard, put in a dark, cold cell with mice and woodlice, exactly like the one in which Princess Tarakanova[1] was confined. Who will stand up for her? Her parents live far away in the provinces; they have no money to come to her. She is alone in the capital, as in an empty field, with no relations or acquaintances. They can do whatever they like with her.

"I'll run to all the judges and defense attorneys . . . ," Mashenka thought, trembling. "I'll explain to them, swear an oath . . . They'll believe that I couldn't be a thief!"

Mashenka remembered that in the basket under the linen were some sweets, which, by an old boarding-school habit, she had put in her pocket at dinnertime and brought to her room. The thought that this little secret was now known to the masters threw her into a fever, she felt ashamed, and from all of it together—fear, shame, and offense—her heart began to beat hard, so that she felt it in her temples, her hands, the pit of her stomach.

"Come and eat, please!" they called Mashenka.

"Shall I go or not?"

Mashenka straightened her hair, wiped her face with a wet towel, and went to the dining room. There the dinner had already begun . . . At one end of the table sat Fedosya Vassilyevna, pompous, with a stupid, serious face; at the other—Nikolai Sergeich. On the sides sat the guests and the children. Dinner was served by two lackeys in tailcoats and white gloves. Everyone knew that there was commotion in the house, that the mistress was in grief, and they kept silent. All that could be heard was chewing and the clink of spoons against plates.

The mistress herself started the conversation.

"What do we have for the third course?" she asked the lackey in a soulful, suffering voice.

"*Esturgeon à la Russe!*"[2] the lackey replied.

"I ordered it, Fenya . . . ," Nikolai Sergeich hastily put in. "I felt like having fish. If you don't like it, *ma chère*, let them not serve it. I did it just . . . by the way . . ."

Fedosya Vassilyevna disliked food that she did not order herself, and now her eyes filled with tears.

"Well, let's not get upset," Mamikov, her personal physician, said in a sweet voice, touching her hand slightly and smiling just as sweetly. "We're nervous enough without that. Let's forget about the brooch! Good health is worth more than two thousand!"

"I'm not sorry about the two thousand!" the mistress replied, and a big tear rolled down her cheek. "I'm shocked by the fact itself! I will not suffer thieves in my house. I'm not sorry, not sorry about anything, but to steal from me—it's such ingratitude! That's how they repay me for my kindness . . ."

They all looked down at their plates, but it seemed to Mashenka that, after the mistress's words, they all glanced at her. She suddenly felt a lump in her throat, burst into tears, and pressed a handkerchief to her face.

"*Pardon,*" she murmured. "I can't. I have a headache. I'll leave."

And she got up from the table, awkwardly scraping the chair, which embarrassed her still more, and quickly went out.

"God knows what's going on!" said Nikolai Sergeich, wincing. "As if there was any need to search her room! It's really so . . . inappropriate."

"I'm not saying she took the brooch," Fedosya Vassilyevna said, "but can you vouch for her? I confess, I have little faith in these educated poor folk."

"Really, Fenya, it's inappropriate . . . Forgive me, Fenya, but by law you have no right to carry out searches."

"I don't know your laws. I only know that my brooch has disappeared, that's all. And I will find that brooch!" She banged her fork on her plate, and her eyes flashed wrathfully. "Eat now and don't interfere in my affairs."

Nikolai Sergeich meekly lowered his eyes and sighed. Meanwhile Mashenka came to her room and collapsed on the bed. She was no longer afraid or ashamed, but she was tormented by a strong desire to go and give this callous, this arrogant, stupid, lucky woman a slap in the face.

She lay there, breathing into the pillow and dreaming of how good it would be to go now, buy the most expensive brooch, and throw it in this female tyrant's face. Or if God should grant that Fedosya Vassilyevna be ruined, go out into the world and learn all the horror of poverty and the servile condition, and the insulted Mashenka should give her alms. Oh, if only she could receive a rich inheritance, buy a carriage, and drive noisily past her windows, making her envious!

But these were all dreams; in reality only one thing remained for her—to leave quickly, not to stay there even an hour longer. True, it was frightening to lose her job, to go back to her parents, who had nothing, but what was she to do? Mashenka could no longer bear the sight of her mistress, nor her little room; it felt stifling there, and spooky. Fedosya Vassilyevna, obsessed with her ailments and her imaginary aristocracy, disgusted her so much that it seemed everything in the world became coarse and unsightly because this woman lived in it. Mashenka jumped up from the bed and started to pack.

"May I come in?" Nikolai Sergeich asked outside the door. He had approached the door inaudibly and spoke in a quiet, gentle voice. "May I?"

"Come in."

He came in and stopped by the door. His gaze was dull, and his red little nose glistened. He had drunk beer after dinner, and it could be noticed by his gait and his weak, limp hands.

"What's this?" he said, pointing to the basket.

"I'm packing. Forgive me, Nikolai Sergeich, but I can no longer remain in your house. I have been deeply insulted by this search!"

"I understand . . . Only you needn't do this . . . Why? So you've been searched . . . What is it to you? There's no harm done."

Mashenka said nothing and went on packing. Nikolai Sergeich plucked at his moustache, as if thinking up what else to say, and went on in an ingratiating voice:

"I understand, of course, but you must be charitable. You know my wife is nervous, hysterical; you mustn't judge her severely . . ."

Mashenka said nothing.

"If you're so insulted," Nikolai Sergeich went on, "very well then, I'm ready to apologize to you. I apologize."

Mashenka made no reply, and only bent lower over her suitcase. This haggard, irresolute man meant precisely nothing in the house. He played the pathetic role of a sponger and a hanger-on even for the servants; and his apology also meant nothing.

"Hm . . . So you're silent? It's not enough for you? In that case I apologize for my wife. In my wife's name . . . She behaved tactlessly, I acknowledge it as a gentleman . . ."

Nikolai Sergeich paced up and down, sighed, and went on.

"So you also want me to have pangs here, in my heart . . . You want me to suffer remorse . . ."

"I know you're not to blame, Nikolai Sergeich," said Mashenka, looking him straight in the face with her big, tearful eyes. "Why should you suffer?"

"Of course . . . But anyhow . . . don't leave . . . I beg you."

Mashenka shook her head negatively. Nikolai Sergeich stopped by the window and started drumming on the glass.

"For me such misunderstandings are sheer torture," he said. "Should I go on my knees before you, or what? Your pride has been insulted, and here you are weeping, preparing to leave, but I also have my pride, and you don't spare it. Or do you want me to tell you something I wouldn't say even at confession? Do you want me to? Listen, do you want me to confess something I wouldn't confess to even on my deathbed?"

Mashenka said nothing.

"I took my wife's brooch!" Nikolai Sergeich said quickly. "Are you pleased now? Satisfied? Yes, I . . . took it . . . Only, of course, I'm counting on your discretion . . . For God's sake, not a word to anyone, not half a hint!"

Mashenka, astonished and frightened, went on packing; she grabbed her things, crumpled them, and stuffed them haphazardly into the suitcase and basket. Now, after Nikolai Sergeich's candid confession, she could not stay even another minute, and she no longer understood how she could have lived in this house before.

"Nothing surprising . . . ," Nikolai Sergeich went on after a brief silence. "An ordinary story. I need money, and she . . . doesn't give me any. This house and everything in it was acquired by my father, Marya Andreevna! It's all mine! And the brooch belonged to my mother, and . . . it's all mine! And she took it, she made it all hers . . . I can't take her to court, you must agree . . . I ask you earnestly, forgive and . . . and stay. *Tout comprendre, tout pardonner.*[3] Will you stay?"

"No!" Mashenka said resolutely, starting to tremble. "Leave me, I beg you."

"Well, God help you." Nikolai Sergeich sighed, sitting down on a little stool by the suitcase. "I confess I like people who are still capable of being insulted, disdainful, and all that. I could spend an eternity gazing at your indignant face . . . Well, so you won't stay? I understand . . . That's how it ought to be . . . Yes, of course . . . Good for you, but for me it's—who-o-a! Not a step outside this cellar. I could go to one of our country estates, but there are all my wife's crooks sitting everywhere . . . managers, agronomists, devil take them. They mortgage, remortgage . . . No fishing, no stepping on the grass, no breaking branches."

"Nikolai Sergeich!" Fedosya Vassilyevna's voice came from the drawing room. "Agnia, call the master!"

"So you won't stay?" asked Nikolai Sergeich, quickly getting up and going to the door. "Why not stay, by God. I'd come and see you some evenings . . . We'd talk. Eh? Stay! You'll leave and there won't be a single human face left in the whole house. It's terrible!"

Nikolai Sergeich's pale, haggard face pleaded, but Mashenka shook her head negatively, and he waved his hand and left.

Half an hour later she was already on the road.

1886

THE WITCH

NIGHT WAS FALLING. The sexton Savely Gykin lay at home in the chuch warden's hut on an enormous bed and did not sleep, though he had the habit of falling asleep at the same time as the chickens. From under one end of a greasy quilt sewn together from motley cotton scraps peeked his stiff red hair, from the other stuck his big, long-unwashed feet. He was listening . . . His little hut was built into the fence, and its only window looked onto the field. And in the field a veritable war was going on. It was hard to figure out who was hounding who to death and for whose sake this calamity had brewed up in nature, but, judging by the ceaseless, sinister din, someone was having a very hard time of it. Some invincible force was chasing someone around the field, rampaging through the forest and over the church roof, angrily beating its fists on the window, ripping and tearing, and something vanquished wept and howled . . . Pitiful weeping was heard now outside the window, now over the roof, now on the stove. No call for help could be heard in it, but anguish, the awareness that it was too late, there was no salvation. Snowdrifts were covered by a thin crust of ice; teardrops trembled on them and on the trees, and along the roads and paths flowed a dark swill of mud and melting snow. In short, on earth there was a thaw, but the sky, through the dark night, did not see that and with all its might poured flakes of new snow onto the thawing ground. And the wind caroused like a drunk man . . . It would not let the snow settle on the ground and whirled it through the darkness as it pleased.

Gykin listened to this music and frowned. The thing was that he knew, or at least guessed, what all this racket outside the window was about and whose handiwork it was.

"I kno-o-ow!" he murmured, shaking his finger under the covers at somebody. "I know everything!"

On a stool by the window sat his wife, Raissa Nilovna. A tin lamp, standing on another stool, timorously, as if not believing in its own power, cast a thin, flickering light over her broad shoulders, the beautiful, appetizing reliefs of her body, the thick braid that reached to the ground. She was sewing burlap sacks. Her hands moved swiftly, but her whole body, the expression of her eyes, eyebrows, plump lips, white neck, were still, immersed in the monotonous mechanical work, and seemed to be asleep. Only occasionally she raised her head, to give her tired neck a rest, glanced for a moment at the window, outside which a blizzard raged, and then bent again over the burlap. Neither desire, nor sorrow, nor joy—nothing expressed itself on her beautiful face with its upturned nose and dimpled cheeks. Just so a beautiful fountain expresses nothing when it is not spouting.

But here she finished one sack, flung it aside, and, stretching sweetly, rested her dull, fixed gaze on the window . . . Teardrops flowed down the windowpanes and short-lived snowflakes dotted them with white. A snowflake would land on the pane, glance at the woman, and melt . . .

"Go to bed," the sexton muttered. His wife said nothing. But suddenly her eyelashes stirred and attention flickered in her eyes. Savely, who had been watching the expression of her face all the while from under the blanket, stuck his head out and asked:

"What is it?"

"Nothing . . . Seems like somebody's driving . . . ," his wife replied softly.

The sexton threw off the blanket with his hands and feet, knelt on the bed, and looked dully at his wife. The lamp's timid light shone on his hairy, pockmarked face and flitted over his coarse, matted head.

"Do you hear it?" asked his wife. Through the monotonous howling of the blizzard he heard a barely audible, high-pitched, ringing moan, like the buzzing of a mosquito when it wants to land on your cheek and is angry at being prevented.

"It's the postman . . . ," Savely muttered, sitting back on his heels.

The post road lay two miles from the church. In windy weather, when it blew from the road towards the church, the inhabitants of the house could hear a jingling.

"Lord, who wants to drive in such weather!" the sexton's wife sighed.

"It's a government job. Like it or not, you have to go . . ." The moan lingered in the air and died away.

"It passed by!" said Savely, lying down.

But he had not managed to cover himself with the blanket before the distinct sound of a bell reached his ears. The sexton glanced anxiously at his wife, jumped off the bed, and started waddling back and forth beside the stove. The sound of the bell went on for a little while and died away again, as if broken off.

"I can't hear it . . . ," the sexton muttered, stopping and squinting at his wife. But just then the wind rapped on the window, bearing the high-pitched, ringing moan . . . Savely turned pale, grunted, and again his bare feet slapped against the floor.

"The postman's going in circles!" he croaked, casting a spiteful sidelong glance at his wife. "Do you hear? The postman's going in circles! . . . I . . . I know! As if I . . . don't understand!" he muttered. "I know everything, curse you!"

"What do you know?" his wife asked softly, not taking her eyes from the window.

"I know this, that it's all your doing, you she-devil! It's your doing, curse you! This blizzard, and the postman going in circles . . . You caused it all! You!"

"You're raving, you silly man," his wife observed calmly.

"I noticed it about you long ago! When we were just married, in the first days, I saw you had a bitch's blood in you!"

"Pah!" Raissa was surprised, shrugged, and crossed herself. "Cross yourself, too, dimwit!"

"A witch, you're a witch!" Savely went on in a hollow, tearful voice, hastily blowing his nose on the hem of his shirt. "Though you're my wife, though you're also of the clerical estate, I'll even tell at confession what you are . . . What else? Lord, save us and have mercy on us! Last year on the day of the prophet Daniel and the three holy youths,[1] there was a blizzard and—what then? A foreman stopped by to get warm. Then on the day of St. Alexei the man of God,[2] the ice on the river broke up, and the constable dropped by . . . He spent the whole night here jabbering with you, curse him, and when he appeared in the morning, and I looked at him, he had black rings around his eyes and his cheeks were all sunken! Eh? During the Dormition fast[3] there were thunderstorms twice, and both times the huntsman came to spend the night. I saw it all, curse him! All! Oh, you've turned red as a crayfish! Hah!"

"You didn't see anything . . ."

"Oh, no! And this winter, before Christmas, on the day of the Ten Martyrs of Crete,[4] when a blizzard went on all day and night . . . Remember?—when the marshal's clerk lost his way and wound up here, the dog . . . And what were you tempted by! Phoo, a clerk! It wasn't worth riling up God's weather on his account! A puny devil, a runt, a mere speck, his mug all in blackheads, his neck bent . . . Maybe if he was handsome, but him—pah—a satan!"

The sexton caught his breath, wiped his lips, and listened. There was no bell to be heard, but the wind tore over the roof, and in the darkness outside the window something clanged again.

"And now, too!" Savely went on. "It's not for nothing this postman is circling! Spit in my eye if the postman isn't looking for you! Oh, the devil knows his business, he's a good helper! He'll make him circle and circle and lead him here. I kno-o-ow! I see-e-e! You can't hide it, you devil's chatterbox, you fiend's lust! As soon as the blizzard started, I immediately understood your thoughts."

"What a dimwit!" his wife smirked. "So, to your foolish mind, I can cause bad weather?"

"Hm . . . Go on, smirk! You or not you, only I notice as soon as your blood begins to act up, there's bad weather, and once there's bad weather, whatever madman is around comes racing here. It happens each time. So it's you!"

For greater persuasiveness, the sexton put a finger to his brow, closed his left eye, and said in a sing-song voice:

"O, madness! O, Judas's fiendishness! If you are indeed a human being and not a witch, you should have thought in your head: What if those were not a foreman, a huntsman, or a clerk, but the devil in their guise! Eh? You'd have thought that."

"How stupid you are, Savely!" his wife sighed, looking at him with pity. "When my papa was alive and lived here, all sorts of people used to come to him to be treated for ague: from the village, from the settlements, from the Armenian farmsteads. It seems they came every day, and nobody called them devils. And with us, if somebody comes once to warm up in bad weather, you, you stupid man, start wondering and getting all sorts of ideas."

Savely was affected by his wife's logic. He stood with his legs apart, his head bent, thinking. He was not yet firmly convinced of his suppositions, and his wife's sincere, indifferent tone threw him off completely, but, even so, after thinking a little, he shook his head and said:

"It's not old men or some sort of bandylegs, it's all young ones that are asking to spend the night . . . Why's that? And they don't just get warm, they play the devil's own games. No, woman, there's no creature in this world slyer than your womankind. Of true reason there's none in you, less than in a starling, but of demonic slyness— o-o-oh!—Queen of Heaven, save us! There, the postman's ringing! The blizzard had only just begun when I already knew all your thoughts! You witched it all up, you spider!"

"Why are you badgering me, curse you?" His wife lost all patience. "Why are you badgering me, you beast?"

"I'm badgering you because if, God forbid, something happens tonight . . . you listen! . . . If something happens, tomorrow at the crack of dawn I'll go to Father Nikodim in Dyadkino and tell him everything. Thus and so, I'll say, Father Nikodim, mercifully forgive me, but she's a witch. Why? Hm . . . you want to know why? All right . . . Thus and so . . . And woe to you, woman! You'll be punished not only at the Last Judgment, but also in this earthly life! It's not for nothing there are prayers against your kind in the service book."

Suddenly there was a knocking on the window, so loud and unusual that Savely turned pale and crouched down in fear. His wife jumped up and also turned pale.

"For God's sake, let us in to warm up!" A quavering, low bass was heard. "Is anyone there? Be so kind! We've lost our way!"

"And who are you?" asked the sexton's wife, afraid to look out the window.

"The postmen!" answered another voice.

"Your devilry wasn't in vain!" Savely waved his hand. "There it is! The truth's mine . . . Watch out now!"

The sexton bounced twice in front of the bed, fell onto the mattress, and, breathing angrily, turned his face to the wall. Soon there was a draft of cold air on his back. The door creaked, and a tall human figure appeared on the threshold, covered with snow from head to foot. Behind him flashed another, also white . . .

"Shall I bring the pouches in?" the second one asked in a hoarse bass.

"We can't leave them there!" Having said this, the first began to unwind his bashlyk, and, not waiting until it was undone, tore it from his head along with the visored cap and angrily flung it towards the stove. Then he pulled off his coat, threw it the same way, and, without any greeting, paced up and down the hut. He was a blond young postman in a shabby uniform jacket and dirty reddish boots. Having warmed himself by walking, he sat down at the table, stretched his dirty feet towards the pouches, and propped his head on his fist. His pale face with red blotches bore the signs of recent pain and fear. Distorted by anger, with fresh traces of physical and moral suffering, with melting snow on its eyebrows, moustache, and rounded beard, it was handsome.

"A dog's life!" the postman growled, passing his gaze over the walls as if not believing he was in warmth. "We nearly perished. If it hadn't been for your light, I don't know what would have happened . . . And devil knows when all this will end! There's no end to this dog's life! Where have we come to?" he asked, lowering his voice and glancing up at the sexton's wife.

"To Gulyaevo Knoll, General Kalinovsky's estate," the woman replied, rousing herself and blushing.

"Hear that, Stepan?" The postman turned to the coachman, who got stuck in the doorway with a big leather pouch on his back. "We've made it to Gulyaevo Knoll!"

"Yes . . . a long way!" Having uttered this phrase in the form of a hoarse, gasping sigh, the coachman went out and a little later brought in another, smaller pouch, then went out again and this time brought in the postman's saber on a wide belt, resembling in form that long, flat sword with which Judith is portrayed on popular prints at the bedside of Holofernes. Having placed the pouches along the wall, he went to the entryway, sat down, and lit his pipe.

"Maybe you'd like some tea after the road?" the sexton's wife asked.

"No tea drinking for us!" the postman frowned. "We've got to warm up quickly and go, otherwise we'll be late for the mail train. We'll stay for ten minutes and then be on our way. Only be so good as to show us the road . . ."

"It's God's punishment, this weather!" sighed the sexton's wife.

"M-m, yes . . . And who are you, then?"

"Us? Local people, attached to the church . . . Of the clerical estate . . . That's my husband lying there! Savely, stand up, come and say hello! There used to be a parish here, but a year and a half ago it was abolished. Of course, when the masters lived here, there were people around, it was worth having a parish, but now, without the masters, judge for yourselves, how can the clergy live, if the nearest village is Markovka, and it's three miles away! Savely's retired now and . . . is a sort of watchman. He's charged with watching over the church . . ."

And here the postman learned that if Savely were to go to the general's wife and ask for a note to his grace the archbishop, he would be given a good post; that he does not go to the general's wife because he is lazy and afraid of people.

"After all, we're from the clerical estate . . . ," the sexton's wife added.

"What do you live on?" asked the postman.

"There's haymaking and vegetable gardens that go with the church. Only we get very little from it . . . ," sighed the sexton's wife. "Father Nikodim from Dyadkino has a greedy eye. He serves here on Saint Nicholas in the summer and Saint Nicholas in the winter,[5] and takes almost all of it for that. There's nobody to defend us."

"Lies!" Savely croaked. "Father Nikodim is a saintly soul and a bright light of the Church, and if he takes, it's according to the rules!"

"What an angry one you've got!" smiled the postman. "Have you been married long?"

"It'll be three years come this Forgiveness Sunday.[6] My papa used to be the sexton here, and when it came time for him to die, he wanted to keep the place for me, so he went to the consistory and asked that some unmarried sexton be sent here. And I married him."

"Aha, so you killed two flies with one swat!" the postman said, looking at Savely's back. "Got a post and took a wife."

Savely twitched his leg impatiently and moved closer to the wall. The postman got up from the table, stretched, and sat on the mail pouch. Having thought a little, he felt the pouches with his hand, moved the sword to another place, and stretched out, one leg hanging on the floor.

"A dog's life . . . ," he muttered, putting his hands behind his head and closing his eyes. "I wouldn't wish such a life even on a wicked Tartar."

Soon silence fell. Only Savely could be heard puffing and the now sleeping postman breathing rhythmically and slowly, emitting at each exhalation a thick, prolonged "k-kh-kh-kh . . ." From time to time some little wheel squeaked in his throat and a twitching leg brushed against the pouch.

Savely stirred under the blanket and slowly turned over. His wife sat on the stool, her cheeks pressed between her palms, and gazed at the postman's face. Her gaze was fixed, as of someone surprised or frightened.

"Well, what are you staring for?" Savely whispered angrily.

"What is it to you? Lie there!" replied his wife, not taking her eyes from the blond head.

Savely angrily exhaled all the air from his chest and turned abruptly to the wall. After some three minutes, he again stirred restlessly, knelt on his bed, and, propping himself on the pillow, looked sidelong at his wife. She was still unmoving and gazed at the guest. Her cheeks were pale, and her gaze was now lit with some strange fire. The sexton grunted, slid off the bed on his stomach, went up to the postman, and covered his face with a handkerchief.

"Why did you do that?" asked his wife.

"So the light doesn't shine in his eyes."

"Just put it out, then!"

Savely looked mistrustfully at his wife, thrust his lips towards the lamp, but at once thought better of it and clasped his hands.

"Well, isn't that the devil's own cunning?" he exclaimed. "Eh? Well, is there any creature more cunning than womankind?"

"Ah, you long-skirted satan!" his wife hissed, wincing with vexation. "Just you wait!" And, settling herself more comfortably, she again stared at the postman. Never mind that his face was covered. She was interested not so much in the face as in the general look, the novelty of the man. His chest was broad, powerful, his hands handsome, fine, and his muscular, shapely legs were more handsome and masculine than Savely's two "stubs." There was even no comparison.

"Maybe I am a long-skirted satan," Savely said, after standing there a little while, "but they have no business sleeping here. Yes . . . They're on official business, we'll be answerable if we keep them here. You deliver mail, so go and deliver it, don't sleep . . . Hey, you!" Savely shouted into the entryway. "You, coachman, what's your name? Shall I show you the way out? Get up, you can't sleep on the job!" And coming unhinged, Savely jumped over to the postman and pulled him by the sleeve.

"Hey, your honor! If it's go, it's go; if not, then . . . It's no good sleeping."

The postman gave a start, sat up, passed a dull gaze around the cottage, and lay back down.

"When are you going to go?" Savely rattled on, pulling him by the sleeve. "The mail's got to be delivered in good time, that's what it's for, do you hear? I'll see you off."

The postman opened his eyes. Warmed up and listless from the first sweet sleep, not yet fully awake, he saw as in a fog the sexton's wife's white neck and her fixed, unctuous gaze, closed his eyes and smiled as if for him it was all a dream.

"Well, where can you go in such weather!" He heard a soft feminine voice. "You might as well go on sleeping to your heart's content."

"And the mail?" Savely became alarmed. "Who'll deliver the mail? Or maybe you're going to deliver it? You?"

The postman opened his eyes again, saw the dimples moving on the woman's cheeks, remembered where he was, and understood Savely.

The thought that he was faced with driving through the cold darkness sent chills from his head all over his body, and he scrunched up.

"We could sleep five little minutes more," he yawned. "We're late anyway."

"And maybe we'll get there just in time!" a voice came from the entryway. "With any luck the train will also be late."

The postman got up and, stretching sweetly, began to put his coat on. Savely, seeing that the visitors were getting ready to leave, even snickered with pleasure.

"Help me, will you!" the coachman shouted to him, lifting the pouch from the floor. The sexton ran over, and together they carried the load of mail outside. The postman began to disentangle the knot of his bashlyk. And the sexton's wife peered into his eyes as if she were about to get into his soul.

"You could have some tea . . . ," she said.

"I wouldn't mind . . . ," he agreed, "but they're all ready. We're late as it is."

"Why don't you stay!" she whispered, lowering her eyes and touching his sleeve.

The postman finally undid the knot and hesitantly threw the bashlyk over his elbow. He felt warm standing next to the sexton's wife.

"What a . . . neck . . . you have . . ." And he touched her neck with two fingers. Seeing that there was no resistance, he stroked her neck, her shoulder with his hand . . . "Oh-h, what a . . ."

"You could stay . . . have some tea."

"Where are you putting it? You soggy pancake!" The coachman's voice came from outside. "Put it crosswise."

"You could stay . . . Look how the weather's howling!"

And not yet quite awake, still under the spell of youthful, languorous sleep, the postman was suddenly overcome by a desire for the sake of which one forgets mail pouches, trains . . . everything in the world. Fearfully, as if wishing to flee or hide, he glanced at the door, seized the sexton's wife by the waist, and was already bending down to put out the lamp, when boots stomped in the entryway and the coachman appeared in the doorway . . . Savely peeked over his shoulder. The postman quickly lowered his arms and stood as if in thought.

"Everything's ready!" said the coachman.

The postman stood there for a while, briskly shook his head as if completely awake at last, and followed the coachman. The sexton's wife remained alone.

"So, get in, show us the road!" she heard.

There was a lazy sound of one bell, then of another, and the jingling raced on in a quick, long chain away from the watchman's hut. When it gradually died down, the sexton's wife tore from her place and started pacing nervously from corner to corner. First she was pale, then she turned all red. Her face was distorted by hatred, she gasped for breath, her eyes gleamed with a savage, ferocious anger, and, pacing as in a cage, she resembled a she-tiger frightened by a red-hot iron.

For a moment she stopped and glanced around her room. Almost half of it was taken up by the bed, which went along the whole wall and consisted of a dirty feather mattress, hard gray pillows, a blanket, and various nameless rags. This bed looked like a shapeless, ugly lump, almost the same as the one sticking up on Savely's head whenever he took a fancy to oil his hair. From the bed to the door leading to the cold entryway stretched the dark stove, with pots and hanging rags. Everything, not excluding the just-stepped-out Savely, was utterly dirty, greasy, sooty, so that it was strange to see, in the midst of such surroundings, the white neck and fine, tender skin of a woman. The sexton's wife ran to the bed, stretched out her arms, as if wishing to scatter it all, trample on it, and reduce it to dust; but then, as if afraid to touch the dirt, she jumped back and started pacing again . . .

When Savely returned a couple of hours later, all covered with snow and worn out, she was already lying undressed in bed. Her eyes were closed, but by the small tremors that passed over her face, he guessed that she was not asleep.

On his way home he promised himself to keep silent until the next day and not to touch her, but now he could not help prodding her.

"Your sorcery was wasted: he's gone!" he said with a gleeful grin. His wife was silent; only her chin twitched.

Savely slowly undressed, climbed over his wife, and lay by the wall.

"And tomorrow I'll explain to Father Nikodim what sort of wife you are!" he muttered, curling up. His wife quickly turned to face him and flashed her eyes at him.

"It's enough that you've got a job," she said. "As for a wife, go and look for one in the forest! What kind of wife am I to you, blast you! What a clodpate, what a slug-a-bed they've hung on my neck, God forgive me!"

"All right, all right . . . Sleep!"

"Miserable me!" his wife sobbed. "If it weren't for you, I might have married a merchant, or some nobleman! If it weren't for you, I might love my husband now! And you weren't buried in the snow, you didn't freeze there on the high road, you Herod!"

The sexton's wife wept for a long time. At last she sighed deeply and quieted down. Outside the window, the blizzard went on raging. In the stove, in the chimney, behind all the walls something wept, and to Savely it seemed that it was inside him and in his ears that it wept. Tonight he was finally confirmed in his suppositions about his wife. He no longer doubted that his wife, with the help of unclean powers, controlled the winds and the post roads. But to his greater grief, this mysteriousness, this savage supernatural power endowed the woman who lay beside him with a special, incomprehensible charm that he had never noticed before. Because, in his stupidity, he poeticized her, not noticing it himself, she became as if whiter, smoother, more unapproachable . . .

"Witch!" he said indignantly. "Tphoo, disgusting!"

And yet, having waited until she quieted down and began to breathe evenly, he touched her nape with his finger . . . held her thick braid in his hand. She did not feel it . . . Then he grew bolder and stroked her neck.

"Leave me alone!" she cried and hit the bridge of his nose so hard that sparks flew out of his eyes. The pain in his nose soon went away, but his torment continued.

1886

A Little Joke

A BRIGHT WINTER NOON . . . The air is bitter cold, and Nadenka, who holds on to my arm, has silvery frost all over the curls at her temples and the down on her upper lip. We are standing on a high hill. From our feet to the very bottom stretches a slope, in which the sun looks as if into a mirror. Beside us stands a small sled upholstered in bright red flannel.

"Let's slide down, Nadezhda Petrovna!" I beg her. "Just once! I promise you we'll make it in one piece."

But Nadenka is afraid. The space from her small galoshes to the foot of the icy hill seems to her like a terrible, bottomless abyss. Her heart sinks and her breath stops when she looks down, when I merely suggest getting into the sled; what will happen if she risks plunging into the abyss! She'll die, she'll go out of her mind.

"I beg you!" I say. "You shouldn't be afraid! You know that's just cowardice, faintheartedness!"

Nadenka finally gives in, but I can see by her face that she gives in with fear for her life. I seat her, pale and trembling, in the sled, put my arms around her, and together with her fling myself into the abyss.

The sled flies like a bullet. As we cut through the air it hits our faces, roars, whistles in our ears, rips, pinches painfully in anger, wants to tear our heads from our shoulders. It pushes so that it's hard to breathe. It seems like the devil himself is grabbing us with his paws, roaring and dragging us into hell. The separate things around us merge into one long, swiftly running strip . . . Another moment and it seems we'll perish!

"I love you, Nadya!" I say in a low voice.

The sled gradually slows down, the roaring of the wind and the swishing of the runners are not as frightening now, the heart stops sinking, and we are finally at the bottom. Nadenka is more dead than alive. She's pale, barely able to breathe. I help her to stand up.

"I wouldn't do that again for anything," she says, looking at me, her wide-open eyes filled with terror. "Not for anything in the world! I nearly died!"

A little later she recovers and is now peeking questioningly into my eyes: did I say those four words, or had she just imagined hearing them in the noise of the wind? I stand beside her, smoking and attentively studying my glove.

She leans on my arm, and we walk for a long time around the foot of the hill. The riddle obviously troubles her. Were those words spoken or not? Yes or no? Yes or no? It's a question of pride, honor, life, happiness, a very important question, the most important in the world. Nadenka looks into my face impatiently, sadly, with searching eyes, answers me at random, waits for me to speak. Oh, what play on that sweet face, what play! I see she's struggling with herself, she needs to say something, to ask something, but she can't find the words, she feels awkward, frightened, hindered by joy . . .

"You know what?" she says, not looking at me.

"What?" I ask.

"Let's slide down . . . again."

We climb the steps up the hill. Again I seat the pale, trembling Nadenka in the sled, again we go flying into the terrible abyss, again the wind roars and the runners swish, and again at the swiftest and noisiest moment I say in a low voice:

"I love you, Nadenka!"

When the sled stops, Nadenka looks back at the hill we only just slid down, then peers into my face for a long time, listens to my voice, indifferent and passionless, and her whole little figure, all of it, even her muff and bashlyk, expresses extreme perplexity. And written on her face is:

"What's happening? Who said *those* words? Was it him, or did it only seem so?"

This uncertainty troubles her; she's losing patience. The poor girl doesn't answer my questions, frowns, and is about to burst into tears.

"Shouldn't I take you home?" I ask.

"I . . . I like this sledding," she says, blushing. "Can we do it one more time?"

She "likes" it, and yet, as she gets into the sled, as on the previous occasions, she is pale, trembling, barely able to breathe from fear.

We go down a third time, and I see how she looks me in the face, watches my lips. But I hold a handkerchief to my lips, cough, and when we're halfway down the hill, I manage to bring out:

"I love you, Nadya!"

And the riddle remains a riddle! Nadenka is silent, she's thinking about something . . . I take her home from the sliding hill. She tries to walk slowly and keeps waiting for me to say those words. And I see how her soul suffers, how she tries to keep herself from saying:

"It can't be that the wind said it! And I don't want it to be the wind that said it!"

The next morning I receive a note: "If you go to the sliding hill today, come by for me. N." From that day on, Nadenka and I go to the sliding hill every day, and each time, flying down on the sled, I say the same words in a low voice:

"I love you, Nadya!"

Soon Nadenka gets used to this phrase, as to wine or morphine. She can't live without it. True, to go flying down the hill is as frightening as before, but now fear and danger lend a special allure to the words of love, words that constitute as much of a riddle as before and torment her soul. The suspects are the same two: myself and the wind . . . Which of the two has declared his love for her she doesn't know, but apparently it makes no difference to her; whichever vessel she drinks from makes no difference to her, so long as she gets drunk.

Once at noon I went to the sliding hill alone; mixing with the crowd, I saw Nadenka going to the hill, saw her searching for me with her eyes . . . Then she timidly goes up the steps . . . It's scary to go alone, oh, how scary! She's pale as the snow, trembling, as if she were going to her execution, but she's going, going resolutely, without looking back. She has obviously decided, finally, to try it: will she hear those amazing, sweet words when I'm not there? I see how, pale, mouth open in terror, she climbs into the sled, closes her eyes, and, bidding farewell to this world forever, sets off . . . "Swish-sh-sh . . ." swish the runners. Whether Nadenka hears those words, I don't know . . . I only see how she gets out of the sled, exhausted, weak. And it's clear from her face that she herself doesn't know whether she heard anything or not. Fear, as she was sliding down, robbed her of the ability to hear, to distinguish sounds, to understand . . .

But now comes the spring month of March . . . The sun turns gentler. Our ice hill grows darker, loses its sheen, and finally melts. We stop sledding. Poor Nadenka can't hear those words anywhere now, nor is there anyone to speak them, for there's no wind to be heard, and I am preparing to go to Petersburg—for a long time, probably forever.

Once, a day or two before my departure, in the evening, I'm sitting in the garden, which is separated from the yard where Nadenka lives by a high, nail-studded fence . . . It is still rather cold, there is still snow under the dung heap, the trees are dead, but there is already the smell of spring, and the rooks make a big racket settling for the night. I go up to the fence and look through a crack for a long time. I see Nadenka come out to the porch and fix a sad, anguished gaze on the sky . . . The spring wind blows directly into her pale, mournful face . . . It reminds her of the wind that roared for us then on the hill, when she heard those four words, and her face turns sad, sad, a tear trickles down her cheek . . . And the poor girl raises her hands up to that wind, as if asking it to bring her those words one more time. And I, having waited for the wind, say in a low voice:

"I love you, Nadya!"

My God, what happens to Nadenka! She cries out, her whole face bursts into a smile, and she reaches her hands up to meet the wind, joyful, happy, so beautiful.

And I go to pack . . .

That was already long ago. Now Nadenka is married; she married, or was married to—it makes no difference—the secretary of the nobility trusteeship,[1] and now has three children. She has not forgotten how we went to the sliding hill and how the wind brought her the words "I love you, Nadenka." For her it is now the happiest, the most touching and beautiful memory of her life . . .

As for me, now that I'm older, I no longer understand why I said those words, why I was joking . . .

1886

AGAFYA

WHEN I WAS LIVING in the S——m district, I often used to go to the Dubovsky kitchen gardens, tended by the gardener Savva Stukach, or simply Savka. These gardens were my favorite place for so-called "general" fishing, when, on leaving home, you do not know the day and hour of your return, and you take along all your fishing gear and a stock of provisions. In fact, I was not as interested in fishing as I was in carefree loafing, eating at odd times, talking with Savka, and prolonged encounters with the quiet summer nights. Savka was a lad of about twenty-five, tall, handsome, strong as flint. He was reputed to be a reasonable and sensible person, was literate, drank vodka rarely, but as a worker this young and strong fellow was not worth a red cent. Along with strength, his taut, rope-like muscles were filled with inert, invincible laziness. He lived, like all of us, in the village, in his own cottage, had a plot of land, but did not plow, did not sow, and did not practice any craft. His old mother went begging under people's windows, and he himself lived like a bird of the air: he did not know in the morning what he would eat at noon. It was not that he was lacking in willpower, energy, or pity for his mother, but simply so, one sensed no wish to work in him and no awareness of its benefit . . . His whole figure had an aura of serenity, of an inborn, almost artistic passion for living idly, any old way. When Savka's young, healthy body felt a physiological need for muscle work, for a short while the lad would give himself up entirely to some free but worthless occupation, like whittling totally useless pegs or running races with the village women. His favorite position was concentrated immobility. He was able to stand in one place for hours at a time, not budging and gazing at one spot. He moved by inspiration, and then only when the chance presented itself for making some sort of quick, impetuous movement: grabbing a running dog by the tail, tearing the kerchief off a woman, jumping over a wide ditch. Needless to say, being so sparing in movement, Savka was poor as a church mouse and lived worse than any pauper. In the course of time he accumulated arrears, and, healthy and young as he was, the village sent to him an old man's post, as a watchman and scarecrow over the common kitchen gardens. However much people laughed at his premature old age, he did not give a hoot. That spot, quiet, good for motionless contemplation, exactly suited his nature.

I happened to be with this same Savka one fine May evening. I remember I was lying on a tattered, shabby travel rug almost up against a hutch, which gave off a dense and stifling smell of dry grass. Putting my hands behind my head, I looked straight in front of me. At my feet lay a wooden pitchfork. Beyond it was the sharply outlined black patch of Savka's little dog Kutka, and no more than fifteen feet from Kutka the ground fell away into the steep riverbank. Lying there, I could not see the river. All I saw were the tops of the willows growing thickly on this bank, and the meandering, as if gnawed-away, edge of the bank opposite. Far beyond the bank, on a dark knoll, like frightened young partridges, the cottages of the village where my Savka lived huddled together. Beyond the knoll the evening sunset was dying out. Only a pale crimson strip was left, and it was beginning to be covered by small clouds, like coals with ash.

To the right of the kitchen gardens a dark alder grove softly whispered, shuddering occasionally under chance gusts of wind; to the left stretched a boundless field. There, where in the darkness the eye could no longer distinguish field from sky, a bright light glimmered. A short distance from me sat Savka. His legs tucked under Turkish fashion, and his head hanging, he pensively gazed at Kutka. Our hooks with live bait had long been dropped in the river, and we had nothing left to do but give ourselves up to rest, which the never-tiring and ever-resting Savka loved so much. The evening glow had not quite died out, but the summer night was already enveloping nature with its tender, lulling caress.

Everything was lapsing into the first deep sleep, only some night bird, unknown to me, drawlingly and lazily kept repeating in the grove a long, articulate sound, resembling the phrase: "Is Ni-ki-ta here?" and immediately answered himself: "He is! He is! He is!"

"Why isn't the nightingale singing now?" I asked Savka.

He slowly turned to me. The features of his face were large, but clean-cut, expressive, and soft, like a woman's. Then he looked with his meek, pensive eyes at the grove, at the willow thicket, slowly drew a reed pipe from his pocket, put it to his lips, and peeped like a female nightingale. And at once, as if in response to his peeping, a corncrake on the opposite bank crexed.

"There's your nightingale . . ." Savka laughed. "Crex-crex! Crex-crex! Just like a door creaking, but he must think he's singing, too."

"I like that bird . . . ," I said. "You know, during migration corncrakes don't fly, they run along the ground. They only fly over rivers and seas, otherwise they walk."

"Good dog . . . ," Savka muttered, glancing with respect in the direction of the crexing corncrake.

Knowing how much Savka liked to listen, I told him all I knew about the corncrake from books on hunting. From the corncrake I gradually went on to migration. Savka listened to me attentively, without blinking, smiling with pleasure all the while.

"Which country is the birds' native one?" he asked. "Ours or over yonder?"

"Ours, of course. The birds themselves are born here, and hatch their young here in their native land, and only fly there so as not to freeze."

"Interesting!" Savka stretched. "Whatever you talk about, it's all interesting. Birds now, or people . . . or take this little stone here—everything's got its sense! . . . Ah, if I'd known, master, that you'd come along, I wouldn't have told that peasant girl to come . . . There's one that asked to come now . . ."

"No, please, I won't interfere!" I said. "I can sleep in the grove . . ."

"Ah, what next! It wouldn't have killed her to come tomorrow . . .

If only she could sit here and listen to our talk, but no, she'll just get all slobbery. With her there's no talking seriously."

"Is it Darya you're waiting for?" I asked after some silence.

"No . . . A new one asked to come . . . Agafya, the switchman's wife . . ."

Savka said this in his usual dispassionate, somewhat hollow voice, as if he were talking about tobacco or kasha, but I jumped with surprise. I knew this Agafya . . . She was a peasant girl, still quite young, about nineteen or twenty, who no more than a year ago had married a railroad switchman, a dashing young fellow. She lived in the village, and the husband came to her from the railroad every night.

"All these stories of yours with women will end badly, brother!" I sighed.

"So, let them . . ."

And, having pondered a little, Savka added:

"I told them, they don't listen . . . The fools couldn't care less!"

Silence ensued . . . Meanwhile the darkness was deepening, and things were losing their outlines. The strip beyond the knoll faded away entirely, and the stars were becoming brighter, more radiant . . . The monotonously melancholic chirr of the grasshoppers, the crex of the corncrake, and the call of the quail did not disrupt the night's silence, but, on the contrary, lent it still greater monotony. It seemed that the soft sounds that enchanted our hearing came not from the birds, not from the insects, but from the stars that looked down on us from the sky . . .

Savka was the first to break the silence. He slowly shifted his eyes from the black Kutka to me and said:

"I see you're bored, master. Let's have supper."

And, not waiting for my consent, he crawled into the hutch on his belly, rummaged around, which made the whole hutch tremble like a single leaf; then crawled back out and set before me my vodka and a clay bowl. In the bowl were baked eggs, rye griddle-cakes cooked in lard, hunks of black bread, and something else . . . We drank from a crooked little glass that could not stand up and began to eat . . . The coarse gray salt, the dirty, greasy griddle-cakes, the eggs chewy as rubber—but how tasty it all was!

"You live like a pauper, but look at the amount of goods you've got!" I said, pointing to the bowl. "Where do you get it all?"

"Women bring it . . . ," Savka murmured.

"Why do they bring it to you?"

"Just . . . out of pity . . ."

Not only the menu but Savka's clothes also bore evidence of the women's "pity." For instance, that evening I noticed he was wearing a new worsted belt and a bright red ribbon on which a copper cross hung from his dirty neck. I knew that the fair sex had a weakness for Savka, and I knew how reluctantly he talked about it, and therefore I did not continue my interrogation. Besides, there was no time for talk . . . Kutka, who lingered near us, patiently waiting for scraps, suddenly pricked up her ears and growled. A remote, intermittent splashing of water could be heard.

"Somebody's wading across . . . ," said Savka.

About three minutes later Kutka growled again and produced a sound that resembled coughing.

"Hush!" her master shouted at her.

In the darkness there was a muffled sound of timid footsteps, and from the grove appeared the silhouette of a woman. I recognized her despite the darkness. It was Agafya, the switchman's wife. She warily approached us, stopped, and struggled to catch her breath. She was panting not so much from the wading as, probably, from fear and the unpleasant feeling everyone has when they wade across a river at night. Seeing two men by the hutch, she cried out weakly and stepped back.

"Ah . . . it's you!" said Savka, stuffing a griddle-cake into his mouth.

"Me . . . me, sir," she muttered, dropping a bundle with something in it on the ground and glancing sidelong at me. "Yakov sends his greetings and asked me to give you . . . There's something here . . ."

"Well, why go lying: Yakov!" Savka grinned. "No need for lying, the master knows what you came for! Sit down, be our guest."

Agafya cast a sidelong glance at me and hesitantly sat down.

"And I got to thinking you wouldn't come tonight," Savka said after a prolonged silence. "Why just sit there? Eat! Or shall I give you a little nip of vodka?"

"What an idea!" said Agafya. "Found yourself some sort of drunkard . . ."

"Have a drink . . . It'll warm up your soul . . . Here!"

Savka handed Agafya the crooked little glass. She drank the vodka slowly, and ate nothing after it, but just exhaled loudly.

"You brought something . . . ," Savka went on, untying the bundle and giving his voice a condescendingly jocular tone. "A woman can't do without bringing something. Ah, a pie and some potatoes . . . They live well!" he sighed, turning his face to me. "They're the only ones in the village who still have potatoes after winter!"

In the darkness I could not see Agafya's face, but from the movements of her head and shoulders it seemed to me that she never took her eyes off Savka's face. So as not to be the third at their tryst, I decided to take a stroll and got up to go. But at that moment a nightingale in the grove unexpectedly produced two low contralto notes. Half a minute later he let out a high trill and, having thus tested his voice, began to sing. Savka jumped up and listened.

"It's yesterday's!" he said. "Hold on! . . ."

And, tearing from his place, he ran noiselessly to the grove.

"What do you need him for?" I called out behind him. "Let him be!"

Savka waved his hand—meaning "don't shout"—and disappeared into the darkness. When he wished, Savka could be an excellent hunter and fisherman, but here, too, his talents, like his strength, went to waste. He was too lazy for the standard ways, and all his hunting passion was spent on empty tricks. He caught nightingales not otherwise than with his bare hands, he killed pike with birdshot, or he would stand for long hours on the riverbank, trying with all his might to snag a small fish on a big hook.

Left with me, Agafya coughed and wiped her hand across her forehead several times . . . She was beginning to feel the effect of the vodka she had drunk.

"How's your life, Agasha?" I asked her after a prolonged silence, when it finally became awkward to keep silent.

"Good, thank God . . . Don't tell anybody, master . . . ," she suddenly added in a whisper.

"Come now," I reassured her. "You're so fearless, Agasha . . . What if Yakov finds out?"

"He won't . . ."

"Well, but what if!"

"No . . . I'll be home before him. He's at the tracks now and will come back once he sees off the mail train, and you can hear the train coming from here . . ."

Agafya wiped her hand across her forehead again and looked towards where Savka had gone. The nightingale was singing. Some night bird flew low over the ground and, noticing us, got frightened, swished its wings, and flew off across the river.

Soon the nightingale fell silent, but Savka did not come back. Agafya stood up, took a few uneasy steps, and sat down again.

"What's he doing?" she burst out. "The train's not coming tomorrow! I've got to go now!"

"Savka!" I called. "Savka!"

Not even an echo answered. Agafya shifted restlessly and stood up again.

"It's time for me to go!" she said in a nervous voice. "The train's coming now! I know when the trains run!"

The poor girl was not mistaken. Before a quarter of an hour went by, there came a distant noise.

Agafya fixed her gaze on the grove for a long time and moved her hands impatiently.

"Well, where is he?" she said, laughing nervously. "Where the deuce has he gone to? I'll leave! By God, master, I'll leave!"

Meanwhile the noise was becoming more distinct. It was already possible to tell the clatter of the wheels from the heavy sighing of the steam engine. A whistle was heard, the train hollowly clattered over the bridge . . . Another minute, and everything became still.

"I'll wait another little minute . . . ," Agafya sighed, resolutely sitting down. "So be it, I'll wait!"

Finally Savka appeared from the darkness. He noiselessly stepped barefoot over the loose soil of the kitchen gardens and was softly murmuring something.

"There's luck, thank you very much!" he laughed merrily. "I was just coming up to that same bush, and was just aiming my hand, and he shut up! Ah, dash it all! I waited and waited for him to sing again, then spat on it . . ."

Savka dropped clumsily to the ground beside Agafya and, to keep his balance, grabbed her by the waist with both hands.

"And what are you scowling at, as if some old witch gave birth to you?" he asked.

For all his kind-heartedness and ingenuousness, Savka scorned women. He treated them casually, haughtily, and even lowered himself so far as to laugh scornfully at their feelings for his own person. God knows, maybe this casual, scornful treatment was one of the causes of the intense, insuperable charm he had for the village dulcineas? He was handsome and well-built, and his eyes always shone with quiet tenderness even at the sight of women he scorned, but it was impossible to explain this charm by external qualities alone. Besides his fortunate appearance and original manner of treating them, it must be thought that it was also Savka's touching role as a universally recognized failure and unfortunate exile from his own cottage to the kitchen gardens that influenced the women.

"Now tell the master why you've come here!" Savka went on, still holding Agafya by the waist. "Go on, tell him, you husband's wife! Ho-ho . . . What do you say, good old Agasha, shall we have another nip of vodka?"

I got up and, making my way between the beds, walked along the garden. The dark beds looked like big, flattened graves. They gave off a smell of tilled soil and the delicate dampness of the plants that were beginning to be covered with dew . . . To the left the little red light still shone. It blinked affably and seemed to smile. I heard happy laughter. It was Agafya laughing.

"And the train?" I remembered. "The train came long ago."

Having waited a little, I went back to the hutch. Savka was sitting motionless, Turkish fashion, and quietly, barely audibly, murmuring some song that consisted only of one-syllable words, something like "Phoo-you, to-you . . . me and you . . ." Agafya, drunk on the vodka, Savka's scornful caress, and the stifling night, lay beside him on the ground and pressed her face hard against his knee. She was so far gone in her feeling that she did not notice my coming.

"Agasha, you know the train came long ago!" I said.

"It's time, it's time." Savka picked up my thought, shaking his head. "What are you doing lying around here? You're shameless!"

Agafya roused herself, glanced at me, and pressed her head to his knee again.

"It's long been time!" I said.

Agafya stirred and got to one knee . . . She was suffering . . . For half a minute her whole figure, as far as I could make it out in the dark, expressed struggle and hesitation. There was a moment when, as if coming to her senses, she raised herself so as to get to her feet, but then some invincible and implacable force pushed her whole body, and she pressed herself to Savka again.

"Ah, forget him!" she said with wild, deep-throated laughter, and in that laughter you could hear reckless resolution, powerlessness, pain.

I slowly trudged off to the grove and from there went down to the river, where our fishing rods were standing. The river was asleep. Some soft, fluffy flower on a tall stem tenderly touched my cheek, like a child who wants to let you know he is not asleep. Having nothing to do, I felt for one line and pulled it. It responded limply and hung down—nothing had been caught . . . I could not see the other bank and the village. A little light glimmered in one cottage, but soon went out. I felt around on the bank, found a depression I had already noticed during the day, and sat down in it as in an armchair. I sat for a long time . . . I saw how the stars began to fade and lose their brightness, how a slight breath of coolness passed over the earth, touching the leaves of the awakening willows . . .

"A-ga-fya! . . ." Someone's muffled voice reached me from the village. "Agafya!"

It was the returned and alarmed husband, looking for his wife in the village. And in the kitchen gardens I heard unrestrained laughter: the wife had forgotten herself, was drunk, and with the happiness of a few hours was trying to offset the suffering that awaited her the next day.

I fell asleep.

When I woke up, Savka was sitting beside me, lightly shaking me by the shoulder. The river, the grove, both banks, green and washed, the village, and the field—all was flooded with bright morning light.

The rays of the just-risen sun struck my back through the thin trunks of the trees.

"So that's how you fish?" Savka smiled. "Well, up you get!"

I stood up, stretched sweetly, and my awakened chest eagerly began to drink in the moist, fragrant air.

"Agasha left?" I asked.

"There she is," Savka pointed in the direction of the ford.

I looked and saw Agafya. Tucking up her skirts, disheveled, her kerchief askew on her head, she was crossing the river. Her legs could barely move . . .

"The cat knows she ate the canary!" Savka muttered, narrowing his eyes at her. "There she goes, tail between her legs . . . These women are mischievous as cats, and cowardly as hares . . . The foolish woman, she should have gone when she was told! Now she's going to get it, and me, too, at the local precinct . . . another flogging on account of a woman . . ."

Agafya stepped onto the bank and went off across the field to the village. At first she walked rather boldly, but then agitation and fear claimed their own: she turned in fright, stopped, and caught her breath.

"See, it's scary!" Savka smiled sadly, looking at the bright green stripe Agafya left on the dewy grass. "She doesn't want to go! The husband's been standing there waiting for a whole hour . . . Did you see him?"

Savka said these last words with a smile, but they chilled my heart. In the village, by the last cottage, on the road, Yakov stood and stared fixedly at his returning wife. He did not stir and was still as a post. What was he thinking as he looked at her? What words had he prepared for their meeting? Agafya stood for a time, looked back once, as if expecting help from us, and went on. I had never yet seen anyone walk like that, either drunk or sober. It was as if Agafya writhed under her husband's gaze. She walked in zigzags, then stamped in place, her knees bending and her arms spreading, then backed up a little. Having gone some hundred steps forward, she looked back again and sat down.

"You should at least hide behind a bush," I said to Savka. "What if the husband sees you . . ."

"He knows who Agasha's coming from anyway . . . It's not for cabbage that women go to the kitchen gardens at night—everybody knows that."

I looked at Savka's face. It was pale and wincing from squeamish pity, as with people when they see an animal tortured.

"The cat laughs, the mouse weeps . . . ," he sighed.

Agafya suddenly jumped to her feet, shook her head, and, stepping boldly, went to meet her husband. She had evidently gathered her forces and made up her mind.

1886

Spring

THE SNOW HAS NOT YET LEFT THE GROUND, but spring is already calling on the soul. If you have ever convalesced from a grave illness, you know the blissful state when you swoon from vague presentiments and smile without any reason. Evidently that is the state nature is experiencing now. The ground is cold, mud mixed with snow sloshes under your feet, but everything around is so cheerful, affectionate, friendly! The air is so clear and transparent that it seems if you climbed up on a dovecot or a belfry you could see the whole universe from end to end. The sun shines brightly, and its rays, playing and smiling, bathe in the puddles along with the sparrows. The river swells and darkens; it is already awake, and will start roaring any day now. The trees are bare, but already living, breathing.

In that season it feels good to drive dirty water along the gutters with a broom or a shovel, to send toy boats down the streams, or crack the stubborn ice with your heels. It also feels good to drive pigeons high up into the heavens, or to climb trees and tie birdhouses in them. Yes, everything feels good in that happy time of year, especially if you're young, love nature, and if you're not capricious, hysterical, and your job does not oblige you to sit between four walls from morning till evening. It's not good if you're sick, if you're pining away in an office, if you keep company with the muses.

Yes, in spring one should not keep company with the muses.

Just look how good, how nice ordinary people feel. Here's the gardener Pantelei Petrovich, bright and early, sporting a broad-brimmed straw hat, and quite unable to part with the little stub of a cigar he picked up this morning on the path; look at him standing, arms akimbo, outside the kitchen window, telling the cook about the boots he bought the day before. His whole long and narrow figure, for which the servants call him "scrimpy," expresses self-satisfaction and dignity. He looks upon nature with the awareness of his superiority over it, and there is in his gaze something proprietary, peremptory, and even supercilious, as if, sitting in his greenhouse or pottering in the garden, he has learned about the vegetable kingdom something that no one else knows.

It would be useless to explain to him that nature is majestic, awesome, and filled with wondrous charms, before which the proud man should bow his head. It seems to him that he knows everything, all the secrets, charms, and wonders, and for him the beautiful spring is as much of a slave as the narrow-chested, haggard woman who sits in the shed of the greenhouse and ladles out meatless cabbage soup to his children.

And the huntsman Ivan Zakharov? This one, in his tattered woollen coat and with galoshes on his bare feet, sits by the stable on an overturned barrel and makes wads out of old corks. He's preparing for woodcock season. In his imagination he pictures the way he will take, with all its footpaths, ice-filled hollows, brooks; closing his eyes, he sees a long, straight row of tall, slender trees, under which he will stand with his gun, trembling from the evening coolness, from sweet excitement, and straining his keen hearing; he imagines the hoarse sounds of a woodcock; he already hears all the bells ringing away in the nearby monastery after the vigil, while he stands at the hunt . . . He feels good, he is boundlessly, senselessly happy.

But now take a look at Makar Denisych, a young man who works for General Stremoukhov as not quite a clerk, not quite a junior manager. His salary is twice that of the gardener, he wears a white shirt front, smokes expensive tobacco, is always well-fed and well-dressed, and on meeting the general always has the pleasure of shaking his plump white hand with its big diamond ring, but despite all that how unhappy he is! He is eternally among books, subscribes to twenty-five roubles' worth of magazines, and writes, writes . . . He writes every evening, every afternoon, while the rest are napping, and he puts all he writes into his big trunk. At the very bottom of that trunk lie his neatly folded trousers and waistcoats; on top of them are an unsealed packet of tobacco, a dozen or so pillboxes, a crimson scarf, a cake of glycerine soap in a yellow wrapper, and many other such goods, and to the side of the trunk timidly cling stacks of written-upon paper, as well as two or three issues of *Our Province*, in which stories and reports by Makar Denisych have been published. The whole district considers him a writer, a poet; they all see something peculiar in him, do not like him, say he talks differently, walks differently, smokes differently, and once, at a general court session to which he had been summoned as a witness, he let slip inappropriately that he was occupied with literature, and blushed as deeply as if he had stolen a chicken.

Here he is, in a dark blue coat, a plush hat, and with a cane in his hand, slowly walking down the drive . . . He takes five steps, stops, and fixes his eyes on the sky or on an old rook sitting in a fir tree.

The gardener stands, arms akimbo, sternness is written on the huntsman's face, and Makar Denisych stoops, coughs timidly, and looks around sourly, as if spring crushes and stifles him with its vapors, its beauty! . . . His soul is filled with timidity. Instead of ecstasies, joys, and hopes, spring evokes in him only some sort of vague desires, which trouble him, and so he walks along, unable to figure out what he needs. In fact, what does he need?

"Ah, greetings, Makar Denisych!" He suddenly hears the voice of General Stremoukhov. "So, has the mail come yet?"

"Not yet, Your Excellency," replies Makar Denisych, looking at the carriage in which the hale and hearty general sits with his little daughter.

"Splendid weather! Spring is here!" says the general. "Going for a stroll? Getting inspired?"

But in his eyes is written: "Giftlessness! Mediocrity!"

"Ah, my dear fellow!" says the general, taking up the reins. "What a wonderful little piece I read today over coffee! A trifle, just two pages, but so charming! Too bad you don't know French, I'd give it to you to read . . ."

The general hastily, sketchily retells the content of the story he read, and Makar Denisych listens and feels embarrassed, as if it is his fault that he is not a French writer who writes little pieces.

"I don't understand what he found good in it," he thinks, following the disappearing carriage with his eyes. "The content is banal, hackneyed . . . My stories are much more substantial."

A worm begins to gnaw at Makar. Authorial vanity is painful, it is an infection of the soul; whoever suffers from it no longer hears the singing of the birds, nor sees the shining of the sun, nor sees the spring . . . It takes only the slightest touch of this sore spot for the whole body to shrink with pain. The poisoned Makar walks on further and through the garden gate comes out onto the dirty road. There, his whole body jouncing on a high britzka, Mr. Bubentsov is hurrying somewhere.

"Ah, Mister Writer!" he cries. "Hello there!"

If Makar Denisych were merely a clerk or a junior manager, no one would dare speak to him in such a condescending, casual tone, but he is a "writer," he is giftlessness, mediocrity!

Such people as Mr. Bubentsov understand nothing about art and have little interest in it, but when they happen to meet up with giftlessness and mediocrity, they are implacable, merciless. They are ready to forgive anyone you like, only not Makar, this wretched misfit whose manuscripts are lying in a trunk. The gardener broke an old ficus and has let many expensive plants rot; the general does nothing and lives off of other people's work; Mr. Bubentsov, when he was justice of the peace, heard cases only once a month and, in hearing them, stammered, confused the laws, and poured out drivel, but all this is forgiven, goes unnoticed; but not to notice the giftless Makar, who writes mediocre poetry and stories, to pass him over in silence without saying something offensive—is impossible. The general's daughter-in-law slaps her maids in the face and gets as foul-mouthed as a washerwoman during card games, the priest's wife never pays her card-playing debts, the landowner Flyugin stole a dog from the landowner Sivobrazov—nobody cares. But the fact that *Our Province* recently returned a third-rate story to Makar is known to the whole district, and gives rise to mockery, long conversations, opprobrium, and instead of Makar Denisych he is now called Makarka.

If there's something wrong with his writing, they don't try to explain why it's "wrong," they simply say:

"Again that son of a bitch wrote some rubbish!"

Makar is prevented from enjoying the spring by the thought that they do not understand him, do not wish to and cannot understand him. For some reason it seems to him that if they were to understand him, everything would be wonderful. But how can they understand whether he is talented or not, if no one in the whole district reads anything, or else they read in such a way that it would be better not to read at all. How instill in General Stremoukhov that that little French piece is a worthless, flat, banal, hackneyed little piece, how instill it in him, if he has never read anything else but such flat, worthless little pieces?

And how the women annoy Makar!

"Ah, Makar Denisych!" they usually say to him. "What a pity you weren't at the marketplace today! If you'd seen how comically those two peasants fought, you'd certainly have written about it!"

All this is trifles, of course, and a philosopher would pay no attention, would disregard it, but Makar feels as if he's on hot coals. His soul is filled with a feeling of loneliness, orphanhood, anguish, the same anguish that is experienced only by very lonely people and great sinners. Never, not once in his life, has he stood arms akimbo the way the gardener stands. Only rarely, maybe once in five years, somewhere in the forest, or on the road, or on a train, meeting another misfit as wretched as himself, and looking him in the eye, does he suddenly revive for a moment, and the other man revives as well. They talk for a long time, argue, admire, praise, laugh, so that, looking at them, you might take them for madmen.

But usually even these rare moments do not come without poison. As if for a laugh, Makar and the wretched fellow he meets deny each other's talent, do not accept each other, envy, hate, become vexed, and finally part as enemies. And so their youth wears out, melts away, joyless, loveless, friendless, without inner peace, and without all that sullen Makar so loves to describe in the evenings, in moments of inspiration.

And with youth spring also passes.

1886

A Nightmare

A PERMANENT MEMBER of the local committee on peasant affairs, Kunin, a young man of about thirty, who had just come back from Petersburg to his native Borisovo, first of all sent a mounted messenger to the village of Sinkovo for the priest there, Father Yakov Smirnov.

Five hours later Father Yakov appeared.

"Very glad to make your acquaintance!" said Kunin, meeting him in the front hall. "I've been living and serving here for a year now, I think it's time we became acquainted. Kindly come in! But . . . you're so young!" Kunin was surprised. "How old are you?"

"Twenty-eight, sir . . . ," Father Yakov replied, weakly shaking the proffered hand and blushing for some reason.

Kunin took the guest to his study and began to examine him.

"What a crude, peasant woman's face!" he thought.

In fact, there was in Father Yakov's face a good deal of the "peasant woman": an upturned nose, bright red cheeks, and big gray-blue eyes with sparse, barely visible eyebrows. Long red hair, dry and smooth, descended to his shoulders like straight sticks. His moustache was just beginning to take the shape of a real masculine one, and his little beard belonged to that good-for-nothing sort that seminarians, for some reason, call "skippish": sparse, quite transparent; it could not be smoothed or combed, it could only be plucked . . .

All this meager vegetation sat there unevenly, in clumps, as if Father Yakov, deciding to make himself up as a priest and starting by gluing on a beard, was interrupted halfway through. He was wearing a cassock the color of weak chicory coffee with large patches on both elbows.

"A strange specimen . . . ," thought Kunin, looking at his mud-splashed skirts. "He comes to the house for the first time and can't dress more decently."

"Have a seat, Father," he began, more casually than affably, moving an armchair to the desk. "Have a seat, please!"

Father Yakov coughed into his fist, lowered himself awkwardly onto the edge of the chair, and placed his palms on his knees. Under-sized, narrow-chested, his face sweaty and flushed, from the first moment he made a very unpleasant impression on Kunin. Previously Kunin simply could not have conceived of there being such unre-spectable and pathetic-looking priests in Russia, and he saw in Father Yakov's pose, in this holding his palms on his knees and sitting on the edge, a lack of dignity and even obsequiousness.

"I have invited you on business, Father . . . ," Kunin began, set-tling against the back of his armchair. "It has fallen to my lot to have the pleasant duty of assisting you in your useful undertaking . . . The thing is that, on coming back from Petersburg, I found a letter on my desk from our marshal of the nobility.[1] Egor Dmitrievich proposes to me that I take under my trusteeship the parish school that is about to open in your Sinkovo. I'm very glad, Father, with all my heart . . . Even more: I am delighted to accept this proposal!"

Kunin stood up and began to pace the study.

"Of course, it is known to Egor Dmitrievich, and probably to you, that I have no great means at my disposal. My estate is mortgaged, and I live only on my salary as a permanent member. Which means that you cannot count on great help from me, but that I will do everything in my power . . . And when do you think of opening your school, Father?"

"When there's money . . . ," Father Yakov replied.

"Do you have any means at your disposal now?"

"Almost none, sir . . . The peasant assembly decided to pay thirty kopecks annually for every male soul,[2] but that's only a promise! At least two hundred roubles are needed to get started . . ."

"Hm . . . yes . . . Unfortunately, I don't have such a sum now . . ." Kunin sighed. "I spent all I had on my trip and . . . even went into debt. Let's try to think something up together."

Kunin started thinking out loud. He gave his views and watched Father Yakov's face, seeking approval or agreement in it. But that face was passionless, immobile, and expressed nothing except timidity and uneasiness. Looking at it, one might have thought that Kunin was talking about such abstruse things that Father Yakov did not understand them, listened only out of delicacy and at the same time fearing that he might be accused of not understanding.

"The fellow is obviously not very bright . . . ," Kunin thought. "Much too timid and a bit simple-minded."

Father Yakov became slightly more animated and even smiled when a servant came into the study bringing a tray with two cups of tea and a plate of cookies. He took his glass and immediately began to drink.

"Shouldn't we write to the bishop?" Kunin went on reasoning aloud. "As a matter of fact, it was not the district council, not us, but the high clerical authorities who raised the question of parish schools. It is really they who should specify the means. I remember reading that there was even a certain sum of money allocated for that purpose. Do you know anything about it?"

Father Yakov was so immersed in tea-drinking that he did not answer this question at once. He raised his gray-blue eyes to Kunin, thought a little, and, as if recalling his question, shook his head negatively. An expression of pleasure and of the most ordinary, prosaic appetite was spreading over his unattractive face from ear to ear. He was drinking and relishing every gulp. Having drunk it all to the last drop, he set his glass on the table, then picked it up again, studied the bottom, and set it down again. The expression of pleasure slipped from his face. Then Kunin saw his guest take a cookie from the plate, bite off a little piece, then turn it around in his fingers and quickly stick it in his pocket.

"Well, that is entirely un-clerical!" thought Kunin, shrugging squeamishly. "What is it, priestly greed or childishness?"

Having let his guest drink a cup of tea and accompanied him to the front hall, Kunin lay down on the sofa and surrendered himself entirely to the unpleasant feeling evoked in him by Father Yakov's visit.

"What a strange, uncouth man!" he thought. "Dirty, slovenly, coarse, stupid, and probably a drunkard . . . My God, and this is a priest, a spiritual father! A teacher of the people! I can imagine how much irony there must be in the deacon's voice as he intones before every liturgy: 'Bless, master!' A fine master! A master who doesn't have a drop of dignity, ill-bred, hiding cookies in his pocket like a schoolboy . . . Ugh! Good Lord, where was the bishop looking when he ordained this man? What do they think of the people, if they give them such teachers? What's needed here is people who . . ."

And Kunin began to think about what Russian priests should be like . . .

"If I, for instance, were a priest . . . A well-educated priest who loves what he does can achieve a great deal . . . I'd have opened a school long ago. And sermons? If a priest is sincere and inspired by love for his work, what wonderful, fiery sermons he could give!"

Kunin closed his eyes and began mentally composing a sermon. A little later he was sitting at his desk and quickly writing it down.

"I'll give it to that redhead, let him read it in church . . . ," he thought.

The next Sunday, in the morning, Kunin was riding to Sinkovo to finish with the question of the school and incidentally become acquainted with the church, where he was considered a parishioner. In spite of the muddy season, the morning was glorious. The sun shone brightly, and its rays cut into the sheets of residual snow showing white here and there. The snow, bidding farewell to the earth, shimmered with such diamonds that it was painful to look at, and next to it the young winter rye was hurriedly turning green. Rooks sedately circled over the earth. A rook flies, then descends to the ground and, before coming to a standstill, hops several times . . .

The wooden church that Kunin rode up to was dilapidated and gray; the little columns on the porch, once painted white, had peeled and were now completely bare and resembled two ugly shafts. The icon over the door looked like a single dark spot. But this poverty touched and moved Kunin. Modestly lowering his eyes, he entered the church and stopped by the door. The service had just begun. An old, crook-backed sexton was reading the hours in a hollow, indistinct tenor. Father Yakov, who served without a deacon, went around censing the church. If it had not been for the humility Kunin felt on entering the beggarly church, the sight of Father Yakov would certainly have made him smile. The undersized priest was wearing a wrinkled and much-too-long vestment of some shabby yellow fabric. The lower edge of the vestment dragged on the ground.

The church was not full. Glancing at the parishioners, Kunin was struck at first by a strange circumstance: he saw only old people and children . . . Where were those of working age? Where were youth and manhood? But, having stood there longer and looked more attentively at the old people's faces, Kunin saw that he had mistaken the young ones for old. However, he ascribed no special significance to this small optical illusion.

The inside of the church was as dilapidated and gray as the outside. On the iconostasis and on the brown walls there was not a single spot that had not been blackened and scratched by time. There were many windows, but the general coloration was gray, and therefore it was dusky in the church.

"For the pure in soul, it's good to pray here . . . ," thought Kunin. "As in St. Peter's in Rome one is struck by the grandeur, so here one is touched by this humility and simplicity."

But his prayerful mood scattered like smoke when Father Yakov entered the altar and began the liturgy. A young man, ordained to the priesthood straight from the seminary, Father Yakov had had no time to adopt a definite manner of serving. While reciting, it was as if he were choosing what sort of voice to use—a high tenor or a flimsy bass; he bowed clumsily, walked quickly, opened and closed the Royal Doors abruptly . . .[3] The old sexton, obviously sick and deaf, heard his exclamations poorly, which did not fail to result in minor misunderstandings. He would start to sing his part before Father Yakov had finished his, or else Father Yakov would have finished long ago and the old man would still be trying to hear him and would be silent until he was pulled by the cassock. The old man had a hollow, sickly voice, short-winded, trembling and lisping . . . To crown the unseemliness, the sexton was joined by a very young boy, whose head was barely visible over the rail of the choir loft. The boy sang in a high, shrill soprano and as if deliberately out of tune. Kunin stood for a while listening, then stepped outside to smoke . . . He was already disappointed and looked at the gray church almost with hostility.

"They complain about the decline of religious feeling among people . . . ," he sighed. "What else! Why don't they stick us with more priests like this one!"

Kunin went into the church three more times after that, and each time was strongly drawn back out into the open air. Having waited for the end of the service, he went off to Father Yakov's. The priest's house from the outside was no different from the peasant cottages, only the thatching on the roof was more evenly laid and there were white curtains in the windows. Father Yakov led Kunin into a small, bright room with a clay floor and walls hung with cheap wallpaper. Despite some attempts at luxury, like framed photographs and a clock with scissors tied to its weights, the setting was striking in its penury. Looking at the furniture, you might think that Father Yakov had gone around the courtyards and collected it piecemeal. In one place they gave him a round table on three legs, in another a stool, in a third a chair with a back sharply tilted backwards, in a fourth a chair with a straight back but a sagging seat, and in a fifth they generously gave him some semblance of a divan with a flat back and a latticework seat. This semblance had been painted a dark red and smelled strongly of the paint. Kunin first wanted to sit on one of the chairs, but thought better of it and sat on the stool.

"Is this the first time you've been to our church?" Father Yakov asked, hanging his hat on a big, ugly nail.

"Yes, the first. I tell you what, Father . . . Before we get down to business, give me some tea, my soul is completely dry."

Father Yakov blinked, grunted, and went behind the partition. There was some whispering . . .

"Must be with his wife . . . ," Kunin thought. "I'd be interested to see what sort of wife the redhead's got . . ."

A little later Father Yakov came from behind the partition, red-faced, sweaty, and, forcing a smile, sat facing Kunin on the edge of the divan.

"The samovar will be started presently," he said, without looking at his guest.

"My God, they haven't started the samovar yet!" Kunin was inwardly horrified. "I must kindly wait now!"

"I've brought you the draft of the letter I've written to the bishop," he said. "I'll read it after tea . . . Maybe you'll find something to add . . ."

"Very well, sir."

Silence ensued. Father Yakov cast a frightened glance at the partition, smoothed his hair, and blew his nose.

"Wonderful weather, sir . . . ," he said.

"Yes. Incidentally, I read something interesting yesterday . . . The district council of Volsk has decreed the handing over of all the schools to the care of the clergy. That's just like them."

Kunin got up, started pacing the clay floor and voicing his reflections.

"That doesn't matter," he said, "if only the clergy is up to its calling and clearly understands its responsibilities. To my misfortune, I know priests who in their development and moral qualities aren't fit to be army clerks, to say nothing of priests. You must agree that a bad teacher does much less harm to a school than a bad priest."

Kunin glanced at Father Yakov. He sat hunched over, thinking hard about something, and was apparently not listening to his guest.

"Yasha, come here!" A woman's voice was heard from behind the partition.

Father Yakov roused himself and went behind the partition. There was more whispering.

Kunin longed desperately for tea.

"No, I won't get any tea here!" he thought, glancing at his watch. "It seems I'm not entirely a welcome guest. The host hasn't deigned to say a single word to me, he just sits and blinks."

Kunin took his hat, waited for Father Yakov, and said goodbye to him.

"I just wasted the whole morning!" he fumed on the way back. "A blockhead! A dolt! He's as interested in the school as I am in last year's snow. No, I can't get anywhere with him! Nothing will come of it! If the marshal knew what sort of priest we've got here, he'd be in no hurry to bother with a school. First we have to see about a good priest, and then about the school!"

Kunin almost hated Father Yakov now. The man, his pathetic caricature of a figure in its long, wrinkled vestment, his peasant woman's face, his manner of serving, his style of life and clerkish, timid deference offended that small bit of religious feeling that still remained in Kunin's breast and quietly flickered there along with other old wives' tales. And it was hard for his vanity to bear the coldness and inattention with which the priest met Kunin's sincere, fervent concern for his own cause . . .

In the evening of that same day, Kunin paced his room for a long time and thought, then resolutely sat down at his desk and wrote a letter to the bishop. Having requested money for the school and his blessing, he candidly explained, among other things, as a spiritual son should, his opinion about the Sinkovo priest. "He is young," he wrote, "not sufficiently developed, seems to be leading a drunken life, and generally does not satisfy the requirements which over the centuries have developed among the Russian people regarding their pastors." Having written this letter, Kunin sighed with relief and went to bed with the consciousness that he had done a good deed.

On Monday morning, while he was still lying in bed, he was told that Father Yakov had come. He did not feel like getting up, and he told them to say he was not at home. On Tuesday he left for the assembly and, returning on Saturday, he learned from the servants that during his absence Father Yakov had come every day.

"Well, so he really liked my cookies!" thought Kunin.

On Sunday, towards evening, Father Yakov came. This time not only the hem of his cassock, but even his hat was spattered with mud. Just as on his first visit, he was red-faced and sweaty, and he sat, as then, on the edge of the armchair. Kunin decided not to start discussing the school, not to cast pearls.

"I've come, Pavel Mikhailovich, to bring you a little list of school manuals . . ." Father Yakov began.

"Thank you."

But by all tokens it could be seen that Father Yakov had not come for the sake of the little list. His whole figure expressed deep embarrassment, but at the same time resolution was written on his face, as on a man upon whom an idea has suddenly dawned. He was struggling to say something important, extremely necessary, and was now trying to overcome his timidity.

"Why is he silent?" Kunin thought angrily. "Sitting around here! As if I have time to bother about him!"

In order to smooth over the awkwardness of his silence somehow and conceal the struggle that was going on in him, the priest began to force a smile, and this smile, prolonged, squeezed out through the sweat and redness of his face, conflicting with the fixed gaze of his gray-blue eyes, made Kunin turn away. He was disgusted.

"Excuse me, Father, I have to leave . . . ," he said.

Father Yakov roused himself, like a sleepy man who has just been punched, and, without ceasing to smile, began in his embarrassment to wrap the skirts of his cassock around him. Despite all his revulsion at this man, Kunin suddenly felt sorry for him, and he wanted to soften his cruelty.

"Please, Father, another time . . . ," he said, "and before you go I have a request to make of you . . . I recently felt inspired, you know, and wrote two sermons . . . I give them to you for your consideration . . . If they're suitable, deliver them."

"Very well, sir . . . ," Father Yakov said, covering Kunin's sermons, which lay on the table, with his palm. "I'll take them, sir . . ."

He stood for a moment, hesitated, still trying to close his cassock, and then suddenly stopped forcing a smile and resolutely raised his head.

"Pavel Mikhailovich," he said, obviously trying to speak loudly and clearly.

"What can I do for you?"

"I've heard that you were pleased . . . sort of . . . to fire your clerk and . . . and are now looking for a new one . . ."

"Yes . . . Do you have someone you can recommend?"

"You see, I . . . I . . . Couldn't you give this post to . . . me?"

"So you're abandoning the priesthood?" Kunin was amazed.

"No, no," Father Yakov said quickly, turning pale for some reason and trembling all over. "God save me from that! If you doubt me, then never mind, never mind. I meant it sort of in my spare time . . . to increase my dividends . . ."

"Hm . . . dividends! . . . But I pay my clerk only twenty roubles a month!"

"Lord, and I'd take ten!" Father Yakov whispered, glancing over his shoulder. "Ten's enough! You're . . . you're amazed . . . and everybody's amazed. Greedy, money-grubbing priest, what does he do with all his money? I myself feel I'm greedy . . . I accuse myself, condemn myself . . . I'm ashamed to look people in the eye . . . To you, Pavel Mikhailovich, in all conscience . . . I call the true God as my witness . . ."

Father Yakov paused to catch his breath and went on:

"On the way here I prepared a whole confession for you, but . . . I forgot it all, I can't find the right words now. I get a hundred and fifty roubles a year from the parish, and everybody . . . wonders what I do with this money . . . But I'll explain it all to you honestly . . . I pay forty roubles a year to the seminary for my brother Pyotr. He gets room and board, but paper and pens are on me . . ."

"Ah, I believe you, I believe you! Well, why all this?" Kunin waved his hand, feeling terribly oppressed by his guest's candor and not knowing where to hide from the tearful glistening of his eyes.

"And then, sir, I have yet to pay off my debt to the chancery. They charged me two hundred roubles for this post, to be paid off ten roubles a month . . . Judge for yourself now, what's left? And besides that I have to give Father Avramy at least three roubles a month!"

"What Father Avramy?"

"Father Avramy who was the priest in Sinkovo before me. He was removed from the position on account of . . . weakness, but he lives in Sinkovo even now! Where can he go? Who will feed him? He's old, but still he needs a corner, and bread, and some clothes! I can't allow that he, with his holy order, should go begging! It would be my sin if something happened! My sin! He . . . owes money to everybody, but it's my sin if I don't pay for him."

Father Yakov tore from his place and, staring madly at the floor, began pacing from corner to corner.

"My God! My God!" he muttered, now raising his arms, now lowering them. "Lord, save us and have mercy! And why did you take such an order upon yourself, if you're of little faith and have no strength? There's no end to my despair! Queen of Heaven, save me."

"Calm down, Father," said Kunin.

"We're starving, Pavel Mikhailovich!" Father Yakov went on. "Kindly forgive me, but it's beyond my strength . . . I know if I ask, if I bow my head, everyone will help me, but . . . I can't! I'm ashamed! How am I going to ask from peasants? You work here, you know . . . How can I hold out my hand and ask from beggars? And I can't ask from those who are richer, from the landowners! Pride! I'm ashamed!"

Father Yakov waved his arm and scratched his head nervously with both hands.

"Ashamed! God, how ashamed! I'm proud, I can't stand it that people see my poverty. When you visited us, we simply had no tea, Pavel Mikhailovich! Not a speck of tea, but my pride kept me from telling you! I'm ashamed of my clothes, of these patches . . . Ashamed of my vestments, of my hunger . . . And is pride a proper thing for a priest?"

Father Yakov stopped in the middle of the study and, as if not noticing Kunin's presence, began reasoning with himself.

"Well, let's say I can bear with the hunger and the shame, but, Lord, I also have a wife! I took her from a good family! She's not used to hard work, she's sensitive, she's used to tea, and white bread, and bedsheets . . . She played the piano in her parents' house . . . She's young, not yet twenty . . . No doubt she would like to dress up, and frolic a bit, and go visiting . . . And with me . . . she's worse off than any kitchen maid, she's ashamed to show herself outside. My God, my God! The only pleasure she has is when I come home from my visits with an apple or a little cookie . . ."

Father Yakov again began to scratch his head with both hands.

"And as a result what we have isn't love, it's pity . . . I can't see her without compassion! And, Lord, what's going on in the world. If somebody writes about it in the newspapers, people won't believe it . . . And when will there be an end to it all!"

"Enough now, Father!" Kunin almost cried out, frightened by his tone. "Why look at life so darkly?"

"Kindly forgive me, Pavel Mikhailovich . . . ," Father Yakov muttered, as if drunk. "Forgive me, it's all nothing, pay no attention . . . And I only blame myself and will go on blaming myself . . . I will!"

Father Yakov glanced over his shoulder and began to whisper:

"Early one morning I was walking from Sinkovo to Luchkovo; I look, and there's a woman standing on the riverbank doing something . . . I come closer and don't believe my eyes . . . Terrible! Doctor Ivan Sergeich's wife is there rinsing laundry . . . A doctor's wife, who finished boarding school! It means she went early in the morning and half a mile from the village, so that people wouldn't see her . . . Invincible pride! When she saw I was near her and had noticed her poverty, she blushed all over . . . I was taken aback, frightened, I ran up to her, wanted to help, but she tried to hide the laundry from me so that I wouldn't see her tattered undershirts . . ."

"This is all somehow even unbelievable . . . ," said Kunin, sitting down and looking at Father Yakov's pale face almost with horror.

"Precisely unbelievable! It's never happened before, Pavel Mikhailovich, that doctors' wives rinsed their linen in the river! Not in any country! As a pastor and a spiritual father, I should not have allowed her to do it, but what can I do? What? I myself always try to be treated by her husband free of charge. You were right to be so good as to declare it unbelievable! The eyes refuse to believe it! You know, during the liturgy I sometimes peek out from the altar, and when I see all my public, the hungry Avramy and my wife, and remember the doctor's wife, her hands blue from the cold—believe me, I'm at a loss and stand there like a fool, oblivious, until the sacristan calls to me . . . Terrible!"

Father Yakov started pacing again.

"Lord Jesus!" He waved his arms. "Saints alive! I can't even serve . . . There you're telling me about the school, and I'm like a wooden idol, I understand nothing and can only think about food . . . Even before the altar . . . But . . . what am I doing?" Father Yakov caught himself. "You have to leave. Excuse me, it's just that I'm so . . . Forgive me . . ."

Kunin silently shook Father Yakov's hand, accompanied him to the front hall, and, going back to his study, stood by the window. He saw Father Yakov come out of the house, put on his shabby broad-brimmed hat, and, his head hanging, as if embarrassed by his own candor, slowly walk down the road.

"I don't see his horse," thought Kunin.

The thought that the priest had been coming to him on foot all these days frightened Kunin: Sinkovo was five or six miles away, and mud made the roads impassable. Then Kunin saw the coachman Andrei and the boy Paramon, leaping over puddles and splashing Father Yakov with mud, run up to him to receive his blessing. Father Yakov took off his hat and slowly blessed Andrei, then blessed the little boy and stroked his head.

Kunin wiped his hand over his eyes, and it seemed to him that his hand became wet from it. He stepped away from the window and passed a clouded gaze around the room, in which he could still hear the timid, stifled voice . . . He glanced at his desk . . . Fortunately, Father Yakov in his haste had forgotten to take his sermons . . . Kunin ran to them, tore them to shreds, and flung them under the desk in disgust.

"And I didn't know!" he moaned, collapsing on the sofa. "I, who for more than a year have been serving here as a permanent member, an honorary justice of the peace, a member of the high school board! A blind puppet! A fop! Quickly come to their aid! Quickly!"

He thrashed about painfully, pressed his temples, and strained his mind.

"I'll receive my salary of two hundred roubles on the twentieth . . . On some plausible pretext I'll give some to him and to the doctor's wife . . . I'll invite him to offer a prayer service, and I'll feign an illness for the doctor . . . That way their pride won't be offended. And I'll help Avramy . . ."

He counted his money on his fingers and was afraid to admit to himself that these two hundred roubles would barely be enough to pay the steward, the servants, the peasant who delivered meat . . . He could not help remembering the recent past, when he senselessly wasted his father's wealth, when, still a twenty-year-old milksop, he gave expensive fans to prostitutes, paid the coachman Kuzma ten roubles a day, offered gifts to actresses out of vanity. Ah, how useful they would be now, all those squandered roubles, three roubles, ten roubles!

"Father Avramy can eat on only three roubles a month," thought Kunin. "For a rouble the priest's wife can make herself an undershirt and the doctor's wife can hire a washerwoman. But anyhow I'll help them! I'll certainly help them!"

Here Kunin suddenly remembered the denunciation he had written to the bishop, and he cringed all over as if from a sudden blast of cold. This memory filled his whole soul with a sense of oppressive shame before himself and before the invisible truth . . .

Thus began and ended the sincere impulse towards useful activity of one of those well-intentioned but all-too-sated and unreasoning human beings.

1886

GRISHA

GRISHA, A CHUBBY LITTLE BOY, born two years and eight months ago, is strolling with his nanny along the boulevard. He is wearing a long padded coat, a scarf, a big hat with a fuzzy button, and warm galoshes. He feels stifled and hot, and the shiny April sun adds to it by shining straight into his eyes and stinging his eyelids.

His whole clumsy figure, stepping timidly and uncertainly, expresses the utmost perplexity.

Up to now Grisha has known only a rectangular world, where his bed stands in one corner, his nanny's trunk in another, a chair in a third, and in the fourth an icon lamp burns. If you peek under the bed, you see a doll with a broken-off arm and a drum, and behind the nanny's trunk there are a great many different things: empty spools, scraps of paper, a lidless box, and a broken toy clown. Besides the nanny and Grisha, this world is often visited by Mama and the cat. Mama looks like a doll, and the cat like Papa's fur coat, only the fur coat has no eyes or tail. From this world, which is called the children's room, a door leads to a space where they have dinner and drink tea. There Grisha's chair stands on its long legs and a clock hangs, which exists only in order to swing its pendulum and chime. From the dining room you can go on to a room with red armchairs. Here there is a dark spot on the rug, for which they still shake their fingers at Grisha.

Beyond this room there is yet another, where he is not allowed to go and where Papa lurks—a person mysterious in the highest degree! The nanny and Mama are understandable: they dress Grisha, feed him, and put him to bed, but what Papa exists for—nobody knows. There is yet another mysterious person—the aunt who gave Grisha the drum. She appears and then disappears. Where does she disappear to? More than once Grisha looked under the bed, behind the trunk, and under the sofa, but she was not there . . .

In this new world, where the sun dazzles his eyes, there are so many papas, mamas, and aunts that you do not know who to run to. But most strange and absurd of all are the horses. Grisha looks at their moving legs and cannot understand anything. He looks at the nanny, so that she can resolve his perplexity, but she is silent.

Suddenly he hears a terrible stomping . . . Down the boulevard, at a measured pace, a crowd of soldiers with red faces and with bath besoms[1] under their arms moves straight towards him. Grisha turns cold all over with terror and looks questioningly at the nanny: is this dangerous? But the nanny does not flee and does not cry, meaning it is not dangerous. Grisha follows the soldiers with his eyes and starts marching in step himself.

Two big cats with long muzzles, tongues hanging out and tails sticking up, run across the boulevard. Grisha thinks that he, too, has to run, and he runs after the cats.

"Stop!" cries the nanny, seizing him roughly by the shoulders. "Where are you going? Who told you to get up to mischief?"

Here some other nanny sits and holds a little basin of oranges. Grisha passes by her and silently takes an orange.

"What'd you do that for?" cries his companion, slapping him on the hand and snatching the orange from him. "Fool!"

Now Grisha would very happily pick up a little piece of glass that is lying at his feet and shining like an icon lamp, but he is afraid his hand will be slapped again.

"My greetings to you!" Grisha suddenly hears someone's loud, deep voice just by his ear, and he sees a tall man with shiny buttons.

To his great pleasure, this man gives the nanny his hand, stops beside her, and starts to talk. The brightness of the sun, the noise of the carriages, the horses, the shiny buttons—it is all so strikingly new and not frightening that Grisha's soul is filled with a feeling of delight, and he bursts out laughing.

"Let's go, let's go," he cries to the man with the shiny buttons, pulling at the skirt of his coat.

"Go where?" the man asks.

"Let's go!" Grisha insists.

He would like to say that it would be nice to take Papa, Mama, and the cat along, but his tongue simply does not say what it should.

A little later the nanny turns off the boulevard and leads Grisha into a big courtyard, where there is still snow. And the man with the shiny buttons also goes with them. They carefully avoid the piles of snow and the puddles, then go up a dirty, dark stairway to a room. Here there is a lot of smoke, the smell of a roast, and some woman is standing by a stove and frying beef patties. The cook and the nanny exchange kisses and, along with the man, sit down on a bench and begin to talk softly. Grisha, all bundled up, feels unbearably hot and stifled.

"Why all this?" he thinks, looking around.

He sees a dark ceiling, an oven fork with two prongs, the stove which looks like a big, black hole . . .

"Ma-a-ma!" he drawls.

"Now, now, now!" shouts the nanny. "You can wait!"

The cook puts a bottle, two glasses, and a pie on the table. The two women and the man with the shiny buttons clink and drink several times, and the man embraces now the nanny, now the cook. And then all three begin to sing softly.

Grisha reaches out for the pie, and they give him a piece. He eats and watches the nanny drink . . . He, too, wants to drink.

"Give! Give, Nanny!" he asks.

The cook lets him take a sip from her glass. He rolls his eyes, winces, coughs, and waves his hands for a long time afterwards, and the cook looks at him and laughs.

On returning home, Grisha begins to tell Mama, the walls, and the bed where he was and what he saw. He speaks not so much with his tongue as with his face and hands. He shows how the sun shines, how the horses run, how the frightening stove stares, and how the cook drinks . . .

In the evening he simply cannot fall asleep. Soldiers with besoms, big cats, horses, a piece of glass, a basin of oranges, the shiny buttons—it all gathers in a heap and presses down on his brain. He tosses from side to side, babbles, and finally, unable to bear his agitation, he starts to cry.

"You have a fever!" says his mama, putting her palm to his forehead. "What could have caused it?"

"Stove!" weeps Grisha. "Go away, stove!"

"He must have eaten something . . . ," his mama decides.

And Grisha, bursting with the impressions of the new life he has just experienced, receives from his mama a spoonful of castor oil.

1886

LADIES

FYODOR PETROVICH, DIRECTOR OF PUBLIC EDUCATION of N——sky Province, who considered himself a fair and magnanimous man, was once meeting with the teacher Vremensky in his chancellery.

"No, Mr. Vremensky," he was saying, "your dismissal is unavoidable. With such a voice you cannot go on working as a teacher. How did you lose it?"

"I was sweaty and drank cold beer . . . ," the teacher wheezed.

"What a pity! A man works for fourteen years, and suddenly such a calamity! Devil knows, to go and ruin your career for such a trifling thing. What do you intend to do now?"

The teacher did not reply.

"Do you have a family?" asked the director.

"A wife and two children, Your Excellency . . . ," the teacher wheezed.

Silence ensued. The director got up from the desk and paced from corner to corner in agitation.

"I have no idea what to do with you!" he said. "You cannot be a teacher, you haven't reached pension age . . . to abandon you to the mercy of fate, to the four winds, is somehow awkward. You're one of our people, you've worked for fourteen years, which means it's our duty to help you . . . But how? What can I do for you? Put yourself in my place: what can I do for you?"

Silence ensued. The director paced and kept thinking, and Vremensky, crushed by his grief, sat on the edge of the chair and also thought. Suddenly the director brightened up and even snapped his fingers.

"I'm surprised I didn't think of it sooner!" he began speaking quickly. "Listen, here's what I can offer you . . . Next week the clerk at our orphanage is going to retire. If you like, you can take his post! There you are!"

Vremensky, who had not expected such a favor, also brightened up.

"Excellent!" said the director. "Write an application today . . ."

Having dismissed Vremensky, Fyodor Petrovich felt relieved and even pleased: the stooping figure of the wheezing pedagogue was no longer sticking up in front of him, and it was pleasant to realize that in offering Vremensky the vacant post he had acted fairly and conscientiously, as a kind, perfectly decent man. But this good mood did not last long. When he came home and sat down to dinner, his wife, Nastasya Ivanovna, suddenly remembered:

"Ah, yes, I almost forgot! Yesterday Nina Sergeevna came to see me and solicited for a young man. They say there's a vacancy opening up in the orphanage . . ."

"Yes, but that post has already been promised to someone else," the director said and frowned. "And you know my rule: I never make appointments through connections."

"I know, but for Nina Sergeevna I suppose you could make an exception. She loves us like her own, and we have yet to do anything good for her. So don't even think of refusing her, Fedya. With your caprices you'll offend both her and me."

"Who is she recommending?"

"Polzukhin."

"What Polzukhin? The one who played Chatsky at the New Year assembly?[1] That fop? Not for anything!"

The director stopped eating.

"Not for anything!" he repeated. "God forbid!"

"Why not?"

"You see, my dear, if a young man doesn't act directly, but through women, it means he's trash! Why doesn't he come to me himself?"

After dinner the director lay down on the sofa in his study and began to read the newspapers and letters he had received.

"Dear Fyodor Petrovich," wrote the mayor's wife, "you once said I was a reader of hearts and a knower of human nature. Now you can test that in practice. One of these days a young man will come to you to solicit the post of a clerk in our orphanage, a certain K. N. Polzukhin, whom I know to be an excellent young man. He is very likeable. Once you concern yourself with him, you will discover . . . ," etc.

"Not for anything!" the director said. "God forbid!"

After that not a day went by without the director receiving letters recommending Polzukhin. One fine morning Polzukhin himself appeared, a young man, portly, with a clean-shaven jockey's face, in a new two-piece black suit . . .

"For matters of business I receive in the office, not here," the director said drily, having heard out his request.

"Forgive me, Your Excellency, but our mutual acquaintances advised me to come precisely here."

"Hm! . . . ," the director grunted, staring with hatred at the man's sharp-toed shoes. "As far as I know," he said, "your father is wealthy and you are not a pauper: why do you need to ask for this post? The salary is paltry!"

"It's not for the salary, but just . . . After all, it's government service . . ."

"Well, sir . . . It seems to me you'll be bored with this position after a month and will quit, and meanwhile there are candidates for whom the post would be a life's career . . . Poor people for whom . . ."

"I won't be bored, Your Excellency," Polzukhin interrupted. "My word of honor, I'll do my best!"

The director blew up.

"Listen," he asked, smiling contemptuously, "why is it you didn't turn directly to me, but found it necessary to trouble the ladies first?"

"I didn't know you would find that disagreeable," Polzukhin replied and became embarrassed. "But, Your Excellency, if you attach no importance to letters of recommendation, I can supply you with an attestation . . ."

He took a paper from his pocket and handed it to the director. Beneath the attestation, written in bureaucratic style and script, was the signature of the governor. Everything suggested that the governor had signed it without reading it, just to get rid of some importunate lady.

"Nothing to be done, I bow down . . . I obey . . . ," said the director, having read the attestation, and he sighed. "Submit your application tomorrow . . . Nothing to be done."

When Polzukhin left, the director gave himself up entirely to the feeling of loathing.

"Trash!" he hissed, pacing from corner to corner. "So he got what he wanted, worthless lickspittle! Vermin! Women's pet! Vile creature!"

The director spat loudly at the door through which Polzukhin had left, then suddenly became embarrassed, because a lady was just coming into his study, the wife of the town treasurer . . .

"Only a moment, a moment . . . ," the lady began. "Sit yourself down, my friend, and listen to me carefully . . . They say you have a vacancy . . . Tomorrow or even today a young man will come to see you, a certain Polzukhin . . ."

The lady went on chirping, and the director gazed at her with dull, bleary eyes, like a man who is about to fall into a faint, gazed and smiled out of politeness.

The next day, receiving Vremensky in his office, the director took a long time before venturing to tell him the truth. He hemmed and hawed, became confused, could not find where to begin, what to say. He would have liked to apologize to the teacher, to tell him the whole truth, but his tongue, like a drunk man's, would not obey him, his ears burned, and he suddenly felt hurt and vexed at having to play such an absurd role—in his own office, before his subordinates. He suddenly pounded the table, jumped up, and shouted angrily:

"I have no post for you! None, none! Leave me alone! Don't torment me! Let me be, finally, do me a favor!"

And he walked out of the office.

1886

Romance with a Double Bass

The musician Bowsky was walking from town to the dacha[1] of Prince Bibulov, where on the occasion of a wedding engagement an evening of music and dance was "to be held." On his back rested an enormous double bass in a leather case. Bowsky walked beside the river, which rolled its cool waters along, if not majestically, at least quite poetically.

"Why not go for a swim?" he thought.

Without further thinking, he undressed and immersed his body in the cool stream. The evening was magnificent. Bowsky's poetic soul began to tune in with the harmony of his surroundings. But what a sweet feeling came over his soul when, having swum some hundred yards, he saw a beautiful girl sitting on the steep bank and fishing. He held his breath and stopped under an influx of heterogeneous feelings: memories of childhood, pining for the past, awakened love . . . God, and here he thought he was no longer capable of love! After losing faith in humankind (his ardently loved wife had run off with his friend, the bassoon Muttkin), his breast had been filled with a sense of emptiness, and he had turned into a misanthrope.

"What is life?" he had asked himself more than once. "What do we live for? Life is a myth, a dream . . . ventriloquism . . ."

But, standing before this sleeping beauty (it was not hard to notice she was asleep), suddenly, against his will, he felt in his breast something resembling love. He stood before her for a long time, devouring her with his eyes . . .

"But enough . . . ," he thought, letting out a deep sigh. "Farewell, wondrous vision! It's time I went to His Excellency's ball . . ."

And glancing once more at the beauty, he was just about to swim back when an idea flashed in his mind.

"I must leave her something to remember me by!" he thought. "I'll attach something to her line. It will be a surprise from 'the unknown one.'"

Bowsky quietly swam to the bank, picked a big bouquet of field and water flowers, and, binding it with a stalk of goosefoot, attached it to the line.

The bouquet sank to the bottom and dragged the pretty float down with it.

Discretion, the laws of nature, and our hero's social situation demand that the romance should end at this point, but—alas!—the author's fate is implacable: owing to circumstances beyond his control, the romance did not end with the bouquet. Counter to common sense and the nature of things, the poor and unaristocratic double bassist was to play an important role in the life of an aristocratic and rich beauty.

Swimming to the bank, Bowsky was astounded: he did not see his clothes. They had been stolen . . . While he was admiring the beauty, unknown villains had stolen everything except the double bass and top hat.

"Damnation!" exclaimed Bowsky. "Oh, people, you brood of vipers! I am not so much indignant at the loss of the clothes (for clothes are perishable) as at the thought that I shall have to go naked, thereby trespassing against public morality."

He sat down on the case of his double bass and started thinking about how to get out of his terrible situation.

"I can't very well go naked to Prince Bibulov's!" he thought. "There'll be ladies there! And besides, along with my trousers, the thieves stole the rosin in my pocket!"

He thought for a long time, tormentingly, until his temples hurt.

"Hah!" he remembered at last. "In the bushes near the bank there's a little bridge . . . I can sit under that little bridge until night falls, and in the evening, under cover of darkness, I'll make my way to the nearest cottage . . ."

Clinging to that thought, Bowsky put on his top hat, hoisted the double bass on his back, and trudged off to the bushes. Naked, with a musical instrument on his back, he resembled some ancient mythical demigod.

Now, reader, while my hero is sitting under the bridge, giving himself up to sorrow, let us leave him for a time and turn to the girl who was fishing. What became of her? The beauty, waking up and not seeing the float in the water, hastily pulled on the line. The line tautened, but the float and hook did not come to the surface. Apparently Bowsky's bouquet had soaked up water, swelled, and become heavy.

"Either a big fish got caught," thought the girl, "or the hook got snagged."

Having pulled at the line a little more, the girl decided that the hook got snagged.

"What a pity!" she thought. "And fish bite so well in the evening. What am I to do?"

And without further thought, the eccentric girl threw off her ethereal clothes and immersed her beautiful body in the stream up to her marble shoulders. To undo the line, the hook, and the bouquet was not easy, but patience and effort won out. After some quarter of an hour, the beauty, radiant and happy, emerged from the water, holding the hook in her hand.

But ill fate lay in wait for her. The scoundrel who had stolen Bowsky's clothes also stole her dress, leaving her only the can of worms.

"What am I to do now?" she wept. "Can I go looking like this? No, never! Better to die! I'll wait till it gets dark; then, in the darkness, I'll go to Aunt Agafya and send her home for a dress . . . And meanwhile I'll go and hide under the little bridge."

My heroine, choosing where the grass was higher and crouching down, scurried to the little bridge. Slipping under it, she saw a naked man with a musician's mane and a hairy chest, cried out and fainted.

Bowsky was also frightened. At first he took the girl for a naiad.

"Isn't she a river siren come to entice me?" he thought, and that surmise flattered him, because he had always had a high opinion of his looks. "If she's not a siren, but a human being, how explain this strange transformation? Why is she here under the bridge? And what's the matter with her?"

While he was debating all these questions, the beauty came to her senses.

"Don't kill me!" she whispered. "I'm Princess Bibulova. I beseech you! You'll be given a lot of money! I was untangling my fishing line in the water, and some thieves stole my new dress, shoes, and everything!"

"Miss!" said Bowsky in a pleading voice. "I also had my clothes stolen. And along with my trousers they also made off with the rosin that was in my pocket!"

Those who play double basses and trombones are usually unresourceful, but Bowsky was a pleasant exception.

"Miss!" he said a while later. "I see you're embarrassed at the sight of me. But you must agree that I have the same grounds for not leaving this place as you do. Here's what I've come up with: how would you like to lie in the case of my double bass and cover yourself with the lid? That will conceal me from you . . ."

Having said that, Bowsky took the instrument out of the case. For a moment it seemed to him that by yielding up the case he was blaspheming against the sacredness of art, but his hesitation did not last long. The beauty lay down in the case and curled up, and he tightened the straps and rejoiced that nature had endowed him with such intelligence.

"Now, miss, you don't see me," he said. "Lie there and be at peace. When it gets dark, I'll carry you to your parents' home. I can come back here later for my double bass."

When darkness fell, Bowsky hoisted the case with the beauty on his shoulders and trudged to Bibulov's dacha. His plan was this: he will come to the first cottage and obtain some clothing, then he will go on . . .

"There's no bad without some good," he thought, stirring up the dust with his bare feet and bending under the burden. "For the heartfelt share I've taken in the princess's fate, Bibulov is sure to reward me generously."

"Are you comfortable, miss?" he asked in the tone of a *cavalier galant* inviting her to a quadrille. "Kindly do not stand on ceremony: treat my case as if it were your own home."

Suddenly the gallant Bowsky fancied that ahead of him, shrouded in darkness, two human figures were walking. He peered intently and realized that this was not an optical illusion: the figures were indeed walking and even carrying some bundles in their hands . . .

"Aren't these the thieves?" flashed through his mind. "They're carrying something. It's probably our clothes!"

Bowsky set the case down by the roadside and ran after the figures. "Stop!" he shouted. "Stop! Seize them!"

The figures turned and, seeing the pursuit, took to their heels . . . The princess heard the quick footsteps and the shouts of "Stop!" for a long time. Finally, all fell silent.

Bowsky got carried away by the pursuit, and the beauty might well have spent a long time lying in the field by the roadside had it not been for a lucky play of chance. It chanced that just then Bowsky's colleagues, the flute Buzzkin and the clarinet Wavarmov, came along the same road. Stumbling upon the case, they looked at each other in surprise and spread their arms.

"A double bass!" said Buzzkin. "Hah, it's our Bowsky's double bass! How did it wind up here?"

"Something probably happened to Bowsky," decided Wavarmov. "Either he got drunk, or he was robbed . . . In either case, it wouldn't be right to leave the instrument here. Let's take it with us."

Buzzkin hoisted the case on his back, and the musicians went on.

"It's heavy, damn it!" the flute grumbled on the way. "Not for anything in the world would I agree to play such a monster . . . Oof!"

On arriving at Prince Bibulov's dacha, the musicians put the case in the area reserved for the orchestra and went to the buffet.

Just then the chandeliers and sconces were being lit. The fiancé, Court Councillor Flunkeyich, a handsome and affable official from the Ministry of Transportation, was standing in the middle of the reception room, his hands in his pockets, talking with Count Flaskov. They were discussing music.

"In Naples, Count," Flunkeyich was saying, "I was personally acquainted with a fiddler who literally performed miracles. You won't believe it! On a double bass . . . on an ordinary double bass, he pulled off such devilish trills, it was simply awful! He played Strauss waltzes."

"Come now, that's impossible . . ." The count doubted him.

"I assure you! He even performed a Liszt rhapsody. I lived in the same room with him and having nothing to do I even learned from him to play a rhapsody of Liszt on the double bass."

"A rhapsody of Liszt . . . Hm . . . you're joking . . ."

"You don't believe it?" Flunkeyich laughed. "I'll prove it to you right now! Let's go to the orchestra!"

The fiancé and the count went to the orchestra. They approached the double bass, quickly started undoing the straps . . . and—oh, horror!

But here, while the reader, giving free rein to his imagination, pictures the outcome of the musical dispute, let us turn back to Bowsky . . . The poor musician, having failed to catch the thieves and gone back to the place where he left the case, could not locate the precious burden. Totally at a loss, he walked up and down the road several times and, not finding the case, decided that he had come to the wrong road . . .

"This is awful!" he thought, clutching his hair and turning cold. "She'll suffocate in the case! I'm a murderer!"

Until midnight Bowsky walked the road and looked for the case, but finally, out of strength, he headed back to the little bridge.

"I'll search at dawn," he decided.

The search at dawn produced the same result, and Bowsky decided to wait under the bridge till nightfall . . .

"I'll find her!" he muttered, taking off his top hat and seizing his hair. "I may look for a whole year, but I'll find her!"

To this day peasants living in the area we have described tell that, at night, by the little bridge, one can see a naked man, overgrown with hair and wearing a top hat. Every now and then under the little bridge the wheezing of a double bass can be heard.

1886

The Chorus Girl

ONCE, WHEN SHE WAS YOUNGER, prettier, more full voiced, her admirer, Nikolai Petrovich Kolpakov, was sitting in the mezzanine of her dacha. It was unbearably hot and stifling. Kolpakov had just finished dinner and, having drunk a whole bottle of bad port, felt out of sorts and ill. They were both bored and were waiting for it to cool off in order to go for a walk.

Suddenly and unexpectedly the doorbell rang. Kolpakov, who was in his shirtsleeves and wearing slippers, jumped up and looked questioningly at Pasha.

"Must be the mailman, or maybe one of my girlfriends," said the singer.

Kolpakov was not embarrassed either by Pasha's friends or by mailmen, but, just in case, he grabbed his clothes and went to the next room, while Pasha ran to open the door. To her great surprise, it was neither a mailman nor a girlfriend who stood at the door, but an unknown woman, young, beautiful, elegantly dressed, and, by all appearances, of a respectable sort.

The unknown woman was pale and breathing heavily, as if after climbing a steep stairway.

"What can I do for you?" asked Pasha.

The lady did not answer at once. She took a step forward, slowly looked around the room, and sat down as if she were too tired or unwell to go on standing; then she moved her pale lips for a long time, trying to utter something.

"Is my husband here?" she asked, finally, raising to Pasha her big eyes with their red, tear-stained eyelids.

"What husband?" Pasha whispered and suddenly became so frightened that her hands and feet went cold. "What husband?" she repeated, beginning to tremble.

"My husband . . . Nikolai Petrovich Kolpakov."

"N-no, madam . . . I . . . I don't know any husband."

A minute passed in silence. The unknown woman wiped her pale lips several times with a handkerchief, holding her breath to overcome her inner trembling, while Pasha stood motionless before her as if rooted to the spot and looked at her with perplexity and fear.

"So you say he's not here?" the lady asked in a firm voice now and smiling somehow strangely.

"I . . . I don't know who you're asking about."

"You're vile, mean, repulsive . . . ," the stranger muttered, looking at Pasha with hatred and loathing. "Yes, yes . . . you're vile. I'm very, very glad that I can finally tell you so!"

Pasha felt that she made on this lady in black, with angry eyes and slender white fingers, the impression of something vile and ugly, and she became ashamed of her plump red cheeks, the pockmarks on her nose, and the fringe on her forehead that refused to stay combed back. And it seemed to her that if she were thin, unpowdered, and without the fringe, it would be possible to conceal that she was not a respectable girl, and it would not be so frightening and shameful to stand before this unknown, mysterious lady.

"Where is my husband?" the lady went on. "However, whether he's here or not makes no difference to me, but I must tell you that the embezzlement has been discovered and they're looking for Nikolai Petrovich . . . They're going to arrest him. That's what you have done!"

The lady got up and paced the room in strong agitation. Pasha looked at her and was too frightened to understand.

"They'll find him today and arrest him," the lady said and sobbed, and in that sound could be heard both offense and vexation. "I know who drove him to such horror! Vile, repulsive! Loathsome, bought woman!" (The lady's lips twisted and her nose wrinkled with loathing.) "I'm powerless . . . listen, you mean woman! . . . I'm powerless, you're stronger than I am, but there's someone who will intercede for me and my children! God sees everything! He is just! He will punish you for each of my tears, for all my sleepless nights! The time will come, and you will remember me!"

Again there was silence. The lady paced the room wringing her hands, and Pasha went on looking at her dully, with perplexity, not understanding and expecting something dreadful from her.

"I don't know anything, madam!" she said and suddenly began to cry.

"You're lying!" the lady shouted and flashed her eyes spitefully. "I know everything! I've known about you for a long time now! I know over this past month he spent every day with you!"

"Yes. So what? What of it? I have many guests, but I don't force anybody. Free is as free does."

"I tell you: there's been an embezzlement! He embezzled other people's money at the office! For the sake of a person . . . like you, for your sake he committed a crime. Listen," the lady said in a resolute tone, stopping in front of Pasha. "You cannot have any principles, you live only to do evil, that is your goal, but it's unthinkable that you have fallen so low as to have no trace of human feeling left! He has a wife, children . . . If he is condemned and exiled, I and the children will die of hunger . . . Understand that! But there is a way to save him and us from poverty and disgrace. If I deposit nine hundred roubles today, he will be left in peace. Just nine hundred roubles!"

"What nine hundred roubles?" Pasha asked softly. "I . . . I don't know . . . I didn't take . . ."

"I'm not asking you for nine hundred roubles . . . you have no money, and I have no need of what is yours. I am asking for something else . . . Men usually give expensive things to the likes of you. Just give me back the things my husband has given you!"

"Madam, he never gave me anything!" Pasha shrieked, beginning to understand.

"Then where is the money? He squandered his, mine, and other people's . . . Where did it all go? Listen, I beg you! I was indignant and said all kinds of unpleasant things to you, but I apologize. You must hate me, I know, but if you're capable of compassion, put yourself in my place! I implore you, give me back those things!"

"Hm . . . ," said Pasha, and she shrugged her shoulders. "I'd be glad to, but, God strike me dead, he never gave me anything. In all conscience. Though, to tell the truth," the singer became embarrassed, "he once brought me two little things. Here, I'll give them to you, if you like . . ."

Pasha pulled open one of the little drawers in her dressing table and took out a hollow gold bracelet and a cheap little ring with a ruby.

"Here!" she said, giving these things to the visitor.

The lady flushed deeply, and her face quivered. She was insulted.

"What's this you're giving me?" she said. "I'm not asking for alms, but for what does not belong to you . . . what you, profiting from your situation, extracted from my husband . . . that weak, unfortunate man . . . On Thursday, when I saw you and my husband at the pier, you were wearing expensive brooches and bracelets. So there's no point in playing the innocent lamb. I ask you for the last time, will you give me those things or not?"

"You're a strange one, by God . . . ," said Pasha, beginning to be offended. "I assure you that, apart from this bracelet and ring, I haven't seen a thing from your husband. He only brought me little pastries."

"Little pastries . . . ," the woman smirked. "At home the children have nothing to eat, and here it's little pastries. So you flatly refuse to return the things?"

Receiving no reply, the lady sat down and, pondering something, fixed her eyes on one spot.

"What am I to do now?" she said. "If I don't find nine hundred roubles, he will perish, and I and the children will perish, too. Shall I kill this loathsome creature or go on my knees to her?"

The lady pressed her handkerchief to her face and burst into sobs.

"I beg you!" could be heard through her sobs. "You bankrupted and ruined my husband. Save him . . . You have no compassion for him, but the children . . . the children . . . What are the children guilty of?"

Pasha imagined little children standing in the street and crying from hunger, and burst into sobs herself.

"What can I do, madam?" she said. "You say I'm a loathsome creature and I've ruined Nikolai Petrovich, but, as God is my witness . . . I assure you I have never profited from him . . . In our chorus, only Motya has a rich patron, and the rest of us get by on bread and kvass. Nikolai Petrovich is a cultivated and delicate man, well, so I received him. We can't do without it."

"I'm asking for the things! Give me the things! I weep . . . I humiliate myself . . . If you like, I'll go on my knees to you! If you like!"

Pasha cried out in fear and waved her hands. She sensed that this pale, beautiful lady, who spoke nobly, as in a theater, was actually capable of going on her knees to her, precisely out of pride, out of nobility, to elevate herself and humiliate the chorus girl.

"All right, I'll give you the things!" Pasha started bustling about, wiping her eyes. "If you like. Only they don't come from Nikolai Petrovich . . . I got them from my other guests. As you please, ma'am . . ."

Pasha pulled open the upper drawer of the chest, took out a brooch with diamonds, a coral necklace, several rings, a bracelet, and gave them all to the lady.

"Take them, if you wish, only I haven't made any profit from your husband. Take them, get rich!" Pasha went on, insulted by the threat of going on her knees. "And if you're his noble . . . lawful wife, you should have kept him by you. So there! I didn't invite him, he came on his own . . ."

Through her tears the lady looked over the things presented to her and said:

"This isn't all . . . It wouldn't make even five hundred roubles."

Pasha impulsively flung a gold watch, a cigarette case, and a pair of cufflinks at her and said, spreading her arms:

"I have nothing else left . . . Go on and search me!"

The visitor sighed, wrapped the things in a handkerchief with trembling hands, and not saying a word, not even nodding her head, went out.

The door to the next room opened, and Kolpakov came in. He was pale and shook his head nervously, as if he had just swallowed something bitter. Tears glistened in his eyes.

"What things did you bring me?" Pasha fell upon him. "When, if I may ask?"

"Things . . . That's nonsense—things!" Kolpakov said and shook his head. "My God! She wept, she humiliated herself before you . . ."

"I'm asking you: what things did you bring me?" cried Pasha.

"My God, she, decent, proud, pure . . . even wanted to go on her knees before . . . before this slut! And I drove her to it! I made it happen!"

He clutched his head and moaned:

"No, I'll never forgive myself! Never! Get away from me, you . . . trash!" he cried in revulsion, stepping back from Pasha and pushing her away from him with trembling hands. "She wanted to go on her knees and . . . before whom? Before you! Oh, my God!"

He dressed quickly and, squeamishly avoiding Pasha, went to the door and left.

Pasha lay down and began to cry loudly. She was sorry now for the things she had given away on an impulse, and she was offended. She remembered how a shopkeeper had given her a beating three years ago for no reason at all, and she cried even louder.

1886

The First-Class Passenger

A FIRST-CLASS PASSENGER, who had just had dinner at the station and was slightly tipsy, sprawled on the velvet seat, stretched out sweetly, and dozed off. After dozing for no more than five minutes, he looked with oily eyes at his *vis-à-vis*, grinned, and said:

"My father, of blessed memory, liked to have his heels scratched by a peasant wench after dinner. I'm exactly the same, with the only difference that each time after dinner I scratch not my heels but my tongue and brain. Sinner that I am, I love to babble on a full stomach. Will you allow me to chat with you a little?"

"By all means," the *vis-à-vis* agreed.

"After a good dinner, it takes only the most insignificant pretext for devilishly big thoughts to come into my head. For instance, you and I just saw two young men at the buffet, and you heard one of them congratulate the other on becoming a celebrity. 'Congratulations,' he said, 'you're already a celebrity and are beginning to be famous.' Obviously actors or microscopic journalists. But they're not the point. I, sir, am now interested in the question of what, in fact, should be understood by the words 'fame' and 'celebrity.' What's your opinion, sir? Pushkin called fame a bright patch on rags;[1] we all understand it Pushkin fashion, that is, more or less subjectively, but no one has yet given a clear, logical definition of this word. I'd give a lot for such a definition."

"Why do you need it so much?"

"You see, if we knew what fame is, we might also know the ways of winning it," the first-class passenger said after some thought. "I must point out to you, sir, that when I was younger I strove for celebrity with every fiber of my soul. Popularity was, so to speak, my madness. For the sake of it I studied, worked, didn't sleep nights, didn't eat enough, and ruined my health. And it seems, insofar as I can judge impartially, that I had all the qualifications for it. First of all, sir, I am an engineer by profession. In my lifetime I've built a couple of dozen splendid bridges in Russia, I've constructed water supply systems for three towns, I've worked in Russia, in England, in Belgium . . . Second, I've written many specialized articles in my line. Third, my dear sir, I've had a weakness for chemistry since childhood; devoting my leisure to this science, I have discovered methods for obtaining certain organic acids, so that you will find my name in all foreign chemistry textbooks. All this while I held a position, rose to the rank of actual state councillor, and have a spotless record. I won't impose on your attention by listing all my honors and achievements, and will only say that I did much more than some celebrities. And what then? I'm already old, on my last legs, one might say, and I'm as much a celebrity as that black dog running along the embankment."

"How can you tell? Maybe you are a celebrity."

"Hm! . . . We'll test it right now . . . Tell me, have you ever heard the name Krikunov?"

The *vis-à-vis* looked up at the ceiling, thought a little, and laughed.

"No, never heard it . . . ," he said.

"It's my last name. You, an educated and elderly man, have never heard of me—conclusive proof! Obviously, in striving to become a celebrity, I didn't do what I should have done at all. I didn't know the proper methods, and, wishing to catch fame by the tail, I started from the wrong end."

"What are the proper methods?"

"Devil knows! You say: talent? genius? originality? Not at all, my dear sir . . . Parallel with me people lived and pursued their careers who, compared to me, were empty, worthless, and even trashy. They worked a thousand times less than I did, didn't turn inside out, didn't sparkle with talent or strive for fame, but look at them! Their names turn up in the newspapers and in conversations all the time! If you're not tired of listening, I'll clarify with an example. Several years ago I built a bridge in the town of K. I must tell you that this shabby K. was a terribly boring town. If it hadn't been for women and cards, I probably would have gone out of my mind. Well, sir, it's all long past: out of boredom there I took up with a little singer. Devil knows why, everybody went into raptures over this little singer, but in my view— how shall I put it to you?—she was an ordinary, commonplace little type, like many others. An empty, capricious, greedy girl, and a fool besides. She ate a lot, drank a lot, slept till five in the afternoon—and nothing more, it seems. She was considered a *cocotte*—that was her profession—and when they wanted to refer to her more literarily, they called her an actress and singer. I used to be an inveterate the-atergoer, and therefore this fraudulent toying with the title of actress outraged me terribly! My little singer didn't have the least right to be called an actress or even a singer. This was a being totally devoid of talent, devoid of feeling, one might even say pathetic. To my under-standing, her singing was disgusting, and the whole charm of her 'art' was that she kicked up her leg when necessary and was not embar-rassed when someone came into her dressing room. She usually chose translated vaudevilles, with songs, the sort in which she could show off in a tightly fitting male costume. In a word—pfui! Now, sir, I ask for your attention. I remember as if it were today, a solemn ceremony was held for the opening of the newly built bridge to traffic. There was a prayer service, speeches, telegrams, and all the rest. I, you know, was hovering around this child of mine, and kept worrying that my heart would burst from authorial excitement. It's all long past, there's no need to play modest, so I'll tell you that my bridge turned out to be magnificent! Not a bridge, but a picture, simply splendid! Just try not being excited when the whole town comes to the opening. 'Well,' I thought, 'now the public will stare all eyes at me. Where can I hide?' But, my dear sir, I worried over nothing—alas! Apart from the officials, no one paid the slightest attention to me. The crowd of them stood on the bank, gazing at the bridge like sheep, and not caring at all about the one who built it. And, devil take them, from that time on, by the way, I began to hate this most esteemed public of ours. But to go on. Suddenly the public stirred: psst, psst, psst . . . Faces smiled, shoulders moved. 'They must have spotted me,' I thought. Oh, yes, fat chance! I look: my little singer is making her way through the crowd, with a bunch of wags behind her; the eyes of the crowd hasten to follow the whole procession. A thousand-voiced whispering began: 'It's So-and-So . . . Lovely! Enchanting!' It was then that they noticed me . . . Two milksops—must have been local amateurs of the scenic art—looked at me, exchanged glances, and whispered: 'That's her lover!' How do you like that? And some sort of runty figure in a top hat, with a long-unshaven mug, shuffled beside me for a long time, then turned to me with these words:

" 'Do you know the lady who's walking on the other bank? It's So-and-So . . . Her voice is beneath criticism, but she masters it to perfection! . . .''

" 'Might you tell me,' I asked the runty figure, 'who built this bridge?'

" 'I really don't know,' he replied. 'Some engineer.'

" 'And who,' I asked, 'built the cathedral in your K.?'

" 'I can't tell you that either.'

"Then I asked who in K. is considered the best pedagogue, who the best architect, and to all my questions the runty figure professed ignorance.

" 'And tell me, please,' I asked in conclusion, 'who does this singer live with?'

" 'With some engineer named Krikunov.'

"Well, my dear sir, how do you like that? But to go on . . . There are no minnesingers or bards in the wide world now, and celebrities are created almost exclusively by the newspapers. The day after the blessing of the bridge, I eagerly snatch up the local *Messenger* and search through it for something about my own person. I spend a long time looking over all four pages and, finally—there it is! Hurrah! I start reading: 'Yesterday, the weather being excellent, an enormous gathering of people, in the presence of His Excellency Governor So-and-So and other authorities, attended the blessing of the newly constructed bridge . . . ,' etc. And it ended: 'Present at the blessing, incidentally, radiant with beauty, was the darling of the K. public, our talented actress So-and-So. Needless to say, her appearance caused a sensation. The star was dressed . . . ,' etc. And not a single word about me! Not even half a word! It was very petty, but, believe me, I was so angry I even wept!

"I calmed myself with the thought that the province is stupid, there's nothing to be expected from it, and for celebrity one must go to the intellectual centers, the capitals.[2] It so happened that one of my little projects was in Petersburg just then, sent to a competition. The date of the competition was approaching.

"I bade farewell to K. and went to Petersburg. The road from K. to Petersburg is long, so, not to be bored, I took a private compartment and . . . well, of course, the little singer. We rode along and all the way ate, drank champagne, and—tra-la-la! But here we arrive at the intellectual center. I arrived there on the very day of the competition, and had the pleasure, my dear sir, of celebrating a victory: my project was awarded the first prize. Hurrah! The next day I go to Nevsky Prospect and buy seventy kopecks' worth of various newspapers. I hasten to my hotel room, lie down on the sofa, and, trying not to tremble, hasten to read. I look through one newspaper—nothing! I look through another—not a hint! Finally, in the fourth, I come across this news: 'Yesterday on the express train the famous provincial actress So-and-So arrived in Petersburg. We are pleased to point out that the southern climate has had a beneficial effect on our acquaintance; her beautiful stage appearance . . .' and I don't remember what else! Far below this news, in the smallest typeface, was printed: 'Yesterday in such-and-such competition the first prize was awarded to the engineer So-and-So.' That's all! And, to top it off, my last name was distorted: instead of Krikunov they wrote Kirkunov. There's an intellectual center for you. But that's not all . . . When I was leaving Petersburg a month later, the newspapers all vied with each other telling about 'our incomparable, divine, highly talented' and called my mistress not by her last name, but by her first name and patronymic. . . .

"Several years later I was in Moscow. I was summoned there by a personal letter from the mayor, on business which Moscow and its newspapers had already been shouting about for more than a hundred years. Among other things, I delivered in one of the museums there five public lectures for charitable purposes. That seems like enough to make one a celebrity in the city, if only for three days, doesn't it? But, alas! Not a single Moscow newspaper mentioned it. Fires, operettas, sleeping councillors, drunken merchants—they mention everything, but about me, my project, my lectures—not a peep. Ah, that dear old Moscow public! I get into a horse tram . . . The wagon is packed full: there are ladies and officers and students of both sexes—two and two.

" 'They say the Town Council has invited an engineer on such-and-such business!' I say to my neighbor, loudly enough so that the whole wagon can hear. 'Do you know his name?'

"The neighbor shook his head. The other people all glanced fleetingly at me, and in their eyes I read: 'I don't know.'

" 'They say someone's giving lectures in such-and-such museum!' I pester the public, wishing to strike up a conversation. 'I've heard it's interesting.'

"No one even nodded. Obviously not all of them had heard about the lectures, and the esteemed ladies didn't even know about the existence of the museum. That was all still nothing, but imagine, my dear sir, the public suddenly jumped up and rushed to the windows. What is it? What's the matter?

" 'Look, look!' my neighbor nudged me. 'See that dark-haired man getting into the cab? That's the famous sprinter King!' And the whole wagon, spluttering, began to talk about the sprinters, who then occupied the minds of Moscow.

"I could give you many other examples, but I suppose these are enough. Now I allow that I'm deluded about myself, that I'm giftless and a braggart, but, besides myself, I could point out to you many of my contemporaries, people remarkable for their talents and hard work, but who died in obscurity. All these Russian navigators, chemists, physicists, mechanics, agronomists—are they popular? Are Russian painters, sculptors, men of letters known to our educated masses? Some old literary dog, hardworking and talented, wears out the publishers' doorsteps for thirty-three years, uses up the devil knows how much paper, is taken to court twenty times for defamation, and still never steps further than his anthill! Name for me at least one coryphaeus of our literature who became a celebrity before the rumor spread in the world that he had been killed in a duel, gone mad, been exiled, or cheated at cards!"

The first-class passenger got so carried away that the cigar dropped from his mouth and he rose from his seat.

"Yes, sir," he went on fiercely, "and parallel to these people I can cite you hundreds of little singers of all sorts, acrobats, and buffoons who are known even to nursing babies. Yes, sir!"

The door creaked, there was a gust of air, and a person of sullen appearance, wearing a greatcoat, a top hat, and blue spectacles, came into the car. The person examined the seats, frowned, and went on.

"Do you know who that is?" a timid whisper came from the far corner of the car. "That's N. N., the famous Tula cardsharp, who was taken to court in the Y. bank affair."

"There you are!" the first-class passenger laughed. "He knows the Tula cardsharp, but ask him if he knows Semiradsky, Tchaikovsky, or the philosopher Soloviev, he'll just shake his head . . . Swinishness!"

Some three minutes passed in silence.

"Allow me to ask you in my turn," the *vis-à-vis* coughed timidly, "is the name Pushkov known to you?"

"Pushkov? Hm! . . . Pushkov . . . No, I don't know it."

"It's my name . . ." the *vis-à-vis* said shyly. "So you don't know it? And I've been a professor at one of the Russian universities for thirty-five years . . . a member of the Academy of Science, sir . . . have published extensively . . ."

The first-class passenger and the *vis-à-vis* looked at each other and burst out laughing.

1886

DIFFICULT PEOPLE

S HIRYAEV, EVGRAF IVANOVICH, a petty landowner and priest's son (his late parent, Father Ioann, had received 274 acres of land as a gift from General Kuvshinnikov's wife), was standing in the corner in front of a copper washstand, washing his hands. As usual, he looked glum and preoccupied, and his beard was dishevelled.

"Well, some weather!" he said. "It's not weather, it's divine punishment. Raining again!"

He was grumbling, and his family was sitting at the table and waiting until he finished washing his hands so as to begin dinner. His wife, Fedosya Semyonovna; their son Pyotr, a student; their daughter Varvara; and the three little boys had long been sitting at the table and waiting. The boys—Kolka, Vanka, and Arkhipka—pug-nosed, grimy, with fleshy faces and coarse, long-untrimmed hair, fidgeted impatiently on their chairs, while the adults sat without stirring, and it seemed it was all the same to them whether they ate or waited . . .

As if testing their patience, Shiryaev slowly dried his hands, slowly said a prayer, and unhurriedly sat down at the table. Cabbage soup was served at once. From the yard came the rapping of carpenters' axes (a new barn was being built at Shiryaev's) and the laughter of the farmhand Fomka, who was teasing a turkey. Few but big drops of rain struck the window.

The student Pyotr, in spectacles and round-shouldered, was eating and exchanging glances with his mother. He set his spoon down several times and coughed, wishing to begin talking, but, taking a close look at his father, fell to eating again. Finally, when the kasha was served, he coughed resolutely and said:

"I should take the evening train tonight. It's long been time, I've already missed two weeks. The lectures started on the first of September!"

"Go, then," Shiryaev consented. "What are you waiting around here for? Just up and go with God!"

A minute passed in silence.

"He'll need money for the road, Evgraf Ivanych," the mother said softly.

"Money? Oh, well! You can't travel without money. Take it right now, since you need it. Could have taken it long ago!"

The student sighed with relief and exchanged cheerful glances with his mother. Shiryaev unhurriedly took the wallet from his side pocket and put on his spectacles.

"How much?" he asked.

"In fact, the trip to Moscow costs eleven roubles forty-two . . ."

"Ah, money, money!" the father sighed (he always sighed when he saw money, even receiving it). "Here's twelve for you. There'll be some change, boy, it'll come in handy during the trip."

"Thank you."

After a few moments, the student said:

"Last year I didn't find lessons right away. I don't know how it will be this year; I probably won't earn any money for a while. I'd like to ask you to give me maybe fifteen roubles for room and board."

Shiryaev pondered and sighed.

"Ten'll be enough for you," he said. "Here, take it!"

The student thanked him. He should have requested more for clothes, to pay for attending lectures, for books, but, having looked closely at his father, he decided not to pester him any more. But his mother, unpolitic and unreasonable, as all mothers are, could not help herself and said:

"Give him another six roubles, Evgraf Ivanovich, so he can buy boots. No, just look, how can he go to Moscow in such tatters?"

"He can take my old ones. They're still quite new."

"Give him some for trousers, too. It's a shame to look at him . . ."

And immediately after that appeared a precursor of the storm before which the entire family trembled: Shiryaev's short, thick neck suddenly turned Turkey red. The color slowly spread to his ears, from his ears to his temples, and gradually covered his whole face. Evgraf Ivanych fidgeted on his chair and unbuttoned the collar of his shirt so as not to suffocate. He was evidently struggling with the feeling that was coming over him. A dead silence ensued. The children held their breath, but Fedosya Semyonovna, as if not understanding what was happening with her husband, went on:

"He's not a little boy. He's ashamed to go around badly dressed."

Shiryaev suddenly jumped up and with all his might hurled his fat wallet into the middle of the table, knocking a piece of bread off the plate. On his face flared up a repulsive expression of wrath, offense, greed—all of it together.

"Take it all!" he shouted in a voice not his own. "Rob me! Take it all! Strangle me!"

He jumped away from the table, clutched himself by the head, and ran stumbling around the room.

"Bleed me dry!" he shouted in a shrieking voice. "Squeeze me to the last drop! Rob me! Strangle me by the throat!"

The student turned red and dropped his eyes. He was no longer able to eat. Fedosya Semyonovna, who in twenty-five years had not grown used to her husband's difficult character, shrank into herself and murmured something in her own defense. On her haggard birdlike face, always dumb and frightened, appeared an expression of astonishment and dumb fear. The boys and the older daughter Varvara, an adolescent girl with a pale, unattractive face, set down their spoons and froze.

Shiryaev, growing more and more furious, uttering words one more terrible than the other, ran to the table and started shaking the money out of his wallet.

"Take it!" he muttered, trembling all over. "You've eaten, you've drunk, so take the money, too! I need nothing! Make yourselves new boots and uniforms!"

The student turned pale and stood up.

"Listen, Papa," he began, gasping for breath. "I . . . I beg you to stop, because . . ."

"Silence!" the father shouted at him, so loudly that his spectacles fell off his nose. "Silence!"

"Before I . . . I could put up with these scenes, but now . . . I've lost the habit! Understand! I've lost the habit!"

"Silence!" the father shouted and stamped his feet. "You must listen to what I say! I say what I like, and you—keep silent! At your age I earned my own money, and you, you scoundrel, do you know how much you cost me? I'll throw you out! Parasite!"

"Evgraf Ivanych!" Fedosya Semyonovna murmured, nervously twitching her fingers. "But he . . . but Petya . . ."

"Silence!" Shiryaev shouted at her, and wrath even brought tears to his eyes. "It's you who spoiled them! You! You're to blame for it all! He doesn't respect us, he doesn't pray to God, he doesn't earn any money! There's ten of you and one of me. I'll throw you out of the house!"

The daughter Varvara stared open-mouthed at her mother for a long time, then shifted her dumb gaze to the window, turned pale, and, with a loud cry, threw herself against the back of the chair. Her father waved his hand, spat, and ran outside.

This was how family scenes usually ended at the Shiryaevs'. But this time, unfortunately, an insurmountable anger suddenly came over the student Pyotr. He was as hot-tempered and difficult as his father, and as his grandfather, an archpriest who used to hit his parishioners on the head with a stick. Pale, his fists clenched, he went up to his mother and screamed in the highest tenor notes he was capable of producing:

"I find these reproaches vile and repulsive! I need nothing from you! Nothing! I'd sooner die of hunger than eat even one more crumb of yours! Here's your wretched money! Take it!"

The mother pressed herself against the wall and started waving her hands, as if it were not her son standing before her, but a phantom.

"What have I done wrong?" she wept. "What?"

The son waved his hand, just like his father, and ran outside. Shiryaev's house stood isolated by a gully that cut through the steppe for three miles. Its edges were overgrown with young oaks and alders, and a stream ran along the bottom. One side of the house looked onto the gully, the other onto the open field. There were no wooden or wattle fences. Instead there were all sorts of outbuildings, pressing close to each other as they surrounded the small space in front of the house, which was considered the yard and where chickens, ducks, and pigs walked about.

Having gone outside, the student went down the muddy road to the field. A penetrating autumnal dampness filled the air. The road was muddy, little puddles glistened here and there, and from the grass of the yellow field peered autumn itself: dismal, putrid, dark. On the right side of the road was a kitchen garden, all dug up, gloomy, with occasional sunflowers rising from it, their downcast heads already black.

Pyotr thought it would not be a bad thing to go to Moscow on foot, to go as he was, without a hat, in tattered boots, and without a kopeck. At the hundredth mile, his dishevelled and frightened father would catch up with him, start begging him to come back or to accept the money, but he would not even glance at him, and would keep going, going . . . Bare forests would be supplanted by dismal fields, the fields by forests; soon the earth would turn white with the first snow and the streams would be covered with sheet ice . . . Somewhere near Kursk or Serpukhov, exhausted and starving, he would fall down and die. His body would be found, and in all the newspapers the report would appear that in such-and-such place the student so-and-so had died of hunger . . .

A white dog with a dirty tail, who had been wandering about the kitchen garden looking for something, glanced at him and trudged after him . . .

He walked along the road and thought about his death, about his family's grief, his father's moral torment, and at the same time he pictured to himself all sorts of adventures on the road, one more whimsical than the other, picturesque places, scary nights, chance encounters. He imagined a procession of women pilgrims, a hut in the forest with one little window, which shone brightly in the darkness; he stands by the window, asks for a night's lodging . . . they let him in and—suddenly he sees robbers. Or better still: he comes upon a big manor house, where, on learning who he is, they give him food and drink, play the piano for him, listen to his complaints, and the owner's beautiful daughter falls in love with him.

Preoccupied with his grief and similar thoughts, young Shiryaev kept walking and walking . . . Far, far ahead against a background of gray clouds an inn appeared darkly; still further beyond the inn, right on the horizon, a small bump could be seen; that was the railroad station. This bump reminded him of the connection that existed between the place where he now stood and Moscow, in which streetlights burned, carriages rattled, lectures were given. He nearly burst into tears from anguish and impatience. This solemn nature with its order and beauty, this deathly silence all around, disgusted him to the point of despair, of hatred!

"Watch out!" he heard a loud voice behind him.

An old lady landowner of his acquaintance drove by him in a light, elegant landau. He bowed to her and smiled with his whole face. And he immediately caught himself in this smile, which did not go at all with his dark mood. Where had it come from, if his whole soul was filled with vexation and anguish?

And he thought that nature herself probably gave man this ability to lie, so that even in difficult moments of inner tension he could keep the secrets of his nest, the way a fox or a wild duck keeps them. Every family has its joys and its horrors, but however great they are, it is hard for an outsider's eye to see them; they are secret. For instance, on account of some falsehood, the father of the lady landowner who had just driven by bore the wrath of Tsar Nicholas for half his life, her husband had been a gambler, of her four sons not one of them had made anything of himself. One can imagine how many terrible scenes took place in her family, how many tears were shed. And yet the old woman seemed happy, content, and responded to his smile with a smile. The student remembered his friends who talked reluctantly about their families, remembered his mother, who almost always lied when she had to talk about her husband and children . . .

Until nightfall Pyotr walked around on roads far from home, abandoning himself to cheerless thoughts. When rain began to sprinkle, he headed for home. On his way back, he decided to talk with his father at all costs, to make him understand once and for all that it was difficult and frightening to live with him.

At home he found silence. His sister Varvara lay behind the partition, moaning sightly from a headache. His mother, with a surprised and guilty look, sat beside her on a trunk, mending Arkhipka's trousers. Evgraf Ivanych paced from window to window, frowning at the weather. From his gait, his cough, and even the crown of his head, one could see that he felt guilty.

"So you've changed your mind about leaving today?" he asked.

The student felt sorry for him, but, overcoming that feeling, he said at once:

"Listen . . . I must talk seriously with you . . . Yes, seriously . . . I've always respected you and . . . never dared to talk with you in this tone, but your behavior . . . your latest act . . ."

The father looked out the window and said nothing. The student, as if searching for words, rubbed his forehead and went on in strong agitation:

"Not a dinner or a tea goes by without you raising a ruckus. Your bread sticks in all of our throats. There's nothing more insulting, more humiliating than being reproached by a crust of bread . . . You may be our father, but nobody, neither God nor nature, gave you the right to insult and humiliate us so deeply, to vent your own bad spirits on the weak. You torment my mother, depersonalize her, my sister is hopelessly downtrodden, and I . . ."

"It's not your business to teach me," the father said.

"No, it is my business! You can bully me as much as you like, but leave Mother alone! I won't allow you to torment Mother!" the student went on, flashing his eyes. "You're spoiled because nobody has ever dared to go against you. We trembled, we went dumb, but that's all over now! Crude, ill-bred man! You're crude . . . understand? Crude, difficult, callous! The peasants can't stand you either!"

The student had lost his thread by then and no longer spoke, but seemed to fire off separate words. Evgraf Ivanovich listened and said nothing, as if stunned; but suddenly his neck turned purple, color crept over his face, and he stirred.

"Keep silent!" he yelled.

"Fine!" His son would not be stopped. "You don't like listening to the truth? Excellent! All right! Start shouting! Excellent!"

"Keep silent, I tell you!" Evgraf Ivanovich roared.

Fedosya Semyonovna appeared in the doorway with an astonished face, very pale; she wanted to say something and could not, but only moved her fingers.

"It's your fault!" Shiryaev yelled at her. "You brought him up this way!"

"I don't want to live in this house anymore!" the student yelled, weeping and looking spitefully at his mother. "I don't want to live with you!"

The daughter Varvara cried out behind the partition and burst into loud sobs. Shiryaev waved his hand and ran out of the house.

The student went to his room and quietly lay down. Until midnight he lay motionless and without opening his eyes. He did not feel anger or shame, but some sort of indefinite inner pain. He did not blame his father, did not pity his mother, did not suffer remorse; it was clear to him that everyone in the house now felt the same sort of pain, but who was to blame, who suffered more, who less, God only knew . . .

At midnight he woke up the farmhand and told him to prepare a horse by five in the morning to go to the station, then undressed and covered himself, but could not fall asleep. Until morning he could hear how his sleepless father quietly paced from window to window and sighed. Nobody slept; they all spoke little, only in whispers. Twice his mother came to him behind the partition. With the same astonished and dumb expression, she made the sign of the cross over him many times, twitching nervously . . .

At five in the morning the student tenderly said goodbye to them all and even wept a little. Passing by his father's room, he looked through the door. Evgraf Ivanovich, still dressed, not having gone to bed, stood at the window and drummed on the glass.

"Goodbye, I'm leaving," said the son.

"Goodbye . . . The money's on the little round table . . . ," the father replied, not turning.

As the farmhand drove him to the station, a disgusting cold rain fell. The sunflowers drooped their heads still more, and the grass looked even darker.

1886

ON THE ROAD

A golden cloudlet spent the night
Upon the breast of a giant cliff . . .

LERMONTOV[1]

IN THE ROOM which the innkeeper himself, the Cossack Semyon Spitcleanov, calls "the traveling room," that is, set aside exclusively for travelers, at a big unpainted table, sat a tall, broad-shouldered man of about forty. He was asleep, his elbow on the table, his head propped on his fist. The stub of a tallow candle, stuck into a jar of pomade, lit up his brown beard, his broad, fat nose, his tanned cheeks, and the thick, black eyebrows hanging over his closed eyes. His nose, his cheeks, his brows, all of his features, taken separately, were crude and heavy, like the furniture and the stove in the "traveling room," but together they resulted in something harmonious and even handsome. Such is the fortuity, as they say, of the Russian face: the larger and sharper its features, the gentler and kindlier it seems. The man was dressed in a gentleman's suit jacket, much-worn but trimmed with a wide new band, a velvet waistcoat, and wide black trousers tucked into big boots.

On one of the benches that stood in an unbroken line along the wall, on a fox-fur coat, slept a girl of about eight, in a brown dress and long black stockings. Her face was pale, her hair blond, her shoulders narrow, her whole body thin and frail, but her nose protruded in the same fat and unattractive lump as the man's. She was fast asleep and did not feel how the curved comb, fallen from her head, was cutting her cheek.

The "traveling room" had a festive look. The air smelled of freshly washed floors, the line that stretched diagonally across the entire room did not have the usual rags hanging on it, and in the corner, over the table, an icon lamp flickered, casting a patch of red light on the icon of St. George. Observing the most strict and careful gradation in the transition from the divine to the secular, from the icon, on both sides of the corner, stretched two rows of popular prints. In the dim light of the candle stub and the red light of the icon lamp, the pictures appeared as continuous strips covered with black blotches. But when the tile stove, wishing to sing in unison with the weather, breathed air into itself with a howl, and the logs, as if awakened, burst brightly into flame and growled angrily, then ruddy patches began to leap on the timber walls, and above the head of the sleeping man one could see now St. Seraphim, now Shah Nasr-Eddin, now a fat brown baby, goggling his eyes and whispering something into the ear of a girl with an extraordinarily dull and indifferent face . . .[2]

Outside a storm was raging. Something fierce, malicious, but deeply unhappy was rushing around the inn with savage ferocity, trying to burst inside. Banging on the doors, knocking on the windows and the roof, clawing at the walls, it threatened and then pleaded, then calmed down for a while, then plunged with a gleeful, treacherous howling down the chimney, but here the logs flared up and the fire, like a guard dog, rushed fiercely to meet the enemy; a fight started, followed by sobbing, shrieking, angry roaring. In all of it there was the sound of malicious anguish, and unquenched hatred, and the offended impotence of someone who had been accustomed to winning . . .

Enchanted by this wild, inhuman music, the "traveling room" seemed to be transfixed forever. But then the door creaked and a servant boy in a new calico shirt came into the room. Limping on one leg and blinking his sleepy eyes, he snuffed the candle with his fingers, added logs to the stove, and left. Just then the bell of the church in Rogachi, which is three hundred paces from the inn, began to strike midnight. The wind played with the ringing as it did with the flakes of snow; chasing after the bell's sounds, it whirled them around the huge space, so that some strokes broke off or were drawn into a long, wavy sound, while others vanished completely in the general din. One stroke sounded as clearly in the room as if the bells were ringing just outside the window. The girl who was sleeping on the fox fur gave a start and raised her head. For a moment she gazed senselessly at the dark window, at Nasr-Eddin, over whom the crimson light from the stove danced at that moment, then she shifted her gaze to the sleeping man.

"Papa!" she said.

But the man did not move. The girl knitted her brow crossly, lay down, and tucked her legs under. Behind the door in the inn someone yawned loud and long. Soon after that the door-pulley screeched and indistinct voices were heard. Someone came in and softly stamped his felt boots, shaking off the snow.

"What is it?" a woman's voice asked lazily.

"Miss Ilovaiskaya has arrived," a bass replied.

Again the door-pulley screeched. The noise of the wind bursting in was heard. Someone, probably the lame boy, ran to the door that led to the "traveling room," coughed deferentially, and touched the latch.

"This way, dear miss, if you please," said the woman's singsong voice. "It's clean here, pretty lady . . ."

The door flew open, and a bearded peasant, all plastered with snow from head to foot, appeared on the threshold, in a coachman's kaftan and with a big suitcase on his shoulder. After him came a woman's figure, short, almost half the size of the coachman, with no face or hands, all wrapped up, muffled, looking like a bundle, and also covered with snow. Dampness wafted over the girl from the coachman and the bundle, as if from a cellar, and the candle's flame wavered.

"What stupidity!" the bundle said angrily. "We could have driven perfectly well! There are only eight miles left to go, all through forest, and we wouldn't get lost . . ."

"Lost, no, not lost, but the horses refused to go, miss," the coachman replied. "And it's Thy will, Lord—as if I'd have done it on purpose!"

"God knows where you've brought us . . . But be quiet . . . People seem to be sleeping here. Go now . . ."

The coachman set down the suitcase, which caused whole layers of snow to fall from his shoulders, produced a sobbing sound with his nose, and left. Then the girl saw two small hands come out from inside the bundle, reach upwards, and angrily begin to untangle the tangle of shawls, kerchiefs, and scarves. First a big shawl fell on the floor, then a bashlyk, followed by a white knitted kerchief. Having freed her head, the visitor took off her overcoat and at once became twice narrower. She was now wearing a long gray coat with big buttons and bulging pockets. From one pocket she took something wrapped in paper, from the other a bunch of big, heavy keys, which she set down so carelessly that the sleeping man gave a start and opened his eyes. For some time he looked around dully, as if not understanding where he was, then shook his head, went to the corner, and sat down . . . The traveler took off her coat, which again made her twice narrower, pulled off her velvet boots, and also sat down.

Now she no longer looked like a bundle. She was a small, thin brunette of about twenty, slender as a little snake, with an elongated white face and wavy hair. Her nose was long, sharp, her chin also long and sharp, her eyelashes long, the corners of her mouth sharp, and, thanks to this overall sharpness, the expression of her face seemed prickly. Drawn tightly into a black dress, with masses of lace at the neck and sleeves, with sharp elbows and long pink fingers, she resembled the portraits of medieval English ladies. The serious, concentrated expression of her face increased this resemblance still more . . .

The brunette looked around the room, glanced sidelong at the man and the girl, and, shrugging her shoulders, went to sit by the window. The dark windows were trembling from the damp west wind. Big flakes of snow, sparkling white, settled on the window glass, but disappeared at once, carried off by the wind. The wild music was becoming ever louder . . .

After a long silence, the little girl suddenly stirred and said, angrily rapping out each word:

"Lord! Lord! I'm so unhappy! Unhappier than anybody!"

The man got up and, with a guilty step not at all suited to his enormous height and big beard, went mincing over to the girl.

"You're not asleep, sweetie?" he said in an apologetic voice. "What do you want?"

"I don't want anything! My shoulder hurts! You're a bad man, Papa, and God will punish you! You'll see, he'll punish you!"

"My darling, I know your shoulder hurts, but what can I do, sweetie?" the man said, in the tone in which drunken men apologize to their stern spouses. "Your shoulder hurts from traveling, Sasha. Tomorrow we'll arrive, get some rest, and it will go away . . ."

"Tomorrow, tomorrow . . . You say 'tomorrow' every day. We'll be traveling for another twenty days!"

"But, sweetie, a father's word of honor, we'll arrive tomorrow. I never lie, and it's not my fault if we've been held up by a blizzard!"

"I can't take any more! I can't, I can't!"

Sasha sharply kicked her foot and filled the room with unpleasant, high-pitched crying. Her father waved his hand and gave the brunette a lost look. She shrugged her shoulders and hesitantly went over to Sasha.

"Listen, my dear," she said, "why cry? True, it's not nice that your shoulder hurts, but what can be done?"

"You see, madam," the man began quickly, as if apologizing, "we haven't slept for two nights, and we've been traveling in disgusting conditions. So, of course, she's sick and languishing . . . And then, too, you know, we happened to have a drunken coachman, and our suitcase was stolen . . . a blizzard all the time, but why cry, madam? Then again, this sleeping sitting up has tired me, and it's as if I'm drunk. By God, Sasha, it's sickening even without you, and then you go crying!"

The man shook his head, waved his hand, and sat down.

"Of course, you shouldn't cry," said the brunette. "Only nursing babies cry. If you're sick, my dear, you should get undressed and go to sleep . . . Let's get undressed!"

Once the girl was undressed and calmed down, there was silence again. The brunette sat by the window and looked around perplexedly at the room, the icon, the stove . . . Apparently, it all seemed strange to her—the room, the girl with her fat nose, in her short boy's undershirt, and the girl's father. This strange man was sitting in the corner, bewildered, like a drunk man, glancing around and rubbing his face with his palm. He said nothing, blinked his eyes, and, looking at his guilty figure, it was hard to suppose that he would soon start talking. But he was the first to start talking. He stroked his knees, coughed, then chuckled and said:

"A comedy, by God . . . I look and don't believe my eyes: why the devil has fate driven us to this vile inn? What did it mean to show by it? Life sometimes performs such a *salto mortale* that you're left staring and blinking in perplexity. Are you going far, madam?"

"No, not far," replied the brunette. "I'm going from our estate, some fifteen miles from here, to our farmstead, to my father and brother. I'm Ilovaiskaya myself, and the farmstead is called Ilovaiskoe, it's eight miles on from here. Such unpleasant weather!"

"Couldn't be worse!"

The lame boy came in and stuck a new candle stub in the pomade jar.

"Serve up the samovar for us, laddie," the man turned to him.

"Who drinks tea now?" the lame boy smirked. "It's a sin to drink before the liturgy."[3]

"Never mind, laddie, it's not you who'll burn in hell, it's us . . ."

Over tea the new acquaintances got to talking. Miss Ilovaiskaya learned that her interlocutor's name was Grigory Petrovich Likharev, that he was the brother of the Likharev who was marshal of the nobility in one of the neighboring districts,[4] and that he himself had been a landowner, but had been "ruined in good time." Likharev learned that Miss Ilovaiskaya was named Marya Mikhailovna, that her father's estate was enormous, but that the management fell to her alone, because her father and brother looked at life through their fingers, were carefree and overly fond of borzois.

"At the farmstead my father and brother are all by themselves," said Miss Ilovaiskaya, waving her fingers (she had the habit of waving her fingers in front of her prickly face during a conversation and of licking her lips with her sharp tongue after each phrase). "They're men, carefree folk, and won't move a finger for themselves! I suppose no one will give them Christmas dinner. We have no mother, and our servants are such that they won't even spread a tablecloth properly without me. Just imagine their situation now! They'll go without Christmas dinner, and I have to sit here all night. How strange it all is!"

Miss Ilovaiskaya shrugged her shoulders, took a sip from the cup, and said:

"There are feasts that have their own smell. At Easter, Pentecost, and Christmas there's a particular smell in the air. Even unbelievers love these feasts. My brother, for instance, says there is no God, but at Easter he's the first to run to church."

Likharev raised his eyes to Miss Ilovaiskaya and laughed.

"They say there is no God," Miss Ilovaiskaya went on, also laughing, "but why then, tell me, do all the famous writers, scholars, and intelligent people in general, become believers toward the end of their lives?"

"Anyone who was unable to believe at a young age, madam, will not believe when he's old, even if he's a writer ten times over."

Judging by his cough, Likharev had a bass voice, but, probably from fear of talking loudly or from excessive shyness, he spoke in a tenor. After a brief silence, he sighed and said:

"As I understand it, faith is a spiritual capacity. It's like a talent: you have to be born with it. Insofar as I can judge by myself, by the people I've met in my time, by all that goes on around me, Russian people possess this capacity in the highest degree. Russian life is an uninterrupted series of beliefs and infatuations, and as for unbelief or denial, Russia, if you wish to know, hasn't caught a whiff of it. If a Russian man doesn't believe in God, it means he believes in something else."

Likharev accepted a cup of tea from Miss Ilovaiskaya, swigged half of it at once, and went on:

"I'll tell you about myself. Nature put into my soul an extraordinary ability to believe. For half my life (don't let me spook you!) I've belonged to the ranks of the atheists and nihilists, but there hasn't been a single hour of my life when I haven't believed. Usually all talents reveal themselves in early childhood, and so my ability already made itself known when I was still knee-high. My mother liked her children to eat a lot, and when she fed me, she used to say: 'Eat! The main thing in life is soup!' I believed, I ate that soup, ate it ten times a day, ate like a shark, to the point of loathing and passing out. My nanny told fairy tales, and I believed in house goblins, in wood demons, in all sorts of devilry. I used to steal rat poison from my father, pour it on gingerbread, and carry it up to the attic, so that the house goblins would eat it and drop dead. And when I learned to read and understand what I read, then things really took off! I fled to America, I became a highway robber, I asked to be taken to a monastery, I hired other boys to torture me for the sake of Christ. And notice, my belief was always active, not dead. If I ran away to America, I didn't go alone, I seduced another fool like myself to go with me, and I was glad when I was freezing outside the city gate and when they flogged me; and when I became a highway robber, I never failed to come back with a bloodied mug. A most troubled childhood, I assure you! And when I was sent to school and showered there with all sorts of truths, like that the earth moves around the sun, and that the color white is not white, but consists of seven colors, my poor little head was in a whirl! Everything went topsy-turvy in me: Joshua, who stopped the sun, and my mother, who rejected lightning rods on behalf of the prophet Elijah,[5] and my father, who was indifferent to the truths I learned. My enlightenment inspired me. I went around the house and stables like a lunatic, preaching my truths, horrified by ignorance, burning with hatred for anyone who saw white as merely white . . . However, this is all nonsense and childishness. My serious, so to speak, masculine passions began at the university. Did you study anywhere, madam?"

"In Novocherkassk, at the Donskoy boarding school."

"So you have no higher education? That means you don't know what science is. All the sciences, however many there are in the world, have one and the same passport, without which they consider themselves unthinkable: striving for the truth! Each of them, even some sort of pharmacognosis, has as its aim not usefulness, not the comforts of life, but truth. Remarkable! When you set about the study of some science, you're struck first of all by its beginnings. I'll tell you, there is nothing more fascinating and grandiose, nothing that so astonishes and captivates the human spirit, as the beginnings of some science. After the first five or six lectures, you're already inspired by the brightest hopes, you already fancy yourself the master of truth. And I gave myself to science selflessly, passionately, as to a beloved woman. I was its slave and didn't want to know any other sun. Day and night I studied, never straightening my back, I went broke on books, I wept when before my eyes people exploited science for their personal ends. But I was not passionate for long. The thing is that each science has a beginning, but no end, like a recurrent decimal. Zoology has discovered thirty-five thousand kinds of insects, chemistry numbers sixty elements. If in time ten zeroes are added to the right of these numbers, zoology and chemistry will be as far from their ends as they are now, and all contemporary scientific work consists precisely in increasing the numbers. I caught on to this trick when I discovered the thirty-five-thousand-and-first species and did not feel any satisfaction. Well, ma'am, I had no time to be disappointed, because soon a new faith took hold of me. I threw myself into nihilism with its leaflets, black repartitions, and the like.[6] I went to the people, worked in factories, was an oiler, a hauler. Later, wandering around Russia, I got a taste of Russian life, and turned into an ardent admirer of that life. I loved the Russian people to the point of suffering, loved and believed in their God, their language, their creativity . . . And so on, and so forth . . . For some time I was a Slavophile, pestered Aksakov with letters,[7] was a Ukrainophile, an archaeologist, collected specimens of folk art . . . I was fascinated by ideas, people, events, places . . . endlessly fascinated! Five years ago I served the repudiation of private property; my last belief was in non-resistance to evil."[8]

Sasha sighed fitfully and stirred. Likharev got up and went over to her.

"Would you like some tea, sweetie?" he asked tenderly.

"Drink it yourself!" the girl replied rudely.

Likharev became embarrassed and with a guilty step went back to the table.

"So you've had fun in your life," said Miss Ilovaiskaya. "There's a lot to remember."

"Well, yes, it's all fun, when you sit chattering over tea with a nice fellow talker, but if you ask what this fun cost me? What was the price of this diversity in my life? You see, madam, I did not believe like a German doctor of philosophy, *zierlichmännerlich*,[9] I didn't live in the desert, no, each of my beliefs bowed me down, tore my life to pieces. Judge for yourself. I was as rich as my brothers, but now I'm a beggar. In the whirl of my passions, I ran through my own fortune and my wife's as well—a huge amount of other people's money. I'm now forty-two, old age is at the door, and I'm as homeless as a dog left behind by the baggage train at night. All my life I've known no peace. My soul was constantly pining, suffering even in its hopes . . . I wore myself out with hard, random tasks, I suffered privation, was in prison maybe five times, dragged myself around the provinces of Archangelsk and Tobolsk[10] . . . It's painful to remember! I've lived, but in the whirl I've never felt the process of life itself. Would you believe it, I don't remember a single spring, I never noticed my wife's love, my children's births. What else shall I tell you? I was a misfortune for all those who loved me . . . My mother has been in mourning for me for fifteen years now, and my proud brothers, who, on account of me, had to feel sick at heart, to blush, to bend their backs, to waste their money, in the end came to hate me like poison."

Likharev stood up and sat down again.

"If I were merely unhappy, I'd give thanks to God," he went on, not looking at Miss Ilovaiskaya. "My personal unhappiness falls into the background when I remember how often in my passions I was absurd, far from the truth, unfair, cruel, dangerous! How often I hated and despised with all my soul those I should have loved, and— vice versa. I've been unfaithful a thousand times. Today I believe, I fall on my knees, but tomorrow I already flee in cowardice from my gods and friends of today and silently swallow the 'scoundrel' they send after me. God alone saw how often I wept and chewed the pillow from shame at my passions. Never once in my life have I deliberately lied or done evil, but my conscience isn't clean! I can't even boast of having no one's life on my conscience, madam, because my wife died before my eyes, worn out by my recklessness. Yes, my wife! Listen, in our everyday life there are now two prevailing attitudes towards women. Some measure women's skulls so as to prove that women are inferior to men, seek out their shortcomings so as to deride them, play the original in their eyes and justify their own animality. Others try with all their might to raise women up to them, that is, to make them learn thirty-five thousand species, and speak and write the same stupidities that they themselves speak and write . . ."

Likharev's face darkened.

"But I tell you that woman has always been and will always be man's slave," he began in a bass voice, pounding his fist on the table. "She is tender, soft wax from which man has always molded whatever he liked. Lord God, for two cents' worth of masculine passion, she'll cut her hair, abandon her family, die in a foreign land . . . Among the ideas for which she has sacrificed herself, not one is feminine . . . A selfless, devoted slave! I haven't measured skulls, I'm speaking from hard, bitter experience. The most proud and independent women, once I managed to convey my inspiration to them, followed me without reasoning, without questioning, and did everything I wanted; I turned a nun into a nihilist, who, as I later learned, shot a policeman; my wife never left me for a moment in my wanderings and, like a weathercock, changed her beliefs parallel to how I changed my passions."

Likharev jumped up and began to pace the room.

"Noble, sublime slavery!" he said, clasping his hands. "The lofty meaning of a woman's life consists precisely in that! Of the terrible muddle that has accumulated in my head during all the time of my dealings with women, my memory, like a filter, has retained not the ideas, not the big words, not the philosophy, but this extraordinary obedience to fate, this extraordinary, all-forgiving mercy . . ."

Likharev clenched his fists, fixed his gaze on one point, and with a sort of passionate tension, as if sucking on each word, said through clenched teeth:

"This . . . this magnanimous endurance, faithfulness to the grave, poetry of the heart . . . The meaning of life is precisely in this uncomplaining martyrdom, in tears that can soften stone, in boundless, all-forgiving love, which brings light and warmth into the chaos of life . . ."

Miss Ilovaiskaya slowly got up, took a step towards Likharev, and fixed her eyes on his face. From the tears that glistened on his eyelashes, from his trembling, passionate voice, from his flushed cheeks, it was clear to her that women were not a chance or simple topic of conversation. They were the subject of his new passion or, as he said himself, his new belief! For the first time in her life, Ilovaiskaya saw before her a passionately, ardently believing man. Gesticulating, flashing his eyes, he seemed insane, frenzied to her, but in the fire of his eyes, in his talk, in the movements of his whole big body there was so much beauty, that she, not noticing it herself, stood before him as if rooted to the spot, and looked him rapturously in the face.

"Take my mother!" he said, stretching his arms towards her and making a pleading face. "I poisoned her existence, to her mind I disgraced the Likharev family, I caused her as much harm as only the worst enemy can cause, and—what then? My brothers give her small change for holy bread and prayer services, and she, violating her religious feelings, saves this money and secretly sends it to her wayward Grigory! This one little thing educates and ennobles the soul far more than any theories, big words, or thirty-five thousand species! I can give you a thousand examples. Take you, for instance! Outside a blizzard, night, and you're going to your brother and father to give them tender warmth on the holiday, though maybe they don't think of you, have even forgotten about you. But just wait, you'll fall in love with a man, and then you'll go to the North Pole with him. You will, won't you?"

"Yes, if . . . I fall in love."

"There, you see!" Likharev rejoiced and even stamped his foot. "Oh, God, I'm so glad we've become acquainted! My fate is so good to me, I keep meeting such splendid people. Every day brings such an acquaintance as a man would simply give his soul for. In this world there are many more good people than evil. Just imagine, you and I have talked as candidly and openheartedly as if we've known each other for a hundred years. Sometimes, I must tell you, for ten years you restrain yourself, say nothing, conceal things from your friends and wife, but you meet a cadet on the train and pour your whole life out to him. I've had the honor of seeing you for the first time, and I've confessed to you as I've never confessed before. Why is that?"

Rubbing his hands and smiling cheerfully, Likharev took a turn around the room and again began talking about women. Meanwhile the bell rang for matins.

"Lord!" Sasha wept. "He won't let me sleep with all his talk!"

"Ah, yes!" Likharev caught himself. "I'm sorry, sweetie. Sleep, sleep . . . Besides her, I also have two boys," he whispered. "They live with their uncle, madam, but this one can't survive a day without her father. She suffers, complains, yet she clings to me like a fly to honey. I'm talking away, madam, but it wouldn't hurt if you got some rest. Wouldn't you like me to make a bed for you?"

Without waiting for permission, he shook the wet overcoat and spread it on the bench fur-side up, gathered the scattered kerchiefs and shawls, put the rolled-up coat at the head, and all that silently, with an expression of obsequious reverence on his face, as if he were fussing not with a woman's rags, but with the broken pieces of sacred vessels. In his whole figure there was something guilty, embarrassed, as if he were ashamed of his height and strength in the presence of a weak being . . .

When Miss Ilovaiskaya lay down, he put out the candle and sat on a stool by the stove.

"So it is, madam," he whispered, lighting a fat cigarette and blowing the smoke into the stove. "Nature has endowed the Russian man with an extraordinary capacity for belief, an inquisitive mind, and a gift for thinking, but it is all reduced to dust by carelessness, laziness, and dreamy light-mindedness . . . Yes, ma'am . . ."

Miss Ilovaiskaya peered into the darkness in astonishment and could see only the red patch on the icon and the flickering of light from the stove on Likharev's face. The darkness, the bell-ringing, the howl of the blizzard, the lame boy, the complaining Sasha, the unhappy Likharev and his talk—all of it was mingling, growing into one enormous impression, and God's world seemed to her fantastic, filled with wonders and enchanting powers. Everything she had just heard resounded in her ears, and human life appeared to her as a beautiful, poetic fairy tale, which had no end.

The enormous impression grew and grew, it clouded her consciousness and turned into a sweet sleep. Miss Ilovaiskaya slept, but she saw the icon lamp and the fat nose with the red light playing on it. She heard crying.

"Dear Papa," a child's voice pleaded tenderly, "let's go back to Uncle! There's a Christmas tree! There's Styopa and Kolya!"

"What can I do, sweetie?" a man's soft bass persuaded. "Understand me! Do understand!"

And the child's crying was joined by a man's.

This voice of human grief amid the howling of the storm touched the girl's hearing with such sweet, human music that she could not bear the sweetness and also started crying. She heard later how the big, dark shadow quietly came over to her, picked up a fallen shawl from the floor, and wrapped it around her feet.

Miss Ilovaiskaya was awakened by a strange roar. She jumped up and looked around in surprise. A bluish dawn was looking through the windows half covered with snow. There was a gray twilight in the room, through which the stove, the sleeping girl, and Nasr-Eddin were clearly outlined. The stove and the lamp had already gone out.

Through the wide-open door, the main room of the inn could be seen, with its counter and tables. Some man with a dull, Gypsy face and astonished eyes stood in the middle of the room, in a puddle of melted snow, holding a big red star on a stick. He was surrounded by a group of boys immobile as statues and all plastered with snow. The light of the star, passing through the red paper, reddened their wet faces. The crowd roared confusedly, and in their roar Miss Ilovaiskaya made out one quatrain:

> Hey, you, ragged little kid,
> Take your knife and go,
> We'll kill, we'll kill ourselves a Yid,
> He is the son of woe . . .

Likharev was standing by the counter, gazing tenderly at the singers and beating time with his foot. Seeing Miss Ilovaiskaya, he smiled broadly and went up to her. She also smiled.

"Merry Christmas!" he said. "I noticed you slept well."

Miss Ilovaiskaya looked at him, said nothing, and went on smiling. After the night's conversation, he now seemed to her not tall, not broad-shouldered, but small, just as the biggest steamship seems small to us once we are told that it has crossed the ocean.

"Well, it's time for me to go," she said. "I must get dressed. Tell me, where are you headed for now?"

"Me? To the Klipushki station, from there to Sergievo, and from Sergievo thirty miles by horse to the coal mines of one jackass, a certain General Shashkovsky. My brothers found me the post of superintendent there . . . I'll be digging coal."

"Wait, I know those mines. Shashkovsky is my uncle. But . . . why are you going there?" Miss Ilovaiskaya asked, looking at Likharev with surprise.

"To be superintendent. To superintend the mines."

"I don't understand!" Miss Ilovaiskaya shrugged her shoulders. "You're going to the mines. But it's bare steppe, deserted, so boring you won't last a day there! The coal is wretched, nobody buys it, and my uncle's a maniac, a despot, a bankrupt . . . You won't even get any salary!"

"It's all the same," Likharev said indifferently. "I'm thankful for the mines at least."

Miss Ilovaiskaya shrugged her shoulders and paced the room in agitation.

"I don't understand, I don't understand!" she kept saying, waving her fingers in front of her face. "It's impossible and . . . and unreasonable! You understand, it's . . . it's worse than exile, it's a grave for a living man! Oh, Lord," she said ardently, going up to Likharev and waving her fingers in front of his smiling face; her upper lip trembled and her prickly face grew pale. "Well, imagine the bare steppe, the solitude. There's no one to talk to, and you . . . are passionate about women! Coal mines and women!"

Miss Ilovaiskaya suddenly became embarrassed at her ardor and, turning away from Likharev, went over to the window.

"No, no, you mustn't go there!" she said, quickly moving her fingers over the glass. Not only with her soul, but even with her back she sensed that behind her stood an infinitely unhappy, lost, neglected man, while he, as if unaware of his unhappiness, as if he had not cried at night, looked at her and smiled good-naturedly. It would have been better if he had gone on crying! She paced the room several times in agitation, then stopped in the corner, pondering. Likharev was saying something, but she did not hear him. Her back turned to him, she took a twenty-five-rouble note from her wallet, crumpled it in her hands for a while, then, turning to Likharev, blushed and slipped the note into her pocket.

The coachman's voice was heard through the door. Silently, with a stern, concentrated face, Miss Ilovaiskaya began to dress. Likharev wrapped her up and chattered cheerfully, but his every word weighed heavily on her soul. It is not cheerful to listen to the banter of an unhappy or a dying man.

When the transformation of the living person into a shapeless bundle was completed, Ilovaiskaya took a last look around the "traveling room," stood silently, and slowly left. Likharev went to see her off . . .

Outside, God knows why, winter was still raging. Whole clouds of big, soft snowflakes circled restlessly over the earth and found no place for themselves. Horses, sledges, trees, an ox tied to a post— everything was white and looked soft, fluffy.

"Well, God be with you," Likharev murmured, helping Miss Ilovaiskaya into the sledge. "Don't remember evil . . ."[11] Miss Ilovaiskaya was silent. When the sledge set off and began to skirt a big snowdrift, she turned and looked at Likharev as if she wanted to say something to him. He ran up to her, but she did not say a word to him, but only looked at him through her long eyelashes, on which snowflakes were hanging . . .

Either his sensitive soul had indeed been able to read that gaze, or maybe his imagination deceived him, but it suddenly began to seem to him that, another two or three good, firm strokes, and this girl would forgive him his failures, his age, his misery, and follow him, without asking questions, without reasoning. For a long time he stood as if rooted to the spot and looked at the tracks left by the runners. Snow-flakes avidly settled on his hair, his beard, his shoulders . . . Soon the tracks of the runners disappeared, and he himself, covered with snow, began to look like a white cliff, but his eyes still went on searching for something in the clouds of snow.

1886

The Beggar

"My dear sir! Be so good as to pay attention to an unfortunate, hungry man. I haven't eaten for three days . . . don't have a fiver for a night's lodging . . . I swear to God! Eight years I worked as a village schoolmaster and lost my post owing to local intrigues . . . Fell victim to denunciation . . . I've been out of work for a year now."

The barrister Skvortsov looked at the petitioner's tattered blue-gray coat, his dull, drunken eyes, the red splotches on his cheeks, and it seemed to him that he had already seen this man somewhere before.

"Now they're offering me a post in Kaluga province," the petitioner went on, "but I have no means of getting there. Be so kind as to help me! I'm ashamed to ask, but . . . circumstances make it necessary."

Skvortsov looked at the man's galoshes, one of which was high and the other low, and suddenly remembered.

"Listen, I believe I met you three days ago on Sadovaya Street," he said, "and you told me then that you were an expelled student, not a village schoolmaster. Remember?"

"N-no, it can't be!" the petitioner mumbled in embarrassment. "I'm a village schoolmaster, and, if you wish, I can show you documents."

"Enough lying! You called yourself a student and even told me what you were expelled for. Remember?"

Skvortsov turned red and stepped back from the ragbag with a look of disgust on his face.

"That is mean, my dear sir!" he shouted angrily. "You're a crook! I'll turn you over to the police, devil take you! You're poor, hungry, but that doesn't give you the right to lie so brazenly and shamelessly!"

The ragbag took hold of the door handle and perplexedly, like a caught thief, looked into the entryway.

"I . . . I'm not lying, sir!" he mumbled. "I can show you documents."

"Who's going to believe you?" Skvortsov went on indignantly. "To exploit society's sympathy for village schoolmasters and students— it's so low, mean, nasty! Outrageous!"

Skvortsov got carried away and scolded the petitioner in a most merciless fashion. By his impudent lying, the ragbag had awakened loathing and disgust in him, had insulted in him that which he, Skvortsov, so loved and valued in himself: kindness, a sensitive heart, compassion for the unfortunate; by his lying appeal for mercy, it was as if this "subject" had defiled the alms which he, out of purity of heart, liked to give to the poor. The ragbag began by justifying himself, swearing to God, but then fell silent and hung his head in shame.

"Sir!" he said, putting his hand to his heart. "Indeed, I . . . was lying! I'm not a student or a village schoolmaster. That's all made up! I sang in a Russian choir, and was fired for drunkenness. But what am I to do? By God, it's impossible without lying. When I tell the truth, nobody gives me alms. With the truth you die of hunger and freeze without night quarters! Your reasoning is correct, I understand, but . . . what am I to do?"

"What to do? You ask what you're to do?" Skvortsov cried, going up close to him. "Work, that's what! You must work!"

"Work . . . I understand that myself, but where will I find work?"

"Nonsense! You're young, healthy, strong, and will always find work, if only you want to. But you're lazy, spoiled, drunk! You stink of vodka like a pot-house! You're false and shoddy to the marrow of your bones, and capable only of panhandling and lying! If you deign some day to lower yourself to work, you'll expect it to be in an office, in a Russian choir, or as a billiard marker, where you can do nothing and get money for it! But how would you like to take up physical labor? It's not as if you'd accept to be a street sweeper or a factory worker! You've got pretensions!"

"The way you reason, my God . . ." the petitioner said and smiled bitterly. "Where am I to get physical labor? It's too late for me to be a shopkeeper, because you start such jobs as a boy; nobody will take me as a street sweeper, because I'm the wrong class to talk down to . . . and they won't hire me at a factory, you have to know a skill, and I don't know anything."

"Nonsense! You'll always find a justification! How would you like to chop wood?"

"I wouldn't refuse, but nowadays even real woodchoppers go hungry."

"Well, all parasites reason like that. If you get an offer, you'll refuse. Would you like to chop some wood for me?"

"All right, I will . . ."

"Very well, we'll see . . . Excellent . . . We'll see!"

Skvortsov hurried off and, not without glee, rubbing his hands, summoned the cook from the kitchen.

"Here, Olga," he said to her, "take this gentleman to the shed and have him chop wood."

The ragbag shrugged his shoulders as if in perplexity, and irresolutely followed the cook. From his gait it could be seen that he had agreed to go and chop wood not because he was hungry and wanted to earn some money, but simply out of vanity and shame, having been taken at his word. It was also obvious that he was badly weakened from vodka, was unwell, and felt not the slightest disposition to work.

Skvortsov hurried to the dining room. There, through the windows looking out on the yard, he could see the woodshed and everything that went on in the yard. Standing at the window, Skvortsov saw the cook and the ragbag come out the back door to the yard and make their way through the dirty snow to the shed. Olga, looking crossly at her companion, her elbows thrust out, unlocked the shed and angrily banged the door open.

"We probably interrupted the woman at her coffee," thought Skvortsov. "What a spiteful creature!"

Then he saw the pseudo-teacher and pseudo-student sit down on a block of wood and, propping his red cheeks on his fists, fall to thinking about something. The woman flung the axe at his feet, spat angrily, and, judging by the expression of her lips, began to scold him. The ragbag irresolutely pulled a log towards him, put it between his legs, and timorously tapped it with the axe. The log swayed and fell over. The ragbag pulled it to him, blew on his cold hands, and again tapped it with the axe, as cautiously as if he were afraid to hit his galosh or chop off his toes. The log fell over again.

Skvortsov's anger was gone by then, and he felt a little pained and ashamed that he had made a man who was spoiled, drunk, and maybe ill undertake physical labor outside in the cold.

"Well, never mind, let him . . . ," he thought, going from the dining room to his study. "It's for his own good."

An hour later Olga came and reported that the wood had been chopped.

"Here, give him fifty kopecks," said Skvortsov. "If he wants, let him come to chop wood on the first of each month . . . Work will always be found."

On the first of the month the ragbag came and again earned fifty kopecks, though he could barely stand on his feet. After that he turned up quite often in the yard, and each time work was found for him: he shoveled piles of snow, tidied up the shed, beat the dust from the rugs and mattresses. Each time he earned from twenty to forty kopecks for his labor, and once he was even given a pair of old trousers.

On moving to different lodgings, Skvortsov hired him to help with packing and transporting the furniture. This time the ragbag was sober, sullen, and silent; he barely laid a finger on the furniture, followed the carts with his head hanging down, and did not even try to look active, and only huddled against the cold and became embarrassed when the carters laughed at his idleness, weakness, and tattered gentleman's coat. After the moving, Skvortsov had him summoned.

"Well, I see my words had an effect on you," he said, handing him a rouble. "This is for your labors. I see you're sober and not against doing work. What is your name?"

"Lushkov."

"I can offer you a different sort of work now, Lushkov, cleaner work. Can you write?"

"Yes, sir."

"Then go to my colleague tomorrow with this letter and you'll get to do copying for him. Work, don't drink, and don't forget what I said to you. Goodbye!"

Pleased at having put the man on the right path, Skvortsov amiably patted Lushkov on the shoulder and even offered him his hand as he said goodbye. Lushkov took the letter, left, and no longer came to the yard for work.

Two years went by. One day, standing at a theater ticket window buying his ticket, Skvortsov saw next to him a little man with an astrakhan collar and a shabby sealskin hat. The little man timidly asked for a ticket in the gallery and paid in copper coins.

"Lushkov, is it you?" asked Skvortsov, recognizing the little man as his former woodchopper. "Well, how are you? What are you up to? Is life going well?"

"Not bad . . . I work for a notary now, earn thirty-five roubles, sir."

"Well, thank God. That's excellent! I'm glad for you. Very, very glad, Lushkov! You're my godson in a certain sense. It was I who pushed you onto the proper path. Remember how I reprimanded you, eh? You almost fell through the floor then. Well, thank you, my dear fellow, for not forgetting my words."

"And thank you," said Lushkov. "If I hadn't come to you then, I'd probably still call myself a teacher or a student. Yes, I was saved through you, I jumped out of the pit."

"I'm very, very glad."

"Thank you for your kind words and deeds. You spoke very well then. I'm grateful to you and to your cook—God grant good health to that kind, generous woman. You spoke very well then, I'm obliged to you till my dying day, but in fact it was your cook Olga who saved me."

"How so?"

"Here's how. I'd come to you to chop wood, and she'd start on me: 'Ah, you drunkard! Cursed as you are! There's no punishment good enough for you!' And then she'd sit down, turn sad, look me in the face and lament: 'Miserable man that you are! There's no joy for you in this world, and in the next, you drunkard, you'll burn in hell! Poor wretch!' And all in the same vein, you know. How much she grieved over me and how many tears she shed, I can't even tell you.

But the main thing was—she chopped the wood for me! I didn't split a single piece of your wood, sir, she did it all! Why she saved me, why I changed, looking at her, and stopped drinking, I can't tell you. I only know that from her words and generous acts, a change took place in my soul, she set me right, and I'll never forget it. But it's time, the curtain bell's already ringing."

Lushkov bowed and went to the gallery.

1887

ENEMIES

TOWARDS TEN O'CLOCK on a dark September evening, the only son of the district doctor Kirilov, six-year-old Andrei, died of diphtheria. Just as the doctor's wife sank to her knees before the dead child's little bed and was overcome by the first onslaught of despair, the doorbell in the front hall rang out sharply.

On account of the diphtheria, all the servants had been sent away in the morning. Kirilov, just as he was, without his frock coat and with an unbuttoned waistcoat, not wiping his wet face and his hands scalded with carbolic acid, went to open the door himself. It was dark in the front hall, and all that could be seen of the man coming in was his medium height, his white scarf, and his large, extremely pale face, so pale that its appearance seemed to make the front hall lighter . . .

"Is the doctor at home?" the man asked quickly.

"Yes, I am," Kirilov replied. "What can I do for you?"

"Ah, it's you? I'm very glad!" the man said happily and began feeling in the dark for the doctor's hand, found it, and pressed it firmly in his own. "Very . . . very glad! We know each other! . . . I'm Abogin . . . had the pleasure of meeting you last summer at the Gnuchevs'. I'm very glad to find you at home . . . For God's sake, don't refuse to come with me now . . . My wife is dangerously ill . . . I have a carriage with me . . ."

From the man's voice and movements it was evident that he was in an extremely agitated state. As if frightened by a fire or a rabid dog, he could barely control his rapid breathing and spoke quickly, in a trembling voice, and something unfeignedly candid, something child-ishly fearful sounded in his speech. Like all frightened and stunned people, he spoke in short, abrupt sentences and used many unneces-sary, totally irrelevant words.

"I was afraid I wouldn't find you at home," he went on. "My soul suffered so much on the way here . . . Get dressed and let's go, for God's sake . . . It happened like this. Papchinsky, Alexander Sem-yonovich, whom you know, comes to see me . . . We talked . . . then sat down to tea; suddenly my wife cries out, puts her hand to her heart, and falls back in her chair. We carried her to her bed and . . . I rubbed her temples with sal-ammoniac, sprinkled her with water . . . she lay as if dead . . . I'm afraid it's an aneurysm . . . Let's go . . . Her father also died of an aneurysm . . ."

Kirilov listened and said nothing, as if he did not understand Russian.

When Abogin again referred to Papchinsky and to his wife's father and again began searching for his hand in the darkness, the doctor shook his head and said, apathetically drawing out each word:

"Forgive me, I can't go . . . Five minutes ago . . . my son died . . ."

"Can it be?" Abogin whispered, taking a step back. "My God, what an evil hour I've hit on! An amazingly unfortunate day . . . amazingly! What a coincidence . . . as if on purpose!"

Abogin took hold of the door handle and hung his head, ponder-ing. He evidently hesitated, not knowing what to do: to leave or to go on entreating the doctor.

"Listen," he said heatedly, catching Kirilov by the sleeve, "I under-stand your position perfectly! God knows, I'm ashamed to be trying to hold your attention at such a moment, but what can I do? Judge for yourself, who can I go to? Besides you, there's no other doctor here. Come, for God's sake! I'm not asking for myself . . . It's not me who's sick!"

Silence ensued. Kirilov turned his back to Abogin, stood for a moment, and slowly went from the front hall to the drawing room. Judging by his uncertain, mechanical gait, by the attention with which, on coming to the drawing room, he straightened the fringed lampshade on an unlit lamp and glanced into a fat book lying on the table, in those moments he had neither intentions nor wishes, was not thinking about anything, and probably no longer remembered that a stranger was standing in his front hall. The darkness and quietness of the room apparently intensified his derangement. Going from the drawing room to his study, he raised his right foot higher than necessary, feeling with his hands for the door frames, and all the while there was a sense of some sort of perplexity in his whole figure, as if he found himself in unfamiliar quarters or had gotten drunk for the first time in his life and now yielded with perplexity to this new sensation. A wide strip of light stretched across the bookcases on one wall of the study; along with the heavy, stale smell of carbolic acid and ether, this light came from the slightly ajar door that led from the study to the bedroom . . . The doctor sank into the armchair in front of the desk; for a moment he gazed sleepily at the lighted books, then got up and went to the bedroom.

Here, in the bedroom, a dead silence reigned. Everything to the smallest detail spoke of the recently endured storm, of fatigue, and everything was resting. A candle, which stood on a stool amid a dense crowd of vials, boxes, and jars, and a big lamp on a chest of drawers brightly lit the whole room. On the bed just by the window lay a boy with open eyes and an astonished look on his face. He did not move, but his open eyes seemed to be growing darker and sinking into his skull with every moment. His mother was kneeling beside the bed, her arms lying on his body, her face hidden in the folds of the sheets. Like the boy, she was motionless, but how much living movement could be felt in the curves of her body and in her arms! She pressed herself to the bed with all her being, with force and greed, as if fearing to disturb the calm and comfortable pose she had finally found for her weary body. Blankets, rags, basins, puddles on the floor, brushes and spoons scattered everywhere, a white bottle with lime water, the very air, stifling and heavy—it was all still and seemed immersed in calm.

The doctor stopped beside his wife, put his hands into his trouser pockets, and, inclining his head to the side, turned his gaze to his son. His face expressed indifference, and only by the drops glistening on his beard could one tell that he had recently wept.

That repulsive horror which people think about when speaking of death was absent from the room. In the general stupor, the mother's pose, the indifference of the doctor's face, lay something attractive, touching the heart, precisely that fine, barely perceptible beauty of human grief, which people will not soon learn to understand and describe, and which only music seems able to convey. Beauty could also be felt in the somber silence; Kirilov and his wife were quiet, they did not weep, as if, besides the heaviness of the loss, they were also conscious of the lyrical side of their situation: as once, in its time, their youth had gone, so now, together with this boy, their right to have children had gone forever into eternity! The doctor was forty-four, he was already gray-haired and looked like an old man; his faded and ailing wife was thirty-five. Andrei had been not just their only one, but also their last.

In contrast to his wife, the doctor belonged by nature to those who, at a time of inner pain, feel the need to move. Having stood by his wife for some five minutes, he walked, raising his right foot high, from the bedroom to a small room, half of which was taken up by a big, wide couch; from there he went on to the kitchen. After lingering briefly around the stove and the cook's bed, he bent down and passed through a small door into the front hall.

Here he again saw the white scarf and the pale face.

"At last!" Abogin sighed, taking hold of the door handle. "Let's go, please!"

The doctor gave a start, looked at him, and remembered . . .

"Listen, I already told you that I can't go!" he said, rousing himself. "How strange!"

"Doctor, I'm not a block of wood, I understand your situation very well . . . I feel for you!" Abogin said in a pleading voice, putting his hand to his scarf. "But I'm not asking for myself . . . My wife is dying! If you had heard that scream, seen her face, you'd understand my insistence! My God, I was already thinking you went to get dressed! Doctor, time is precious! Let's go, I beg you!"

"I cannot go!" Kirilov said in a measured tone and stepped into the drawing room.

Abogin followed him and grabbed him by the sleeve.

"You're in grief, I understand that, but I'm not inviting you to treat a toothache or give a diagnosis, but to save a human life!" he went on pleading like a beggar. "That life is higher than any personal grief! So, I'm asking for courage, a brave deed! For the love of humanity!"

"The love of humanity is a stick with two ends," Kirilov said irritably. "I beg you in the name of that same love of humanity not to take me away. And it's so strange, by God! I can barely keep my feet, and you frighten me with the love of humanity! I'm good for nothing now . . . I won't go with you for anything, and who will I leave my wife with? No, no . . ."

Kirilov waved his hands and took several steps back.

"And . . . and don't ask!" he went on in fright. "Excuse me . . . According to volume thirteen of the law, it's my duty to go, and you have the right to drag me by the scruff of the neck . . . All right, drag me, but . . . I'm no good . . . I can't even speak . . . Excuse me . . ."

"There's no point talking to me in that tone, doctor!" Abogin said, again taking the doctor by the sleeve. "Never mind about volume thirteen! I have no right to force your will. If you want to come, come; if you don't—God help you, but I'm not appealing to your will, but to your feelings. A young woman is dying! You told me your son just died—who can understand my horror if not you?"

Abogin's voice trembled with agitation; in that tremor and in that tone there was far more persuasiveness than in his words. Abogin was sincere, but, remarkably, no matter what phrases he spoke, they all came out stiff, soulless, inappropriately florid, and even seemed to insult both the air in the doctor's quarters and the woman who was dying somewhere. He felt it himself, and therefore, afraid he would not be understood, he tried as hard as he could to give his voice softness and tenderness, so as to prevail, if not by words, then at least by sincerity of tone. Generally a phrase, however beautiful and profound, affects only the indifferent, but cannot always satisfy the happy or the unhappy; therefore the highest expression of happiness or unhappiness turns out most often to be silence; lovers understand each other better when they are silent, and an ardent, passionate speech made over a grave moves only the outsiders, while the widow and children of the deceased find it cold and insignificant.

Kirilov stood and was silent. When Abogin said a few more phrases about the high calling of a doctor, about self-sacrifice and so on, the doctor asked sullenly:

"Is it far?"

"Something like nine or ten miles. I've got excellent horses, doctor! On my word of honor, I'll get you there and back in one hour. Just one hour!"

These last words affected the doctor more strongly than the references to the love of humanity or a doctor's vocation. He thought a little and said with a sigh:

"All right, let's go!"

He went quickly, and now with a sure step, to his office and came back a little later in a long frock coat. Mincing and shuffling around him, the cheered-up Abogin helped him into his overcoat and they left together.

Outside it was dark, but brighter than in the front hall. In the darkness, the doctor's tall, stooping figure, his long, narrow beard and aquiline nose, were clearly outlined. Abogin, it could now be seen, besides his pale face, also had a big head and a small visored cap that barely covered the top of it. The white scarf showed only in front, being hidden in back by his long hair.

"Believe me, I'll know how to appreciate your generosity," Abogin muttered, helping the doctor into the carriage. "We'll be there in no time. Luka, my dear fellow, drive as fast as you can! Please!"

The coachman drove quickly. First they went past a row of nondescript buildings that stood along the hospital yard; it was dark everywhere, only from someone's window in the depth of the yard a bright light shone through the front garden, and three windows on the upper floor of the hospital building looked paler than the air. Then the carriage drove into dense darkness; here there was a smell of mushroomy dampness and the whispering of the trees could be heard; crows, awakened by the rumbling of the wheels, stirred in the foliage and raised an anxious, plaintive cawing, as if they knew that the doctor's son had died and Abogin's wife was sick. But now separate trees and bushes flitted by, a pond on which big black shadows slept flashed sullenly—and the carriage rolled over a level plain. The cawing of the crows sounded faintly, far behind, and soon died away completely.

Kirilov and Abogin made almost the whole journey in silence. Only once Abogin sighed deeply and murmured:

"What a painful state! You never love your own so much as at the moment when you risk losing them!"

And when the carriage was slowly crossing the river, Kirilov suddenly roused himself, as if frightened by the splashing, and began to stir.

"Listen, let me go back," he said with anguish. "I'll come to you later. I just want to send my assistant to my wife. She's there alone!"

Abogin was silent. The carriage, rocking and clattering over the stones, drove up the sandy bank and rolled on. Kirilov twisted in anguish and looked around. Behind, through the scant light of the stars, the road and the willows on the riverbank could be seen, merging with the darkness. To the right lay the plain, as level and boundless as the sky; on it here and there, in the distance, probably on the peat bogs, dim lights were burning. To the left, parallel to the road, stretched a hill, all curly with small shrubs, and above the hill a big half-moon hung motionless, red, slightly veiled with mist, and surrounded by small clouds, which seemed to be watching it from all sides and keeping it from going away.

In the whole of nature there was a feeling of something hopeless, sick; the earth, like a fallen woman who sits alone in a dark room trying not to think about her past, languished in memories of spring and summer and waited apathetically for the inevitable winter. Wherever you looked, nature seemed like a dark, infinitely deep and cold pit, from which neither Kirilov nor Abogin nor the red half-moon would ever get out . . .

The closer the carriage came to its goal, the more impatient Abogin grew. He fidgeted, jumped up, peered over the coachman's shoulder. And when the carriage finally stopped by the porch, prettily draped in striped canvas, and he looked at the lighted windows on the first floor, one could hear how his breath quavered.

"If something happens . . . I won't survive it," he said, going into the front hall with the doctor and nervously rubbing his hands. "But I don't hear any commotion, meaning so far everything's all right," he added, listening to the stillness.

In the front hall no sound of voices or footsteps could be heard, and the whole house seemed asleep, despite the bright lights. Now the doctor and Abogin, who until then had been in the dark, could see each other. The doctor was tall, stooped-shouldered, slovenly dressed, and had an unattractive face. Something unpleasantly sharp, unfriendly, and severe was expressed by his lips, thick as a Negro's, his aquiline nose, and his sluggish, indifferent gaze. His disheveled head, sunken temples, the premature gray in his long, narrow beard, through which his chin showed, the pale gray color of his skin, and his careless, awkward manners—the callousness of it all suggested the notion of years of poverty, ill luck, weariness of life and people. Looking at his whole dry figure, it was hard to believe that this man had a wife, that he could weep over a child. Abogin embodied something else. He was a thickset, sturdy blond man, with a big head and large but soft facial features, elegantly dressed in the latest fashion. In his bearing, his tightly buttoned frock coat, his mane, and his face one could sense something noble, leonine; he walked with his head erect and his chest thrust out, spoke in a pleasant baritone, and the way he took off his scarf or touched his hair betrayed a fine, almost feminine elegance. Even his pallor and the childlike fear with which he kept glancing up the stairs as he took his coat off, did not harm his bearing or diminish the satiety, healthiness, and aplomb which his whole figure breathed.

"There's nobody, not a sound," he said, going up the stairs. "No commotion. God grant . . . !"

He led the doctor through the front hall into the big drawing room, where a black grand piano was darkly outlined and a chandelier hung in a white dust cover; from there the two went on to a small, very snug and pretty sitting room, filled with a pleasant rosy half-light.

"Well, you sit here, doctor," said Abogin, "and I . . . right away. I'll go have a look and let them know."

Kirilov remained alone. The luxury of the sitting room, the pleasant half-light, and the very fact of his presence in a stranger's unfamiliar house, which had the character of an adventure, evidently did not move him. He sat in an armchair and examined his hands burnt by carbolic acid. He looked only fleetingly at the bright red lampshade, the cello case, and, leaning towards the side where the clock was ticking, noticed a stuffed wolf as sturdy and sated as Abogin himself.

It was quiet . . . Somewhere far away in the adjoining rooms someone loudly uttered the sound "Ah!" and there was the clinking of a glass door, probably of a cupboard, and everything became quiet again. Having waited for about five minutes, Kirilov stopped studying his hands and raised his eyes to the door behind which Abogin had disappeared.

On the threshold of that door stood Abogin, but not the one who had gone out. His expression of satiety and refined elegance had vanished; his face, his hands, and his posture were distorted by a repulsive expression of something like horror or a tormenting physical pain. His nose, lips, moustache, all his features were moving and seemed to be trying to detach themselves from his face, while his eyes were as if laughing from pain . . .

Abogin stepped with heavy, long strides to the middle of the sitting room, bent over, groaned, and shook his fists.

"She deceived me!" he cried, heavily emphasizing the syllable "-cei-". "Deceived me! Left! Fell ill and sent me for a doctor only so as to run off with that buffoon Papchinsky! My God!"

Abogin strode heavily towards the doctor, brought his soft white fists close to the doctor's face, and, shaking them, went on yelling:

"She left! Deceived me! What need was there for this lie?! My God! My God! Why this dirty, swindling trick, this devilish, viperish game? What did I do to her? She left!"

Tears gushed from his eyes. He turned on one foot and began to pace the sitting room. Now, in his short frock coat and fashionably narrow trousers, which made his legs look too thin for his body, with his big head and mane, he very much resembled a lion. The doctor's indifferent face brightened with curiosity. He stood up and looked at Abogin.

"Excuse me, but where is the sick woman?" he asked.

"The sick woman! The sick woman!" Abogin shouted, laughing, crying, and still shaking his fists. "She's not sick, she's accursed! Meanness! Vileness, nastier than anything Satan himself could think up! She sent me away so as to run off, run off with a buffoon, a stupid clown, an Alphonse![1] Oh, God, it would be better if she'd died! I can't bear it! Can't bear it!"

The doctor straightened up. His eyes blinked, filled with tears, his narrow beard moved right and left together with his jaw.

"Excuse me, but how is that?" he asked, looking around with curiosity. "My child died, my wife is alone in the house, in anguish . . . I myself can barely stand on my feet, I haven't slept for three nights . . . and what then? I've been forced to play in some sort of banal comedy, to play the role of a stage prop! I . . . I don't understand!"

Abogin opened one fist, flung a crumpled note on the floor and stepped on it, as if it was an insect he wanted to squash.

"And I didn't see . . . didn't understand!" He spoke through clenched teeth, shaking one fist next to his face, and with such an expression as if someone had stepped on his callus. "I didn't notice that he came every day, didn't notice that today he came in a carriage! Why in a carriage? And I didn't see! Dunce!"

"I . . . I don't understand!" muttered the doctor. "What is all this! It's a mockery of a living person, a jeering at human suffering! It's something impossible . . . the first time in my life I've seen it!"

With the dull astonishment of a man who has just begun to realize that he has been deeply insulted, the doctor shrugged his shoulders, spread his arms, and, not knowing what to say or do, sank exhaustedly into the armchair.

"So, you fell out of love, fell in love with someone else—God help you, but why this deceit, why this vile, treacherous stunt?" Abogin was saying in a tearful voice. "How come? And what for? What did I do to you? Listen, doctor," he said hotly, going up to Kirilov. "You've been an involuntary witness to my misfortune, and I won't conceal the truth from you. I swear to you that I loved this woman, loved her devotedly, like a slave! I sacrificed everything for her: quarreled with my relations, abandoned my work and music, forgave her things I wouldn't have been able to forgive my mother or my sister . . . Never once did I look askance at her . . . never gave her any reason! So why this lie? I don't insist on love, but why this vile deception? If you don't love me, say so outright, honestly, the more so as you know my views in that regard . . ."

With tears in his eyes, trembling all over, Abogin sincerely poured out his soul before the doctor. He spoke fervently, pressing both hands to his heart, exposed his family secrets without any hesitation, and was even as if glad that these secrets had finally burst from his soul. If he had spoken like that for an hour, two hours, pouring out his soul, he would undoubtedly have felt better. Who knows, if the doctor had heard him out, shown friendly compassion, perhaps, as often happens, he would have been reconciled to his loss without protest, without any unnecessary foolishness . . . But something else happened. As Abogin spoke, the insulted doctor changed noticeably. The indifference and astonishment on his face gradually gave way to an expression of bitter offense, indignation, and wrath. The features of his face became still sharper, harder, and more unpleasant. When Abogin placed before his eyes the photograph of a young woman with a beautiful, but dry and expressionless face, like a nun's, and asked whether it was possible, looking at that face, to allow that it was capable of expressing a lie, the doctor suddenly jumped up, flashed his eyes, and said, rudely rapping out each word:

"Why are you telling me all this? I have no wish to hear it! No wish!" he shouted and banged his fist on the table. "I don't need to know your banal secrets, devil take them! Don't you dare tell me these banalities! Do you think I haven't been insulted enough already? That I'm a lackey who can be insulted endlessly? Eh?"

Abogin backed away from Kirilov and stared at him in astonishment.

"Why did you bring me here?" the doctor went on, his beard shaking. "You go crazy from your fat life and act out melodramas, but why bring me into it? What have I got to do with your love affairs? Leave me alone! Exercise your noble eccentricity, flaunt your humane ideas, play"—the doctor cast a sidelong glance at the cello case—"play your double basses and trombones, fatten up like capons, but don't you dare jeer at a human being! If you can't respect me, at least spare me your attention!"

"Excuse me, but what's the meaning of all this?" Abogin asked, turning red.

"It means that it's base and vile to play with people like that! I'm a doctor, and you consider doctors and workers in general, who don't smell of perfume and prostitution, as your lackeys and in *mauvais ton*[2]—well, go ahead, but no one gave you the right to turn a suffering man into a stage prop!"

"How dare you say that to me?" Abogin asked softly, and his face began to twitch again, this time clearly from wrath.

"No, knowing that I'm in grief, how could you dare bring me here to listen to banalities?" the doctor shouted, and again banged his fist on the table. "Who gave you the right to mock another man's grief like this?"

"You're out of your mind!" shouted Abogin. "That's not magnanimous! I'm profoundly unhappy myself and . . . and . . ."

"Unhappy," the doctor smirked contemptuously. "Don't touch that word, it doesn't concern you. A good-for-nothing who can't pay off his debts also calls himself unhappy, a capon that suffocates from too much fat is also unhappy. Worthless people!"

"My dear sir, you are forgetting yourself!" shrieked Abogin. "Such words . . . call for a beating! Understand?"

Abogin hurriedly went to his side pocket, took out his wallet, and pulling two notes from it, flung them on the table.

"That's for your visit!" he said, his nostrils twitching. "You've been paid!"

"Don't you dare offer me money!" the doctor shouted and swept the notes from the table. "An insult isn't paid for with money!"

Abogin and the doctor stood face to face and went on angrily hurling undeserved insults at each other. It seems that never in their lives, even in delirium, had they said so much that was unfair, cruel, and preposterous. In both men the egotism of the unhappy showed strongly. The unhappy are egotistic, spiteful, unfair, cruel, and less capable than the stupid of understanding each other. Unhappiness does not unite but divides people, and even where it seems that people should be united by the similarity of their grief, there is much more unfairness and cruelty done than in a comparatively contented milieu.

"Kindly send me home!" the doctor shouted, suffocating.

Abogin rang brusquely. When no one appeared at his call, he rang again and angrily threw the bell on the floor; it hit the rug dully and let out a plaintive, as if dying moan. A lackey appeared.

"Where are you all hiding, devil take you?!" The master fell upon him with clenched fists. "Where were you just now? Go, tell them to bring the carriage for this gentleman, and order the coach harnessed for me! Wait!" he shouted, when the lackey turned to go. "Let there not be a single traitor left in the house by tomorrow! Away with all of you! I'll hire new ones. Vermin!"

While waiting for their vehicles, Abogin and the doctor were silent. To the first an expression of satiety and refined elegance had already returned. He paced the sitting room, gracefully shaking his head and obviously planning something. His wrath had not yet cooled down, but he tried to pretend that he did not notice his enemy . . . The doctor stood, holding the edge of the table with one hand and looking at Abogin with that profound, somewhat cynical and unattractive contempt which only grief and misery can express when faced with satiety and elegance.

When, a little later, the doctor got into the carriage and went off, his eyes still had a contemptuous look. It was dark, much darker than an hour earlier. The red half-moon had already gone behind a hill, and the clouds that had watched over it lay in dark spots near the stars. A coach with red lights rumbled down the road and overtook the doctor. It was Abogin going to protest and do stupid things . . .

All the way the doctor thought not about his wife, not about Andrei, but about Abogin and the people who lived in the house he had just left. His thoughts were unjust and inhumanly cruel. He judged Abogin and his wife, and Papchinsky, and all those who live in rosy half-light and the smell of perfume, and all the way he hated them and despised them until his heart ached. And in his mind a firm conviction about these people was formed.

Time will pass, and Kirilov's grief will pass, but this conviction, unjust, unworthy of the human heart, will not pass but will remain in the doctor's mind to the grave.

1887

THE LETTER

THE RURAL DEAN,[1] Father Fyodor Orlov, a fine-looking, well-nourished man of about fifty, imposing and stern as always, with a habitual dignified expression that never left his face, but weary in the extreme, paced his small drawing room from corner to corner and thought strenuously about one thing: when would his visitor finally go away? This thought tormented him and did not leave him for a moment. The visitor, Father Anastasy, a priest in one of the outlying villages, had come to him some three hours earlier on his own business, very unpleasant and boring, had stayed on, and now, leaning his elbow on a thick accounting ledger, sat in the corner at a small, round table, and apparently had no thought of leaving, though it was already past eight o'clock in the evening.

Not everyone knows how to stop talking at the right time and leave at the right time. It often happens that even well-bred, tactful society people do not notice that their presence is provoking in a tired or busy host a feeling not unlike hatred, and that the feeling is being strenuously hidden and covered up by a lie. Father Anastasy saw and understood perfectly well that his presence was burdensome and inappropriate, that the dean, who had served matins late at night and a long liturgy at noon,[2] was tired and wanted to rest; he was on the point of getting up and leaving any moment, but instead of getting up, he went on sitting as if he was waiting for something. He was an old man of sixty-five, decrepit beyond his years, bony and stoop-shouldered, with an age-darkened, haggard face, red eyelids, and a long, narrow back like a fish's; he was dressed in a light-purple cassock, elegant but too ample for him (it had been given to him by the widow of a young priest who recently passed away), a broadcloth kaftan with a wide leather belt, and clumsy boots, the size and color of which clearly showed that Father Anastasy did without galoshes. Despite his clerical dignity and venerable age, something pathetic, downtrodden, and humiliated showed in his dull red eyes, the gray braids with a greenish tinge on his nape, the big shoulder blades on his skinny back . . . He was silent, did not stir, and coughed so discreetly as if he was afraid the sound of coughing would make his presence more conspicuous.

The old man had come to the dean on business. A couple of months earlier he had been forbidden to serve until further notice, and he had been put under investigation. His sins were many. He led an unsober life, did not get along with the clergy nor with the laity, neglected the parish register and the accounting—these were the formal accusations against him; but besides that there had long been rumors that he performed illegal marriages for money and sold certificates of fasting to clerks and officers who came to him from town.[3] These rumors were the more stubborn in that he was poor and had nine children on his neck, who were failures just as he was. His sons were uneducated, spoiled, and sat around doing nothing, and his unattractive daughters were still not married.

Not having strength enough to be candid, the dean paced from corner to corner, saying nothing or speaking only in hints.

"So you're not going home tonight?" he asked, stopping by the dark window and poking his little finger through the cage to the fluffed-up, sleeping canary.

Father Anastasy roused himself, coughed discreetly, and said in a quick patter:

"Home? God help me, no, Fyodor Ilyich. You yourself know that I can't serve, so what am I to do there? I left on purpose so as not to meet peoples' eyes. You yourself know: it's shameful not to serve. And besides I have business here, Fyodor Ilyich. Tomorrow after breaking the fast[4] I want to discuss something thoroughly with the father investigator."

"So . . ." The dean yawned. "And where are you staying?"

"At Zyavkin's."

Father Anastasy suddenly remembered that in a couple of hours the dean was to serve the Easter matins, and he became so ashamed of his unpleasant, inhibiting presence that he decided to go away at once and give the weary man some peace. And the old man got up to go, but before he began to say goodbye he spent a whole minute clearing his throat and looking imploringly, with the same expression of vague expectation in his whole figure, at the dean's back; shame, timidity, and a pathetic, forced laughter typical of people who do not respect themselves, played over his face. Waving his hand somehow resolutely, he said with a wheezing, jittery laughter:

"Father Fyodor, carry your mercy through to the end, tell them to give me before I go . . . a little glass of vodka!"

"This is no time to be drinking vodka," the dean said sternly. "You should be ashamed."

Father Anastasy became even more confused, laughed, and, for-getting his resolve to go home, sank back into the chair. The dean looked at his perplexed, embarrassed face, at his bent body, and felt sorry for the old man.

"God willing, we'll have a drink tomorrow," he said, wishing to soften his stern refusal. "All in good time."

The dean believed in reforming people, but now, as the feeling of pity flared up in him, it began to seem to him that this man who was under investigation, haggard, covered with sins and ailments, was irretrievably lost for life, that there was no longer any power on earth that could unbend his back, give clarity to his gaze, restrain his unpleasant, timid laugh, which he laughed on purpose to smooth over, if only slightly, the repulsive impression he made on people.

The old man now seemed to Father Fyodor not guilty or depraved, but humiliated, insulted, wretched; the dean remembered his wife, his nine children, the dirty, beggarly beds in Zyavkin's inn, remem-bered, for some reason, those who are glad to see drunken priests and exposed superiors, and he thought that the best thing Father Anastasy could do now was die as soon as possible and leave this world forever.

There was the sound of footsteps.

"Father Fyodor, are you resting?" a bass voice asked in the entryway.

"No, deacon, come in."

Orlov's colleague, the deacon Liubimov, came into the drawing room, an old man with a big bald spot on the top of his head, but still sturdy, dark-haired, and with thick black eyebrows, like a Georgian's. He bowed to Father Anastasy and sat down.

"What's the good word?" asked the dean.

"Is there any?" the deacon replied and, after a pause, went on with a smile: "Little children, little grief; big children, big grief. Such things are going on, Father Fyodor, that I can't come to my senses. A comedy, that's all."

He paused again briefly, smiled more broadly, and said:

"Today Nikolai Matveich came back from Kharkov. He told me about my Pyotr. Went to see him twice, he said."

"What did he tell you?"

"Got me worried, God help him. He wanted to give me joy, but when I thought it over, it turned out there wasn't much joy in it. More cause for grief than joy . . . 'Your Petrushka,' he says, 'lives a high life, he's way beyond reach now.' 'Well, thank God for that,' I say. 'I had dinner with him,' he says, 'and saw his whole way of life. He lives grandly,' he says, 'couldn't be better.' I'm curious, of course, so I ask: 'And what did they serve at his dinner?' 'First,' he says, 'a fish dish, something like a soup, then tongue with peas, then,' he says, 'a roast turkey.' 'Turkey during Lent? A fine treat!' I say. Turkey during the Great Lent. Eh?"

"That's not so surprising," said the dean, narrowing his eyes mockingly.

And, tucking both thumbs behind his belt, he straightened up and said in the tone in which he usually delivered sermons or taught catechism in the district high school:

"People who don't observe the fasts can be divided into two different categories: those who don't observe out of light-mindedness, and those who don't out of unbelief. Your Pyotr doesn't observe the fasts out of unbelief. Yes."

The deacon looked timidly at Father Fyodor's stern face and said:

"That's not the worst of it . . . We talked and talked, about this and that, and it also turned out that my unbelieving boy lives with some madame, another man's wife. She's there in his quarters in place of a wife and hostess: pours tea, receives guests, and all the rest, as if they were married. It's already the third year he's been carrying on with this viper. A comedy, that's all. Three years together, and no children."

"Meaning they live in chastity!" Father Anastasy giggled, with a wheezing cough. "There are children, Father Deacon, there are, but they don't keep them at home! They send them to foster care! Ha-ha-ha . . ." (Anastasy had a coughing fit.)

"Don't butt in, Father Anastasy," the dean said sternly.

"So Nikolai Matveich asked him, 'Who is this madame who serves soup at your table?'" the deacon went on, looking darkly at Anastasy's bent body. "And he says to him, 'She's my wife,' he says. And the other asks, 'Have you been pleased to be married long?' And Pyotr replies, 'We were married in Kulikov's pastry shop.'"

The dean's eyes lit up wrathfully, and his temples turned red. Apart from his sinfulness, he found Pyotr unsympathetic in general as a human being. Father Fyodor had what is known as a bone to pick with him. He remembered him when he was still a high school boy, and remembered him distinctly, because even then he had seemed abnormal to him. The schoolboy Petrusha was embarrassed to assist at the altar, was offended when addressed informally, did not cross himself on entering a room, and, most memorably of all, liked to talk much and heatedly, and, in Father Fyodor's opinion, garrulousness in children was improper and harmful; besides that, Petrusha had a scornful and critical attitude towards fishing, of which the dean and the deacon were great enthusiasts. As a student Pyotr did not go to church at all, slept until noon, looked down his nose at people, and, with a sort of special defiance, liked to raise ticklish, unanswerable questions.

"What do you want?" the dean asked, going up to the deacon and looking at him crossly. "What do you want? This was to be expected! I aways knew and was sure that nothing good would come of your Pyotr! I told you and I'm telling you. You're now reaping what you sowed! Reap, then!"

"What did I sow, Father Fyodor?" the deacon asked softly, looking up at the dean.

"And whose fault is it, if not yours? You are the parent, he is your child! It was for you to instruct him, to instill the fear of God in him. You had to teach him! Begot him, yes, you begot him, but instruct him—no, you did not. That's a sin! Bad! Shameful!"

The dean forgot about his weariness, paced about, and went on talking. On the deacon's bare crown and forehead small drops appeared. He raised guilty eyes to the dean and said:

"So I didn't instruct him, Father Fyodor? Lord have mercy, am I not the father of my child? You yourself know I spared nothing for him, all my life I strove and prayed to God to give him a proper education. I sent him to school, and I hired private tutors for him, and he finished university. And if I couldn't guide his mind, Father Fyodor, then, judge for yourself, I simply had no ability for it! He used to come here when he was a student, and I would tell him what I thought, but he didn't listen. I tell him, 'Go to church,' and he says, 'Why should I?' I'd explain, and he says, 'Why? What for?' Or else he pats me on the shoulder and says, 'Everything in this world is relative, approximate, and conventional. I don't know anything, and you don't know a blessed thing either, Papa.' "

Father Anastasy burst into wheezy laughter, had a coughing fit, and waved his fingers in the air as if he was about to say something. The dean glanced at him and said sternly:

"Don't butt in, Father Anastasy."

The old man laughed, beamed, and evidently enjoyed listening to the deacon, as if he was glad there were other sinful people in this world besides himself. The deacon spoke sincerely, with a contrite heart, and tears even came to his eyes. Father Fyodor felt sorry for him.

"It's your fault, Deacon, your fault," he said, but not so sternly and heatedly now. "If you know how to beget, you should know how to instruct. You should have instructed him while he was still a child, but now that he's a student, just try putting him right!"

Silence ensued. The deacon clasped his hands and said with a sigh:

"And I'm the one who must answer for him!"

"There you have it!"

After a brief pause, the dean yawned and sighed at the same time, and asked:

"Who is reading the Acts?"[5]

"Evstrat. Evstrat always reads the Acts."

The deacon got up and, looking imploringly at the dean, asked:

"Father Fyodor, what am I to do now?"

"Do whatever you like. I'm not his father, you are. You know best."

"I know nothing, Father Fyodor! Be so kind as to teach me! Believe me, I'm sick at heart! I can't sleep now, or sit quietly, and the holiday isn't a holiday for me! Tell me what to do, Father Fyodor!"

"Write him a letter."

"What am I going to write to him?"

"Write that he mustn't do this. Write briefly but sternly and specifically, without softening or diminishing his guilt. It's your parental obligation. You'll write, fulfill your duty, and calm down."

"That's true, but what am I to write to him? In what sense? I'll write, and he'll answer: 'Why? What for? How is it a sin?'"

Father Anastasy again laughed wheezily and moved his fingers.

"'Why? What for? How is it a sin?'" he began shrilly. "I was once confessing a certain gentleman and told him that to trust too much in God's mercy is a sin, and he asks: 'Why?' I wanted to answer him, but up here," Anastasy slapped himself on the forehead, "up here I had nothing! Haa-ha-ha-ha . . ."

Anastasy's words, his wheezing, his cackling laughter at something that was not funny, had an unpleasant effect on the dean and the deacon. The dean was about to tell the old man "Don't butt in," but he did not say it and merely winced.

"I can't write to him!" sighed the deacon.

"If you can't, who can?"

"Father Fyodor!" the deacon said, inclining his head to one side and pressing his hand to his heart. "I'm an uneducated, slow-witted man, but to you the Lord has given intelligence and wisdom. You know and understand everything, you grasp it all with your mind, while I don't even know how to speak properly. Be so good, instruct me in the composing of this letter! Teach me what and how . . ."

"What is there to teach? There's nothing to teach. Sit down and write."

"No, do me this kindness, Father Superior! I beg you. I know he'll be frightened of your letter and listen to your advice, because you're also educated. Be so good! I'll sit down, and you dictate. Tomorrow it would be a sin to write,[6] but today is just the right time, and I'll calm down."

The dean looked at the deacon's pleading face, remembered the unsympathetic Pyotr, and agreed to dictate. He sat the deacon at his desk and began:

"So, write . . . 'Christ is risen, my dear son . . . ,'[7] exclamation point. 'Rumors have reached me, your father . . .' then in parentheses . . . 'and from what source does not concern you . . .' parenthesis . . . Written that? . . . 'that you are leading a life consistent neither with divine nor with human law. Neither the comfort, nor the mundane splendor, nor the education with which you cover yourself externally, can conceal your pagan look. In name you are a Christian, but in essence you are a pagan, as pitiful and unfortunate as all other pagans, even more pitiful, because those pagans, not knowing Christ, perish out of ignorance, while you are perishing because, though you possess the treasure, you neglect it. I will not enumerate here all your vices, which are known well enough to you, I will only say that I see the cause of your perdition in your unbelief. You imagine yourself wise, boast of your scholarly knowledge, and yet you refuse to understand that knowledge without faith not only does not elevate a man, but even reduces him to the level of a lowly animal, for . . .'"

The whole letter was in that vein. Having finished writing, the deacon read it aloud, beamed, and jumped up.

"A gift, truly a gift!" he said, looking rapturously at the dean and clasping his hands. "What a godsent gift, really! Eh? Queen of Heaven! Never in a hundred years could I come up with such a letter! Lord save you!"

Father Anastasy was also in raptures.

"Without a gift you won't go writing like that!" he said, getting up and moving his fingers. "You won't! It's such rhetoric, no philosopher could write a little comma of it! A mind! A brilliant mind! If you weren't married, Father Fyodor, you'd have been a bishop long ago, that's the truth!"

Having poured out his wrath in the letter, the dean felt relieved. Fatigue and brokenness came back to him.

The deacon was an old acquaintance, and the dean said to him unceremoniously:

"Well, Deacon, go with God. I'll lie down on the couch for half an hour, I need some rest."

The deacon left and took Anastasy with him. As always happens on the eve of Easter, it was dark outside, but the whole sky shone with bright, radiant stars. In the quiet, motionless air there was a scent of spring and festivity.

"How long was he dictating?" The deacon marveled. "Some ten minutes, not more! Another man would take a month and not compose such a letter. Eh? There's a mind for you! Such a mind, I don't even know what to say! Astonishing! Truly astonishing!"

"Education!" sighed Anastasy, tucking the skirts of his cassock up to his waist as he crossed the muddy street. "We can't compare with him. We're from simple church folk, but he's got learning. A real man, whatever you say."

"You should hear him read the Gospel in Latin tonight during the liturgy![8] He knows Latin and he knows Greek . . . And Petrukha, Petrukha!" The deacon suddenly remembered. "Well, now he'll rub his sores! Bite his tongue! He'll know what's what! Now he won't go asking, 'Why?' He's met his match, that's what! Ha-ha-ha!"

The deacon burst into loud and merry laughter. Once the letter to Pyotr was written, he became cheerful and calmed down. Consciousness of a fulfilled parental duty and faith in the written word brought back his ready laughter and good spirits.

"Pyotr means 'stone' in translation," he said as they approached his house. "My Pyotr's not a stone, he's a rag. That viper took him over, and he coddles her, he can't get rid of her. Pah! There really are such women, God forgive me. Eh? Where's their shame? She latched on to the lad, clings to him, and keeps him at her skirts . . . may the foul one take her where she deserves!"

"Maybe it's not she who holds him, but he her?"

"Anyhow it means she's got no shame! I'm not defending Pyotr . . .

He's going to get it . . . He'll read the letter and scratch his head! He'll burn with shame!"

"It's a fine letter, only . . . better not send it to him, Father Deacon! Let him be."

"Why so?" The deacon was alarmed.

"Just so! Don't send it, Deacon! What's the point? So you send it, he reads it, and . . . and then what? He'll just get all upset. Forgive him, let him be!"

The deacon looked in surprise at Anastasy's dark face, at his thrown-open cassock, resembling wings in the darkness, and shrugged his shoulders.

"How can I forgive him?" he asked. "I'll have to answer to God for him!"

"Even so, forgive him anyway. Really! And God will forgive you for your kindness."

"But isn't he my son? Should I teach him or not?"

"Teach him? Why not? You can teach him, only why call him a pagan? It will hurt him, Deacon . . ."

The deacon was a widower and lived in a small three-window house. His older sister oversaw the housekeeping for him, an unmarried woman who had lost the use of her legs three years ago and therefore never left her bed. He was afraid of her, obeyed her, and did nothing without consulting her. Father Anastasy went home with him. Seeing his table already covered with kulichi and red-dyed eggs,[9] he began to weep for some reason, probably remembering his own house, and to make a joke of those tears he at once laughed wheezily.

"Yes, soon we'll break the fast," he said. "Yes . . . You know, Deacon, even now it would do no harm . . . to drink a little glass. May I? I'll drink it," he whispered with a sidelong glance at the door, "so that the old woman . . . doesn't hear . . . no, no . . ."

The deacon silently pushed the decanter and a glass towards him, unfolded the letter, and began to read it aloud. He liked the letter now as much as he had when the dean dictated it. He beamed with pleasure and wagged his head, as if he had tasted something very sweet.

"Now tha-a-at's a letter!" he said. "Petrukha has never dreamed of getting such a letter. Just what he needs, so that he feels the heat . . . there!"

"You know what, Deacon? Don't send it!" said Anastasy, pouring himself a second glass as if absentmindedly. "Forgive him, let him be! I tell you . . . in all conscience. If his own father won't forgive him, who will? So it means he'll live without forgiveness? And consider, Deacon: punishers will turn up even without you, but just try finding people who'll have mercy on your own son! I . . . I, brother, will have . . . One last one . . . Up and write to him straight out: I forgive you, Pyotr! He'll understa-a-and! He'll fe-e-el it! I, brother . . . I know it from myself, Deacon. When I lived like other people, I didn't mind much, but now, when I've lost the image and likeness,[10] I want only one thing: that good people forgive me. And consider this, that it's not the righteous who need forgiving, it's the sinners. What should you forgive your old woman for, if she's not sinful? No, you forgive the one it's a pity to see . . . that's what!"

Anastasy propped his head with his fist and fell to thinking.

"It's bad, Deacon," he sighed, obviously fighting against the wish to drink. "Bad! In sin did my mother conceive me,[11] in sin I've lived, and in sin I'll die . . . Lord have mercy on me a sinner! I'm confounded, Deacon! There's no salvation for me! And I got confounded not in life, but in old age, just before death . . . I . . ."

The old man waved his hand and had another drink, then got up and sat in a different place. The deacon, not letting go of the letter, paced from corner to corner. He was thinking about his son. Discontent, grief, and fear no longer troubled him: it had all gone into the letter. Now he only imagined Pyotr to himself, pictured his face, recalled the past years, when his son used to visit for the holiday. He thought only of what was good, warm, sad, of what he could even think about all his life without wearying. Longing for his son, he reread the letter one more time and looked questioningly at Anastasy.

"Don't send it!" the latter said, waving his hand.

"No, anyhow . . . I must. Anyhow it will sort of . . . set him to rights. It won't hurt . . ."

The deacon took an envelope from his desk, but, before putting the letter into it, sat down at the desk, smiled, and added something of his own at the bottom of the letter: "And they've sent us a new full-time caretaker. He's livelier than the previous one. He's a dancer, and a babbler, and a jack-of-all-trades, and all the Govorov girls have lost their minds over him. They say the military commander Kostirev will also retire soon. It's high time!" And very pleased with himself, not realizing that by this postscript he had totally ruined the stern letter, the deacon wrote the address on the envelope and placed it in the most conspicuous place on the table.

1887

VOLODYA

ONE SUMMER SUNDAY, at around five o'clock in the evening, Volodya, a seventeen-year-old boy, unattractive, sickly, and timid, was sitting in the gazebo of the Shumikhins' dacha, feeling bored. His cheerless thoughts flowed in three directions. First, the next day, Monday, he was to take an examination in mathematics; he knew that if, the next day, he did not succeed in solving a written problem, he would be expelled, because he was already repeating his senior year and had a very low average in algebra. Second, his stay with the Shumikhins, rich people with a claim to aristocracy, constantly hurt his pride. It seemed to him that *M-me* Shumikhin and her nieces looked upon him and his *maman* as poor relations and spongers, that they did not respect *maman* and laughed at her. Once he accidentally overheard *M-me* Shumikhin on the terrace saying to her cousin Anna Fyodorovna that his *maman* went on pretending that she was still young and prettified herself, that she never paid her debts at cards and had a predilection for other people's shoes and cigarettes. Volodya begged her every day not to visit the Shumikhins, described to her how humiliating a role she played with these gentlefolk, persuaded, spoke rudely, but she, flighty, pampered, having run through two fortunes in her time, her own and her husband's, always drawn to high society, did not understand him, and twice a week Volodya had to accompany her to the hateful dacha.

Third, the boy could not rid himself, even for a moment, of a

strange, unpleasant feeling that was totally new to him . . . It seemed
to him that he was in love with *M-me* Shumikhin's cousin and guest,
Anna Fyodorovna. She was a lively, loud, and laughter-prone little
lady of about thirty, healthy, buxom, rosy, with round shoulders, a
round, plump chin, and a constant smile on her thin lips. She was not
attractive and not young—Volodya knew that perfectly well—but for
some reason he was unable not to think about her, not to look at her
when, playing croquet, she shrugged her round shoulders and moved
her smooth back, or else, after a long time of laughing and running
up and down the stairs, she collapsed into an armchair and, closing
her eyes, her chest heaving, pretended that she was out of breath and
suffocating. She was married. Her husband, a respectable architect,
came to the dacha once a week, had a good night's sleep, and went
back to town. Volodya's strange feeling started with a groundless
hatred of this architect and a rejoicing each time the man returned to
town.

Now, sitting in the gazebo and thinking about the next day's examination and about *maman*, who was laughed at, he felt a strong desire
to see Nyuta (as the Shumikhins called Anna Fyodorovna), to hear
her laughter, the rustling of her dress . . . This desire was not like that
pure, poetic love, which was familiar to him from novels and which
he dreamed about every night going to bed; it was strange, incomprehensible, he was ashamed and afraid of it, as of something very bad
and impure, something hard to admit to himself . . .

"This isn't love," he said to himself. "You don't fall in love with
thirty-year-old married women . . . This is simply a little intrigue . . .
Yes, a little intrigue . . ."

Thinking of the little intrigue, he remembered about his invincible
timidity, his lack of a moustache, his freckles, his narrow eyes, putting
himself in imagination beside Nyuta—and the couple seemed impossible to him; then he hastened to imagine himself handsome, brave,
witty, dressed in the latest fashion . . .

At the very peak of his reverie, when he sat in the dark corner of
the gazebo, hunched over and looking at the ground, there came the
sound of light footsteps. Someone was walking unhurriedly down
the path. Soon the footsteps fell silent and something white flashed at
the entrance.

"Is anyone here?" a woman's voice asked.

Volodya recognized the voice and raised his head timorously.

"Who's here?" Nyuta asked, coming into the gazebo. "Ah, it's you, Volodya? What are you doing here? Thinking? How can you think, think, think all the time . . . you could lose your mind that way!"

Volodya got up and looked perplexedly at Nyuta. She was just coming back from bathing. On her shoulder hung a bath-sheet and a Turkish towel, and a strand of wet hair escaped from under her white silk head scarf and clung to her forehead. She smelled of the moist, cool bathhouse and almond soap. She was breathless from walking quickly. The top button of her blouse was undone, so that the young man saw her neck and bosom.

"Why are you silent?" asked Nyuta, looking Volodya up and down. "It's impolite to be silent when a lady speaks to you. What a lummox you are, Volodya! Always sitting, thinking silently, like some kind of philosopher. There's no life and fire in you at all! You're disgusting, really . . . At your age you should live, jump, chatter, pay court to women, fall in love."

Volodya was looking at the bath-sheet held up by a plump white hand and thinking . . .

"Not a word!" Nyuta was surprised. "It's even strange . . . Listen, be a man! Well, smile at least! Pfui, disgusting philosopher!" she laughed. "You know why you're such a lummox, Volodya? Because you don't pay court to women. Why don't you? True, there are no young misses here, but nothing keeps you from paying court to the ladies. Why don't you pay court to me, for instance?"

Volodya listened and in heavy, strained reflection scratched his temple.

"Only very proud people are silent and love solitude," Nyuta went on, pulling his hand away from his temple. "You're proud, Volodya. Why do you look at me surreptitiously? Kindly look me straight in the face! Ah, come on, you lummox!"

Volodya decided to speak. Wishing to smile, he moved his lower lip, blinked, and again put his hand to his temple.

"I . . . I love you!" he brought out.

Nyuta raised her eyebrows in surprise and laughed.

"What is this I hear?" she sang, as opera singers do when they hear something terrible. "How's that? What did you say? Repeat it, repeat it . . ."

"I . . . I love you!" Volodya repeated.

And now without any participation of his will, neither understanding nor reflecting on anything, he made a half step towards Nyuta and took her by the arm above the wrist. His eyes went dim and tears rose in them; the whole world turned into one big Turkish towel that smelled of the bathhouse.

"Bravo, bravo!" He heard merry laughter. "Why are you silent? I'd like you to speak! Well?"

Seeing that she did not prevent him from holding her arm, Volodya looked at Nyuta's laughing face and clumsily, awkwardly put his arms around her waist, both hands coming together behind her back. He held her by the waist with both arms, while she, raising both hands to the back of her head and showing the dimples in her elbows, straightened her hair under the scarf and said in a calm voice:

"You should be adroit, gracious, affable, Volodya, and one can be like that only under the influence of women's society. But what an unpleasant . . . angry face you have. You should talk, laugh . . . Yes, Volodya, don't be so mopey, you're young, you'll have a lot of time for philosophizing. Well, let go of me, I'm leaving! Let go!"

Without effort she freed her waist and, humming something, left the gazebo. Volodya remained alone. He smoothed his hair, smiled, and paced three times from corner to corner, then sat on the bench and smiled again. He was unbearably ashamed, so much so that he was even surprised that human shame could reach such acuteness and intensity. From shame he smiled, whispered some incoherent words, and gesticulated.

He was ashamed that he had just been treated like a boy, ashamed of his timidity, and above all that he had dared to take a respectable married woman by the waist, though it seemed to him that neither by his age, nor by his appearance, nor by his social position did he have any right to do so.

He jumped up, left the gazebo, and, without looking back, walked into the depths of the garden, further away from the house.

"Ah, leave here the sooner the better!" he thought, clutching his head. "My God, the sooner the better!"

The train that Volodya and his *maman* were to take departed at eight-forty. There were about three hours until the train, but he would have been very happy to leave for the station right then, without waiting for *maman*.

It was going on eight when he approached the house. His whole figure was the picture of resolution: whatever would be, would be! He decided to go in boldly, look straight ahead, speak loudly, no matter what.

He passed through the terrace, the reception room, the drawing room, and stopped there to catch his breath. From there he could hear tea being served in the adjacent dining room. *M-me* Shumikhin, *maman*, and Nyuta were talking about something and laughing.

Volodya listened.

"I assure you!" Nyuta was saying. "I couldn't believe my eyes. When he began to declare his love and even, imagine, took me by the waist, I didn't recognize him. And you know, he has this manner! When he said he was in love with me, there was something wild in his face, like in a Circassian."

"Really!" *maman* gasped, dissolving in drawn-out laughter. "Really! How he reminds me of his father!"

Volodya ran back and out into the fresh air.

"And how can they talk about it out loud!" He suffered, clasping his hands and looking at the sky with horror. "Out loud, coolheadedly . . . And *maman* laughed . . . *maman*! My God, why did you give me such a mother? Why?"

But he had to go into the house no matter what. He paced up and down the path three times, calmed himself a little, and went in.

"Why didn't you come in time for tea?" *M-me* Shumikhin asked sternly.

"I'm sorry, I . . . it's time for me to leave," he murmured without raising his eyes. "*Maman*, it's already eight o'clock!"

"Go by yourself, my dear," *maman* said languidly, "I'm staying the night at Lily's. Goodbye, my pet . . . Let me bless you . . ."

She made the sign of the cross over her son and said in French, turning to Nyuta:

"He looks a little like Lermontov[1] . . . Isn't it so?"

Having hurriedly said goodbye, without looking anyone in the face, Volodya left the dining room. Ten minutes later he was already marching down the road to the station and was glad of it. Now he was no longer either frightened or ashamed; he breathed lightly and freely.

A quarter of a mile from the station he sat down on a stone by the roadside and began to look at the sun, which was more than half hidden behind the embankment. At the station lights were already lit here and there, one dim green light was flickering, but there was no train in sight yet. Volodya liked sitting, not moving, and listening to how the evening gradually approached. The darkness of the gazebo, the footsteps, the smell of the bathhouse, the laughter, and the waist—it all rose up with astonishing clarity in his imagination, and it was all no longer as frightening and significant as before . . .

"Nonsense . . . She didn't pull her hand away, and she laughed when I held her by the waist," he thought, "which means she liked it. If it disgusted her, she would have gotten angry . . ."

Now Volodya was annoyed that there, in the gazebo, he had not been bold enough. He was sorry that he was going away so stupidly, and he was now certain that, if the chance repeated itself, he would look on things more boldly and simply.

And the chance could easily repeat itself. The Shumikhins took long strolls after supper. If Volodya went for a stroll in the dark garden with Nyuta—that would be a chance!

"I'll go back," he thought, "and take the morning train tomorrow . . . I'll say I was late for the train."

And he went back . . . *M-me* Shumikhin, *maman*, Nyuta, and one of the nieces were sitting on the terrace playing whist. When Volodya lied to them that he had been late for the train, they worried that he would be late for the examination the next morning, and advised him to get up early. All the while they played cards, he sat to one side, greedily looking at Nyuta and waiting . . . In his head a plan was already formed: he would approach Nyuta in the darkness, take her by the hand, then embrace her; there would be no need for talk, because they would both understand everything without talking.

But after supper the ladies did not go for a stroll in the garden, but went on playing cards. They played until one in the morning and then went to bed.

"How stupid this all is!" Volodya thought vexedly, going to bed.

"But never mind, I'll wait till tomorrow . . . Tomorrow again in the gazebo. Never mind . . ."

He did not try to fall asleep, but sat on the bed, his arms around his knees, thinking. The thought of the examination was loathsome to him. He had already decided that he would be expelled and that there would be nothing terrible in his expulsion. On the contrary it was all good, even very good. Tomorrow he would be free as a bird, he would change out of his uniform, smoke openly, come here and court Nyuta whenever he liked; and he would no longer be a high school boy, but a "young man." And the rest, what is known as a career and a future, was quite clear: Volodya would volunteer for the army, or become a telegrapher, or get a job in a pharmacy, where he would work his way up to chief dispenser . . . as if there weren't enough occupations! An hour or two went by, and he was still sitting and thinking . . .

It was past two o'clock and dawn was breaking, when the door creaked cautiously and *maman* came in.

"You're not asleep?" she asked, yawning. "Sleep, sleep, I'll leave at once . . . I'll just take the drops . . ."

"What for?"

"Poor Lily's having spasms again. Sleep, my child, you have an examination tomorrow . . ."

She took a vial of something from the medicine chest, went to the window, read the label, and left.

"Marya Leontyevna, these are the wrong drops!" Volodya heard a woman's voice a minute later. "This is convallaria, and Lily's asking for morphine. Is your son asleep? Ask him to find it . . ."

It was Nyuta's voice. Volodya turned cold. He quickly put on his trousers, threw his coat over his shoulders, and went to the door.

"You understand? Morphine!" Nyuta was explaining in a whisper. "It should be written on it in Latin. Wake Volodya up, he'll find it . . ."

Maman opened the door, and Volodya saw Nyuta. She was in the same blouse in which she had gone to bathe. Her hair was not done up, but strewn over her shoulders; her face was sleepy, swarthy in the darkness . . .

"Here's Volodya, not asleep . . . ," she said. "Volodya, dearest, look for the morphine in the medicine chest! What a punishment this Lily is . . . She's always got something."

Maman muttered something, yawned, and left.

"Go and look," Nyuta said, "don't just stand there."

Volodya went to the medicine chest, knelt by it, and started rummaging through vials and boxes of medications. His hands trembled, and in his chest and stomach there was a feeling as if cold waves were running all through his insides. The smell of ether, carbolic acid, and various herbs, which his trembling hands seized and crumbled without any need, stifled him and made his head spin.

"*Maman* seems to have gone," he thought. "That's good . . . good . . ."

"Why so slow?" Nyuta asked, drawing out the words.

"Right away . . . This seems to be morphine . . . ," said Volodya, having read the word "morph . . ." on one of the labels. "Here you are!"

Nyuta stood in the doorway so that one foot was in the corridor, the other in his room. She was straightening her hair, which was hard to do—so thick and long it was!—and looking absently at Volodya. In an ample blouse, sleepy, with loose hair, in the scant light that came into the room from the white but not yet sunlit sky, Volodya found her fascinating, resplendent . . . Enchanted, trembling all over, recalling with pleasure how he had embraced that wonderful body in the gazebo, he handed her the drops and said:

"You're so . . ."

"What?"

She came into the room.

"What?" she asked, smiling.

He said nothing and looked at her, then, as before in the gazebo, took her by the arm . . . And she looked at him, smiled, and waited for what would come next.

"I love you . . . ," he whispered.

She stopped smiling, pondered, and said:

"Wait, I think someone's coming. Oh, these schoolboys!" she said in a low voice, went to the door, and peeked out to the corridor. "No, nobody to be seen . . ."

She came back . . .

Then it seemed to Volodya that the room, Nyuta, the dawn, and his own self—all merged into one sensation of keen, extraordinary, unheard-of happiness, for which one could give one's whole life and go to eternal torment, but half a minute went by and it all suddenly vanished. Volodya saw only a plump, unattractive face, distorted by an expression of disgust, and he himself suddenly felt a loathing for what had happened.

"Anyhow I must go," said Nyuta, looking Volodya over squeamishly. "What an unattractive, pathetic . . . phoo, an ugly duckling!"

How repulsive her long hair, her ample blouse, her footsteps, her voice now seemed to Volodya! . . .

" 'Ugly duckling,' " he thought after she left. "In fact, I am ugly . . . Everything's ugly."

Outside the sun was already rising, the birds sang loudly; the gardener's footsteps were heard in the garden and the creaking of his wheelbarrow . . . A little later came the mooing of cows and the sounds of a shepherd's pipe. The sunlight and the sounds were saying that somewhere in this world there exists a pure, refined, poetic life. But where is it? Neither *maman* nor all those people around him had ever spoken of it to Volodya.

When a lackey came to wake him up for the morning train, he pretended to be asleep . . .

"Ah, to hell with it all!" he thought.

He got up between ten and eleven. Brushing his hair before the mirror and looking at his unattractive face, pale after a sleepless night, he thought:

"Quite right . . . an ugly duckling."

When *maman* saw him and was horrified that he was not at the examination, Volodya said:

"I overslept, *maman* . . . But don't worry, I'll present a medical excuse."

Madame Shumikhin and Nyuta woke up at noon. Volodya heard *M-me* Shumikhin noisily open her window and Nyuta responding to her coarse voice with ringing laughter. He saw the door open and a string of nieces and spongers (*maman* in the crowd of the latter) come filing out of the drawing room for lunch. He saw Nyuta's washed, laughing face, and next to her face the black eyebrows and beard of the just-arrived architect.

Nyuta was wearing a Ukrainian costume, which did not suit her at all and made her ungainly; the architect's jokes were trite and flat; in the beef patties served at lunch there was far too much onion—so it seemed to Volodya. It also seemed to him that Nyuta guffawed loudly on purpose and kept glancing in his direction to let him know that the memory of the night before did not trouble her in the least and that she did not notice the ugly duckling's presence at the table.

At three o'clock Volodya rode to the station with *maman*. The sordid memories, the sleepless night, the impending expulsion from school, the pangs of conscience—it all now aroused in him a heavy, dark anger. He looked at *maman*'s gaunt profile, at her little nose, at the rain cape Nyuta had given her, and muttered:

"Why do you use powder? At your age it's unbecoming! You prettify yourself, you don't pay your card debts, you smoke other people's cigarettes . . . disgusting! I don't love you . . . don't love you!"

He insulted her, and she rolled her frightened eyes, clasped her little hands, and whispered in horror:

"What are you saying, dear? My God, the coachman will hear you! Be quiet, or the coachman will hear you! He can hear everything!"

"Don't love you . . . don't love you!" he went on breathlessly. "You're immoral, soulless . . . Don't you dare go around in that rain cape! Do you hear me? I'll tear it to shreds . . ."

"Calm down, child!" *Maman* began to cry. "The coachman will hear you!"

"Where's my father's fortune? Where's your money? You squandered it all! I'm not ashamed of my poverty, but I am ashamed to have such a mother . . . When my comrades ask about you, I always blush."

By train the town was two stops away. Volodya stood all the while at the rear of the car and trembled all over. He did not want to go into the car, since his mother, whom he hated, was sitting there. He hated himself, the conductors, the smoke of the engine, the cold, which he thought was the cause of his trembling . . . And the heavier his heart became, the more strongly he felt that somewhere in this world, among some people, there was a pure, noble life, warm, refined, filled with love, tenderness, gaiety, freedom . . . He felt it, and his yearning was so strong that one of the passengers, looking him closely in the face, even asked:

"Maybe you have a toothache?"

In town *maman* and Volodya lived with Marya Petrovna, a gentlewoman who rented a big apartment and took in tenants. *Maman* rented two rooms: in the one with windows, where her bed stood and two paintings in gilt frames hung on the walls, she herself lived; and in the other, adjacent, small and dark, lived Volodya. Here stood the sofa he slept on, and there was no other furniture; the whole room was taken up by hampers full of clothes, hat boxes, and all sorts of junk that *maman* kept for some reason. Volodya did his homework in his mother's room or the "common room"—so the large room was called where the tenants all gathered at dinnertime and in the evenings.

Returning home, he lay down on the sofa and covered himself with a blanket to calm his trembling. The hat boxes, hampers, and junk reminded him that he had no room of his own, no shelter where he could hide from *maman*, from her guests, and from the voices that were now coming from the common room; the satchel and books scattered in the corners reminded him of the examination he had not taken . . . For some reason, quite beside the point, he recalled Menton, where he had lived with his late father when he was seven years old; he remembered Biarritz and two little English girls he used to run with in the sand . . . He wanted to refresh his memory of the color of the sky and the ocean, the height of the waves, and his mood at that time, but he did not succeed; the little English girls flashed in his imagination as if alive, but all the rest became confused and dissolved in disorder . . .

"No, it's cold here," Volodya thought, got up, put on his overcoat, and went to the common room.

In the common room they were having tea. Three people were sitting by the samovar: *maman*; a music teacher, a little old lady in tortoiseshell pince-nez; and Avgustin Mikhailych, an elderly, very fat Frenchman, who worked at a perfume factory.

"I had no lunch today," *maman* was saying. "We'll have to send the maid for bread."

"*Douniache!*" the Frenchman cried.

It turned out that the landlady had sent the maid somewhere.

"Oh, that signifies nothing," the Frenchman said with a big smile. "I'll go myself right now for bread. Oh, it's nothing!"

He laid his strong, stinking cigar in a conspicuous place, put on his hat, and left. On his departure, *maman* started telling the music teacher how she had visited the Shumikhins and how well she had been received there.

"Lily Shumikhin is my relative . . . ," she said. "Her late husband, General Shumikhin, was my husband's cousin. She herself was born Baroness Kolb . . ."

"*Maman*, that's not true!" Volodya said irritably. "Why lie?"

He knew perfectly well that *maman* was telling the truth: there was not a single lying word in her story about General Shumikhin and the born Baroness Kolb, but nonetheless he still felt she was lying. The lie was felt in her manner of speaking, in the expression of her face, in her gaze, in everything.

"You're lying!" Volodya repeated and pounded on the table so hard that all the china trembled and *maman*'s tea splashed out. "Why do you go telling about generals and baronesses? It's all lies!"

The music teacher was taken aback and coughed into her handkerchief, making it look as if she was choking, and *maman* burst into tears.

"Where can I go?" thought Volodya.

He had already been outside; he was ashamed to go to his school friends. Again, beside the point, he remembered the two little English girls . . . He walked up and down the common room and went into Avgustin Mikhailych's room. Here it smelled strongly of essential oils and glycerine soap. On the table, in the windows, and even on the chairs stood a multitude of bottles, little tumblers, and shot glasses with liquids of various colors. Volodya took a newspaper from the table, unfolded it, and read the title: *Figaro*. The newspaper had a strong and pleasant smell. Then he took a revolver from the table . . .

"Enough now, don't pay any attention!" The music teacher was comforting *maman* in the next room. "He's still so young! At his age men always allow themselves excesses. You must reconcile yourself to that."

"No, Evgenia Andreevna, he's too spoiled!" *maman* said in a singsong voice. "There's no older man over him, and I'm weak and can't do anything. No, I'm unhappy!"

Volodya put the muzzle of the revolver into his mouth, felt something like a trigger or catch, and pressed it with his finger . . . Then he felt some other sort of protuberance and pushed that as well. Taking the muzzle out of his mouth, he wiped it on the skirt of his overcoat and studied the lock; never before in his life had he held a weapon in his hands . . .

"Seems it should be raised . . . ," he figured. "Yes, it seems so . . ."

Avgustin Mikhailych came into the common room and laughingly began telling about something. Volodya again put the muzzle into his mouth, clenched it with his teeth, and pressed something with his finger. A shot rang out . . . Something struck Volodya in the back of the head with terrible force, and he fell onto the table, face down on the glasses and bottles. Then he saw his late father, in a top hat with a wide black band, dressed in mourning for some lady in Menton, suddenly embrace him with both arms, and they both fell into a very dark, deep abyss.

Then everything became confused and disappeared . . .

1887

Luck

To Y. P. Polonsky[1]

B Y THE WIDE STEPPE ROAD known as the highway a herd of sheep was spending the night. It was watched over by two shepherds. One, an old man of around eighty, toothless, with a quivering face, was lying on his stomach just by the road, resting his elbows on the dusty leaves of a plantain; the other, a young fellow with bushy black eyebrows and no moustache, dressed in the burlap from which cheap sacks are made, lay on his back, his hands behind his head, looking up into the sky, where, just over his face, the Milky Way stretched and stars were drowsing.

The shepherds were not alone. Some two yards from them, in the darkness that covered the road, loomed the dark outline of a saddled horse, and beside it, leaning against the saddle, stood a man in high boots and a short jacket, by all appearances a landlord's overseer. Judging by his erect and motionless figure, his manners, his treatment of the shepherds, the horse, he was a serious, reasonable man and knew his own worth; even in the darkness traces of military bearing were discernible in him and that grandly condescending expression which is acquired from frequent dealing with masters and stewards.

The sheep were sleeping. Against the gray background of the dawn, which was already beginning to cover the eastern part of the sky, the silhouettes of those that were not asleep could be seen; they stood with their heads lowered, thinking about something. Their thoughts, long, drawn-out, evoked only by impressions of the wide steppe and the sky, of days and nights, probably astonished and oppressed them to the point of stupefaction, and, standing now as if rooted to the spot, they noticed neither the stranger's presence nor the restlessness of the dogs.

In the sleepy, static air hung a monotonous noise, without which there could be no summer steppe night; grasshoppers chirred incessantly, quails sang, and a half mile or so from the herd, in a ravine, where a brook flowed and pussywillows grew, young nightingales whistled languidly.

The overseer had stopped to ask the shepherds for fire to light his pipe. He silently lit up, smoked the whole pipe, then, without saying a word, leaned his elbow against the saddle and fell to thinking. The young shepherd paid no attention to him; he went on lying there and looking at the sky, but the old man studied the overseer for a long time and then asked:

"Might you be Pantelei from the Makarov estate?"

"Himself," the overseer replied.

"Now I see. I couldn't tell—so you'll be a rich man.[2] Where did God fetch you from?"

"The Kovylevsky tract."

"That's far off. Is it let out for sharecropping?"

"Various things. Some for sharecropping, some on lease, some for melon patches. In fact, I just went to the mill."

A big old sheepdog of a dirty white color, shaggy, with clumps of fur around its eyes and nose, trying to seem indifferent to the presence of strangers, calmly circled the horse three times and suddenly, unexpectedly, with a vicious old dog's wheezing, attacked the overseer from behind. The other dogs could not control themselves and jumped up from their places.

"Shush, damn you!" the old man shouted, rising on his elbow. "Ah, go burst, you fiendish creature!"

When the dogs calmed down, the old man assumed his former pose and said in a calm voice:

"And in Kovyli, right on Ascension Day, Efim Zhmenya died. Shouldn't say it before sleep, it's a sin to think of such people—he was a vile old man. You must have heard."

"No, I haven't."

"Efim Zhmenya, Styopka the blacksmith's uncle. Everybody around here knew him. Oh, yes, a cursed old man! Some sixty years I knew him, ever since the tsar Alexander, the one who drove the French out, was being brought from Taganrog to Moscow in a wagon.[3] We went together to meet the dead tsar, and back then the high road didn't go through Bakhmut, but from Esaulovka to Gorodishche, and where Kovyli is now there were bustards' nests—you take a step and there's a bustard's nest. I noticed then that Zhmenya had given up his soul, and there was an unclean spirit in him. I've observed: if a man of the peasant order mostly keeps quiet, is interested in old women's things, and prefers to live by himself, there's little good in it, and this Efim, it so happens, was always silent, silent, ever since childhood, and looked askance at you, and kept pouting and puffing himself up, like a rooster in front of a hen. So that going to church, or hanging out with the lads in the street, or in a pot-house, just wasn't his style, and he mostly sat alone or gossiping with old women. He was young, but already hired himself out to the beekeepers and melon-growers. It so happened good people would come to him at the melon patches, and his watermelons and muskmelons would whistle. Or once he caught a pike in front of people, and—ho-ho-ho!—it burst out laughing . . ."

"It happens," said Pantelei.

The young shepherd turned on his side and, raising his black eyebrows, looked intently at the old man.

"Did you ever hear watermelons whistle?" he asked.

"Me, no, God spared me," the old man sighed, "but people tell about it. It's no great wonder . . . If unclean powers want to, they'll whistle in a stone. Before the freedom,[4] we had a rock humming for three days and three nights. I heard it myself. And the pike laughed because Zhmenya caught a demon, not a pike."

The old man remembered something. He quickly got up on his knees and, huddling as if from the cold, nervously tucking his hands into his sleeves, murmured through his nose an old woman's patter:

"God save us and have mercy! Once I was going along the riverbank to Novopavlovka. A thunderstorm was gathering, and there was such a gale, save us, Queen of Heaven, Holy Mother . . . I'm hurrying as fast as I can, and I see a white ox going down the path among the blackthorn bushes. The blackthorns were in bloom then. And I think: Whose ox is it? What ill wind brought him here? He goes along, swinging his tail and moo-o-o! Only this same ox, brothers, when I caught up with him, got close, and looked!—it was no ox now, it was Zhmenya. Holy, holy, holy! I made the sign of the cross, and he looks at me and mutters, his eyes bugging out. I was frightened, terribly! We walked side by side, I'm afraid to say a word to him—thunder rolls, lightning streaks the sky, the pussywillows bend down right to the water—suddenly, brothers, God punish me, so I die without repentance, a hare runs across our path . . . He runs, stops, and says in human language: 'Hello, boys!' Away, damn you!" the old man yelled at the shaggy dog, who was circling the horse again. "Ah, go croak!"

"It happens," the overseer said, still leaning against the saddle and not stirring; he said it in a soundless, muted voice, the way people speak who are sunk in thought.

"It happens," he repeated meaningfully and with conviction.

"Ohh, a fiendish old man he was!" the old man went on, not so heatedly now. "Five years after the freedom, we all flogged him in the village office, and to show his anger, he sent a throat ailment to everybody in Kovyli. A host of people died then, no counting them, like from cholera . . ."

"How did he send this ailment?" the young shepherd asked after a pause.

"As if we don't know. No need for great wisdom here, if there's the will. Zhmenya did people in with viper fat. It's such stuff that, not just the fat itself, but even the smell kills people."

"That's right," Pantelei agreed.

"Our boys wanted to kill him then, but the old men wouldn't allow it. It was forbidden to kill him; he knew where the treasure was. Apart from him, not a single soul knew. Around here treasures have a spell on them, so that even if you happen on it, you don't see it—but he saw it. He'd go along a riverbank or through a wood, and there would be little fires, fires, fires under the bushes or rocks . . . Little fires, as if from sulfur. I saw them myself. Everybody waited for Zhmenya to point the places out to people, or dig them up himself, but he—a real dog in the manger—went and died: didn't dig it up himself, didn't show anybody else."

The overseer lit his pipe and for a moment revealed his big moustache and a sharp, stern, respectable-looking nose. Small circles of light jumped from his hands to his visored cap, flitted across the saddle over the horse's back, and disappeared in the mane by its ears.

"In these parts there are many treasures," he said.

And, slowly drawing on his pipe, he looked around, rested his gaze on the brightening east, and added:

"There must be treasures."

"What's there to talk about," sighed the old man. "By the looks of it there are, brother, only there's nobody to dig them up. Nobody knows the real places, and nowadays, most likely, all the treasures have a spell on them. To find them and see them, you've got to have a talisman, and without a talisman, my lad, you can't do anything. Zhmenya had talismans, but was there any wheedling them out of him? The bald devil held on to them so nobody could get them."

The young shepherd crept a couple of paces toward the old man, and, propping his head on his fists, fixed his unmoving gaze on him. A childlike expression of fear and curiosity lit up in his dark eyes and, as it seemed in the twilight, stretched and flattened the large features of his coarse young face. He listened intently.

"And in writings it's written that there are many treasures here," the old man went on. "What's there to talk about . . . there's nothing to say. An old soldier from Novopavlovsk was shown a tag in Ivanovka, and printed on this tag was the place, and even how many pounds of gold, and in what sort of vessel; this treasure could have been found long ago, only there's a spell on it so you can't get to it."

"Why can't you get to it, grandpa?" asked the young one.

"Must be there's some reason, the soldier didn't say. There's a spell . . . You need a talisman."

The old man spoke with enthusiasm, as if he were pouring out his soul before the passerby. Being unused to speaking much and quickly, he maundered, stammered, and, sensing the deficiency of his speech, tried to make up for it by gesticulating with his head, hands, and scrawny shoulders. With each movement, his sackcloth shirt crumpled, pulled up to the shoulders, and bared his back, blackened from sunburn and old age. He pulled it down, but it pulled up again at once. Finally, as if driven beyond all patience by the disobedient shirt, he jumped up and said bitterly:

"There is luck, but what's the use of it if it's buried in the ground? And so the good will perish for nothing, uselessly, like chaff or sheep dung! Yet there's a lot of luck out there, such a lot, boy, that it would be enough for the whole district, but not a soul sees it! If people go on waiting, the masters will dig it up or the government will take it. The masters have already started digging up the barrows[5] . . . They've sniffed it out! They envy the peasants' luck! The government also keeps its own counsel. In the law it's written that if a peasant finds a treasure, he must report it to the authorities. Well, they'll have a good wait! There's stew, but not for you."

The old man laughed contemptuously and sat down on the ground. The overseer listened with attention and nodded, but from the expression of his whole figure and from his silence it was obvious that nothing the old man was telling was new to him, that he had been thinking about it for a long time and knew much more than the old man did.

"In my lifetime, I must confess, I've sought out luck maybe a dozen times," the old man said, scratching himself bashfully. "I searched in the right places, but it must be I kept hitting on treasures with a spell on them. My father also searched, and my brother—didn't even find a blessed thing, so they just died luckless. A certain monk revealed to my brother Ilya, may he rest in peace, that in Taganrog, in the fortress, in a place under three stones, there is a treasure, and that the treasure has a spell on it, and back then—I remember, it was the year 'thirty-eight—there was an Armenian living in the Matveev Barrow who sold talismans. Ilya bought a talisman, took two lads with him, and went to Taganrog. Only he, my brother, comes to the place in the fortress, and in that same place stands a soldier with a gun."

A sound burst through the still air and scattered over the steppe. Something far away made a terrible bang, struck against the stone, and raced over the steppe, going "takh! takh! takh! takh!" When the sound died away, the old man looked questioningly at the indifferent, motionlessly standing Pantelei.

"That was a bucket falling down a mineshaft," said the young shepherd on reflection.

Dawn was breaking. The Milky Way was growing paler and gradually melted like snow, losing its contours. The sky was becoming somber and dull, so that it was impossible to tell whether it was clear or completely covered with clouds, and only by a clear, glossy strip in the east and the remaining stars here and there could you tell which it was.

The first morning breeze, without a murmur, went flitting down the road, cautiously stirring the spurge and the tall brown stems of last year's weeds.

The overseer awoke from his thoughts and shook his head. He tugged at the saddle with both hands, felt the girth, and, as if undecided about mounting the horse, again stood thinking.

"Yes," he said, "so near and yet so far . . . Luck is there, but there's no knowing how to find it."

And he turned his face to the shepherds. His stern face was sad and scornful, as in a disappointed man.

"Yes, so you die without seeing what this luck amounts to . . . ," he said slowly, raising his left foot to the stirrup. "Those who are younger might live to see it, but for us it's time we stopped thinking about it."

Stroking his long, dew-covered moustache, he seated himself heavily on the horse and, with a look as if he had forgotten something or not finished speaking, narrowed his eyes toward the distance. In the bluish distance, where the furthest visible hill merged with the mist, nothing stirred; the lookout and burial mounds that rose here and there on the horizon and the boundless steppe kept a severe and deathly watch; in their stillness and silence one sensed long ages and a total indifference to man; another thousand years will pass, billions of people will die, and they will stand there as they stand now, without the least regret for the dead or interest in the living, and not a single soul will know why they stand and what secret of the steppe is hidden beneath them.

Rooks awoke and flew silently and solitarily over the earth. Neither in the lazy flight of these long-lived birds, nor in the morning that was punctually repeated each day, nor in the boundlessness of the steppe—in none of it was any sense to be seen. The overseer grinned and said:

"Such vastness, Lord have mercy! Go find your luck! Here," he went on, lowering his voice and making a serious face, "here for sure two treasures are buried. The masters don't know about them, but the old peasants, especially the soldiers, have precise knowledge of them. Somewhere on that ridge" (the overseer pointed out the direction with his whip) "robbers once fell upon a caravan with gold; this gold was being transported from Petersburg to the emperor Peter, who was in Voronezh then building the fleet.[6] The robbers killed the drivers and buried the gold, and later couldn't find it. Our Don Cossacks buried the other treasure. In the year 'twelve they plundered no end of silver, and gold, and all sorts of goods from the French.[7] On their way home, they heard that the authorities wanted to take all the gold and silver from them. Rather than give it to the authorities for nothing, the fine lads went and buried it, so that their children at least would get it, but where they buried it—nobody knows."

"I've heard about those treasures," the old man muttered sullenly.

"Yes." Pantelei again fell to thinking. "So . . ."

Silence ensued. The overseer pensively looked into the distance, grinned, and touched the reins, still with that same expression as if he had forgotten something or not finished speaking. The horse set off reluctantly at a slow pace. Having gone about a hundred steps, Pantelei shook his head resolutely, awoke from his thoughts, and, whipping up his horse, went on at a canter.

The shepherds remained alone.

"That was Pantelei from the Makarov estate," the old man said. "Gets a hundred and fifty roubles a year, plus grub. An educated man . . ."

The sheep—there were some three thousand of them—woke up and reluctantly, having nothing else to do, began grazing on the low, half-trampled grass. The sun was not up yet, but the barrows were all visible already, as was Saur's Grave with its pointed peak,[8] far off, looking like a cloud. If you climb up that grave, from it you can see the plain, as flat and boundless as the sky, you can see manor houses, German and Molokan farmsteads, villages, and a keen-sighted Kalmuk[9] will even see the town and the railroad trains. Only from there can you see that in this world, besides the silent steppe and the age-old barrows, there is another life, which has nothing to do with buried treasure and sheep's thoughts.

The old man felt around him, found his "gerlyga," a long staff with a hook at the upper end, and stood up. He was silent and thoughtful. The childlike expression of fear and curiosity had not yet left the young man's face. He was under the impression of what he had heard and waited impatiently for new stories.

"Grandpa," he said, getting up and taking his gerlyga, "what did your brother Ilya do with that soldier?"

The old man did not hear the question. He glanced absently at the young man and replied, munching his lips:

"And you know, Sanka, I keep thinking about that tag they showed the soldier in Ivanovka. I didn't tell Pantelei, God help him, but there was a place indicated on that tag that even an old woman could find. Do you know what place? Rich Ravine, at that place, you know, where it splits like a goose foot into three gullies. It's in the middle one."

"So you're going to dig?"

"I'll try my luck . . ."

"And what will you do with the treasure, grandpa, once you find it?"

"Who, me?" The old man grinned. "Hm! . . . Just let me find it, and then . . . I'll give them all a hot time . . . Hm! . . . I know what to do . . ."

The old man was not able to say what he would do with the treasure if he found it. The question had probably presented itself to him that morning for the first time in his life, and judging by the expression of his face, carefree and indifferent, it did not seem important to him and worthy of reflection. In Sanka's head another perplexity was stirring: why did only old men look for treasure, and what was the use of such earthly luck to people who might die of old age any day? But Sanka was unable to turn this perplexity into a question, and it was unlikely the old man would have found an answer for him.

Surrounded by a light haze, the enormous crimson sun appeared. Wide strips of light, still cold, bathing in the dewy grass, stretching out and looking cheerful, as if trying to show that they were not sick of it, began to spread over the ground. Silvery wormwood, the light blue flowers of wild onion, yellow rapeseed, cornflowers—all this multicolored joyfulness took the sunlight for its own smile.

The old man and Sanka split up and went to stand at the edges of the flock. They both stood like posts, not moving, looking at the ground and thinking. The former was still gripped by thoughts of luck, while the latter was thinking about what had been talked about during the night; he was interested not in luck itself, which he did not need or understand, but in the fantastic and fairy-tale nature of human luck.

A hundred or so sheep gave a start and, in some incomprehensible terror, as if at a signal, rushed away from the flock. And Sanka, as if the sheep's thoughts, long and drawn-out, momentarily communicated themselves to him, also rushed away in the same incomprehensible animal terror, but at once came to his senses and shouted:

"Pah, you loonies! Gone hog wild, dad blast you!"

And when the sun, promising a long, invincible heat, began to scorch the earth, everything alive, that had moved and produced sounds during the night, sank into slumber. The old man and Sanka stood with their staffs at opposite ends of the herd, stood without moving, like fakirs at prayer, fixed on their thoughts. They no longer noticed each other, and each of them lived his own life. The sheep were also thinking . . .

1887

The Siren

After one of the sessions of the N. justice of the peace court, the justices gathered in the assembly room to take off their uniforms, have a moment's rest, and go home for dinner. The chairman of the session, a very imposing man with fluffy side-whiskers, who held "a particular opinion" on one of the cases just examined, was sitting at a desk and hurriedly writing out his opinion. A local justice of the peace, Milkin, a young man with a languid, melancholy face, reputed to be a philosopher, displeased with his milieu and seeking a purpose in life, stood by the window and looked sorrowfully outside. Another local justice and one of the honorary justices had already left. The remaining honorary justice, a flabby, heavily breathing fat man, and an associate prosecutor, a young German with a catarrhal face, were sitting on a little sofa, waiting for the chairman to finish writing so that they could go to dinner together. Before them stood the secretary of the session, Zhilin, a small man with little side-whiskers around his ears and an expression of sweetness on his face. With a honeyed smile, looking at the fat man, he was saying in a low voice:

"We all want to eat now, because we're tired and it's already past three o'clock, but this, my dear friend Grigory Savvich, is not a real appetite. A real, voracious appetite, when it seems you could eat your own father, comes only after physical exercise, for instance, hunting with hounds, or when you've whipped through some fifty miles non-stop on hired horses. Imagination also means a lot, sir. If, say, you're coming home from a hunt and you wish to dine with a good appetite, never think about clever things; clever and learned things rob you of your appetite. As you're pleased to know, philosophers and scholars are the last people when it comes to eating, and, forgive me, even worse eaters than pigs. Going home, you should try to have your head think only of a little decanter and a nibble. Once on my way home I closed my eyes and pictured to myself a suckling pig with horseradish, and felt such a craving that it gave me hysterics. Well, sir, and when you drive into your courtyard, there should be such a smell coming from the kitchen just then, you know . . ."

"Roast goose has an exquisite smell," said the honorary justice, breathing heavily.

"Don't talk, my dear Grigory Savvich: duck or snipe can give a ten-point handicap to a goose. In the goose bouquet there's no tenderness and delicacy. The headiest of all is the smell of young onion when it starts to brown and hisses, the scoundrel, for the whole house to hear. And so, sir, when you enter the house, the table should be laid, and when you sit down, tuck the napkin behind your tie at once and reach out unhurriedly for the little decanter of vodka. And you should pour the dearie not into a glass, but into some prediluvian grandfather's silver tumbler or one of those fat-bellied ones with the inscription 'even monks partake of it,' and you shouldn't drink it at once, but first take a deep breath, rub your hands, cast an indifferent glance at the ceiling, then unhurriedly bring it, I mean the vodka, to your lips and—instantly sparks fly from your stomach all over your body . . ."

The secretary's sweet face was a picture of bliss.

"Sparks . . . ," he repeated, screwing up his eyes. "The moment you drink, you have to nibble something."

"Listen," said the chairman, raising his eyes to the secretary, "speak more softly! I've already ruined this page twice on account of you."

"Ah, I'm sorry, Pyotr Nikolaich! I'll talk softly," said the secretary, and he went on in a half-whisper: "Well, sir, for nibbling, my dear Grigory Savvich, you also have to have a knack. You must know what to nibble. The best nibble, if you wish to know, is pickled herring. Once you've eaten a piece, with onion and in mustard sauce, then right away, my benefactor, while there are still sparks in your stomach, eat some caviar by itself or, if you wish, with a bit of lemon, then some plain black radish with salt, then again some pickled herring, but best of all, my benefactor, are pickled mushrooms, chopped finely like caviar, with onion and olive oil . . . delicious! But burbot liver— that is a tragedy!"

"Hm—yes . . ." the honorary justice of the peace agreed, screwing up his eyes. "For a nibble, another good thing is . . . sautéed wild mushrooms."

"Yes, yes, yes . . . with onion, you know, with bay leaf and various spices. You open the pot, and there's steam, mushroom breath . . . sometimes tears even come to your eyes! Well, sir, and as soon as they fetch the kulebiak[1] from the kitchen, right then, immediately, you should have a second shot."

"Ivan Guryich!" the chairman said in a tearful voice. "I've ruined the page a third time on account of you!"

"Devil take him, he only thinks about food!" the philosopher Milkin growled, making a contemptuous face. "Are there no other interests in life besides mushrooms and kulebiak?"

"Well, sirs, so drink before the kulebiak," the secretary went on in a low voice; he was so carried away by now that, like a singing nightingale, he heard nothing but his own voice. "The kulebiak should be appetizing, shameless, in all its nakedness, so that there's real temptation. You wink at it, you cut a slice this big and move your fingers over it like this, from an abundance of feelings. You start eating it, and there's butter on it like tears, the stuffing's greasy, juicy, with eggs, giblets, onion . . ."

The secretary rolled his eyes and stretched his mouth to his ears. The honorary justice of the peace grunted and moved his fingers, probably imagining the kulebiak.

"Devil knows what this is . . . ," grumbled the local justice, retiring to another window.

"You eat two pieces and save a third for the cabbage soup," the inspired secretary went on. "As soon as you finish the kulebiak, right then, so as not to lose your appetite, you have the cabbage soup served . . . The cabbage soup should be hot, fiery. But best of all, my benefactor, is a nice beet borscht in Ukrainian style, with ham and sausage. You add sour cream, fresh parsley, and dill. Another splendid thing is pickled cabbage soup with giblets and young kidney, and if you like soup very much, the best is with various roots and greens: carrots, asparagus, cauliflower, and suchlike jurisprudence."

"Yes, a splendid thing . . . ," the chairman sighed, tearing his eyes from the paper, but he immediately caught himself and groaned: "Have some fear of God! This way I won't finish my notes before nightfall! I've ruined it for the fourth time!"

"I'll stop, I'll stop! Sorry, sir!" the secretary apologized and went on in a whisper. "As soon as you finish the borscht or other soup, order the fish course at once. Of all voiceless fish, the best is a fried carp in sour cream; only so that it loses the smell of slime and acquires delicacy, you must keep it alive in milk for twenty-four hours."

"Equally good is a sterlet in a ring," said the honorary justice, closing his eyes, but at once, unexpectedly for everyone, he tore from his seat, made a ferocious face, and roared in the direction of the chairman: "Pyotr Nikolaich, will you be done soon? I can't wait any longer! I can't!"

"Let me finish!"

"Then I'll go by myself! To hell with you!"

The fat man waved his hand, grabbed his hat, and ran out of the room without saying goodbye. The secretary sighed and, leaning toward the ear of the associate prosecutor, went on in a low voice:

"Pike perch or carp is also good with a sauce of tomatoes and mushrooms. But fish, Stepan Frantsych, is not filling; it's not substantial food, the main thing in a dinner is not fish, not sauces, but a roast. What's your favorite fowl?"

The associate prosecutor made a sour face and said with a sigh:

"Unfortunately, I cannot sympathize with you: I have a stomach catarrh."

"Come now, sir! Stomach catarrh is a doctor's invention! Free-thinking and pride are more to blame for this illness! Don't pay it any attention. Let's say you don't want to eat or feel nauseous, but you pay no attention and eat. If, let's say, they serve you a pair of roast snipe, and if they add to that a partridge or a pair of fat quail, you'll forget about any catarrh, on my word of honor. And a roast turkey? So white, fat, juicy, you know, just like a nymph . . ."

"Yes, it's probably tasty," the prosecutor said with a sad smile. "I could most likely eat some turkey."

"Lord, and duck? If you take a young duck, that's only just felt the first frost, and you put it in a frying pan along with some potatoes, and the potatoes should be cut in small pieces, so they turn golden brown and get steeped in duck fat, and so that . . ."

The philosopher Milkin made a ferocious face and apparently wanted to say something, but suddenly smacked his lips, probably imagining the fried duck, and without saying a word, drawn by an unknown force, grabbed his hat and ran out.

"Yes, most likely I could also eat some duck . . . ," the associate prosecutor sighed.

The chairman stood up, paced back and forth, and sat down again.

"After the roast, you become sated and fall into a sweet oblivion," the secretary went on. "At this point your body feels good and your soul is tender. For the pleasure of it you could drink some three little glasses of honey-spice vodka."

The chairman grunted as he crossed out yet another page.

"I've ruined it for the sixth time," he said angrily. "This is shameless!"

"Write, write, my benefactor!" the secretary whispered. "I'll stop! I'll speak softly. I'm telling you in all honesty, Stepan Frantsych," he went on in a barely audible whisper, "homemade honey-spice vodka is better than any champagne. After the first glass, your whole soul is engulfed in a sort of fragrant mirage, and it seems that you're not at home in your armchair, but somewhere in Australia, on some sort of ultrasoft ostrich . . ."

"Ah, let's go, Pyotr Nikolaich!" the prosecutor said, jerking his leg impatiently.

"Yes, sir!" the secretary went on. "During the honey-spice vodka it's good to light up a cigar and blow smoke rings, and it's then that such dreamy thoughts come to your head, as if you're a field marshal, or married to the foremost beauty in the world, and this beauty swims all day in front of your windows in a pool full of goldfish. She swims, and you say to her: 'Come kiss me, sweetie!' "

"Pyotr Nikolaich!" the assistant prosecutor moaned.

"Yes, sir!" the secretary went on. "After smoking, you pick up the skirts of your dressing gown, and it's off to bed! You lie down on your back, belly up, and take a newspaper in your hands. When your eyes start closing and your whole body is filled with drowsiness, it's a pleasure to read about politics: here Austria made a slip-up, there France failed to hit it off with somebody, here the pope of Rome was at cross-purposes—you read, and it's a pleasure."

The chairman jumped up, flung his pen away, and grabbed his hat with both hands. The assistant prosecutor, who forgot about his catarrh and was swooning with impatience, also jumped up.

"Let's go!" he cried.

"Pyotr Nikolaich, my benefactor, what about the particular opinion?" The secretary was alarmed. "When will you write it? You have to go to town at six o'clock!"

The chairman waved his hand and rushed to the door. The assistant prosecutor also waved his hand and, grabbing his briefcase, disappeared along with the chairman. The secretary sighed, followed them with a reproachful gaze, and began to gather up the papers.

1887

THE SHEPHERD'S PIPE

S LUGGISH FROM THE SULTRINESS of the dense firs, covered
with cobwebs and pine needles, the steward of the Demen-
tyevs' farmstead, Meliton Shishkin, carrying his gun, was making his way to the edge of the forest. His Damka—a cross between
a mutt and a setter—extraordinarily skinny and pregnant, her wet
tail between her legs, trudged after her master, trying her best not
to prick her nose. The morning was unpleasant, overcast. From the
trees, enveloped in light mist, and from the ferns heavy spatters fell,
and the forest dampness gave off a pungent smell of rot.

Ahead, where the forest ended, stood birches, and through their
trunks and branches the misty distance could be seen. Beyond the
birches someone was playing a homemade shepherd's pipe. The
player hit no more than five or six notes, lazily drawing them out, not
trying to connect them into a tune, but nonetheless something stern
and extremely mournful could be heard in his piping.

When the forest thinned out and the firs mixed with young birches,
Meliton saw the herd. Hobbled horses, cows, and sheep wandered
among the bushes, making the twigs crackle, and sniffing at the forest grass. At the edge of the forest, leaning against a wet birch, stood
an old shepherd, skinny, in tattered homespun and without a hat. He
looked at the ground, thought about something, and played his pipe
as if mechanically.

"Good day, grandpa! God be with you!" Meliton greeted him in a high, husky little voice, which was not at all suited to his enormous height and big, fleshy face. "And you play the pipe so nicely! Whose herd are you tending?"

"The Artamonovs'," the shepherd replied reluctantly and put the pipe into his bosom.

"So the forest is also the Artamonovs'?" Meliton asked, looking around. "And in fact it is, mercy me . . . I was completely lost. My mug's all scratched up from the brush."

He sat down on the wet ground and began to roll a cigarette from a scrap of newspaper.

Like his feeble little voice, everything about this man was small and out of proportion with his height, breadth, and fleshy face: his smile, his eyes, his buttons, his little visored cap, which barely clung to his fat, close-cropped head. When he spoke and smiled, his plump, clean-shaven face and his whole figure had the feeling of something womanish, timid, and humble.

"What weather, God help us!" he said and shook his head. "The oats haven't been harvested yet, and the rain's like it's been hired full time, God help it."

The shepherd glanced at the sky, where the drizzle was coming from, at the forest, at the steward's wet clothes, thought a moment, and said nothing.

"It's been like this all summer . . ." Meliton sighed. "Bad for the peasants and no pleasure for the masters."

The shepherd glanced once more at the sky, thought a moment, and said measuredly, as if chewing over each word:

"It's all headed the same way . . . Don't expect anything good."

"How is it with you here?" Meliton asked, lighting up his cigarette. "Have you seen any coveys of black grouse in the Artamonovs' clearing?"

The shepherd did not reply at once. He glanced again at the sky and to both sides, thought a moment, blinked his eyes . . . Apparently he attached no little significance to his words, and in order to increase their value, he tried to utter them in a drawn-out way, with a certain solemnity. The expression of his old face was keen, grave, and his nose, crossed by a saddle-shaped groove and with upturned nostrils, gave it a sly and mocking look.

"No, seems I haven't," he replied. "Our hunter, Eremka, did say he scared off a covey by Empty Lot on St. Elijah's day,[1] but it must be he's lying. There's few birds."

"Yes, brother, few . . . Few everywhere! Hunting, if we reason soberly, is insignificant and unprofitable. There's almost no game, and whatever there is right now isn't worth dirtying your hands for—it hasn't grown yet. So small it's shameful to look at!"

Meliton grinned and waved his hand.

"Such things go on in this world, it's simply laughable, that's all. Birds nowadays have become so inconsistent, they lay eggs late, and there's some that are still sitting them on St. Peter's day.[2] By God!"

"It's all headed the same way," said the shepherd, raising his face. "Last year there was little game, this year there's still less, and in five years, most like, there won't be any. As I see it, soon there'll be, not just no game birds, but no birds left at all."

"Yes," Meliton agreed after some thought. "True enough."

The shepherd smiled bitterly and shook his head.

"Astonishing!" he said. "Where has it all gone to? Some twenty years ago, I remember, there were geese, and cranes, and ducks, and black grouse—huge flocks! When the masters got together for the hunt, all you heard was poom-poom-poom! poom-poom-poom! Great snipe, common snipe, jack snipe all over, and little teal and sandpipers, the same as starlings, say, or sparrows—no end of them! And where has it all gone? Even the birds of prey are nowhere to be seen. Eagles, and falcons, and owls—all gone for naught . . . And there are fewer beasts. Nowadays, brother, wolves and foxes are rare, to say nothing of bears or minks. We even used to have elk! For forty years, year after year, I've been keeping an eye on God's works, and my understanding is it's all headed the same way."

"Which way?"

"The bad way, man. To ruin, I can only think . . . It's come time for God's world to perish."

The old man put his cap on and started looking at the sky.

"It's a pity!" he sighed after some silence. "God, such a pity! Of course, it's God's will, we didn't make the world, but all the same, dear brother, it's a pity. If one tree withers, or, say, one cow dies, you pity them, but how is it, my good man, to look on while the whole world goes to naught? So much that's good, Lord Jesus! The sun, and the sky, and the forests, and the rivers, and the creatures—it's all been created, arranged, fitted together. Each thing is suited to its task and knows its place. And it all has to perish!"

The shepherd's face broke into a sad smile, and his eyelids blinked.

"You say the world is perishing," Meliton said, pondering. "The end may even come soon, only you can't judge by the birds. It's unlikely that birds can signify anything."

"It's not just the birds," said the shepherd. "It's also the beasts, and the cattle, and the bees, and the fish . . . If you don't believe me, ask the old folk; they'll all tell you that the fish aren't the same now as they used to be. In the seas, and in the lakes, and in the rivers there are fewer and fewer fish every year. I remember in our Peschanka there were three-foot pike to be caught, and burbot to be taken, and ide, and bream, and each fish was a fair sight. But now, thank God if you catch a little pike or perch a foot long. There aren't even any real perch. It gets worse and worse every year, and if you wait a little, there won't be any fish at all. And take today's rivers . . . The rivers are drying up for sure!"

"True enough, they're drying up."

"So there it is. Every year they get shallower and shallower, and, dear brother, there are no more of those deep pools there used to be. See those bushes over there?" the old man asked, pointing to one side. "Beyond them there's an old riverbed, known as the backwater; in my father's day the Peschanka flowed there, but today look where the devil's sent it! It keeps changing its bed, and, you'll see, it'll go on doing it till it dries up completely. Beyond Kurgasavo there were swamps and ponds, and now where are they? Where have the brooks gone to? Here in our forest a brook used to run, and in that brook peasants set nets and caught pike, wild duck wintered by it, and now, even in flood time, there's no real water. Yes, brother, no matter where you look, it's bad everywhere. Everywhere!"

Silence ensued. Meliton fell to thinking and fixed his eyes on one spot. He wanted to recall at least one place in nature that had not yet been touched by all-encompassing doom. Bright patches began to glide over the mist and the slanting streaks of rain, as if over frosted glass, and immediately faded away—it was the rising sun trying to break through the clouds and look down at the earth.

"And the forests as well . . . ," Meliton murmured.

"The forests as well . . . ," the shepherd repeated. "They get cut down, they burn, they dry up, and new ones don't grow. What does grow gets cut down at once; today it's there, and tomorrow, you'll see, people cut it down—and it goes on endlessly, till there's nothing left. I, my good man, have been tending the communal flock since the freedom,[3] and before that I was a shepherd for my masters, tended in this same place, and in all my life I don't remember a summer day when I wasn't here. And all this while I've been observing God's works. I've kept an eye out in my time, brother, and so now I understand that all plants are in decline. Take rye, or some vegetable, or some flower, it's all headed the same way."

"But people have become better," the manager observed.

"Better how?"

"Smarter."

"Smarter, maybe so, man, but what's the good of it? What use is intelligence to people who are doomed? You can perish without any intelligence. What's intelligence to a hunter if there's no game? The way I reason, God gave man intelligence, but took away his strength. Folk have become weak, extremely weak. Take me, for instance . . . I'm barely worth a penny, I'm the lowest peasant in the whole village, but even so, man, I've got strength. Look, I'm past sixty, and I tend all day long, and I also look after horses during the night for twenty kopecks, and I don't sleep and I don't get cold. My son's smarter than me, but put him in my place and tomorrow he'll ask for a raise or go to the doctor. So there. I eat nothing but bread, because give us this day our daily bread, and my father ate nothing but bread, and the same with my grandfather, but today's peasant wants tea, and vodka, and white rolls, and to sleep all night, and to go to the doctor, and all sorts of indulgence. And why? He's grown weak, he's got no strength to bear up. He'd be glad not to sleep, but his eyes stick shut—nothing to be done."

"True enough," Meliton agreed. "Today's peasant is worthless."

"Let's say it straight out, it's getting worse year by year. If we consider masters now, they've weakened worse than the peasants. The masters nowadays are ahead in everything, they know things that shouldn't even be known, but what's the good of it? You look at him and feel such pity . . . Skinny, puny, like some Hungarian or Frenchman, no importance in him, no look—a master in name only. The poor dear has no position, no work, and there's no telling what he wants. Either it's sitting with a rod fishing, or lying belly-up reading a book, or hanging around with peasants and saying all sorts of things, and then going hungry and getting hired as a clerk. So he lives a piddling life, and it doesn't occur to him to set himself up in some real work. In the old days the masters were half of them generals, but nowadays—sheer trash!"

"They've grown really poor," said Meliton.

"They've grown poor because God took their strength away. You can't go against God."

Meliton again fixed his eyes on one spot. Having thought a little, he sighed, the way staid, reasonable people sigh, shook his head, and said:

"And why so? We've sinned a lot, we've forgotten God . . . and it means the time has come for everything to end. That is to say, the world can't last forever—enough's enough."

The shepherd sighed and, as if wishing to break off the unpleasant conversation, stepped away from the birch and began to count the cows with his eyes.

"Hyah-yah-yah!" he shouted. "Hyah-yah-yah! Ah, there's no keeping you back! The fiend's driven you into the gorse! Hoo-loo-loo!"

He made an angry face and went into the bushes to gather the herd. Meliton got up and walked slowly along the edge of the forest. He looked under his feet and thought; he still wanted to recall at least something that had not been touched by death. Bright patches again glided along the slanted streaks of rain; they leaped up to the treetops and faded among the wet leaves. Damka found a hedgehog under a bush and, wishing to draw her master's attention, raised a whiny barking.

"Did you have the eclipse or not?" the shepherd cried from the bushes.

"We did!" replied Meliton.

"So. Folk everywhere are complaining that it happened. Meaning, dear brother, that there's disorder in the heavens, too! It's not for nothing . . . Hyah-yah-yah! Hyah!"

Having driven the herd to the edge of the forest, the shepherd leaned on the birch tree, looked at the sky, unhurriedly took the pipe from his bosom, and began to play. He played mechanically, as before, no more than five or six notes; as if he were holding the pipe for the first time, the sounds flew out of it irresolutely, in disorder, not merging into a melody, but Meliton, thinking about the world perishing, heard something very anguished and repugnant in his playing, which he would prefer not to listen to. The highest squeaky notes trembled and broke off and seemed to weep inconsolably, as if the pipe were sick and frightened, and the lowest notes for some reason were reminiscent of the mist, the dreary trees, the gray sky. Such music seemed suited to the weather, and the old man, and his talk.

Meliton felt like complaining. He went up to the old man and, looking at his sad, mocking face, and at his pipe, began to mutter:

"Life's grown worse, too, grandpa. It's totally unbearable to live. Bad harvests, poverty . . . cattle plague time and again, diseases . . . Overwhelmed by need."

The manager's plump face turned purple and acquired an anguished, womanish expression. He moved his fingers, as if searching for words to convey his indefinite feeling, and went on:

"Eight children, a wife . . . a mother still living, and a salary of a mere ten roubles a month without grub. My wife's gone frenzied from poverty . . . and me, I drink. I'm a sensible, staid man, I've got education. I'd like to sit at home, in peace and quiet, but I'm out all day like a dog, with my rifle, because I just can't do it: I hate my home!"

Sensing that what his tongue was muttering was not at all what he meant to express, the manager waved his hand and said bitterly:

"If the world is to perish, then let it be soon! There's no use dragging it out and making people suffer uselessly . . ."

The old man took the pipe from his lips and, narrowing one eye, looked into its small mouth hole. His face was sad and covered with big drops like tears. He smiled and said:

"It's a pity, dear brother! God, such a pity! The earth, the forest, the sky . . . every creature—all of it was created, arranged, there's reasonableness in it all. It will all perish for nothing. And it's a pity about people most of all."

From a distance, moving towards the edge of the forest, came the sound of heavy rain. Meliton glanced in the direction of the sound, buttoned up his coat, and said:

"I'll head for the village. Goodbye, grandpa. What's your name?"

"Luka the Poor."

"Well, goodbye, Luka! Thanks for your kind words. Damka, *ici*!"

Having taken leave of the shepherd, Meliton trudged along the edge of the forest, then down across the meadow, which gradually turned into a swamp. Water squelched under his feet, and rusty sedge, still green and lush, bent towards the ground, as if in fear of being trampled underfoot. Beyond the swamp, on the bank of the Peschanka, of which the old man had spoken, stood willows, and beyond the willows a threshing barn showed blue in the mist. One could sense the nearness of that miserable, in no way avertable time when the fields become dark, the earth dirty and cold, when the weeping willow looks still more sorrowful and tears flow down its trunk, and only cranes escape the general disaster, and even they, as if fearing to offend dreary nature by expressing their happiness, fill the sky with their sad, melancholy song.

Meliton trudged towards the river and listened to the sounds of the pipe gradually dying away behind him. He still felt like complaining. He glanced sorrowfully around and felt an unbearable pity for the sky, and the earth, and the sun, and the forest, and his Damka, and when the highest drawn-out note of the pipe swept through the air and trembled like the voice of a weeping man, he felt extremely bitter and upset at the disorder he observed in nature.

The high note trembled, broke off, and the pipe fell silent.

1887

COSTLY LESSONS

FOR AN EDUCATED MAN an ignorance of foreign languages amounts to a great inconvenience. Vorotov felt it strongly when, having graduated from the university with an advanced degree, he began a small scholarly work.

"It's terrible!" he said breathlessly (despite his twenty-six years, he was plump, heavy, and suffered from shortness of breath). "It's terrible! Without languages I'm like a bird without wings. I might just as well drop my work."

And he decided at all costs to overcome his innate laziness and learn French and German, and he started looking for tutors.

One winter noon, when Vorotov was sitting in his study working, his valet told him that a young lady was asking to see him.

"Show her in," said Vorotov.

A young woman, elegantly dressed in the latest fashion, came into the study. She introduced herself as Alisa Osipovna Enquête, a teacher of French,[1] and said that she had been sent to Vorotov by one of his friends.

"Very nice! Sit down!" Vorotov said breathlessly, concealing the collar of his nightshirt with his hand. (To breathe more easily, he always worked in his nightshirt.) "Pyotr Sergeich sent you to me? Yes, yes . . . I asked him . . . Very glad!"

While making arrangements with Mlle Enquête, he kept glancing at her shyly and with curiosity. She was a real Frenchwoman, very graceful and still very young. From her pale and languid face, her short, curly hair, and unnaturally slim waist, he could give her no more than eighteen years; but looking at her broad, well-developed shoulders, her beautiful back and stern eyes, Vorotov thought she was certainly no less than twenty-three, maybe even all of twenty-five; but then again it seemed to him that she was only eighteen. Her expression was cold, businesslike, as in someone who has come to discuss money. She never once smiled or frowned, and only once did perplexity flicker on her face, when she learned that she was being invited not to teach children, but a grown-up, fat man.

"So, Alisa Osipovna," Vorotov said to her, "we'll study every day from seven to eight in the evening. As concerns your wish to receive one rouble per lesson, I have no objection. If it's a rouble, it's a rouble . . ."

He also asked her if she wanted tea or coffee, if it was nice out, and with a good-natured smile, stroking the felt desktop with his palm, he affably inquired who she was, where she had studied, and how she earned her living.

Alisa Osipovna, with a cold, businesslike expression, replied that she had finished her studies in a private boarding school and had a license as a tutor, that her father had died recently of scarlet fever, that her mother was alive and made silk flowers, that she, Mlle Enquête, was employed in a private boarding school until lunchtime, and after lunch, until evening, went around to respectable homes and gave lessons.

She left, and behind her lingered the light, very delicate fragrance of a woman's dress. Vorotov spent a long time afterwards not working, but sitting at his desk, stroking the green felt with his palms, and reflecting.

"It's very pleasant to see girls who earn their crust of bread," he thought. "On the other hand, it's very unpleasant to see that need doesn't spare even such elegant and pretty girls as this Alisa Osipovna, and that she, too, has to struggle for existence. Too bad! . . ."

He, who had never seen a virtuous Frenchwoman, also thought that this elegantly dressed Alisa Osipovna, with her well-developed shoulders and exaggeratedly slender waist, in all probability did something else besides teach.

The next evening, when the clock showed five minutes to seven, Alisa Osipovna came in, rosy from the cold; she opened Margot,[2] which she had brought with her, and began without any preliminaries:

"In French grammar is twenty-six letters. First letter is called A, second B . . ."

"Excuse me," Vorotov interrupted her, smiling. "I must warn you, mademoiselle, that you will have to change your method slightly to teach me. The thing is that I know Russian, Latin, and Greek very well . . . I studied comparative linguistics, and it seems to me that we can skip Margot and go directly to reading some author."

And he explained to the Frenchwoman how grown-up people study languages.

"An acquaintance of mine," he said, "wishing to learn new languages, placed French, German, and Latin gospels before him and read them in parallel, analyzing each word meticulously—and what then? He achieved his goal in less than a year. Let's do the same. We'll take some author and read him."

The Frenchwoman looked at him in perplexity. Apparently Vorotov's suggestion seemed quite naïve and absurd to her. If this strange suggestion had been made by an underage person, she would probably have gotten angry and scolded him, but since this was a grown-up and extremely fat man, whom she could not scold, she merely gave a barely noticeable shrug and said:

"As you wish."

Vorotov rummaged in his bookcase and took from it a tattered French book.

"Will this do?" he asked.

"It makes no difference."

"In that case let's begin. Lord bless us. We'll begin with the title . . . *Mémoires.*"

"Reminiscences . . . ," Mlle Enquête translated.

"Reminiscences . . . ," Vorotov repeated.

Smiling good-naturedly and breathing heavily, he spent a quarter of an hour on the word *mémoires*, and as long again on the word *de*, and this wore Alisa Osipovna out. She answered his questions list-lessly, became confused, and apparently had a poor understanding of her pupil and did not try to understand him. Vorotov asked her questions, and meanwhile kept looking at her blond head and thinking:

"Her hair isn't naturally curly, she curls it. Amazing! She works from morning to night, and still has time to curl her hair."

At exactly eight o'clock she stood up and, saying a dry, cold "*Au revoir, monsieur*," left the study; after her lingered that same delicate, subtle, tantalizing fragrance. Again for a long time the pupil did nothing, sat at the desk, and thought.

In the following days he became convinced that his tutor was a nice, serious, and punctual young lady, but that she was very ignorant and did not know how to teach adults; and he decided not to waste his time, to let her go and invite another tutor. When she came for the seventh time, he took an envelope with seven roubles from his pocket and, holding it in his hands, became very abashed and began thus:

"Forgive me, Alisa Osipovna, but I must tell you . . . by force of necessity . . ."

Seeing the envelope, the Frenchwoman realized what it was about, and for the first time since they began their lessons, her face quivered, and the cold, businesslike expression vanished. She blushed slightly and, lowering her eyes, nervously began to finger her fine gold chain. And Vorotov, looking at her embarrassment, realized how much a rouble meant to her and how hard it would be for her to lose this income.

"I must tell you . . . ," he murmured, still more embarrassed, and in his breast something skipped a beat; he hastily shoved the envelope into his pocket and went on. "Forgive me, I . . . I'll leave you for ten minutes . . ."

Pretending that he did not intend to dismiss her, but was only asking her permission to leave her for a short time, he went to another room and sat out the ten minutes. Then he returned more embarrassed still; he realized that she might have interpreted his brief absence in her own way, and he felt awkward.

The lessons began again.

Vorotov studied now without any enthusiasm. Knowing that the sessions were of no use, he gave free rein to the Frenchwoman, no longer asked her anything, and did not interrupt. She translated as she liked, up to ten pages per lesson, and he did not listen, breathed heavily, and, having nothing to do, studied her curly head, or her neck, or her soft white hands, inhaled the fragrance of her dress . . .

He caught himself having improper thoughts, was ashamed, or else he waxed tender-hearted, and was then upset and annoyed that she was so cold and businesslike with him, as with a pupil, never smiling and as if afraid he might accidentally touch her. He kept wondering how he could inspire her trust, become closer friends with her, and then help her, give her to understand how badly she teaches, poor thing.

Once Alisa Osipovna appeared at a lesson in a fancy pink dress with a slight décolleté, and she gave off such a fragrance that it seemed she was wrapped in a cloud, that if you blew on her, she would fly off into the air or scatter like smoke. She apologized and said she could teach for only half an hour, because after the lesson she would be going straight to a ball.

He looked at her neck and at her back, bare behind her neck, and understood, as it seemed to him, why Frenchwomen enjoyed a reputation as frivolous and easily yielding creatures; he was drowning in this cloud of fragrance, beauty, nakedness, while she, unaware of his thoughts and most likely not interested in them in the least, quickly turned the pages and translated at full steam:

"He was walking on the street and was meeting his mister acquaintance, and said: 'Where are you precipitating to, seeing your face so pale, it does me hurt.'"

The *Mémoires* had long been finished, and now Alisa was translating some other book. Once she came to the lesson an hour early, excusing herself with having to go to the Maly Theater[3] at seven. Having seen her out after the lesson, Vorotov dressed and also went to the theater. He went, as it seemed to him, only in order to relax, to amuse himself, and he did not even think about Alisa. He could not allow that a serious man, preparing for a scholarly career, so hard to budge, dropped everything and went to the theater only so as to meet there an unintelligent, poorly educated girl whom he barely knew . . .

But for some reason during the intermissions his heart pounded, and, not noticing it himself, he ran around the foyer and the corridors like a boy, impatiently searching for someone; and he felt disheartened when the intermission drew to an end; but when he saw the familiar pink dress and the beautiful shoulders under the tulle, his heart was wrung, as if in anticipation of happiness, he smiled joyfully, and for the first time in his life experienced the feeling of jealousy.

Alisa was walking with a pair of unattractive students and an officer. She laughed and talked loudly, was clearly flirting; Vorotov had never seen her like that. She was obviously happy, content, sincere, warm. How so? Why? Perhaps because these people were close to her, from the same circle as she was ... And Vorotov sensed a dreadful abyss between himself and that circle. He bowed to his tutor, but she coldly nodded to him and quickly went by; evidently she did not want her cavaliers to know that she had pupils and that she gave lessons out of poverty.

After the meeting in the theater, Vorotov realized that he was in love ... In the subsequent lessons, devouring his elegant teacher with his eyes, he no longer fought with himself, but gave free rein to his pure and impure thoughts. The face of Alisa Osipovna never ceased to be cold, at exactly eight o'clock each night she calmly said "*Au revoir, monsieur,*" and he felt that she was indifferent to him, and would remain indifferent, and that his position was hopeless.

Occasionally during a lesson he began to dream, to hope, to make plans, mentally composed a declaration of love, recalled that Frenchwomen were light-minded and yielding, but it needed only a look at his tutor's face for his thoughts to be instantly extinguished, as a candle is extinguished when you take it out to the terrace of your dacha on a windy night. Once, inebriated, forgetting himself, as if in delirium, he lost control and, barring her way as she was leaving the study and going to the front hall after the lesson, suffocating and stammering, he began to declare his love:

"You're dear to me! I ... love you! Allow me to speak!"

Alisa turned pale—probably out of fear, figuring that after this declaration she would no longer be able to come here and get a rouble per lesson; she made frightened eyes and whispered loudly:

"Ah, you mustn't do this! Don't speak, I beg you! You mustn't!"

After that Vorotov did not sleep all night, suffered from shame, scolded himself, thought hard. It seemed to him that he had offended the girl by his declaration, that she would never come to him again.

He decided to find out her address at the information bureau the next morning and write her a letter of apology. But Alisa came without a letter. At first she felt awkward, but then she opened the book and began to translate as quickly and glibly as ever:

"Oh, young sir, do not rip these flowers from my garden, which I wish to be giving to my sick daughter . . ."

She comes to this day. Four books have been translated, and Vorotov knows nothing except the word "*mémoires*," and when people ask him about his scholarly work, he waves his hand and, not answering the question, begins to talk about the weather.

1887

THE KISS

O N THE TWENTIETH OF MAY, at eight o'clock in the evening, all six batteries of the N—— reserve artillery brigade, on their way to camp, halted overnight in the village of Mestechki. At the very height of the turmoil, when some officers were busy with the cannon, while others, gathered on the square by the church wall, were listening to the quartermasters, a rider appeared from behind the church, in civilian dress and on a strange horse. The horse, dun-colored and small, with a beautiful neck and a short tail, did not walk straight but somehow sideways, and performed little prancing movements, as if it were being whipped on the legs. Going up to the officers, the rider raised his hat and said:

"His Excellency Lieutenant General von Rabbek, a local landowner, invites the gentlemen officers to call on him presently for tea..."

The horse bowed, pranced, and backed up sideways; the rider raised his hat again and instantly, together with his strange horse, disappeared behind the church.

"What the devil is this?" some officers grumbled, dispersing to their quarters. "You want to sleep, and here's this von Rabbek with his tea! We know what this tea means!"

The officers of all six batteries vividly recalled last year's incident, when, during maneuvers, and with the officers of a Cossack regiment, they were invited to tea in the same way by a landowner-count, a retired soldier; the hospitable and cordial count welcomed them, wined and dined them, and would not let them go to their quarters in the village, but made them stay overnight with him. This was all very good, of course, nothing better was needed, but the trouble was that the retired soldier was all too happy to be with young men. He went on until dawn telling the officers episodes from his good past life, took them around the house, showed them expensive paintings, old prints, rare weapons, read them original letters from high-placed persons, while the worn-out, weary officers listened, looked, and, longing for their beds, cautiously yawned into their sleeves. When the host finally let them go, it was already too late to sleep.

Was this von Rabbek not the same sort? But whether he was or not, there was nothing to be done. The officers dressed up, brushed themselves off, and the throng of them went in search of the landowner's house. On the square by the church they were told that they could get to the gentleman by the lower way—going down behind the church to the river and walking along the bank to the garden, and from there along the paths to the house; or by the upper way—straight from the church along the road that leads to the barns of the estate a half mile from the village. The officers decided to take the upper way.

"Which von Rabbek is this?" they discussed on the way. "The one who commanded the N—— cavalry division at Plevna?"[1]

"No, that one wasn't von Rabbek, he was just Rabbe, and without the von."

"What fine weather!"

By the first barn the road divided in two: one branch went straight and disappeared into the evening murk; the other led to the right, to the manor house. The officers turned right and began to speak softly . . . On both sides of the road stretched stone barns with red roofs, heavy and stern, very much like the barracks of the provincial capital. Ahead shone the windows of the manor house.

"A good omen, gentlemen," said one of the officers. "Our setter has gone ahead of us all; it means he senses there'll be quarry! . . ."

Ahead of them all walked Lieutenant Lobytko, tall and thickset but quite moustacheless (he was over twenty-five, but for some reason no growth appeared on his round, well-fed face), famous in the brigade for his intuition and proficiency in divining the presence of women from a distance. He turned around and said:

"Yes, there should be women here. I sense it instinctively."

On the doorstep of the house the officers were met by von Rabbek himself, a fine-looking old man of about sixty, in civilian dress. Shaking his guests' hands, he said he was very glad and delighted, but earnestly, for God's sake, asked the gentlemen officers to forgive him for not inviting them to stay the night; two sisters with children, brothers, and neighbors had come to visit, so that there was not a single spare room left.

The general shook hands with them all, apologized and smiled, but from his face it could be seen that he was far from being as glad of his guests as last year's count, and that he had invited the officers only because, in his opinion, propriety demanded it. And the officers themselves, going up the carpeted stairs and listening to him, felt that they had been invited to this house only because it was awkward not to invite them, and at the sight of the servants, who were hurriedly lighting candles downstairs by the entrance and upstairs in the front hall, it began to seem to them that, along with themselves, they had brought unrest and anxiety. In the house, where, probably on account of some family celebration or event, two sisters with children, brothers, and neighbors had gathered, how could anyone be pleased by the presence of nineteen unknown officers?

Upstairs, at the entrance to the reception room, the guests were met by a tall and slender old woman with a long, dark-browed face, very much resembling the empress Eugénie.[2] With a welcoming and majestic smile, she said she was glad and delighted to see guests in her house, and apologized that she and her husband were deprived this time of the possibility of inviting the gentlemen officers to stay the night with them. By her beautiful, majestic smile, which instantly disappeared from her face each time she turned away from her guests for some reason, one could see that she had seen many gentlemen officers in her time, that she could not be bothered with them right now, and if she invited them to her house and apologized, it was only because her upbringing and social position demanded it.

In the large dining room that the officers entered, at one end of a long table, some dozen men and women, old and young, sat at tea. Further behind their chairs, a group of men enveloped in light cigar smoke showed darkly; in the middle of it stood a lean young man with red sideburns, speaking loudly in English and rolling his *r*'s. Beyond the group, through a doorway, a bright room with light blue furniture could be seen.

"Gentlemen, there are so many of you that it's impossible to introduce you!" the general said loudly, trying to seem very cheerful. "Simply introduce yourselves, gentlemen!"

The officers—some with very serious, even stern faces, others with forced smiles, all of them feeling very awkward—somehow made their bows and sat down to tea.

The one who felt most awkward of all was Staff-Captain Ryabovich, a short, stoop-shouldered officer in spectacles and with side-whiskers like a lynx. While some of his comrades put on serious faces and others forced smiles, his face, his lynx side-whiskers, and his spectacles seemed to say: "I'm the most timid, the most modest, and the most colorless officer in the whole brigade!" At first, coming into the dining room and then sitting at tea, he could not fix his attention on any one face or object. Faces, dresses, cut-glass decanters of cognac, steam from the tea-glasses, molded cornices—it all merged into one enormous general impression, which aroused anxiety in Ryabovich and a wish to hide his head. Like a reciter appearing before the public for the first time, he saw everything that was before his eyes, but somehow understood it poorly (in physiology such a state, when the subject sees but does not understand, is known as "psychic blindness"). A little later, feeling more at ease, Ryabovich recovered his sight and began to observe. For him, as a timid and unsociable man, what struck his eyes first of all was something he had never possessed, namely—the extraordinary courage of his new acquaintances. Von Rabbek, his wife, two elderly ladies, a certain young lady in a lilac dress, and the young man with red sideburns, who turned out to be Rabbek's younger son, very cleverly, as if they had rehearsed it beforehand, positioned themselves among the officers and immediately got into a heated argument, which their guests could not fail to mix into. The lilac young lady began to insist heatedly that an artillerist had a much easier life than a cavalry or infantry man, while Rabbek and the elderly ladies maintained the opposite. Cross-talk began. Ryabovich looked at the lilac young lady, who was arguing very heatedly about something alien and totally uninteresting to her, and watched insincere smiles appear and disappear on her face.

Von Rabbek and his family artfully drew the officers into the argument, and meanwhile kept a close eye on their glasses and mouths, to see if they were all drinking, if they had sugar, and why this or that one was not eating biscuits or drinking cognac. And the more Ryabovich looked and listened, the more he liked this insincere but perfectly disciplined family.

After tea the officers went to the reception room. Lieutenant Lobytko's intuition had not deceived him: there were many young ladies, married and unmarried, in the room. The setter-lieutenant was already standing beside a very young blond girl in a black dress and, dashingly bending over, as if leaning on an invisible sword, smiled and flirtatiously twitched his shoulders. He was probably saying some very interesting nonsense, because the blond girl looked indulgently at his well-fed face and asked indifferently: "Really?" And from this impassive "Really?" the setter, had he been intelligent, might have concluded that he was unlikely to hear the call "Fetch!"

A grand piano thundered; a melancholy waltz flew out of the reception room through the wide-open windows, and for some reason everyone remembered that outside the windows it was now spring, a May evening. Everyone sensed that the air smelled of young poplar leaves, roses, and lilacs. Ryabovich, in whom, under the effect of the music, the cognac he had drunk began to tell, looked askance at the window, smiled, and started to follow the women's movements, and it now seemed to him that the smell of roses, poplars, and lilacs came not from the garden, but from the women's faces and dresses.

Rabbek's son invited some skinny girl and made two turns with her. Lobytko, gliding over the parquet, flew up to the lilac young lady and whirled around the room with her. The dancing began ... Ryabovich stood by the door among the non-dancers and watched. He had never once danced in his life and had never once held his arms around the waist of a respectable woman. He was terribly pleased when a man, before everyone's eyes, took hold of an unknown girl's waist and offered his shoulder to her hand, but he was unable to imagine himself in this man's place. There was a time when he envied his comrades' boldness and pluck, and his heart ached; the awareness that he was timid, stoop-shouldered, and colorless, that he had a long waist and lynx side-whiskers, was deeply humiliating, but with the years this awareness became habitual, and now, looking at the dancing or loudly talking people, he no longer envied them, but only felt sadly moved.

When the quadrille began, the young von Rabbek approached the non-dancers and invited two officers to a game of billiards. The officers accepted and left the reception room with him. Ryabovich, having nothing to do, and wishing to take at least some part in the general activity, trudged after them. From the reception room they went to the drawing room, then down a narrow glass corridor, from there to a room where, when they appeared, three sleepy servants jumped up from the sofas. Finally, having gone through a whole string of rooms, the young Rabbek and the officers entered a small room where the billiard table stood. The game began.

Ryabovich, who had never played anything but cards, stood by the billiard table and looked indifferently at the players, and they, in unbuttoned coats, with cues in their hands, walked about, made puns, and shouted unintelligible words. The players did not notice him, and only occasionally one of them, having shoved him with an elbow or caught him accidentally with a cue, would turn and say, *"Pardon!"* The first game was not yet over, but he was already bored, and it began to seem to him that he was superfluous and a nuisance . . . He felt drawn back to the reception room, and he left.

On the way back he was to meet with a little adventure. At some point he noticed that he was not going where he should. He remembered very well that on the way he should meet three sleepy servants, but he went through five or six rooms and those figures had vanished without a trace. Noticing his mistake, he went a little way back, turned to the right, and wound up in a semi-dark parlor that he had not seen when he went to the billiard room; he stood there for half a minute, then resolutely opened the first door he happened upon and entered a totally dark room. Straight ahead of him he could see a crack in a door through which bright light shone; from behind the door came the muted sounds of a melancholy mazurka. Here, as in the reception room, the windows were wide open and there was a smell of poplars, lilacs, and roses . . .

Ryabovich paused to reflect . . . Just then, unexpectedly, he heard hasty footsteps and the rustling of a dress, a breathless feminine voice whispered "At last!" and two soft, fragrant, unquestionably feminine arms embraced his neck; a warm cheek pressed itself to his cheek and simultaneously came the sound of a kiss. But the kissing woman gave a small cry at once and, as it seemed to Ryabovich, recoiled from him in disgust. He, too, all but cried out and dashed for the bright crack in the door . . .

When he returned to the reception room, his heart was pounding and his hands trembled so visibly that he hurriedly hid them behind his back. At first he suffered from shame and fear that the whole room knew he had just been embraced and kissed by a woman. He fidgeted and looked about anxiously, but, satisfying himself that the people in the room were dancing and chattering as calmly as before, he gave himself entirely to this new sensation, which until then he had never experienced in his life. Something strange was happening to him . . . It seemed to him that his neck, which had just been embraced by soft, fragrant arms, had been smeared with oil; his cheek, by the left moustache, where the unknown woman had kissed him, trembled with a light, pleasant coolness, as if from menthol drops, and the more he rubbed that spot, the more intensely he felt the coolness, and his whole being from head to foot was filled with a strange new sensation that kept growing, growing . . . He wanted to dance, to talk, to run out to the garden, to laugh loudly . . . He completely forgot that he was stoop-shouldered and colorless, and had lynx side-whiskers and an "indefinite appearance" (so his appearance had once been described in a ladies' conversation, which he accidentally overheard). When Rabbek's wife walked past him, he gave her such a broad and tender smile that she stopped and looked at him questioningly.

"I like your house terribly! . . . ," he said, straightening his spectacles.

The general's wife smiled and told him that this house had belonged to her father, then she asked if his parents were living, if he had been in the service long, why he was so skinny, and so on . . . Having received answers to her questions, she went on her way, and he, after talking with her, began to smile still more tenderly and to think that he was surrounded by splendid people . . .

At dinner Ryabovich mechanically ate everything he was offered, drank, and, not listening to anything, tried to explain the recent adventure to himself. This adventure had a mysterious and romantic character, but explaining it was not difficult. Probably some young miss or lady had arranged an assignation with somebody in the dark room, had waited for a long time, and, being in nervous agitation, had taken Ryabovich for her hero; this was the more likely since Ryabovich, as he passed through the dark room, had paused to reflect, that is, had looked like a person who was also expecting something . . . Thus Ryabovich explained to himself the received kiss.

"But who is she?" he thought, looking around at the women's faces. "She must be young, because old women don't go to assignations. Then, too, she must be cultivated, that could be sensed from the rustling of her dress, her fragrance, her voice . . ."

He rested his gaze on the lilac young lady, and he liked her very much; she had beautiful shoulders and arms, an intelligent face, and a lovely voice. Looking at her, Ryabovich wanted precisely her, and not anyone else, to be his unknown one . . . But she laughed somehow insincerely and wrinkled her long nose, which made her look old; then he shifted his gaze to the blond girl in the black dress. This one was younger, more simple and sincere, had lovely temples, and drank very prettily from her glass. Ryabovich now wanted her to be the one. But soon he found that her face was flat, and he shifted his gaze to the girl next to her . . .

"It's hard to guess," he thought dreamily. "If you were to take just the shoulders and arms from the lilac one, add the blond one's temples, and the eyes of the one sitting to the left of Lobytko, then . . ."

He performed the composition mentally and came up with an image of the girl who had kissed him, the image he wanted but could not find at the table.

After supper the guests, sated and tipsy, started to take their leave and say thank you. The hosts again began to apologize that they could not have them stay the night.

"Very, very glad, gentlemen!" the general was saying, this time sincerely (probably because people are usually much more sincere and kind when seeing guests off than when receiving them). "Very glad! You're welcome to stop by on your way back! Without ceremony! Which way? You want to go up? No, go through the garden, the lower path—it's shorter."

The officers went out into the garden. After the bright light and the noise, the garden seemed very dark and quiet. They went as far as the gate in silence. They were half-drunk, cheerful, content, but the darkness and quiet gave them pause for a moment. Each of them, like Ryabovich, probably had one and the same thought: would there come a time when they, like Rabbek, would have a big house, a family, a garden, and when they would be able, even if insincerely, to regale people, to make them sated, drunk, and content?

After going through the gate, they all immediately started talking and laughing loudly for no reason. Now they were already walking along the path that went down to the river and then ran just by the water, skirting the bushes that grew on the bank, the pools, and the willows hanging over the water. The bank and the path were barely visible, and the opposite bank was all drowned in darkness. Here and there stars were reflected in the dark water; they quivered and blurred—and only by that could one tell that the current was swift. It was quiet. On the opposite bank drowsy snipe moaned, and on this bank, in one of the bushes, a nightingale, paying no attention to the crowd of officers, was trilling loudly. The officers stopped by the bush, touched it, but the nightingale went on singing.

"How about that!" came exclamations of approval. "We stand right here and he ignores us completely! What a rascal!"

Towards the end, the path went uphill and joined the road by the church wall. Here the officers, weary from walking up the hill, sat down and smoked. A dim red light appeared on the opposite bank, and, having nothing better to do, they spent a long time discussing whether it was a bonfire, or a light in a window, or something else . . . Ryabovich also looked at the light, and it seemed to him that the light smiled and winked at him, as if it knew about the kiss.

On coming to his quarters, Ryabovich quickly undressed and lay down. He shared a cottage with Lobytko and with Lieutenant Merzlyakov, a quiet, taciturn fellow, who in his own circle was considered a well-educated officer, and who, wherever possible, always read *The*

Messenger of Europe,[3] which he carried with him everywhere. Lobytko undressed, paced back and forth for a long time, with the look of a man who is dissatisfied, and sent his orderly for beer. Merzlyakov lay down, put a candle by the head of the bed, and immersed himself in reading *The Messenger of Europe.*

"Who is she?" thought Ryabovich, staring at the sooty ceiling.

His neck, as it seemed to him, was still smeared with oil, and near his mouth he felt a coolness, as from menthol drops. The shoulders and arms of the lilac young lady, the temples and sincere eyes of the blond girl in black, waists, dresses, brooches flitted through his imagination. He tried to fix his attention on these images, but they leaped, blurred, flickered. On the wide black background that every person sees when he closes his eyes, these images disappeared entirely, and he began to hear hasty footsteps, the rustling of a dress, the sound of the kiss, and—an intense, causeless joy came over him . . . As he surrendered himself to that joy, he heard the orderly come back and report that there was no beer. Lobytko was terribly indignant and again began to pace.

"Well, isn't he an idiot?" he said, stopping in front of Ryabovich, then in front of Merzlyakov. "You'd have to be a blockhead and a fool not to find any beer! Eh? Well, isn't he a *canaille?*"[4]

"Of course you can't find beer here," said Merzlyakov, without taking his eyes from *The Messenger of Europe.*

"Really? You don't think so?" Lobytko persisted. "Lord God, drop me on the moon, and right away I'll find you beer and women! Look, I'll go right now and find it . . . Call me a scoundrel if I don't!"

He spent a long time getting dressed and pulling on his big boots, then silently smoked a cigarette and left.

"Rabbek, Grabbek, Labbek," he muttered, stopping in the front hall. "I don't like going alone, devil take it. Ryabovich, wouldn't you like to make a *promenazh?* Eh?"

Receiving no reply, he came back, slowly undressed, and lay down. Merzlyakov sighed, set aside *The Messenger of Europe,* and blew out the candle.

"Hm—yes, sir . . . ," Lobytko murmured, lighting up a cigarette in the dark.

Ryabovich pulled the covers over his head, curled up, and began gathering together the images flitting through his imagination and uniting them into a single whole. But nothing came of it. Soon he fell asleep, and his last thought was that someone had caressed him and made him happy, that in his life something extraordinary, stupid, but extremely good and joyful had happened. This thought did not leave him even in sleep.

When he woke up, the sensation of oil on his neck and of menthol coolness near his lips was not there, but the wave of joy surged up in his breast as the day before. He gazed rapturously at the window frames gilded by the rising sun and listened to the movement outside. There was loud talk just by the window. Ryabovich's battery commander, Lebedetsky, had just caught up with the brigade, and, being unaccustomed to speaking softly, was talking very loudly with his sergeant.

"And what else?" shouted the commander.

"During yesterday's shoeing, Your Honor, Golubchik got pricked. The paramedic applied clay and vinegar. They lead him to one side now on a bridle. And also, Your Honor, the workman Artemyev got drunk yesterday, and the lieutenant punished him by sitting him on the front of a spare gun carriage."

The sergeant also reported that Karpov forgot about new cords for the bugles and stakes for the tents, and that last night the officers visited General von Rabbek. In the middle of the conversation, the red-bearded head of Lebedetsky appeared in the window. He squinted at the officers' sleepy physiognomies and greeted them.

"All well?" he asked.

"The shaft horse has a sore on his withers from the new yoke," Lobytko said, yawning.

The commander sighed, thought a moment, and said loudly:

"And I think I'll still go to see Alexandra Evgrafovna. I must call on her. Well, goodbye. I'll catch up with you in the evening."

A quarter of an hour later the brigade set out on its way. As it moved down the road past the barns of the estate, Ryabovich looked to the right at the house. The blinds were drawn. Evidently the house was still asleep. Asleep, too, was the girl who had kissed Ryabovich yesterday. He wanted to picture her sleeping. The bedroom window wide open, green branches peeking through the window, the morning freshness, the smell of poplars, lilacs, and roses, a bed, a chair, and on it the dress that had rustled yesterday, little shoes, a watch on the table—all this he portrayed to himself clearly and distinctly, but the features, the sweet, sleepy smile, precisely what was important and specific, evaded his imagination, like quicksilver under a finger. Having gone half a mile, he turned to look back: the yellow church, the house, the river, and the garden were flooded with light; the river with its bright green banks reflected the blue sky and, silvery here and there from the sun, was very beautiful. Ryabovich looked at Mestechki for the last time and felt as sad as if he were parting with something very near and dear.

And before his eyes on the road lay only long familiar, uninteresting scenes . . . To right and left fields of young rye and buckwheat, with hopping rooks; look ahead—you see dust and napes, look behind—you see the same dust and faces . . . In front march four men with sabers—this was the vanguard. Behind them a crowd of singers, and behind them buglers on horseback. The vanguard and the singers, like torchbearers in a funeral procession, keep forgetting about the regulation distance and march far ahead . . . Ryabovich is placed by the first gun of the fifth battery. He can see all four of the batteries marching ahead of him. For a civilian, this long, heavy file formed by the moving brigade looks like an intricate and incomprehensible mess; it is incomprehensible why one gun is surrounded by so many people, and why it is pulled by so many horses, entangled in strange harness, as if it were indeed so frightening and heavy. For Ryabovich it was all comprehensible, and therefore extremely uninteresting. He had long known why, at the head of each battery, beside the officer, rides an imposing firemaster, and why he is called the carrier; behind the back of this firemaster he can see the riders of the first, then of the middle team; Ryabovich knows that the horses to the left, which they ride on, are called saddle horses, and to the right, helpers—all very uninteresting. After the riders come two shaft horses. One of them is mounted by a rider with yesterday's dust on his back and with a clumsy, extremely ridiculous piece of wood on his right leg; Ryabovich knows the purpose of this piece of wood, and to him it does not seem ridiculous. The riders, all of them, mechanically swing their whips and shout now and then. The gun itself is ugly. In front lie sacks of oats covered with canvas, and the gun itself is all hung with kettles, kit bags, pouches, and has the look of a small, harmless animal, surrounded for some unknown reason by people and horses. At its flank, on the leeward side, swinging their arms, march six gunners. Following the gun, new carriers, riders, shaft horses begin again, and behind them drags another gun, as ugly and unimpressive as the first. The second is followed by a third, a fourth; by the fourth an officer, and so on. There are six batteries in a brigade, and four guns in each battery. The file stretches out for half a mile. It ends with a supply train, next to which, his long-eared head thoughtfully lowered, marches a highly sympathetic character—the donkey Magar—whom one of the battery commanders brought from Turkey.

Ryabovich looked indifferently ahead and behind, at the napes and at the faces; any other time he would have dozed off, but now he was all immersed in his new, pleasant thoughts. At first, when the brigade had just set out, he wanted to persuade himself that the incident with the kiss was interesting only as a small, mysterious adventure, that it was essentially worthless, and to think seriously about it was stupid, to say the least; but he soon waved logic away and gave himself up to dreaming . . . Now he imagined himself in Rabbek's drawing room next to a girl who resembled the lilac young lady and the blond girl in black; then he closed his eyes and saw himself with another totally unknown girl with very indefinite features; mentally he talked to her, caressed her, leaned down to her shoulder, imagined to himself war and separation, then reunion, a supper with his wife, children . . .

"Mind the swingletrees!" The command rang out each time they went down a hill.

He, too, cried, "Mind the swingletrees!" and worried that this cry might break up his dream and bring him back to reality . . .

Passing by some landowner's estate, Ryabovich looked through the paling into the garden. His eyes caught sight of a long alley, straight as a ruler, sprinkled with yellow sand and lined with young birches . . . With the avidity of a daydreamer, he pictured to himself a woman's small feet walking on the yellow sand, and, quite unexpectedly, in his imagination there clearly appeared the girl who had kissed him and whom he had managed to picture to himself yesterday at dinner. This image had stayed in his brain and now did not leave him.

At noon a cry came from the rear by the supply train:

"Attention! Eyes left! Officers!"

In a carriage with a pair of white horses, the brigade general rolled by. He stopped at the second battery and shouted something nobody understood. Several officers rode up to him, Ryabovich among them.

"How's things? Eh?" asked the general, blinking his red eyes. "Any sick?"

Having received answers, the general, short and skinny, munched, pondered, and said, turning to one of the officers:

"The shaft rider of the third carriage took his knee-guard off and hung it on the front, the *canaille*. Slap a penalty on him."

He raised his eyes to Ryabovich and went on:

"And your breeching strap looks much too long . . ."

After making several more dull observations, the general looked at Lobytko and grinned.

"And you, Lieutenant Lobytko, look very sad today," he said. "Missing Lopukhova, eh? Gentlemen, he's missing Lopukhova!"

Lopukhova was a very corpulent and very tall lady, well past forty. The general, who nursed a predilection for large women, whatever age they might be, suspected this same predilection in his officers. The officers smiled deferentially. The general, pleased that he had said something very funny and caustic, laughed loudly, tapped his driver's back, and saluted. The carriage rolled on . . .

"Everything I'm dreaming about now, and that now seems impossible and unearthly to me, is essentially quite ordinary," thought Ryabovich, looking at the clouds of dust in the wake of the general's carriage. "It's all quite ordinary and experienced by everyone . . . For instance, this general loved in his time, is married now, has children. Captain Vakhter is also married and loved, though he has a very ugly red nape and no waist . . . Salmanov is brutish and too much of a Tartar, but he, too, had a love affair that ended in marriage . . . I'm like everybody else, and sooner or later will experience the same thing everybody does . . ."

And the thought that he was an ordinary man and had an ordinary life gladdened and encouraged him. Now he boldly pictured *her* and his happiness as he wished, and nothing hindered his imagination . . .

When the brigade reached its destination in the evening and the officers were resting in their tents, Ryabovich, Merzlyakov, and Lobytko sat around a trunk having supper. Merzlyakov ate unhurriedly and, chewing slowly, read *The Messenger of Europe*, holding it on his knees. Lobytko talked incessantly and kept topping up his glass of beer, while Ryabovich, who had a fog in his head from dreaming all day long, said nothing and drank. After three glasses, he became tipsy, weak, and had an irrepressible desire to share his new sensations with his comrades.

"A strange happening happened to me at those Rabbeks' . . . ," he began, trying to give his voice an indifferent and mocking tone. "I went to the billiard room, you know . . ."

He started telling in great detail about the incident with the kiss and after a minute fell silent . . . In that minute he had told everything, and he was terribly surprised that it had taken so little time to tell it. It had seemed to him that he could tell about the kiss till morning. Having heard him out, Lobytko, who lied a lot and therefore did not believe anyone, looked at him mistrustfully and smirked. Merzlyakov raised his eyebrows and calmly, not tearing his eyes from *The Messenger of Europe*, said:

"God knows! . . . Throwing herself on your neck without any warning . . . Must be some kind of psychopath."

"Right, must be a psychopath . . . ," Ryabovich agreed.

"Something similar once happened to me . . . ," said Lobytko, making frightened eyes. "I was going to Kovno last year . . . I had a second-class ticket . . . The car was overcrowded, it was impossible to sleep. I gave the conductor fifty kopecks . . . He took my luggage and brought me to a separate compartment . . . I lie down and cover myself with a blanket . . . It's dark, you see. Suddenly I feel somebody touch my shoulder and breathe into my face. I move my hand and feel somebody's elbow . . . I open my eyes and, can you imagine—a woman! Dark eyes, red lips like fine salmon, nostrils breathing passion, bosom—a buffer . . ."

"Excuse me," Merzlyakov interrupted calmly, "I understand about the bosom, but how could you see the lips if it was dark?"

Lobytko began to dodge and laughed at Merzlyakov's obtuseness. This jarred on Ryabovich. He left the trunk, lay down, and promised himself never to be openhearted.

Camp life began . . . Days flowed by, one very much like another. During all those days, Ryabovich felt, thought, and behaved like a man in love. Every morning, when the orderly brought him a full washbasin, he poured the cold water over his head, remembering each time that there was something good and warm in his life.

In the evenings, when his comrades started talking about love and women, he listened, moved closer, and assumed the expression that the faces of soldiers have when they hear stories of battles they themselves took part in. And on those evenings when carousing officers, with setter-Lobytko at their head, made donjuanesque raids on the "outskirts," Ryabovich, taking part in the raids, was sad each time, felt himself deeply guilty, and mentally asked *her* forgiveness . . . In leisure hours or on sleepless nights, when the urge came over him to remember his childhood, father, mother, all that was near and dear, he unfailingly remembered Mestechki, the strange horse, Rabbek, his wife, who resembled the empress Eugénie, the dark room, the bright crack in the door . . .

On the thirty-first of August he was returning from camp, now not with his brigade, but with two batteries. He dreamed all the way and was excited, as if he were going to his native land. He passionately wanted to see again the strange horse, the church, the insincere Rabbek family, the dark room; the "inner voice" that so often deceives lovers whispered to him for some reason that he was sure to see her . . . And he was tormented by questions: How would he meet her? What would he talk about with her? Would she not have forgotten about the kiss? In the worst outcome, he thought, even if he did not run into her, it would already be pleasant enough for him to walk through the dark room and remember . . .

Towards evening the familiar church and white barns appeared on the horizon. Ryabovich's heart began to pound . . . He was not listening to the officer who was riding next to him and saying something. He forgot about everything and greedily peered at the river glistening in the distance, the roof of the house, the dovecot over which pigeons circled, lit by the setting sun.

Approaching the church and then listening to the quartermaster, he waited every second for a rider to appear from behind the wall and invite the officers to tea, but . . . the quartermaster's report ended, the officers dismounted and wandered off to the village, and the rider did not appear . . .

"Rabbek will find out at once from his peasants that we have come and will send for us," Ryabovich thought, going into the cottage and not understanding why his comrade was lighting a candle and the orderlies were hurrying to start the samovars . . .

A heavy anxiety came over him. He lay down, then got up again and looked out the window to see if the rider was coming. But there was no rider. He lay down again, got up half an hour later, and, unable to bear his anxiety, went outside and walked towards the church. The square by the wall was dark and deserted . . . Three soldiers stood in a row at the very top of the slope and were silent. Seeing Ryabovich, they roused themselves and saluted. He returned the salute and started down the familiar path.

On the other bank, the whole sky was flooded with crimson color: the moon was rising; two peasant women, talking loudly, walked about in the kitchen garden tearing off cabbage leaves; beyond the kitchen garden, several cottages showed darkly . . . On the near bank everything was the same as in May: the path, the bushes, the willows hanging over the water . . . only the brave nightingale was not singing and there was no smell of poplars and young grass.

On reaching the garden, Ryabovich looked through the gate. The garden was dark and quiet . . . He could only see the white trunks of the nearest birches and a small part of the alley; the rest all merged into a black mass. Ryabovich greedily listened and peered, but after standing there for a quarter of an hour and not hearing or seeing anything, he trudged back . . .

He approached the river. Before him the general's bathhouse and the sheets hanging on the rails of the little bridge showed white. He went up on the little bridge, stood there, and without any need touched a sheet. The sheet turned out to be rough and cold. He looked down at the water . . . The river flowed swiftly and the gurgling around the pilings of the bathhouse was barely audible. The red moon was reflected near the left bank; little ripples ran across its reflection, spreading it, tearing it to pieces, and, it seemed, wishing to carry it off . . .

"How stupid! How stupid!" thought Ryabovich, looking at the flowing water. "Not smart at all!"

Now, when he expected nothing, the incident with the kiss, his impatience, vague hopes, and disappointment appeared to him in a clear light. It no longer seemed strange to him that he had not gone on waiting for the general's rider and that he would never see the one who had accidentally kissed him instead of someone else; on the contrary, it would be strange if he were to see her . . .

The water flowed who knows where and why. It had flowed the same way in May; from the small river in the month of May it had poured into a big river, from the river into the sea, then it evaporated, turned into rain, and maybe that same water was now flowing again before Ryabovich's eyes . . . What for? Why?

And the whole world, the whole of life appeared to Ryabovich as an incomprehensible, pointless joke . . . And taking his eyes from the water and looking at the sky, he again recalled how fate in the person of an unknown woman had unwittingly been kind to him, recalled his summer dreams and images, and his life seemed to him extraordinarily meager, miserable, and colorless . . .

When he went back to his cottage, he did not find any of his comrades. The orderly reported that they had all gone to "General Fontryabkin," who had sent a rider for them . . . For a moment joy rose in Ryabovich's breast, but he extinguished it at once, went to bed, and to spite his fate, as if wishing to vex it, did not go to the general's.

1887

BOYS

"VOLODYA'S HERE!" someone shouted outside.

"Volodechka's here!" hollered Natalya, running into the dining room. "Oh, my God!"

The whole Korolyov family, who had been expecting their Volodya to come any moment, rushed to the windows. At the entrance stood a wide sledge, and from the troika of white horses a thick mist rose. The sledge was empty, because Volodya was already standing in the front hall and undoing his bashlyk with red, cold fingers.[1] His school coat, cap, galoshes, and the hair at his temples were covered with rime, and the whole of him from head to foot gave off such a tasty, frosty smell that, looking at him, you wanted to get chilled and say "Brrr!" His mother and aunt rushed to embrace and kiss him, Natalya fell at his feet and began pulling off his felt boots, his sisters let out squeals, doors creaked and slammed, and Volodya's father, in his shirtsleeves and with scissors in his hand, ran to the front hall and cried out in alarm:

"We've been expecting you since yesterday! A good trip? All's well? Lord God, let the boy greet his father! What, am I not his father?"

"Bow-wow!" bellowed the bass voice of Milord, a huge black dog, his tail knocking against the walls and furniture.

Everything merged into one general, joyful noise that went on for about two minutes. When the first impulse of joy passed, the Korolyovs noticed that, besides Volodya, there was another small person in the front hall, wrapped in kerchiefs, shawls, and bashlyks, and covered with rime. He stood motionless in the corner, in the shadow of a big fox-fur overcoat.

"Volodechka, who is this?" his mother asked in a whisper.

"Ah!" Volodya caught himself. "I have the honor of introducing my friend Lentilkin, a junior in my school . . . I've brought him for a visit."

"How nice, you're very welcome!" the father said joyfully. "Excuse me, I'm in my house clothes . . . Come in! Natalya, help Mr. Ventilkin out of his coat! My God, chase this dog away! What a punishment!"

A short time later Volodya and his friend Lentilkin, stunned by the noisy reception and still rosy from the cold, were sitting at the table having tea. The winter sun, passing through the snow and frosty patterns on the windows, glimmered on the samovar and bathed its pure rays in a rinsing bowl. The room was warm, and the boys felt how, unwilling to yield to each other, warmth and frost both tickled their chilled bodies.

"Well, soon it will be Christmas!" the father said in a singsong voice, rolling a cigarette of reddish-brown tobacco. "It feels like no time since it was summer, and your mother wept seeing you off! Yet here you are again! Time flies, lad! Before you can say 'Ah!' old age will be upon you. Mr. Mentilkin, help yourself, don't be shy! We're simple folk."

Volodya's three sisters, Katya, Sonya, and Masha—the eldest was eleven—sat at the table and did not take their eyes off the new acquaintance. Lentilkin was the same age and height as Volodya, but not so plump and white; he was thin, swarthy, and covered with freckles. His hair was bristly, his eyes narrow, his lips thick; generally he was quite unattractive, and if he had not been wearing a school jacket, by his appearance he might have been taken for a scullery maid's son. He was sullen, silent all the time, and never once smiled. Looking at him, the girls immediately figured out that he must be a very intelligent and educated man. He was thinking about something all the time, and was so taken up with his thoughts that, when he was asked about something, he gave a start, shook his head, and asked them to repeat the question.

The girls noticed that Volodya, always cheerful and talkative, also spoke little this time, did not smile at all, and did not even seem glad that he had come home. While they sat over tea, he addressed his sisters only once, and that with somehow strange words. He pointed to the samovar and said:

"In California they drink gin instead of tea."

He, too, was taken up with some thoughts, and, judging by the glances he exchanged with his friend Lentilkin, the boys' thoughts were the same.

After tea they all went to the children's room. The father and the girls sat down at the table and went on with the work interrupted by the boys' arrival. They were making flowers and Christmas tree garlands from different colored papers. It was fascinating and noisy work. The girls met each newly made flower with rapturous cries, even cries of awe, as if the flower had fallen from the sky; Papa also went into raptures and occasionally threw the scissors on the floor, angry with them for being dull. The mother kept running into the children's room with a very anxious look and asking:

"Who took my scissors? Ivan Nikolaich, did you take my scissors again?"

"Lord God, they won't even give me scissors!" Ivan Nikolaich would reply in a tearful voice and, heaving himself against the back of his chair, would assume the pose of an insulted man, but a minute later he would again be in raptures.

During his previous visits, Volodya had also busied himself with preparing the Christmas tree or had run out to the yard to see the coachman and the shepherd piling up the snow, but this time he and Lentilkin paid no attention to the colored paper and did not go to the stable even once, but sat by the window and started whispering about something; then the two of them opened a geographical atlas and started studying some map.

"First to Perm . . . ," Lentilkin said in a low voice, ". . . from there to Tyumen . . . then Tomsk . . . then . . . to Kamchatka . . . From there the Samoyeds[2] will take us in a boat across the Bering Strait . . . And there's America for you . . . They've got a lot of fur-bearing animals."

"And California?" asked Volodya.

"California's further down . . . Just get to America, and Califor-

nia's right around the corner. We can provide for ourselves by hunting and robbery."

Lentilkin avoided the girls all day and looked at them mistrustfully.
After the evening tea it happened that he was left alone with them
for five minutes. It was awkward to be silent. He cleared his throat
sternly, rubbed his left arm with his right palm, glanced sullenly at
Katya, and asked:

"Have you read Mayne Reid?"[3]

"No, I haven't . . . Listen, do you know how to skate?"

Immersed in his thoughts, Lentilkin made no reply to this question,
and only puffed his cheeks and sighed, as if he felt very hot. He raised
his eyes to Katya and said:

"When a herd of bison runs across the pampas, the earth trembles,
and then the mustangs get frightened, kick, and whinny . . ."

Lentilkin smiled sadly and added:

"And the Indians also attack trains. But worst of all are the mosquitoes and termites."

"What are they?"

"They're like ants, but with wings. They bite very painfully. Do
you know who I am?"

"Mr. Lentilkin."

"No. I'm Montigomo Hawk's Claw, chief of the invincibles."

Masha, the smallest of the girls, looked at him, then at the window,
outside which evening was descending, and said pensively:

"And yesterday they cooked lentils for us."

Lentilkin's totally incomprehensible words, and that he constantly
whispered with Volodya, and that Volodya did not play but kept
thinking about something—all this was mysterious and strange. And
the two older girls, Katya and Sonya, began to keep a sharp eye on
the boys. In the evening, when the boys were going to bed, the girls
crept up to the door and eavesdropped on their conversation. Oh,
what they found out! The boys were going to run away to America
somewhere to dig for gold; they had everything ready for the journey: a pistol, two knives, rusks, a magnifying glass to start a fire, a
compass, and four roubles in cash. They learned that the boys were
to go several thousand miles on foot, fighting tigers and savages on
the way, then dig for gold and hunt for ivory, kill enemies, become

sea robbers, drink gin, and finally marry beauties and cultivate plantations. Volodya and Lentilkin talked enthusiastically, interrupting each other. Lentilkin called himself "Montigomo Hawk's Claw" and Volodya "my paleface brother."

"Watch yourself, don't tell Mama," Katya said to Sonya as they were going to bed. "Volodya will bring us gold and ivory from America, and if you tell Mama, he won't be allowed to go."

Lentilkin spent the whole day before Christmas Eve studying the map of Asia and writing things down, while Volodya, languid, puffy, as if stung by a bee, sullenly paced the rooms and ate nothing. Once, in the children's room, he even stopped in front of an icon, crossed himself, and said:

"Lord, forgive me, a sinner! Lord, watch over my poor, unhappy mama!"

In the evening he burst into tears. On going to bed, he spent a long time embracing his father, mother, and sisters. Katya and Sonya understood what it was all about, but the youngest, Masha, understood nothing, decidedly nothing, and, looking at Lentilkin, only pondered, and said with a sigh:

"When it's Lent, nanny says, we should eat peas and lentils."

Early in the morning of Christmas Eve, Katya and Sonya quietly got out of bed and went to see how the boys would run away to America. They crept up to the door.

"So you won't go?" Lentilkin asked angrily. "Speak: you won't go?"

"Lord!" Volodya wept quietly. "How can I go? I feel sorry for Mama."

"My paleface brother, I beg you, let's go! You assured me you'd go, you enticed me, and when the time comes to go you turn coward!"

"I . . . I haven't turned coward, but I . . . I feel sorry for Mama."

"Just tell me: will you go or not?"

"I'll go, only . . . only wait. I want to live at home for a while."

"In that case I'll go by myself!" Lentilkin decided. "I'll manage without you. And you, who wanted to hunt tigers, to fight! If that's how it is, give me back my percussion caps."

Volodya wept so bitterly that the sisters could not bear it and also quietly wept. Silence ensued.

"So you're not going?" Lentilkin asked once more.

"I . . . I'm going."

"Get dressed, then!"

And to persuade Volodya, Lentilkin praised America, roared like a tiger, imitated a steamboat, cursed, promised to give Volodya all the ivory and all the lion and tiger skins.

And to the girls this thin, swarthy boy with bristly hair and freckles seemed extraordinary, remarkable. He was a hero, a resolute, fearless man, and by the way he roared you might have thought, standing outside the door, that it was a real tiger or lion.

When the girls went back to their room and were getting dressed, Katya, her eyes filled with tears, said:

"Ah, I'm so frightened!"

Until two o'clock, when they sat down to dinner, everything was quiet, but at dinner it suddenly turned out that the boys were not at home. They were sent for to the servants' quarters, the stables, the steward's office—they were not there. They were sent for to the village—they were not found there either. The family had tea without the boys, and when they sat down to supper, Mama was very worried and even wept. During the night they went again to the village, searched, went with lanterns to the river. God, what turmoil arose!

The next day a policeman came; some sort of paper was written out in the dining room. Mama wept.

But then a wide sledge stopped at the porch, and steam billowed up from the troika of white horses.

"Volodya's here!" someone shouted outside.

"Volodechka's here!" hollered Natalya, running into the dining room.

And Milord barked "Bow-wow!" in his bass voice. It turned out that the boys had been detained in town, in the Shopping Arcade (where they had gone around asking everyone where to buy gunpowder). As soon as Volodya entered the front hall, he burst into tears and threw himself on his mother's neck. The girls, trembling, thought with horror of what would happen now, listening as Papa took Volodya and Lentilkin to his study and talked with them for a long time; and Mama also talked and wept.

"How is it possible?" Papa admonished. "God help us, if they find out at school, you'll be expelled. And shame on you, Mr. Lentilkin! It's bad, sir! You're the instigator, and I hope your parents will punish you. How is it possible? Where did you spend the night?"

"At the train station!" Lentilkin proudly replied.

Then Volodya lay down, and they put a towel soaked in vinegar to his head. A telegram was sent somewhere, and the next day a lady came, Lentilkin's mother, and took her son away.

As Lentilkin was leaving, his face was stern, haughty, and, in parting with the girls, he did not say a single word; he only took Katya's notebook and wrote as a memento:

"Montigomo Hawk's Claw."

1887

KASHTANKA

A young, rusty-red dog, half dachshund and half mutt, her muzzle very much resembling a fox's, was running up and down the sidewalk, looking anxiously in all directions. Every once in a while she stopped and whined, shifting from one frozen paw to the other, trying to figure out how she could have gotten lost.

She remembered perfectly well the events of the day that had brought her to this unfamiliar sidewalk.

The day had begun when her master, the cabinetmaker Luka Alexandrych, put on his hat, took some wooden thing wrapped in a red handkerchief under his arm, and hollered:

"Kashtanka, let's go!"

Hearing her name, the half dachshund half mutt came out from under the workbench where she slept on the wood shavings, stretched sweetly, and ran after her master.

Luka Alexandrych's customers lived terribly far apart, so on his way from one to the other he had to stop several times at a tavern to fortify himself. Kashtanka remembered that on the way she had behaved very improperly. She was so overjoyed to be going for a walk that she jumped about, barked at trolley cars, dashed into backyards, and chased other dogs. The cabinetmaker kept losing sight of her and would stop and shout angrily at her. Once, with an avid expression on his face, he even grabbed her foxlike ear in his fist, tugged at it, and said slowly, "Drop . . . dead . . . you . . . pest!"

Having seen his customers, Luka Alexandrych had stopped at his sister's, where he had a bite to eat and a few more drinks. From his sister's, he went to see a bookbinder he knew; from the bookbinder's, he went to a tavern; from the tavern to a friend's house, and so on. In short, by the time Kashtanka found herself on the unfamiliar sidewalk, it was getting dark and the cabinetmaker was as drunk as a fish. He waved his arms and, sighing deeply, moaned:

"In sin did my mother conceive me in my womb! Oh, my sins, my sins! So now we're going down the street and looking at the streetlights, but when we die, we'll burn in the fiery hyena . . ."[1]

Or else he fell into a good-natured tone, called Kashtanka to him, and said:

"You, Kashtanka, are an insect creature and nothing more. Compared to a man, you're like a carpenter compared to a cabinetmaker . . ."

While he was talking to her in that fashion, suddenly there had come a burst of music. Kashtanka looked around and saw a regiment of soldiers marching down the street straight at her. She couldn't stand music, which upset her nerves, and she rushed around and howled. But to her great surprise, the cabinetmaker, instead of being frightened, yelping and barking, grinned broadly, stood at attention, and gave a salute. Seeing that her master did not protest, Kashtanka howled even louder, then lost her head and rushed to the other side of the street.

When she came to her senses, the music had already stopped and the regiment was gone. She rushed back across the street to where she had left her master, but alas, the cabinetmaker was also gone. She rushed ahead, then back, ran across the street once more, but it was as if the cabinetmaker had vanished into thin air . . . Kashtanka began sniffing the sidewalk, hoping to find her master by the smell of his tracks, but some scoundrel had just walked past in new galoshes, and now all the delicate scents were mixed with the strong smell of rubber, so that it was impossible to tell one from the other.

Kashtanka ran here and there but could not find her master, and meanwhile night was falling. The lamps were lit on both sides of the street, and lights appeared in the windows. Big, fluffy snow-flakes were falling, painting the sidewalks, the horses' backs, and the coachmen's hats white, and the darker it grew, the whiter everything became. Unknown customers ceaselessly walked back and forth past Kashtanka, obstructing her field of vision and shoving her with their feet. (Kashtanka divided the whole of mankind into two very unequal parts: the masters and the customers; there was an essential difference between them: the first had the right to beat her, the second she herself had the right to nip on the calves.) The customers were hurrying somewhere and did not pay the slightest attention to her.

When it was quite dark, Kashtanka was overcome by fear and despair. She huddled in some doorway and began to weep bitterly. She was tired from her long day's travels with Luka Alexandrych, her ears and paws were cold, and besides she was terribly hungry. Only twice in the whole day had she had anything to eat: at the book-binder's she had lapped up some paste, and in one of the taverns she had found a sausage skin near the counter—that was all. If she had been a human being, she would probably have thought:

"No, it's impossible to live this way! I'll shoot myself!"

CHAPTER TWO / A MYSTERIOUS STRANGER

But she did not think about anything and only wept. When soft, fluffy snow had completely covered Kashtanka's back and head, and she had sunk into a deep slumber from exhaustion, suddenly the door clicked, creaked, and hit her on the side. She jumped up. A man came out, belonging to the category of customers. As Kashtanka squealed and got under his feet, he could not help noticing her. He leaned down and asked:

"Where did you come from, pooch? Did I hurt you? Oh, poor thing, poor thing. . . . Well, don't be angry, don't be angry . . . I'm sorry."

Kashtanka looked up at the stranger through the snowflakes that stuck to her eyelashes and saw before her a short, fat little man with a plump, clean-shaven face, wearing a top hat and an unbuttoned fur coat.

"Why are you whining?" the man went on, brushing the snow from her back. "Where is your master? You must be lost. Oh, poor pooch! What shall we do now?"

Catching a warm, friendly note in the stranger's voice, Kashtanka licked his hand and whined even more pitifully.

"You're a nice, funny one!" said the stranger. "A real fox! Well, nothing to be done. Come with me, maybe I'll find some use for you . . . Well, phweet!"

He whistled and made a gesture to Kashtanka which could only mean: Let's go! Kashtanka went.

In less than half an hour she was sitting on the floor of a large, bright room, with her head cocked, looking tenderly and curiously at the stranger, who was sitting at the table eating supper. He ate and tossed her some scraps . . . At first he gave her bread and the green rind of cheese, then a small piece of meat, half of a dumpling, some chicken bones, and she was so hungry that she gobbled them up without tasting anything. And the more she ate, the hungrier she felt.

"Your master doesn't feed you very well," said the stranger, seeing with what fierce greed she swallowed the unchewed pieces. "And what a scrawny one! Skin and bones . . ."

Kashtanka ate a lot, yet she didn't feel full, only groggy. After supper she sprawled in the middle of the room, stretched her legs and, feeling pleasantly weary all over, began wagging her tail. While her new master sat back in an armchair, smoking a cigar, she wagged her tail and kept trying to decide where she liked it better—at this stranger's or at the cabinetmaker's. At the stranger's the furnishings were poor and ugly. Apart from the armchairs, the sofa, the lamp, and the rugs, he had nothing, and the room seemed empty. At the cabinetmaker's, the whole place was chock-full of things: he had a table, a workbench, a pile of wood shavings, planes, chisels, saws, a basin, a goldfinch in a cage. . . . The stranger's room had no particular smell, while at the cabinetmaker's there was always a fog and the wonderful smell of glue, varnish, and wood shavings. Still, being with the stranger had one great advantage: he gave her a lot to eat—one must give him full credit—and when she sat by the table with a sweet look on her face, he never once hit her or stamped his foot or shouted: "Get ou-u-ut, curse you!"

When he finished his cigar, her new master went out and came back a moment later carrying a small mattress.

"Hey, pooch, come here!" he said, putting the mattress in the corner near the sofa. "Lie down! Go to sleep!"

Then he turned off the lamp and went out. Kashtanka lay down on the mattress and closed her eyes. She heard barking outside and wanted to answer it, but suddenly she became unexpectedly sad. She remembered Luka Alexandrych, his son Fedyushka, and her cozy place under the workbench . . . She remembered how on long winter evenings while the cabinetmaker was planing a board or reading the newspaper aloud, Fedyushka used to play with her . . . He would drag her from under the workbench by her hind legs and do such tricks with her that everything turned green in her eyes and all her joints hurt. He would make her walk on her hind legs, turn her into a bell by pulling her tail hard, until she squealed and barked, or give her tobacco to sniff. Especially tormenting was the following trick: Fedyushka would tie a piece of meat to a string and give it to Kashtanka; then, once she had swallowed it, with loud laughter he would pull it out of her stomach. And the more vivid her memories became, the more loudly and longingly Kashtanka whined.

But weariness and warmth soon overcame her sadness . . . She began to fall asleep. In her mind's eye dogs ran past, among them a shaggy old poodle she had seen that day in the street, sore-eyed, with tufts of fur around his nose. Fedyushka was chasing the poodle with a chisel in his hand; then all at once he too was covered with shaggy fur, and barked merrily beside Kashtanka. Kashtanka and he sniffed each other's noses good-naturedly and ran off down the street . . .

CHAPTER THREE / NEW AND VERY PLEASANT ACQUAINTANCES

It was already light when Kashtanka woke up, and noise came from the street, as only happens in daytime. There was nobody in the room. Kashtanka stretched, yawned, and began nosing around in a grumpy mood. She sniffed the corners and the furniture, glanced into the entryway and found nothing interesting. Besides the door to the entryway, there was one other door. Kashtanka thought for a moment, then scratched at the door with both paws, opened it, and went into the next room. There on the bed, under a flannel blanket, a customer lay sleeping, whom she recognized as last night's stranger.

"Grrr . . . ," she growled. Then, remembering yesterday's supper, she wagged her tail and began sniffing.

She sniffed the stranger's clothes and boots and found that they smelled strongly of horse. In the bedroom was another door, also closed. Kashtanka scratched at this door, too, then leaned her chest against it, opened it, and was immediately aware of a strange, very suspicious smell. Anticipating an unpleasant encounter, growling and glancing around, Kashtanka went into the small room with dirty wallpaper and drew back in fear. She saw something unexpected and frightening. A gray goose, with its head and neck low to the floor and its wings outstretched, was coming straight at her, hissing. Nearby, on a little mat, lay a white tomcat. Seeing Kashtanka, he jumped up, arched his back, stiffened his tail, and with his fur standing on end, also hissed. Frightened in earnest, but not wanting to show it, the dog barked loudly and rushed at the cat . . . The cat arched his back even more, hissed, and smacked the dog on the head with his paw. Kashtanka jumped back, crouched down on all fours and, stretching her muzzle toward the cat, let out a burst of shrill barking. The goose, meanwhile, came from behind and pecked her painfully on the back. Kashtanka jumped up and lunged at the goose . . .

"What's going on!" shouted an angry voice, and into the room came the stranger, wearing a robe, with a cigar between his teeth. "What's the meaning of all this? Go to your places!"

He went up to the cat, gave him a flick on his arched back, and said, "Fyodor Timofeyich, what's the meaning of this? You started a fight, eh? You old rapscallion! Lie down!"

And turning to the goose, he shouted, "Ivan Ivanych, to your place!"

The cat obediently lay down on his mat and closed his eyes. From the expression on his face and whiskers, he himself seemed displeased at losing his temper and getting into a fight. Kashtanka whined, offended, and the goose stretched his neck and began explaining something quickly, ardently, distinctly, but quite incomprehensibly.

"All right, all right," said his master, yawning. "One must live in peace and friendship." He patted Kashtanka and said, "Don't be afraid, rusty . . . They're nice folks, they won't hurt you. What are we going to call you, anyway? You can't go around without a name, brother."

The stranger thought for a moment, and then he said, "I've got it! We'll call you Auntie! Understand . . . ? Auntie!"

And having repeated the word "Auntie" several times, he went out. Kashtanka sat down and kept her eyes open. The cat lay still on his mat, pretending to sleep. The goose, stretching his neck and stamping in place, went on talking about something quickly and ardently. Apparently he was a very smart goose. After each long harangue, he would step back with a look of amazement, as if he were delighted by his own speech. Kashtanka listened to him for a while, answered him with a "grrr," and began sniffing around the corners of the room.

In one corner stood a small trough in which she saw some soaked peas and rye crusts. She tried the peas—no good, tried the crusts—and began to eat. The goose was not offended in the least that a strange dog was eating his feed, and, on the contrary, started talking still more ardently, and, to show his confidence, went to the trough himself and ate a few peas.

CHAPTER FOUR / FEATS OF WONDER

After a while, the stranger came back in carrying an odd thing that looked like a sawhorse. A bell hung from the crosspiece of this wooden, crudely made sawhorse, and there was also a pistol tied to it. Strings were tied to the clapper of the bell and the trigger of the pistol. The stranger set the sawhorse down in the middle of the room, spent a long time tying and untying something, then turned to the goose and said:

"Ivan Ivanych, you're on!"

The goose came up to him and stood with a look of anticipation.

"All right," said the stranger, "let's begin from the very beginning. First, bow and make a curtsy. Quick, now!"

Ivan Ivanych stretched his neck, nodded his head all around, and scraped the floor with his foot.

"Good boy . . . Now, play dead!"

The goose turned on his back with his feet sticking up in the air. After a few more simple tricks of this sort, the stranger suddenly clutched his head with an expression of horror and cried, "Fire! Help! The house is burning!"

Ivan Ivanych ran to the sawhorse, took the string in his beak, and rang the bell.

The stranger was very pleased. He stroked the goose's neck and said:

"Good boy, Ivan Ivanych! Now imagine that you're a jeweler and sell gold and diamonds. Imagine now that you come to your shop one day and find robbers there. What would you do in that case?"

The goose took the other string in his beak and pulled. A deafening shot rang out. Kashtanka, who had liked the bell ringing very much, was so delighted by the pistol shot that she ran around the sawhorse barking.

"Auntie, sit!" the stranger shouted. "No barking!"

The shooting was not the end of Ivan Ivanych's workout. For a whole hour more, the stranger drove the goose around him on a tether, cracking his whip while the goose had to leap over a hurdle, jump through a hoop, and rear up on his tail with his feet waving in the air. Kashtanka couldn't keep her eyes off of Ivan Ivanych, howled with delight, and several times started to run after him, yelping. Having worn out the goose and himself as well, the stranger mopped his brow and shouted:

"Marya, tell Khavronya Ivanovna to come here!"

A moment later, grunting was heard. Kashtanka growled, put on a brave expression, and moved closer to the stranger, just in case. The door opened and an old woman looked in, muttered something, and let in a very ugly black pig. Paying no attention at all to Kashtanka's growling, the pig raised her snout and grunted happily. She seemed very pleased to see her master, Ivan Ivanych, and the cat. She came up to the cat and gently nudged him under his stomach with her snout, then struck up a conversation with the goose. Her movements, her voice, and the quivering of her tail expressed nothing but good nature. Kashtanka realized at once that it was useless to growl and bark at such a character.

The master took away the sawhorse and shouted:

"Fyodor Timofeyich, you're on!"

The cat got up, stretched lazily, and reluctantly, as if doing a favor, went over to the pig.

"We'll start with the Egyptian Pyramid," said the master.

He spent a long time explaining something, then gave the command, "One . . . two . . . three!" At the word "three," Ivan Ivanych flapped his wings and jumped up onto the pig's bristly back . . . When he had steadied himself by balancing with his wings and neck, Fyodor Timofeyich slowly and lazily, with obvious scorn, looking as if he despised his art and would not give a penny for it, climbed onto the pig's back, then reluctantly got up on the goose and stood on his hind legs. The result was what the stranger called the "Egyptian Pyramid." Kashtanka yapped with delight, but at that moment the old tomcat yawned, lost his balance, and tumbled off the goose. Ivan Ivanych wobbled and fell off, too. The stranger yelled, waved his arms, and began explaining again. After working for a whole hour on the pyramid, the untiring master began teaching Ivan Ivanych to ride the cat, then he started teaching the cat to smoke, and so on.

The lessons ended, the stranger mopped his brow and went out. Fyodor Timofeyich sniffed scornfully, lay down on his mat, and closed his eyes. Ivan Ivanych went to the trough, and the pig was led away by the old woman. The day was so full of new impressions that Kashtanka did not notice where the time went. In the evening, she and her mattress were installed in the room with the dirty wallpaper, where she spent the night in the company of Fyodor Timofeyich and the goose.

CHAPTER FIVE / TALENT! TALENT!

A month went by.

Kashtanka was already used to having a nice dinner every evening and to being called Auntie. She was used to the stranger and to her new companions. Life went on smoothly.

Each day began in the same way. Ivan Ivanych usually woke up first, and he immediately went over to Auntie or the cat, curved his neck, and began talking ardently and persuasively but, as ever, incomprehensibly. Sometimes he held his head high and delivered a long monologue. At first, Kashtanka thought he talked so much because he was very smart, but after a while she lost all respect for him. When he came up to her with his endless speeches, she no longer wagged her tail but treated him as an annoying babbler who wouldn't let anyone sleep, and answered him unceremoniously with a "grrr . . . !"

Fyodor Timofeyich, however, was a gentleman of a very different sort. When he woke up, he didn't make any noise, he didn't move, he didn't even open his eyes. He would have been glad not to wake up at all, for he was obviously none too fond of life. Nothing interested him, he treated everything sluggishly and carelessly, despised everything, and even snorted squeamishly at his delicious dinners.

On waking up, Kashtanka would start walking around the room and sniffing in the corners. Only she and the cat were allowed to walk all over the apartment; the goose had no right to cross the threshold of the little room with dirty wallpaper, and Khavronya Ivanovna lived somewhere in a shed out back and only appeared for lessons. The master slept late, had his tea, and immediately started working on his tricks. Every day the sawhorse, the whip, and the hoops were brought into the room, and every day almost the same things were repeated. The lessons lasted for three or four hours and sometimes left Fyodor Timofeyich so exhausted that he staggered like a drunk man, while Ivan Ivanych opened his beak and gasped for breath and the master got red in the face and couldn't mop the sweat from his brow fast enough.

Lessons and dinner made the days very interesting, but the evenings were rather boring. Usually, in the evening, the master went out somewhere and took the goose and the cat with him. Left alone, Auntie would lie down on her mattress, feeling sad . . . Sadness crept up on her somehow imperceptibly and came over her gradually, as darkness falls upon a room. She would lose all desire to bark, to eat, to run through the rooms, or even to look. Then two vague figures would appear in her imagination, not quite dogs, not quite people, with sympathetic, dear, but incomprehensible physiognomies; but when they appeared, Auntie began wagging her tail, and it seemed to her that somewhere, sometime, she had known and loved them . . .

And each time, as she was falling asleep, these figures brought to mind the smell of glue, wood shavings, and varnish.

One day, when she was already accustomed to her new life, and had turned from a skinny, bony mutt into a sleek, well-cared-for dog, her master came to her, stroked her and said:

"Auntie, it's time you got to work. Enough of this sitting around. I want to make an artiste out of you . . . Would you like to be an artiste?"

And he began teaching her all sorts of things. The first lesson she learned was to stand and walk on her hind legs, which she enjoyed greatly. For the second lesson, she had to jump on her hind legs and catch a piece of sugar that her teacher held high above her head. In the lessons that followed, she danced, ran on the tether, howled to music, rang the bell, and fired the pistol, and in a month she could successfully take Fyodor Timofeyich's place in the "Egyptian Pyramid." She was an eager student and was pleased with her own achievements; running, her tongue hanging out, on a tether, jumping through a hoop, and riding on old Fyodor Timofeyich afforded her the greatest pleasure. She followed each successful trick with a loud, delighted yapping. Her teacher was surprised and also delighted!

"Talent! Talent!" he said, rubbing his hands. "Unquestionable talent! You'll be a positive success!"

And Auntie got so used to the word "talent" that she jumped up each time her master said it, and looked around as if it was her name.

CHAPTER SIX / A TROUBLED NIGHT

Auntie had a dog dream one night that a janitor was chasing her with a broom, and she woke up in a fright.

Her little room was quiet, dark, and very stuffy. The fleas were biting. Auntie had never been afraid of the dark before, but now for some reason she was terrified and felt like barking. In the next room, her master sighed loudly, then, a little later, the pig grunted in her shed, and then everything was silent again. One always feels easier at heart when thinking about food, and so Auntie began thinking about a chicken leg she had stolen from Fyodor Timofeyich that day and hidden in the living room between the cupboard and the wall, where there were many cobwebs and a lot of dust. It might not be a bad idea to go and see if the leg was still there. It was quite possible that her master had found it and eaten it. But she was forbidden to leave the room before morning—that was the rule. Auntie closed her eyes, hoping to fall asleep quickly, because she knew from experience that the sooner one falls asleep, the sooner morning comes. But suddenly, not far from her, a strange cry rang out that made her shudder and jump to her feet. It was Ivan Ivanych, and the cry was not his usual persuading babble but a wild piercing and unnatural shriek, like the creaking of a gate opening. Unable to see or understand anything in the darkness, Auntie felt all the more frightened and growled:

"Gr-r-r . . ."

Some time passed, as long as it takes to gnaw a good bone, but the scream was not repeated. Auntie gradually calmed down and dozed off. She dreamed of two big black dogs with clumps of last year's fur on their haunches and flanks; they were greedily eating mash from a big basin, which gave off white steam and a very delicious smell. Every once in a while they turned around to Auntie, bared their teeth, and snarled, "We won't give you any!" Then a peasant in a sheepskin coat ran out of the house and chased them away with a whip. Auntie went over to the basin and started to eat, but no sooner had the peasant gone out the gate than the two black dogs rushed growling at her, and suddenly, there was another piercing scream.

"Ka-ghee! Ka-ghee-ghee!" cried Ivan Ivanych.

Auntie woke up, jumped to her feet, and, not leaving her mattress, broke into a howling bark. This time it seemed to her that it was not Ivan Ivanych but someone else, some stranger, who was screaming. For some reason, the pig grunted again in her shed.

There was the sound of shuffling slippers, and the master came into the room in his robe, carrying a candle. The wavering light danced over the dirty wallpaper and the ceiling and chased away the darkness. Auntie saw that there was no stranger in the room. Ivan Ivanych was sitting on the floor. He was not asleep. His wings were spread wide, his beak was open, and he generally looked as if he were very tired and thirsty. Old Fyodor Timofeyich was not asleep either. He, too, must have been awakened by the scream.

"What's wrong, Ivan Ivanych?" the master asked the goose. "Why are you screaming? Are you sick?"

The goose was silent. The master felt his neck, stroked his back, and said:

"You're a funny one. You don't sleep yourself, and you won't let anyone else sleep."

When the master went out and took the light with him, darkness came again. Auntie was afraid. The goose did not scream, but again it began to seem to her that a stranger was standing in the dark. The most frightening thing was that she could not bite this stranger, because he was invisible and had no form. And for some reason she thought that something very bad was bound to happen that night. Fyodor Timofeyich was restless too. Auntie heard him stirring on his mat, yawning and shaking his head.

Somewhere outside there was a knocking at a gate, and the pig grunted in the shed. Auntie whined, stretched her front paws out, and put her head on them. In the knocking at the gate, in the grunting of the pig, who for some reason was not asleep, in the darkness and silence, she imagined something as anguished and terrifying as Ivan Ivanych's scream. Everything was uneasy and anxious, but why? Who was this stranger who could not be seen? Now next to Auntie two dull green sparks lit up. It was Fyodor Timofeyich, who approached her for the first time in their acquaintance. What did he want? Auntie licked his paw and, not asking why he had come, howled softly in different tones.

"Ka-ghee!" cried Ivan Ivanych. "Ka-ghee-ghee!"

The door opened again, and the master came in with the candle. The goose was still in the same position, with his beak open and his wings spread. His eyes were shut.

"Ivan Ivanych!" the master called.

The goose did not move. The master sat down on the floor in front of him, looked at him silently for a moment, and said, "Ivan Ivanych, what's the matter? Are you dying or something? Ah, now I remember, I remember!" he cried, clutching his head. "I know what it is! It's because that horse stepped on you today! My God! My God!"

Auntie did not understand what her master was saying, but from the look on his face she saw that he, too, was expecting something terrible. She stretched her muzzle towards the dark window, through which it seemed to her some stranger was looking, and howled.

"He's dying, Auntie!" her master said, clasping his hands. "Yes, yes, dying! Death has come to your room! What are we to do?"

Pale and disturbed, the master went back to his bedroom, sighing and shaking his head. Auntie dreaded being left in the dark, so she followed him. He sat down on his bed and said several times, "My God! What are we going to do?"

Auntie walked around his feet and, not understanding what was causing him such anguish and where all this agitation came from, but trying to understand, she watched his every movement. Fyodor Timofeyich, who rarely left his mat, also came into the master's bedroom and began rubbing against his legs. He shook his head, as if he wanted to shake the painful thoughts out of it, and looked suspiciously under the bed.

The master took a saucer, poured some water into it from a washstand, and went back to the goose.

"Drink, Ivan Ivanych," he said tenderly, setting the saucer down in front of him. "Drink, my dear."

But Ivan Ivanych did not move or open his eyes. The master brought his head down to the saucer and dipped his beak in the water, but the goose did not drink, he only spread his wings wider and let his head lie in the saucer.

"No, there's nothing we can do!" the master sighed. "It's all over. Ivan Ivanych is done for!"

And glittering drops, such as one sees on windowpanes when it rains, ran down his cheeks. Not understanding what was wrong, Auntie and Fyodor Timofeyich huddled close to him, staring in horror at the goose.

"Poor Ivan Ivanych!" said the master, sighing mournfully. "And I was dreaming of how I'd take you to the country in the spring, and we'd go for a walk in the green grass. Dear animal, my good comrade, you're no more! How can I manage now without you?"

It seemed to Auntie that the same thing was going to happen to her, that she, too, for some unknown reason, would close her eyes, stretch out her paws, open her mouth, and everybody would look at her with horror. Apparently, similar thoughts were wandering through Fyodor Timofeyich's head. Never before had the old cat been so sullen and gloomy as now.

Dawn was breaking, and the invisible stranger who had frightened Auntie so much was no longer in the room. When it was already quite light, the janitor came, picked the goose up by the legs, and carried him out. Later the old woman came and took away the trough.

Auntie went to the living room and looked behind the cupboard. The master hadn't eaten her chicken leg; it was still there, covered with dust and cobwebs. But Auntie felt dull, sad, and wanted to cry. She didn't even sniff the leg. She got under the sofa, lay down, and began to whine softly in a thin voice:

"Hnnn . . . hnnn . . . hnnn . . ."

CHAPTER SEVEN / AN UNSUCCESSFUL DEBUT

One fine evening the master walked into the room with the dirty wallpaper and, rubbing his hands, said:

"Well . . ."

He wanted to say something more, but did not say it and left. Auntie had made a close study of his face and voice during her lessons, and she could tell that he was disturbed, worried, maybe even angry. A little later he came back and said:

"Today I'll take Auntie and Fyodor Timofeyich with me. Today, in the Egyptian Pyramid, you, Auntie, will replace the late Ivan Ivanych. Devil knows what will come of it! Nothing's ready, nothing's been learned by heart, we haven't rehearsed enough! It'll be a disgrace, a flop!"

Then he went out again and came back after a minute in a fur coat and top hat. Going over to the cat, he picked him up by the front paws and put him on his chest inside the fur coat, to which Fyodor Timofeyich seemed very indifferent and did not even bother opening his eyes. For him, clearly, it was decidedly all the same: to lie down, or to be picked up by the feet, to sprawl on his mat, or to rest on his master's chest under the fur coat . . .

"Let's go, Auntie," said the master.

Understanding nothing, Auntie wagged her tail and followed him. Soon she was sitting in a sleigh at her master's feet, and heard him say, shivering with cold and worry:

"It'll be a disgrace! A flop!"

The sleigh pulled up in front of a large, peculiar building that looked like a turned-over soup tureen. The long, wide entrance of the building with its three glass doors was lighted by a dozen bright lanterns. The doors opened with a loud clang and, like mouths, swallowed up the people who were milling around by the entrance. There were many people; horses, too, trotted up to the entrance, but there were no dogs to be seen.

The master picked Auntie up and shoved her under his coat with Fyodor Timofeyich. It was dark and stuffy there, but it was warm. Two dull green sparks flashed for a second—the cat, disturbed by his neighbor's cold, rough paws, opened his eyes. Auntie licked his ear and, trying to make herself comfortable, squirmed and crushed the cat under her cold paws and accidentally stuck her head out of the fur coat, but at once gave an angry growl and ducked back inside. She thought she had seen a huge, poorly lit room full of monsters. Horrible heads peered out from the partitions and bars that lined both sides of the room: horses with horns or with enormous ears, and one huge fat mug with a tail where its nose should be and two long gnawed bones sticking out of its mouth.

The cat meowed hoarsely under Auntie's paws, but at that moment the coat was thrown open, the master said, "Hup!" and Fyodor Timofeyich and Auntie jumped to the floor. They were now in a little room with gray plank walls; here, besides a small table with a mirror, a stool, and rags hung in a corner, there was no furniture at all, and instead of a lamp or a candle, a fan-shaped light attached to a little tube in the wall was burning brightly. Fyodor Timofeyich licked his fur where Auntie had rumpled it, got under the stool and lay down. The master, still nervous and rubbing his hands, began to undress . . . He undressed in the same way he usually did at home, preparing to lie down under the flannel blanket, that is, he took off everything except his underclothes, then sat on the stool and, looking in the mirror, started doing the most amazing things to himself. First he put on a wig with a part down the middle and two tufts of hair sticking up like horns. Then he smeared a thick coat of white stuff on his face, and over the white he painted eyebrows, a moustache, and red spots on his cheeks. But his antics did not stop there. Having made such a mess of his face and neck, he began getting into an outlandish, incongruous costume, unlike anything Auntie had ever seen before, either at home or outside. Imagine a pair of the baggiest trousers, made out of chintz with a big flowery print such as is used in tradesmen's houses for curtains or slipcovers, trousers that came up to the armpits, one leg of brown chintz, the other of bright yellow. Having sunk into them, the master then put on a short chintz jacket with a big ruffled collar and a gold star on the back, socks of different colors, and green shoes . . .

Auntie's eyes and soul were dazzled. The white-faced, baggy figure smelled like her master, the voice was her master's familiar voice, yet at moments she had great doubts and almost wanted to back away and bark at this colorful figure. The new place, the fan-shaped light, the smell, the metamorphosis that had come over her master—all this instilled a vague fear in her and a presentiment that she was sure to meet some horror like a fat mug with a tail in place of a nose. What's more, they were playing hateful music somewhere outside the wall and every now and then an incomprehensible roar was heard. Only Fyodor Timofeyich's calmness reassured her. He was most quietly napping under the stool, and didn't open his eyes even when the stool was moved.

A man in a tailcoat and white vest looked into the room and said:

"Miss Arabella is just going on. You're next."

The master didn't answer. He took a small suitcase from under the table, sat down, and waited. From his trembling lips and hands one could see that he was nervous, and Auntie could hear him breathing in short gasps.

"Monsieur Georges, you're on!" someone called outside the door. The master stood up, crossed himself three times, took the cat from under the stool, and put him in the suitcase.

"Come, Auntie," he said softly.

Auntie, who had no idea what was happening, went up to him. He kissed her on the head and put her in next to Fyodor Timofeyich. Then it became dark. Auntie stepped all over the cat, and clawed at the sides of the suitcase, but she was so frightened that she couldn't utter a sound. The suitcase rocked and swayed as if it were floating on water . . .

"Here I am!" the master shouted loudly. "Here I am!" After this shout, Auntie felt the suitcase hit against something solid and stop swaying. There was a loud, deep roar. It sounded as if someone were being slapped, and someone—probably the fat mug with a tail where its nose should be—roared and laughed so loudly that the latch on the suitcase rattled. In response to the roar, the master laughed in a shrill, squeaky voice, not at all the way he laughed at home.

"Ha!" he yelled, trying to outshout the roar. "Most esteemed public! I've just come from the station! My granny dropped dead and left me an inheritance! The suitcase is very heavy—gold, obviously . . . Ha-a! And suddenly we've got a million here! Let's open it right now and have a look . . ."

The latch clicked. Bright light struck Auntie's eyes. She jumped out of the suitcase and, deafened by the roar, ran around her master as fast as she could go, yelping all the while.

"Ha!" shouted the master. "Uncle Fyodor Timofeyich! Dear Auntie! My nice relatives, devil take you all!"

He fell down on the sand, grabbed Auntie and the cat, and started hugging them. Auntie, while he was squeezing her in his embrace, caught a glimpse of that world which fate had brought her to and, struck by its immensity, froze for a moment in amazement and rapture, then tore herself from his arms and, from the keenness of the impression, spun in place like a top. This new world was big and full of bright light, and everywhere she looked from floor to ceiling there were faces, faces, nothing but faces.

"Auntie, allow me to offer you a seat!" the master shouted.

Remembering what that meant, Auntie jumped up on the chair and sat. She looked at her master. His eyes were serious and kind, as usual, but his face, especially his mouth and teeth, were distorted by a wide, fixed grin. He himself guffawed, leaped about, hunched his shoulders, and pretended to be very happy in front of the thousands of faces. Auntie believed in his happiness, and suddenly felt with her whole body that those thousands of faces were all looking at her, and she raised her foxlike head and howled joyfully.

"Sit there, Auntie," the master said to her, "while Uncle and I dance a kamerinsky."

Fyodor Timofeyich, while waiting until he was forced to do stupid things, stood and glanced about indifferently. He danced sluggishly, carelessly, glumly, and by his movements, by his tail and whiskers, one could see that he deeply despised the crowd, the bright lights, his master, and himself . . . Having done his part, he yawned and sat down.

"Well, Auntie," said the master, "now you and I will sing a song, and then we'll dance. All right?"

He took a little flute from his pocket and started playing. Auntie, who couldn't stand music, fidgeted on her chair uneasily and howled. Roars and applause came from all sides. The master bowed, and when things quieted down, he continued playing . . . Just as he hit a very high note, someone high up in the audience gasped loudly.

"Daddy!" a child's voice cried. "That's Kashtanka!"

"Kashtanka it is!" confirmed a cracked, drunken little tenor. "Kashtanka! Fedyushka, so help me God, it's Kashtanka! Phweet!"

A whistle came from the top row, and two voices, one a boy's and the other a man's, called out:

"Kashtanka! Kashtanka!"

Auntie was startled, and looked in the direction of the voices. Two faces—one hairy, drunk, and grinning and the other chubby, pink-cheeked, and frightened—struck her eyes as the bright light had done earlier . . . She remembered, fell off the chair, floundered in the sand, jumped up, and with a joyful yelp ran toward those faces. There was a deafening roar, pierced by whistles and the shrill shout of a child:

"Kashtanka! Kashtanka!"

Auntie jumped over the barrier, then over someone's shoulder, and landed in a box seat. To get to the next tier, she had to leap a high wall. She leaped, but not high enough, and slid back down the wall. Then she was picked up and passed from hand to hand, she licked hands and faces, she kept getting higher and higher, and at last she reached the top row . . .

Half an hour later, Kashtanka was walking down the street, following the people who smelled of glue and varnish. Luka Alexandrych staggered as he went, and instinctively, having been taught by experience, kept as far as possible from the gutter.

"Lying in the abyss of sinfulness in my womb . . . ," he muttered. "And you, Kashtanka, are a bewilderment. Compared to a man, you're like a carpenter compared to a cabinetmaker."

Fedyushka walked beside him wearing his father's cap. Kashtanka watched their backs, and it seemed to her that she had been happily following them all this time, and that her life had not been interrupted for a single moment.

She remembered the little room with dirty wallpaper, the goose, Fyodor Timofeyich, the tasty dinners, the lessons, the circus, but it all now seemed to her like a long, confused, and painful dream . . .

1887

THE NAME-DAY PARTY

I

After her husband's name-day dinner, with its eight courses and endless conversation, his wife, Olga Mikhailovna, went out to the garden. The obligation of constant smiling and talking, the clatter of dishes, the witlessness of the servants, the long breaks between courses, and the corset she had put on to conceal her pregnancy from the guests, had wearied her to the point of exhaustion. She wanted to get far away from the house, to sit in the shade and rest in thoughts of the baby who was to be born to her in about two months. She was used to having these thoughts come to her when she turned from the big avenue to the narrow path on the left; there, in the dense shade of plum and cherry trees, dry branches scratched her shoulders and neck, cobwebs clung to her face, and in her thoughts arose the image of a little person of indefinite sex, with vague features, and it would begin to seem to her that it was not the cobwebs tenderly tickling her face and neck, but that little person; and when, at the end of the path, a flimsy wattle fence appeared, and beyond it fat-bellied beehives with tile lids, when the motionless, stagnant air began to smell of hay and honey, and she could hear the meek buzzing of bees, the little person would take complete possession of Olga Mikhailovna. She would sit down on the bench by a hut of woven willow and begin to think.

This time, too, she came to the bench, sat down, and began to think; but instead of the little person, her imagination pictured the big people whom she had just left. It troubled her deeply that she, the hostess, had abandoned her guests; she also remembered how at dinner her husband Pyotr Dmitrich and her uncle Nikolai Nikolaich had argued over trial by jury, publishing, and women's education. Her husband, as usual, had argued in order to show off his conservative views before the guests, and above all in order to disagree with her uncle, whom he disliked. Her uncle had contradicted him and picked on his every word, in order to show the guests that he, the uncle, in spite of his fifty-nine years, still preserved a youthful freshness of spirit and freedom of thought. And towards the end of the dinner Olga Mikhailovna herself could not hold back and began a lame defense of women's education, not because such education needed defending, but simply because she wanted to annoy her husband, who, in her opinion, was not right. The guests were tired of the argument, but they all found it necessary to mix in and talked a great deal, though none of them cared either about trial by jury or about women's education . . .

Olga Mikhailovna was sitting on the near side of the wattle fence by the hut. The sun was hidden behind the clouds, the trees and the air were overcast, as before rain, but despite that it was hot and stifling. The hay that had been cut under the trees on the eve of St. Peter's day[1] had not been gathered and lay sadly, dotted with faded flowers, giving off a heavy, sickly smell. It was quiet. Beyond the wattle fence bees buzzed monotonously . . .

Unexpectedly, she heard footsteps and voices. Someone was walking down the path to the apiary.

"It's stifling!" a woman's voice said. "Do you think it will rain?"

"It will, my sweet, but not before nightfall," languidly replied a very familiar male voice. "There'll be a good downpour."

Olga Mikhailovna decided that if she quickly hid in the hut, they would not notice her and would pass by, and she would not have to talk and force herself to smile. She picked up her skirt, bent over and went into the hut. Instantly she felt hot, stifling air, like steam, on her face, neck, and arms. Had it not been for the stuffiness and the stale smell of rye bread, dill, and willow, which took her breath away, here, under the thatched roof and in the semi-darkness, would have been an excellent place to hide from the guests and think about the little person. Cozy and quiet.

"What a nice little spot this is!" said the woman's voice. "Let's sit here a while, Pyotr Dmitrich."

Olga Mikhailovna began to look through a gap between two willow switches. She saw her husband, Pyotr Dmitrich, and a guest, Lyubochka Scheller, a seventeen-year-old girl who had recently graduated from boarding school. Pyotr Dmitrich, his hat pushed back on his head, languid and lazy from having drunk a lot at dinner, slouched about by the wattle fence, raking the hay into a pile with his foot; Lyubochka, rosy from the heat and as pretty as ever, stood with her hands behind her back and followed the lazy movements of his big, handsome body.

Olga Mikhailovna knew that her husband was pleasing to women, and—did not like to see him with them. There was nothing special about Pyotr Dmitrich lazily raking up hay so as to sit on it with Lyubochka and chat about trifles; there was nothing special about pretty Lyubochka looking meekly at him; and yet Olga Mikhailovna was annoyed with her husband, and felt frightened and pleased to be able to eavesdrop now.

"Sit down, enchantress," said Pyotr Dmitrich, lowering himself onto the hay and stretching. "That's right. Well, so tell me something."

"Oh, yes! I'll start telling, and you'll fall asleep."

"Me fall asleep? *Allah kerim!*[2] Could I fall asleep when such pretty eyes are looking at me?"

Neither in her husband's words, nor in his sprawling with his hat pushed back in the presence of a guest, was there anything unusual. He was spoiled by women, knew that they liked him, and adopted a special tone in dealing with them, which everyone said was becoming to him. With Lyubochka he was behaving just as he did with all women. But Olga Mikhailovna was still jealous.

"Tell me, please," Lyubochka began after a brief silence, "is it true what they say about you being taken to court?"

"Me? Yes, it's true . . . I've been numbered among the transgressors,[3] my sweet."

"But what for?"

"For nothing, just . . . more from politics," Pyotr Dmitrich yawned.

"The struggle between left and right. I, an obscurantist and routineer, dared to use expressions in official papers that were insulting to such infallible Gladstones[4] as Vladimir Pavlovich Vladimirov and our local justice of the peace, Kuzma Grigoryevich Vostryakov."

Pyotr Dmitrich yawned again and went on:

"The way things are with us, you can speak disapprovingly about the sun, the moon, anything you like, but God forbid you touch the liberals! God forbid! A liberal is the same as one of those nasty dry toadstools that, if you accidentally touch it with your finger, showers you with a cloud of dust."

"What happened to you?"

"Nothing special. The whole to-do flared up over a mere trifle. Some teacher, a runty fellow with a churchy background, addressed Vostryakov with a complaint against a tavernkeeper, accusing him of offensive words and acts in a public place. By all tokens, both the teacher and the tavernkeeper were drunk as fish, and both behaved themselves equally badly. If there was an offense, in any case it was mutual. Vostryakov should have fined them both for disturbing the peace and kicked them out of court—that's all. But how is it with us? With us what always comes first is not the person, the fact, but the trademark and the label. A teacher, no matter how rascally he is, is always right, because he's a teacher; a tavernkeeper is always guilty, because he's a tavernkeeper and a moneygrubber. Vostryakov sentenced the tavernkeeper to jail, so the man turned to the appellate court. The appellate court solemnly confirmed Vostryakov's sentence. Well, I stuck to my own opinion . . . Got a little worked up . . . That's all."

Pyotr Dmitrich spoke calmly, with casual irony. In fact, the impending trial worried him greatly. Olga Mikhailovna remembered how, on returning from the ill-fated appellate court, he had tried his best to conceal from the family how hard it was for him and how displeased he was with himself. As an intelligent man, he could not help feeling that he had gone too far in his own opinion, and how much deception he needed to hide this feeling from himself and from other people! So many unnecessary conversations, so much grumbling and insincere laughter at something that was not funny! Having learned that he was being taken to court, he suddenly felt tired and lost heart, slept poorly, stood at the window more often than usual and drummed on the glass with his fingers. And he was ashamed to admit to his wife that it was hard for him, and that annoyed her . . .

"They say you were in Poltava province?" asked Lyubochka.

"Yes, I was," replied Pyotr Dmitrich. "I came back two days ago."

"It must be nice there?"

"Nice. Even very nice. I must tell you, I got there just during the haymaking, and in the Ukraine, haymaking is the most poetic time. Here we have a big house, a big garden, lots of people and fuss, so you don't see them making hay; here everything goes by imperceptibly. On my farm there, the forty acres of fields are like in the palm of your hand; whichever window you stand at, you see the mowers from everywhere. They mow the field, they mow in the garden, there are no guests, no fuss either, so that like it or not all you hear, see, and feel is the haymaking. The yard and the rooms smell of hay, from dawn to dusk the scythes ring. Generally Khokhlandia[5] is a nice country. Would you believe it, when I was drinking water from the wells, or foul vodka in the Jews' taverns, when the sounds of a Ukrainian fiddle and tambourine reached me on a quiet evening, an enchanting thought tempted me—to settle on my farm and live there as long as I could stand it, away from these court sessions, clever conversations, philosophizing women, drawn-out dinners . . ."

Pyotr Dmitrich was not lying. It was hard for him and he really wanted to rest. He had gone to Poltava province only so as not to see his study, servants, acquaintances, and all that could remind him of his wounded vanity and his mistakes.

Lyubochka suddenly jumped up and waved her arms in fright.

"Ah, a bee, a bee!" she shrieked. "It'll sting me!"

"Nonsense, it won't sting!" said Pyotr Dmitrich. "What a coward you are!"

"No, no, no!" cried Lyubochka and, looking back at the bee, she quickly walked away.

Pyotr Dmitrich walked behind her and followed her with his eyes tenderly and sadly. Looking at her, he must have been thinking of his farm, of solitude, and—who knows?—maybe even of how warm and cozy his life on the farm would be if his wife were this girl—young, pure, fresh, unspoiled by education, not pregnant . . .

When the voices and footsteps died away, Olga Mikhailovna came out of the hut and headed for the house. She felt like crying. She was now intensely jealous over her husband. She understood that Pyotr Dmitrich was tired, displeased with himself, and ashamed, and when people are ashamed they hide first of all from their near ones and confide in strangers; she also understood that Lyubochka was not a threat, no more so than all the women who were now having coffee in the house. But in general everything was incomprehensible, frightening, and it now seemed to Olga Mikhailovna that Pyotr Dmitrich only half belonged to her . . .

"He has no right!" she murmured, trying to make sense of her jealousy and her vexation with her husband. "He has no right at all! I'll speak my mind to him at once!"

She decided to find her husband at once and speak her mind to him: it was vile, utterly vile, that he pleased other women and sought it out like manna from heaven; it was unfair and dishonest that he gave to others what by right belonged to his wife, that he hid his soul and conscience from his wife and revealed them to the first pretty face that came along. What wrong had his wife done him? Where was her fault? Finally, she had long been sick of his lying: he was constantly showing off, mincing, flirting, saying things he did not mean, and trying to appear as other than what he was and what he ought to be. Why this lying? Was it becoming in a decent man? If he lied, he insulted himself and those to whom he lied, and showed no respect for the things he lied about. Did he not understand that if he minced and posed at the court bench or theorized over dinner about the prerogatives of authority only so as to spite her uncle—did he not understand that by doing that he was belittling the court, and himself, and all those who heard and saw him?

Coming out to the big avenue, Olga Mikhailovna put on an expression as if she had just gone about some household necessity. On the terrace the men were drinking liqueur and eating berries; one of them, a court prosecutor, a stout old man, a banterer and wit, must have been telling some dirty joke, because, seeing the hostess, he suddenly clapped his hand to his fat lips, goggled his eyes, and hunched over. Olga Mikhailovna did not like provincial functionaries. She did not care for their clumsy, ceremonious wives, who gossiped, paid frequent visits, and flattered her husband, whom they all hated. And now, when they were drinking, had eaten well, and were not about to leave, she felt their presence wearisome to the point of anguish, but, so as not to appear ungracious, she smiled affably to the prosecutor and shook her finger at him. She crossed the reception room and the drawing room smiling and with a look as if she were going to give orders and take care of things. "God forbid someone stops me!" she thought, but she forced herself to stop in the drawing room and out of politeness listened to the young man who was playing the piano. She stood there for a moment, cried, "Bravo, Monsieur Georges!" and, after clapping twice, went on.

She found her husband in his study. He was sitting at his desk and thinking about something. His face was stern, pensive, and guilty. This was no longer the Pyotr Dmitrich who had argued over dinner and whom his guests knew, but a different one—tired, guilty, and displeased with himself—who was known only to his wife. He must have gone to his study to get cigarettes. Before him lay an open cigarette case full of cigarettes, and one hand was lowered into the desk drawer. As he was taking out cigarettes, he had frozen like that.

Olga Mikhailovna felt sorry for him. It was clear as day that the man was anguished and on edge, perhaps struggling with himself. Olga Mikhailovna silently approached the desk; wishing to show that she had forgotten the dinnertime argument and was no longer angry, she closed the cigarette case and put it in his pocket.

"What shall I say to him?" she thought. "I'll say that lying is like a forest: the further in you go, the more difficult it is to get out. I'll say: you got carried away with your false role and went too far; you offended people who are attached to you and have done you no wrong. Go and apologize to them, laugh at yourself, and you'll feel better. And if you want peace and solitude, we'll go away together."

Meeting his wife's eyes, Pyotr Dmitrich suddenly gave his face the expression it had had at dinner and in the garden—indifferent and slightly mocking—yawned, and stood up.

"It's past five," he said, glancing at his watch. "If our guests are merciful and leave at eleven, we've still got another six hours to wait. Good fun, to say the least!"

And, whistling some tune, slowly, with his usual dignified gait, he left the study. She could hear his dignified footsteps as he walked through the reception room, then through the drawing room, laughed dignifiedly at something, and said "Bra-o! Bra-o!" to the young man at the piano. Soon his footsteps died away: he must have gone out to the garden. And now it was not jealousy or vexation, but a real hatred of his footsteps, his insincere laughter and voice, that came over Olga Mikhailovna. She went to the window and looked out at the garden. Pyotr Dmitrich was already walking down the avenue. One hand in his pocket, snapping the fingers of the other, his head thrown slightly back, he walked with dignity, looking as if he were quite satisfied with himself, his dinner, his digestion, and nature . . .

Two small schoolboys appeared in the avenue, the children of the landowner Madame Chizhevskaya, who had just arrived, and with them a student-tutor in a white tunic and very tight trousers. Going up to Pyotr Dmitrich, the children and the student stopped and probably congratulated him on his name-day. Handsomely moving his shoulders, he patted the children's cheeks and casually shook the student's hand without looking at him. The student probably praised the weather and compared it with Petersburg, because Pyotr Dmitrich said loudly and in a tone as if he were talking not to a guest, but to a court usher or a witness:

"Well, sir, so it's cold in your Petersburg? And here, my good man, we have seasonable weather and abundance of the fruits of the earth.[6] Eh? What?"

And, putting one hand in his pocket and snapping the fingers of the other, he walked on. All the while, until he disappeared behind the hazelnut bushes, Olga Mikhailovna gazed at the back of his head in perplexity. Where did this thirty-four-year-old man get such a dignified generalissimo's gait? Where did he get such a weighty, handsome way of walking? Where did he get such a superior vibration in his voice—"well, sir," "hm-yes, sir," "my good man," and all that?

Olga Mikhailovna recalled how, in the first months of marriage, so as not to be bored alone at home, she had driven to the appellate court, where Pyotr Dmitrich occasionally presided in place of her godfather, Count Alexei Petrovich. On the presidential chair, in his uniform, with a chain on his chest, he was totally transformed. Majestic gestures, a thundering voice, "well, sir" and "hm-yes, sir," the condescending tone . . . All that was ordinarily human, his own, that Olga Mikhailovna was used to seeing in him at home, was swallowed up in grandeur, and it was not Pyotr Dmitrich who sat in the chair, but some other man, whom everyone called Mister President. The consciousness that he was in power kept him from sitting calmly in his place, and he looked for an occasion to ring the bell, glance sternly at the public, shout . . . Whence came this nearsightedness and deafness, when he would suddenly begin to see and hear poorly, and, wincing majestically, demanded that people speak louder and come closer to the table. From the height of his grandeur he poorly distinguished faces and sounds, so it seemed that if Olga Mikhailovna herself had come up to him in those moments, even to her he would have shouted, "What is your last name?" He spoke familiarly to peasant witnesses, yelled so loudly at the public that his voice could be heard outside, and behaved impossibly with lawyers. If an attorney happened to speak, Pyotr Dmitrich sat slightly sideways to him and squinted at the ceiling, wishing to show thereby that there was no need for any attorney here and that he did not recognize or listen to him; if a gray-clad local attorney spoke, Pyotr Dmitrich was all ears, and looked the attorney up and down with a mocking, annihilating gaze: now here's a real lawyer for you! "What do you mean to say by that?" he would interrupt. If a grandiloquent attorney used some sort of foreign word and, for instance, said "factitious" instead of "fictitious," Pyotr Dmitrich would suddenly perk up and ask: "How's that, sir? What? Factitious? What might that mean?"—and then observe didactically: "Do not use words you don't understand." And the attorney, finishing his speech, would leave the table red-faced and all in a sweat, while Pyotr Dmitrich, with a self-contented smile, would throw himself against the back of his chair in celebration of his victory. In his treatment of lawyers he imitated Count Alexei Petrovich somewhat, but when the count said, for instance, "Defense, keep quiet for a little!" it came out unaffectedly and with elderly good nature, while from Pyotr Dmitrich it sounded rude and forced.

II

Applause was heard. The young man had finished playing. Olga Mikhailovna remembered about her guests and hastened to the drawing room.

"Listening to you, I forgot myself," she said, going to the piano. "I forgot myself. You have an astonishing ability! But don't you find our piano out of tune?"

At that moment the two schoolboys came into the drawing room and the student along with them.

"My God, Mitya and Kolya?" Olga Mikhailovna said drawlingly and joyfully, going to meet them. "How big you've become! I hardly recognized you! And where is your mama?"

"Congratulations on your husband's name-day," the student began casually. "I wish you all the best. Ekaterina Andreevna sends her best wishes and her apologies. She's not feeling well."

"How unkind of her! I've been waiting all day for her. And did you come from Petersburg long ago?" Olga Mikhailovna asked the student. "How's the weather there now?" And without waiting for an answer, she looked tenderly at the boys and repeated, "How big you've grown! Just recently they came here with a nanny, and now they're already schoolboys! The old grow older, and the young grow up . . . Have you eaten?"

"Ah, don't go to any trouble, please!" said the student.

"So you haven't eaten?"

"For God's sake, don't go to any trouble!"

"But don't you want to eat?" Olga Mikhailovna asked in a rude and harsh voice, impatiently and with vexation—it came out of her inadvertently, but she immediately coughed, smiled, and blushed. "How big you've grown!" she said softly.

"Don't go to any trouble, please!" the student said again.

The student asked her not to go to any trouble, the children said nothing; obviously, all three wanted to eat. Olga Mikhailovna took them to the dining room and told Vassily to set the table.

"Your mother is unkind!" she said, seating them. "She's completely forgotten me. Unkind, unkind, unkind . . . Tell her so. And what are you studying?" she asked the student.

"Medicine."

"Well, and I have a weakness for doctors, just imagine. I'm very sorry my husband isn't a doctor. What courage one must have, for instance, to do surgery or cut up corpses! Terrible! You're not afraid? I think I'd die of fear. You'll have some vodka, of course?"

"Don't go to any trouble, please."

"After traveling, you need a drink. I'm a woman, but I sometimes drink, too. Mitya and Kolya will have Malaga. It's weak wine, don't worry. What fine fellows, really! Fit to be married off."

Olga Mikhailovna talked non-stop. She knew from experience that, in entertaining guests, it was much easier and more relaxing to talk than to listen. When you talk, there is no need to strain your attention, to invent answers to questions and change the expression of your face. But she had inadvertently asked a serious question, the student began to reply at length, and like it or not she had to listen. The student knew that she had once taken some courses, and therefore, in addressing her, he tried to seem serious.

"What are you studying?" she asked, forgetting that she had already asked this question.

"Medicine."

Olga Mikhailovna remembered that she had not been with the ladies for a long time.

"Are you? Meaning you're going to be a doctor?" she said, getting up. "That's good. I'm sorry I didn't take courses in medicine. So have your dinner here, gentlemen, and then come out to the garden. I'll introduce you to the young ladies."

As she went out, she glanced at her watch: it was five minutes to six. She was surprised that time passed so slowly and dreaded the thought that midnight, when the guests would leave, was still six hours away. How to kill those six hours? What phrases to speak? How to behave with her husband?

There was not a soul in the drawing room or on the terrace. All the guests had wandered off to the garden.

"I'll have to offer them a stroll in the birch grove before tea, or a boat ride," Olga Mikhailovna thought, hurrying to the croquet ground, where voices and laughter could be heard. "And the old ones can sit and play whist . . ."

The footman Grigory came walking towards her from the croquet ground carrying empty bottles.

"Where are the ladies?" she asked.

"In the raspberry patch. The master's there, too."

"Oh, my God!" someone shouted in exasperation on the croquet ground. "I've told you the same thing a thousand times! To know the Bulgars, you have to see them! You can't judge by the newspapers!"

Owing to this shout, or to something else, Olga Mikhailovna suddenly felt a great weakness all through her body, especially in her legs and shoulders. She suddenly wanted not to speak, not to hear, not to move.

"Grigory," she said wearily and with effort, "when you're serving tea or whatever, please don't address me, don't ask, don't speak about anything . . . Do everything yourself and . . . and don't stamp your feet. I beg you . . . I can't, because . . ."

She did not finish and walked off to the croquet ground, but on the way she remembered the ladies and turned to the raspberry patch. The sky, the air, and the trees were still overcast and promised rain; it was hot and sultry; huge flocks of crows, anticipating bad weather, circled cawing over the garden. The closer to the kitchen garden, the more overgrown, dark, and narrow were the pathways; in one of them, which was hiding in a thicket of wild pear trees, crabapples, young oaks, and hops, whole clouds of tiny black flies surrounded Olga Mikhailovna; she covered her face with her hands and forced herself to imagine the little person . . . In her mind's eye flashed Grigory, Mitya, Kolya, the faces of the peasants who had come in the morning with congratulations . . .

She heard someone's footsteps and opened her eyes. Her uncle Nikolai Nikolaich was quickly walking towards her.

"It's you, dear? I'm very glad . . . ," he began breathlessly. "Just a couple of words . . ." He wiped his clean-shaven red chin with a hand-kerchief, then suddenly stepped back, clasped his hands, and rolled his eyes. "My dear, how long will this go on?" he said quickly, sputtering. "I ask you: where are the limits? I'm not even saying that his overbearing views demoralize the milieu, that he insults all that is best and most sacred in me and in any honest, thinking man—I'm not saying that, but let him at least be decent! What is it? He shouts, he roars, he minces, he acts like some sort of Bonaparte, won't let anyone say a word . . . devil knows about him! Some sort of majestic gestures, generalissimo laughter, condescending tone! Allow me to ask: Who is he? I ask you: Who is he? His wife's husband, a small landowning titular councillor, who had the luck to marry a rich girl! An upstart, a junker, like so many others! Shchedrin described the type![7] I swear to God, it's one of two things: either he's suffering from megalomania, or that imbecilic old rat, Count Alexei Petrovich, is right when he says that today's children and young people take a long time growing up, and play at being cabbies or generalissimos till they're forty years old!"

"That's true, true . . . ," Olga Mikhailovna agreed. "Let me pass."

"Now judge for yourself, what will come of it?" her uncle went on, blocking her way. "How will this playing the conservative and the generalissimo end? He's already being taken to court! To court! I'm very glad! His shouting and showing off have landed him in the dock! And not in the circuit court or whatever, but in the appellate court! It's hard to think up anything worse! Second, he's quarreled with everybody! Today is his name-day and, look, neither Vostryakov, nor Yakhontov, nor Vladimirov, nor Shevud, nor the count has come . . . It seems there's nobody more conservative than Count Alexei Petrovich—and even he hasn't come. And he'll never come again! You'll see, he won't come!"

"Ah, my God, but what have I got to do with it?" Olga Mikhailovna asked.

"What do you mean, what? You're his wife! You're intelligent, you've taken courses, it's in your power to make an honest worker of him!"

"My courses didn't teach how to influence difficult people. It seems I'll have to apologize to you all for having taken courses!" Olga Mikhailovna said sharply. "Listen, Uncle, if you heard the same scales being played right in your ear all day long, you wouldn't just sit and listen, you'd run away. All year round, all day long, I hear the same thing over and over. You must finally take pity, gentlemen!"

Her uncle assumed a very serious expression, then looked at her inquisitively and twisted his lips into a mocking smile.

"So that's how it is!" he intoned in an old-womanish voice. "Sorry, ma'am!" he said and bowed ceremoniously. "If you yourself have fallen under his influence and changed your convictions, you should have told me sooner. Sorry, ma'am!"

"Yes, I've changed my convictions!" she cried. "Rejoice!"

"Sorry, ma'am!"

Her uncle bowed ceremoniously for a last time, somehow sideways, and, hunching up, scraped his foot and went back inside.

"Fool," thought Olga Mikhailovna. "Let him take himself home."

She found the ladies and the young people in the raspberry patch by the kitchen garden. Some were eating raspberries; others, who were already sick of raspberries, wandered through the beds of strawberries or rummaged among the sweet peas. A little to one side of the raspberry patch, by a sprawling apple tree, propped up all around with palings pulled from an old fence, Pyotr Dmitrich was mowing the grass. His hair fell over his forehead, his necktie was untied, his watch chain hung from the buttonhole. His every step and swing of the scythe showed skill and the presence of enormous physical strength. Next to him stood Lyubochka and the daughters of a neighbor, Colonel Bukreev, Natalya and Valentina, or, as everybody called them, Nata and Vata, anemic and unhealthily fat blond girls of about sixteen or seventeen, in white dresses, looking remarkably alike. Pyotr Dmitrich was teaching them to mow.

"It's very simple . . . ," he was saying. "You need only know how to hold the scythe and not get too excited, that is, not use more strength than necessary. Like this . . . Want to give it a try?" He offered the scythe to Lyubochka. "Go on!"

Lyubochka clumsily took hold of the scythe, suddenly blushed and laughed.

"Don't be shy, Lyubov Alexandrovna!" Olga Mikhailovna shouted loudly enough for the other ladies to hear her and know she was with them. "Don't be shy! You must learn! You'll marry a Tolstoyan, and he'll make you mow."[8]

Lyubochka raised the scythe, but burst out laughing again and, weak from laughter, lowered it at once. She was embarrassed and pleased to be spoken to as a grown-up. Nata, not smiling and not embarrassed, with a cold, serious face, took the scythe, swung it, and got it tangled in the grass; Vata, also not smiling, cold and serious like her sister, silently took the scythe and stuck it into the ground. Having accomplished that, the two sisters linked arms and silently went off to the raspberry patch.

Pyotr Dmitrich laughed and frolicked like a little boy, and this childishly frolicksome mood, when he became exceedingly good-natured, suited him much more than any other. Olga Mikhailovna loved him like that. But his boyishness usually did not last long. And this time, too, having frolicked with the scythe, he found it necessary for some reason to give a serious tinge to his frolicking.

"When I'm mowing, I feel myself more healthy and normal," he said. "If I were forced to be content only with intellectual life, I think I'd go out of my mind. I feel that I wasn't born a cultivated man! I want to mow, to plow, to sow, to break in horses . . ."

And a conversation began between Pyotr Dmitrich and the ladies about the advantages of physical work, about culture, then about the harmfulness of money, of property. Listening to her husband, Olga Mikhailovna for some reason remembered about her dowry.

"The time will come," she thought, "when he will not forgive me for being richer than he is. He's proud and touchy. He may well come to hate me because he owes me so much."

She stopped near Colonel Bukreev, who was eating raspberries and also taking part in the conversation.

"Come," he said, making way for Olga Mikhailovna and Pyotr Dmitrich. "The ripest are here . . . And so, sir, according to Proudhon," he went on, raising his voice, "property is theft.[9] But I must confess that I don't acknowledge Proudhon and don't consider him a philosopher. For me the French have no authority, God help them!"

"Well, when it comes to these Proudhons and various Buckles, I'm a washout," said Pyotr Dmitrich. "Concerning philosophy, address yourself to her, my spouse. She took some courses and knows all these Schopenhauers and Proudhons inside out . . ."[10]

Olga Mikhailovna felt bored again. She again went through the garden, down the narrow path, past the apple and pear trees, and again she looked as if she were going about a very important chore. Here was the gardener's cottage . . . On the porch sat the gardener's wife, Varvara, and her four small children with big, close-cropped heads. Varvara was also pregnant and was to give birth, by her calculations, around the day of Elijah the prophet.[11] Having greeted her, Olga Mikhailovna silently looked at her and her children and asked:

"Well, how do you feel?"

"All right . . ."

Silence ensued. It was as if the two women silently understood each other.

"It's scary giving birth for the first time," Olga Mikhailovna said, after some thought. "I keep feeling I won't come through it, I'll die."

"It seemed that way to me, too, but here I am alive . . . We imagine all sorts of things!"

Varvara, already pregnant for the fifth time and experienced, looked down somewhat on her mistress and spoke to her in a didactic tone, and Olga Mikhailovna could not help feeling her authority; she wanted to talk about her fear, about the baby, about her feelings, but she was afraid that to Varvara it would seem petty and naïve. And she kept silent and waited for Varvara to say something herself.

"Olya, let's go home!" Pyotr Dmitrich called from the raspberry patch.

Olga Mikhailovna liked keeping silent, waiting, and looking at Varvara. She would have agreed to stand like that, silently and needlessly, until nightfall. But she had to go. She no sooner stepped away from the cottage than Lyubochka, Nata, and Vata came running to meet her. The latter two stopped a few feet away and stood as if rooted to the spot, but Lyubochka ran up to her and hung on her neck.

"My dearest! My darling! My precious!" She started kissing her face and neck. "Let's go and have tea on the island!"

"On the island! On the island!" the identical Nata and Vata both said at once without smiling.

"But it's going to rain, my dears."

"It won't, it won't!" Lyubochka cried, making a tearful face. "Everybody's agreed to go! My dearest, my darling!"

"They're all going to go and have tea on the island," said Pyotr Dmitrich, coming up. "Give the orders . . . We'll all go by boat, and the samovars and the rest should be sent with the servants in a carriage."

He walked beside his wife and took her under the arm. Olga

Mikhailovna wanted to say something unpleasant to her husband, something sharp, maybe even to mention the dowry—the harsher the better, she felt. She thought a little and said:

"Why is it Count Alexei Petrovich didn't come? Such a pity!"

"I'm very glad he didn't come," Pyotr Dmitrich lied. "That holy fool bores me stiff."

"But you waited for him so impatiently before dinner!"

III

Half an hour later all the guests were already crowding on the bank by the piling where the boats were moored. They all talked and laughed a lot, and fussed about so much that they were unable to settle into the boats. Three boats were already crammed full of passengers, and two stood empty. The keys for these two had disappeared somewhere, and messengers kept running from the river to the house in search of them. Some said Grigory had the keys, others that they were with the steward, and a third group advised sending for a blacksmith and breaking the locks. They all talked at once, interrupting and drowning each other out. Pyotr Dmitrich paced up and down the bank and shouted:

"Devil knows what's going on! The keys should always lie on the windowsill in the entryway! Who dared take them from there? The steward can get his own boat if he wants!"

The keys were finally found. Then it turned out that two oars were missing. There was more turmoil. Pyotr Dmitrich, who was bored with pacing up and down, jumped into a long, narrow dugout made from a poplar trunk, rocked, nearly fell into the water, and pushed off. One by one the other boats set out after him, to the loud laughter and shrieking of the young ladies.

The white cloudy sky, the riverbank trees, the bulrushes, and the boats with people and oars were reflected in the water as in a mirror; under the boats, far down in the depths, in the bottomless abyss, there was also a sky and flying birds. One bank, on which the manor house stood, was high, steep, and all covered with trees; on the other, gently sloping, wide water-meadows showed greenly and creeks glistened.

The boats went some hundred yards and, beyond the mournfully drooping willows, on the sloping bank, appeared cottages and a herd of cows; there was singing, drunken shouting, and the sounds of a concertina.

Boats darted here and there on the river with fishermen going to set their nets for the night. In one little boat sat some reveling music-lovers, playing homemade violins and cellos.

Olga Mikhailovna sat at the tiller. She smiled affably and talked a lot to entertain her guests, while casting sidelong glances at her husband. He floated in his dugout ahead of everybody, standing and working one oar. His light, sharp-prowed little dugout, which the guests all called a deathtrap, and Pyotr Dmitrich for some reason called *Penderaklia*,[12] raced along quickly; it had a lively, cunning expression and seemed to hate the heavy Pyotr Dmitrich, waiting for an appropriate moment to slip from under his feet. Olga Mikhailovna kept glancing at her husband, and was repulsed by his good looks, which everyone admired, the nape of his neck, his pose, his familiar manner with women; she hated all the women sitting in her boat, was jealous, and at the same time kept jumping every moment, afraid that the unsteady little dugout might turn over and cause a disaster.

"Easy, Pyotr!" she cried, her heart sinking with fear. "Get into the boat. We believe you're brave without that!"

She was also uneasy about the people sitting in the boat with her. They were all ordinary people, not bad, like many others, but now each of them seemed extraordinary and bad to her. In each of them she saw nothing but falseness. "Take," she thought, "that brown-haired young man with gold-rimmed spectacles and a handsome little beard, now working an oar: he's a rich, well-nourished, and eternally happy mama's boy, whom everyone considers an honest, freethinking, progressive man. It's not even a year since he finished university and came to live in the district, but he already says of himself: 'We zemstvo activists.'[13] But a year will go by, and he, like so many others, will get bored, leave for Petersburg, and, to justify his flight, will go around saying that the zemstvo is good for nothing and he's disappointed. And from the other boat his young wife never takes her eyes off him, and believes that he's a 'zemstvo activist,' just as she'll believe a year from now that the zemstvo is good for nothing. Or take that plump, clean-shaven gentleman in the straw hat with a wide ribbon and with an expensive cigar in his teeth. That one likes to say: 'It's time we abandoned fantasies and got down to business!' He has Yorkshire pigs, Butlerov's beehives,[14] rapeseed, pineapples, an oil press, a cheese dairy, and Italian double-entry bookkeeping. Yet every summer, in order to spend the fall with his mistress in Crimea, he sells some forest for felling and mortgages his land bit by bit. Or take Uncle Nikolai Nikolaich, who is angry with Pyotr Dmitrich and yet for some reason doesn't go home!"

Olga Mikhailovna kept looking at the other boats, and saw in them only uninteresting cranks, play-actors or small-minded people. She recalled all those she knew in the district, and could not recall a single person of whom she could say or think anything good. To her they all seemed giftless, bland, limited, narrow-minded, false, heartless, they all said what they did not think and did what they did not want. Boredom and despair stifled her; she wanted to suddenly stop smiling, jump up and shout: "I'm sick of you!" and then leap from the boat and swim ashore.

"Gentlemen, let's take Pyotr Dmitrich in tow!" someone shouted.

"In tow! In tow!" all the others chimed in. "Olga Mikhailovna, take your husband in tow."

To take him in tow, Olga Mikhailovna, who was sitting at the tiller, had to seize the moment and deftly catch hold of the *Penderaklia* by the chain at the bow. As she leaned over for the chain, Pyotr Dmitrich winced and looked at her in alarm.

"I hope you won't catch cold here!" he said.

"If you fear for me and the child, why do you torment me?" thought Olga Mikhailovna.

Pyotr Dmitrich admitted defeat and, not wishing to be towed, jumped from the *Penderaklia* into the boat, which was already crammed with passengers, and he jumped so carelessly that the boat heeled over badly and everyone cried out in terror.

"He jumped like that to please the women," Olga Mikhailovna thought. "He knows it looks good . . ."

From boredom, as she thought, from vexation, forced smiles, and the discomfort she felt in her whole body, her hands and feet began to tremble. To conceal this trembling from the guests, she tried to speak louder, to laugh, to move . . .

"If I suddenly happen to burst into tears," she thought, "I'll say I have a toothache . . ."

But here, finally, the boats pulled in at the island of "Good Hope." That was the name of the peninsula formed by a sharp bend in the river, covered by an old grove of birches, oaks, willows, and poplars. Tables were already standing under the trees, there was smoke from the samovars, and Vassily and Grigory, in tailcoats and white knitted gloves, were already busy setting the places. On the other bank, across from "Good Hope," stood the wagons that had delivered the provisions. The baskets and bags of provisions were ferried across from the wagons to the island in a little dugout closely resembling the *Penderaklia*. The footmen, the drivers, even the peasant who sat in the dugout had solemn name-day expressions on their faces, such as only children and servants have.

While Olga Mikhailovna was brewing the tea and filling the first glasses, the guests busied themselves with liqueurs and sweets. Then the turmoil set in that is usual during the tea-drinking at picnics, very boring and tiresome for hostesses. Grigory and Vassily had barely had time to serve when hands were already reaching out to Olga Mikhailovna with empty glasses. One asked for it without sugar, another wanted it stronger, another weaker, another said no thank you. Olga Mikhailovna had to remember and then call out: "Ivan Petrovich, it was you without sugar?" or "Gentlemen, who asked for it weak?" But the one who asked for it weak or without sugar no longer remembered and, carried away by a pleasant conversation, took the first glass that came along. A short distance from the table, dejected figures wandered about like shadows, pretending to be looking for mushrooms in the grass or reading the labels on boxes— they were those for whom there were not enough glasses. "Have you had tea?" Olga Mikhailovna would ask, and the one to whom she addressed the question would beg her not to worry and say, "I can wait," though for the hostess it was better if the guests did not wait, but hurried.

Some, caught up in conversation, drank their tea slowly, clinging to their glasses for half an hour, while others, especially those who had drunk a lot at dinner, stood by the table and drank off glass after glass, so that Olga Mikhailovna barely had time to refill them. One young joker drank his tea through a lump of sugar and kept saying: "Sinner that I am, I love to indulge in the Chinese herb." Again and again he asked with a deep sigh: "One more little shardful, please!" He drank a lot, bit his sugar loudly, and thought it was all funny and original and that he imitated a merchant perfectly. No one realized that all these trifles were a torment for the hostess, and it was hard to realize, because Olga Mikhailovna smiled affably all the while and babbled nonsense.

And she was not feeling well . . . She was vexed by the crowd, the laughter, the questions, the joker, the dazed servants who were run off their feet, the children's fidgety presence by the table; she was vexed that Vata looked like Nata, Kolya like Mitya, and it was impossible to tell which of them had had tea and which had not. She felt that her forced welcoming smile was turning into an angry expression, and it seemed to her that she might burst into tears any moment.

"Rain, ladies and gentlemen!" someone shouted.

They all looked up at the sky.

"Yes, rain indeed . . . ," Pyotr Dmitrich confirmed and wiped his cheek.

The sky let fall only a few drops, there was no real rain yet, but the guests abandoned the tea and began to hurry. At first they all wanted to go in the carriages, but they changed their minds and headed for the boats. Olga Mikhailovna, on the pretext of having to quickly make arrangements for supper, asked permission to leave the company behind and drive home in a carriage.

Sitting in the carriage, first of all she let her face rest from smiling. She drove through the village with an angry face, and with an angry face responded to the bowing of the peasants she met. On reaching home, she went by the back door to the bedroom and lay down on her husband's bed.

"Good God," she whispered, "why this forced labor? Why do these people mill around here and pretend they're having fun? Why do I smile and lie? I don't understand, I don't understand!"

She heard footsteps and voices. It was the guests returning.

"Let them," thought Olga Mikhailovna. "I'll lie here a while longer."

But a maid came into the bedroom and said:

"Marya Grigorievna's leaving, ma'am."

Olga Mikhailovna leaped up, straightened her hair, and hurried out.

"What's this, Marya Grigorievna?" she began in an offended voice, going up to Marya Grigorievna. "Where are you rushing off to?"

"I must, darling, I must! I've stayed too long as it is. I have children waiting at home."

"That's unkind! Why didn't you bring your children with you?"

"My dear, if you'll allow me, I'll bring them to you some weekday, but today . . ."

"Ah, please do," Olga Mikhailovna interrupted. "I'll be very glad! Your children are so sweet! Kiss them all for me . . . But, really, you hurt my feelings! Why the hurry, I don't understand."

"I must, I must . . . Goodbye, dear. Take care of yourself. Knowing the condition you're in now . . ."

The two women kissed. After accompanying the guest to her carriage, Olga Mikhailovna went to the ladies in the drawing room. There the lamps were already lit, and the gentlemen were sitting down to play cards.

IV

The guests began to leave after supper, at a quarter past midnight. Seeing her guests off, Olga Mikhailovna stood on the porch and said:

"You really should take a shawl! It's getting a bit chilly. God forbid you should catch cold!"

"Don't worry, Olga Mikhailovna," the guests replied, seating themselves. "Well, goodbye! Mind yourself, we'll be expecting you! Don't disappoint us!"

"Who-o-a!" The coachman held back the horses.

"Off we go, Denis! Goodbye, Olga Mikhailovna!"

"Kiss the children for me!"

The carriage set off and disappeared at once into the darkness. In the red circle that the lamp cast on the road a new pair or troika of impatient horses would appear, and the silhouette of a driver with his arms stretched forward. Again kisses and reproaches began, and entreaties to come again or to take a shawl. Pyotr Dmitrich kept running out from the front hall to help the ladies get into the carriages.

"You go by Efremovshchina now," he instructed the coachman. "It's closer by Mankino, but the road is worse. God forbid you should overturn the carriage . . . Goodbye, my sweet! *Mille compliments* to your artist!"

"Goodbye, Olga Mikhailovna, darling! Go inside or you'll catch cold! It's damp!"

"Who-o-a! Behave yourself!"

"What horses have you got here?" asked Pyotr Dmitrich.

"Bought from Khaidarov during Lent," the coachman replied.

"Fine horsies . . ."

And Pyotr Dmitrich patted the outrunner on the rump.

"Well, off you go! God be with you!"

Finally the last guest left. The red circle on the road swayed, floated to one side, shrank, and went out—this was Vassily taking the lamp from the porch. On previous occasions, after seeing off their guests, Pyotr Dmitrich and Olga Mikhailovna usually began leaping about face to face in the reception room, clapping their hands and singing: "Gone! gone! gone!" But this time Olga Mikhailovna was not up to it. She went to the bedroom, undressed, and got into bed.

It seemed to her that she would fall asleep at once and sleep soundly. Her legs and shoulders ached, her head was heavy from talking, and, as earlier, she felt some sort of discomfort all over her body. She covered her head, lay there for some three minutes, then peeked from under the blanket at the icon lamp, listened to the silence, and smiled.

"Very nice, very nice . . . ," she whispered, bending her legs, which seemed longer to her because she had walked so much. "Sleep, sleep . . ."

Her legs refused to lie still, her whole body felt ill at ease, and she turned on the other side. A big fly buzzed around the bedroom, restlessly beating against the ceiling. There were also the sounds of Grigory and Vassily in the reception room, stepping cautiously as they cleared the tables. It seemed to Olga Mikhailovna that she would fall asleep and feel comfortable only when these noises died down. And she again turned impatiently on the other side.

Her husband's voice reached her from the drawing room. Someone must have stayed for the night, because Pyotr Dmitrich was addressing whoever it was and speaking loudly:

"I wouldn't say that Count Alexei Petrovich is a false man. But he can't help seeming to be, because you gentlemen are all trying to see him as not what he really is. In his play-acting you see an original mind; in his unceremonious manners—good nature; in his total lack of opinion you see conservatism. Let's even allow that he is indeed a sterling conservative. But what essentially is conservatism?"

Pyotr Dmitrich, angry with Count Alexei Petrovich, and with his guests, and with himself, was now unburdening his heart. He denounced the count and the guests, and, in vexation with himself, was ready to say and preach anything at all. Having bid the guest good night, he paced up and down the drawing room, walked through the dining room, the corridor, the study, the drawing room again, and went into the bedroom. Olga Mikhailovna was lying on her back, covered with the blanket only up to her waist (it now seemed hot to her), and with an angry face was watching the fly as it knocked against the ceiling.

"Has someone stayed for the night?" she asked.

"Egorov."

Pyotr Dmitrich undressed and got into his bed. He silently lit a cigarette and also started watching the fly. His gaze was stern and troubled. For about five minutes Olga Mikhailovna silently looked at his handsome profile. It seemed to her for some reason that if her husband suddenly turned his face to her and said, "Olya, it's hard for me," she would burst out crying or laughing, and would feel better. She thought that her legs ached and her whole body was ill at ease because her soul was strained.

"Pyotr, what are you thinking about?" she asked.

"Nothing really . . . ," her husband replied.

"You've been keeping some sort of secrets from me lately. That's not good."

"Why is it not good?" Pyotr Dmitrich replied drily and not at once. "Each of us has a personal life, so we must also have secrets."

"Personal life . . . secrets . . . That's all just words! Understand that you're insulting me!" said Olga Mikhailovna, sitting up on her bed. "If your soul is heavy, why do you conceal it from me? Why do you find it more comfortable to be open with other women, and not with your wife? I heard you pour yourself out today to Lyubochka."

"Well, congratulations. I'm very glad you heard me."

This meant: Leave me alone, don't interfere when I'm thinking! Olga Mikhailovna was indignant. The vexation, hatred, and anger that had accumulated in her in the course of the day suddenly boiled over: she wanted to tell her husband everything at once, not put it off till the next day, to insult him, to take her revenge . . . Trying hard not to shout, she said:

"Know, then, that this is all vile, vile, vile. I've been hating you all day today—that's what you've done!"

Pyotr Dmitrich also sat up.

"Vile, vile, vile!" Olga Mikhailovna went on, beginning to tremble all over. "Don't go congratulating me! Better if you congratulate yourself! A shame, a disgrace! You've been lying so much that you're ashamed to be in the same room with your wife! False man! I see through you and understand your every step!"

"Olya, when you're out of sorts, please warn me. Then I'll sleep in my study."

Having said that, Pyotr Dmitrich took his pillow and left the bedroom. Olga Mikhailovna had not foreseen that. For several minutes, her mouth open and her whole body trembling, she silently stared at the door through which her husband had disappeared and tried to understand what it meant. Was it one of the methods that false people use in arguments when they're wrong, or was it an insult deliberately inflicted on her pride? How was she to understand it? Olga Mikhailovna recalled her cousin, an officer, a merry fellow, who often told her laughingly that when, during the night, his "dear spouse began to carp at him," he usually took his pillow and went whistling off to his study, leaving his wife in a stupid and ridiculous position. This officer was married to a rich, capricious, and stupid woman, whom he did not respect but merely tolerated.

Olga Mikhailovna leaped out of bed. In her opinion, only one thing was left for her now: to dress quickly and leave this house forever.

The house belonged to her, but so much the worse for Pyotr Dmitrich. Without considering whether or not there was any need for it, she quickly went to the study to inform her husband of her decision ("Women's logic!" flashed through her mind), and to say something insulting and sarcastic to him in farewell . . .

Pyotr Dmitrich was lying on the sofa pretending to read a newspaper. On a chair beside him a candle was burning. His face was hidden behind the newspaper.

"Would you care to explain the meaning of this? I ask you, sir!"

"Sir . . . ," Pyotr Dmitrich repeated mockingly, not showing his face. "I'm sick of it, Olga! Honestly, I'm tired and can't deal with it right now . . . We can quarrel tomorrow."

"No, I understand you perfectly well!" Olga Mikhailovna went on. "You hate me! Yes, yes! You hate me for being wealthier than you! You'll never forgive me for it and will always lie to me!" ("Women's logic!" again flashed through her mind.) "Right now, I know, you're laughing at me . . . I'm even sure you married me only so as to have property qualifications,[15] and those trashy horses . . . Oh, I'm so unhappy!"

Pyotr Dmitrich dropped the newspaper and sat up. The unexpected insult startled him. With a childishly helpless smile he gave his wife a lost look, and, as if shielding himself from a blow, reached his arms out to her and said pleadingly:

"Olya!"

And expecting her to say something else terrible, he pressed himself to the back of the sofa, and his big figure now seemed as helplessly childish as his smile.

"Olya, how could you say that?" he whispered.

Olga Mikhailovna came to her senses. She suddenly felt her mad love for this man, remembered that he was her husband, Pyotr Dmitrich, without whom she could not live a single day, and who also loved her madly. She burst into loud sobs, in a voice not her own, clutched her head, and ran back to the bedroom.

She fell on the bed, and her short, hysterical sobs, which hindered her breathing and caused cramps in her arms and legs, filled the bedroom. Remembering that three or four rooms away a guest was spending the night, she hid her head under the pillow to stifle her sobs, but the pillow fell on the floor, and she herself nearly fell leaning over to pick it up; she pulled the blanket towards her face, but her hands did not obey her and tore convulsively at everything she took hold of.

It seemed to her that all was already lost, that the lie she had told to insult her husband had broken her whole life to smithereens. Her husband would not forgive her. The insult she had inflicted on him was of the sort that cannot be smoothed over by any caresses or oaths . . . How would she persuade her husband that she herself did not believe what she had said?

"It's all over, all over!" she cried, not noticing that the pillow had fallen on the floor again. "For God's sake, for God's sake!"

The guest and the servants must already have been awakened by her cries; tomorrow the whole district would know that she had had hysterics, and everyone would blame Pyotr Dmitrich. She made efforts to restrain herself, but her sobs grew louder and louder every minute.

"For God's sake!" she cried in a voice not her own, not understanding why she cried it. "For God's sake!"

It seemed to her that the bed collapsed under her and her feet got entangled in the blanket. Pyotr Dmitrich came into the bedroom in a dressing gown and with a candle in his hand.

"Come now, Olya!" he said.

She rose and, kneeling on the bed, squinting at the candle, managed to say through her sobs:

"Understand . . . understand . . ."

She wanted to say that she was worn out from the guests, from his lying, her lying, that it was seething inside her, but all she could produce was:

"Understand . . . understand!"

"Here, drink!" he said, offering her water.

She obediently took the glass and started to drink, but spilled the water on her hands, breast, knees . . . "I must be terribly ugly now!" she thought. Pyotr Dmitrich silently laid her back in bed and covered her with the blanket, then took the candle and went out.

"For God's sake!" Olga Mikhailovna cried again. "Pyotr, understand, understand!"

Suddenly something pressed her below the stomach and in the back with such force that her weeping broke off and she bit the pillow from pain. But the pain soon left her and she started sobbing again.

A maid came in and, straightening her blanket, asked in alarm:

"Mistress, dearest, what's the matter?"

"Get out of here!" Pyotr Dmitrich said sternly, going to the bed.

"Understand, understand . . . ," Olga Mikhailovna began.

"Olya, I beg you, calm down!" he said. "I didn't mean to offend you. I wouldn't have left the bedroom if I knew it would affect you like this. It was simply hard for me. I'm telling you as an honest man . . ."

"Understand . . . You lied, I lied . . ."

"I understand . . . Well, well, come now! I understand . . . ," Pyotr Dmitrich said tenderly, sitting down on her bed. "You said it in a fit of temper, it's understandable . . . I swear to God I love you more than anything in the world, and when I married you, I never once gave a thought to your being rich. I loved you boundlessly—that's all . . . I assure you. I was never poor and never knew the value of money, and so I never felt any difference between your fortune and mine. It always seemed to me that we were equally rich. But it's true, of course, that I was false in small things. My life so far has been organized so frivolously that it was somehow impossible to do without petty lies. I myself find it hard now. Let's drop this conversation, for God's sake! . . ."

Olga Mikhailovna again felt intense pain and seized her husband by the sleeve.

"It hurts, it hurts, it hurts," she said quickly. "Oh, it hurts!"

"Devil take these guests!" Pyotr Dmitrich muttered, getting up. "You shouldn't have gone to the island today!" he cried. "And how is it I didn't stop you, fool that I am? Lord God!"

He scratched his head in vexation, waved his hand, and left the bedroom.

Afterwards he came back a few times, sat by her on the bed, and talked a lot, now very tenderly, now angrily, but she hardly heard him. Her sobbing alternated with terrible pain, and each new pain was stronger and lasted longer. At first during the pain she held her breath and bit the pillow, but then she started to scream in an indecent, rending voice. Once, seeing her husband by her, she remembered that she had insulted him and, without considering whether it was delirium or the real Pyotr Dmitrich, she seized his hand in both of hers and started kissing it.

"You lied, I lied . . . ," she began to justify herself. "Understand, understand . . . I was exhausted, driven out of all patience . . ."

"Olya, we're not alone here!" said Pyotr Dmitrich.

Olga Mikhailovna raised her head and saw Varvara, who was kneeling by the chest of drawers, pulling open the lowest drawer. The upper ones were already open. Finishing with the drawers, Varvara stood up and, red from the strain, her face cold and solemn, set about opening a little box.

"Marya, I can't open it!" she said in a whisper. "Maybe you can try."

The maid Marya, who was poking in a candlestick with scissors so as to put in a new candle, came over to Varvara and helped her to open the little box.

"There should be nothing closed . . . ," Varvara whispered. "Open this box, too, old girl. Master," she turned to Pyotr Dmitrich, "send word to Father Mikhail, tell him to open the Royal Doors![16] You must!"

"Do whatever you like," said Pyotr Dmitrich, gasping for breath, "only, for God's sake, quickly bring a doctor or a midwife! Has Vassily gone? Send someone else. Send your husband!"

"I'm giving birth," Olga Mikhailovna realized. "Varvara," she moaned, "but he won't be born alive."

"It's all right, it's all right, ma'am . . . ," Varvara whispered. "God willing, he'll be borned alive!" (That was how she said it.) "Borned alive."

The next time Olga Mikhailovna recovered from pain, she no longer sobbed and thrashed, but only moaned. She could not keep from moaning even in the intervals when there was no pain. The candles were still burning, but morning light was already breaking through the blinds. It was probably about five o'clock in the morning. In the bedroom, at a round table, sat an unknown woman in a white apron and with a very modest physiognomy. By the way she was sitting, one could see that she had been there for a while. Olga Mikhailovna guessed that she was the midwife.

"Will it be over soon?" she asked, and in her voice she heard a sort of special, unfamiliar note, such as had never been there before. "I must be dying in childbirth," she thought.

Pyotr Dmitrich, dressed for daytime, warily came into the bedroom and stood by the window, his back to his wife. He raised the blind and looked out the window.

"Heavy rain!" he said.

"What time is it?" Olga Mikhailovna asked, in order to hear the unfamiliar note in her voice again.

"A quarter to six," the midwife answered.

"What if I really am dying?" Olga Mikhailovna thought, looking at her husband's head and at the window panes, against which the rain was beating. "How will he live without me? With whom will he drink tea, have dinner, talk in the evening, sleep?"

And he looked small to her, orphaned; she felt sorry for him and wanted to say something nice, gentle, comforting. She remembered that in the spring he had intended to buy some hounds, and that she, considering hunting a cruel and dangerous pastime, had prevented him from doing it.

"Pyotr, buy yourself those hounds!" she moaned.

He lowered the blind and went to the bed, was about to say something, but just then Olga Mikhailovna felt pain and cried out in an indecent, rending voice.

The pain, the frequent cries and moans, stupefied her. She could hear, see, she sometimes spoke, but she understood little, and only knew that she was in pain, or was about to be in pain. It seemed to her that the name-day party was long, long past, not yesterday, but maybe a year ago, and that her new life of pain had lasted longer than her childhood, boarding school, studies, marriage, and would still go on for a long, long time, endlessly. She saw how the midwife was served tea, how she was invited to have lunch at noon, and then to have dinner; she saw how Pyotr Dmitrich got accustomed to coming in, standing by the window for a long time, then going out; saw how some unknown men, the maid, Varvara got accustomed to coming in . . . Varvara just repeated "borned alive," and got angry when somebody closed the drawers. Olga Mikhailovna saw how the light changed in the room and in the windows: it would be twilight, then murky, like fog, then bright daylight, as it had been the day before at dinner, then twilight again . . . And each of these changes lasted a long time, like childhood, studies at boarding school, the institute . . .

In the evening two doctors—one bony, bald, with a broad red beard, the other with a Jewish face, swarthy and in cheap spectacles— performed some sort of surgery on Olga Mikhailovna. She remained totally indifferent to the fact that strange men were touching her body. She no longer had any shame, any will, and people could do whatever they wanted with her. If at that time someone had attacked her with a knife, or insulted Pyotr Dmitrich, or taken away her right to the little person, she would not have said a word.

During the operation she was given chloroform. When she woke up later, the pain still went on and was unbearable. It was night. And Olga Mikhailovna remembered that there had already been exactly such a night, with silence, with an icon lamp, with a midwife sitting motionless by her bed, with open drawers, with Pyotr Dmitrich standing by the window, but sometime very, very long ago . . .

V

"I didn't die . . . ," thought Olga Mikhailovna, when she began to recognize her surroundings again and there was no longer any pain.

A bright summer day looked through the two wide-open windows of the bedroom; in the garden outside the windows, sparrows and magpies chattered without stopping for a second.

The drawers of the chest were now closed, her husband's bed was made. The midwife, Varvara, and the maid were not in the bedroom; only Pyotr Dmitrich stood motionless at the window as before, looking out into the garden. No baby's crying was heard, no one offered congratulations or rejoiced: evidently the little person had not been born alive.

"Pyotr!" Olga Mikhailovna called to her husband.

Pyotr Dmitrich turned to look. It must have been a very long time since the last guest had left and Olga Mikhailovna had insulted her husband, because Pyotr Dmitrich had grown noticeably haggard and thin.

"What is it?" he asked, going to the bed.

He looked aside, moved his lips, and gave a childishly helpless smile.

"Is it all over?" Olga Mikhailovna asked.

Pyotr Dmitrich wanted to reply, but his lips trembled, and his mouth twisted like an old man's, like her toothless uncle Nikolai Nikolaich's.

"Olya!" he said, wringing his hands, and big tears suddenly welled up in his eyes. "Olya! I don't need any qualifications, or court sessions" (he sobbed) ". . . or special opinions, or guests, or your dowry . . . I don't need anything! Why didn't we take care of our baby? Ah, what's there to talk about!"

He waved his hand and left the bedroom.

But for Olga Mikhailovna nothing mattered anymore. There was a fog in her head from the chloroform, her soul was empty . . . That dull indifference to life, which she had felt when the two doctors performed the operation, still had not left her.

1888

A BREAKDOWN

I

Mayer, a medical student, and Rybnikov, studying in the Moscow School of Painting, Sculpture, and Architecture, went one evening to their friend, the law student Vassilyev, and invited him to go with them to S——v Lane. Vassilyev first protested for a long time, then got dressed and went with them.

He knew of fallen women only by hearsay and from books, and never once in his life had been in the houses where they lived. He knew that there were such immoral women, who, under the pressure of fatal circumstances—milieu, bad upbringing, poverty, and so on—were forced to sell their honor for money. They do not know pure love, have no children, no legal rights; their mothers and sisters lament over them like the dead, science treats them as evil, men speak familiarly to them. Yet, despite all that, they do not lose the image and likeness of God.[1] They are all conscious of their sin and hope for salvation. They could employ the means leading to salvation on the most vast scale. It is true that society does not forgive people their past, but for God Saint Mary of Egypt is considered no lower than the other saints.[2] Whenever Vassilyev happened to recognize a fallen woman in the street by her dress or manners, or saw one portrayed in a satirical magazine, he remembered a story he once read somewhere: a certain young man, pure and self-sacrificing, fell in love with a fallen woman and offered to make her his wife, and she, considering herself unworthy of such happiness, poisoned herself.

Vassilyev lived in one of the lanes off Tverskoy Boulevard. When he and his friends left the house, it was about eleven o'clock. The first snow had fallen a little earlier, and everything in nature was under the sway of this young snow. The air smelled of snow, snow softly crunched underfoot, the ground, the roofs, the trees, the benches on the boulevards—everything was soft, white, young, and that made the houses look different than the day before, the lamps shone brighter, the air became more transparent, the clatter of the carriages was muffled, and a feeling that resembled this white, young, fluffy snow asked to enter one's soul along with the fresh, light, frosty air.

" 'Without my will to these sad shores,' " the medic began to sing in a pleasant tenor, " 'a mysterious force doth draw me . . .' "[3]

" 'Behold the mill . . . ,' " the artist joined in. " 'Already 'tis in ruin . . .' "

" 'Behold the mill . . . Already 'tis in ruin . . . ,' " repeated the medic, raising his eyebrows and sadly shaking his head.

He fell silent, rubbed his forehead, trying to remember the words, then sang loudly and so well that the passersby turned to look at him:

" 'Here once I would freely meet with my free love . . .' "

The three men stopped at a restaurant and, without taking off their overcoats, drank two glasses of vodka each at the bar. Before drinking his second, Vassilyev noticed a piece of cork in his vodka, brought the glass up to his eyes, and looked at it for a long time, frowning nearsightedly. The medic misunderstood his expression and said:

"Well, what are you staring at? Please, no philosophy! Vodka's given us to be drunk, sturgeon to be eaten, women to be visited, snow to be walked on. Live for at least one evening as a human being!"

"But I didn't mean . . . ," said Vassilyev, laughing. "Did I refuse?"

The vodka warmed his insides. He looked tenderly at his friends, admired and envied them. How balanced everything was in these healthy, strong, cheerful people, how everything in their minds and souls was finished and smooth! They sing, and they passionately love the theater, and they draw, and they talk and drink a lot, and don't have a headache the next day; they are poetic, and dissolute, and tender, and

bold; they know how to work, to be indignant, to laugh for no reason, to say silly things; they are hot-headed, honest, self-sacrificing,
and, as human beings, no worse in any way than he, Vassilyev, who
watches his every step and every word, is self-conscious, prudent,
and ready to elevate the least trifle to the level of a problem. And he
wished to live like his friends for at least one evening, to let himself
go, to free himself from his own self-control. Must he drink vodka?
Then he will drink, even if his head splits with pain tomorrow. They
take him to the women? He goes. He will laugh, fool around, respond
merrily to the comments of passersby . . .

He stepped out of the restaurant laughing. He liked his friends—
one in a crumpled broad-brimmed hat with a pretense to artistic disorder, the other in a sealskin cap, not a poor man, but with the pretense
of belonging to the educated bohemians; he liked the snow, the pale
light of the lamps, the sharply outlined black tracks left by the soles
of passersby on the first snow; he liked the air and especially that
transparent, tender, naïve, as if virginal hue which can be observed
in nature only twice a year: when everything gets covered with snow,
and in spring on clear days or moonlit evenings when the ice is breaking up on the river.

" 'Without my will to these sad shores,' " he sang in a low voice,
" 'an unknown force doth draw me . . .' "

And all along the way for some reason he and his friends could not
free their tongues of this motif, and all three sang it mechanically, not
in time with each other.

Vassilyev's imagination pictured how he and his friends, in about
ten minutes, knock on the door, how they steal to the women through
dark corridors and dark rooms, how he lights a match in the darkness
and suddenly sees a suffering face and a guilty smile. The unknown
blonde or brunette will probably have her hair down and be wearing
a white bed jacket; she will be frightened by the light, become terribly
embarrassed, and say: "For God's sake, what are you doing! Blow it
out!" All this was scary, but intriguing and new.

II

From Trubnaya Square the friends turned off to Grachevka Street and soon entered the lane which Vassilyev knew of only by hearsay. Seeing two rows of houses with brightly lit windows and wide-open doors, hearing the merry sounds of pianos and fiddles—sounds that flew out of all the doors and mixed into a strange confusion, as if in the darkness above the roofs an invisible orchestra were tuning up. Vassilyev was surprised and said:

"So many houses!"

"That's nothing!" said the medic. "In London there are ten times more. There's around a hundred thousand such women there."

Cabbies sat on their boxes as calmly and indifferently as in all lanes; the same people walked along the sidewalks as on other streets. No one hurried, no one hid his face in his collar, no one shook his head reproachfully . . . And in this indifference, in the sonorous confusion of pianos and fiddles, in the bright windows, in the wide-open doors, one felt something quite overt, brazen, bold, and sweeping. In the old days it must have been just as merry and noisy at the slave markets, and people's faces and gaits must have expressed the same indifference.

"Let's begin right from the beginning," said the artist.

The friends entered a narrow corridor lit by a lamp with a reflector. When they opened the door to the front hall, a man in a black frock coat, with an unshaven lackey face and sleepy eyes, rose lazily from a yellow divan. It smelled like a laundry and of vinegar as well. From the front hall, the door led to a brightly lit room. The medic and the artist stopped in the doorway and, craning their necks, both looked in at once.

"Bona-serra, signori, rigoletto-ugonotti-traviata!" the artist began, bowing theatrically.

"Havanna-tarakana-pistoletto!" said the medic, pressing his hat to his chest and making a low bow.

Vassilyev stood behind them. He, too, would have liked to make a theatrical bow and say something silly, but he merely smiled, felt an awkwardness that resembled shame, and waited impatiently for what would follow. In the doorway appeared a little blonde of seventeen or eighteen, with bobbed hair, in a short light-blue dress with a white aiglet on her breast.

"Why are you standing in the doorway?" she said. "Take your coatses off and come in."

The medic and the artist, still speaking Italian, went into the reception room. Vassilyev hesitantly followed them.

"Take your coatses off, gentlemen!" the lackey said sternly. "It's not done like that."

Besides the blonde there was another woman in the room, very plump and tall, with a non-Russian face and bare arms. She was sitting by the piano and laying out a game of patience on her knees. She paid no attention at all to the visitors.

"Where are the other young ladies?" asked the medic.

"They're having tea," said the blonde. "Stepan," she shouted, "go tell the young ladies that some students have come!"

A little later a third girl came into the room. This one was wearing a bright red dress with blue stripes. Her face was made up heavily and ineptly, her forehead was hidden behind her hair, her eyes stared unblinking and frightened. On coming in, she immediately began to sing a song in a loud, crude contralto. Behind her appeared a fourth young lady, then a fifth . . .

In all this Vassilyev saw nothing either new or intriguing. It seemed to him that this room, the piano, the mirror in its cheap gilt frame, the aiglet, the dress with blue stripes, and these dull, indifferent faces, he had already seen somewhere, and more than once. But of the darkness, the silence, the secrecy, the guilty smile that he had expected to meet here and that frightened him, he saw not even a trace.

Everything was ordinary, prosaic, and uninteresting. Only one thing slightly aroused his curiosity—the terrible, as if purposely contrived tastelessness that could be seen in the cornices, the absurd paintings, the dresses, the aiglet. In this tastelessness there was something characteristic, distinctive.

"How poor and stupid it all is!" thought Vassilyev. "What in all this rubbish I see now can tempt a normal man, urge him to commit a terrible sin—to buy a living human being for a rouble? I can understand any sin for the sake of glamour, beauty, grace, passion, taste, but here what is there? For the sake of what do people sin here? However . . . better not to think!"

"Beardy, treat me to some porter!" the blonde addressed him.

Vassilyev suddenly became embarrassed.

"With pleasure . . . ," he said, bowing politely. "Only pardon me, ma'am, but I . . . I won't drink with you. I don't drink."

Five minutes later the friends were already on their way to another house.

"So, why did you order porter?" the medic said angrily. "Some millionaire! To throw away six roubles just like that, for nothing, to the wind!"

"If she wants it, why not give her that pleasure?" Vassilyev justified himself.

"You gave pleasure not to her, but to the madam. The madams get them to ask for treats, because they profit from it."

" 'Behold the mill . . . ,' " the artist sang. " 'Already 'tis in ruin . . .' "

On coming to the second house, the friends only stood in the front hall, but did not go into the reception room. Just as in the first house, a figure in a frock coat and with a sleepy lackey face rose from a divan in the front hall. Looking at this lackey, at his face and shabby frock coat, Vassilyev thought: "How much must an ordinary, simple Russian man live through before fate brings him here as a lackey? Where was he before, and what did he do? What awaits him? Is he married? Where is his mother, and does she know that he works here as a lackey?" And now in each house Vassilyev involuntarily paid attention first of all to the lackey. In one of the houses, the fourth in line it seemed, the lackey was a small, scrawny, dried-up man with a watch chain on his waistcoat. He was reading *The Leaflet*[4] and paid no attention to the men coming in. Looking at his face, Vassilyev thought for some reason that a man with such a face could steal, and kill, and lie under oath. And in fact the face was interesting: a big forehead, gray eyes, a flattened little nose, thin, tight lips, and a dull and at the same time insolent expression, like a young hound chasing down a hare. Vassilyev thought it would be nice to touch this lackey's hair: was it stiff or soft? Most likely stiff, like a dog's.

III

The artist, having tossed off two glasses of porter, somehow suddenly became drunk and unnaturally animated.

"Let's go to another!" he commanded, waving his arms. "I'll take you to the best one!"

Having brought his friends to the house which in his opinion was the best, he expressed a firm desire to dance a quadrille. The medic began to grumble about having to pay the musicians a rouble, but agreed to be his *vis-à-vis*. They began to dance.

The best house was just as bad as the worst one. There were the same mirrors and paintings, the same hairstyles and dresses. Looking at the furnishings and costumes, Vassilyev now saw that this was not tastelessness, but something that might be called the taste or even the style of S——v Lane, and that could not be found anywhere else, something of a piece with its ugliness, not accidental but developed over time. After having been in eight houses, he was no longer astonished by the colors of the dresses, or the long trains, or the bright bows, or the sailor suits, or the thick purplish rouge on the cheeks; he realized that here it had to be that way, that if even one of these women were to dress like a human being, or if a decent etching were hung on the wall, the general tone of the whole lane would suffer.

"How ineptly they sell themselves!" he thought. "Can they possibly not understand that vice is captivating only when it is beautiful and hidden, when it wears the cover of virtue? Modest black dresses, pale faces, sad smiles, and darkness have a stronger effect than these gaudy adornments. Stupid women! If they don't understand it themselves, their visitors might have taught them . . ."

A girl in a Polish costume with white fur trim came and sat beside him.

"Nice dark-haired boy, why aren't you dancing?" she asked. "Why are you so bored?"

"Because it's boring."

"Just treat me to some Lafite. Then it won't be boring."

Vassilyev made no reply. He kept silent, then asked:

"What time do you go to sleep?"

"Towards six."

"And when do you get up?"

"Sometimes at two, and sometimes at three."

"What do you do when you get up?"

"We drink coffee, then at six we have dinner."

"And what do you have for dinner?"

"The usual things . . . Cabbage soup or some other, beefsteak, dessert. Our madam treats the girls well. Why are you asking all this?"

"Just to make conversation . . ."

Vassilyev wanted to talk with the girl about many things. He felt a strong desire to find out where she was born, whether her parents were living, and if they knew she was here; how she wound up in this house, whether she was happy and content or sad and oppressed by dark thoughts; and whether she had hopes of ever getting out of her present situation . . . But he simply could not think up what to begin with and how to formulate the question so as not to appear indiscreet. He thought for a long time and then asked:

"How old are you?"

"Eighty," the young lady joked, laughing as she watched the capers the dancing artist performed with his arms and legs.

Suddenly she burst out laughing at something and uttered a long, cynical phrase, so loudly that everyone could hear it. Vassilyev was taken aback, and, not knowing what expression to give his face, forced himself to smile. He was the only one to smile; all the others—his friends, the musicians, and the women—did not even glance at his companion, as if they had not heard.

"Treat me to some Lafite," the girl said again.

Vassilyev felt an aversion to her white fur trim and her voice and walked away from her. It now seemed stuffy and hot to him, and his heart began to pound slowly but hard, like a hammer: one! two! three!

"Let's leave here!" he said, pulling the artist's sleeve.

"Wait, let us finish."

While the artist and the medic were finishing the quadrille, Vassilyev, so as not to look at the women, studied the musicians. The piano was played by a fine-looking old man in spectacles, whose face resembled Marshal Bazaine's;[5] the violin by a young man with a brown little beard, dressed in the latest fashion. The young man's face was not stupid, not wasted, but, on the contrary, intelligent, young, fresh. He was dressed fastidiously and with taste, he played with feeling. A puzzle: how did he and this decent, fine-looking old man wind up here? Why weren't they ashamed to be here? What did they think about when they looked at the women?

If the people playing the piano and violin had been bedraggled, hungry, gloomy, drunk, with wasted or stupid faces, their presence might have been understandable. Now, though, Vassilyev understood nothing. He recalled a story he had read once about a fallen woman, and he now thought this human image with a guilty smile had nothing in common with what he was seeing here. It seemed to him that he was seeing not fallen women, but some other, totally separate world, alien and incomprehensible to him; if he had seen this world earlier on the stage of a theater or read about it in a book, he would not have believed it . . .

The woman with the white fur trim burst out laughing again and loudly uttered a repulsive phrase. A squeamish feeling came over him. He blushed and left the room.

"Wait, we're coming too!" the artist called after him.

IV

"Just now, while we were dancing, I had a conversation with my partner," the medic said, when all three of them came outside. "It was about her first romance. He, her hero, was some kind of bookkeeper in Smolensk, who had a wife and five children. She was seventeen and lived with her father and mother, who traded in soap and candles."

"How did he win over her heart?" asked Vassilyev.

"He bought her fifty roubles' worth of underwear. What the hell!"

"Anyhow he managed to worm her romance out of his partner," Vassilyev thought about the medic. "And I don't know how . . ."

"Gentlemen, I'm going home!" he said.

"Why?"

"Because I don't know how to behave here. Besides, I'm bored and disgusted. Where's the fun of it? If only they were human beings, but they're savages and animals. I'm leaving, do as you like."

"Now, Grisha, Grigory, dear heart . . . ," said the artist in a tearful voice, snuggling up to Vassilyev. "Come on! We'll go to one more, and curse them all . . . Please! Grigoriants!"

They talked Vassilyev into it and led him up the stairs. In the carpeting, in the gilt banisters, in the porter who opened the door, and in the panels that decorated the front hall, the same S——v Lane style could be felt, but improved, more impressive.

"Really, I'm going home!" Vassilyev said, taking off his coat.

"Now, now, dear heart . . . ," said the artist, kissing him on the neck. "Don't throw a tantrum . . . Be a good friend, Gri-Gri! We've come together, and we'll leave together. What a brute you are, really."

"I can wait for you outside. By God, it disgusts me here."

"Now, now, Grisha . . . It disgusts you, but just observe it! Understand? Observe!"

"One must look at things objectively," the medic said seriously.

Vassilyev went into the reception room and sat down. Besides him and his two friends, there were many visitors in the room: two infantry officers, a gray-haired and balding gentleman in gold-rimmed spectacles, two moustacheless students from the land-surveying institute, and a very drunk man with an actor's face. The girls were all occupied with these visitors and paid no attention to Vassilyev. Only one of them, dressed like Aïda,[6] glanced sideways at him, smiled at something, and said, yawning:

"Here's a dark-haired boy . . ."

Vassilyev's heart was pounding and his face was burning. He felt ashamed before the visitors for his presence there, and also disgusted and tormented. He was tormented by the thought that he, a decent and affectionate man (as he had considered himself until then), hated these women and felt nothing but loathing for them. He was not sorry for these women, or for the musicians, or for the lackeys.

"It's because I'm not trying to understand them," he thought. "They all resemble animals more than people, but still they are people, they have souls. I must understand them and only then judge them . . ."

"Grisha, don't go, wait for us!" the artist shouted and disappeared. Soon the medic also disappeared.

"Yes, I must try to understand, not do like this . . . ," Vassilyev went on thinking.

And he started peering intently into each woman's face and searching for a guilty smile. But either he did not know how to read faces, or none of these women felt any guilt: on each face he read only a dull expression of humdrum, banal boredom and contentment. Stupid eyes, stupid smiles, sharp, stupid voices, insolent gestures—and nothing else. Apparently each of them in the past had a romance with a bookkeeper and fifty roubles of underwear, and in the present no delight in life except coffee, a three-course dinner, wine, the quadrille, and sleeping until two in the afternoon . . .

Not finding a single guilty smile, Vassilyev began to search for an intelligent face. And his attention fixed on a pale, slightly sleepy, tired face . . . It was a brunette, no longer young, dressed in an outfit covered with sequins; she was sitting in an armchair, looking down and thinking about something. Vassilyev walked back and forth and, as if accidentally, sat down beside her.

"I should begin with something banal," he thought, "and then gradually go on to the serious . . ."

"What a pretty little outfit you have," he said and touched the golden fringe of her shawl with his finger.

"I wear what I've got . . . ," the brunette said listlessly.

"What province are you from?"

"Me? From far away . . . Chernigov."

"That's a good province. Life's good there."

"It's always good where we're not."

"A pity I'm not able to describe nature," Vassilyev thought. "I could move her by descriptions of nature in Chernigov. She must love it, since she was born there."

"Are you bored here?" he asked.

"Of course I'm bored."

"Why don't you leave this place, if you're bored?"

"Where should I go? Begging, or something?"

"Begging is better than living here."

"How do you know? Do you beg?"

"I did, when I couldn't pay for my schooling. But even if I didn't beg, it's clear anyway. A beggar, whatever else, is a free man, and you're a slave."

The brunette stretched and followed with her sleepy eyes a waiter who was carrying glasses and seltzer water on a tray.

"Treat me to some porter," she said and yawned again.

"Porter . . . ," thought Vassilyev. "And what if your brother or your mother came in here now? What would you say? And what would they say? There'd be porter then, I can just picture it . . ."

Suddenly he heard weeping. A fair-haired gentleman with a red face and angry eyes quickly came out of the room where the lackey had carried the seltzer water. He was followed by the tall, plump madam, who was shouting in a shrill voice:

"No one has allowed you to slap girls in the face! We have better visitors than you, and they don't go hitting people! Charlatan!"

A row ensued. Vassilyev became frightened and turned pale. In the next room someone was sobbing, genuinely, as an insulted person does. And he realized that in fact people lived here, real people, who, as everywhere, get insulted, suffer, weep, ask for help . . . The intense hatred and feeling of disgust gave way to a sharp feeling of pity and anger at the offender. He rushed to the room where the weeping came from; behind the row of bottles that stood on the marble tabletop, he made out a suffering, tear-drenched face, reached his arms out to it, took a step towards the table, but recoiled at once in horror. The weeping girl was drunk.

Making his way through the noisy crowd that surrounded the fair-haired man, he lost heart, turned chicken like a little boy, and it seemed to him that in this alien, incomprehensible world he would be hunted down, beaten, showered with dirty words . . . He tore his coat from the rack and rushed headlong down the stairs.

V

Pressing against the fence, he stood by the house waiting for his comrades to come out. The sounds of pianos and fiddles, merry, rollicking, impudent, and sad, mingled in the air into a sort of chaos, and this mingling as before resembled an invisible orchestra tuning up in the darkness above the roofs. If you looked up into this darkness, the whole black background was speckled with white, moving dots: it was snowing. Snowflakes, falling into the light, circled lazily in the air like down, and still more lazily fell to the ground. Snow whirled densely around Vassilyev and clung to his beard, eyelashes, eyebrows . . . The cabbies, the horses, the passersby were white.

"How can it snow in this lane?" Vassilyev thought. "Curse these houses!"

His legs, weary from having run down the stairs, were giving way under him; he was breathless, as if he had been climbing a mountain; his heart was pounding so hard he could hear it. He was tormented by the desire to get out of the lane quickly and go home, but he wanted still more to wait for his comrades and vent his painful feeling on them.

There was much in those houses he did not understand, the souls of the perishing women still remained a mystery to him, but it was clear to him that things were much worse than one might have thought. If that guilty woman who had poisoned herself was called fallen, then it was hard to find a suitable name for all the ones who were now dancing to that muddle of sounds and uttering long, repulsive phrases. They were not perishing, they had already perished.

"There is vice," he thought, "but there is no consciousness of guilt or hope for salvation. They are bought and sold, drowned in wine and vileness, but, like sheep, they are dumb, indifferent, and without understanding. My God, my God!"

It was also clear to him that here everything that is called human dignity, personhood, the image and likeness of God, is defiled to its very foundation, "totaled," as drunkards say, and that the fault for it was not only with the lane and the stupid women.

A crowd of students, white with snow, went past him, laughing and talking merrily. One of them, tall and thin, stopped, looked into Vassilyev's face, and said in a drunken voice:

"One of ours! Smashed, brother? A-ha-ha, brother! Never mind, live it up! Go on! Keep at it, old boy!"

He took Vassilyev by the shoulders and pressed his wet, cold moustache to his cheeks, then slipped, staggered, and, waving both arms, cried:

"Hold on! Don't fall!"

And, laughing, he ran to catch up with his comrades.

Through the noise the artist's voice was heard:

"Don't you dare beat women! I won't allow it, devil take you! What scoundrels!"

The medic appeared in the doorway of the house. He looked around and, seeing Vassilyev, said in alarm:

"You're here? Listen, by God, it's decidedly impossible to go anywhere with Egor! I don't understand what got into him! He started a scandal! Do you hear? Egor!" he shouted into the doorway. "Egor!"

"I won't allow you to beat women!" the artist's piercing voice came from above.

Something heavy and bulky rolled down the stairs. It was the artist flying down headlong. He had obviously been thrown out.

He got up from the ground, dusted off his hat, and with an angry, indignant face shook his fist up the stairs and shouted:

"Scoundrels! Butchers! Bloodsuckers! I won't allow it! To beat a weak, drunken woman! Ahh, you . . ."

"Egor . . . Come on, Egor . . ." the medic started pleading. "I give you my word of honor, I'll never go with you again. Word of honor!"

The artist gradually calmed down, and the friends went home.

" 'Without my will to these sad shores,' " the medic began to sing, " 'a mysterious force doth draw me . . .' "

" 'Behold the mill . . .' " the artist joined in a little later. " 'Already 'tis in ruin . . .' Holy Mother, the snow's really pouring down! Grishka, why did you leave? You're a coward, an old woman, and nothing more."

Vassilyev walked behind his friends, looked at their backs, and thought:

"One of two things: either it only seems to us that prostitution is evil, and we exaggerate, or, if prostitution is in fact as evil as we commonly think, then these dear friends of mine are as much slave-owners, rapists, and murderers as those residents of Syria and Cairo portrayed in *Niva*.[7] Now they sing, laugh, reason sensibly, but didn't they just exploit hunger, ignorance, and stupidity? They did—I witnessed it. What has their humaneness, medicine, art got to do with it?

The learning, art, and lofty feelings of these murderers remind me of a joke about lard. Two robbers killed a beggar in the forest. They started dividing up his clothes and found a piece of pork lard in his bag. 'What luck,' says the one, 'let's have a bite.' 'No, how can we?' the other says in horror. 'Have you forgotten it's Wednesday?'[8] And they didn't eat it. Having killed a man, they left the forest convinced that they were good observers of the fast. The same with these two: they buy women, and go off thinking they're artists and scholars . . ."

"Listen, you two!" he said angrily and sharply. "Why do you come here? Don't you understand how terrible it is? Your medicine says that each of these women dies prematurely of consumption or something else; art tells us that morally she dies even before that. Each of them dies, because in the course of her life she receives an average of, let's say, five hundred men. Each woman is killed by five hundred men. And you are among those five hundred! Now, if you both go to this and other similar places two hundred and fifty times in your life, the two of you will have killed one woman! Isn't that clear? Isn't that terrible? The two of you, or three, or five, kill one stupid, hungry woman! Ah, my God, isn't that terrible?"

"I just knew it would end like this," the artist said, wincing. "We should have nothing to do with this fool and blockhead! So you think you've got great thoughts and ideas in your head now? No, devil knows what, only not ideas! You're looking at me now with hatred and disgust, but in my opinion you'd do better to build twenty more of these houses than look like that. There's more vice in this look of yours than in this whole lane! Let's go, Volodya, to hell with him! A fool, a blockhead, and nothing more . . ."

"We human beings do kill each other," the medic said. "It's immoral, of course, but philosophy won't help here. Goodbye!"

At Trubnaya Square the friends said goodbye and parted. Left alone, Vassilyev walked quickly down the boulevard. He was afraid of the darkness, afraid of the snow that poured down in big flakes and seemed intent on covering the whole world; he was afraid of the streetlamps, palely glimmering through the billows of snow. His soul was seized by an unaccountable, fainthearted fear. There were some rare passersby, but he timorously avoided them. It seemed to him that women, only women, were coming from everywhere and looking at him from everywhere . . .

"It's beginning," he thought. "The breakdown is beginning . . ."

VI

At home he lay on the bed and said, shuddering all over:

"Alive! Alive! My God, they're alive!"

He fantasized, trying very hard to imagine to himself now the brother of the fallen woman, now her father, now the fallen woman herself, with her painted cheeks, and it all horrified him.

It seemed to him for some reason that he had to resolve this question immediately, at all costs, and that it was not someone else's question, but his own. With great effort, he overcame his despair and, sitting on his bed, holding his head in his hands, began to think: how to save all the women he had seen that day? As an educated man, he knew the method for resolving various questions very well. And, agitated as he was, he held strictly to this method. He recalled the history of the question, the literature about it, and by three o'clock he was already pacing up and down trying to remember all the attempts put into practice at the present time for saving women. He had a great many good friends and acquaintances who lived in the furnished rooms of Falzfein, Galyashkin, Nechaev, Echkin. Among them were not a few honest and self-sacrificing men. Some of them had attempted to save women . . .

"All of these not very numerous attempts," thought Vassilyev, "can be divided into three groups. Some, having bought a woman out of the brothel, would rent her a room, buy her a sewing machine, and she would become a seamstress. And having bought her out, willy-nilly, he made her his kept woman; then, on finishing his studies, he would leave and hand her over to some other decent man, like some sort of object. And the fallen woman remained fallen. Others, having bought her out, also rented her a furnished room, bought the inevitable sewing machine, and set about on literacy, sermonizing, reading books. The woman lived and sewed as long as it was interesting and new, but then, getting bored, she would start receiving men in secret from the preacher, or would run away and go back to where she could sleep until three o'clock, drink coffee, and have good dinners. The third group, the most ardent and self-sacrificing, took a bold, resolute step. They married. And when the insolent, spoiled, or stupid down-trodden animal became a wife, a homemaker, and then a mother, it turned her life and worldview upside down, so that in the wife and mother it was hard to recognize the former fallen woman. Yes, marriage is the best and perhaps the only way."

"But it's impossible!" Vassilyev said aloud and fell back on the bed. "I'm the first who couldn't marry! For that you need to be a saint, to know no hatred and feel no revulsion. But suppose that I, the medic, and the artist overcome ourselves and get married, and they all marry us. What would be the result? The result? The result would be that while they're getting married here, in Moscow, the bookkeeper from Smolensk will be corrupting a new batch, and that batch will swarm here to the vacant places, along with others from Saratov, Nizhni-Novgorod, Warsaw . . . And where to put the hundred thousand from London? From Hamburg?"

The lamp, which was running out of kerosene, began to smoke. Vassilyev did not notice it. He started pacing again and went on thinking. Now he put the question differently: What must be done so that fallen women are no longer needed? For that it is necessary that the men who buy them and do them in feel all the immorality of their slave-owning role and are horrified. The men must be saved.

"Science and the arts are obviously no help . . . ," thought Vassilyev. "The only solution here is to become an apostle."

And he began to dream of how, the very next evening, he would stand at the corner of the lane and say to every passerby:

"Where are you going and for what? Have fear of God!"

He would turn to the indifferent cabbies and say to them:

"Why are you standing here? Why aren't you indignant, outraged? You believe in God, and you know that it's sinful, that people will go to hell for that, so why are you silent? True, they're strangers to you, but they, too, have fathers, brothers, just as you do . . ."

One of his friends once said of Vassilyev that he was a talented

man. There are talents for writing, acting, painting, but he had a special talent—for *being human*. He possessed a refined, superb sense of
pain in general. As a good actor reflects other people's movements
and voices in himself, so Vassilyev could reflect other people's pain
in his soul. Seeing tears, he wept; next to a sick person, he himself
became sick and moaned; if he saw violence, it seemed to him that the
violence was being done to him, he became afraid like a little boy and,
turning coward, ran for help. Other people's pain chafed him, roused
him, brought him to a state of ecstasy, and so on.

Whether this friend was right, I don't know, but what Vassilyev experienced when it seemed to him that the question had been
resolved was very much like inspiration. He wept, laughed, recited
aloud the words he would speak the next day; he felt an ardent love for
the people who would listen to him and stand beside him at the corner
of the lane in order to preach; he sat down to write letters, made vows
to himself . . .

All this was like inspiration also in that it did not last long. Vassilyev soon became tired. The London, Hamburg, and Warsaw women
weighed on him in their mass as mountains weigh upon the earth; he
quailed before this mass, felt at a loss; he remembered that he had no
gift for words, that he was cowardly and fainthearted, that indifferent people would hardly want to listen to him and understand him,
a third-year law student, a timid and insignificant man, that a true
apostolic calling consisted not only in preaching, but also in acts . . .

When it became light and carriages were already clattering in the
street, Vassilyev lay motionless on the divan staring at a single spot.
He was no longer thinking about women, or men, or becoming an
apostle. All his attention was concentrated on the inner pain that tormented him. It was a dull, aimless, indefinite pain, which resembled
both anguish and fear in the highest degree, and also despair. He
could point to where it was: in his chest, under his heart; but he had
nothing to compare it with. In the past he had had a bad toothache,
had had pleurisy and neuralgia, but it was all nothing compared to
this inner pain. In the face of this pain, life appeared disgusting. His
dissertation, an excellent piece of work, already written, the people
dear to him, the saving of perishing women—all that still yesterday

he had loved or been indifferent to, now, on recollection, annoyed him in the same way as the noise of the carriages, the running of the floor boys, the daylight . . . If right now, before his eyes, someone were to perform a deed of mercy or of outrageous violence, either would have made an equally disgusting impression on him. Of all the thoughts that lazily wandered in his head, only two did not annoy him: one, that at every moment it was in his power to kill himself; the other, that the pain would not last longer than three days. The second he knew from experience.

After lying there for a while, he got up and, wringing his hands, paced, not up and down as usual, but in a square along the walls. In passing he looked at himself in the mirror. His face was pale and pinched, his temples sunken, his eyes had become bigger, darker, more fixed, as if they were someone else's, and expressed an unbearable inner suffering.

At noon the artist knocked on the door.

"Grigory, are you there?" he asked.

Receiving no answer, he stood for a minute, pondered, and answered himself in Ukrainian:

"Nobody. Went off to the university, curse him."

And he left. Vassilyev lay down on the bed and, hiding his head under the pillow, began to weep from pain, and the more his tears flowed, the more terrible his inner pain became. When it grew dark, he remembered about the tormenting night ahead of him, and was overcome by terrible despair. He quickly got dressed, ran out of his room, and, leaving his door wide open, with no need or purpose went outside. Not asking himself where to go, he walked quickly along Sadovaya Street.

Snow poured down as the day before; it was a thaw. Thrusting his hands into his sleeves, trembling and afraid of noises, of horsecar bells, and of passersby, Vassilyev went along Sadovaya to the Sukharev Tower, then to the Red Gate, and from there turned onto Basmannaya Street. He stopped at a pot-house and drank a big glass of vodka, but felt no better for that. On reaching Razgulyai, he turned right and set off along lanes he had never been on in his life before. He came to the old bridge where the Yauza flows and from where you can see long rows of lights in the windows of the Red Barracks. To divert his inner pain with some new sensation or a different pain, not knowing what to do, weeping and trembling, Vassilyev unbuttoned his overcoat and his frock coat and offered his bared chest to the wet snow and wind. But that also did not lessen the pain. Then he bent over the railing of the bridge and looked down at the black, turbulent Yauza, and he felt like throwing himself down headlong, not out of revulsion for life, not to commit suicide, but at least to hurt himself and divert one pain with another. But the black water, the darkness, the deserted banks covered with snow, were frightening. He shuddered and went on. He went along the Red Barracks, then back and descended into some sort of grove, from the grove to the bridge again . . .

"No, home, home!" he thought. "At home it seems better . . ."

And he went back. On returning home, he tore off his wet overcoat and hat, began to pace along the walls, and went on pacing tirelessly until morning.

VII

When the artist and the medic came to see him the next day, he rushed about the room, in a torn shirt and with bitten hands, groaning with pain.

"For God's sake!" he sobbed, seeing his friends. "Take me wherever you like, do whatever you know, but for God's sake save me quickly! I'll kill myself!"

The artist turned pale and was at a loss. The medic also nearly wept, but, in the belief that medics must in all circumstances remain coolheaded and serious, said coldly:

"You're having a breakdown. But never mind. We'll go to the doctor right now."

"Wherever you like, only quickly, for God's sake!"

"Don't get worked up. You've got to control yourself."

Their hands trembling, the artist and the medic dressed Vassilyev and led him outside.

"Mikhail Sergeich has been wanting to meet you for a long time," said the medic as they went. "He's a very nice man and knows his business extremely well. He graduated in 'eighty-two and already has a huge practice. With students he behaves like he's one of them."

"Quickly, quickly . . . ," Vassilyev urged.

Mikhail Sergeich, a plump, fair-haired doctor, met the friends courteously, professionally, coldly, and smiled with only one cheek.

"The artist and Mayer have already told me about your illness," he said. "I'm very glad to be of help. Well, sir? I humbly invite you to sit down . . ."

He seated Vassilyev in a big armchair by the desk and moved a box of cigarettes towards him.

"Well, sir?" he began, stroking his knees. "Let's get to work . . . How old are you?"

He asked questions, and the medic answered them. He asked whether Vassilyev's father had any particular illnesses, whether he was given to bouts of drinking, was notably cruel or in any way odd. He asked the same things about his grandfather, mother, sisters and brothers. On learning that Vassilyev's mother had an excellent voice and occasionally performed in the theater, he suddenly perked up and asked:

"Sorry, sir, but can you recall whether the theater was your mother's passion?"

Twenty minutes went by. Vassilyev was tired of the way the doctor kept stroking his knees and saying the same things all the time.

"As far as I understand from your questions, doctor," he said, "you would like to know if my illness is hereditary. It is not."

After that, the doctor asked whether at a young age Vassilyev had had any secret vices, head injuries, passions, oddities, particular predilections. Half the questions usually asked by diligent doctors can be ignored without any detriment to one's health, but Mikhail Sergeich, the medic, and the artist looked as though if Vassilyev failed to answer even one question all would be lost. Receiving answers, the doctor for some reason wrote them down on a piece of paper. On learning that Vassilyev had already completed courses in natural science and was now studying law, the doctor fell to thinking . . .

"Last year he wrote an excellent paper . . . ," said the medic.

"Sorry, don't interrupt me, you keep me from concentrating," the doctor said and smiled with one cheek. "Yes, of course, and this plays

a role in anamnesis. Intense mental effort, overstrain . . . Yes, yes . . .
Do you drink vodka?" he addressed Vassilyev.

"Very rarely."

Another twenty minutes went by. The medic began in a low voice
to express his opinion about the immediate causes of the breakdown
and told how two days ago he, the artist, and Vassilyev had gone to
S——v Lane.

The indifferent, restrained, cold tones in which his friends and the
doctor talked about the women and about the wretched lane seemed
strange to him in the highest degree . . .

"Doctor, tell me just one thing," he said, restraining himself so as
not to be rude, "is prostitution evil or not?"

"Who's disputing it, dear boy?" said the doctor, looking as if he
had resolved all these questions for himself long ago. "Who's disputing it?"

"You're a psychiatrist?" Vassilyev asked rudely.

"Yes, sir, a psychiatrist."

"Maybe you've all got it right!" Vassilyev said, getting up from
the chair and starting to pace up and down. "Maybe so! But to me all
this seems astonishing! I studied in two departments—that's seen as a
great feat; I wrote a paper which three years from now will be thrown
out and forgotten, and for that I'm praised to the skies; but because
I can't speak of fallen women as coolheadedly as about these chairs,
you send me to the doctor, call me crazy, feel sorry for me!"

For some reason, Vassilyev suddenly felt an unbearable pity for
himself, and his comrades, and all those he had seen two days ago,
and for this doctor. He burst into tears and fell back into the armchair.

The friends looked questioningly at the doctor. He, with the
expression of someone who understood perfectly well his tears and
his despair, as if he felt himself an expert in this line, went up to Vassilyev and silently gave him some drops to drink, and then, when he
calmed down, undressed him and started testing the sensitivity of his
skin, his knee reflexes, and all the rest.

And Vassilyev felt better. On leaving the doctor's office, he already
felt embarrassed, the noise of the carriages did not seem so annoying,
and the heaviness under his heart was getting lighter and lighter, as
if it was melting away. In his hand he had two prescriptions: one for

potassium bromide, the other for morphine . . . He had taken it all before!

Outside he stood for a while, pondered, and, saying goodbye to his friends, lazily trudged off to the university.

1889

THE BET

I

It was a dark autumn night. The old banker paced up and down his study remembering how fifteen years ago, in the autumn, he had given a party. At this party there were many intelligent people and they had interesting conversations. Among other things they talked about capital punishment. The guests, who included not a few scholars and journalists, for the most part had a negative view of capital punishment. They found this mode of punishment outdated, unsuitable to Christian states, and immoral. In the opinion of some, capital punishment should be universally replaced by life imprisonment.

"I disagree with you," said the banker-host. "I have never experienced either capital punishment or life imprisonment, but if one may judge *a priori*, in my opinion capital punishment is more moral and humane than imprisonment. Capital punishment kills at once, and life imprisonment slowly. Which executioner is more humane? The one who kills you in a few moments, or the one who draws life out of you over the course of many years?"

"Both are equally immoral," observed one of the guests, "because they have one and the same goal—to take away life. The state isn't God. It has no right to take away what it cannot give back if it wants to."

Among the guests was a lawyer, a young man of about twenty-five. When asked his opinion, he said:

"Capital punishment and life imprisonment are equally immoral, but if I were offered the choice between execution and life in prison, I would of course choose the second. To live somehow is better than not to live at all."

An animated discussion followed. The banker, who was then younger and more high-strung, suddenly lost his temper, pounded his fist on the table, and shouted at the young lawyer:

"That's not true! I'll bet two million roubles that you couldn't sit out even five years in a prison cell."

"If you're serious," said the lawyer, "I'll bet I can sit out not five but fifteen."

"Fifteen? You're on!" shouted the banker. "Gentlemen, I stake two million!"

"I accept! You stake your millions, and I stake my freedom!" said the lawyer.

And this wild, senseless bet was made! The banker, who back then had untold millions, a spoiled and light-minded man, was delighted with the bet. At supper he made fun of the lawyer and said:

"Come to your senses, young man, before it's too late. For me two million is a trifle, but you risk losing three or four of the best years of your life. I say three or four, because you won't sit it out longer. And also don't forget, poor fellow, that voluntary confinement is much harder than compulsory. The thought that you have the right every moment to go out into freedom will poison your whole existence in the cell. I pity you!"

And now the banker, pacing up and down, recalled it all and asked himself:

"Why this bet? What's the use of the lawyer losing fifteen years of his life and me throwing away two million? Can it prove to people that capital punishment is worse or better than life imprisonment? No, no. Stuff and nonsense. It was the whim of a satiated man on my part, and on the lawyer's part a simple lust for money."

Then he recalled what happened after that evening. It was decided that the lawyer would serve his confinement under strict surveillance in a cottage built in the banker's garden. It was agreed that in the course of fifteen years he would be deprived of the right to cross the threshold of the cottage, to see living people, to hear human voices, to receive letters and newspapers. He was allowed to have a musical instrument, to read books, to write letters, drink wine, and smoke. With the outside world, by agreement, he could make contact only silently, through a small window made especially for that purpose. He could obtain everything he needed—books, scores, wine, and so on—in any quantities, by means of notes, but only through that window. The contract specified all the small details that made the confinement strictly solitary, and it obliged the lawyer to sit out *exactly* fifteen years, from twelve noon on November 14, 1870, to twelve noon on November 14, 1885. The slightest attempt on the lawyer's part to break the contract, even two minutes before the term was up, would free the banker of the obligation to pay him the two million.

In his first year of confinement the lawyer, judging by his brief notes, suffered greatly from solitude and boredom. The sounds of the piano were heard coming from the cottage constantly day and night! He renounced wine and tobacco. Wine, he wrote, awakens desires, and desires are a prisoner's worst enemies; besides, nothing is more boring than drinking good wine and seeing nobody. And tobacco befouled the air in his room. In the first year the lawyer was predominantly sent books of light content: novels with complex love plots, crime or fantastic stories, comedies, and so on.

In the second year the music in the shed fell silent, and the lawyer requested only classics in his notes. In the fifth year music was heard again, and the prisoner requested wine. Those who kept watch on him through the window said that all that year he only ate, drank, and lay in bed, yawned frequently, and talked angrily to himself. He did not read books. Sometimes during the night he sat down to write, wrote for a long time, and in the morning tore up everything he had written. More than once they heard him weep.

In the second half of the sixth year the prisoner began an assiduous study of languages, philosophy, and history. He took it up so eagerly that the banker barely had time to order books for him. In the course of four years some six hundred volumes were ordered at his request. During the period of this passion the banker received, incidentally, the following letter from his prisoner: "My dear jailer! I am writing these lines to you in six languages. Show them to knowledgeable persons. Let them read them. If they do not find a single mistake, then, I beg you, have a shot fired in the garden. That will let me know that my efforts have not been in vain. The geniuses of all ages and countries speak in different languages, but the same fire burns in them. Oh, if you knew what unearthly happiness now fills my soul because I am able to understand them!" The prisoner's wish was fulfilled. The banker ordered two shots to be fired in the garden.

Then, after the tenth year, the lawyer sat motionless at a desk and read nothing but the Gospel. It seemed strange to the banker that a man who, in the course of four years, had gone through six hundred sophisticated volumes, could spend nearly a year reading one easily understandable and not very thick book. After the Gospel came the history of religions and theology.

In the last two years of confinement the prisoner read a great deal, without any discrimination. First he studied natural science, then requested Byron or Shakespeare. There were notes from him asking to be sent at the same time chemistry and medical textbooks, and a novel, and some philosophical or theological treatise. His reading made it seem as if he was swimming in the sea in the midst of a shipwreck and, wishing to save his life, was greedily clutching at one piece of wreckage, then another!

II

The old banker remembered all that and thought:

"Tomorrow at twelve noon he will be set free. According to the contract, I must pay him two million. If I pay it, all is lost: I'll be utterly ruined . . ."

Fifteen years ago he had had untold millions, but now he was afraid to ask himself which he had more of—money or debts? Playing the stock market, risky speculations, and a hotheadedness which he could not get rid of even in old age, gradually led to a decline in his affairs, and the fearless, confident, proud rich man turned into a middling sort of banker, trembling at every rise or fall of the rates.

"Accursed bet!" the old man muttered, clutching his head in despair. "Why didn't the man die? He's only forty. He'll take my last money, get married, enjoy life, play the stock market, while I, like a beggar, will look on enviously and hear the same phrase from him every day: 'I owe you the happiness of my life, allow me to help you!' No, that's too much! The only salvation from bankruptcy and disgrace is—this man's death!"

It struck three. The banker listened: everyone in the house was asleep, and he could hear only the rustling of the chilled trees outside the windows. Trying to make no noise, he took from a safe the key to the door that had not been opened for fifteen years, put on his coat, and went out.

In the garden it was dark and cold. Rain was falling. A sharp, damp wind was howling all over the garden and gave the trees no peace. The banker strained his eyes, but could not see the ground, nor the white statues, nor the cottage, nor the trees. Coming to the place where the cottage was, he called twice to the watchman. There was no answer. Obviously the watchman had taken refuge from the bad weather and was now sleeping somewhere in the kitchen or the hothouse.

"If I have courage enough to carry out my intention," the old man thought, "the suspicion will fall first of all on the watchman."

He felt for the steps and the door in the darkness and entered the front hall of the cottage, then felt his way into a small corridor and lit a match. Not a soul was there. There was someone's bed without covers, and the dark outline of an iron stove in the corner. The seals on the door leading to the prisoner's room were intact.

When the match went out, the old man, trembling with agitation, peeked through the small window.

A candle was burning dimly in the prisoner's room. He was sitting at the table. Only his back, his hair, and his arms could be seen. On the table, on two armchairs, and on the rug by the table lay open books.

Five minutes went by, and not once did the prisoner stir. Fifteen years of imprisonment had taught him to sit motionlessly. The banker tapped on the window with his finger, but the prisoner did not respond to this tapping with the least movement. Then the banker carefully tore the seals off the door and put the key into the keyhole.

The rusty lock produced a rasping sound and the door creaked. The banker expected to hear a cry of astonishment and footsteps at once, but some three minutes went by, and behind the door it was as quiet as before. He decided to go into the room.

Motionless at the table sat a man who looked nothing like ordinary people. He was a skeleton covered in skin, with long womanish curls and a shaggy beard. The color of his face was yellow with a sallow tinge, his cheeks were sunken, his back long and narrow, and the arm that supported his unshorn head was so thin and bony it was scary to look at. His hair was already a silvery gray, and glancing at his aged, emaciated face, no one would have believed he was only forty years old. He was asleep . . . On the table in front of his bowed head lay a sheet of paper on which something was written in small script.

"Pathetic man!" the banker thought. "He sleeps and probably sees millions in his dreams! All I need to do is take this half-corpse, throw him onto the bed, and gently smother him with a pillow, and the most conscientious expertise will find no signs of a violent death. But first let's read what he's written here . . ."

The banker took the paper from the table and read the following:

"Tomorrow at twelve noon I will be granted freedom and the right to associate with people. But before I leave this room and see the sun, I find it necessary to say a few words. With a clear conscience and before God who sees me, I declare to you that I scorn freedom, and life, and health, and all that is known in your books as worldly blessings.

"For fifteen years I have attentively studied earthly life. True, I have seen neither earth nor people, but in your books I have drunk fragrant wine, sung songs, chased deer and wild boar in the forests, loved women . . . Beauties, airy as clouds, created by the magic of poets of genius, have visited me by night and whispered wondrous tales that intoxicated me. In your books I climbed the peaks of Elbrus and Mont Blanc, and from there I saw the sun rise in the mornings and in the evenings flood the sky, the ocean, and the mountain peaks with crimson gold; from there I saw flashes of lightning cleave the clouds above me; I saw green forests, fields, rivers, lakes, cities; I heard sirens sing and shepherds' pipes play; I touched the wings of beautiful devils, who flew to me to talk about God . . . In your books I threw myself into bottomless abysses, performed miracles, killed, burned cities, preached new religions, conquered whole kingdoms . . .

"Your books gave me wisdom. Everything that tireless human thought has created in the course of centuries is compressed in my skull into a small lump. I know that I am more intelligent than all of you.

"And I scorn your books, I scorn all the world's blessings and its wisdom. It is all paltry, fleeting, illusory, and as deceptive as a mirage. You may be proud, wise, and beautiful, but death will wipe you from the face of the earth the same as cellar mice, and your descendants, history, the immortality of your geniuses will freeze or burn along with the terrestrial globe.

"You have lost your minds and are following the wrong path. You take falsehood for truth and ugliness for beauty. You would be amazed if, owing to certain circumstances, apple and orange trees suddenly produced frogs and lizards instead of fruit, or roses smelled of horse sweat; so am I amazed at you, who have exchanged the sky for the earth. I do not want to understand you.

"To show you in practice my scorn for what you live by, I renounce the two million that I once dreamed of as of paradise, and which I now scorn. To deprive myself of my right to it, I will leave here five hours before the agreed term, thereby breaking the contract . . ."

Having read that, the banker put the paper on the table, kissed the strange man on the head, wept, and left the cottage. Never before, even after losing heavily on the stock market, had he felt such scorn for himself as he did now. On coming home, he went to bed, but for a long time agitation and tears did not let him sleep . . .

The next morning the pale-faced watchmen came running and informed him that they had seen the man who lived in the cottage climb out the window into the garden, go to the gate, and then disappear somewhere. Together with the servants, the banker went at once to the cottage and verified his prisoner's escape. To avoid unnecessary discussions, he took the paper with the renunciation from the table and, returning home, locked it in a safe.

1889

THE PRINCESS

THROUGH THE BIG, so-called "Red" gate of the N——sky Monastery drove a carriage and a foursome of fine, sleek horses. The hieromonks and novices who crowded near the gentry side of the guest house already recognized from afar, by the coachman and the horses, the lady who sat in the carriage as their good acquaintance, Princess Vera Gavrilovna.

An old man in livery jumped down from the box and helped the princess out of the carriage. She raised her dark veil, unhurriedly went up to each of the hieromonks to be blessed, then nodded affectionately to the novices and went into the house.

"What, have you been missing your princess?" she said to the monks who carried her things inside. "It's a whole month since I was here. Well, so I've come, look at your princess. And where is the Father Archimandrite?[1] My God, I'm burning with impatience! A wonderful, wonderful old man! You should be proud to have such an archimandrite."

When the archimandrite came in, the princess cried out rapturously, crossed her arms on her breast, and went to receive his blessing.

"No, no! Allow me to kiss it!" she said, seizing his hand and greedily kissing it three times. "How glad I am, holy father, to see you finally! You have no doubt forgotten your princess, but mentally I have lived every moment in your dear monastery. How good it is here! In this life for God, far from the vain world, there is some special charm, holy father, that I feel with all my soul, though I cannot convey it in words!"

The princess's cheeks flushed and tears welled up in her eyes. She talked without a pause, heatedly, while the archimandrite, an old man of about seventy, serious, homely, and shy, was silent, and only said from time to time, abruptly, in military fashion: "Just so, Your Excellency . . . yes, ma'am . . . I see, ma'am . . ."

"How long will you be staying with us?" he asked.

"I'll spend the night tonight, and tomorrow I'll go to see Klavdia Nikolaevna—we haven't seen each other for a long time—and the day after tomorrow I'll come back and stay for three or four days. I want my soul to rest here, holy father . . ."

The princess liked visiting the N———sky Monastery. Over the past two years it had been her favorite place, and during the summers she came there almost every month and spent two or three days, sometimes a week. The timid novices, the quiet, the low ceilings, the smell of cypress, the humble meals, the cheap curtains on the windows—it all touched her, moved her, and disposed her to contemplation and good thoughts. Spending half an hour there was enough for her to start feeling that she, too, was timid and humble, that she, too, smelled of cypress; the past became remote, lost its value, and the princess would begin to think that, despite her twenty-nine years, she very much resembled the old archimandrite and that, like him, she had been born not for riches, not for earthly greatness and love, but for a quiet life, hidden from the world, a life of twilight, like her rooms here . . .

It sometimes happens that a ray of sunlight suddenly peeks into the dark cell of an ascetic immersed in prayer, or a little bird alights in the window of the cell and sings its song; the severe ascetic smiles involuntarily, and in his breast, from under the heavy sorrow of his sins, as from under a stone, a stream of quiet, sinless joy suddenly begins to flow. It seemed to the princess that she had brought with her from outside just such a consolation as the ray of sunlight or the little bird. Her amiable, cheerful smile, meek eyes, voice, jokes, the whole of her in general, small, well-built, wearing simple black dresses, could not help arousing by her appearance a feeling of tenderness and joy in simple, stern people. Each of them, looking at her, could not help thinking: "God has sent us an angel . . ." And, sensing that each of them involuntarily thought that, she smiled still more amiably and tried to resemble a bird.

Having had her tea and rested, she went out for a stroll. The sun had already set. The princess smelled the fragrant moisture of the just-watered mignonettes coming from the monastery flower garden, and from the church came the quiet singing of male voices, which from a distance seemed very pleasant and sad. The vigil was in progress. In the dark windows where icon lamps meekly flickered, in the shadows, in the figure of the old monk who sat by an icon on the porch holding a cup for alms, there was inscribed so much serene peace that the princess somehow felt like weeping . . .

Outside the gate, on the footpath between the wall and the birches, where benches stood, it was already evening. The air was darkening very quickly . . . The princess strolled along the footpath, sat down on a bench, and fell to thinking.

She thought that it would be good to settle for her whole life in this monastery, where life was as quiet and serene as a summer evening; it would be good to forget completely about her ungrateful and libertine prince, about her enormous fortune, about the creditors who bothered her every day, about her misfortunes, about the maid Dasha, who had an insolent expression on her face that morning. It would be good to sit here on the bench for her whole life and look through the trunks of the birches at how wisps of evening mist hover at the foot of the hill; at how, far away over the forest, in a black cloud like a veil, rooks fly to their night roost; at how two novices—one mounted on a piebald horse, the other on foot—drive the horses to their night pasture and, rejoicing in their freedom, frolic like little children, their young voices ringing out in the motionless air so that you can catch every word. It was good to sit and listen to the silence: now the wind blows and stirs the tops of the birches, now a frog rustles in last year's leaves, now the bell behind the wall strikes the quarter hour . . . To sit motionless, listen, and think, think, think . . .

An old woman with a sack went by. The princess thought it would be good to stop this woman and say something tender, soulful, to help her . . . But the old woman turned the corner without looking at her even once.

A little later a tall man with a gray beard and wearing a straw hat appeared on the footpath. Coming up to the princess, he took off his hat and bowed, and by his big bald spot and sharp, hooked nose the princess recognized him as Doctor Mikhail Ivanovich, who some five years earlier had worked for her in Dubovki. She remembered someone telling her that the doctor's wife had died a year ago, and she wanted to show him sympathy, to comfort him.

"You probably don't recognize me, Doctor?" she asked, smiling affably.

"No, Princess, I did recognize you," the doctor said, taking off his hat again.

"Well, thank you, and here I thought you'd forgotten your princess. People only remember their enemies, not their friends. So you've come to pray?"

"I'm here overnight every Saturday, on duty. I treat people."

"Well, how are you?" the princess asked, sighing. "I heard that your wife passed away! What a misfortune!"

"Yes, Princess, for me it is a great misfortune."

"What can be done? We should humbly bear our misfortunes. Not a single hair falls from a man's head without the will of Providence."

"Yes, Princess."

To the princess's meek, affable smile and her sighs, the doctor replied coldly and drily: "Yes, Princess." And the expression on his face was cold and dry.

"What else should I tell him?" thought the princess.

"It's so long since we've seen each other, though!" she said. "Five years! So much water has flowed under the bridge in that time, so many changes have occurred, it's even frightening to think of it! You know I got married . . . from a countess I've become a princess. And I'm already separated from my husband."

"Yes, I heard."

"God has sent me many trials! You've probably also heard that I'm almost ruined. To pay my unfortunate husband's debts, my estates in Dubovki and Kiryakovo and Sofyino have been sold. I have only Baranovo and Mikhaltsevo left. It's frightening to look back: so many changes, all sorts of misfortunes, so many mistakes!"

"Yes, Princess, many mistakes."

The princess was slightly embarrassed. She knew her mistakes; they were all of such an intimate sort that she alone could think and speak of them. She could not help herself and asked:

"What mistakes are you thinking of?"

"You've mentioned them, which means you know . . . ," the doctor replied and smiled wryly. "Why talk about them?"

"No, tell me, Doctor. I'll be very grateful to you! And please don't stand on ceremony with me. I love hearing the truth."

"I'm not your judge, Princess."

"My judge? If you speak in such a tone, it means you know something. Tell me!"

"If you wish, I will. Only, unfortunately, I'm not a good speaker, and it's not always possible to understand me."

The doctor thought a little and began:

"There are many mistakes, but in fact the main one, in my opinion, was the general spirit that . . . that reigned in all your estates. You see, I'm not good at expressing myself. The main thing was this—a dislike, an aversion to people, which was felt in positively everything. Your whole system of life was built on this aversion. Aversion to the human voice, to faces, the backs of heads, ways of walking . . . in short, to everything that makes up a human being. In all the doorways and on the stairs stand well-fed, crude and lazy lackeys in livery, to keep improperly dressed people from entering the house; the chairs in the front hall have high backs, so that during balls and receptions the servants won't soil the wallpaper with their heads; there are thick rugs in all the rooms, so that human footsteps will not be heard; whoever enters is warned to talk little and softly, and to avoid saying anything that might affect the imagination or the nerves. And in your study a visitor does not get a handshake and is not invited to sit down, just as now you did not shake my hand or invite me to sit down . . ."

"Very well, if you want!" said the princess, holding out her hand and smiling. "To be angry over such a trifle, really . . ."

"Do I seem angry?" The doctor laughed, but immediately flushed, took off his hat, and, waving it, began to speak heatedly. "Frankly speaking, I've been waiting a long time for a chance to tell you everything, everything . . . That is, I want to tell you that you look at all people Napoleonically, as cannon fodder. But Napoleon at least had an idea of some sort, while you have nothing except an aversion to people!"

"So I have an aversion to people!" the princess smiled, shrugging her shoulders in amazement. "Do I!"

"Yes, you do! You need facts? Very well! In your Mikhaltsevo three of your former cooks live by begging. They went blind in your kitchens from the heat of the stoves. On your many thousands of acres, all that there is of healthy, strong, and handsome, all of it has been taken by you and your hangers-on as servants, lackeys, coachmen. All this two-legged livestock is being bred for lackeydom; they overeat, grow crude, lose the image and likeness,[2] in short . . . Young doctors, agronomists, teachers, intelligent workers in general, my God, they're taken from their work, from honest labor, and forced for the sake of a crust of bread to participate in all sorts of puppet comedies that are an embarrassment for any decent person! Before three years go by, a young man in your service turns into a hypocrite, a lickspittle, a squealer . . . Is that good? Your Polish managers, these lowdown spies, all these Kasimirs and Kaetans, prowl over your thousands of acres from morning to night and try to take three hides off one ox just to please you. Sorry, I'm not putting things very systematically, but never mind! Simple people on your estates don't count as human beings. And those princes, counts, and bishops who visited you, you considered as décor, not as living people. But the main thing . . . the main thing, which outrages me most of all—you have a fortune of over a million, and you do nothing for people, nothing!"

The princess sat there astonished, frightened, offended, not knowing what to say or how to behave. No one had ever spoken to her in such a tone. The doctor's unpleasant, angry voice, his awkward, faltering speech, produced in her ears and head a sharp, rapping noise, and after a while it seemed to her that the gesticulating doctor was hitting her on the head with his hat.

"That's not true!" she brought out in a soft and pleading voice. "I did a lot of good for people, you know that yourself!"

"Oh, enough!" cried the doctor. "Can you still go on considering your charity work as something serious and useful, and not as a puppet comedy? It was a comedy from beginning to end, it was a performance of loving one's neighbor, such an obvious performance that

even children and stupid peasant women understood it! Take your—
what was it?—hospice for homeless old women, where you made me
something like the head doctor, and you yourself were an honorary
trustee. Oh, Lord God, what a splendid institution! You had a house
built, with parquet floors and weathervanes on the roof, then a dozen
old women were found in the villages and forced to sleep under flannel blankets, on Dutch linen sheets, and eat fruit drops."

The doctor snorted maliciously into his hat and went on quickly,
stammering:

"That was a performance! The lower-ranking hospice workers put
the blankets and sheets under lock and key so that the old women
wouldn't dirty them, and let the old hags sleep on the floor! The old
women didn't dare sit on the beds, or put on bed jackets, or walk
on the polished parquet. Everything was kept for display and hidden
from the old women, as if from thieves, and the old women secretly
went begging for food and clothing, and prayed to God day and night
to get out of this jail as soon as possible and to be rid of the sancti-
monious admonishments of the well-fed scoundrels you appointed to
look after them. And what were the higher ranks up to? That was simply delightful! About twice a week, in the evening, thirty-five thousand messengers came galloping³ to announce that the next day the
princess—you, that is—would come to the hospice. That meant that
the next day I had to abandon my patients, dress up, and go to the
parade. Very well, I arrive. The old women, all fresh and clean, are
already lined up and waiting. Around them walks the retired garrison
rat—the supervisor, with his sweet, lickspittle smile. The old women
yawn and exchange glances, but they're afraid to murmur. We wait.
The junior manager comes galloping. Half an hour later the senior
manager, then the head manager of the accounting office, then someone else, then someone else . . . no end to the galloping! They all have
mysterious, solemn faces. We wait and wait, we shift our feet, we keep
glancing at our watches—all this in sepulchral silence, because we all
hate each other and are at daggers drawn . . . An hour goes by, then
another, and now, finally, a carriage appears in the distance, and . . .
and . . ."

The doctor dissolved in high-pitched laughter and in a high little
voice squeaked:

"You step out of the carriage, and the old hags, at the command of the garrison rat, start to sing: 'How glorious is our Lord in Zion, the tongue cannot tell . . .'[4] Not bad, eh?"

The doctor guffawed in a bass voice and waved his hand, as if wishing to show that he could not utter a word more from laughter. He laughed painfully, sharply, with tightly clenched teeth, as unkind people laugh, and by his voice, his face, and his gleaming, slightly impudent eyes one could tell that he deeply despised the princess, and the hospice, and the old women. There was nothing funny or merry in anything he told so ineptly and crudely, but he guffawed with pleasure and even with glee.

"And the school?" he went on, breathing heavily from laughter. "Remember how you wanted to teach the peasant children yourself? You must have taught them very well, because soon all the boys ran away, so that they had to be whipped and then given money to come to you. And remember how you wanted to give bottles with your own hands to the nursing babies whose mothers worked in the fields? You went around the village lamenting that these babies were not at your service—the mothers had all taken them to the fields with them. Then the headman ordered the mothers to take turns leaving their babies for you to have fun with. It's amazing! Everyone fled from your good deeds like mice from a cat! And why? Very simple! Not because our people are ignorant and ungrateful, as you always explained, but because in all your escapades—forgive me the expression—there was not a pennyworth of love and mercy! There was only a wish to amuse yourslf with living dolls and nothing else . . . Somebody who is unable to distinguish people from lapdogs should not get involved in charitable works. I assure you, there's a big difference between people and lapdogs!"

The princess's heart was pounding terribly, there was a throbbing in her ears, and she still felt as if the doctor was hammering her on the head with his hat. The doctor spoke quickly, heatedly, and unpleasantly, stammering and gesticulating excessively; she could only understand that this was a rude, ill-bred, spiteful, ungrateful man talking to her, but what he wanted from her and what he was talking about she did not understand.

"Go away!" she said in a tearful voice, raising her hands to protect her head from the doctor's hat. "Go away!"

"And how you deal with your employees!" the doctor went on indignantly. "You don't consider them human beings and treat them like the worst swindlers. For instance, allow me to ask, what did you fire me for? I worked ten years for your father, then for you, honorably, with no holidays, no vacations; I earned the love of everyone for a hundred miles around, and suddenly one fine day it was announced to me that I was no longer employed! What for? I still don't understand! I, a doctor of medicine, a well-born man, a graduate of Moscow University, the father of a family, am such an insignificant little pipsqueak that I can be chucked out with no explanations! Why stand on ceremony with me? I heard later that my wife, without my knowledge, secretly went to you three times to plead for me, and you didn't receive her even once. They say she wept in the front hall. And for that I can never forgive the late woman! Never!"

The doctor fell silent and clenched his teeth, straining to think of something else very unpleasant and vengeful to say. He remembered something, and his scowling, cold face suddenly brightened.

"Or take your relation with this monastery!" he began eagerly. "You never spared anybody, and the holier the place, the greater the chance that it will get the full dose of your loving kindness and angelic meekness. Why do you keep coming here? What do you need from the monks here, if I may ask? What is Hecuba to you, or you to Hecuba?[5] Again it's an amusement, a game, a blasphemy against human beings, and nothing else. You don't believe in the monks' God, you have your own God in your heart, whom you arrived at with your own mind at spiritualistic séances; you look condescendingly at church rites, you don't go to the liturgies or vigils, you sleep till noon . . . Why do you come here? . . . You come with your own God to other people's monastery, and you imagine the monastery considers it a great honor! Oh, yes, of course! Have you ever asked, incidentally, what your visits cost the monks? You were pleased to arrive here tonight, but two days ago a messenger already came here on horseback, sent from your estate to warn them you were coming. Yesterday they spent the whole day preparing rooms for you and waiting. Today the advance guard arrived—an impudent maid, who keeps running around the yard, rustling, pestering with questions, giving orders . . . I can't stand it! Today the monks have been on the lookout all day: If you're not met with ceremony—it's bad! You'll complain to the bishop! 'Your Grace, the monks don't love me. I don't know what I've done to deserve it. True, I'm a great sinner, but I'm so unhappy!' One monastery already got a roasting because of you. The archimandrite is a busy, learned man who doesn't have a free moment, and you keep on summoning him to your rooms. No respect either for his old age or for his cloth. It would be one thing if you donated a lot, it wouldn't be so bad, but in all this time the monks haven't received even a hundred roubles from you!"

When the princess was upset, not understood, offended, and when she did not know what to say or do, she usually began to weep. And now she finally covered her face and began to weep in a thin, childish voice. The doctor suddenly fell silent and looked at her. His face darkened and became stern.

"Forgive me, Princess," he said hollowly. "I yielded to a spiteful feeling and forgot myself. That's not good."

And, with an embarrassed cough, forgetting to put his hat on, he quickly walked away from the princess.

Stars were already twinkling in the sky. On the other side of the monastery, the moon was probably rising, because the sky was clear, transparent, and tender. Bats raced noiselessly along the white monastery wall.

The clock slowly struck three-quarters of some hour, probably past eight. The princess stood up and slowly went to the gate. She felt hurt and was weeping, and it seemed to her that the trees, and the stars, and the bats were sorry for her; and the clock struck melodiously only in order to sympathize with her. She was weeping and thinking how good it would be to go into the monastery for the rest of her life. On quiet summer evenings she would stroll in solitude down the footpaths, hurt, insulted, misunderstood, and only God and the starry sky would see the suffering woman's tears. In the church the vigil was still going on. The princess stopped and listened to the singing; how good this singing sounded in the still, dark air! How sweet it was to weep and suffer to this singing!

Coming to her rooms, she looked at her tear-stained face in the mirror and powdered it, then sat down to supper. The monks knew that she liked pickled sterlet, tiny mushrooms, Malaga, and simple honey-cakes that leave a taste of cypress in the mouth, and each time she came they served her all that. Eating the mushrooms and following them with Malaga, the princess dreamed of how she would be utterly ruined and abandoned, how all these stewards, agents, clerks, and maids, for whom she had done so much, would betray her and start saying rude things; how all the people on earth would attack her, revile her, laugh at her; she would renounce her title of princess, renounce luxury and society, and go into the monastery without a word of reproach; she would pray for her enemies, and then everyone would suddenly understand her, would come to ask her forgiveness, but it would be too late . . .

After supper she knelt in the corner before an icon and read two chapters from the Gospel. Then the maid prepared her bed and she lay down. Stretching out under the white coverlet, she sighed sweetly and deeply, as one sighs after weeping, closed her eyes, and began to drift off into sleep . . .

In the morning she woke up and looked at her watch: it was half past nine. On the rug beside the bed stretched a narrow, bright strip of light from a ray that came through the window and just barely lit up the room. Behind the black window curtain flies were buzzing.

"It's early!" the princess thought and closed her eyes.

Stretching and luxuriating in the bed, she recalled yesterday's encounter with the doctor and all the thoughts she had fallen asleep with last night; she recalled that she had been unhappy. Then came the memory of her husband, who lived in Petersburg, then of her stewards, doctors, neighbors, official acquaintances . . . A long line of familiar men's faces passed by in her imagination. She smiled and thought that, if these people had been able to penetrate her soul and understand her, they would all be at her feet . . .

At a quarter past eleven she summoned the maid.

"Get me dressed, Dasha," she said languorously. "But first go and tell them to hitch up the horses. I must go to see Klavdia Nikolaevna."

Coming out of her rooms to get into the carriage, she squinted from the brightness of the daylight and laughed with pleasure: it was a wonderful day! Looking with her narrowed eyes at the monks who had gathered by the porch to see her off, she nodded affably and said:

"Goodbye, my friends! See you in two days."

She was pleasantly surprised to see the doctor among the monks by the porch. His face was pale and stern.

"Princess," he said, taking off his hat and smiling guiltily, "I've already been waiting here a long time for you. Forgive me, for God's sake . . . I was carried away yesterday by a mean, vengeful feeling, and I said a lot of . . . stupid things. In short, I ask your forgiveness."

The princess smiled affably and offered him her hand. He kissed it and blushed.

Trying to resemble a little bird, the princess fluttered into the carriage and nodded her head on all sides. Her heart was cheerful, serene, and warm, and she herself felt that her smile was unusually affectionate and gentle. As the carriage drove to the gate, then down the dusty road past the sheds and gardens, past long trains of Ukrainian carts and pilgrims walking in files to the monastery, she kept squinting and smiling gently. She thought there was no higher delight than to bring warmth, light, and joy everywhere, to forgive offenses, and to smile affably at one's enemies. The passing peasants bowed to her, the carriage softly whished by, the wheels raised clouds of dust which the wind carried over to the golden rye, and it seemed to the princess that her body was rocking, not on the cushions of the carriage, but on those clouds, and that she herself resembled a light, transparent cloud . . .

"I'm so happy!" she whispered, closing her eyes. "So happy!"

1889

After the Theater

NADYA ZELENINA CAME BACK with her mama from the theater, where there had been a performance of *Evgeny Onegin*, and, going to her room, quickly took off her dress, loosened her braid, and, wearing only a petticoat and a white bed jacket, hurriedly sat down at the table to write the sort of letter Tatiana wrote.[1]

"I love you," she wrote, "but you do not love me, you do not love me!"

She wrote it and laughed.

She was only sixteen and had never loved anyone yet. She knew that the officer Gorny and the student Gruzdev loved her, but now, after the opera, she felt like doubting their love. To be unloved and unhappy—how interesting! When the one loves much and the other is indifferent, there is something beautiful, touching, and poetic about it. Onegin is interesting in that he does not love at all, and Tatiana is enchanting because she loves so much, and if they loved each other equally and were happy, they might seem dull.

"So stop assuring me that you love me," Nadya went on writing, thinking about the officer Gorny. "I cannot believe you. You are very intelligent, cultivated, serious, you have great talents, and it may be that a brilliant future awaits you, while I am an uninteresting, worthless girl, and you know perfectly well that I will only be a hindrance in your life. True, you took a fancy to me, and you thought that in me you had met your ideal, but that was a mistake, and now you are already asking yourself in despair: why did I meet this girl? And only your kindness keeps you from admitting it! . . ."

Nadya felt sorry for herself, started to cry, and went on:

"It is painful for me to leave Mama and my brother, otherwise I would put on a nun's habit and go wherever my feet took me. And you would be free and would fall in love with someone else. Ah, if only I could die!"

Through her tears she could not make out what she was writing; brief rainbows trembled on the table, the floor, the ceiling, as if Nadya were looking through a prism. She could not write, so she leaned back in her armchair and started thinking about Gorny.

My God, how interesting, how charming men are! Nadya recalled what a wonderful expression—ingratiating, guilty, and gentle—the officer had when someone argued with him about music, and how he tried at the same time to keep his voice from sounding passionate. In society, where cool haughtiness and indifference are considered signs of good upbringing and noble character, one must hide one's passion. And so he does, but he doesn't succeed, and everybody knows perfectly well that he loves music passionately. Endless arguments about music, the bold opinions of uncomprehending people, keep him under constant strain; he becomes frightened, shy, taciturn. He plays the piano magnificently, like a true pianist, and if he were not an officer, he would probably be a famous musician.

The tears dried up in her eyes. Nadya recalled that Gorny had declared his love at a symphony concert and then downstairs by the cloakroom, where drafts were blowing from all sides.

"I am very glad that you have finally made the acquaintance of the student Gruzdev," she went on writing. "He is a very intelligent person, and you will probably like him. Yesterday he visited us and stayed until two. We were all delighted, and I was sorry you did not come. He said many remarkable things."

Nadya put her arms on the desk and lowered her head onto them, and her hair covered the letter. She recalled that the student Gruzdev also loved her and that he had the same right to a letter from her as Gorny. In fact, hadn't she better write to Gruzdev? Joy stirred in her breast for no reason at all: at first the joy was small and rolled around in her breast like a rubber ball; then it became wider, bigger, and surged up like a wave. Nadya had already forgotten about Gorny and Gruzdev, her thoughts were confused, and the joy was growing, growing, it spread from her breast into her arms and legs, and it seemed as if a light, cool breeze blew on her head and ruffled her hair. Her shoulders shook with quiet laughter, the table also shook, and the glass of the lamp, and tears from her eyes spattered the letter. She was unable to stop this laughter, and to show herself that she was not laughing for no reason, she hurriedly recalled something funny.

"What a funny poodle!" she said, feeling as if she was choking with laughter. "What a funny poodle!"

She remembered how, after tea yesterday, Gruzdev had frolicked with the poodle Maxim and then told about a very smart poodle who chased a raven in the yard, and the raven turned to him and said:

"Ah, you scallywag!"

The poodle, who did not know he was dealing with a learned raven, was terribly embarrassed and backed off in perplexity, then started barking.

"No, I'd better love Gruzdev," Nadya decided and tore up the letter.

She started thinking about the student, about his love, about her love, but it turned out that the thoughts in her head became blurred and she thought about everything: about Mama, about the street, about her pencil, about the grand piano . . . She was thinking joyfully and it turned out that everything was good, splendid, and her joy told her that this was not all, that a little later it would be still better. Soon it would be spring, summer, time to go with Mama to Gorbiki, Gorny will come for vacation, he will be strolling with her in the garden and courting her. Gruzdev will also come. He will play croquet and skittles with her, tell her funny or astonishing things. She passionately longed for the garden, the darkness, the clear sky, the stars. Again her shoulders shook with laughter, and it seemed to her that the room smelled of wormwood and a branch was knocking on the window.

She went to her bedroom, sat on the bed, and, not knowing what to do with her immense joy, which wearied her, gazed at the icon that hung at the head of her bed and kept saying:

"Lord! Lord! Lord!"

1892

History of a Business Enterprise

ANDREI ANDREEVICH SIDOROV inherited four thousand roubles from his mother and decided to open a bookshop with this money. Such a shop was extremely necessary. The town was drowning in ignorance and prejudice; the old people went to the bathhouse, the officials played cards and guzzled vodka, the ladies gossiped, the young people lived without ideals, the girls spent their days dreaming of getting married and eating buckwheat kasha, husbands beat their wives, and pigs walked in the streets.

"Ideas! More ideas!" thought Andrei Andreevich. "Ideas!"

He rented a space for the shop, went to Moscow, and brought back many old and recent authors and many textbooks, and he put all these goods on the shelves. For the first three weeks, no buyers came. Andrei Andreevich sat behind the counter reading Mikhailovsky[1] and tried to think honestly. When it inadvertently came to his head, for example, that it might be nice right now to eat some bream with kasha, he immediately caught himself: "Ah, how banal!" Every morning a chilled wench in a kerchief and leather galoshes over bare feet rushed into the shop and said:

"Gimme two kopecks' worth of vinegar!"

And Andrei Andreevich replied disdainfully:

"You've picked the wrong door, madam!"

When one of his friends came by, he would assume a significant and mysterious air, take from the furthest shelf the third volume of

Pisarev,[2] blow the dust off it, and looking as if he had something else in his shop but was afraid to show it, would say:

"Yes, my dear fellow . . . This thing, I must tell you, is not . . . Yes . . . Here, in a word, my dear fellow, I must point out, is something, you understand, that you read and just spread your arms . . . Yes."

"Watch out, brother, you may catch hell!"

After three weeks, the first customer came. He was a fat, gray-haired gentleman with side-whiskers, wearing a peaked cap with a red band, in all likelihood a landowner. He requested the second volume of the textbook *Russian Literature*.

"And do you have lead pencils?" he asked.

"I don't carry them."

"Too bad . . . A pity. Who wants to drive to the market for a trifle . . ."

"In fact, it's too bad I don't carry lead pencils," Andrei Andreevich thought when the customer left. "Here in the provinces, you shouldn't have a narrow specialization, you should sell everything related to education and contributing to it in one way or another."

He wrote to Moscow, and before the month was out there was in his shop window a display of pens, pencils, notebooks, slates, and other school supplies. Boys and girls began coming to him occasionally, and there was even one day when he made a rouble and forty kopecks. Once the wench in leather galoshes came flying headlong to him; he had already opened his mouth to tell her disdainfully that she had picked the wrong door, but she shouted:

"Give me a kopeck's worth of paper and a seven-kopeck stamp!"

After that Andrei Andreevich began to carry postage and revenue stamps, and promissory note forms along with them. Some eight months later, counting from the day he opened, a lady came to buy pens.

"And might you have school satchels?" she asked.

"Alas, ma'am, I don't carry them!"

"Ah, what a pity! In that case show me what dolls you have, only of the cheaper sort."

"I have no dolls, either, ma'am!" Andrei Andreevich said sorrowfully.

Without thinking twice, he wrote to Moscow, and soon satchels, dolls, drums, sabers, harmonicas, balls, and all sorts of toys appeared in his shop.

"That's all nothing!" he said to his friends. "Just wait till I start selling training manuals and intelligence games! In my shop, you understand, the educational section will be grounded, as they say, in the finest achievements of science, in a word . . ."

He ordered dumbbells, croquet, backgammon, children's billiards, gardening tools for children, and some two dozen very sophisticated games of reasoning. Then the inhabitants, walking past his shop, to their great delight saw two bicycles: one big, the other smaller. And the trade went famously. It went especially well before Christmas, when Andrei Andreevich put a notice in the window that he was selling Christmas tree ornaments.

"I'm going to slip some hygiene in for them, you understand," he said to his friends, rubbing his hands. "Just wait till I get to Moscow! I'll have such filters and scientific advancements of every sort, you'll all lose your minds, in a word. Science, my dear fellow, cannot be ignored! No-o-o!"

Having made a lot of money, he went to Moscow and bought all sorts of merchandise for five thousand roubles, in cash and on credit. There were filters, and exquisite desk lamps, and guitars, and hygienic underwear for children, and pacifiers, and wallets, and zoological collections. Besides that he also bought five hundred roubles' worth of exquisite china, and was glad to have bought it, because beautiful objects develop refined taste and soften morals. On returning home from Moscow, he started placing the new merchandise on the shelves and on stands. And it somehow happened that, when he climbed up to clear an upper shelf, there was some sort of tremor, and ten volumes of Mikhailovsky fell from the shelf one after another. One volume hit him on the head, the rest fell down right on the lamps and broke two glass spheres.

"Anyhow, that's . . . heavy writing!" Andrei Andreevich murmured, scratching himself.

He gathered up all the books, tied them with string, and hid them under the counter. A couple of days later he was informed that his neighbor the grocer had been sentenced to a penal battalion for torturing his nephew, and that his shop was for rent. Andrei Andreevich was very happy about it and asked to rent the shop himself. Soon a doorway was broken through the wall, and the two shops, united into one, were chock-full of merchandise. Since the customers who came to the other half of the shop were in the habit of asking for tea, sugar, and kerosene, Andrei Andreevich, without thinking twice, introduced groceries as well.

Nowadays he is one of the most prominent shopkeepers in our town. He sells china, tobacco, tar, soap, pretzels, fabric, haberdashery and chandlery, guns, hides, and hams. He has rented a wine cellar at the market, and they say he is going to open a family bathhouse with private rooms. The books that used to stand on his shelves, including volume three of Pisarev, were sold long ago at one rouble five kopecks per thirty pounds.

At birthday parties or weddings, former friends, whom Andrei Andreevich now mockingly styles "Americans," occasionally start talking to him about progress, literature, and other lofty matters.

"Have you read the latest issue of *The Messenger of Europe*?"[3] they ask him.

"No, sirs, I haven't . . . ," he replies, narrowing his eyes and playing with a heavy watch chain. "That doesn't concern us. We're taken up with more positive things."

1892

NEIGHBORS

PYOTR MIKHAILYCH IVASHIN was badly out of sorts. His sister, a young girl, had gone off to Vlasich, a married man. To rid himself somehow of the oppressive, dejected mood that never left him either at home or in the fields, he called upon the help of his sense of justice, his good, honorable convictions—for he had always stood for free love!—but that did not help, and each time he involuntarily arrived at the same conclusion as the stupid nanny, that is, that his sister had behaved badly, and Vlasich had stolen her away. And that was painful.

Their mother spent whole days without leaving her room, the nanny spoke in a whisper, the aunt was at the point of leaving each day, and her suitcases were first carried to the front hall, then back to her room. In the house, in the yard, and in the garden there was a hush, as in the house of a dead person. It seemed to Pyotr Mikhailych that the aunt, the servants, and even the peasants looked at him mysteriously and with perplexity, as if they wanted to say: "Your sister has been seduced, why don't you do something?" And he reproached himself for not doing something, though he did not know what, in fact, the something should consist in.

Six days went by this way. On the seventh—it was on Sunday after lunch—a mounted messenger brought a letter. The address was written in a familiar woman's handwriting: "To Her Excel. Anna Nikolaevna Ivashina." For some reason it seemed to Pyotr Mikhailych that there was something challenging, feisty, liberal in the look of the letter, the handwriting, the abbreviated word "Excel." And women's liberalism was stubborn, implacable, cruel . . .

"She'd sooner die than show indulgence to her poor mother by asking for her forgiveness," Pyotr Mikhailych thought, going to his mother with the letter.

His mother was lying in bed, fully dressed. Seeing her son, she got up impetuously and, tucking back the gray hair that had strayed from under her bonnet, quickly asked:

"What is it? What is it?"

"This was sent . . . ," the son said, handing her the letter.

Zina's name, and even the word "she," was not pronounced at home; they spoke of Zina impersonally: "was sent," "left" . . . The mother recognized her daughter's handwriting, and her face became unattractive, unpleasant, and her gray hair again strayed from under the bonnet.

"No!" she said, drawing her hands back as if the letter had burned her fingers. "No, no, never! Not for anything!"

The mother sobbed hysterically from grief and shame; she obviously wanted to read the letter, but was hindered by her pride. Pyotr Mikhailych knew that he should open the letter and read it aloud, but he was suddenly overcome with such anger as he had never felt before. He ran out to the yard and shouted to the messenger:

"Say there'll be no reply! No reply! Say just that, you brute!"

And he tore up the letter; then tears came to his eyes, and feeling himself cruel, guilty, and miserable, he went out to the fields.

He was only twenty-seven, but he was already fat, dressed like an old man in loose and baggy clothes, and suffered from shortness of breath. He already had all the makings of an old bachelor landowner. He did not fall in love, did not think of marrying, and loved only his mother, his sister, the nanny, and the gardener Vassilyich; he loved to eat well, loved his after-dinner nap and talking about politics and lofty matters . . . In his day he had finished university, but he now looked at it as if he had gone through mandatory service for young men from eighteen to twenty-five; at any rate the thoughts that now wandered through his head every day had nothing to do with the university and the disciplines he had studied.

In the fields it was hot and still, as before rain. In the forest it was sultry, and a heavy, fragrant smell came from the pine trees and the rotting leaves. Pyotr Mikhailych stopped frequently and wiped his wet forehead. He looked over his winter and summer crops, went around the clover field, and twice disturbed a partridge and her chicks on the edge of the forest; and all the while he was thinking that this unbearable situation could not last forever, and that it had to be ended one way or another. Ended anyhow, stupidly, wildly, but ended without fail.

"But how? What am I to do?" he asked himself, glancing pleadingly at the sky and at the trees, as if begging them for help.

But the sky and the trees were silent. Honorable convictions were no help, and common sense suggested that there was no resolution for the tormenting question except something stupid, and that today's scene with the messenger was not the last of its kind. What else might happen—it was frightening to think!

As he returned home, the sun was already setting. It now seemed to him that the question could in no way be resolved. To reconcile with the accomplished fact was impossible, not to reconcile was also impossible, and there was nothing in between. As he walked down the road, taking off his hat and fanning himself with his handkerchief, and still over a mile from home, he heard the jingle of bells behind him. It was an intricate and quite successful combination of big and little bells, which produced a glassy sound. This jingle could belong only to the police chief Medovsky, a former hussar officer, who had squandered his fortune and gone to seed, an ailing man, a distant relation to Pyotr Mikhailych. He was a familiar at the Ivashins', had a tender paternal feeling for Zina and admired her.

"I'm on my way to your place," he said, catching up with Pyotr Mikhailych. "Get in, I'll give you a lift."

He was smiling and looked cheerful; evidently he did not know yet that Zina had gone off to Vlasich; or maybe he had been told, but did not believe it. Pyotr Mikhailych felt himself in an embarrassing position.

"You're quite welcome," he murmured, blushing to the point of tears and not knowing what and how to lie. "I'm very glad," he went on, trying to smile, "but . . . Zina has gone and Mama is sick."

"What a pity!" the police chief said, looking pensively at Pyotr Mikhailych. "And I was planning to spend the evening with you. Where did Zinaida Mikhailovna go?"

"To the Sinitskys', and from there, I think, to the monastery. I don't know for sure."

The police chief talked a little longer, then turned back. Pyotr Mikhailych walked home and thought with horror of how the police chief would feel when he learned the truth. Pyotr Mikhailych pictured that feeling to himself and went into the house experiencing it.

"Help us, Lord, help us," he thought.

In the dining room his aunt was sitting alone over evening tea. On her face, as usual, there was an expression which said that, though she was weak and defenseless, she would not allow anyone to offend her. Pyotr Mikhailych sat at the other end of the table (he did not like his aunt) and silently began to drink his tea.

"Your mother had no dinner again today," the aunt said. "You should pay attention, Petrusha. Starving yourself to death doesn't help anything."

It seemed absurd to Pyotr Mikhailych that his aunt should interfere in what was none of her business and think her departure was connected with Zina's leaving. He wanted to say something insolent, but restrained himself. And, as he restrained himself, he felt that the time had come to act, and that he could no longer stand it. To act at once, or to fall down, scream, and beat his head on the floor. He imagined Vlasich and Zina, two self-satisfied liberals, kissing each other somewhere under a maple tree, and everything oppressive and malignant that had accumulated in him over the past seven days heaped itself on Vlasich.

"One seduced and stole my sister," he thought, "another will come and put a knife in my mother, a third will set my house on fire or rob me . . . And all that in the guise of personal friendship, lofty ideas, suffering!"

"No, it will never be!" Pyotr Mikhailych suddenly cried out and banged his fist on the table.

He jumped up and ran out of the dining room. In the stable stood the steward's saddled horse. He mounted it and galloped off to Vlasich.

A whole storm rose up in his soul. He felt the need to do something outrageous, drastic, even if he would repent of it for the rest of his life. Call Vlasich a scoundrel, slap him in the face, and challenge him to a duel? But Vlasich was not the sort to fight a duel; the scoundrel and the slap would make him still more miserable, and he would withdraw still more deeply into himself. These miserable, uncomplaining people are the most unbearable, the most oppressive people. They can do anything with impunity. When such a miserable person, in response to a deserved reproach, looks at you with deep, guilty eyes, smiles painfully, and obediently offers his head, it seems that justice itself will be unable to raise a hand against him.

"Never mind. I'll hit him with my whip in front of her and say all sorts of insolent things to him," Pyotr Mikhailych decided.

He rode through his woods and wastelands, and imagined how Zina, to justify her act, would talk about women's rights, about personal freedom, and about there being no difference between religious and civil marriage. She would argue in her womanly way about things she does not understand. And probably in the end she would ask: "How do you enter into it? What right have you got to interfere?"

"Yes, I have no right," Pyotr Mikhailych muttered. "So much the better . . . The more rude, the less right, the better."

It was stifling. Swarms of mosquitoes hung low over the ground, and in the wastelands lapwings wept pitifully. Everything portended rain, but there was not a single cloud. Pyotr Mikhailych crossed his boundary and galloped over a smooth, level field. He often took this road and knew every little bush, every pothole on it. What now in the twilight looked like a dark cliff far ahead of him in the twilight was a red church; he could picture it to himself in minute detail, even the stucco of the front gate and the calves that always grazed inside the fence. Half a mile to the right of the gate was a dark grove that belonged to Count Koltovich. And beyond the grove Vlasich's land already began.

From behind the church and the count's grove an enormous black cloud was looming up, with pale lightning flashing in it.

"Here it comes!" thought Pyotr Mikhailych. "Help us, Lord, help us!"

The horse soon became tired from going so quickly, and Pyotr

Mikhailych was tired as well. The dark cloud looked at him angrily, as if advising him to go back home. He felt a little frightened.

"I'll prove to them that they're not right!" he tried to encourage himself. "They'll say that this is free love, personal freedom; but freedom is in abstinence, not in subjection to passions. What they have is depravity, not freedom!"

Here was the count's big pond; the cloud turned it dark blue and gloomy, it smelled of dampness and slime. By the dam two willows, an old one and a young one, leaned tenderly towards each other. Two weeks earlier, Pyotr Mikhailych and Vlasich had come there on foot, singing in low voices the old student song: "Not to love means to bury your young life . . ." A pathetic song!

There was a rumble of thunder as Pyotr Mikhailych rode through the grove, and the trees rustled and bent in the wind. He had to hurry. There was no more than a mile left to go from the grove across the meadow to Vlasich's estate. Here old birches stood on both sides of the road. They looked as sad and miserable as their master Vlasich, and were as gaunt and lanky as he. Big raindrops splashed on the birches and the grass; the wind died down at once, and there was a smell of wet soil and poplars. Then Vlasich's fence appeared with its yellow acacia, which was also gaunt and lanky; where the grillwork had fallen down, you could see the neglected orchard.

Pyotr Mikhailych was no longer thinking of the slap in the face or the whip, and did not know what he was going to do at Vlasich's. He turned coward. He feared for himself and for his sister, and was frightened that he was about to see her. How would she behave with her brother? What would the two of them talk about? Shouldn't he turn back before it was too late? With these thoughts he rode down the linden alley towards the house, skirted the thick bushes of lilacs, and suddenly saw Vlasich.

Vlasich, hatless, in a cotton shirt and high boots, stooping under the rain, was walking from the corner of the house towards the porch; behind him came a workman carrying a hammer and a box of nails. They must have been repairing a shutter that was banging in the wind. Seeing Pyotr Mikhailych, Vlasich stopped.

"Is it you?" he said and smiled. "Well, that's nice."

"Yes, I've come, as you see . . . ," Pyotr Mikhailych said softly, shaking off the rain with both hands.

"Well, that's good. I'm very glad," Vlasich said, but did not offer his hand: evidently he hesitated and waited for a hand to be offered him. "It's good for the oats!" he said and looked up at the sky.

"Yes."

They silently went into the house. The door to the right from the front hall led to another hallway and then to the reception room, the door to the left to a small room where the steward lived in winter. Pyotr Mikhailych and Vlasich went into that room.

"Where did you get caught by the rain?" Vlasich asked.

"Not far away. Almost by the house."

Pyotr Mikhailych sat down on the bed. He was glad that the rain made noise and that the room was dark. It was better that way: not so frightening, and there was no need to look his interlocutor in the face. He was no longer angry, but only fearful and vexed with himself. He felt that he had begun badly and that this visit of his would come to nothing.

The two were silent for a time and pretended to be listening to the rain.

"Thank you, Petrusha," Vlasich began, clearing his throat. "I'm very grateful to you for coming. It is magnanimous and noble on your part. I understand that, and, believe me, I value it highly. Believe me."

He looked out the window and went on, standing in the middle of the room.

"It all happened somehow in secret, as if we were concealing it from you. The consciousness that you might be offended and angry with us put a stain on our happiness all these days. But allow me to justify myself. We acted in secret not because we had little trust in you. In the first place, it all happened suddenly, by some sort of inspiration, and there was no time to reason things out. Secondly, this is an intimate, ticklish matter . . . it was awkward to mix a third person into it, even such a close one as you. But the main thing is that in all this we counted strongly on your magnanimity. You are a very magnanimous, very noble person. I'm infinitely grateful to you. If you ever need my life, come and take it."[1]

Vlasich spoke in a quiet, muffled bass, all on the same note, as if he were humming; he was obviously nervous. Pyotr Mikhailych sensed that it was his turn to speak, and that to listen and say nothing would mean that in fact he was playing the part of a magnanimous and noble simpleton, and that was not what he had come there for. He quickly stood up and said in a low voice, breathlessly:

"Listen, Grigory, you know I loved you and never wished my sister a better husband; but what's happened is terrible! It's awful to think of it!"

"Why awful?" Vlasich asked in a faltering voice. "It would be awful if we had acted badly, but that isn't so!"

"Listen, Grigory, you know I'm without prejudice; but, forgive my frankness, in my opinion you both acted egocentrically. Of course, I wouldn't say this to Zina, it would upset her, but you should know: Mother is suffering so much, it's hard to describe."

"Yes, that's sad." Vlasich sighed. "We foresaw it, Petrusha, but what were we to do? If your action upsets someone, that doesn't mean it's bad. Nothing to be done! Any serious step you take is inevitably going to upset someone. If you go to fight for freedom, that will also make your mother suffer. Nothing to be done! Anyone who places the peace of his family above all else must completely renounce the life of ideas."

There was a bright flash of lightning outside the window, and this flash seemed to change the course of Vlasich's thinking. He sat down beside Pyotr Mikhailych and began saying something completely uncalled for.

"I'm in awe of your sister, Petrusha," he said. "When I used to visit you, I had the feeling each time as if I was on a pilgrimage, and I actually prayed before Zina. Now my awe increases with each day. She is higher than a wife for me! Higher!" (Vlasich raised his arms.) "She is sacred to me. Since she's been living here, I enter my house as if it were a temple. She's a rare, extraordinary, noble woman!"

"So, he's grinding away on his barrel-organ!" thought Pyotr Mikhailych. He did not like the word "woman."

"Why don't you really get married?" he asked. "How much does your wife want for a divorce?"

"Seventy-five thousand."

"That's a bit steep. What if you bargain?"

"She won't yield a kopeck. She's a terrible woman, brother!" Vlasich sighed. "I never told you about her before, it was disgusting to recall, but since there's now an occasion, I will. I married her under the influence of a good, honest impulse. In our regiment, if you want the details, a battalion commander took up with an eighteen-year-old girl, that is, he simply seduced her, lived with her for a couple of months, and abandoned her. She ended up in the most terrible situation. She was ashamed to go back to her parents, and they wouldn't take her; her lover had abandoned her—so go and sell yourself at the barracks. The comrades in the regiment were indignant. They weren't saints themselves, but the baseness here was too offensive. Besides, everyone in the regiment detested this battalion commander. And, to do him dirt, you see, the indignant lieutenants all started a subscription to raise money for the unfortunate girl. Well, so, when we young subalterns met together and started laying out five or ten roubles, I suddenly had a brainstorm. The situation seemed all too suitable for a heroic deed. I hurried to the girl and in ardent phrases expressed my commiseration to her. And while going to her and then talking to her, I loved her ardently, as someone humiliated and insulted.[2] Yes . . . Well, it so happened that a week after that I proposed to her. My superiors and my comrades found my marriage incompatible with the dignity of an officer. That inflamed me still more. So, you see, I wrote a long letter in which I asserted that my action ought to be written down in the history of the regiment in golden letters, and so on. I sent the letter to my commander and copies to my comrades. Well, of course, I was agitated, and did not do it without some sharpness. I was asked to leave the regiment. I put the draft away somewhere, I'll give it to you to read some day. It's written with great feeling. You'll see what honorable, bright moments I lived through. I handed in my resignation and came here with my wife. My father left some debts, I had no money, and my wife made acquaintances from day one, started dressing up and playing cards, so I had to mortgage the estate. She led a bad life, you see, and of all my neighbors you alone were not her lover. A couple of years later I gave her smart money—all I had then—and she left for the city. Yes . . . And now I pay her twelve hundred a year. A terrible woman! There's a fly, brother, that sticks a larva on a spider's back, so that it can't shake it off; the larva attaches itself to the spider and drinks its heart's blood. In just the same way this woman is attached to me and drinks my heart's blood. She hates and despises me for doing such a stupid thing, that is, marrying a woman like her. She finds my magnanimity pathetic. 'An intelligent man dropped me,' she says, 'and a fool picked me up.' In her opinion, only a pathetic idiot could act as I did. It's unbearably painful for me, brother. Generally, brother, I'll say parenthetically, fate weighs me down. It really weighs me down."

Pyotr Mikhailych listened to Vlasich and asked himself in perplexity: How could Zina like this man so much? None too young—he was already forty-one—skinny, gangly, narrow-chested, with a long nose and some gray in his beard. His talk is like humming, his smile is sickly, and when he talks he waves his arms awkwardly. No health, no handsome masculine manners, no social grace, no gaiety, and on the outside something lackluster and indefinite. He dresses tastelessly, his furniture is depressing, he doesn't acknowledge poetry or painting, because "they don't respond to the needs of the day," meaning he doesn't understand them; music doesn't touch him. He is a bad landowner. His estate is in total disorder and is mortgaged; he pays twelve percent on his second mortgage, and on top of that owes about ten thousand in promissory notes. When the time comes to pay interest or send money to his wife, he begs loans from everybody with a look as if his house is burning down, and at the same time he rushes headlong to sell his entire winter stock of kindling for five roubles, or a haystack for three roubles, and then orders that they stoke the stoves with garden fencing or old hotbed frames. His meadows are destroyed by pigs, in the woods peasant cattle eat the young growth, and with every winter there are fewer and fewer old trees; beehives and rusty buckets lie about in his garden and vegetable patch. He has no talents or gifts, nor even the ordinary ability to live as people live. In practical life he is a naïve, weak man, whom it is easy to deceive and offend, and it's not for nothing that his peasants call him "a bit simple."

He is a liberal and in the district is considered a red, but that, too, comes out boring in him. There is no originality or pathos in his freethinking; he is outraged, indignant, or joyful somehow all in the same tone, unimpressively and listlessly. Even in moments of great inspiration, he does not raise his head and remains stoop-shouldered. But most boring of all is that he even manages to express his good, honorable ideas in such a way that they come out banal and retrograde. It reminds you of something old, read long ago, when he begins, slowly and with an air of profundity, to talk about his honest, bright moments, his best years, or when he extols the young, who have always gone and still go in advance of society, or denounces Russian men for putting on their dressing-gowns at the age of thirty and forgetting the precepts of their *alma mater*. When you stay overnight, he puts Pisarev or Darwin on your night table. If you tell him you've read them, he goes and brings you Dobrolyubov.[3]

In the district this was known as freethinking, and many regarded this freethinking as an innocent and harmless eccentricity; for him, however, it was a cause of profound unhappiness. It was that larva he had just been talking about: it attached itself firmly to him and drank his heart's blood. In the past a strange marriage in Dostoevsky's taste,[4] long letters and their copies, in poor, illegible handwriting, but with great feeling; endless misunderstandings, explanations, disappointments; then debts, a second mortgage, payments to his wife, monthly loans—and all that of no use to anyone, neither himself nor other people. And in the present, as before, he keeps bustling, seeks a heroic deed, meddles in other people's affairs; as before, at every favorable opportunity there are long letters and copies, tiresome commonplace conversations about communes or the developing of arts and crafts, or establishing the cheese-making industry—conversations that resemble each other, as if he prepared them not in his living brain, but by machine. And, finally, this scandal with Zina, the outcome of which is as yet unknown!

And meanwhile his sister Zina is young—only twenty-two—good-looking, graceful, cheerful. She is a giggler, a chatterbox, an arguer, a passionate musician; she is a connoisseur of clothes, of books, and of good furniture, and she would not suffer having a room like this at home, smelling of boots and cheap vodka. She is also liberal-minded, but in her freethinking one senses an abundance of force, the ambition of a young, strong, brave girl, a passionate desire to be better and more original than others . . . How could it happen that she fell in love with Vlasich?

"He's a Don Quixote, a stubborn fanatic, a maniac," Pyotr Mikhailych thought, "and she's as slack, weak-willed, and yielding as I am . . . We both surrender quickly and without resistance. She fell in love with him; but don't I love him myself, in spite of it all . . ."

Pyotr Mikhailych considered Vlasich a good, honest, but narrow and one-sided man. In his worries and sufferings and in his whole life he did not see any lofty aims, either immediate or distant, but only boredom and an inability to live. His self-denial and all that Vlasich called heroic deeds or honest impulses seemed to him a useless waste of strength, unnecessary blank shots, which used up a great deal of powder. That Vlasich believed fanatically in the extraordinary honesty and infallibility of his thinking, seemed to him naïve and even morbid; and that all his life Vlasich had somehow managed to confuse the worthless with the lofty, that he had married stupidly and considered it a heroic deed, and then had taken up with women and saw in it the triumph of some idea—that was simply incomprehensible.

But Pyotr Mikhailych still loved Vlasich, sensed in him the presence of some force, and for some reason never had the heart to contradict him.

Vlasich sat down quite close to him, so as to talk under the noise of the rain, in the dark, and had already cleared his throat, prepared to tell something long, like the story of his marriage; but Pyotr Mikhailych found it unbearable to listen; he was tormented by the thought that he was about to see his sister.

"Yes, you weren't lucky in life," he said gently, "but, forgive me, we've strayed from the main thing. We're talking about something else."

"Yes, yes, indeed. So let's get back to the main thing," Vlasich said and stood up. "I'm telling you, Petrusha, our conscience is clear. We weren't married in church, but our marriage is perfectly legitimate— it's not for me to prove and not for you to judge. Your thinking is as free as mine, and, thank God, we can't have any disagreement on that account. As for our future, that shouldn't alarm you. I'll work till I sweat blood, I won't sleep nights—in short, I'll pour all my strength into making Zina happy. Her life will be beautiful. You ask if I'll be able to do it? I will, brother! When a man thinks about one and the same thing every moment, it's not hard for him to achieve what he wants. But let's go to Zina. She'll be so glad!"

Pyotr Mikhailych's heart pounded. He got up and followed Vlasich into the front hall and from there into the reception room. In this enormous, gloomy room there was only a piano and a long row of old chairs with bronze trimming, on which no one ever sat. On the piano one candle was burning. From the reception room they silently passed into the dining room. It was also vast and uninviting. In the middle of the room stood a round extension table on six fat legs, and only one candle. The clock, in a big red case that resembled an icon case, showed half past two.

Vlasich opened the door to the next room and said:

"Zinochka, Petrusha's here!"

At once there was the sound of hurrying footsteps and Zina came into the dining room, tall, buxom, and very pale, dressed the way Pyotr Mikhailych had last seen her at home—in a black skirt and a red blouse with a big buckle at the waist. She embraced her brother with one arm and kissed him on the temple.

"Such a thunderstorm!" she said. "Grigory went out somewhere, and I was left alone in the whole house."

She was not embarrassed and looked at her brother candidly and directly, as at home. Looking at her, Pyotr Mikhailych also stopped feeling embarrassed.

"But you're not afraid of a thunderstorm," he said, sitting down at the table.

"No, but the rooms here are enormous, the house is old and jingles all over from the thunder, like a cupboard full of dishes. A charming little house, generally," she went on, sitting down facing her brother. "Here, in any room you like, there's some sort of pleasant memory. In my room, just imagine, Grigory's grandfather shot himself."

"In August there'll be money, we'll renovate the cottage in the garden," said Vlasich.

"For some reason during thunderstorms I remember the grandfather," Zina went on. "And in this dining room a man was flogged to death."

"That's an actual fact," Vlasich confirmed and looked wide-eyed at Pyotr Mikhailych. "In the 'forties this estate was rented by a certain Olivier, a Frenchman. His daughter's portrait is still lying here in the attic. A very pretty girl. This Olivier, my father told me, despised Russians for their ignorance and mocked them cruelly. So, for instance, he demanded that the priest take off his hat a half mile before he passed the manor house, and that church bells be rung each time the Olivier family drove through the village. With the serfs and the lowly of the world in general, of course, he showed even less ceremony. Once a man came down the road here, one of the most kindhearted sons of wandering Russia, something like Gogol's seminarian Khoma Brut.[5] He asked to spend the night, the clerks liked him, and they kept him on in the office. There are many variations. Some say the seminarian stirred up the peasants, others that Olivier's daughter supposedly fell in love with him. I don't know which is right, but one fine evening Olivier summoned him here and interrogated him, then ordered him beaten. You see, he was sitting at this table drinking Bordeaux, and the stablemen were beating the seminarian. It must have been real torture. By morning the man died from it, and they hid the body somewhere. They say it was thrown into Count Koltovich's pond. A case was opened, but the Frenchman paid several thousand to the proper person and left for Alsace. Incidentally, the term of his lease was also up, so the matter ended there."

"What scoundrels!" Zina said and shuddered.

"My father remembered Olivier and his daughter very well. He said she was a remarkable beauty and an eccentric besides. I think that that seminarian did all of it at once: stirred up the peasants and enticed the daughter. Maybe he wasn't a seminarian, but some sort of incognito."

Zina fell to thinking: the story of the seminarian and the beautiful French girl carried her far away in her imagination. It seemed to Pyotr Mikhailych that externally she had not changed at all in the last week, only become a little more pale. She looked calm and the same as ever, as if she had come to visit Vlasich along with her brother. But Pyotr Mikhailych felt that some sort of change had taken place in himself. Indeed, before, when she lived at home, he could talk to her about decidedly anything, while now he could not bring himself to ask even the simple question: "How do you like living here?" The question seemed awkward and unnecessary. The same change must have taken place in her as well. She was in no hurry to talk about their mother, about home, about her affair with Vlasich; she did not justify herself, did not say that civil marriage was better than religious, was not nervous, and calmly pondered the story of Olivier . . . And why had they suddenly started talking about Olivier?

"You've both got wet shoulders from the rain," Zina said and smiled joyfully. She was touched by this slight resemblance between her brother and Vlasich.

And Pyotr Mikhailych felt all the bitterness and all the horror of his situation. He remembered his now empty house, the closed grand piano, and Zina's bright room, which no one went into anymore; he remembered that there were no small footprints on the garden paths now, and that no one went swimming now, laughing loudly, before evening tea. What he had been so attached to since early childhood, what he had liked to think about when he sat in a stuffy classroom or lecture hall—brightness, purity, joy—all that had filled the house with life and light, was gone irretrievably, vanished, and mixed up with a crude, uncouth story of some battalion commander, a magnanimous lieutenant, a depraved woman, a grandfather who had shot himself . . . And to start talking about their mother, or thinking that the past could come back, meant not to understand what was clear.

Pyotr Mikhailych's eyes filled with tears, and his hand, resting on the table, trembled. Zina guessed what he was thinking about, and her eyes also turned red and glistened.

"Grigory, come here!" she said to Vlasich.

They walked over to the window and started discussing something in a whisper. And by the way Vlasich bent towards her and the way she looked at him, Pyotr Mikhailych realized once again that everything was already irretrievably finished and that there was no need to talk about anything. Zina went out.

"So it goes, brother," Vlasich began after some silence, rubbing his hands and smiling. "I just called our life happiness, but that was to obey literary requirements, so to speak. As a matter of fact, there has been no sense of happiness yet. Zina has been thinking all the time about you, about her mother, and she's suffered. Looking at her, I suffered, too. She has a free, bold nature, but when you're unaccustomed, you know, it's hard, and besides she's young. The servants call her 'miss'; it seems like a trifle, but it upsets her. So it goes, brother."

Zina brought a bowl of strawberries. She was followed by a little maid, who looked meek and downtrodden. The maid put a jug of milk on the table and made a very low bow . . . She had something in common with the old furniture, just as torpid and dull.

There was no more sound of rain. Pyotr Mikhailych was eating strawberries, and Vlasich and Zina silently watched him. The time of the needless but inevitable conversation was drawing near, and it already weighed on the three of them. Pyotr Mikhailych's eyes again filled with tears; he pushed the bowl aside and said it was time he went home, or else it would be late and it might well rain again. The moment came when Zina, out of propriety, ought to say something about home and her new life.

"How are things at our place?" she asked quickly, and her pale face quivered. "How is Mama?"

"You know Mama . . . ," Pyotr Mikhailych replied without looking at her.

"Petrusha, you've long been thinking about what's happened," she said, taking her brother by the sleeve, and he realized how hard it was for her to speak. "You've long been thinking. Tell me, can we count on Mama reconciling with Grigory some day . . . and generally with this situation?"

She stood close to her brother, face to face, and he was astonished that she was so beautiful and that he seemed not to have noticed it before; and that his sister, whose face resembled their mother's, pampered, refined, was living in Vlasich's house, and with Vlasich, along with the torpid maid, along with the six-legged table, in a house where a living man had been flogged to death, and that she would not ride home with him now, but would stay here for the night—that struck him as incredibly absurd.

"You know Mama . . . ," he said without answering the question. "In my opinion, you ought to observe . . . to do something, to ask her forgiveness, or whatever . . ."

"But to ask her forgiveness means to make it look as if we acted badly. I'm ready to lie for the sake of Mama's peace, but that wouldn't lead to anything. I know Mama. Well, what will be, will be!" Zina said, cheering up because what was most unpleasant had already been said. "We'll wait five, ten years, bear with it, and then it's as God wills."

She took her brother under the arm and, when they went through the dark front hall, she pressed herself to his shoulder.

They came out to the porch. Pyotr Mikhailych said goodbye, mounted his horse, and rode at a walk; Zina and Vlasich went a little of the way to see him off. It was quiet, warm, and there was a wonderful smell of hay; stars shone brightly between the clouds in the sky. Vlasich's old garden, which had witnessed so many unhappy stories in its time, slept, wrapped in darkness, and for some reason it was sad to ride through it.

"After dinner today Zina and I spent several truly bright moments!" Vlasich said. "I read aloud to her an excellent article on the question of resettlement. Read it, brother! It's necessary for you! The article is remarkable in its honesty. I couldn't help myself and wrote the publisher a letter to be forwarded to the author. I wrote just one line: 'I thank you and firmly press your honest hand!'"

Pyotr Mikhailych wanted to say: "Please don't meddle in what's none of your business!"—but he kept silent.

Vlasich walked by the right stirrup, Zina by the left; they both seemed to forget that they had to go back home, and it was damp and they were already not far from Koltovich's grove. Pyotr Mikhailych felt that they were waiting for something from him, though they themselves did not know what, and he felt an unbearable pity for them. Now, as they walked beside the horse, with a submissive look and lost in thought, he was deeply convinced that they were unhappy and could not be happy, and their love seemed to him a sad, irreparable mistake. From pity and the awareness that he could not help them in any way, he was overcome by that state of inner laxity in which, to rid himself of the painful feeling of compassion, he was ready for any sacrifice.

"I'll come to stay the night with you," he said.

But that sounded as if he was making a concession, and it did not satisfy him. When they stopped at Koltovich's grove to say goodbye, he bent down to Zina, touched her shoulder, and said:

"You're right, Zina! You did well!"

And, so as not to say more and not to burst into tears, he whipped up his horse and galloped into the grove. Going into the darkness, he turned and saw Vlasich and Zina walking home down the road—he with big strides, and she beside him with a hurrying, skipping gait—and talking animatedly about something.

"I'm just an old woman," Pyotr Mikhailych thought. "I went to resolve the question, but I've confused it even more. Well, God be with it all!"

His heart was heavy. When the grove ended, he rode on at a walk and then stopped the horse by the pond. He wanted to sit motionless and think. The moon was rising, and was reflected in a red column on the other side of the pond. There was a muted rumbling of thunder somewhere. Pyotr Mikhailych looked at the water without blinking and imagined his sister's despair, the suffering paleness and dry eyes with which she would hide her humiliation from people. He imagined her pregnancy, their mother's death, her funeral, Zina's horror . . . The proud, superstitious old woman could not end otherwise than in death. Terrible pictures of the future loomed before him on the dark, smooth water, and among pale women's figures he saw himself, faint-hearted, weak, with a guilty face . . .

A hundred paces away, on the right bank of the pond, something dark stood motionless: was it a man or a tall stump? Pyotr Mikhailych remembered about the seminarian who had been killed and thrown into this pond.

"Olivier behaved inhumanly, but in any case he resolved the question, and I haven't resolved anything, but only confused it," he thought, peering at the dark figure, which looked like a phantom. "He said and did what he thought, while I say and do what I do not think; and I don't even know for certain what I actually think . . ."

He rode up to the dark figure: it was a rotten old post left from some construction.

A strong scent of lily-of-the-valley and honeyed herbs came from the grove and Koltovich's estate. Pyotr Mikhailych rode along the bank of the pond and gazed sorrowfully at the water, and, looking back on his life, was becoming convinced that up to then he had always said and done what he did not think, and people had repaid him in kind, and therefore the whole of life now looked to him as dark as this water in which the night sky was reflected and waterweeds were entangled. And it seemed to him that it could not be set right.

1892

FEAR

My Friend's Story

DMITRI PETROVICH SILIN finished his studies at the university and entered government service in Petersburg, but at the age of thirty he abandoned the service and took up farming. His farming went rather well, but it still seemed to me that this was not the right place for him and that he would do well to go back to Petersburg. When, sunburnt, gray with dust, worn out from work, he met me at the gate or by the porch, and then at supper struggled with drowsiness, and his wife led him off to bed like a child, or when, overcoming his drowsiness, he began in his soft, soulful, as if pleading voice to explain his good thoughts, I saw in him not a farmer and not an agronomist, but only a weary man, and it was clear to me that he did not need any farming, but needed only for the day to be over—and thanks be to God.

I liked to visit him and, occasionally, to spend two or three days on his estate. I liked his house, and the park, and the big orchard, and the river, and his philosophizing, a bit languid and flowery, but clear. It must be that I also liked the man himself, though I cannot say so for certain, since to this day I'm unable to sort out my feelings of that time. He was an intelligent, kind, sincere man, and not boring, but I remember very well that when he confided his innermost secrets to me and called our relations friendship, it disturbed me unpleasantly, and I felt awkward. In his friendship towards me there was something troubling, burdensome, and I would sooner have preferred ordinary comradely relations with him.

The thing was that I had a great liking for his wife, Maria Sergeevna. I was not in love with her, but I liked her face, her eyes, her voice, her gait, I missed her when I had not seen her for a long time, and then my imagination pictured no one more eagerly than that beautiful and refined young woman. I had no definite intentions regarding her, nor did I dream of any, but for some reason each time she and I were left alone together, I remembered that her husband considered me his friend, and I felt awkward. When she played my favorite pieces on the piano or told me something interesting, I listened with pleasure, and at the same time for some reason thoughts crept into my head that she loved her husband, that he was my friend, and that she herself considered me his friend, and my mood would be spoiled, and I would become listless, awkward, and bored. She would notice this change and usually say:

"You're bored without your friend. We must send to the fields for him."

And when Dmitri Petrovich came, she would say:

"Well, your friend has come now. Be glad."

So it went for a year and a half.

Once on a Sunday in July, Dmitri Petrovich and I, having nothing to do, went to the big village of Klushino to buy some things for supper. While we made the round of the shops, the sun went down and evening came on, an evening I will probably never forget all my life. We bought cheese that resembled soap and petrified sausage that smelled of tar, then went to the inn to ask if they had beer. Our coachman drove to the smithy to have the horses shod, and we told him we would wait for him by the church. We walked, talked, laughed at our purchases, and behind us, silently and with a mysterious look, like a sleuth, followed a man known to us in the district by the rather strange nickname of Forty Martyrs. This Forty Martyrs was none other than Gavrila Severov, or simply Gavryushka, who had worked for a short time as my valet and had been fired for drunkenness. He had also worked for Dmitri Petrovich and had been fired by him for exactly the same sin. He was a hardened drunkard, and in general his whole life was as drunken and wayward as himself. His father had been a priest and his mother a noblewoman, meaning that by birth he had belonged to the privileged class, but however much I studied his wasted, deferential, eternally sweaty face, his red, already graying beard, his pathetic, ragged suit jacket and loose red shirt, I simply could not find even a trace of what is known in our society as privilege. He called himself educated and told of how he had studied at a seminary, where he did not finish his courses because he was expelled for smoking, then sang in a bishop's choir and lived for two years in a monastery, from which he had also been expelled, not for smoking this time, but for "the weakness." He had gone on foot all over two provinces, had made some sort of petitions to the consistory and various offices, had been tried four times. Finally, having landed in our district, he had worked as a servant, a forester, a huntsman, a beadle, had married a wanton widow—a scullery maid—and had sunk definitively into a subservient life. He became so accustomed to its squalor and squabbles that he himself spoke of his privileged origins with a certain mistrust, as of some sort of myth. At the time I am describing, he hung around without work, passing himself off as a farrier and a huntsman, and his wife vanished somewhere without a trace.

From the inn we went to the church and sat down on the porch to wait for the coachman. Forty Martyrs stood at a distance and put his hand to his mouth, so that he could cough into it respectfully when necessary. It was already dark; there was a strong smell of evening dampness and the moon was preparing to rise. In the clear, starry sky there were only two clouds just over our heads: one big, the other smaller; solitary, like a mother and child, they ran one after the other in the direction where the evening glow was fading.

"A fine day today," said Dmitri Petrovich.

"In the extreme . . . ," Forty Martyrs agreed and coughed respectfully into his hand. "How is it, Dmitri Petrovich, that you kindly thought of coming here?" he began in an ingratiating voice, evidently trying to strike up a conversation.

Dmitri Petrovich did not reply. Forty Martyrs sighed deeply and said in a low voice, not looking at us:

"I suffer solely because of the matter for which I must answer to almighty God. Of course, I'm a lost man and without ability, but believe my conscience: without a crust of bread and worse off than a dog . . . Forgive me, Dmitri Petrovich!"

Silin was not listening and, propping his head on his fists, was thinking about something. The church stood at the end of the street, on a high bank, and through the grill of the fence we could see the river, the water-meadows on the other side, and the bright, crimson light of a bonfire, with dark people and horses moving around it. And further on from the bonfire more lights: this was a village . . . They were singing a song there.

On the river and here and there on the water-meadows mist was rising. High, narrow wisps of mist, thick and white as milk, hovered over the river, covering the reflections of the stars and catching at the willows. They changed their look every moment, and it seemed as if some embraced, others bowed, still others raised their arms to the sky in wide, clerical sleeves, as if praying . . . They probably suggested to Dmitri Petrovich a thought about ghosts and dead people, because he turned his face to me and asked, smiling sadly:

"Tell me, my dear fellow, why is it that when we want to tell something frightening, mysterious, and fantastic, we draw material not from life but inevitably from the world of ghosts and shades from beyond the grave?"

"What's frightening is what's incomprehensible."

"And is life comprehensible to you? Tell me: do you understand life better than the world beyond the grave?"

Dmitri Petrovich moved quite close to me, so close that I could feel his breath on my cheek. In the evening darkness his pale, lean face seemed still more pale, and his dark beard blacker than soot. His eyes were sad, earnest, and a bit afraid, as if he were about to tell me something frightening. He looked me in the eye and went on in his habitual pleading voice.

"Our life and the world beyond the grave are equally incomprehensible and frightening. Whoever is afraid of ghosts should also be afraid of me, and of those fires, and of the sky, because all of it, if you think well, is no less incomprehensible and fantastic than apparitions from the other world. Prince Hamlet did not kill himself, because he feared the visions that might come in that sleep of death.[1] I like his famous soliloquy, but, frankly speaking, it never touched my soul. I'll confess to you as a friend, in moments of anguish I've sometimes pictured to myself the hour of my death, my fantasy has invented thousands of the most gloomy visions, and I've managed to drive myself to tormenting exaltation, to nightmare, and that, I assure you, did not seem more frightening to me than reality. Needless to say, visions are frightening, but life is frightening, too. I, my dear friend, do not understand and am afraid of life. I don't know, maybe I'm a sick, demented person. It seems to a normal, healthy person that he understands everything he sees and hears, whereas I've lost that 'it seems,' and day after day I poison myself with fear. There exists a sickness—the fear of spaces—well, so I'm sick with the fear of life. When I lie in the grass and look for a long time at a bug that was born yesterday and doesn't understand anything, it seems to me that its whole life consists of nothing but horror, and I see myself in it."

"What is it that actually frightens you?" I asked.

"Everything frightens me. I'm not a profound man by nature and I have little interest in such questions as life after death, the destiny of mankind, and generally I rarely soar into the heavenly heights. I'm frightened mainly by the commonplace, which none of us can escape from. I'm unable to tell what in my actions is true or false, and they bother me; I'm aware that the conditions of life and my upbringing confined me to a narrow circle of lies, and that my whole life is nothing but a daily worry about deceiving myself and others and not noticing it, and I'm frightened by the thought that till death I won't get out of this lie. Today I do something, and tomorrow I don't understand why I did it. I entered the service in Petersburg and got scared, I came here to take up farming and also got scared . . . I see that we know little and therefore make mistakes every day, we are often unfair, we slander, we prey on other people's lives, we expend all our strength on nonsense that we don't need and that hinders our lives, and that frightens me, because I don't understand who needs it and why. I don't understand people, my dear friend, and I'm afraid of them. I'm frightened looking at peasants, I don't know for what higher purposes they suffer and what they live for. If life is pleasure, they are superfluous, unnecessary people; but if the goal and meaning of life is need and unmitigated, hopeless ignorance, I don't understand who needs this inquisition and why. I understand no one and nothing. Kindly try to understand this subject here!" said Dmitri Petrovich, pointing to Forty Martyrs. "Set your mind to it!"

Noticing that we were both looking at him, Forty Martyrs coughed respectfully into his fist and said:

"I was always a faithful servant to good masters, but the main reason is alcoholic beverages. If you were to honor me now, an unfortunate man, and give me a post, I would kiss an icon. My word is firm."

The sexton walked by, looked at us in perplexity, and started pulling the rope. The bell, abruptly breaking the evening silence, slowly and protractedly rang ten.

"Anyhow it's already ten o'clock," said Dmitri Petrovich. "Time for us to go. Yes, my dear friend," he sighed, "if you only knew how afraid I am of my humdrum, everyday thoughts, in which it seems there should be nothing frightening. So as not to think, I divert myself with work and try to wear myself out, so as to sleep soundly at night. Children, wife—for others it's ordinary, but how hard it is for me, my dear friend!"

He rubbed his face with his hands, grunted, and laughed.

"If I could tell you what a fool I've played in my life!" he said. "Everybody says to me: you have a nice wife, lovely children, and you're an excellent family man. They think I'm very happy, and they envy me. Well, since we're at it, I'll tell you in secret: my happy family life is nothing but a sad misunderstanding, and I'm afraid of it."

A strained smile made his pale face unsightly. He put his arm around my waist and went on in a low voice:

"You're my true friend, I trust you and I deeply respect you. Friendship is sent to us by heaven so that we can speak ourselves out and be saved from the secrets that oppress us. Allow me to take advantage of your friendly disposition and tell you the whole truth. My family life, which seems so delightful to you, is my main misfortune and my main fear. I married strangely and stupidly. I must tell you that before the wedding I loved Masha madly, and I courted her for two years. I proposed to her five times and she rejected me, because she was totally indifferent to me. The sixth time, when I crawled on my knees before her, stupefied by love, begging for her hand as if for alms, she accepted . . . This is what she said to me: 'I don't love you, but I will be faithful to you . . .' I accepted that condition rapturously. I understood then what it meant, but now, I swear to God, I don't. 'I don't love you, but I will be faithful to you'—what does that mean? It's fog, darkness . . . I love her now just as deeply as on the first day of our marriage, and she, it seems to me, is as indifferent as before and must be glad when I leave the house. I don't know for certain whether she loves me or not, I don't know, I don't know, but we live under the same roof, we talk intimately, we sleep together, we have children, our property is held in common . . . What does it mean? What for? Do you understand any of it, my dear friend? A cruel torture! Because I understand nothing in our relationship, I hate now her, now myself, now both of us, everything is mixed up in my head, I torment myself and turn stupid, and she, as if on purpose, gets prettier every day, she becomes astonishing . . . I think she has wonderful hair, and she smiles like no other woman. I love her and I know that I love her hopelessly. A hopeless love for a woman with whom you already have two children! Can that be understood and not be frightening? Isn't it more frightening than ghosts?"

He got into such a state that he could have gone on talking for a very long time, but fortunately we heard the coachman's voice. Our horses came. We got into the carriage, and Forty Martyrs, taking off his hat, helped us both in with such a look as if he had long been waiting for a chance to touch our precious bodies.

"Dmitri Petrovich, allow me to come to you," he said, blinking hard and tilting his head to the side. "Show me divine mercy! I'm perishing from hunger!"

"Oh, all right," Silin said. "Come, stay for three days, and then we'll see."

"Yes, sir!" Forty Martyrs was overjoyed. "I'll come today, sir."

It was four miles to the house. Dmitri Petrovich, pleased that he had finally spoken everything out to a friend, held me by the waist all the way and, now without bitterness and without fright, but cheerfully, said to me that, if everything had been well with him in his family, he would have gone back to Petersburg and taken up science. The trend, he said, which had driven so many gifted young people to the countryside, was a deplorable trend. There was a great deal of rye and wheat in Russia, but there was a dearth of cultivated people. Gifted, healthy youths should take up science, the arts, and politics; to do otherwise was even wasteful. He philosophized with pleasure and expressed regret that he must part from me early the next morning, because he had to go to a woodlot auction.

But I felt awkward and sad, and it seemed to me that I was deceiving the man. And at the same time I was pleased. I looked at the enormous crimson moon, which was rising, and pictured to myself a tall, slender blonde, pale, always smartly dressed, fragrant with some special perfume like musk, and for some reason I was cheered by the thought that she did not love her husband.

We came home and sat down to supper. Maria Sergeevna, laughing, served us our purchases, and I found that she did in fact have wonderful hair and that she smiled like no other woman. I watched her, and I wanted to see in her every movement and glance that she did not love her husband, and it seemed to me that I did see it.

Dmitri Petrovich soon began fighting off drowsiness. After supper he sat with us for some ten minutes, then said:

"Do as you like, my friends, but I have to get up tomorrow at three in the morning. Allow me to leave you."

He tenderly kissed his wife, shook my hand firmly, with gratitude, and made me promise that I would come next week without fail. So as not to oversleep the next morning, he went to spend the night in the cottage.

Maria Sergeevna stayed up late, Petersburg fashion, and now for some reason I was glad of it.

"And so?" I began, when we were left alone. "And so, you're going to be kind and play something for me."

I didn't want any music, but I didn't know how to begin the conversation. She sat down at the piano and played, I don't remember what. I sat near her, looked at her plump white hands, and tried to read something in her cold, indifferent face. But then she smiled for some reason and looked at me.

"You're bored without your friend," she said.

I laughed.

"For the sake of friendship, it would be enough to come here once a month, but I come here more than once a week."

Having said that, I got up and paced the room in agitation. She also got up and went to the fireplace.

"What do you mean to say by that?" she asked, raising her big, clear eyes to me.

I said nothing.

"You weren't telling the truth," she went on after reflecting. "You come here only for the sake of Dmitri Petrovich. Well, I'm very glad. In our time one rarely sees such friendship."

"Aha!" I thought, and, not knowing what to say, I asked: "Would you like to take a stroll in the garden?"

"No."

I stepped out on the terrace. My scalp was tingling, and I was chilled with excitement. I was already certain that our conversation would be very insignificant and that we would not be able to say anything special to each other, but that during that night what I did not even dare to dream of would certainly take place. Certainly, that night, or never.

"What fine weather!" I said loudly.

"For me it's decidedly all the same," came the answer.

I went into the drawing room. Maria Sergeevna was standing by the fireplace as before, her hands behind her back, thinking about something and looking away.

"Why is it decidedly all the same for you?" I asked.

"Because I'm bored. You're only bored without your friend, but I'm always bored. However . . . that doesn't interest you."

I sat down at the piano and played several chords, waiting for what she would say.

"Please don't stand on ceremony," she said, looking at me angrily and as if she were about to weep with vexation. "If you want to go to bed, go. Don't think that, if you're Dmitri Petrovich's friend, you're obliged to be bored with his wife. I don't want any sacrifices. Please go."

I didn't go, of course. She went out to the terrace, and I stayed in the drawing room and spent some five minutes leafing through the scores. Then I, too, went out. We stood next to each other in the shadow of the curtains, and below us were the steps flooded with moonlight. The black shadows of trees stretched across the flower beds and over the yellow sand of the paths.

"I also have to leave tomorrow," I said.

"Of course, if my husband isn't home, you can't stay here," she said mockingly. "I can imagine how miserable you'd be if you fell in love with me! Just wait, someday I'll up and throw myself on your neck . . . I'll watch how you flee from me in terror. It will be interesting."

Her words and her pale face were angry, but her eyes were filled with the most tender, passionate love. I already looked upon this beautiful creature as my property, and now I noticed for the first time that she had golden eyebrows, lovely eyebrows, such as I had never seen before. The thought that I could now draw her to me, caress her, touch her wonderful hair, suddenly seemed so monstrous to me that I laughed and shut my eyes.

"However, it's already time . . . Sleep well," she said.

"I don't want to sleep well," I said, following her to the drawing room. "I'll curse this night if I sleep at all."

Pressing her hand and walking her to the door, I could see from her face that she understood me and was glad that I also understood her.

I went to my room. On my desk by the books lay Dmitri Petrovich's cap, and that reminded me of his friendship. I took a walking stick and went out to the garden. Here the mist was already rising, and around the trees and bushes, embracing them, wandered the same high and narrow apparitions I had just seen on the river. What a pity I couldn't speak with them!

In the extraordinarily transparent air, every little leaf, every drop of dew stood out distinctly—it all smiled to me in silence, half awake, and, passing by the green benches, I recalled words from some play of Shakespeare's: how sweetly sleeps the moonlight upon this bench![2]

There was a small hummock in the garden. I went up it and sat down. An enchanting feeling came over me. I knew for certain that I was about to embrace her luxurious body, to press myself to it, to kiss those golden eyebrows, and I wanted not to believe it, to excite myself, and was sorry that she had tormented me so little and yielded so soon.

But here I suddenly heard heavy footsteps. A man of average height appeared in the path, and I immediately recognized him as Forty Martyrs. He sat down on a bench and sighed deeply, then crossed himself three times and lay down. A minute later he sat up and turned on the other side. Mosquitoes and the night's dampness kept him from sleeping.

"Ah, life!" he said. "Miserable, bitter life!"

Looking at his scrawny, bent body and hearing deep, hoarse sighs, I remembered the other miserable, bitter life confessed to me that day, and my blissful state became eerie and frightening to me. I left the hummock and headed home.

"Life, in his opinion, is frightening," I thought, "so don't stand on ceremony with it, break it, and, before it crushes you, take all you can grab from it."

Maria Sergeevna was standing on the terrace. I silently embraced her and greedily started kissing her eyebrows, temples, neck . . .

In my room she told me that she had loved me for a long time, more than a year. She swore her love for me, wept, begged me to take her away with me. I kept bringing her to the window, so as to see her face in the moonlight, and she seemed like a beautiful dream to me, and I hurried to embrace her tightly, so as to believe in its reality. I had not experienced such raptures for a long time . . . But all the same, far off somewhere in the depths of my soul, I felt a certain awkwardness, and I was out of sorts. There was something troubling and burdensome in her love for me, as there was in Dmitri Petrovich's friendship. It was a great, serious love, with tears and oaths, while I didn't want anything serious—no tears, no oaths, no talk about the future. Let this moonlit night flash by in our lives like a bright meteor—and basta.

At exactly three o'clock she left my room, and as I followed her with my gaze, standing in the doorway, Dmitri Petrovich suddenly appeared at the end of the corridor. Running into him, she gave a start and made way for him, and disgust was written all over her. He smiled somehow strangely, coughed, and came into my room.

"I forgot my cap here yesterday," he said, not looking at me.

He found his cap, put it on with both hands, then looked at my embarrassed face, at my slippers, and said in a strange, husky voice, not quite his own:

"I was probably predestined not to understand anything. If you understand something, then . . . I congratulate you. It's all dark in my eyes."

And he went out with a little cough. Then I saw through the window how he hitched up the horses by the stable. His hands were trembling, he was in a hurry and kept glancing at the house; he was probably frightened. Then he got into the tarantass and with a strange expression, as if fearing pursuit, whipped up the horses.

A little later I myself left. The sun was already rising, and the previous day's mist timidly pressed itself to the bushes and hummocks. Forty Martyrs, who had already managed to have a drink somewhere, sat on the box and mouthed drunken nonsense.

"I'm a free man!" he cried to the horses. "Hey, you beauties! I'm a hereditary, honorary citizen, if you want to know!"

Dmitri Petrovich's fear, which was on my mind, communicated itself to me. I thought about what had happened and understood nothing. I looked at the rooks, and found it strange and frightening that they were flying.

"Why did I do it?" I asked myself in bewilderment and despair. "Why did it happen precisely like this, and not some other way? To whom and for what was it necessary that she should love me seriously and that he should come to the room to get his cap? What has the cap got to do with it?"

That same day I left for Petersburg, and since then I have not seen Dmitri Petrovich and his wife even once. People say they're still living together.

1892

BIG VOLODYA AND LITTLE VOLODYA

L ET ME! I WANT TO DRIVE MYSELF! I'll sit beside the coachman!" Sofya Lvovna said loudly. "Coachman, wait, I'll sit on
the box with you."

She was standing up in the sledge, and her husband Vladimir Nikitych and her childhood friend Vladimir Mikhailych were holding her
by the arms to keep her from falling. The troika raced along quickly.

"I said not to give her cognac," Vladimir Nikitych whispered
vexedly to his companion. "What a one, really!"

The colonel knew from experience that in such women as his wife
Sofya Lvovna violent, slightly drunken gaiety is usually followed by
hysterical laughter and then tears. He was afraid that now, when they
came home, instead of sleeping, he would have to fuss with compresses and drops.

"Whoa!" cried Sofya Lvovna. "I want to drive!"

She was genuinely happy and triumphant. Over the past two
months, ever since her wedding day, she had been beset by the thought
that her marriage to Colonel Yagich was of convenience and, as they
say, *par dépit*.[1] Tonight, in a suburban restaurant, she had finally
become convinced that she loved him passionately. In spite of his
fifty-four years, he was so trim, adroit, supple, he quipped and sang
along with the Gypsies so nicely. Really, nowadays older people are a
thousand times more interesting than the young, and it looks as if old
age and youth have exchanged roles. The colonel was two years older

than her father, but could this circumstance have any meaning, if, in all conscience, there was immeasurably more of life's force, vigor, and freshness in him than in her, though she was only twenty-three?

"Oh, my dearest!" she thought. "My wonderful one!"

In the restaurant she had also become convinced that there was not even a spark of the former feeling left in her heart. To her childhood friend Vladimir Mikhailych, or simply Volodya, whom still yesterday she had loved to the point of madness, of despair, she now felt herself totally indifferent. All that evening he had seemed listless to her, sleepy, uninteresting, insignificant, and this time the coolness with which he usually avoided paying the check in restaurants had outraged her, and she had barely kept herself from saying to him: "If you're poor, stay home." The colonel alone had paid.

Maybe because trees, telegraph poles, and snowdrifts kept flashing by her eyes, the most varied thoughts came into her head. She thought: a hundred and twenty to pay the check in the restaurant, and a hundred for the Gypsies, and tomorrow, if she likes, she can throw even a thousand roubles to the wind, yet two months ago, before the wedding, she didn't have even three roubles to her name, and had to turn to her father for every trifle. What a change in life!

Her thoughts were confused, and she recalled how, when she was around ten years old, Colonel Yagich, now her husband, had paid court to her aunt, and everyone in the house said he ruined her, and in fact the aunt often came to dinner with tearful eyes and kept driving somewhere, and people said that the poor thing didn't know what to do with herself. He was very handsome then and had extraordinary success with women, so that the whole town knew him, and the story went that he visited his lady admirers every day, the way a doctor visits his patients. And even now, despite the gray hair, the wrinkles, and the spectacles, his lean face sometimes looked very handsome, especially in profile.

Sofya Lvovna's father was an army doctor and had once served in the same regiment with Yagich. Volodya's father was also an army doctor and had also served in the same regiment with her father and Yagich. In spite of love adventures, often very complex and troublesome, Volodya was an excellent student; he finished his studies at the university with great success, chose foreign literature as his specialization, and is now said to be writing his dissertation. He lives in the barracks with his father, the army doctor, and has no money of his own, though he is already thirty. In childhood he and Sofya Lvovna lived in different apartments, but under the same roof, and he often came to play with her, and they took dancing and French lessons together. But when he grew up and became a slim, very handsome young man, she began to feel bashful with him, then fell madly in love with him, and loved him until quite recently, when she married Yagich. He, too, had extraordinary success with women, almost since the age of fourteen, and the ladies who were unfaithful to their husbands with him excused themselves by saying that Volodya was little. Not long ago someone told of him that, supposedly, when he was a student, he lived in furnished rooms close to the university, and each time someone knocked on his door, his footsteps would be heard and then a low-voiced apology: "*Pardon, je ne suis pas seul.*"[2] Yagich went into raptures over him, gave him his blessing for the future, as Derzhavin had Pushkin,[3] and apparently loved him. For hours at a time they silently played billiards or blackjack together, and if Yagich went somewhere in a troika, he took Volodya with him, and Volodya initiated Yagich alone into the mysteries of his dissertation. Earlier, when the colonel was younger, they often wound up in the position of rivals, but they were never jealous of each other. In society, where they appeared together, Yagich was called big Volodya and his friend little Volodya.

Besides big Volodya, little Volodya, and Sofya Lvovna, there was one more person in the sledge—Margarita Alexandrovna, or, as everyone called her, Rita, Madame Yagich's cousin, a girl already over thirty, very pale, with black eyebrows, in a pince-nez, who chain-smoked cigarettes, even outside in freezing weather. Her breast and knees were always covered with ashes. She spoke nasally, drawing out each word, was cold-tempered, could drink any quantity of liqueurs and cognac without getting drunk, told off-color jokes flatly, insipidly. At home she read intellectual journals from morning till night, sprinkling them with ashes, or else ate frozen apples.

"Sonya, stop acting up," she said in a singsong voice. "It's really stupid."

In sight of the city gates, the troika slowed its pace, houses and people flashed by, and Sofya Lvovna quieted down, pressed herself to her husband, and gave herself up to her thoughts. Little Volodya sat facing her. Now her happy, bright thoughts already began to mingle with gloomy ones. She thought: This man who sits facing her was aware that she had loved him, and of course he believed the gossip that she had married the colonel *par dépit*. She had never once confessed her love to him, and did not want him to know, and she hid her feeling, but by his face it could be seen that he understood her perfectly—and her vanity suffered. The most humiliating thing about her position was that after the wedding this little Volodya suddenly started paying attention to her, which had never happened before. He would sit with her for long hours silently, or chatting about trifles, and now, in the sledge, he did not talk to her, but only stepped lightly on her foot, or pressed her hand. Obviously, all he had needed was that she get married; and it was obvious that he despised her, and that she aroused in him only an interest of a certain kind, as a bad and dishonorable woman. And when triumph and love for her husband mingled in her soul with a feeling of humiliation and offended pride, she became defiant and wanted to sit on the box and shout, whistle . . .

Just as they were driving past a convent, they heard the stroke of the big twenty-ton bell. Rita crossed herself.

"Our Olya is in this convent," Sofya Lvovna said, also crossing herself and shuddering.

"Why did she go to the convent?" asked the colonel.

"*Par dépit*," Rita replied angrily, obviously alluding to the marriage of Sofya Lvovna and Yagich. "This *par dépit* is fashionable nowadays. A challenge to the whole world. She loved to laugh, was a desperate flirt, only liked balls and her cavaliers, and suddenly—there, take that! Surprise!"

"That's not true," said little Volodya, turning down the collar of his fur coat and showing his handsome face. "There's no *par dépit* in it, but sheer horror, if you wish. Her brother Dmitri was sent to hard labor and now nobody knows where he is. And her mother died of grief."

He turned up his collar again.

"And Olya did well," he added hollowly. "To live in the position of a ward, and with such a treasure as Sofya Lvovna—give that some thought!"

Sofya Lvovna heard the contemptuous tone of his voice and wanted to say something insolent to him, but she kept silent. She again became defiant; she got to her feet and shouted in a tearful voice:

"I want to go to matins! Coachman, turn back! I want to see Olya!"

They turned back. The ringing of the convent bell was deep, and, as it seemed to Sofya Lvovna, there was something in it reminiscent of Olya and her life. Bells were ringing in the other churches as well. When the coachman reined in the troika, Sofya Lvovna jumped out of the sledge and alone, without escort, quickly walked to the gateway.

"Hurry up, please!" called her husband. "It's already late."

She walked through the dark gateway, then down the avenue that led from the gates to the main church, and the snow crunched under her feet, and the ringing now came from right over her head and seemed to penetrate her whole being. Here was the church door, three steps down, then the vestibule with icons of saints on both sides, a smell of juniper and incense, another door, and a dark little figure opened it and bowed low, very low . . . Inside the church, the service had not begun yet. One nun was walking around the iconostasis lighting candles on the stands, another was lighting the big chandelier. Here and there, close to the columns and to the side chapels, dark figures stood motionless. "The way they're standing now, it means they won't budge till morning," Sofya Lvovna thought, and to her the place seemed dark, cold, boring—more boring than at the cemetery. With a feeling of boredom she looked at the motionless, frozen figures, and suddenly her heart was wrung. Somehow in one of the nuns, small, with narrow shoulders and a black headcloth, she recognized Olya, though Olya, when she left for the convent, had been plump and had seemed taller. Hesitantly, extremely agitated for some reason, Sofya Lvovna went up to the novice, looked over her shoulder, and saw it was Olya.

"Olya!" she said and clasped her hands, and could no longer speak from agitation. "Olya!"

The nun recognized her at once, raised her eyebrows in surprise, and her pale, recently washed, clean face, and even, as it seemed, her white coif, which could be seen under the headcloth, brightened with joy.

"This is a God-sent miracle," she said, and also clasped her thin, pale hands.

Sofya Lvovna embraced her tightly and kissed her, fearing as she did so that she smelled of drink.

"We were just driving by and remembered about you," she said, breathless as if from walking quickly. "Lord, you're so pale! I . . . I'm very glad to see you. Well, so? How is it? Do you miss us?"

Sofya Lvovna glanced at the other nuns and went on in a low voice:

"We've had so many changes . . . You know, I married Yagich, Vladimir Nikitych. You surely remember him . . . I'm very happy with him."

"Well, thank God. And your papa is in good health?"

"Yes. He often speaks of you. Come to see us during the holidays, Olya. You hear?"

"I will," Olya said and smiled. "I'll come on the second day."

Sofya Lvovna began to cry, not knowing why herself, and for a minute she cried silently, then wiped her eyes and said:

"Rita will be very sorry not to have seen you. She's also with us. And Volodya's here. They're by the gate. They'd be so glad to see you! Let's go to them, the service hasn't started yet."

"Let's go," Olya agreed.

She crossed herself three times and walked to the door together with Sofya Lvovna.

"So you say you're happy, Sonechka?" she asked when they were outside the gate.

"Very."

"Well, thank God."

Big Volodya and little Volodya, seeing the nun, got out of the sledge and greeted her respectfully. They were both visibly moved by her pale face and black monastic habit, and they were both pleased that she remembered them and came to greet them. To keep her warm, Sofya Lvovna wrapped her in a plaid and put the skirt of her fur coat around her. Her recent tears had eased and brightened her heart, and she was glad that this noisy, restless, and essentially impure night had unexpectedly ended so purely and meekly. In order to keep Olya beside her for longer, she suggested:

"Let's take her for a ride! Get in, Olya, just for a little."

The men expected that she would refuse—nuns don't ride in troikas—but to their surprise she accepted and got into the sledge. And as the troika raced to the gate, they were all silent and only tried to make sure she was comfortable and warm, and each of them thought of how she had been before and how she was now. Her face now was impassive, expressionless, cold and pale, transparent, as if water flowed in her veins instead of blood. Yet two or three years ago she had been plump, red-cheeked, talked about suitors, laughed at the merest trifle . . .

By the gate the troika turned back; ten minutes later, when it stopped at the convent, Olya got out of the sledge. The bells were already chiming.

"God save you," said Olya, and she bowed low, in monastic fashion.

"So come to see us, Olya."

"I will, I will."

She quickly walked away and soon disappeared through the dark gateway. And after that, for some reason, when the troika drove on, everything became very sad. They were all silent. Sofya Lvovna felt weak all over and lost heart; that she had made the nun get into the sledge and go for a ride, in tipsy company, now seemed stupid to her, tactless, and all but blasphemous; along with intoxication, the wish to deceive herself also went away, and it was clear to her that she did not and could not love her husband, that it was all nonsense and stupidity. She had married out of convenience, because he, as her boarding-school friends put it, was insanely rich, and because she was afraid to be left an old maid, like Rita, and because she was sick of her doctor father and wanted to annoy little Volodya. If she could have foreseen, when she married, that it would be so oppressive, scary, and ugly, she would not have agreed to the marriage for anything in the world. But now the harm could not be set right. She had to reconcile to it.

They came home. Getting into her warm, soft bed and covering herself with a blanket, Sofya Lvovna remembered the dark side chapel, the smell of incense, and the figures by the columns, and it was scary for her to think that those figures would stand motionless all the while she slept. There would be the long, long matins, then the hours, then the liturgy, the prayer service . . .

"But there is God, surely there is, and I will certainly die, which means that sooner or later I must think about my soul, about eternal life, like Olya. Olya is saved now, she has resolved all the questions for herself . . . But what if there is no God? Then her life is lost. But how is it lost? Why lost?"

After a moment a thought again came to her head:

"There is God, death will certainly come, one must think of one's soul. If Olya sees her death now, she won't be frightened. She's ready. And above all, she has already resolved the question of life for herself. There is God . . . yes . . . But can it be that there's no other solution than going into a convent? Going into a convent means renouncing life, ruining it . . ."

Sofya Lvovna felt a little frightened; she hid her head under the pillow.

"I mustn't think about it," she whispered. "I mustn't . . ."

Yagich was walking on the carpet in the next room, softly jingling his spurs, and thinking about something. It occurred to Sofya Lvovna that this man was near and dear to her only for one thing: he was also named Vladimir. She sat up in bed and called out tenderly:

"Volodya!"

"What is it?" her husband replied.

"Nothing."

She lay down again. She heard ringing, maybe from the same convent, she again recalled the side chapel and the dark figures, in her head wandered thoughts about God and inevitable death, and she covered her head with the blanket so as not to hear the bells. She reflected that, before the arrival of old age and death, there would drag out a long, long life, and day after day she would have to reckon with the intimacy of an unloved man, who had already come into the bedroom and was getting into bed, and to stifle in herself a hopeless love for another—young, charming, and, as it seemed to her, extraordinary. She glanced at her husband and was about to wish him good night, but instead she suddenly began to cry. She was vexed with herself.

"Well, here comes the music!" said Yagich, stressing the *mu*.

She calmed down, but late, only by ten o'clock in the morning; she stopped crying and trembling all over, but instead she was beginning to have a bad headache. Yagich was hurrying to the late liturgy and grumbled at his orderly, who was helping him to dress in the next room. He came into the bedroom once, softly jingling his spurs, and took something, then once more, already in his epaulettes and medals, limping slightly from rheumatism, and for some reason it seemed to Sofya Ivanovna that he walked and looked like a predator.

She heard Yagich make a telephone call.

"Please connect me with the Vassilyevsky Barracks!" he said, and a minute later: "Vassilyevsky Barracks? Please call Doctor Salimovich to the phone . . ." And after another minute: "Who is that on the phone? You, Volodya? Very glad. My dear boy, ask your father to come to the phone now. My spouse has gone quite to pieces after last evening. Not home, you say? Hm . . . Thank you. Excellent . . . much obliged . . . *Merci*."

Yagich came into the bedroom for a third time, bent down to his wife, made a cross over her, let her kiss his hand (women who loved him kissed his hand, and he was used to it), and said he would be back for dinner. And he left.

Sometime after eleven o'clock the maid announced that Vladimir Mikhailych had come. Sofya Lvovna, reeling from fatigue and the headache, quickly put on her astonishing new mauve housecoat trimmed with fur and hurriedly did up her hair somehow. She felt an inexpressible tenderness in her soul, and trembled from joy and the fear that he might leave. She wanted at least to have a look at him.

Little Volodya had come to visit, properly dressed in a tailcoat and white tie. When Sofya Lvovna came in, he kissed her hand and said he sincerely regretted that she was not well. Then, when they sat down, he praised her housecoat.

"Yesterday's meeting with Olya upset me," she said. "At first I was terrified, but now I envy her. She's an indestructible rock, she can't be moved from her place; but can it be, Volodya, that she had no other way out? Can it be that to bury yourself alive is to resolve the question of life? It's death, not life."

At the mention of Olya, tenderness appeared on little Volodya's face.

"Look, Volodya, you're an intelligent person," said Sofya Lvovna. "Teach me to act just as she has. Of course, I'm an unbeliever, and I wouldn't go into a convent, but I could do something tantamount. My life isn't easy," she went on after a brief pause. "Do teach me . . . Say something persuasive to me. Say at least one word."

"One word? All right: tararaboomdeay."

"Why do you despise me, Volodya?" she asked quickly. "You speak to me in some sort of peculiar—forgive me—foppish language, such as one doesn't use with friends and respectable women. You're a success as a scholar, you're fond of learning, why don't you ever talk to me about your learning? Why? Am I not worthy?"

Little Volodya winced peevishly and said:

"Why do you suddenly want learning? Maybe you want a constitution? Or maybe sturgeon with horseradish?"

"Well, all right, I'm worthless, trashy, without principles, and none too bright. I've made no end of mistakes, I'm a psychopath, I'm spoiled, and I ought to be despised for it. But you're ten years older than me, Volodya, and my husband is thirty years older. I grew up in your presence, and if you wanted, you could have made whatever you like out of me, even an angel. But you . . ." (her voice quavered) "behave terribly with me. Yagich married me when he was already old, but you . . ."

"Well, enough, enough," said Volodya, sitting close to her and kissing both of her hands. "Let the Schopenhauers philosophize and prove whatever they like, but we will kiss these little hands."

"You despise me, and if you only knew how I suffer from it!" she said hesitantly, knowing beforehand that he would not believe her. "And if you only knew how I want to change, to start a new life! I think of it with rapture," she said, and she actually shed a few tears of rapture. "To be a good, honest, pure human being, not to lie, to have a goal in life."

"Now, now, now, please don't pretend! I don't like it!" said Volodya, and his face acquired an annoyed expression. "By God, just as if you're onstage! Let's behave like human beings."

So that he would not get angry and leave, she began to apologize and, to please him, even forced herself to smile, and again talked about Olya and about her own wish to resolve the question of her life, to become a human being.

"Tara . . . ra . . . boomdeay . . . ," he sang in a low voice. "Tara . . . ra . . . boomdeay!"

And suddenly he took her by the waist. And she, not knowing herself what she was doing, put her hands on his shoulders and for a moment, as if in a daze, stared with admiration at his intelligent, mocking face, his brow, his eyes, his handsome beard . . .

"You've known for a long time that I love you," she confessed and blushed painfully, feeling that her lips had even twisted convulsively from shame. "I love you. Why do you torment me?"

She shut her eyes and kissed him firmly on the lips; and for a long time, perhaps a full minute, she could not end the kiss, though she knew it was improper, that he himself might disapprove of her, or a servant might come in . . .

"Oh, how you torment me!" she repeated.

When, half an hour later, having obtained what he wanted, he was sitting in the dining room and eating, she knelt before him and greedily looked into his face, and he told her she looked like a little dog waiting to be thrown a piece of ham. Then he sat her on his knee and, rocking her like a child, sang:

"Tara . . . raboomdeay . . . Tara . . . raboomdeay!"

When he was preparing to leave, she asked him in a passionate voice:

"When? Today? Where?"

And she reached both hands out to his mouth, as if wishing to seize the answer even with her hands.

"Today is hardly convenient," he said on reflection. "Maybe tomorrow."

And they parted. Before dinner Sofya Lvovna went to the convent to see Olya, but they told her Olya was somewhere reading the psalter over a dead person. From the convent she went to her father and also did not find him at home. Then she changed cabs and started going aimlessly around the streets and lanes, and went on driving like that until evening. And for some reason she kept remembering that same aunt with the tearful eyes, who didn't know what to do with herself.

At night they again drove off in the troika and listened to the Gypsies in the suburban restaurant. And when they went past the convent again, Sofya Lvovna remembered about Olya, and she felt eerie at the thought that for the girls and women of her circle there was no solution except to keep driving around in troikas and lying, or to go into a convent to mortify the flesh . . . The next day there was a rendezvous, and again Sofya Lvovna rode around town alone in a cab and remembered her aunt.

A week later little Volodya abandoned her. And after that, life went on as before, just as uninteresting, dreary, and sometimes even tormenting. The colonel and little Volodya played long rounds of billiards and piquet, Rita told jokes insipidly and flatly, Sofya Lvovna kept riding around in a cab and asked her husband to give her a ride in the troika.

She stopped by the convent almost every day, bothered Olya, complaining about her unbearable sufferings, wept, and felt all the while that something impure, pathetic, and shabby had entered the cell with her, while Olya kept telling her, mechanically, in the tone of a lesson learned by rote, that it was all nothing, it would all pass, and God would forgive.

1893

THE TEACHER OF LITERATURE

I

There was a drumming of horse hooves on the timber floor: first they led the black Count Nulin[1] from the stable, then the white Giant, then his sister Maika. They were all excellent and expensive horses. Old Shelestov saddled Giant and said, turning to his daughter Masha:

"Well, Maria Godefroi,[2] mount up. Hopla!"

Masha Shelestova was the youngest in the family; she was already eighteen, but the family was still in the habit of considering her little, and therefore they all called her Manya or Manyusya; and after a circus came to town, which she eagerly went to, they all started calling her Maria Godefroi.

"Hopla!" she cried, mounting Giant.

Her sister Varya got on Maika, Nikitin on Count Nulin, the officers on their own horses, and the long, elegant cavalcade, mottled with white officers' tunics and black riding habits, slowly filed out of the yard.

Nikitin noticed that, as they were mounting their horses and then riding out to the street, Manyusya for some reason paid attention only to him. She anxiously examined him and Count Nulin and said:

"Keep him on the bit all the time, Sergei Vassilyich. Don't let him shy. He's pretending."

And either because her Giant was great friends with Count Nulin, or it came about by chance, she rode next to Nikitin all the time, as she had yesterday and the day before. And he looked at her small, shapely body, seated on the proud white animal, at her fine profile, her top hat, which did not suit her and made her look older than she was, looked with joy, with tenderness, with rapture, listened to her, understood little, and thought:

"On my word of honor, I swear to God, I won't be timid, I'll propose to her today . . ."

It was past six in the evening—that time when the scent of white acacia and lilacs is so intense that it seems the air and the trees themselves swoon from it. Music was already playing in the town garden. The horses drummed resoundingly on the pavement; on all sides there was the sound of laughter, talk, the slamming of gates. Passing soldiers saluted the officers, schoolboys greeted Nikitin; and the promenaders, who were hurrying to the garden to listen to the music, were all obviously very pleased to see the cavalcade. And how warm it was, how soft the clouds looked, scattered in disorder across the sky, how meek and homey the shadows of the poplars and acacias— shadows that stretched all the way across the wide street and covered the houses on the other side up to the balconies and second floors!

They rode out of town and went at a trot down the high road. Here there was no scent of acacias and lilacs, no sound of music; instead there was the smell of the fields, the green growth of young rye and wheat, the squealing of gophers, the cawing of rooks. It was green everywhere you looked, with dark melon patches here and there and far to the left, by the cemetery, the white strip of a fading apple orchard.

They rode past the slaughterhouses, then past the brewery, overtook a crowd of military musicians hurrying to a park outside town.

"Polyansky has a very good horse, I don't dispute it," Manyusya said to Nikitin, indicating with her eyes the officer who was riding beside Varya. "But it's flawed. That white blotch on its left leg is totally out of place, and look how it tosses its head. There's no way to break it now, it will go on tossing its head till it drops dead."

Manyusya was as passionate about horses as her father. She suffered when she saw someone with a fine horse, and was glad when she found defects in other people's horses. Nikitin understood nothing about horses, and for him it was decidedly all the same to hold a horse by the reins or by the bit, to ride at a trot or a gallop; he only felt that his posture was unnatural, strained, and therefore officers who knew how to seat a horse must be more pleasing to Manyusya than he was. And he felt jealous of those officers.

As they rode past the park, someone suggested they stop and drink some seltzer water. So they did. The only trees in the park were oaks; they had begun to leaf out only recently, so that for now, through the young foliage, the whole park could be seen, with its bandstand, tables, swings, and with all its crows' nests, which looked like big hats. The horsemen and their ladies dismounted by one of the tables and ordered seltzer water. Some acquaintances who were strolling in the park came up to them. Among others there was the army doctor in high boots and the choirmaster, who was waiting for his musicians. The doctor must have taken Nikitin for a student, because he asked:

"Are you here on vacation?"

"No, I live here permanently," Nikitin replied. "I teach in the high school."

"Really?" the doctor was surprised. "So young and already a teacher?"

"Why young? I'm twenty-six . . . Thank God."

"You have a beard and moustache, but all the same you look no more than twenty-two or twenty-three. So youthful!"

"What swinishness!" thought Nikitin. "This one, too, considers me a milksop!"

He disliked it very much when someone turned the conversation to his youth, especially in the presence of women or schoolboys. Since coming to this town and taking up his post, he had begun to hate his youthfulness. The schoolboys were not afraid of him, the old men called him a youngster, women much preferred dancing with him to listening to his long discourses. And he would have given a lot to age by ten years or so.

From the park they rode further on, to the Shelestovs' farm. There they stopped at the gate, sent for the steward's wife Praskovya, and asked for some fresh milk. No one tasted the milk; they all looked at each other, laughed, and rode home. On their way back, music was already playing in the park; the sun had hidden behind the cemetery, and half the sky was crimson with sunset.

Manyusya again rode beside Nikitin. He would have liked to talk about how passionately he loved her, but he was afraid that the officers and Varya would hear him and kept silent. Manyusya was also silent, and he sensed what kept her silent and why she rode beside him, and was so happy that the earth, the sky, the lights of the town, the black silhouette of the brewery—all merged in his eyes into something very good and affectionate, and it seemed to him that his Count Nulin was riding on air and wanted to climb up into the crimson sky.

They came home. On the table in the garden the samovar was already boiling, and old Shelestov was sitting at one end of the table with his friends, the officials of the circuit court, and criticizing something as usual.

"That's boorishness!" he said. "Boorishness and nothing but! Yes, sirs, boorishness!"

Since Nikitin fell in love with Manyusya, he had liked everything at the Shelestovs': the house, the garden by the house, the evening tea, the wicker chairs, the old nanny, and even the word "boorishness," which the old man loved to pronounce all the time. The only things he did not like were the abundance of dogs and cats and the Egyptian doves that moaned mournfully in a big cage on the terrace. There were so many yard dogs and house dogs that in the course of his acquaintance with the Shelestovs he had learned to recognize only two: Mushka and Som. Mushka was a small, mangy dog with a shaggy muzzle, wicked and spoiled. She hated Nikitin. Each time she saw him, she cocked her head to one side, bared her teeth, and went "grrr . . . nya-nya-nya-nya . . . grrr . . ."

Then she would get under his chair. When he tried to chase her out from under his chair, she would dissolve into shrill barking, and the owners would say:

"Don't be afraid. She doesn't bite. She's a good dog."

Som was a huge black dog with long legs and a tail as stiff as a stick. During dinner and tea, he usually walked silently under the table and beat his tail against the boots and table legs. He was a kindly, stupid dog, but Nikitin could not stand him, because he had the habit of putting his muzzle on the diners' knees and slobbering on their trousers. More than once Nikitin tried to hit him on his big forehead with a knife handle, gave him flicks on the nose, yelled at him, complained, but nothing saved his trousers from the spots.

After the promenade on horseback, the tea, preserves, rusks and butter seemed very tasty. They all drank the first glass with great appetite and in silence, but before the second they began to argue. The arguments at tea and at dinner were started each time by Varya. She was already twenty-three, good-looking, prettier than Manyusya, was considered the most intelligent and educated one in the house, and behaved importantly, sternly, as befitted an older daughter who had taken the place in the house of the late mother. By right as hostess she came before the guests in a smock, called the officers by their last names, looked at Manyusya as a little girl, and talked to her in the tone of a headmistress. She called herself an old maid—meaning she was sure she would marry.

Every conversation, even about the weather, she unfailingly turned into an argument. It was some sort of passion with her—to catch everyone at their words, to expose their contradictions, to pick on phrases. You would start telling her something, and she would already be peering intently into your face, and would suddenly interrupt: "Excuse me, excuse me, Petrov, but two days ago you said just the opposite!"

Or else she would smile mockingly and say: "However, I notice you're beginning to preach the principles of the Third Department.[3] My congratulations."

If you said something witty or produced a quip, you would immediately hear her voice: "That's old hat!" or "That's banal!" If an officer joked, she would make a contemptuous grimace and say: "An arrrmy joke!"

And she would bring out that "grrr" so impressively that Mushka never failed to respond from under the chair: "Grrr...nya-nya-nya..."

This time the argument over tea began with Nikitin talking about school examinations.

"Excuse me, Sergei Vassilyich," Varya interrupted him. "Here you're telling us it's difficult for the students. But whose fault is that, may I ask? For instance, you assigned your students a composition on the theme 'Pushkin as Psychologist.' First of all, you shouldn't assign such difficult topics, and second, what kind of psychologist is Pushkin? Well, Shchedrin[4] or, let's say, Dostoevsky—that's another matter, but Pushkin is a great poet and nothing more."

"Shchedrin is one thing, and Pushkin is another," Nikitin replied sullenly.

"I know, you schoolteachers don't recognize Shchedrin, but that's not the point. Tell me, what kind of psychologist is Pushkin?"

"So he's not a psychologist? If you like, I'll give you examples."

And Nikitin recited several passages from *Onegin,* then from *Boris Godunov.*[5]

"I see no psychology here," Varya sighed. "A psychologist is someone who describes the twists of the human soul, but this is just beautiful verse and nothing more."

"I know what kind of psychology you want!" Nikitin was offended. "You want someone to saw my finger with a dull saw and me to scream at the top of my lungs—that's what you call psychology."

"Banal! However, you still haven't proven it to me: what makes Pushkin a psychologist?"

When Nikitin had to dispute what he found commonplace, narrow-minded, or something of that sort, he usually jumped up, clutched his head with both hands, and started groaning and rushing up and down. And now he did the same: he jumped up, clutched his head, and walked groaning around the table, then sat down further off.

The officers took his side. Staff-Captain Polyansky started assuring Varya that Pushkin really was a psychologist, and to prove it produced two verses from Lermontov;[6] Lieutenant Gernet said that if Pushkin were not a psychologist, they would not have set up a monument to him in Moscow.

"That's boorishness!" came from the other end of the table. "As I said to the governor: that, Your Excellency, is boorishness!"

"I won't argue any more!" cried Nikitin. "Of his kingdom there shall be no end![7] Basta! Ah, get away, you vile dog!" he shouted at Som, who put his head and paw on his knees.

"Grrr . . . nya-nya-nya . . ." came from under the chair.

"Admit you're wrong!" shouted Varya. "Admit it!"

But some young ladies came calling, and the argument stopped by itself. They all went to the reception room. Varya sat down at the grand piano and began to play dances. First they danced a waltz, then a polka, then a quadrille with a *grand rond* through all the rooms led by Staff-Captain Polyansky, then they danced another waltz.

During the dancing, the old men sat in the reception room, smoked, and watched the young people. Among them was Shebaldin, director of the municipal credit society, known for his love of literature and the theater arts. He was the founder of the local "Music and Drama Circle," and took part in performances himself, for some reason playing only funny lackeys or reciting "The Sinful Woman"[8] in singsong. In town they called him a mummy, because he was tall, very lean, sinewy, and always had a solemn expression on his face and dull, fixed eyes. He loved the theater arts so sincerely that he shaved his moustache and beard, and that made him look still more like a mummy.

After the *grand rond*, he came up to Nikitin hesitantly, somehow sideways, coughed, and said:

"I had the pleasure of being present at tea during the argument. I fully share your opinion. You and I are like-minded, and I would be very pleased to talk with you. Have you read Lessing's *Hamburg Dramaturgy?*"[9]

"No, I haven't."

Shebaldin was horrified and waved his hands as if he had burned his fingers, and, saying nothing, backed away from Nikitin. Shebaldin's figure, his question, and his astonishment seemed ridiculous to Nikitin, but all the same he thought:

"In fact it's embarrassing. I'm a teacher of literature, and I still haven't read Lessing. I must read him."

Before supper everyone, young and old, sat down to play "fate." They took two decks of cards: one was dealt out equally among them, the other was placed facedown on the table.

"Whoever holds this card," old Shelestov solemnly began, lifting the top card from the second deck, "is fated to go right now to the nursery and kiss the nanny."

The pleasure of kissing the nanny fell to Shebaldin. They all surrounded him, flocked to the nursery, and, laughing and clapping their hands, made him kiss the nanny. There was noise, shouting . . .

"Not so passionately!" Shelestov shouted, weeping with laughter. "Not so passionately!"

Nikitin's fate was to confess them all. He sat on a chair in the middle of the reception room. They brought a shawl and covered him head and all. The first to come for confession was Varya.

"I know your sins," Nikitin began, looking at her stern profile in the darkness. "Tell me, my lady, why on earth do you go strolling with Polyansky every day? Oh, not in vain, 'tis not in vain, that she with a hussar doth remain."[10]

"That's banal," said Varya and she left.

Then big, motionless eyes gleamed under the shawl, a dear profile outlined itself in the darkness, and there was the scent of something cherished, long familiar, which reminded Nikitin of Manyusya's room.

"Maria Godefroi," he said and did not recognize his own voice, so tender and soft it was, "what are your sins?"

Manyusya narrowed her eyes and showed him the tip of her tongue, then burst out laughing and left. A moment later she was standing in the middle of the reception room, clapping her hands and calling out:

"Supper, supper, supper!"

And they all flocked to the dining room.

At supper Varya argued again, this time with her father. Polyansky ate heartily, drank red wine, and told Nikitin how once in wintertime, during the war, he stood all night up to his knees in a swamp; the enemy was so close that they were not allowed to talk or smoke; it was a cold, dark night, a piercing wind was blowing. Nikitin listened and glanced sidelong at Manyusya. She was gazing fixedly at him, not blinking, as if deep in thought or lost in reverie . . . For him it was both pleasant and agonizing.

"Why is she looking at me like that?" he agonized. "It's embarrassing. People may notice. Ah, she's still so young, so naïve!"

The guests began to disperse at midnight. When Nikitin went out the gate, a window on the first floor banged open and Manyusya appeared.

"Sergei Vassilyich," she called.

"What are your orders?"

"The thing is . . . ," Manyusya said, obviously trying to think up what to say. "The thing is . . . Polyansky has promised to come one of these days with his photography and take a picture of us all. We'll have to get together."

"All right."

Manyusya disappeared, the window banged shut, and at once someone in the house started playing the piano.

"What a house!" Nikitin thought as he crossed the street. "A house where only Egyptian doves moan, and then only because they don't know how else to express their joy!"

But the Shelestovs were not the only ones who lived merrily. Nikitin had not gone two hundred paces before he heard the sounds of a piano in another house. He went on a little further and saw a peasant in a gateway playing a balalaika. In the garden an orchestra struck up a potpourri of Russian songs . . .

Nikitin lived half a mile from the Shelestovs, in an eight-room apartment he rented for three hundred roubles a year together with his colleague, the teacher of geography and history, Ippolit Ippolitych. This Ippolit Ippolitych, an older man, with a red beard, pug-nosed, with a coarse and uncultivated face like a workman's, but good-natured, was sitting at his desk when Nikitin came home, correcting students' maps. He considered the drawing of maps the most necessary and important thing in geography, and in history the knowledge of chronology. He spent whole nights correcting his students' maps with a blue pencil, or putting together chronological tables.

"What splendid weather today!" Nikitin said, going into his room. "I'm amazed that you can sit inside like this."

Ippolit Ippolitych was a taciturn man; he either was silent, or said only what had long been known to everyone. Now he made this reply:

"Yes, fine weather. It's May now, soon it will be real summer. Summer isn't the same as winter. In winter we have to light the stoves, but in summer it's warm without the stoves. In summer you open the windows at night and it's still warm, but in winter—double-paned windows, and it's still cold."

Nikitin sat by the desk for no more than a minute and became bored.

"Good night!" he said, getting up and yawning. "I was about to tell you something romantic concerning myself, but you're—geography! Someone starts talking to you about love, and you immediately say: 'What year was the battle of Kalka?' To hell with you with your battles and your Chukotsky Noses!"[11]

"Why are you angry?"

"It's annoying!"

And, annoyed that he still had not proposed to Manyusya and that he now had no one to talk with about his love, he went to his study and lay down on the sofa. The study was dark and quiet. As he lay there and looked into the darkness, Nikitin began for some reason to think about how, in two or three years, he would go to Petersburg for something, how Manyusya would accompany him to the station and weep; in Petersburg he would receive a long letter from her, in which she would beg him to come home quickly. And he would write to her . . . His letter would begin: "My dearest rat . . ."

"Precisely, my dearest rat," he said and laughed.

It was uncomfortable for him lying there. He put his hands behind his head and lifted his left leg onto the back of the sofa. Then it was comfortable. Meanwhile the window became noticeably pale, sleepy roosters started squawking in the yard. Nikitin went on thinking of how he would come back from Petersburg, how Manyusya would meet him at the station, cry out with joy, and throw herself on his neck; or, better still, he would pull a trick: he would come home at night on the quiet, the cook would open the door, he would tiptoe into the bedroom, silently undress, and—plop into bed! She would wake up and—oh, joy!

The air turned completely pale. There was no longer any study or window. On the porch of the brewery, the same one they rode past that day, Manyusya was sitting and saying something. Then she took Nikitin under the arm and went with him to the park. There he saw the oaks and the crows' nests that looked like hats. One of the nests shook, Shebaldin looked down from it and shouted: "You haven't read Lessing!"

Nikitin shuddered all over and opened his eyes. In front of the sofa stood Ippolit Ippolitych, his head thrown back, tying his necktie.

"Get up, it's time for work," he said. "And you shouldn't sleep in your clothes. It's bad for the clothes. You should sleep in your own bed, undressed . . ."

And, as usual, he began speaking at length and with pauses about something that had long been known to everyone.

Nikitin's first lesson was in Russian language for the second-year students. When he entered the classroom at exactly nine o'clock, there were two big letters written in chalk on the blackboard: M. S. They probably meant Masha Shelestov.

"They've already sniffed it out, the rascals . . . ," thought Nikitin. "How do they know everything?"

The second lesson in literature was for the fifth-year students. Here, too, M. S. was written on the blackboard, and when he finished the lesson and was leaving the classroom, he was followed by a cry, as if from a theater gallery:

"Hurrah! Shelestova!!"

Sleeping in his clothes had given him a slight headache and left his body feeling weary and lazy. The students, who were waiting every day for the break before examinations, did nothing, languished, became mischievous out of boredom. Nikitin also languished, did not notice the mischief, and kept going to the window. He could see the street, brightly lit by the sun. Above the houses a transparent blue sky, birds, and far away, beyond the green gardens and the houses, a vast, endless distance with bluish groves and the smoke of a racing train . . .

Now two officers in white tunics came walking down the street in the shade of the acacias, brandishing their whips. Now a group of Jews with gray beards and visored caps drove by in a wagon. A governess strolled with the headmaster's granddaughter . . . Som ran somewhere with two yard dogs . . . Now Varya came along, in a simple gray dress and red stockings, holding *The Messenger of Europe* in her hand.[12] She must have visited the town library . . .

And the lessons would not end soon—only at three o'clock! After the lessons he had to go, not home and not to the Shelestovs', but to Wolf's for a lesson. This Wolf, a rich Jew who had embraced Lutheranism, did not send his children to school, but invited schoolteachers to them and paid five roubles per lesson . . .

"Boring, boring, boring!"

At three o'clock he went to Wolf's and sat it out there through what seemed like a whole eternity. He left them at five o'clock, and after six he already had to go to school for a faculty meeting—to set up oral examinations for the fourth- and sixth-year students!

When, late in the evening, he walked from school to the She-lestovs', his heart was pounding and his face was burning. A week ago and a month ago, each time he had intended to propose, he had prepared a whole speech with a preface and a conclusion, but this time he had not prepared a single word, everything was confused in his head, and he knew only that today he would *certainly* propose to her and that to wait any longer was absolutely impossible.

"I'll invite her to the garden," he reflected, "stroll a little, and propose . . ."

There was not a soul in the front hall; he went into the reception room, then the drawing room . . . There was no one there either. Varya could be heard arguing with someone upstairs, on the first floor, and the hired seamstress clicking her scissors in the children's room.

There was a little room in the house that bore three epithets: small, pass-through, and dark. In it stood a big old cupboard with medicines, gunpowder, and other hunting accessories. From there a narrow wooden stairway, on which the cats always slept, led to the first floor. Here there were doors: one to the children's room, the other to the drawing room. When Nikitin came in to go upstairs, the door to the children's room opened and made such a bang that the stairs and the cupboard shook; Manyusya ran in wearing a dark dress, with a length of blue fabric in her hands, and, not noticing Nikitin, darted for the stairs.

"Wait . . ." Nikitin stopped her. "Good evening, Godefroi . . . Allow me . . ."

He was breathless, he did not know what to say; with one hand he held her by the hand, with the other by the blue fabric. She was either frightened or surprised and looked at him with big eyes.

"Allow me . . . ," Nikitin went on, afraid she might leave. "I must tell you something . . . Only . . . it's awkward here. I can't, I'm not able . . . Understand, Godefroi, I just can't . . . that's all . . ."

The blue fabric fell to the floor, and Nikitin took Manyusya by the other hand. She turned pale, moved her lips, then backed away from Nikitin and ended up in the corner between the wall and the cupboard.

"My word of honor, I assure you . . . ," he said softly. "Manyusya, my word of honor . . ."

She threw her head back, and he kissed her on the lips, and, to make the kiss last longer, he took her by the cheeks with his fingers; and it somehow turned out that he himself ended up in the corner between the cupboard and the wall, and she put her arms around his neck and pressed her head to his chin.

Then they ran out to the garden.

The Shelestovs' garden was big, a good ten acres. In it grew a couple of dozen old maples and lindens, there was one spruce, the rest were all fruit trees: cherries, apples, pears, horse chestnuts, silvery olives . . . There were also many flowers.

Nikitin and Manyusya silently ran along the footpaths, laughed, occasionally asked each other disjointed questions, which they did not answer, while a half-moon shone over the garden, and on the ground, from the dark grass, dimly lit by this half-moon, sleepy tulips and irises grew upwards, as if also asking for a declaration of love.

When Nikitin and Manyusya returned to the house, the officers and young ladies were all there, dancing a mazurka. Again Polyansky led the *grand rond* through all the rooms, again after dancing they played "fate." Before supper, when the guests went from the reception room to the dining room, Manyusya, remaining alone with Nikitin, pressed herself to him and said:

"You talk with Papa and Varya yourself. I'm embarrassed . . ."

After supper he talked with the old man. Having heard him out, Shelestov reflected and said:

"I'm very grateful to you for the honor you are showing me and my daughter, but allow me to speak with you as a friend. I'll speak not as a father, but as a gentleman to a gentleman. Tell me, please, why do you wish to marry so early? Only peasants marry early, but with them, of course, it's boorishness, but what about you? What is the pleasure of putting yourself in fetters at such a young age?"

"I'm not all that young!" Nikitin was offended. "I'm twenty-six years old."

"Papa, the farrier's here!" Varya shouted from the other room.

And the conversation ended. Varya, Manyusya, and Polyansky went to see Nikitin home. When they came to his gate, Varya said:

"Why is it your mysterious Mitropolit Mitropolitych never shows himself anywhere? Let him come to see us."

The mysterious Ippolit Ippolitych was sitting on his bed and taking off his trousers when Nikitin came to his room.

"Don't go to bed, my dear friend!" Nikitin said breathlessly. "Wait, don't go to bed!"

Ippolit Ippolitych quickly put on his trousers and asked worriedly: "What's the matter?"

"I'm getting married!"

Nikitin sat down beside his colleague and, looking at him in surprise, as if he were surprised at himself, said:

"Imagine, I'm getting married! To Masha Shelestova! I proposed today!"

"Really? She seems like a nice girl. Only very young."

"Yes, young!" Nikitin sighed and shrugged worriedly. "Very, very young!"

"She was my student in school. I know her. She wasn't bad in geography, but in history—very poor. And she was inattentive in class."

For some reason Nikitin suddenly felt sorry for his colleague and wanted to say something gentle and comforting to him.

"My dear friend, why don't you get married?" he asked. "Why not marry Varya, for instance—eh, Ippolit Ippolitych? She's a wonderful, superlative girl! She loves to argue, true, but her heart . . . such a heart! She just asked about you. Marry her, my dear friend! Eh?"

He knew perfectly well that Varya would never marry this dull, pug-nosed man, but he still went on persuading him to marry her. Why?

"Marriage is a serious step," Ippolit Ippolitych said on reflection. "One must discuss everything, ponder, it's not done just like that. Good sense never hurts, especially in marriage, when a man ceases to be a bachelor and starts a new life."

And he went on talking about things that had long been known to everyone. Nikitin stopped listening to him, said good night, and went to his room. He quickly undressed and quickly went to bed, the sooner to start thinking about his happiness, about Manyusya, about the future, smiled, and suddenly remembered that he had not yet read Lessing.

"I'll have to read him . . . ," he thought. "Though why should I read him? To hell with him!"

And, wearied by his happiness, he immediately fell asleep and went on smiling till morning.

He dreamed about the drumming of horse hooves on the timber floor; dreamed of how they had first led the black Count Nulin from the stable, then the white Giant, then his sister Maika . . .

II

"The church was very crowded and noisy, and someone even cried out once, and the archpriest, who was marrying Manyusya and me, looked at the crowd through his spectacles and said sternly:

" 'Do not walk around in the church and do not make noise, but stand quietly and pray. You must have the fear of God.'

"My best men were two of my colleagues, and Manya's were Staff-Captain Polyansky and Lieutenant Gernet. The bishop's choir sang magnificently. The sputtering of the candles, the brilliance, the finery, the officers, the multitude of happy, pleased faces, and Manya's especially ethereal look, and the whole situation in general, and the words of the marriage prayers moved me to tears, filled me with festive feeling. I thought: how my life has blossomed, how poetically beautiful it has come to be recently! Two years ago I was still a student, I lived in cheap furnished rooms on Neglinny Passage, with no money, no family, and, as it seemed then, no future. Yet now I am a high school teacher in one of the best provincial capitals, I am secure, loved, pampered. It is for me, I thought, that this crowd has now gathered, for me that three chandeliers are burning, the protodeacon is bellowing, the singers are outdoing themselves, and for me that she is so young, elegant, and joyful—this young being who will soon be called my wife. I remembered our first meetings, our rides out of town, my declaration of love, and the weather which, as if on purpose, had been wondrously fine all summer; and that happiness which, when I lived on Neglinny Passage, had seemed possible to me only in novels and stories, I now experienced in reality, as if I were taking it in my hands.

"After the wedding everyone crowded in disorder around Manya and me and expressed their sincere pleasure, congratulated us, and wished us happiness. The brigadier general, an old man of about seventy, congratulated only Manyusya and said in an old man's rasping voice, so loudly that it resounded all through the church:

" 'I hope, my dear, that even after the wedding you will remain the same rose you are now.'

"The officers, the headmaster, and all the teachers smiled politely, and I also felt on my face a pleasant, insincere smile. Dearest Ippolit Ippolitych, the teacher of history and geography, who always says what everyone already knows, firmly shook my hand and said with feeling:

" 'Up to now you weren't married and lived alone, but now you're married and will live as two.'

"From the church we drove to the two-story unstuccoed house I received as a dowry. Besides this house, Manya comes with twenty thousand in cash and also some vacant lot in Melitonovo with a watch house, where they say there are lots of chickens and ducks that are untended and have gone wild. On coming back from church, I stretched out, sprawled on the Turkish divan in my new study, and smoked: it felt soft, comfortable, and cozy, like never before in my life, and just then the guests shouted 'Hurrah' and in the front room a bad orchestra played flourishes and all sorts of nonsense. Varya, Manya's sister, came running into the study with a wineglass in her hand and with some sort of strange, tense expression, as if her mouth was full of water; it looked as if she wanted to run on further, but suddenly she started laughing and sobbing, and the wineglass fell to the floor with a clank. We took her under the arms and led her out.

" 'Nobody can understand!' she muttered afterwards in the farthest room, lying on the wet-nurse's bed. 'Nobody, nobody! My God, nobody can understand!'

"But everybody understood perfectly well that she was four years older than her sister Manya and was still unmarried, and that she wept not out of envy, but out of a sad awareness that her time was passing and might already have passed. When they were dancing the quadrille, she was already in the reception room, with a tearful, heavily powdered face, and I saw how Staff-Captain Polyansky held a dish of ice cream out for her, and she ate it with a little spoon . . .

"It is already past five in the morning. I sat down with my diary in order to describe my full and varied happiness, and I thought I would write some six pages and read them to Manya tomorrow, but, strangely enough, everything got confused in my head, became vague, dreamlike, and the only thing I remember with clarity is that episode with Varya, and I want to write: poor Varya! I could just sit here and write: poor Varya! What's more, the trees are rustling: it's going to rain; the crows are cawing, and for some reason my Manya, who just fell asleep, has a sad face."

Then for a long time Nikitin did not touch his diary. In early August there were repeat examinations and entrance examinations, and after the Dormition classes started.[13] He usually went to work by eight o'clock, and by nine he had already begun to pine for Manya and his new house and kept glancing at his watch. In the lower grades he would make one of the boys dictate, and while the youngsters were writing, he would sit on the windowsill with his eyes shut, dreaming; whether he dreamed of the future or remembered the past, it all came out equally beautiful, like in a fairy tale. In the higher grades they read Gogol or Pushkin's prose aloud, and that made him drowsy; people, trees, fields, saddle horses rose up in his imagination, and he said with a sigh, as if admiring the author:

"How good!"

During the noon recess Manya sent him lunch wrapped in a snow-white napkin, and he ate it slowly, with pauses, to prolong the pleasure, and Ippolit Ippolitych, who usually lunched on nothing but a roll, watched him with respect and envy and said something well-known, like:

"Without food people cannot exist."

From school Nikitin went to give private lessons, and when, after five o'clock, he was finally on his way home, he felt both joy and anxiety, as if he had not been home for a whole year. He ran up the stairs, out of breath, found Manya, embraced her, kissed her, swore that he loved her, could not live without her, assured her that he had missed her terribly, and in fear asked her if she was well and why her face was so cheerless. Then they both had supper. After supper he lay on the divan in his study and smoked, and she sat beside him and talked in a low voice.

The happiest days for him now were Sundays and holidays, when he stayed home from morning till evening. On those days he partook of a naïve but extraordinarily pleasant life, which reminded him of pastoral idylls. He ceaselessly observed how his sensible and positive Manya was making their nest, and, wishing to show that he was not superfluous in the house, he did something useless—for instance, he rolled the charabanc out of the shed and examined it all over. With three cows Manyusya started a veritable dairy farm, and had many jugs of milk and pots of sour cream in the cellar and cold pantry, and all of it she kept for making butter. Occasionally, as a joke, Nikitin would ask for a glass of milk; she would get frightened, because it was against the rules, but, laughing, he would hug her and say:

"Now, now, I was joking, my treasure! Joking!"

Or else he would chuckle at her punctiliousness, when, for instance, she would find a forgotten scrap of sausage or cheese in the cupboard, hard as a rock, and say pompously:

"They will eat it in the kitchen."

He would point out to her that such a small scrap was good only for a mousetrap, and she would start insisting hotly that men understand nothing about housekeeping, and that servants are surprised at nothing, even if you send a hundred pounds of snacks to them in the kitchen, and he would agree and embrace her rapturously. What was right in her words seemed to him extraordinary, amazing; and what went against his convictions was, in his opinion, naïve and touching.

Occasionally a philosophical mood came over him, and he would start reflecting on an abstract subject, and she would listen and look into his face with curiosity.

"I'm endlessly happy with you, my joy," he would say, playing with her fingers or undoing her braid and braiding it again. "But I don't look upon this happiness of mine as something that has fallen upon me accidentally, as if from the sky. This happiness is a wholly natural phenomenon, consistent, logically correct. I believe that man is the creator of his own happiness, and now I am taking precisely what I myself have created. Yes, I say it without affectation, I created this happiness and I own it by right. You know my past. Orphanhood, poverty, unhappy childhood, dreary youth—all that struggle was the path I was laying down to happiness . . ."

In October the school suffered a heavy loss: Ippolit Ippolitych fell ill with erysipelas of the head and died. For the two last days before his death he was unconscious and delirious, but even in delirium he said only what was known to everyone:

"The Volga flows into the Caspian Sea . . . Horses eat oats and hay . . ."

On the day of his burial there were no classes at the school. Colleagues and students carried the lid and the coffin, and the school choir sang "Holy God" all the way to the cemetery.[14] In the procession there were three priests, two deacons, the entire boys' school, and the archbishop's choir in festive caftans. And, looking at the solemn funeral, passersby crossed themselves and said:

"God grant everyone such a death."

On coming home from the cemetery, the deeply moved Nikitin found his diary in his desk and wrote:

"Just lowered Ippolit Ippolitovich Ryzhitsky into his grave.

"Rest in peace, humble laborer! Manya, Varya, and all the women who attended the funeral wept sincerely, maybe because they knew that this uninteresting, downtrodden man had never been loved by a single woman. I wanted to say some warm words at my colleague's grave, but I had been warned that it might displease the headmaster, because he did not like the deceased. Since my wedding, it seems this is the first day that my soul has not felt light . . ."

After that there were no special events for the whole school year.

Winter was mild, without frosts, with wet snow; on the eve of Theophany,[15] for instance, the wind howled pitifully all night as in autumn and the roofs were dripping, and in the morning, during the blessing of the water, the police did not allow anyone to go to the river, because, they said, the ice was swollen and dark. But, despite the bad weather, Nikitin's life was as happy as in summer. One extra diversion was even added: he learned to play whist. Only one thing occasionally upset and angered him, and seemed to keep him from being fully happy: this was the cats and dogs that came with the dowry. The rooms always smelled like a zoo, especially in the morning, and nothing could stifle that smell; the cats often fought with the dogs. Wicked Mushka was fed ten times a day, and she still did not acknowledge Nikitin and growled at him:

"Grrr . . . nya-nya-nya . . ."

Once during the Great Lent,[16] at midnight, he was coming home from the club, where he had been playing cards. Rain was falling, it was dark and muddy. Nikitin had an unpleasant aftertaste in his soul and could not understand why: was it because he had lost twelve roubles at the club, or because, as they were settling accounts, one of his partners said that Nikitin was rolling in money, apparently alluding to the dowry? He was not sorry about the twelve roubles, and there was nothing offensive in his partner's words, but all the same it was unpleasant. He did not even feel like going home.

"Pah, how disagreeble!" he said, stopping by a streetlight.

It occurred to him that he was not sorry about the twelve roubles, because they had come to him gratis. If he were a worker, he would know the value of every kopeck and would not have been indifferent to a gain or a loss. And his whole happiness, he went on reasoning, had come to him gratis, for nothing, and was in fact a luxury for him, like medicine for a healthy man; if he, like the vast majority of people, were weighed down by anxiety over a crust of bread, were struggling for existence, if his back and chest ached from work, then supper, a warm, cozy apartment and family happiness would be a necessity, a reward, and the adornment of his life; while now it all had a strange, indefinite significance.

"Pah, how disagreeable!" he repeated, understanding perfectly well that this reasoning itself was already a bad sign.

When he got home, Manya was in bed. She was breathing evenly, smiling, and apparently sleeping with great pleasure. Beside her lay a white cat curled up and purring. While Nikitin was lighting a candle and smoking, Manya woke up and greedily drank a glass of water.

"I ate a lot of marmalade," she said and laughed. "Were you with our people?" she asked after a pause.

"No, I wasn't."

Nikitin already knew that Staff-Captain Polyansky, whom Varya had recently been counting on very much, was being transferred to one of the western provinces and was paying farewell visits, and therefore it was dreary at his father-in-law's.

"Varya came by this evening," Manya said, sitting up. "She didn't say anything, but you could see by her face how hard it is for her, poor thing. I can't stand Polyansky. Fat, flabby, when he walks or dances, his cheeks flop . . . Not my ideal. But still I considered him a decent man."

"Even now I consider him a decent man."

"And why did he act so badly with Varya?"

"Why badly?" Nikitin asked, beginning to be annoyed by the white cat, who stretched and arched his back. "As far as I know he made no proposals and gave no promises."

"Then why did he come to the house so often? If you have no intention to marry, don't come."

Nikitin put out the candle and lay down. But he had no wish either to sleep or to lie down. It seemed to him that his head was huge and empty, like a barn, and that new, somehow special thoughts were wandering through it in the form of long shadows. He thought that, apart from the soft light of an icon lamp, smiling upon his quiet family happiness, apart from this little world in which he lived so peacefully and sweetly, along with this cat, there exists another world . . . And he suddenly wanted passionately, desperately, to be in that other world, so that he himself could work somewhere in a factory or a big workshop, speak from a podium, write, publish, make a noise, wear himself out, suffer . . . He wanted something that would absorb him to the point of self-forgetfulness, of indifference to his personal happiness, the sensations of which are so monotonous. And suddenly there rose up in his imagination, as if alive, the clean-shaven Shebaldin, who said with horror:

"You haven't even read Lessing! You're so far behind! My God, how low you've sunk!"

Manya again drank some water. He looked at her neck, her full shoulders and breast, and remembered what the brigadier general once said in church: a rose.

"A rose," he murmured and laughed.

In reply the sleepy Mushka growled under the bed:

"Grrr . . . nya-nya-nya . . ."

Heavy spite, like a cold hammer, stirred in his soul, and he wanted to say something rude to Manya and even to jump up and hit her. His heart began to pound.

"You mean," he asked, restraining himself, "that if I visited your house, I necessarily had to marry you?"

"Of course. You understand that perfectly well."

"Nice."

And a moment later he said again:

"Nice."

To hold his tongue and quiet his heart, Nikitin went to his study and lay down on the divan without a pillow, then lay on the floor, on the carpet.

"What nonsense!" He tried to calm himself. "You're a pedagogue, you work at a most noble profession . . . What need do you have of some other world? That's all rubbish!"

But at once he told himself confidently that he was not a pedagogue at all, but a functionary, just as giftless and faceless as the Czech who taught Greek; he had never had any calling to be a teacher, was unfamiliar with pedagogy and had no interest in it, and did not know how to deal with children; the significance of what he taught was unknown to him, and he might even be teaching things that were not needed. The late Ippolit Ippolitych was plainly stupid, and all his colleagues and students knew who he was and what to expect of him; while he, Nikitin, like the Czech, was able to conceal his stupidity and cleverly deceive everybody, making it seem that with him, thank God, everything was going well. These new thoughts frightened Nikitin; he rejected them, called them foolish, and believed it was all caused by nerves, that he himself would come to laugh at himself.

And, indeed, by morning he was already laughing at his nervousness, called himself an old woman, but it was already clear to him that peace was lost, probably forever, and that in the two-story unstuccoed house happiness was already impossible for him. He felt that the illusion was exhausted, and that a new, nervous, conscious life was beginning, which was not in tune with peace and personal happiness.

The next day, Sunday, he went to the school church and met there with the headmaster and his colleagues. It seemed to him that they were all busy only with carefully concealing their ignorance and dissatisfaction with life, and he himself, so as not to betray his anxiety to them, smiled pleasantly and talked about trifles. Then he went to the station and saw the mail train come and go, and he was pleased to be alone and not to have to talk to anyone.

At home he found his father-in-law and Varya, who had come for dinner. Varya had tearful eyes and complained of a headache, and Shelestov ate a lot and talked about present-day young men being unreliable and having little of the gentleman about them.

"That's boorishness!" he said. "I'll tell him straight out: that's boorishness, my dear sir!"

Nikitin smiled pleasantly and helped Manya to serve the guests, but after dinner he went to his study and shut the door.

The March sun was shining brightly, and hot rays fell on the desk through the windowpanes. It was still only the twentieth, but wheels were already rolling on the roads and starlings were making noise in the garden. It seemed as if Manyusya would now come in, put her arm around his neck, and say that saddle horses or the charabanc should be brought to the porch, and ask him what she should wear so as not to get chilled. Spring was beginning, as wonderful as the year before, and promising the same joys . . . But Nikitin was thinking how good it would be to take a vacation and go to Moscow and stay in the familiar furnished rooms on Neglinny Passage. In the next room they were drinking coffee and talking about Staff-Captain Polyansky, but he tried not to listen and wrote in his diary: "My God, where am I? I'm surrounded by banality upon banality. Boring, worthless people, pots of sour cream, jugs of milk, cockroaches, stupid women . . . There's nothing more terrible, more insulting, more dreary than banality. I must flee from here, flee today, or I'll go out of my mind!"

1894

IN A COUNTRY HOUSE

P AVEL ILYICH RASHEVICH walked about, stepping lightly on the floor covered with Ukrainian rugs, and casting a long, narrow shadow on the wall and ceiling, while his guest, Meier, the acting examining magistrate, sat on the Turkish divan, one leg tucked under, smoking and listening. The clock already showed eleven, and there were sounds of the table being set in the room next to the study.

"As you like, sir," Rashevich was saying, "from the point of view of brotherhood, equality, and all that, the swineherd Mitka may be as much of a human being as Goethe or Frederick the Great; but put yourself on a scientific footing, have the courage to look facts straight in the face, and it will be obvious to you that blue blood is not a prejudice, not an old wives' tale. Blue blood, my dear fellow, has a natural-historical justification, and to deny it, in my opinion, is as strange as to deny that a deer has antlers. We must reckon with the facts! You're a jurist and haven't sampled any other studies than the humanities, and you may still deceive yourself with illusions concerning equality, brotherhood, and all that. I'm an incorrigible Darwinist, and for me words like race, aristocratism, noble blood are not empty sounds."

Rashevich was excited and spoke with feeling. His eyes flashed, his pince-nez refused to stay on his nose, he twitched his shoulders nervously, winked, and at the word "Darwinist" glanced dashingly in the mirror and stroked his gray beard with both hands. He was dressed in a very short, much-worn jacket and narrow trousers; his quick movements, dashing air, and this curtailed jacket somehow did not suit him; and it seemed that his big, long-haired, fine-looking head, reminiscent of a bishop or a venerable poet, had been attached to the body of a tall, lean, and affected adolescent. When he spread his legs wide, his long shadow resembled a pair of scissors.

Generally he liked to talk, and it always seemed to him that he was saying something new and original. In the presence of Meier, he felt an extraordinary inspiration and influx of thoughts. He found the magistrate sympathetic and was inspired by his youth, health, excellent manners, seriousness, and above all by his cordial attitude towards himself and his family. Generally acquaintances did not like Rashevich, avoided him, and, as he knew, told of him that he had supposedly driven his wife into the grave by his talk, and behind his back called him a hate-monger and a toad. Only Meier, a new and unprejudiced man, visited him frequently and willingly, and even said somewhere that Rashevich and his daughters were the only people in the district with whom he felt as warm as with his own family. Rashevich also liked him, because he was a young man who might make a suitable match for Zhenya, his older daughter.

And now, enjoying his thoughts and the sound of his own voice, and glancing with pleasure at the moderately plump, handsomely cropped, respectable Meier, Rashevich dreamed of how he would set his daughter up with a good man, and how the cares of the estate would then pass to his son-in-law. Unpleasant cares! The interest to the bank had not been paid for the last two periods, and over two thousand were owing in various fines and penalties!

"For me it is not subject to doubt," Rashevich went on, becoming more and more inspired, "that if some Richard the Lionhearted or Frederick Barbarossa, say, is brave and magnanimous, those qualities will be inherited by his son along with the bumps and convolutions of the brain. And if this bravery and magnanimity are protected in his son by means of upbringing and exercise, and if he marries a princess who is also brave and magnanimous, those qualities will be passed on to the grandson, and so on, until they become a particularity of the species and are transmitted organically, so to speak, in flesh and blood. Owing to the strict sexual selection by means of which noble families instinctively protected themselves from unequal marriages and high-born young men did not marry the devil knows who, lofty inner qualities were passed on from generation to generation in all their purity, were protected, and in the course of time, by being exercised, became more perfect and lofty. Whatever good there is in mankind we owe precisely to nature, to the regular natural-historical, purposeful course of things, which carefully, over the centuries, has separated blue blood from common blood. Yes, my dear man! It was not some unwashed commoner, some scullery maid's son, who gave us literature, science, the arts, law, the notions of honor, duty . . . Mankind owes all this exclusively to blue blood, and in that sense, from the natural-historical point of view, a bad Sobakevich,[1] solely by being of blue blood, is more useful and lofty than the best of merchants, even one who builds fifteen museums. Say what you like, sir! And if I don't offer my hand to an unwashed commoner, a scullery maid's son, and don't seat him at my table, I thereby protect what is best on earth and fulfill one of the highest designs of Mother Nature, who leads us to perfection . . ."

Rashevich paused, stroking his beard with both hands; on the wall his shadow, which looked like a pair of scissors, also paused.

"Take our Mother Russia," he went on, putting his hands in his pockets and standing now on his heels, now on his toes. "Who are her best people? Take our first-class artists, writers, composers . . . Who are they? All of them, my dear, were representatives of blue blood. Pushkin, Gogol, Lermontov, Turgenev, Goncharov, Tolstoy—they were no sexton's kids!"

"Goncharov[2] was a merchant," said Meier.

"What of it! Exceptions only prove the rule. And concerning Goncharov's genius we could also have a hot debate. But let's drop the names and get back to the facts. For instance, what will you say, my dear sir, of this eloquent fact: as soon as a commoner gets where he wasn't allowed before—to high society, the sciences, literature, local government, the courts—notice, nature herself stands up for the highest human rights and is the first to declare war on this rabble. Indeed, as soon as the commoner gets into the wrong sled, he begins to mope, to languish, to lose his mind and degenerate, and you'll never meet so many neurasthenics, psychological cripples, consumptives, and other wimps as among these sweethearts. They die like flies in autumn. If it weren't for this saving degeneration, there would long since have been no stone left upon stone of our civilization, the unwashed would have gobbled everything up. Kindly tell me: What has this infestation given us so far? What have the unwashed brought with them?" Rashevich made a mysterious, frightened face and went on: "Never before have our science and literature been on such a low level as now! The modern-day ones, my dear sir, have no ideas, no ideals, and all their dealings are pervaded by one spirit: to rip off as much as possible and take the last shirt from whoever they can. All these modern-day ones, who pass themselves off as progressive and honest, can be bought for a rouble, and the contemporary intellectual has this special quality, that when you talk to him, you must keep a strong grip on your pocket, or else he'll snatch your wallet." Rashevich winked and burst out laughing. "By God, he will!" he went on in a gleefully high voice. "And morals? What about morals?" Rashevich glanced at the door. "Nowadays nobody's surprised when a wife robs and abandons her husband—it's nothing, mere trifles! Nowadays, my dear man, a twelve-year-old girl aims at having a lover, and all these amateur theatricals and literary evenings have been invented only to make it easier to hook up with a moneybag and be kept by him . . . Mothers sell their daughters, and husbands are asked outright about their wives' going price, and can even haggle over it, my dear fellow . . ."

Meier, who had been silent all the while and sat motionless, suddenly got up from the divan and looked at his watch.

"Sorry, Pavel Ilyich," he said, "it's time I went home."

But Pavel Ilyich, who had not yet finished talking, embraced him and, forcing him to sit back down on the divan, swore he would not let him go without supper. And Meier again sat and listened, but now kept glancing at Rashevich in perplexity and apprehension, as if he were only now beginning to understand him. Red blotches appeared on his face. And when the maid finally came in and said that the young ladies invited them to supper, he sighed with relief and was the first to leave the study.

At the table in the next room sat Rashevich's daughters, Zhenya and

Iraida, twenty-four and twenty-two years old, both dark-eyed, very pale, of identical height. Zhenya with her hair down, and Iraida with a tall hairdo. Before eating they both drank a glass of bitter liqueur, looking as if they had drunk it accidentally, for the first time in their life, and they both became embarrassed and burst into laughter.

"Don't be mischievous, girls," said Rashevich.

Zhenya and Iraida spoke French with each other, and Russian with their father and the guest. Interrupting each other and mixing Russian with French, they quickly began telling how, in former years, they used to leave for boarding school precisely then, in August, and what a happy time it was. Now there was nowhere to go, and they had to live there in the country without leaving all summer and winter. What boredom!

"Don't be mischievous, girls," Rashevich repeated.

He wanted to talk himself. When others talked in his presence, he experienced a feeling similar to jealousy.

"So it goes, my dear fellow . . . ," he began again, looking affectionately at the magistrate. "In our kindness and simplicity, and also for fear of being suspected of backwardness, we fraternize, forgive me, with all sorts of trash, we preach brotherhood and equality with moneybags and tavernkeepers; but if we cared to think about it, we would see to what degree this kindness of ours is criminal. The result of it is that our civilization is hanging by a hair. My dear fellow! That to which our ancestors devoted centuries will be desecrated and destroyed today or tomorrow by these latter-day Huns . . ."

After supper they all went to the drawing room. Zhenya and Iraida lit the candles on the grand piano, prepared the scores . . . but their father went on talking, and there was no knowing when he would stop. They already looked with anguish and annoyance at their egoist-father, for whom the pleasure of babbling and showing off his intelligence was obviously more valuable and important than his daughters' happiness. Meier was the only young man who frequented their house, frequented it—this they knew—for the sake of their sweet feminine company, but the irrepressible old man took him over and would not let him go even a step away.

"Just as the western knights repelled the attacks of the Mongols, so we, before it's too late, should rally and attack our enemy with a united front," Rashevich went on in a preacherly tone, raising his right arm. "Let me appear before the commoner not as Pavel Ilyich, but as the terrible and mighty Richard the Lionhearted. Let us cease all this delicacy with them—enough! Let us decide all together that as soon as a commoner comes near us, we will hurl words of contempt right in his mug: 'Hands off! Know your place!' Right in his mug!" Rashevich went on in ecstasy, jabbing in front of him with a bent finger. "In his mug! In his mug!"

"I can't do it," Meier said, looking away.

"Why not?" Rashevich asked briskly, looking forward to an interesting and prolonged argument. "Why not?"

"Because I'm a commoner myself."

Having said that, Meier turned red, his neck even swelled, and tears even glistened in his eyes.

"My father was a simple worker," he added in a rough, jerky voice, "but I see nothing wrong with it."

Rashevich was terribly embarrassed, stunned, and, as if he had been caught redhanded, looked at Meier in perplexity, not knowing what to say. Zhenya and Iraida blushed and bent over their music; they were ashamed of their tactless father. A moment passed in silence, and the shame was becoming unbearable, when all at once—morbidly, stiffly, and inappropriately—words rang out in the air:

"Yes, I'm a commoner and proud of it."

Then Meier, awkwardly stumbling into the furniture, took his leave and quickly went to the front hall, though the horses had not yet been brought.

"You'll be driving in the dark tonight," Rashevich muttered, going after him. "The moon rises late now."

They both stood on the porch in the dark waiting for the horses to be brought. It was chilly.

"A star just fell . . . ," Meier said, wrapping himself in his coat.

"A lot of them fall in August."

When the horses were brought, Rashevich looked attentively at the sky and said with a sigh:

"A phenomenon worthy of the pen of Flammarion . . ."[3]

Having seen his guest off, he strolled through the garden, gesticulating in the darkness and not wishing to believe that such a strange, stupid misunderstanding had just occurred. He was ashamed and annoyed with himself. First, it had been extremely imprudent and tactless on his part to bring up this cursed question of blue blood without having first found out whom he was dealing with; something similar had happened to him before; once on a train he had started to denounce the Germans, and it had turned out that all his fellow travelers were German. Second, he sensed that Meier would never call on them again. These cultivated ones who rise from the common people are painfully touchy, stubborn, and unforgiving.

"Not nice, not nice . . . ," murmured Rashevich, spitting. He felt embarrassed and disgusted, as if he had eaten soap. "No, not nice!"

From the garden, through the window, he could see Zhenya by the piano in the drawing room, her hair down, extremely pale, frightened, talking very, very quickly about something . . . Iraida paced up and down, deep in thought; but then she, too, began talking, also quickly, with an indignant look. They talked at the same time. Not a word could be heard, but Rashevich could guess what they were talking about. Zhenya was probably complaining that her father frightened off all decent people with his talk, and today had deprived them of the only acquaintance who might have been a suitor, and now the poor young man had no place in the whole district where he could find rest for his soul. And Iraida, judging by the way she threw up her arms in despair, was probably talking on the theme of their boring life, their ruined youth . . .

On coming to his room, Rashevich sat on his bed and slowly began to undress. He was in a depressed state of mind, and was tormented by that same feeling of having eaten soap. He was ashamed. He undressed, looked at his long, sinewy, old man's legs, and recalled that in the district he was known as "the toad," and that he had been ashamed after every long conversation. In some sort of fatal way it came about that he would begin softly, gently, with good intentions, calling himself an old student, an idealist, a Don Quixote, but, unbeknownst to himself, would gradually go on to abuse and slander and, most surprising of all, would quite sincerely criticize science, art, and morals, though it was already twenty years since he had read a single book or gone further than the provincial capital, and in fact he had no idea of what was happening in the wide world. If he sat down to write anything, be it only a congratulatory letter, abuse would appear in the letter as well. And all this was strange, because in fact he was a sentimental, tearful man. Was it some demon sitting in him, who hated and slandered in him against his will?

"Not nice . . . ," he sighed, lying under the blanket. "Not nice!"

His daughters also did not sleep. He heard loud laughter and shouting, as if someone were being pursued: it was Zhenya having hysterics. A little later Iraida also began to sob. A barefoot maid ran down the corridor several times . . .

"Lord, what a mishap . . . ," Rashevich muttered, sighing and tossing from side to side. "Not nice!"

In sleep he was oppressed by a nightmare. He dreamed that he was standing in the middle of the room, naked, tall as a giraffe, jabbing his finger in front of him and saying:

"In the mug! In the mug! In the mug!"

He woke up in fright and first of all remembered that a misunderstanding had occurred the day before, and that Meier, of course, would not call on them any more. He also remembered that he had to pay the interest to the bank, marry off his daughters, had to eat and drink, and that illness, old age, troubles were near, it would soon be winter, there was no firewood . . .

It was already past nine in the morning. Rashevich slowly got dressed, had tea, and ate two big slices of bread with butter. His daughters did not come out for tea; they did not want to meet him, and that offended him. He lay on the divan in his study for a while, then sat down at the desk and started writing a letter to his daughters. His hand trembled, and his eyes itched. He wrote that he was already old, nobody needed him, and that nobody loved him, and he asked his daughters to forget him and, when he died, to bury him in a simple pine coffin, without ceremony, or send his body to the anatomical theater in Kharkov. He sensed that his every line breathed out spite and histrionics, but he could no longer stop and kept on writing, writing . . .

"The toad!" suddenly reached him from the neighboring room; it was the voice of his older daughter, an indignant, rasping voice. "The toad!"

"The toad!" the younger repeated like an echo. "The toad!"

1894

THE PECHENEG

IVAN ABRAMYCH ZHMUKHIN, [1] a retired Cossack officer, who had once served in the Caucasus and now lived on his farmstead, who had once been young, healthy, strong, and was now old, dry, and bent, with shaggy eyebrows and a greenish-gray moustache, was coming back from town to his farmstead on a hot summer day. In town he went to confession and wrote a will at the notary's (he had had a slight stroke two weeks earlier), and now, all the while he rode on the train, sad, serious thoughts about the imminence of death, about the vanity of vanities, about the transience of all earthly things never left him. At the Provalye station—there is such a station on the Donetsk line [2]—a fair-haired gentleman entered the car, middle-aged, plump, with a scuffed briefcase, and sat down across from him. They fell to talking.

"Yes, sir," Ivan Abramych said, pensively looking out the window. "It's never too late to marry. I myself married when I was forty-eight. People said it was late, but as it turned out it was neither late nor early, but it would have been better not to marry at all. Everybody soon gets bored with his wife, but not everybody will tell you the truth, because, you know, people are ashamed of unhappy family life and they hide it. Around his wife it's 'Manya this' and 'Manya that,' but if he had his way, he'd stuff this Manya in a sack and drown her. With a wife it's boredom, sheer stupidity. And with the children it's no better, I hasten to assure you. I've got two of them, the scoundrels. There's nowhere to educate them here in the steppe. I've got no money to send them to Novocherkassk,[3] so they live here like wolf cubs. Look out or they'll knife somebody on the high road."

The fair-haired gentleman listened attentively, answered questions briefly and in a low voice, and was apparently a man of quiet, modest character. He said he was an attorney and was going to the village of Duyevka on business.

"Lord God, that's six miles from me!" Zhmukhin said, sounding as if someone were arguing with him. "Sorry, but you won't find any horses at the station. I think the best thing for you, you know, would be to come to my place now, spend the night, and in the morning go with God on my horses."

The attorney thought it over and accepted.

When they arrived at the station, the sun already stood very low over the steppe. They were silent all the way to the farmstead: the jolting drive hindered speaking. The tarantass bounced, squeaked, and seemed to sob, as if the bouncing caused it great pain, and the attorney, who was seated very uncomfortably, looked ahead in anguish to see if the farmstead was in sight. They drove for about five miles and in the distance a low house appeared, with a yard surrounded by a dark flagstone wall; the roof of the house was green, the stucco was chipping off, and the windows were small and narrow, like squinting eyes. The farmstead stood open to the heat of the sun, and no water or trees could be seen anywhere around. The neighboring landowners and peasants called it "the Pecheneg's Farmstead." Many years earlier some passing surveyor, staying overnight at the farmstead, had spent the whole night talking with Ivan Abramych, ended up displeased, and in the morning, on leaving, said to him sternly: "You, my good sir, are a Pecheneg." Hence "the Pecheneg's Farmstead," and the nickname became still more entrenched when Zhmukhin's children grew up and started raiding the neighboring orchards and melon patches. Ivan Abramych himself was called "You Know," because he habitually talked a great deal and often used the phrase "you know."

In the yard by the shed stood Zhmukhin's sons: one about nineteen years old, the other younger, both barefoot, without hats; and just as the tarantass drove into the yard, the younger one tossed a chicken up high; it clucked and flew, describing an arc in the air, the older one fired his gun, and the killed chicken went crashing to the ground.

"It's my boys learning to shoot on the wing," said Zhmukhin.

In the front hall the arrivals were met by a woman, small, thin, with a pale face, still young and pretty; from her clothes she might have been taken for a servant.

"And this, allow me to introduce her," said Zhmukhin, "is the mother of my sons-of-a-bitch. Well, Lyubov Osipovna," he turned to her, "get a move on, old girl, see to our guest. Serve supper! Look lively!"

The house consisted of two halves. In one was the "reception room," and next to it old Zhmukhin's bedroom—both stuffy, with low ceilings, and with multitudes of flies and wasps. The other was the kitchen, where the cooking and laundry were done, and workers were fed; right there, under the benches, geese and turkeys hatched their eggs, and there, too, were the beds of Lyubov Osipovna and her two sons. The furniture in the reception room was unpainted, knocked together, obviously, by a carpenter; on the walls hung rifles, hunting bags, whips, and all that old trash had rusted long ago and gone gray with dust. Not a single painting; in one corner a dark board that had once been an icon.

A young Ukrainian woman set the table and served ham, then borscht. The guest declined vodka and ate only bread and cucumbers.

"How about some ham?" Zhmukhin asked.

"No, thank you, I don't eat it," the guest replied. "I generally don't eat meat."

"Why not?"

"I'm a vegetarian. Killing animals is against my convictions."

Zhmukhin thought for a moment and then said slowly, with a sigh:

"Yes . . . So . . . In town I also saw a man who doesn't eat meat. There's this belief going around now. Well, so? It's a good thing. Can't keep slaughtering and shooting, you know, someday you've got to back off and give the animals some peace. It's a sin to kill, a sin—no disputing it. Sometimes you wound a hare, hit him in the leg, and he screams like a baby. That means it hurts!"

"Of course it hurts. Animals suffer just as people do."

"That's true," Zhmukhin agreed. "I understand it all very well," he went on, still thinking, "only, I confess, there's one thing I can't understand: suppose, you know, if people all stop eating meat, then what will become of domestic animals, for instance chickens and geese?"

"Chickens and geese will live freely, like the wild ones."

"Now I see. In fact, crows and jackdaws live and get along without us. Yes . . . And chickens, and geese, and hares, and sheep will all live in freedom, you know, they'll rejoice and praise God, and they won't be afraid of us. There'll be peace and quiet. Only, you know, there's one thing I can't understand," Zhmukhin went on, glancing at the ham. "What do you do with the pigs? Where do you put them?"

"They'll be like all the rest, that is, they'll be free, too."

"Yes. Right. But, excuse me, if they're not slaughtered, they'll multiply, you know, and then say goodbye to your meadows and vegetable gardens. If a pig is set free and not watched over, he'll destroy everything in a single day. A pig's a pig, and it's not for nothing he's called a pig . . ."

They finished supper. Zhmukhin got up from the table and walked around the room for a long time and kept talking, talking . . . He liked to talk about important and serious things and liked to think; and he wished in his old age to settle on something, to put his mind at rest, so that it would not be so frightening to die. He wished for such meekness, inner peace, self-confidence, as this guest had, who ate his fill of cucumbers and bread and thought it made him more perfect; he sits there on a chest, healthy, plump, silent, patiently bored, and in the twilight, when you look at him from the hallway, he resembles a big immoveable boulder. The man has an anchor in life—and all's well with him.

Zhmukhin walked out through the front hall to the porch, and then could be heard sighing and saying broodingly to himself: "Yes . . . so." It was already getting dark, and stars appeared here and there in the sky. Inside they had not yet brought lights. Someone came into the reception room noiselessly, like a shadow, and stopped by the door. It was Lyubov Osipovna, Zhmukhin's wife.

"Are you from town?" she asked timidly, without looking at the guest.

"Yes, I live in town."

"Maybe you're in the teaching line, sir, so kindly teach us. We need to make an application."

"Where?" asked the guest.

"We have two sons, good sir, and we should have sent them to study long ago, but nobody visits us and there's no one to advise us. And I don't know anything myself. Because if they don't study, they'll be taken into the army as simple Cossacks. It's not good, sir! They're illiterate, worse than peasants, and Ivan Abramych himself scorns them and won't allow them in his room. But is it their fault? At least the younger one could be sent to study, really, or it's such a pity!" she said, drawing out the words, and her voice quivered; and it seemed incredible that such a small and young woman already had grown-up children. "Ah, such a pity!"

"You don't understand anything, Mother, and it's none of your business," Zhmukhin said, appearing in the doorway. "Don't pester the guest with your wild talk. Go away, Mother!"

Lyubov Osipovna left and in the front hall repeated in a high voice: "Ah, such a pity!"

They made a bed for the guest on the sofa in the reception room and lit an icon lamp so that he would not be in the dark. Zhmukhin lay down in his bedroom. And, lying there, he thought about his soul, about old age, about the recent stroke, which had frightened him so much and had vividly reminded him of death. He liked to philosophize, left by himself, in silence, and then it seemed to him that he was a very serious, profound man, and in this world he was concerned only with important questions. And now he kept thinking, and he wished to settle on some one thought, unlike the others, a significant one, that would be a guidance in life, and he wished to think up some rules for himself, so as to make his life as serious and profound as he himself was. For instance, it would be good if an old man like him could give up meat and various excesses entirely. The time when people stop killing animals and each other would come sooner or later, it could not be otherwise, and he imagined that time to himself, and clearly pictured himself living in peace with all animals, and suddenly he again remembered about the pigs, and everything became confused in his head.

"Lord have mercy, what a puzzle!" he muttered, sighing heavily. "Are you asleep?" he asked.

"No."

Zhmukhin got out of bed and stood in the doorway in nothing but his nightshirt, showing the guest his legs, sinewy and dry as sticks.

"Nowadays, you know," he began, "all sorts of telegraphs, telephones, and various wonders, in a word, have come along, but people haven't gotten better. They say that in our time, some thirty or forty years ago, people were coarse, cruel; but isn't it the same now? Actually, in my time we lived without ceremony. I remember, in the Caucasus, when we spent a whole four months by the same little river with nothing to do—I was still a sergeant then—a story happened, something like a novel. Right on the bank of that little river, you know, where our squadron was stationed, they buried a little prince we had killed earlier. And by night, you know, the widowed princess came to his grave and wept. She howled and howled, moaned and moaned, and annoyed us so much that we couldn't sleep at all. We didn't sleep one night, we didn't sleep another night; well, enough of that! And, reasoning from common sense, in fact one shouldn't lose sleep on account of the devil knows what, forgive the expression. We took that princess, gave her a whipping—and she stopped coming. There you have it. Now, of course, people are no longer of that category, and nobody gets whipped, and they live cleaner, and there's more learning, but, you know, the soul's still the same, there's no change. So, kindly see, we've got a landowner living here. He owns mines, you know. He's got people working for him who have nowhere to go: all sorts of vagrants, without passports.[4] On Saturdays he was supposed to pay his workers, but he didn't want to pay them, you know, he was sorry for the money. So he found this clerk, also a bum, though he went around in a hat. 'Pay them nothing,' he said, 'not a kopeck. They'll beat you, but let them beat you,' he said, 'bear with it, and I'll pay you ten roubles for it every Saturday.' So on Saturday evening the workers, in good order, as usual, come for their pay; the clerk tells them, 'No money.' Well, one thing leads to another, they start a fight, a brawl . . . They beat him, beat him and kick him—you know, the folk are brutal from hunger—they beat him unconscious, and then go their ways. The owner has the clerk doused with water, then shoves ten roubles at him, which he gladly takes, because in fact he'd do anything, even put his head in a noose, for three roubles, let alone ten. Yes . . . And on Monday a new party of workers comes; they come, no way out of it . . . On Saturday, the same story all over again . . ."

The guest turned on his other side, facing the back of the sofa, and murmured something.

"And here's another example," Zhmukhin went on. "Once there was anthrax here, you know; cattle dropping like flies, let me tell you, and veterinarians came here, and there were strict orders to bury the dead animals further, deeper in the ground, and to pour lime on them, you know, on a scientific basis. A horse dropped dead on me, too. I buried it with all the precautions and poured three hundred pounds of lime on it. And what do you think? My fine fellows, you know, these dear sons of mine, dug up the horse at night, skinned it, and sold the skin for three roubles. There you have it. Meaning people haven't gotten better, and meaning once a wolf, always a wolf. There you have it. There's something to think about! Eh? How does that strike you?"

In the windows on one side, through the chinks in the shutters, lightning flashed. It was stifling before the storm, mosquitoes were biting, and Zhmukhin, lying in his room and reflecting, groaned, moaned, and said to himself: "Yes . . . so"—and it was impossible to fall asleep. Thunder rumbled somewhere very far away.

"Are you asleep?"

"No," the guest replied.

Zhmukhin got up and walked, stomping his heels, through the reception room and the front hall to the kitchen, to have a drink of water.

"The worst thing in the world, you know, is stupidity," he said a little later, returning with a dipper. "My Lyubov Osipovna kneels and prays to God. She prays every night, you know, and bows to the ground, first of all, that the children be sent to study. She's afraid they'll go into the army as simple Cossacks and be whacked across the back with swords. But it takes money for them to study, and where to get it? She can beat her head on the floor, but if there isn't any, there just isn't. Second, she prays because, you know, every woman thinks there's nobody in the world unhappier than she is. I'm a plainspoken man and have no wish to conceal anything from you. She comes from a poor family, a priest's daughter, the bell-ringing class, so to speak. I married her when she was seventeen, and they gave her to me more on account of having nothing to eat, want, dire poverty, and after all, as you see, I have some land, a farm, well, anyhow, I'm an officer after all; it was flattering for her to marry me, you know. On the first day of our marriage she wept, and after that for all of twenty years she's been weeping—there was always a tear in her eye. And she goes on sitting and thinking, thinking. And what's she thinking about, you may ask? What can a woman think about? Nothing. I confess, I don't consider women human beings."

The attorney got up abruptly and sat on the bed.

"Sorry, I feel somehow stifled," he said. "I'll step outside."

Zhmukhin, still talking about women, unbolted the door in the front hall, and they both went out. Just then a full moon was floating in the sky over the yard, and in the moonlight the yard and the sheds looked whiter than during the day; and on the grass between the black shadows stretched bright strips of light, also white. To the right the steppe is visible far away, with stars quietly shining over it—and it is all mysterious, infinitely far away, as if you are looking into a deep abyss; and to the left over the steppe heavy thunderclouds are piled on each other, black as soot; their edges are lit by the moon, and it looks as if there are mountains there with white snow on their peaks, dark forests, the sea; lightning flashes, thunder rumbles softly, and it looks as if there is a battle going on in the mountains . . .

Just by the farmstead a small night owl cries monotonously: "Sleep! Sleep!"

"What time is it now?" the guest asked.

"A little past one."

"Dawn is still a long way off!"

They went back to the house and lay down again. It was time to sleep, and one usually sleeps so well before rain, but the old man wanted to have important, serious thoughts; he wanted not simply to think, but to reflect. And he reflected that it would be good, seeing the imminence of death, for the sake of his soul, to put an end to the idleness that so imperceptibly swallows day after day, year after year, without leaving a trace; to think up some great deed for himself, for instance, to go somewhere on foot far, far away, to give up meat, like this young man. And again he pictured to himself a time when people would not kill animals, pictured it clearly, distinctly, as if he were living in that time; but suddenly everything became confused in his head again and it all became unclear.

The thunderstorm passed by, but the edge of the cloud caught them, rain fell and pattered softly on the roof. Zhmukhin got up and, stretching and groaning from old age, looked into the reception room. Noticing that the guest was not asleep, he said:

"One of our colonels in the Caucasus, you know, was also a vegetarian. He didn't eat meat, never went hunting, didn't allow his men to fish. Of course, I understand. Every animal should live in freedom and enjoy life; only I don't understand how a pig can go wherever it likes, untended . . ."

The guest got up and sat on the bed. His pale, crumpled face expressed vexation and fatigue; he was obviously exhausted, and only his meekness and inner delicacy kept him from voicing his vexation.

"Dawn already," he said meekly. "Please order them to give me a horse."

"What for? Wait a bit, the rain will pass."

"No, I beg you," the guest said pleadingly, in fright. "I need it right now."

And he hastily began to dress.

When the horse was brought, the sun was already rising. The rain stopped, the clouds raced quickly, there were more and more blue spaces in the sky. In the puddles below, the first rays gleamed timidly. The attorney passed through the front hall with his briefcase to get into the tarantass, and at that moment Zhmukhin's wife, pale, and seeming paler than the day before, tearful, looked at him attentively, without blinking, with a naïve expression, like a little girl's. It was obvious from her sorrowful face that she envied his freedom—ah, how delighted she would be to leave here herself!—and that she needed to say something to him, probably to ask for advice about the children. And how pitiful she was! Not a wife, not the mistress of the household, not even a servant, but rather a sponger, a poor relation needed by no one, a nonentity . . . Her husband, bustling about, never stopped talking and kept running ahead, seeing the guest off, and she pressed up against the wall fearfully and guiltily and kept waiting for the right moment to speak.

"You're welcome to come again!" the old man kept saying all the time. "Whatever we have is yours for the asking, you know."

The guest hurriedly got into the tarantass, evidently with great pleasure and as if fearful that he might be detained at any moment. As on the previous day, the tarantass bounced, squeaked, the bucket tied behind rattled furiously. The attorney glanced back at Zhmukhin with a peculiar expression; it looked as if he, like the surveyor once, would have liked to call him a Pecheneg, or something similar, but his meekness won out, he restrained himself and said nothing. But in the gateway, he suddenly could not help himself, rose up, and shouted loudly and angrily:

"I'm sick of you!"

And disappeared through the gate.

By the shed stood Zhmukhin's sons: the older one was holding a rifle, in the younger one's hands was a gray rooster with a beautiful bright comb. The younger one threw the rooster into the air with all his might; the rooster flew up higher than the house and turned over in the air like a pigeon; the older one fired, and the rooster dropped like a stone.

The old man, embarrassed, not knowing how to explain this strange, unexpected outcry of his guest, unhurriedly went into the house. And, sitting there at the table, he reflected for a long time on the present-day turn of mind, on universal immorality, on the telegraph, the telephone, bicycles, and on how it was all not needed, and he gradually calmed down, then unhurriedly had a bite to eat, drank five glasses of tea, and lay down to sleep.

1897

In the Cart

T HEY DROVE OUT OF TOWN at half past eight in the morning.
The road was dry, the wonderful April sun was very warm,
but there was still snow in the ditches and the woods. The
fierce, dark, long winter was still so near, spring had come suddenly,
but for Marya Vassilyevna, who was now sitting in the wagon, there
was nothing new or interesting either in the warmth or in the languid,
transparent woods, thawed by the breath of spring, or in the black
flocks flying in the field over huge puddles that resembled lakes, or
in that sky, wondrous, bottomless, into which it seemed you could
go so joyfully. It was already thirteen years that she had been working as a teacher, and there was no counting how many times in all
those years she had ridden to town for her salary; and whether it was
spring, as now, or a rainy autumn evening, or winter—for her it was
all the same, and she always invariably wanted one thing: to get there
quickly.

It felt to her as if she had been living in those parts for a long, long
time, a hundred years, and it seemed to her that she knew every stone,
every tree on the way from town to her school. Here was her past, her
present, and she was unable to imagine any other future apart from
the school, the road to town and back, and again the school, and again
the road . . .

She had already lost the habit of recalling how things had been in
the past, before she became a teacher—and had forgotten almost all

of it. Once upon a time she had a father and a mother; they lived in a big apartment in Moscow, near the Red Gate, but of all that time there remained in her memory something vague and elusive, like a dream. Her father died when she was ten years old, her mother died soon after . . . There was an officer brother, with whom she exchanged letters at first, but then her brother stopped answering her letters, he lost the habit. Of former things there remained only a photograph of her mother, but it had faded from the dampness of her room at the schoolhouse, and now nothing could be seen but hair and eyebrows.

When they had gone some two miles, old Semyon, who drove the horse, turned around and said:

"They arrested an official in town. Packed him off. Rumor has it that he and some Germans killed the mayor Alexeev in Moscow."

"Who told you that?"

"They read it in a newspaper in Ivan Ionov's tavern."

And again they fell silent for a long time. Marya Vassilyevna was thinking about her school, about how there would soon be an examination and she would present four boys and one girl. And just as she was thinking about the examination, the landowner Khanov overtook her in a coach and four, the same man who had conducted examinations at her school the previous year. Drawing even with her, he recognized her and bowed.

"Greetings!" he said. "Might you be going home?"

This Khanov, a man of about forty, with a worn face and listless expression, was already beginning to age noticeably, but was still handsome and pleasing to women. He lived alone on his big estate, did not work anywhere, and it was said of him that at home he did nothing, but only paced up and down whistling, or played chess with his old valet. It was also said that he drank a lot. In fact, at the last year's examination, even the papers he brought with him smelled of scent and drink. He was wearing all new clothes then, and Marya Vassilyevna liked him very much, and, sitting beside him, she felt quite embarrassed. She was used to having examiners who were cold, sober-minded, but this one did not remember a single prayer, did not know what questions to ask, was polite and tactful, and gave only the highest marks.

"I'm on my way to see Bakvist," he went on, addressing Marya Vassilyevna, "but they say he's not home."

From the highway they turned off onto a dirt road: Khanov went ahead, Semyon followed him. The team of four drove along the road, slowly, straining to pull the heavy coach through the mud. Semyon, avoiding the road, maneuvered now over a hummock, now across a meadow, often jumping off the cart and helping the horse. Marya Vassilyevna kept thinking about school, about whether the math problem at the examination would be difficult or simple. She was also upset with the zemstvo office,[1] where she had not found anyone yesterday. What disorder! It was already two years that she had been asking them to fire the caretaker, who did nothing, was rude to her, and beat the pupils, but no one listened to her. The chairman was hard to catch in his office, and if you did, he said with tears in his eyes that he had no time; the inspector visited the school once in three years and had no idea what he was doing, because he had formerly worked in an excise office and got the job of inspector through connections; the school board met very rarely and no one ever knew where it would meet; the custodian was a barely literate peasant, the owner of a tannery, unintelligent, rude, and great friends with the caretaker—so God only knew who she could turn to with complaints or for information . . .

"He really is handsome," she thought, glancing at Khanov.

But the road was getting worse and worse . . . They rode into the forest. Here there was no way to turn off. The ruts were deep, and water flowed and gurgled in them. And prickly branches kept hitting her in the face.

"Some road, eh?" Khanov asked and laughed.

The teacher looked at him and could not understand: Why does this odd fellow live here? What good can his money, his imposing appearance, his refined politeness do him in this backwoods, with its mud and boredom? He gets no advantages from life, and, just like Semyon, drives slowly over the execrable road, and suffers the same inconveniences. Why live here, if it's possible to live in Petersburg or abroad? And it would seem worth his while, rich man as he is, to make a good road out of this bad one, so as not to suffer and not to see the despair written on the faces of his coachman and Semyon;

but he just laughs, and it seems to make no difference to him, and he needs no better life. He's kind, gentle, naïve, he doesn't understand this coarse life, he doesn't know it, just as he didn't know the prayers at the examination. He only donates globes to the school, and sincerely considers himself a useful person and a prominent activist in the people's education. And who here needs his globes!

"Hold tight, Vassilyevna!" said Semyon.

The cart tilted sharply and nearly overturned; something heavy landed on Marya Vassilyevna's feet—it was her purchases. They climbed steeply uphill, on clay; there noisy streams flowed through meandering ditches, the water seemed to gnaw away at the road—how could you even drive there! The horses snorted. Khanov got out of the carriage and walked along the edge of the road in his long coat. He felt hot.

"Some road, eh?" he said again and laughed. "Bad enough to break the carriage."

"Who told you to drive in such weather!" Semyon said sternly. "Better to stay home."

"Home is boring, grandpa. I don't like staying home."

Next to old Semyon he looked trim, vigorous, but in his gait there was something barely noticeable that betrayed him as being already poisoned, weak, close to ruin. And it was as if the forest suddenly smelled of drink. Marya Vassilyevna became frightened and felt sorry for this man, who was perishing no one knew why, and it occurred to her that if she were his wife or sister, she might give her whole life to save him from ruin. To be a wife? Life was so arranged that he lived alone in a big manor house, she lived alone in a remote village, but for some reason even the notion that he and she could be close and equal seemed impossible, absurd. In fact, all of life was so arranged, and human relations had become complicated to such an incomprehensible degree, that once you thought about it, you felt eerie and your heart sank.

"And it's incomprehensible," she thought, "why God gives this beauty, this affability, these sad, sweet eyes to weak, unhappy, useless people, and why they're so attractive."

"We turn right here," Khanov said, getting into his carriage. "Goodbye! All the best!"

And again she began to think about her pupils, about the examination, the caretaker, the school board; and when the wind from the right brought the sound of the carriage driving away, these thoughts mixed with the others. She wanted to think about beautiful eyes, about love, about the happiness that was never to be . . .

To be a wife? In the morning it is cold, there is no one to light the stove, the caretaker has gone off somewhere; the pupils come at the crack of dawn, bring in snow and mud, make noise; everything is so uncomfortable, uninviting. Her apartment is one room, plus a little kitchen. Every day after classes she has a headache, and after dinner she has heartburn. She has to collect money from the pupils for firewood, for the caretaker, and give it to the custodian, and then beg that well-fed, insolent peasant for God's sake to send the firewood. And at night she dreams about examinations, peasants, snowdrifts. And she has grown old and coarse from such a life, become unattractive, angular, awkward, as if she were filled with lead; and she is afraid of everything; and she stands up and does not dare to sit down in the presence of a member of the board or the custodian; and when she speaks about any of them, it is in deferential terms. And no one likes her, and her life goes by dully, with no gentleness, no friendly concern, no interesting acquaintances. In her situation, how terrible it would be if she fell in love!

"Hold tight, Vassilyevna!"

Again they climbed steeply uphill . . .

She had become a teacher out of necessity, without any sense of vocation; and she never thought about the vocation, about the usefulness of education, and it always seemed to her that the main thing in what she was doing was not the pupils and not the education, but the examinations. And when was she to think about the vocation, about the usefulness of education? Teachers, poor doctors, medical aides, with their enormous workload, do not even have the comfort of thinking they are serving an idea, or the people, because their heads are always crammed with thoughts about a crust of bread, firewood, bad roads, illnesses. It is a hard, uninteresting life, and only silent dray horses like this Marya Vassilyevna could bear it for long; the lively, high-strung, impressionable ones, who talked about their vocation, about serving an idea, soon became tired and dropped out.

Semyon kept choosing the drier and shorter way to go, across meadows, over back roads; but here the peasants would not let them pass, there it was a priest's land and couldn't be crossed, elsewhere Ivan Ionov had bought a plot from his master and surrounded it with a ditch. They kept having to turn back.

They arrived at Nizhny Gorodishche. Carts stood by a tavern, where the lingering snow was covered with dung: they carried big glass jugs full of oil of vitriol. There were many men in the tavern, all coachmen, and there was a smell of vodka, tobacco, and sheepskin. There was loud talk, the slamming of the door on its pulley. In a shop on the other side of the wall, someone was playing a concertina without stopping for a moment. Marya Vassilyevna sat and drank tea, but the peasants at the next table, steamed up by tea and the stifling tavern air, were drinking vodka and beer.

"Listen here, Kuzma!" disorderly voices rang out. "Never mind! God bless! I could do it for you, Ivan Dementyich! Watch it, lad!"

A short peasant with a black beard, pockmarked, long since drunk, suddenly got surprised at something and poured out some foul abuse.

"Why do you go badmouthing! You!" Semyon, who was sitting to one side, responded angrily. "Look, there's a young lady here!"

"A young lady . . . ," someone said mockingly in another corner.

"A swiny crow!"

"Never mind us . . ." The little peasant became embarrassed. "Beg your pardon. We're spending our money, the young lady's spending hers . . . Hello there!"

"Hello," replied the schoolteacher.

"And our heartfelt thanks!"

Marya Vassilyevna was enjoying her tea, and was becoming as red as the peasants herself, and again she thought about the firewood, the caretaker . . .

"Hold on, lad!" reached her from the next table. "She's the teacher from Vyazovye . . . we know her! A nice young lady."

"A decent one!"

The door on the pulley kept slamming, people came in, others went out. Marya Vassilyevna sat and went on thinking about the same things, and the concertina behind the wall went on playing and playing. There were patches of sunlight on the floor, then they moved to the counter, to the wall, and disappeared completely; that meant the sun had gone past noon. The peasants at the next table were preparing to leave. The little peasant, staggering slightly, went up to Marya Vassilyevna and gave her his hand; looking at him, the others all gave her their hands as they left and went out one after the other, and the door on the pulley squealed and slammed nine times.

"Vassilyevna, get ready!" called Semyon.

They set off. And again slowly all the time.

"A while ago they were building a school here, in their Nizhny Gorodishche," said Semyon, turning around. "There was no end of wrongdoing!"

"How so?"

"Seems the chairman put a thousand in his pocket, and the custodian another thousand, and the teacher five hundred."

"The whole school costs a thousand. It's not nice to slander people, grandpa. It's all nonsense."

"I don't know . . . I say what folk say."

But it was clear that Semyon did not believe the teacher. The peasants did not believe her; they had always thought that she received too big a salary—twenty-one roubles a month (five would have been enough)—and that, of the money she collected from the pupils for firewood and the caretaker, she kept the greater part for herself. The custodian thought the same as all the peasants, and he himself made something from the firewood and also got a salary from the peasants for his duties, in secret from the authorities.

The forest ended, thank God, and now there would be level fields all the way to Vyazovye. And there was already not far to go: cross the river, then the railroad tracks, and there was Vyazovye.

"Where are you going?" Marya Vassilyevna asked Semyon. "Take the road to the right over the bridge."

"Wha? We'll cross over this way. It ain't all that deep."

"See you don't drown the horse on us."

"Wha?"

"There's Khanov crossing the bridge," Marya Vassilyevna said, seeing a coach and four to the right. "That's him, isn't it?"

"Y-yes. Must not have found Bakvist. What a dumbbell, Lord help him, going that way, and why, this way's a good two miles shorter."

They drove to the river. In summer it was a shallow little stream that could easily be forded and by August had usually dried up, but now, after the spring floods, it was a river some forty feet wide, swift, muddy, cold; on the bank and right down to the water, fresh tracks could be seen—meaning someone had crossed there.

"Giddap!" Semyon shouted angrily and anxiously, snapping hard on the reins and raising his elbows like a bird its wings. "Giddap!"

The horse went into the water up to its belly and stopped, but went on again at once, straining its forces, and Marya Vassilyevna felt a sharp cold on her legs.

"Giddap!" she also shouted, standing up. "Giddap!"

They drove out onto the bank.

"And what is it, this thing, Lord," Semyon muttered, adjusting the harness. "Sheer punishment, this zemstvo . . ."

Her galoshes and shoes were full of water, the hem of her dress and coat, and one sleeve as well, were wet and dripping; the sugar and flour turned out to be damp—that was the most annoying thing of all, and in her despair Marya Vassilyevna only clasped her hands and said:

"Oh, Semyon, Semyon! . . . You're really something! . . ."

The barrier at the railway crossing was lowered: an express train was coming from the station. Marya Vassilyevna stood at the crossing waiting for it to pass and trembling all over from the cold. Vyazovye could already be seen—the school with its green roof and the church with its crosses ablaze, reflecting the evening sun; and the windows of the station were also ablaze, and the locomotive gave off pinkish smoke . . . And it seemed to her that everything was trembling from the cold.

Here it is—the train; its windows, shot with bright light like the crosses on the church, were painful to look at. On the rear platform of one of the first-class carriages a lady was standing, and Marya Vassilyevna caught a passing glimpse of her: Mother! What a resemblance! Her mother had the same fluffy hair, exactly the same forehead and tilt of the head. And for the first time in those thirteen years she pictured to herself, vividly, with striking clarity, her mother, father, brother, the apartment in Moscow, the aquarium with its fish, and all to the last detail; she suddenly heard the piano playing, her father's voice, she felt herself as she was then, young, beautiful, dressed up, in a bright, warm room, amidst her family; a feeling of joy and happiness suddenly came over her; in ecstasy she pressed her palms to her temples and called out tenderly, imploringly:

"Mama!"

And she began to weep, not knowing why. Just then Khanov drove up in his coach and four, and, seeing him, she imagined such happiness as had never been, and she smiled and nodded to him as an equal and intimate, and it seemed to her that the sky, and all the windows, and the trees shone with her happiness, her triumph. Yes, her father and mother had never died, she had never been a teacher, it had all been a long, strange, oppressive dream, and now she was awake.

"Vassilyevna, get in!"

And suddenly it all vanished. The barrier was slowly rising. Marya Vassilyevna, trembling, freezing cold, got into the cart. The coach and four crossed the rails, Semyon followed them. The watchman at the crossing took off his hat.

"And here's Vyazovye. We've arrived."

1897

About Love[1]

For lunch the next day we were served very tasty little patties, crayfish, and lamb cutlets; and while we were eating, the cook Nikanor came upstairs to ask what the guests would like for dinner. He was a man of medium height, with a puffy face and small eyes, clean-shaven, and it seemed that his moustache was not shaved, but plucked.

Alekhin told us that the beautiful Pelageya was in love with this cook. Since he was a drunkard and had a violent temper, she did not want to marry him, but agreed to live just so. He was very pious, and his religious convictions did not allow him to live just so; he demanded that she marry him, and would not have it otherwise, and he yelled at her when he was drunk and even beat her. When he was drunk, she hid upstairs and wept, and then Alekhin and the servants did not leave the house, so as to defend her if need be.

The talk turned to love.

"How love is born," said Alekhin, "why Pelageya did not fall in love with someone else, who suited her better in her inner and outer qualities, but fell in love precisely with Nikanor, this ugly mug—here everybody calls him 'ugly mug'—insofar as questions of personal happiness are important in love—all this is unknown and can be interpreted any way you like. Up to now only one unquestionable truth has been uttered about love, that 'this is a great mystery,'[2] and all the rest that has been written and said about love is not an answer, but a posing of questions that still remain unanswered. An explanation that seems suited to one case is not suited to a dozen others, and the best thing, in my opinion, is to explain each case separately, without trying to generalize. We ought, as doctors say, to individualize each separate case."

"Absolutely right," Burkin agreed.

"We decent Russian people entertain a partiality for these questions that remain without answers. Love is usually poeticized, adorned with roses, with nightingales, but we Russians adorn our loves with these fatal questions, and on top of that choose the most uninteresting of them. In Moscow, when I was still a student, I had a life companion, a nice lady, who, each time I held her in my arms, thought about how much money I'd allow her a month and what was the price of beef per pound. So we, when we love, never stop asking ourselves questions: Is this honorable or dishonorable, intelligent or stupid, what will this love lead to, and so on. Whether it's a good thing or not, I don't know, but that it's disrupting, unsatisfying, annoying—that I do know."

It looked as though he wanted to tell some story. People who live alone always have something in their hearts that they are eager to tell about. In town, bachelors purposely go to the public baths and to restaurants just in order to talk, and they sometimes tell very interesting stories to the bath attendants and waiters, while in the country they usually pour out their souls to their guests. Now in the window gray sky could be seen and trees wet with rain, and in such weather there was nothing left for us to do but tell and listen.

"I've been living in Sofyino and farming for a long time now," Alekhin began, "ever since I finished university. By upbringing I'm an idler, by inclination an armchair philosopher, but when I came here, there was a big debt on the estate, and since my father had acquired that debt partly because he spent a lot on my education, I decided I wouldn't leave and would work until I'd paid off the debt. I made that decision, and started working here not without a certain aversion, I must confess. The local soil yields little, and for the farming not to suffer losses, you have to employ the labor of serfs or hired hands, which is almost the same, or else do your farming as peasants do, that is, work the fields yourself, with your family. There's no middle ground here. But I didn't enter into such subtleties at the time. I didn't leave a single scrap of land in peace, I rounded up all the peasants and their women from the neighboring villages, and the work here boiled furiously. I myself also plowed, sowed, mowed, and despite all that was bored and winced squeamishly, like a village cat that's so hungry it eats cucumbers in the kitchen garden. My body was in pain, and I slept as I walked. At first it seemed to me that I could easily reconcile this working life with my cultural habits; for that, I thought, I had only to observe a certain external order in my life. I settled upstairs, in the main rooms, and ordered coffee and liqueurs to be served after lunch and dinner, and at night, lying in bed, I read *The Messenger of Europe*.[3] But our priest came once, Father Ivan, and at one go drank all my liqueurs; and *The Messenger of Europe* also went to the priest's daughters, because in summer, especially during the mowing, I never managed to make it to my bed, and fell asleep in a shed, or the sledge, or in a forester's hut somewhere—who can read there? I gradually moved downstairs, began to have dinner in the servants' kitchen, and all that remained of the former luxury was this maid, who had served my father and whom it would have been painful for me to dismiss.

"In those first years here I was elected an honorary justice of the peace. Every now and then I had to go to town and take part in the meetings of the assembly and the circuit court, and that distracted me. When you live here without a break for two or three months, especially in winter, you finally begin to pine for a black frock coat. And in the circuit court there were frock coats, and uniforms, and tailcoats, all lawyers, people who had received a general education; you could talk with them. After sleeping in the sledge, after the servants' kitchen, to sit in an armchair, in a clean shirt, in light shoes, with a chain on your chest—it was such luxury!

"In town they received me cordially, I eagerly made acquaintances. And of these acquaintances the most solid and, to tell the truth, the most agreeable for me was the acquaintance with Luganovich, the associate chairman of the circuit court. You both know him: the dearest person. It was just after the famous case of the arsonists; the trial had gone on for two days, we were exhausted. Luganovich looked at me and said:

" 'You know what? Come to my place for dinner.'

"That was unexpected, because I barely knew Luganovich, only officially, and had never once visited him. I stopped at my hotel room for a moment to change clothes, and went to dinner. And here the chance was presented to me of meeting Anna Alexeevna, Luganovich's wife. She was very young then, no more than twenty-two, and six months earlier her first child had been born to her. It's a thing of the past, and now I would have a hard time explaining what, in fact, was so extraordinary in her, what it was in her that I liked so much, but then, at dinner, it was all irrefutably clear to me. I saw a young woman, beautiful, kind, intelligent, charming, such as I had never met before. I immediately felt in her a close, already familiar being, as if I had already seen that face, those friendly, intelligent eyes sometime in my childhood, in the album of photographs that lay on my mother's chest of drawers.

"In the case of the arsonists, the accused were four Jews, declared to be a gang, in my opinion quite groundlessly. At dinner I was very agitated, it was painful, and I no longer remember what I said, but Anna Alexeevna kept shaking her head and saying to her husband:

" 'Dmitri, how can it be?'

"Luganovich was a kindly man, one of those simplehearted people who firmly hold the opinion that, once a person winds up in court, it means he's guilty, and that expressing doubts about the correctness of a sentence cannot be done otherwise than in the legal way, on paper, and never at dinner or in private conversation.

" 'You and I haven't committed arson,' he said gently, 'so we're not on trial, we're not being sent to prison.'

"And both of them, husband and wife, tried to make me eat and drink more. From certain small details, for instance, from the way the two of them made coffee together, and the way they understood each other at half a word, I was able to conclude that they lived peacefully, happily, and were glad of their guest. After dinner they played piano four hands, then it grew dark and I went home. It was the beginning of spring. After that I spent the whole summer without leaving Sofyino, and had no time even to think about town, but the memory of the slender blond woman stayed with me all those days. I didn't think about her, but it was as if her light shadow lay on my soul.

"In late autumn there was a charity performance in town. I went into the governor's box (where I had been invited during the intermission), I look—there next to the governor's wife is Anna Alexeevna, and again the same irresistible, striking impression of beauty and sweet, tender eyes, and the same feeling of closeness.

"We sat next to each other, then walked in the foyer.

" 'You've grown thinner,' she said. 'Have you been ill?'

" 'Yes. I caught a chill in my shoulder, and I sleep poorly in rainy weather.'

" 'You have a listless look. In the spring, when you came to dinner, you were younger, livelier. You were animated then and talked a lot, you were very interesting, and, I confess, I was even a bit taken with you. For some reason you've often come back to my memory over the summer, and today, as I was getting ready for the theater, I had a feeling I would see you.'

"And she laughed.

" 'But today you have a listless look,' she repeated. 'That ages you.'

"The next day I had lunch at the Luganoviches'; after lunch they went to their dacha to make arrangements for the winter, and I went with them. I also came back to town with them, and at midnight had tea with them in a quiet, family atmosphere, with the fireplace burning and the young mother frequently going to see if her little girl was asleep. And after that, each time I came to town, I never failed to visit the Luganoviches. They got used to me, and I got used to them. I usually came in without being announced, like one of the family.

" 'Who's there?' the drawn-out voice I found so beautiful would reach me from the inner rooms.

" 'It's Pavel Konstantinych,' the maid or nanny would reply.

"Anna Alexeevna would come out to me with a preoccupied look and ask each time:

" 'Why haven't you come for so long? Has anything happened?'

"Her gaze, the graceful, refined hand she held out to me, her everyday dress, hairdo, voice, steps, made the impression on me each time of something new, unusual in my life, and important. We would talk for a long time, and be silent for a long time, each thinking our own thoughts, or else she would play the piano for me. If there was no one home, I stayed and waited, talked with the nanny, played with the child, or lay down on the Turkish divan in the study and read the newspaper, and when Anna Alexeevna came back, I met her in the front hall, took all her purchases from her, and, for some reason, I carried those purchases each time with such love, such triumph, like a little boy.

"There's a proverb: a peasant woman had no troubles, so she bought a pig. The Luganoviches had no troubles, so they befriended me. If I did not come to town for a long time, it meant I was sick or something had happened to me, and they both worried greatly. They worried that I, an educated man, with a knowledge of languages, instead of occupying myself with studies or literary work, lived in a village, ran around like a squirrel on a wheel, worked so much, and was always left without a kopeck. It seemed to them that I suffered, and if I talked, laughed, ate, it was only so as to hide my suffering, and even in cheerful moments, when all was well with me, I sensed their searching eyes on me. They were especially touching when things actually became hard for me, when I was pursued by some creditor, or had no money for an urgent payment; the two of them, husband and wife, would whisper by the window, then he would come to me and say with an earnest look:

"'If you're in need of money right now, Pavel Konstantinovich, my wife and I beg you not to be embarrassed and to take it from us.'

"And his ears would turn red from nervousness. It also happened that, having whispered by the window in the same way, he would come to me with red ears and say:

"'My wife and I insist that you accept this gift from us.'

"And he would give me cuff links, a cigarette case, or a lamp, and in exchange I would send them game, butter, and flowers from the village. Incidentally, they were both well-to-do people. In the beginning I often borrowed money and was none too discriminating, I took wherever I could, but no power could force me to borrow from the Luganoviches. Though why talk about that!

"I was unhappy. At home, and in the fields, and in the shed I thought about her, I tried to understand the mystery of a young, beautiful, intelligent woman who has married an uninteresting man, almost old (the husband was over forty), has children by him—to understand the mystery of this uninteresting man, a kindly, simple soul, who reasoned with such boring sobriety, who kept company at balls with staid people, listless, useless, with a submissive, apathetic expression, as if he had been brought there to be sold, who believed, however, in his right to be happy, to have children with her; and I kept trying to understand why she had met precisely him, and not me, and what made it necessary for such a terrible mistake to happen in our life.

"And coming to town, I saw each time by her eyes that she was expecting me; and she herself would confess to me that she had had some special feeling since morning, that she had guessed I was coming. We had long talks, then fell silent, but we did not declare our love to each other, we concealed it timidly, jealously. We were afraid of everything that might reveal our secret to our own selves. I loved her tenderly, deeply, but I reasoned, I asked myself what our love could lead to, if we had no strength to fight it; it seemed incredible to me that this quiet, sad love of mine should suddenly, crudely interrupt the happy course of the life of her husband, her children, this whole household, where I was so loved and where I was so trusted. Was that honorable? She would have followed me, but where? Where could I take her? It would have been a different thing if I had a beautiful, interesting life, if, for instance, I were fighting for the freedom of my motherland, or was a famous scholar, artist, painter, but as it was I would be taking her from one ordinary, humdrum situation to another just like it, or even more humdrum. And how long would our happiness last? What would become of her in case of my illness, death, or if we simply fell out of love with each other?

"And she apparently reasoned in the same way. She was thinking about her husband, her children, her mother, who loved her husband like her own son. If she were to surrender to her feeling, she would have to lie, or to tell the truth, and in her situation either one would be equally terrible and awkward. And the question tormented her: would her love bring me happiness, would she not complicate my life, difficult and filled with all sorts of misfortunes as it was? It seemed to her that she was no longer young enough for me, not industrious and energetic enough to start a new life, and she often talked with her husband about my needing to marry an intelligent, worthy girl, who would be a good housewife, a helpmate—and immediately added that there was scarcely such a girl to be found in the whole town.

"Meanwhile the years passed. Anna Alexeevna now had two children. When I visited the Luganoviches, the servants smiled affably, the children shouted that Uncle Pavel Konstantinych had come and hung on my neck; everyone was glad. They didn't understand what was going on in my soul, and thought that I was glad, too. They all saw me as a noble being. Both the adults and the children thought that a noble being was walking through the rooms, and that lent a special charm to their attitude towards me, as if in my presence their life became more pure and beautiful. Anna Alexeevna and I went to the theater together, always on foot; we sat next to each other in the stalls, our shoulders touched, I silently took the opera glasses from her hands and at the same time felt that she was close to me, that she was mine, that we could not be without each other, yet, by some strange misunderstanding, on leaving the theater, we said goodbye each time and parted like strangers. God knows what they were already saying about us in town, but there wasn't a word of truth in anything they said.

"In later years Anna Alexeevna started going more often to visit her mother or her sister; she was already having bad moods, resulting from the awareness of an unfulfilled, ruined life, when she didn't want to see either her husband or her children. She was already being treated for a nervous disorder.

"We said nothing, and went on saying nothing, but in front of other people she felt some strange vexation with me; she disagreed with whatever I said, and if I got into an argument, she would take my opponent's side. When I dropped something, she would say coldly:

" 'My congratulations.'

"If I forgot the opera glasses when we went to the theater, she would say afterwards:

" 'I just knew you'd forget them.'

"Fortunately or unfortunately, there's nothing in our life that doesn't end sooner or later. The time came for parting, because Luganovich had been appointed chairman in one of the western provinces. They had to sell the furniture, the horses, the dacha. When we went to the dacha and then, on the way back, turned to look for a last time at the garden, at the green roof, we all felt sad, and I understood that the time had come to say goodbye not only to the dacha. It was decided that at the end of August we would see Anna Alexeevna off to the Crimea, where the doctors were sending her, and a little later Luganovich would leave with the children for his western province.

"A big crowd of us saw Anna Alexeevna off. When she had already said goodbye to her husband and the children, and there was just a moment left before the third bell, I ran into her compartment to put on the rack one of her baskets, which she had almost forgotten; and I had to say goodbye. When our eyes met there in the compartment, our inner forces abandoned us both, I embraced her, she pressed her face to my breast, and tears poured from her eyes. Kissing her face, shoulders, hands, wet with tears—oh, how unhappy we both were!—I confessed my love to her, and with burning pain in my heart I realized how unnecessary, petty, and deceptive was everything that had hindered our love. I realized that, when you love, your reasonings about that love must proceed from something higher, something of greater importance than happiness or unhappiness, sin or virtue in their ordinary sense, or else you shouldn't reason at all.

"I kissed her for the last time, pressed her hand, and we parted—forever. The train was already moving. I went to the next compartment—it was empty—sat there until the first stop, and wept. Then I went on foot to my Sofyino . . ."

While Alekhin was telling his story, it stopped raining and the sun came out. Burkin and Ivan Ivanych went to the balcony; there was a beautiful view from there to the garden and the millpond, which now glistened in the sun like a mirror. They admired it, and at the same time they were sorry that this man with kind, intelligent eyes, who had told them his story with such sincerity, in fact ran around here, on this huge estate, like a squirrel on a wheel, instead of occupying himself with studies or something else that would make his life more agreeable; and they thought of how grief-stricken the young lady's face must have been, when he was saying goodbye to her and kissing her face and shoulders. They had both met her in town, and Burkin was even acquainted with her and found her beautiful.

1898

IONYCH

I

When newcomers to the provincial capital S. complained about the boredom and monotony of life, the local people, as if to justify themselves, said that, on the contrary, life in S. was very good, that there was a library, a theater, a club; there were balls; that, finally, there were intelligent, interesting, agreeable families, with whom one could strike up an acquaintance. And they would point to the Turkin family as the most cultivated and talented.

This family lived on the main street, next door to the governor, in their own house. Ivan Petrovich Turkin himself, a stout, handsome, dark-haired man with side-whiskers, organized amateur theatricals for charitable purposes, and himself played old generals and coughed very amusingly. He knew many anecdotes, charades, sayings, liked to joke and be witty, and always had such an expression that it was impossible to tell whether he was joking or being serious. His wife, Vera Iosifovna, a thin, nice-looking lady in a pince-nez, wrote long stories and novels, and willingly read them aloud to her guests. Their daughter, Ekaterina Ivanovna, a young girl, played the piano. In short, each member of the family had a certain talent. The Turkins received guests cordially and displayed their talents for them cheerfully, with heartfelt simplicity. Their big stone house was spacious and cool in the summer; half the windows looked out on the old, shady garden, where nightingales sang in springtime; when there were guests in the house, there was a chopping of knives in the kitchen, the smell of fried onions in the yard—and each time this presaged an abundant and delicious supper.

And Doctor Dmitri Ionych Startsev, when he had just been appointed zemstvo doctor[1] and settled in Dyalizh, six miles from S., was also told that, as a cultivated man, he must make the acquaintance of the Turkins. One winter day, in the street, he was introduced to Ivan Petrovich; they chatted about the weather, the theater, cholera, and an invitation ensued. In the spring, on a holiday—it was the Ascension[2]—after receiving his patients, Startsev went to town for a little diversion and incidentally to buy something or other. He went on foot, unhurriedly (he did not yet own horses), murmuring a song:

When I'd not yet drunk tears from the cup of life . . .[3]

In town he had dinner, strolled in the garden, then Ivan Petrovich's invitation came to his mind somehow of itself, and he decided to call on the Turkins, to see what sort of people they were.

"Welcome if you please," said Ivan Petrovich, meeting him on the porch. "Very, very glad to see such an agreeable guest. Come, I'll introduce you to my better half. I've been telling him, Verochka," he went on, as he introduced the doctor to his wife, "I've been telling him that he has no right of passage to sit in his hospital, that he should devote his leisure time to society. Don't you agree, dearest?"

"Sit here," Vera Iosifovna said, seating her guest beside her. "You may pay court to me. My husband is a jealous Othello, but we'll try to behave so that he doesn't notice anything . . ."

"Ah, my ducky, my little rascal . . . ," Ivan Petrovich murmured tenderly and kissed her on the forehead. "You've come just in time." He turned back to the guest. "My better half has written a biggy novel, and tonight she'll read it aloud."

"*Jeanchik*," Vera Iosifovna said to her husband, "*dites que l'on nous donne du thé.*"[4]

Startsev was introduced to Ekaterina Ivanovna, an eighteen-year-old girl, who resembled her mother very much, was just as thin and nice-looking. Her expression was still childlike and her waist slender, delicate; and her maidenly, already developed breast, beautiful and healthy, spoke of springtime, a real springtime. Then they drank tea with preserves, with honey, with sweets, and with very tasty cookies that melted in the mouth. With the coming of evening, guests gradually gathered, and Ivan Petrovich looked at each of them with his laughing eyes and said:

"Welcome if you please."

Then they all sat in the drawing room with very serious faces, and Vera Iosifovna read her novel. She began thus: "It was freezing cold . . ." The windows were wide open, one could hear knives chopping in the kitchen, and there was a smell of frying onions . . . The soft, deep armchairs were comfortable, the lamps flickered so soothingly in the twilight of the drawing room; and now, on a summer evening, when voices and laughter drifted in from outside and a whiff of lilacs came from the yard, it was hard to understand how it could be freezing cold and how the setting sun was shining its cold rays on the snowy plain and the lone wayfarer walking down the road. Vera Iosifovna read about how a young, beautiful countess established schools, hospitals, and libraries on her estate, and how she fell in love with an itinerant artist—about something that never happens in life, and yet listening to it was pleasant, comfortable, and such nice, peaceful thoughts came into your head that you had no wish to get up . . .

"None too bad . . . ," Ivan Petrovich pronounced quietly.

And one of the guests, listening and in his thoughts carried off somewhere very far away, said barely audibly:

"Yes . . . indeed . . ."

An hour went by, then another. In the town park nearby an orchestra played and a choir sang. When Vera Iosifovna closed her notebook, they kept silent for some five minutes and listened to "Luchinushka,"[5] which the choir was singing, and this song told of something that was not in the novel and that had happened in real life.

"Do you publish your work in magazines?" Startsev asked Vera Iosifovna.

"No," she said, "I don't publish anywhere. I write and hide it in the bookcase. Why publish?" she explained. "We have means enough."

And for some reason they all sighed.

"Now you play something, Kotik," Ivan Petrovich said to his daughter.

They raised the lid of the grand piano and opened the scores that lay ready there. Ekaterina Ivanovna sat down and struck the keys with both hands; and then at once struck them again with all her might, and again, and again. Her shoulders and breast shook, she stubbornly struck in the same place, and it seemed she would not stop until she had driven the keys into the piano. The drawing room was filled with thunder; everything thundered: the floor, the ceiling, the furniture . . . Ekaterina Ivanovna played a difficult piece, interesting precisely in its difficulty, long and monotonous, and Startsev, listening to it, pictured stones pouring down a high mountain, pouring and pouring, and he would have liked them to stop pouring soon, and at the same time Ekaterina Ivanovna, rosy with effort, strong, energetic, with a lock of hair falling across her forehead, pleased him very much. After the winter spent in Dyalizh, among sick people and peasants, to sit in a drawing room, to look at this young, graceful, and probably pure being, and to listen to these noisy, tedious, but all the same cultivated sounds, was so pleasant, so new . . .

"Well, Kotik, tonight you played better than ever," Ivan Petrovich said with tears in his eyes, when his daughter finished and got up. " 'Die now, Denis, you'll never write better.' "[6]

They all surrounded her, congratulated her, marveled, assured her that it was long since they had heard such music, and she listened silently, smiling slightly, and triumph was written all over her.

"Wonderful! Superb!"

"Wonderful," Startsev said as well, succumbing to the general enthusiasm. "Where did you study music?" he asked Ekaterina Ivanovna. "At the conservatory?"

"No, I'm still just preparing for the conservatory, and meanwhile I've been studying here with Madame Zavlovsky."

"Have you finished your studies in the local high school?"

"Oh, no!" Vera Iosifovna answered for her. "We invited teachers to the house. In high school or boarding school, you'll agree, there may be bad influences; while a girl is growing up, she should remain under the influence of her mother alone."

"But all the same I'm going to the conservatory," said Ekaterina Ivanovna.

"No, Kotik loves her mama. Kotik is not going to upset her papa and mama."

"No, I'm going! I'm going!" Ekaterina Ivanovna said, jokingly and capriciously, and stamped her little foot.

At supper Ivan Petrovich displayed his talents. Laughing with his eyes only, he told anecdotes, cracked jokes, asked amusing questions and answered them himself, and all the while spoke his extraordinary language, elaborated during long exercises in witticism, and obviously long since become habitual to him: biggy, none too bad, I hummingly thank you . . .

But that was not all. When the guests, sated and content, were crowding in the front hall sorting out their coats and canes, bustling about them was the lackey Pavlusha, or Pava, as he was called there, a boy of about fourteen, short-haired, with plump cheeks.

"Go on, Pava, perform!" Ivan Petrovich said to him.

Pava assumed a pose, raised his arm, and said in a tragic tone:

"Die, wretched woman!"

And they all laughed.

"Amusing," thought Startsev, going outside.

He stopped at a restaurant and drank some beer, then went home to Dyalizh on foot. He walked and sang to himself all the way:

"Thy voice for me, affectionate and languid . . ."[7]

Having walked six miles and then gone to bed, he did not feel the least bit tired; on the contrary, it seemed to him that he would gladly have walked another fifteen.

"None too bad . . . ," he remembered, falling asleep, and he laughed.

II

Startsev kept thinking about visiting the Turkins, but there was a great deal of work in the hospital, and he could never find any free time. More than a year went by like that, in toil and solitude; but then a letter in a blue envelope was brought from town . . .

Vera Iosifovna had been suffering from migraine for a long time, but lately, when Kotik threatened every day that she was going to the conservatory, the attacks began to recur more frequently. All the doctors in town visited the Turkins, and finally the zemstvo doctor's turn came. Vera Iosifovna wrote him a touching letter, asking him to come and ease her suffering. Startsev came and after that started visiting the Turkins often, very often . . . In fact he helped Vera Iosifovna a little, and she was already telling all her guests that he was an extraordinary, amazing doctor. But he no longer went to the Turkins' on account of her migraine . . .

A holiday. Ekaterina Ivanovna finished her long, wearisome piano exercises. Then they sat in the dining room for a long time having tea, and Ivan Petrovich was telling some funny story. But the bell rang; he had to go to the front hall to meet some guest; Startsev profited from the moment of confusion and said to Ekaterina Ivanovna in a whisper, greatly agitated:

"For God's sake, I beg you, don't torment me, let's go to the garden!"

She shrugged her shoulders, as if perplexed and wondering what he wanted from her, but she got up and went.

"You spend three or four hours playing the piano," he said, walking after her, "then you sit with Mama, and there's no possibility of talking with you. Grant me at least a quarter of an hour, I beg you."

Autumn was coming, and in the old garden it was quiet, sad, and dark leaves lay along the paths. Dusk fell early.

"I haven't seen you for a whole week," Startsev went on, "and if you only knew what suffering it is! Let's sit down. Listen to me."

They both had a favorite place in the garden: a bench under an old spreading maple. And now they sat down on that bench.

"What can I do for you?" Ekaterina Ivanovna asked in a dry, business-like tone.

"I haven't seen you for a whole week, I haven't heard you for so long. I passionately want, I yearn for your voice. Speak."

He admired her freshness, the naïve expression of her eyes and cheeks. Even in the way her dress sat on her, he saw something extraordinarily sweet, touching in its simple and naïve grace. And at the same time, despite this naïveté, she seemed to him very intelligent and developed beyond her age. He could talk with her about literature, about art, about anything; he could complain to her about life, about people, though it would happen during a serious conversation that she would suddenly start laughing inappropriately or run off into the house. Like nearly all the girls in S., she read a great deal (in general people read little in S., and in the local library they said that if it were not for the girls and the young Jews, they could just as well close the library); that delighted Startsev no end, and he excitedly asked her each time what she had been reading lately and listened, enchanted, as she told him.

"What have you been reading this week, while we haven't seen each other?" he asked now. "Speak, I beg you."

"I've been reading Pisemsky."[8]

"What exactly?"

"*A Thousand Souls*," Kotik replied. "And what a funny name Pisemsky has: Alexei Feofilaktych!"

"Where are you going?" Startsev said, horrified, when she suddenly got up and walked towards the house. "I've got to talk to you, I must tell you . . . Stay with me for at least five minutes! I beseech you!"

She stopped as if she wished to say something, then awkwardly thrust a note into his hand and ran into the house, and there sat down at the piano again.

"Tonight, at eleven o'clock," Startsev read, "be in the cemetery by Demetti's memorial."

"Well, that's not smart at all," he thought, having come to his senses. "Why the cemetery? What for?"

It was clear: Kotik was fooling. Indeed, who would seriously conceive of scheduling a meeting at night, far from town, in a cemetery, when it could easily be arranged on the street, in the town park? And was it fitting for him, a zemstvo doctor, an intelligent, serious man, to sigh, to receive little notes, to drag himself to cemeteries, to do stupid things that even schoolboys would laugh at nowadays? What would this love affair come to? What would his colleagues say when they learned of it? So Startsev was thinking as he wandered among the tables in his club, and at half past ten he suddenly up and drove to the cemetery.

He already had his own pair of horses and the coachman Panteleimon in a velvet waistcoat. The moon was shining. It was quiet, warm, but warm in an autumnal way. In the outskirts, by the slaugh-terhouse, dogs were howling. Startsev left the horses at the edge of town, in one of the lanes, and went to the cemetery on foot. "People have their oddities," he thought. "Kotik is also an odd one and—who knows?—maybe she's not joking and will come," and he surrendered to this weak, futile hope, and it intoxicated him.

He walked half a mile across a field. The cemetery appeared in the distance as a dark strip, like a grove or a big garden. He saw the white stone fence, the gate . . . In the moonlight one could read on the gate: "The hour is nigh . . ." Startsev went through the gate, and first of all he saw white crosses and tombstones on both sides of a wide alley, and the dark shadows cast by them and the poplars; and the white and black stretched far around, and sleepy trees bowed their branches over the white. It seemed brighter here than in the field; the maple leaves, looking like paws, were sharply outlined on the yellow sand of the alleys and on the slabs, and the inscriptions on the tombstones were clearly visible. In the first moments, Startsev was struck by what he was now seeing for the first time in his life and would probably not chance to see again: a world unlike anything else—a world where moonlight was so lovely and gentle, as if this were its cradle, where there was no life, no, no, but in each dark poplar, in each grave, one felt the presence of a mystery, promising a quiet, beautiful, eternal life. Along with the scent of autumn leaves, the tombstones and the withered flowers breathed of forgiveness, sorrow, and peace.

All around there was silence; stars looked down from the sky in profound humility, and the sound of Startsev's footsteps was loud and out of place. And only when the clock began to strike in the church and he imagined himself dead, buried there for all eternity, did it seem to him that someone was looking at him, and for a moment he thought that this was not peace and quiet, but the blank anguish of non-being, suppressed despair . . .

The Demetti memorial was in the form of a chapel with an angel on top. Once the Italian opera was passing through S. One of the singers died, was buried, and this memorial was set up. No one in town remembered her, but the lamp over the entrance reflected the moonlight and looked like it was burning.

No one was there. Who would come there at midnight? But

Startsev waited, and, as if the moonlight were warming the passion in him, he waited passionately, his imagination picturing kisses, embraces. He sat by the memorial for about half an hour, then strolled in the side alleys, hat in hand, waiting and thinking about the many women and girls buried here in these graves, who had been beautiful, charming, who had loved, had burned with passion at night, yielding to caresses. What wicked tricks, indeed, Mother Nature plays on human beings, how vexing the awareness of it! So Startsev thought, and at the same time he felt like crying out that he wanted, that he was waiting for love at all costs; it was no longer pieces of marble that showed white before him, but beautiful bodies, he saw shapes that modestly hid in the shade of the trees, he felt warmth, and this languor was becoming oppressive . . .

And like the lowering of a curtain, the moon went behind a cloud, and suddenly everything around became dark. Startsev barely managed to find the gate—it was already as dark as on an autumn night. Then he wandered for an hour and a half, looking for the lane where he had left his horses.

"I'm tired, I can barely keep my feet," he said to Panteleimon.

And, delightedly seating himself in the carriage, he thought: "Oof, I'd better not gain weight!"

III

The next day, in the evening, he went to the Turkins' to propose. But this turned out to be awkward, because Ekaterina Ivanovna was in her room having her hair done by a hairdresser. She was getting ready for an evening dance at the club.

Again he had to sit for a long time in the dining room having tea. Ivan Petrovich, seeing that the guest was pensive and bored, took some notes from his waistcoat pocket and read an amusing letter from a German manager about how all the lockitudes on the estate were broken, and there was a crashing of the wallery.

"And they'll probably provide no small dowry," thought Startsev, listening distractedly.

After a sleepless night, he was in a stunned state, as if he had been given something sweet and somniferous; his heart was foggy, but joyful, warm, and at the same time some cold, heavy little snippet in his head was reasoning:

"Stop before it's too late! Is she any match for you? She's spoiled, capricious, she sleeps till two, and you're a churchwarden's son, a country doctor . . ."

"Well, what then?" he thought. "So be it!"

"Besides, if you marry her," the little snippet went on, "her family will make you drop your zemstvo work and live in town."

"Well, what of it?" he thought. "If it's town, it's town. They'll give a dowry, we'll buy furniture . . ."

Finally Ekaterina Ivanovna came in wearing a ball gown, décolleté, pretty, clean, and Startsev admired her so much and went into such rapture that he could not utter a single word, but only looked at her and laughed.

She started saying goodbye, and he—there was no longer any reason for him to stay—stood up, said it was time he went home: his patients were waiting.

"Nothing to be done," said Ivan Petrovich. "Go, then, and on your way take Kotik to the club."

Outside it was drizzling rain, very dark, and only by Panteleimon's rough coughing could they tell where the horses were. They put up the hood.

"I lie on the rug," said Ivan Petrovich, seating his daughter in the carriage, "he lies like a rug . . . Touch 'em up! Goodbye if you please!"

They drove off.

"I went to the cemetery last night," Startsev began. "That was so ungenerous and unmerciful on your part . . ."

"You went to the cemetery?"

"Yes, I was there and waited for you till nearly two o'clock. I suffered . . ."

"Suffer, then, if you don't understand jokes."

Ekaterina Ivanovna, pleased that she had so cleverly played a joke on the amorous man and that he was so much in love, laughed loudly and suddenly cried out in fright, because just then the horses turned sharply through the gates of the club, and the carriage tilted. Startsev put his arm around Ekaterina Ivanovna's waist, and she, frightened, pressed herself to him. He could not help himself and kissed her passionately on the lips, on the chin, and tightened his embrace.

"Enough," she said drily.

A moment later she was no longer in the carriage, and the policeman by the lit-up entrance of the club yelled at Panteleimon in a disgusting voice:

"What're you stopping for, you old crow? Keep driving!"

Startsev went home, but soon came back. At midnight, in a borrowed tailcoat and a stiff white cravat that somehow kept sticking out and trying to slip from the collar, he was sitting in the club drawing room and saying to Ekaterina Ivanova with enthusisasm:

"Oh, how little they know who have never loved! I think no one has yet described love correctly, and it's hardly possible to describe this tender, joyful, tormenting feeling, and anyone who has experienced it at least once will not try to convey it in words. What's the use of preambles and descriptions? What's the use of unnecessary eloquence? My love is boundless . . . I ask you, I beg you," Startsev finally brought out, "be my wife!"

"Dmitri Ionych," Ekaterina Ivanovna said with a very serious expression, having thought a little. "Dmitri Ionych, I am very grateful to you for the honor, I respect you, but . . ." She stood up and remained standing, "But, I'm sorry, I cannot be your wife. Let's talk seriously, Dmitri Ionych, you know I love art more than anything in the world, I madly love, I adore music, I've devoted my whole life to it. I want to be an artist, I want fame, success, freedom, and you want me to go on living in this town, to go on with this empty, useless life, which has become unbearable to me. To become a wife—oh, no, I'm sorry! A human being should strive for a lofty, brilliant goal, and family life would bind me forever. Dmitri Ionych" (she smiled slightly, because in saying "Dmitri Ionych" she remembered "Alexei Feofilaktych"), "Dmitri Ionych, you are a kind, noble, intelligent man, you are the best . . ." Tears came to her eyes. "I feel for you with all my heart, but . . . but you'll understand . . ."

And, to keep herself from bursting into tears, she turned away and left the drawing room.

Startsev's heart stopped beating anxiously. On leaving the club, he first of all took off the stiff cravat and drew a deep breath. He was slightly ashamed, and his vanity was wounded—he had not expected a refusal—and he could not believe that all his dreams, longings, and hopes had brought him to such a silly end, as in a little amateur play. And he was sorry for his feeling, for his love, so sorry that it seemed he might just burst into tears or whack Panteleimon's broad back as hard as he could with his umbrella.

For three days he was fit for nothing, did not eat, did not sleep, but when the rumor reached him that Ekaterina Ivanovna had gone to Moscow to enter the conservatory, he calmed down and began to live as before.

Afterwards, remembering occasionally how he had wandered in the cemetery, or how he had driven all over town looking for a tail-coat, he stretched lazily and said:

"So much bother, really!"

IV

Four years went by. Startsev already had a large practice in town. Every morning he hurriedly received patients at his hospital in Dya-lizh, then went to his patients in town, went now not with a pair but with a troika with little bells, and came home late at night. He gained weight, grew stout, and did not like going on foot, because he suffered from shortness of breath. Panteleimon, too, gained weight, and the wider he grew, the more pitifully he sighed and complained of his bitter lot: he was sick of driving!

Startsev visited many houses and met many people, but he did not become close with anyone. The local inhabitants' conversations, views of life, and even their looks irritated him. Experience gradually taught him that when you play cards with a local inhabitant or dine with him, he is a peaceable, good-natured, and even rather intelligent man, but the moment you start talking with him about something non-edible, for instance politics or science, he gets nonplussed or goes off into such stupid and spiteful philosophy that all you can do is wave your hand and walk away. Even when Startsev once tried talking with a liberal inhabitant and said that, thank God, mankind was progressing, and that a time would come when they could dispense with passports and capital punishment, the inhabitant looked at him askance and incredulously and asked:

"So anybody could go down the street and put a knife into whoever he wants?" And when Startsev, in company, at supper or tea, said that one must work, that it was impossible to live without working, everybody took it as a reproach and became angry and obnoxiously quarrelsome. With all that, the inhabitants did nothing, decidedly nothing, were not interested in anything, and it was simply impossible to think up something to talk about with them. So Startsev avoided conversation, and only ate and played whist, and when he happened upon a festive dinner in some house, and they invited him to take part, he sat down and ate silently, looking into his plate; and everything they talked about then was uninteresting, unjust, and stupid; he felt irritated, edgy, but he said nothing, and because he was always sternly silent and looked into his plate, he became known in town as "the pouting Pole," though he had never been a Pole.

He avoided such amusements as the theater and concerts, but he did play whist every evening for about three hours, with pleasure. He had another amusement, which he was drawn into imperceptibly, little by little: this was taking from his pocket in the evening the banknotes he had earned from his practice, and it would happen that his pockets were all stuffed with these banknotes—yellow and green, smelling of perfume, or vinegar, or incense, or whale oil—adding up to some seventy roubles; and when he collected several hundred, he took them to the Mutual Credit Society and deposited them in his account.

In all the four years since Ekaterina Ivanovna's departure, he had been to the Turkins' only twice, at the invitation of Vera Iosifovna, who was still being treated for migraine. Each summer Ekaterina Ivanovna came to visit her parents, but he had not seen her once; it somehow did not happen.

But now four years had gone by. On one quiet, warm morning a letter was brought to him in the hospital. Vera Iosifovna wrote to Dmitri Ionych that she missed him very much and urged him to visit them and ease her suffering, and incidentally today was her birthday. Below was a postscript: "I join in Mama's invitation. K."

Startsev thought it over and in the evening went to the Turkins'.

"Ah, welcome if you please!" Ivan Petrovich met him, smiling with his eyes only. "Bonzhurings!"

Vera Iosifovna, already much aged, her hair white, shook Startsev's hand, sighed affectedly, and said:

"You don't want to court me, Doctor, you never visit us, I'm already too old for you. But here a young girl has come, maybe she will have more luck."

And Kotik? She had grown thinner, paler, become more beautiful and shapely; but she was already Ekaterina Ivanovna and not Kotik; the former freshness and expression of childlike naïveté were no longer there. Her gaze and her manners had something new in them— timid and guilty, as if here, in the Turkins' home, she no longer felt herself at home.

"It's been so long!" she said, offering Startsev her hand, and one could see that her heart was beating anxiously; and looking into his face intently, with curiosity, she went on: "How you've filled out! You're tanned, you've matured, but on the whole you've changed very little."

Now, too, he liked her, liked her very much, but there was already something missing in her, or something superfluous—he himself was unable to tell which precisely, but something kept him from feeling as he used to. He did not like her paleness, her new expression, her weak smile, voice, and a little later he no longer liked her dress, the armchair she was sitting in, did not like something in the past, when he had almost married her. He remembered his love, the dreams and hopes that had excited him four years ago—and he became embarrassed.

They had tea with cake. Then Vera Iosifovna read a novel aloud, read about things that never happen in life, and Startsev listened, looked at her beautiful gray head, and waited for her to finish.

"Giftless," he thought, "isn't the one who can't write stories, but the one who writes them and can't conceal it."

"None too bad," said Ivan Petrovich.

Then Ekaterina Ivanovna played the piano long and noisily, and when she finished, she was long thanked and admired.

"It's a good thing I didn't marry her," thought Startsev.

She looked at him, and was apparently waiting for him to invite her to the garden, but he said nothing.

"So, let's talk," she said, going up to him. "How is your life? What are you up to? How are things? I've been thinking about you all these days," she went on nervously. "I wanted to send you a letter, wanted to go myself to see you in Dyalizh, and was already set on going, but then changed my mind—God knows how you feel about me now. I waited for you with such excitement today. For God's sake, let's go to the garden."

They went to the garden and sat there on the bench under the old maple tree, like four years ago. It was dark.

"So how are you getting on?" Ekaterina Ivanovna asked.

"Not bad, inching away," Startsev replied.

And he could not think up anything more. They fell silent.

"I'm excited," Ekaterina Ivanovna said and covered her face with her hands, "but pay no attention. I feel so good at home, I'm so glad to see everybody, and I can't get used to it. So many memories! I thought we'd go on talking till morning."

Now he saw her face up close, her shining eyes, and here, in the darkness, she looked younger than in the room, and it was even as if her former childlike expression had come back to her. And indeed she looked at him with naïve curiosity, as if she wished to examine more closely and understand the man who had once loved her so ardently, with such tenderness and such ill luck; her eyes thanked him for that love. And he remembered everything that had been, all the smallest details, how he had wandered in the cemetery, how later, towards morning, he had come home, exhausted, and he suddenly felt sad and sorry for the past. A little fire lit up in his soul.

"Do you remember how I took you to the club one evening?" he said. "It was raining then, dark . . ."

The little fire was burning brighter in his soul, and now he wanted to talk, to complain about life . . .

"Ahh!" he said with a sigh. "You ask how I'm getting along. How do we get along here? We don't. We age, gain weight, go to seed. Day and night—swift in flight, life goes by drably, without impressions, without thoughts . . . Daytime lucre, and evening the club, the company of cardplayers, alcoholics, poseurs, whom I can't stand. What's the good of it?"

"But you have work, a noble purpose in life. You liked so much to talk about your hospital. I was sort of strange then, I fancied myself a great pianist. Nowadays all girls play the piano, and I also played, like all of them, and there was nothing special in me: I'm as much a pianist as Mama is a writer. And, of course, I didn't understand you then, but later, in Moscow, I often thought of you. I thought only of you. What happiness it is to be a zemstvo doctor, to help those who suffer, to serve people. What happiness!" Ekaterina Ivanovna repeated with enthusiasm. "When I thought of you in Moscow, you appeared to me so ideal, so lofty . . ."

Startsev thought of the banknotes he so enjoyed taking from his pockets in the evenings, and the fire in his soul went out.

He got up to go to the house. She took him under the arm.

"You're the best of the people I've known in my life," she went on. "We'll see each other, we'll talk, won't we? Promise me that. I'm not a pianist, I no longer have any illusions on that account, and I won't play or talk about music in your presence."

When they went into the house, and in the evening light Startsev saw her face and her sad, grateful, searching eyes directed at him, he felt uneasy and thought again:

"It's a good thing I didn't marry then."

He started saying goodbye.

"You have no right of passage to leave without supper," Ivan Petrovich said, seeing him to the door. "It's quite perpendicular on your part. Go on, perform!" he said, addressing Pava in the front hall. Pava, no longer a boy, but a young man with a moustache, assumed a pose, raised his arm, and said in a tragic tone:

"Die, wretched woman!"

All this irritated Startsev. Getting into his carriage and looking at the dark house and garden that had once been so precious and dear to him, he remembered it all at once—Vera Iosifovna's novels, and Kotik's noisy playing, and Ivan Petrovich's witticisms, and Pava's tragic pose—and thought, if the most talented people in the whole town are so giftless, what kind of town can it be.

Three days later Pava brought a letter from Ekaterina Ivanovna.

"You don't come to see us. Why?" she wrote. "I fear you've changed towards us; I fear it, and I'm frightened at the very thought of it. Set me at peace, come and tell me that all is well.

"It's necessary that I speak to you. Yours, E. T."

He read this letter, pondered, and said to Pava:

"Tell them, my dear boy, that I cannot come today, I'm very busy. I'll come, say, in three days or so."

But three days went by, then a week, and he did not go. Once, passing by the Turkins' house, he remembered that he should stop by if only for a minute, but he pondered and . . . did not stop by.

And he never visited the Turkins again.

V

A few more years have gone by. Startsev has gained still more weight, grown fat, breathes heavily, and now walks with his head thrown back. When he rides, plump, red, in his troika with little bells, and Panteleimon, also plump and red, with a beefy neck, sits on the box, stretching his straight, as if wooden, arms out in front of him, and shouts at the passersby: "Keep ri-i-ight!" the picture is impressive, and it looks as if it is not a man riding, but a pagan god. He has an enormous practice in town, has no time to catch his breath, and already owns an estate and two houses in town, and is on the lookout for a third, more profitable one, and when they tell him in the Mutual Credit Society about some house that is up for sale, he goes to the house unceremoniously, and, passing through the rooms, paying no attention to the undressed women and childen who stare at him in astonishment and fear, jabs at all the doors with his stick, and says:

"Is this the study? Is this a bedroom? And what's this?"

And all the while he breathes heavily and wipes the sweat from his forehead.

He has much on his hands, but even so he has not left his post at the zemstvo; he is devoured by greed, he wants to keep it up both here and there. In Dyalizh and in town they now call him simply Ionych. "Where's Ionych off to?" or "Shouldn't we invite Ionych to the consultation?"

Probably because his throat is swollen with fat, his voice has changed and become high and shrill. His character has also changed: he has become difficult, irritable. When he receives patients, he is usually angry, raps his stick impatiently on the floor, and shouts in his unpleasant voice:

"Kindly just answer my questions! No talking!"

He is solitary. His life is dull, nothing interests him.

In all the time he has lived in Dyalizh, the love for Kotik was his only joy, and probably the last. In the evenings he plays whist at the club and then sits alone at a big table and eats supper. The servant Ivan, the oldest and most respected one, waits on him. He is served Lafite No. 17, and everybody—the staff of the club, the chef, and the waiter—already knows what he likes and what he does not like, they try their best to please him, or for all they know he will suddenly get angry and rap his stick on the floor.

While eating supper, he occasionally turns and interferes in some conversation:

"What's that about? Eh? Who?"

And when it so happens that at some neighboring table there is talk of the Turkins, he asks:

"Which Turkins do you mean? The ones whose daughter plays the piano?"

That is all that can be said about him.

And the Turkins? Ivan Petrovich has not aged, has not changed at all, is still witty and tells jokes as before; Vera Iosifovna reads her novels to guests as eagerly as before, with heartfelt simplicity. And Kotik plays the piano for four hours every day. She has aged noticeably, is frequently unwell, and goes to the Crimea every autumn with her mother. Seeing them off at the station, Ivan Petrovich, as the train departs, wipes his tears and calls out:

"Goodbye if you please!"

And waves his handkerchief.

1898

The New Dacha

I

Two miles from the village of Obruchanovo an enormous bridge was being built. From the village, which stood high on a steep bank, its latticed framework could be seen, and in foggy weather, and on quiet winter days, when its thin iron rafters and all the scaffolding around were covered with hoarfrost, it presented a picturesque and even fantastic sight. The engineer Kucherov, the builder of the bridge, a stout, broad-shouldered, bearded man in a soft, crumpled cap, sometimes drove through the village in a racing droshky or a carriage; sometimes on holidays vagabonds who worked on the bridge turned up; they begged for alms, laughed at the peasant women, and occasionally made off with things. But that happened rarely. Ordinarily the days passed quietly and peacefully, as if there were no building at all, and only in the evening, when bonfires were lit by the bridge, did the wind bring the faint sound of the tramps singing. And sometimes during the day a mournful metallic sound was heard: dong . . . dong . . . dong . . .

One day the engineer Kucherov's wife came to visit. She liked the banks of the river and the magnificent view over the green valley with its hamlets, churches, flocks, and she started asking her husband to buy a small plot of land and build a dacha there. The husband obeyed. They bought fifty acres of land, and on the high bank, in a clearing, where the Obruchanovo cows used to graze, they built a beautiful two-story house with a terrace, balconies, a tower and a spire, on which a flag was raised on Sundays—built it in only three months, and then all winter planted big trees, and when spring came and everything around turned green, there were already allées in the new estate, a gardener and two workmen in white aprons were digging near the house, a little fountain spouted, and a mirror globe shone so brightly that it was painful to look at. And this estate already had a name: the New Dacha.

On a clear, warm morning at the end of May, two horses were brought to Rodion Petrov, the Obruchanovo blacksmith, to be re-shod. They were from the New Dacha. The horses were white as snow, sleek, well-fed, and strikingly resembled each other.

"Perfect swans!" Rodion exclaimed, looking at them in awe.

His wife Stepanida, his children and grandchildren came outside to look. A crowd gradually gathered. The Lychkovs came, father and son, both beardless from birth, with swollen faces and hatless. Kozov also came, a tall, skinny old man with a long, narrow beard and a stick with a crook; he kept winking his sly eyes and smiling mockingly, as if he knew something.

"It's only that they're white, otherwise what?" he said. "Feed mine oats and they'll be just as smooth. Hitch 'em to a plow and whip 'em . . ."

The coachman only glanced at him with scorn and did not say a word. And later, while the fire was heating up in the smithy, the coachman stood talking and smoking cigarettes. The peasants learned many details from him: his masters were rich; earlier, before her marriage, the mistress, Elena Ivanovna, had lived in Moscow as a poor governess; she was kind, compassionate, and liked to help the poor. On the new estate, he went on telling them, there will be no plowing, no sowing, they will live only for their own pleasure, only so as to breathe the clean air. When he finished and led the horses back, he was followed by a crowd of boys, dogs barked, and Kozov, following them with his eyes, winked mockingly.

"So-o-ome landowners!" he said. "They build a house, buy horses, but they've probably got nothing to eat. So-o-ome landowners!"

Kozov began somehow at once to hate the new estate, and the

white horses, and the well-fed, handsome coachman. He himself was a single man, a widower; his life was boring (he was prevented from working by some illness which he called now a hoornia, now worms); he received money for subsistence from his son, who worked in a pastry shop in Kharkov, and from early morning till evening he wandered idly along the riverbank or around the village, and if he saw, for instance, a peasant carrying a log or fishing, he would say: "That log's deadwood, rotten," or "Fish don't bite in such weather." During a dry spell, he would say there would be no rain before the frost, and when it rained, he would say now everything in the fields was going to rot and perish. And all the while he kept winking, as if he knew something.

On the estate in the evenings they burned Bengal lights and set off fireworks, and a boat with red lamps went sailing past Obruchanovo. One morning the engineer's wife, Elena Ivanovna, came to the village with her little daughter in a carriage with yellow wheels, drawn by a pair of dark bay ponies; both mother and daughter were wearing straw hats with broad brims bent down to their ears.

This was just the time of the dung carting, and the blacksmith Rodion, a tall, gaunt old man, hatless, barefoot, with a fork on his shoulder, stood by his filthy, ugly cart, looking at the ponies in bewilderment, and his face showed clearly that he had never seen such small horses before.

"It's Kucherov's woman!" people whispered all around. "Look, it's Kucherov's woman!"

Elena Ivanovna kept glancing at the cottages as if she were choosing, then stopped the horses by the poorest cottage, where there were so many children's heads in the windows—blond, dark, red. Stepanida, Rodion's wife, a stout old woman, ran out of the cottage, the kerchief slipped from her gray head, she looked at the carriage against the sun, and her face smiled and winced as if she were blind.

"This is for your children," Elena Ivanovna said and handed her three roubles.

Stepanida suddenly burst into tears and bowed to the ground. Rodion also dropped down, displaying his broad, tanned bald spot and almost snagging his wife's side with his fork. Elena Ivanovna became embarrassed and drove away.

II

The Lychkovs, father and son, caught two workhorses, one pony, and a broad-muzzled Aalhaus bull calf on their meadow, and together with red-headed Volodka, the son of the blacksmith Rodion, led them to the village. They called the headman, took witnesses, and went to look at the damage.

"All right, let 'em!" said Kozov, winking. "Go o-o-on! Let 'em squirm a bit now, these engineers! They think there's no justice? All right! Send for the police, draw up a report! . . ."

"Draw up a report!" Volodka repeated.

"I don't want to leave it like this!" Lychkov the son was shouting, shouting louder and louder, and that seemed to make his beardless face swell even more. "It's some new fashion! If you let them, they'll trample down all the meadows! They've got no full right to bully people! There are no serfs now!"

"There are no serfs now!" Volodka repeated.

"We lived without a bridge," Lychkov the father said sullenly, "we didn't ask for it, what do we need a bridge for? We don't want it!"

"Brothers, good Orthodox people! We can't leave it like this!"

"All right, go o-o-on!" Kozov winked. "Let 'em squirm a bit now! So-o-ome landowners!"

They headed back to the village, and all the while they walked, Lychkov the son beat himself on the chest with his fist and shouted, and Volodka also shouted, repeating his words. And in the village, meanwhile, a whole crowd had gathered around the thoroughbred bull calf and the horses. The bull calf was embarrassed and looked from under his brow, but suddenly he lowered his muzzle to the ground and ran, kicking up his hind legs. Kozov got frightened and waved his stick at him, and they all burst out laughing. Then they locked up the beasts and began to wait.

In the evening the engineer sent five roubles for the damages, and the two horses, the pony, and the bull calf, unfed and unwatered, went back home, hanging their heads like guilty men, as if they were being led out to execution.

Having received five roubles, the Lychkovs, father and son, the headman, and Volodka crossed the river in a boat, and on the other side went to the village of Kryakovo, where there was a pot-house, and reveled there for a long time. Their singing and the young Lychkov's shouting could be heard. In the village the womenfolk worried and did not sleep all night. Rodion also did not sleep.

"It's a bad business," he kept saying, tossing from side to side and sighing. "The master will be angry, he'll have us up in court . . . The master's been offended . . . ohh, offended, it's bad."

One day the peasants, and Rodion in their number, went to their communal forest to do the haymaking, and on the way back they met the engineer. He was wearing a red calico shirt and high boots; behind him followed a pointer, his long tongue hanging out.

"Hello, brothers!" he said.

The peasants stopped and took their hats off.

"I've been meaning to talk with you for a long time now, brothers," he went on. "The thing is this. Every day since early spring your herd has been coming to my garden and woods. Everything gets trampled, the pigs root around in the meadow, muck up the vegetable patch, and all the young trees in the woods have vanished. There's no dealing with your herdsmen; you ask them something, and they get rude. Damage is done every day, and I do nothing, I don't fine you, I don't complain, and meanwhile you penned up my horses and my bull calf and took five roubles from me. Is that good? Do you call it neighborly?" he went on, and his voice was gentle, persuasive, and his look was not severe. "Is this the way decent people behave? A week ago one of you cut down two young oaks in my woods. You dug up the road to Eresnevo, and now I have to make a two-mile detour. Why do you harm me at every step? What wrong have I done you, tell me, for God's sake? My wife and I try very hard to live in peace and harmony with you; we help the peasants all we can. My wife is a kind, warmhearted woman, she doesn't refuse to help, it's her dream to be of use to you and your children. But you repay our good with ill. It's unfair, brothers. Think about it. I ask you earnestly to think about it. We treat you humanely, you should repay us in kind."

He turned and left. The peasants stood there for a while, put on their hats, and went on. Rodion, who understood what was said to him not as it was meant, but always in some way of his own, sighed and said:

"We've got to pay it back. Pay it back, I say, brothers, in kind . . ."

They reached the village in silence. Having come home, Rodion said a prayer, took off his boots, and sat down on the bench beside his wife. When he and Stepanida were at home, they always sat next to each other and outside they always walked next to each other, they always ate, drank, and slept together, and the older they grew, the more they loved each other. Their cottage was crowded, hot, there were children everywhere—on the floor, on the windowsills, on the stove[1] . . . Stepanida, though she was getting on in years, still bore children, and now, looking at the heap of children, it was hard to tell which were Rodion's and which Volodka's. Volodka's wife, Lukerya, an unattractive young woman with bulging eyes and a bird-like nose, was kneading dough in a tub; Volodka himself was sitting on the stove, his legs hanging down.

"On the road by Nikita's buckwheat, you know . . . the engineer and his dog . . . ," Rodion began, after resting, scratching his sides and elbows. "You've got to pay it back, he says . . . In kind, he says . . . In kind or not, but ten kopecks a household it should be. We've harmed the master a lot. I feel sorry . . ."

"We lived without a bridge," Volodka said, not looking at anyone, "and we have no wish."

"Go on! It's a government bridge."

"We have no wish."

"Nobody's asking you. Drop it!"

" 'Nobody's asking' . . . ," Volodka mimicked. "We've got nowhere to go, what do we need a bridge for? When need be, we can cross in a boat."

Someone outside knocked so hard on the window that the whole cottage seemed to shake.

"Is Volodka there?" came the voice of Lychkov the son. "Volodka, come out, let's go!"

Volodka jumped off the stove and started looking for his cap.

"Don't go, Volodya," Rodion said timidly. "Don't go with them, sonny. You're stupid as a little child, and they won't teach you any good. Don't go!"

"Don't go, sonny!" begged Stepanida, and she blinked, getting ready to weep. "They must be calling you to the pot-house."

" 'To the pot-house' . . . ," Volodya mimicked.

"You'll come home drunk again, you Herod-dog!" said Lukerya, looking at him spitefully. "Go, go, and I hope you burn up with vodka, you tail-less Satan!"

"Shut up!" cried Volodka.

"They married me off to a fool, a red-haired drunkard—me, a wretched orphan—they ruined me . . . ," Lukerya wailed, wiping her face with her hand, which was all covered with dough. "I wish I'd never set eyes on you!"

Volodka hit her on the ear and left.

III

Elena Ivanovna and her little daughter came to the village on foot. They were taking a walk. It happened to be Sunday, and the women and girls had come outside in their bright dresses. Rodion and Stepanida, who were sitting next to each other on the porch, bowed and smiled to Elena Ivanovna and her girl as if to acquaintances. Ten or more children looked out at them through the windows; their faces expressed perplexity and curiosity, and whispering was heard.

"Kucherov's woman! It's Kucherov's woman!"

"Hello," Elena Ivanovna said and stopped; after a pause, she asked, "Well, how are you doing?"

"We're doing all right, God be thanked!" Rodion replied in a quick patter. "We live, as you see."

"As if this is a life!" Stepanida smirked. "You can see for yourself, lady, dearest, it's poverty! We're fourteen in the family, and only two breadwinners. They call us blacksmiths, but when a horse is brought to be shod, there's no coal, no money to buy it. It's torment, lady," she went on, and started laughing. "A-ah, what torment!"

Elena Ivanovna sat down on the porch and, embracing her girl, fell to thinking about something, and the girl, too, judging by her face, had some cheerless thoughts wandering in her head; brooding, she toyed with the pretty lace parasol she took from her mother's hands.

"Poverty!" said Rodion. "There's many cares, we work—and

there's no end in sight. Now God isn't sending rain . . . We don't live well, that's for sure."

"In this life it's hard for you," said Elena Ivanovna, "but in the other world you'll be happy."

Rodion did not understand her and only coughed into his fist in response. And Stepanida said:

"Lady, dearest, for a rich man things will be well in the other world, too. A rich man lights candles, offers prayer services, gives alms, but what about a peasant? You've got no time to cross yourself, lowest of the low, there's no way to save yourself. Many sins also come from poverty, out of grief we all quarrel like dogs, never say a decent word, and what doesn't go on, dearest lady—God forbid! It must be there's no happiness for us either in the other world or in this one. All happiness goes to the rich."

She spoke cheerfully; obviously, she had long been used to talking about her hard life. And Rodion also smiled; he was pleased that his old woman was so intelligent and garrulous.

"It only seems that things are easy for the rich," said Elena Ivanovna. "Every person has his grief. We, my husband and I, aren't poor, we have means, but are we happy? I'm still young, but I already have four children; they're sick all the time, and I'm also sick and constantly being treated."

"And what kind of sickness is it?" asked Rodion.

"A woman's. I can't sleep, headaches give me no peace. I'm sitting here, talking, but something's not right in my head, I'm weak all over, and I agree that the hardest work is better than such a condition. And my soul is also not at peace. I constantly worry about the children and my husband. There's some sort of grief in every family, and so there is in ours. I'm not from the gentry. My grandfather was a simple peasant, my father went into trade in Moscow and was also a simple man. But my husband's parents are noble and rich. They didn't want him to marry me, but he disobeyed, quarreled with them, and they still haven't forgiven us. This upsets my husband, worries him, keeps him in constant anxiety. He loves his mother, loves her very much. Well, and I'm upset, too. My soul aches."

Around Rodion's cottage peasants, men and women, were already standing and listening. Kozov also came and stopped, twitching his long, narrow beard. The Lychkovs, father and son, came.

"And, of course, you can't be happy and content unless you feel you're in your own place," Elena Ivanovna went on. "Each of you has his own strip of land, each of you works and knows why he works; my husband builds bridges—in a word, each of you has his own place. And me? I just walk around. I don't have my own land, I don't work, and I feel like a stranger. I'm saying all this so that you won't judge by external appearances. If somebody wears expensive clothes and is well off, that still doesn't mean that he's pleased with his life."

She got up to leave and took her daughter by the hand.

"I like it here with you very much," she said and smiled, and by that weak, timid smile one could tell how unwell she really was, how young she was still, and how attractive. She had a pale, lean face with dark eyebrows, and blond hair. And the girl was just like her mother, lean, blond, and slender. They smelled of perfume.

"I like the river, and the forest, and the village . . . ," Elena Ivanovna went on. "I could live here all my life, and it seems to me that here I would recover my health and find my place. I want, I passionately want to help you, to be useful, to be close to you. I know how needy you are, and what I don't know, I feel, I guess with my heart. I'm sick, weak, and for me it's probably already impossible to change my life as I'd like to. But I have children, I'll try to raise them so that they're accustomed to you and love you. I'll constantly instill in them that their lives belong not to them, but to you. Only I ask you earnestly, I beg you, trust us, be friends with us. My husband is a kind, good man. Don't upset him, don't vex him. He's sensitive about every little thing, and yesterday, for instance, your herd got into our vegetable garden, and one of you broke the wattle fence at our apiary, and this attitude drives my husband to despair. I beg you," she went on in a pleading voice, clasping her hands on her breast, "I beg you, treat us as good neighbors, let us live in peace! They say a bad peace is better than a good quarrel, and 'Don't buy a house, buy a neighbor.' I repeat, my husband is a kind man, a good man; if all goes well, I promise you, we'll do everything in our power; we'll repair the roads, we'll build a school for your children. I promise you."

"We humbly thank you, for sure, lady," said Lychkov the father, looking at the ground. "You're educated, you know better. Only you see, in Eresnevo a rich peasant, Ravenov, promised to build a school, he also said 'I'll do this, I'll do that,' and only put up the frame and quit, and then the peasants were forced to roof it and finish it—a thousand roubles went on it. It was nothing to Ravenov, he just stroked his beard, but it was kind of hurtful for the peasants."

"That was the raven, and now the rook's come flying," Kozov said and winked.

Laughter was heard.

"We don't need a school," Volodka said sullenly. "Our children go to Petrovskoe, and let them. We have no wish."

Elena Ivanovna somehow suddenly became timid. She grew pale, pinched, cringed all over, as if she had been touched by something coarse, and walked off without saying another word. And she walked more and more quickly, without looking back.

"Lady!" Rodion called out, walking after her. "Lady, wait, I've got something to tell you."

He followed right behind her, without his hat, and spoke softly, as if begging for alms.

"Lady! Wait, I've got something to tell you."

They left the village, and Elena Ivanovna stopped in the shade of an old rowan tree, near somebody's cart.

"Don't be offended, lady," said Rodion. "It's nothing! Just be patient. Be patient for a couple of years. You'll live here, you'll be patient, and it'll all come round. Our folk are good, peaceable . . . decent enough folk, I'm telling you as God is my witness. Don't look at Kozov and the Lychkovs, or my Volodka, he's a little fool: he listens to whoever speaks first. The rest are peaceable folk, they keep mum . . . Some would be glad to say a word in all conscience, to stand up for you, I mean, but they can't. There's soul, there's conscience, but they've got no tongue. Don't be offended . . . be patient . . . It's nothing!"

Elena Ivanovna looked at the wide, calm river, thinking about something, and tears flowed down her cheeks. And Rodion was confused by these tears; he all but wept himself.

"Never mind . . . ," he murmured. "Be patient for a couple of little years. The school can be done, and the roads can be done, only not right away . . . Say, for example, you want to sow wheat on that hillock: so first root it up, dig out all the stones, then plow it, go on and on . . . And so, with our folk, I mean . . . it's the same, go on and on, and you'll manage."

The crowd separated from Rodion's cottage and came down the street in the direction of the rowan tree. They struck up a song, a concertina played. And they drew nearer and nearer . . .

"Mama, let's go away from here," said the girl, pale, pressing herself to her mother and trembling all over. "Let's go away, Mama!"

"Where?"

"To Moscow . . . Let's go away, Mama!"

The girl wept. Rodion became totally confused, his face all covered with sweat. He took a cucumber from his pocket, small, bent like a moon sickle, stuck all over with breadcrumbs, and started shoving it into the girl's hands.

"Now, now . . . ," he murmured, frowning sternly. "Take the cucumber, eat it . . . It's no good crying, Mama will beat you . . . at home she'll complain to your father . . . Now, now . . ."

They went on, and he kept following behind them, wishing to tell them something gentle and persuasive. But, seeing that they were both taken up with their own thoughts and their own grief and did not notice him, he stopped and, shielding his eyes from the sun, looked after them for a long time, until they disappeared into their woods.

IV

The engineer apparently became irritable, petty, and now saw every trifle as a theft or an encroachment. The gates were locked even during the day, and at night two watchmen walked in the garden, rapping on boards;[2] no one from Obruchanovo was hired to do day labor any more. As if on purpose, someone (one of the peasants or a tramp—no one knew) took the new wheels off the cart and replaced them with old ones; then, a little later, two bridles and a pair of pincers were taken, and murmuring even began in the village. They said a search should be carried out at the Lychkovs' and Volodka's, after which the pincers and the bridles were found by the fence in the engineer's garden: someone had put them there.

Once a crowd of them came out of the woods and again met the engineer on the road. He stopped and, without greeting them, looking angrily first at one, then at another, began:

"I've asked that the mushrooms not be picked in my park and around the premises, that they be left for my wife and children, but your girls come at dawn, and then there's not a single mushroom left. Asking you or not asking—it's all the same. Requests, kindness, persuasion, I see, are all useless."

He fixed his indignant eyes on Rodion and went on:

"My wife and I treated you as human beings, as equals, and you? Eh, what's there to talk about! It will end, most likely, with us looking down on you. There's nothing else left!"

And making an effort to restrain his wrath, so as not to say something unnecessary, he turned and went on his way.

On coming home, Rodion said a prayer, took off his boots, and sat down on the bench beside his wife.

"Yes . . . ," he began, after resting. "We were going along just now and met Mister Kucherov . . . Yes . . . He's seen the village girls at daybreak . . . He says, 'Why don't they bring mushrooms,' he says . . . 'to my wife and children?' And then he looks at me and says: 'My wife and I,' he says, 'are going to look after you.' I wanted to bow down at his feet, but I turned shy . . . God grant him good health . . . Lord, send them . . ."

Stepanida crossed herself and sighed.

"They're kind masters, sort of simple . . . ," Rodion went on. " 'We'll look after you . . .' he promised in front of everybody. In our old age and . . . it would be nice . . . I'd pray to God for them eternally . . . Queen of Heaven, send them . . ."

The Elevation, on the fourteenth of September, was the church feast.[3] The Lychkovs, father and son, crossed the river in the morning, and came back drunk at lunchtime; they went around the village for a long time, now singing, now abusing each other in foul language; then they got into a fight and went to the estate to complain. First Lychkov the father came into the yard with a long aspen stick in his hand; he stopped hesitantly and took off his hat. Just then the engineer and his family were sitting on the terrace having tea.

"What do you want?" the engineer shouted.

"Your Honor, sir . . . ," Lychkov began and burst into tears. "Show me divine mercy, intercede . . . My son won't let me live . . . He's ruined me, he beats me . . . Your Honor . . ."

Lychkov the son also came in, hatless, also with a stick. He stopped and fixed his drunken, mindless gaze on the terrace.

"It's not my business to sort it out," said the engineer. "Go to the local court or the police."

"I've been everywhere . . . I've petitioned . . . ," said Lychkov the father, and he started sobbing. "Where can I go now? So it means he can kill me now? It means he can do anything? And me his father? His father?"

He raised his stick and hit his son on the head; the son raised his and hit the old man right on his bald spot, so that the stick even bounced off. Lychkov the father did not even sway and again hit his son, again on the head. They stood like that and kept hitting each other on the head, and it looked not like a fight, but like some sort of game. And outside the gate peasant men and women crowded and silently looked into the yard, and their faces were all serious. They had come with wishes for the feast day, but, seeing the Lychkovs, they felt ashamed and did not enter the yard.

The next morning Elena Ivanovna left for Moscow with the children. And the rumor spread that the engineer was selling his dacha . . .

V

The bridge had long been a familiar sight, and it was already hard to imagine the river in that place without it. The heaps of debris left from the construction had long been overgrown with grass, the vagabonds were forgotten, and instead of the song "Dubinushka," the sound of a passing train was heard almost every hour.

The New Dacha was sold long ago; it now belongs to some official, who comes here from town on holidays with his family, has tea on the terrace, and then goes back to town. He has a cockade on his visored cap, he talks and coughs like a very important official, though in rank he is a mere collegiate secretary,[4] and when the peasants bow to him, he does not respond.

In Obruchanovo everyone has aged; Kozov has already died, Rodion has even more children in his cottage, Volodka has grown a long red beard. Life is as poor as before.

In early spring the Obruchanovo peasants saw wood near the train station. Now they are going home after work, going unhurriedly, one by one; the wide saws bend over their shoulders, and the sun is reflected in them. Nightingales sing in the bushes along the riverbank, larks pour out their song in the sky. It is quiet at the New Dacha, not a soul is there, and only golden pigeons, golden because the sun is shining on them, fly over the house. Everyone—Rodion, both Lychkovs, and Volodka—remembers the white horses, the little ponies, the fireworks, the boat with its lamps, remembers how the engineer's wife, beautiful, finely dressed, came to the village and spoke so gently. And it is all as if it never was. All like in a dream or a fairy tale.

They walk one foot after the other, worn out, and they think . . .

In their village, they think, the folk are good, quiet, sensible, they fear God, and Elena Ivanovna was also quiet, kind, meek, it was such a pity to look at her, but why is it that they did not get along and parted as enemies? What was this mist that hid from sight the most important things and let only the damage be seen, the bridles, the pincers, and all those trifles which now in recollection seem like such nonsense? Why is it that they live in peace with the new owner, but could not get along with the engineer?

And, not knowing how to answer these questions for themselves, they all keep silent, and only Volodka mutters something.

"What's that?" asks Rodion.

"We lived without the bridge . . . ," Volodka says glumly. "We lived without the bridge and didn't ask . . . and we've got no need."

Nobody responds to him, and they walk on silently, hanging their heads.

1898

NOTES

JOY

1. Collegiate Registrar: In the table of ranks established by Peter the Great in 1722, there were fourteen grades of government officials, of which collegiate registrar was fourteenth and lowest.

FAT AND SKINNY

1. Nikolaevsky train station: A railway terminal in Moscow and Petersburg, named after the emperor Nicholas I.

2. Herostratus . . . Ephialtes: In the fourth century B.C. the arsonist Herostratus burned down the temple of Artemis in Ephesus, listed by the historian Herodotus as one of the seven wonders of the ancient world. Ephialtes of Trachis betrayed the Greeks to the Persians, enabling the latter to win the battle of Thermopylae in 480 B.C.

3. collegiate assessor . . . a Stanislas: Collegiate assessor was eighth in the table of ranks (see note 1 to "Joy," above). The Polish Order of St. Stanislaus (or Stanislas), founded in 1765, was adopted by Russia in 1832.

4. state councillor . . . privy councillor: State councillor was fifth in the table of ranks; privy councillor was third and brought with it the right to be addressed as "Your Excellency."

AT THE POST OFFICE

1. blini: Thin Russian wheat or buckwheat pancakes served with various accompaniments, sweet or savory.

READING

1. actual state councillor: Or "active state councillor," fourth grade in the table of ranks.

2. *The Count of Monte Cristo*: Well-known adventure novel (1844) by the French author Alexandre Dumas (1802–70).

3. gulps milk all through Lent: Dairy products are forbidden during the forty-day fast (the Great Lent) preceding Easter.

4. *The Wandering Jew*: A multivolume novel (1844–45) by French author Eugène Sue (1804–57), which became an international best seller.

THE COOK GETS MARRIED

1. Chernomor: The name of the wizard who steals Lyudmila on her wedding night, in the poem *Ruslan and Lyudmila* (1820), by Alexander Pushkin (1799–1837).

IN A FOREIGN LAND

1. say tray jolee: crude mispronunciation of the French *c'est très jolie* ("it's very pretty").

THE EXCLAMATION POINT

1. collegiate secretary: The tenth grade in the table of ranks.

2. his Stanislas medal: Decoration of the Order of St. Stanislas (see note 3 to "Fat and Skinny").

AN EDUCATED BLOCKHEAD

1. Sixwingsky: The seraphim, as described in Isaiah 6:2, are angels with six wings. They belong to the highest rank in the Judeo-Christian angelic hierarchy.

A SLIP-UP

1. Nekrasov: Nikolai Alexeevich Nekrasov (1821–78), poet, essayist, editor, and social critic with strong liberal views, was a major figure in mid-nineteenth-century Russian literature.

2. be fruitful . . . multiply: God's words to Adam and Eve in Genesis 1:28.

3. Lazhechnikov: Ivan Ivanovich Lazhechnikov (1792–1869) was a novelist and playwright, credited with introducing the historical novel into Russian literature.

ANGUISH

1. To whom will I impart my sorrow?: The beginning of an anonymous fifteenth- or sixteenth-century Russian poem known as "Joseph's Lament."

2. On the stove . . . : The traditional Russian stove was an elaborate structure which included "shelves" for sleeping on.

A COMMOTION

1. **Princess Tarakanova:** A woman (ca. 1745–75) who claimed to be the daughter of the Russian empress Elizabeth (1709–62). She adopted several names, but her real name is not known. "Tarakanova," which comes from the Russian word for "cockroach," was attached to her after her death in prison. Her story has been the subject of several films and paintings.

2. *Esturgeon à la Russe:* "Russian-style sturgeon."

3. *Tout comprendre, tout pardonner:* An abbreviated version of a French saying, meaning "To understand all is to forgive all."

THE WITCH

1. **the prophet Daniel and the three holy youths:** The story of Daniel and his three fellow princes is told in the first chapter of the Old Testament Book of Daniel. In the Orthodox Church they are commemorated on December 17.

2. **St. Alexei the man of God:** Alexeios, or Alexis, a saint of the early Church, was born in Rome in 380 and, after many adventures, died there in 411. His feast day is March 17.

3. **the Dormition fast:** A two-week fast, August 1–14, preceding the Feast of the Dormition, the "falling asleep" of the Mother of God, celebrated on August 15.

4. **the Ten Martyrs of Crete:** Ten Christian men who suffered martyrdom under the emperor Decius in the third century AD.

5. **Saint Nicholas:** St. Nicholas of Myra (270–342) is commemorated twice in the Orthodox Church, on May 9 and December 6.

6. **Forgiveness Sunday:** The last Sunday before the Great Lent preceding Easter, during which weddings are not celebrated.

A LITTLE JOKE

1. **the nobility trusteeship:** A system of placing the estates of orphans in the hands of trustees until their coming of age; also used in cases of impoverishment or mental instability.

A NIGHTMARE

1. **marshal of the nobility:** Each administrative subdivision of the Russian Empire had an assembly of the nobility, presided over by an elected marshal.

2. **male soul:** A way of referring to male peasants belonging to an estate.

3. **the Royal Doors:** In an Orthodox church, the altar is separated from the nave of the church by a partition, called the iconostasis, which has two smaller side doors and one pair of central doors known as the Royal Doors.

GRISHA

1. bath besoms: branches of birch, eucalyptus, or other trees and bushes, used during a steam bath for a stimulating beating of the bather's skin.

LADIES

1. Chatsky: Alexander Andreevich Chatsky is the young, idealistic protagonist of the play *Woe from Wit*, by the poet and statesman Alexander Griboedov (1795–1829).

ROMANCE WITH A DOUBLE BASS

1. dacha: A country house, often a second home; its residents, known as *dachniki*, are somewhat separated from the local people.

THE FIRST-CLASS PASSENGER

1. Pushkin: Alexander Pushkin (1799–1837) was and remains Russia's greatest poet. The reference is to his poem "A Conversation Between a Bookseller and a Poet."
2. the capitals: Moscow and St. Petersburg were commonly referred to as the "two capitals" of Russia.

ON THE ROAD

1. A golden cloudlet: The opening lines of "The Cliff" (1841), a short lyric poem by the poet Mikhail Lermontov (1814–41).
2. St. Seraphim ... Shah Nasr-Eddin: St. Seraphim of Sarov (1754–1833), one of the most venerated Russian Orthodox saints, lived for twenty-five years as a hermit in the forest outside the monastery of Sarov. Shah Nasr-Eddin (Naser al-Din Shah Qajar, 1831–96) was shah of Persia from 1848 until his assassination in 1896. He visited Europe a number of times.
3. a sin ... liturgy: The Orthodox Church ordains a strict fast before partaking of the eucharist (consecrated bread and wine) at the liturgy.
4. marshal of the nobility: See note 1 to "The Nightmare."
5. Joshua ... Elijah: In the Book of Joshua 10:12–13, Joshua commanded the sun to stand still during his war with the Amorites. In 2 Kings 1:10–12, Elijah twice calls down lightning ("fire from heaven") upon the enemies of Israel.
6. nihilism: Russian nihilism began in the 1860s as an intellectual/political movement that rejected all authority of state and church. The term, which comes from the Latin word *nihil*, meaning "nothing," was introduced in Russia by Ivan Turgenev (1818–83) in his novel *Fathers and Sons* (1862).
7. Slavophile ... Aksakov: Slavophilism was an intellectual movement in nineteenth-century Russia that favored Slavic history and traditions, as opposed to the Europeanizing

tendencies of the radical thinkers called Westernizers. Konstantin Aksakov (1817–60), critic, historian, and playwright, was one of its chief proponents.

8. non-resistance to evil: A teaching with roots in Christian tradition, taken up by Leo Tolstoy in the 1880s and later by Mahatma Gandhi.

9. zierlichmännerlich: "delicate-mannerly" (German).

10. Arkhangelsk and Tobolsk: Arkhangelsk is a city in the north of Russia on the White Sea; Tobolsk, a city east of the Ural Mountains, some fifteen hundred miles from Moscow, was the first Russian capital of Siberia.

11. Don't remember evil . . . : A traditional Russian phrase spoken on parting; the full phrase is "Don't remember evil against me."

ENEMIES

1. an Alphonse: A reference to the character Octave, called Alphonse, in the play *Monsieur Alphonse* (1873) by Alexander Dumas *fils* (1824–95).

2. mauvais ton: Literally "bad tone" in French, meaning "bad form."

THE LETTER

1. rural dean: A priest who supervises several churches in a rural district.

2. matins late at night . . . : Easter matins in the Orthodox Church are celebrated around midnight.

3. certificates of fasting: In the nineteenth century there was strict state and Church control over fasting, confession, and communion. Priests issued certificates to those who fulfilled these obligations.

4. after breaking the fast: i.e., after the Easter liturgy.

5. reading the Acts: The Book of the Acts of the Apostles.

6. Tomorrow it would be a sin to write: i.e., on a holy day.

7. Christ is risen . . . : The traditional Orthodox greeting between Easter and Pentecost.

8. the Gospel in Latin: It is traditional to read the Prologue to the Gospel of St. John in various languages during the Easter liturgy.

9. kulichi and red-dyed eggs: Traditional food for the feast following Easter. A *kulich* (plural *kulichi*) is a sweet cake.

10. the image and likeness: At the creation (Genesis 1:26) God said, "Let us make man in our image, after our likeness."

11. In sin did my mother conceive me: Psalm 51:5.

VOLODYA

1. Lermontov: See note 1 to "On the Road."

LUCK

1. Y. P. Polonsky: Yakov Petrovich Polonsky (1819–98) was a romantic poet of the generation following Pushkin and the first winner of the prestigious Pushkin Prize, established in 1881, for which he successfully nominated Chekhov in 1888.

2. so you'll be a rich man: According to an old Russian superstition, if a person goes unrecognized, it means he will be rich.

3. the tsar Alexander . . . in a wagon: The tsar Alexander I (1777–1825) died of typhus in the town of Taganrog on the Sea of Azov (incidentally Chekhov's birthplace).

4. Before the freedom: meaning the abolition of serfdom, in 1861, by Alexander II (1818–81), known as "the tsar-liberator."

5. digging up the barrows: Barrows are large earth and stone mounds built over burial places in prehistoric times.

6. the emperor Peter . . . building the fleet: Peter the Great (1672–1725) had the first large Russian warships built on the Voronezh River, near the city of the same name, at the turn of the eighteenth century.

7. In the year 'twelve . . . from the French: Napoleon's invasion of Russia, from June to December 1812, ended in the total defeat of the French.

8. Saur's Grave: A high barrow said to be the grave of a legendary Tatar hero.

9. German and Molokan farmsteads . . . Kalmuk . . . : German Mennonites and members of the Christian sect of Molokans ("Milk-drinkers"), which was suppressed in Russia, migrated to the Donbass region of the eastern Ukraine. The Kalmuks (or Kalmyks) are a traditionally Buddhist people who first came to Russia in 1607.

THE SIREN

1. kulebiak: A Russian pastry of a long, rounded form, with various savory fillings.

THE SHEPHERD'S PIPE

1. St. Elijah's day: July 20.

2. St. Peter's day: June 29 (also called the feast of Saints Peter and Paul).

3. since the freedom: See note 4 to "Luck."

COSTLY LESSONS

1. Enquête: French for "inquest" or "investigation" (impossible as a name).

2. Margot: A theoretical and practical grammar book of the French language for advanced high school classes, by D. Margot, lecturer in French at the University of St. Petersburg (third edition, 1875).

3. the Maly Theater: A Moscow drama theater, founded in 1806 and still functioning.

THE KISS

1. at Plevna: The siege of the Bulgarian town of Plevna (July–December 1877) took place during the Russo-Turkish War of 1877–78, and ended with the victory of the Russian-Romanian coalition over the Ottoman forces.

2. the empress Eugénie: Maria Eugenia Ignacia Augustina de Palafox y Kirkpatrick (1826–1920), of high Spanish nobility, was the wife of the French emperor Napoleon III.

3. *The Messenger of Europe:* The most important liberal journal of its time, founded in 1866 and published continually until 1918.

4. *canaille:* French for scoundrel, rascal, rogue.

BOYS

1. bashlyk: A traditional peaked Cossack or Turkic hood with long sides that serve as a scarf.

2. Samoyeds: A general name for several small indigenous peoples of Russia.

3. Mayne Reid: Thomas Mayne Reid (1818–83) was a Scots-Irish writer who spent some ten years in America (1840–50), working in various places at various jobs, then returned to Northern Ireland and began to write novels, producing some seventy-five in his lifetime, often about his American experiences, the cruelty of slavery, the life of American Indians. He was very popular in Russia.

KASHTANKA

1. In sin . . . fiery hyena . . . : See note 11 to "The Letter." By "fiery hyena" the cabinetmaker means "fiery Gehenna," a biblical name for the place of the damned. "Hyena" in Russian begins with a *g* ("giena").

THE NAME-DAY PARTY

1. St. Peter's day: See note 2 to "The Shepherd's Pipe."

2. *Allah kerim!:* "God is gracious!" (Turkish).

3. numbered among the transgressors: A line from Isaiah 53:12, quoted in Mark 15:28 and Luke 22:37.

4. infallible Gladstones: William Ewart Gladstone (1809–98) was a liberal British statesman who served a total of twelve years as prime minister between 1869 and 1894.

5. Khokhlandia: i.e., "land of the Khokhols," a mildly disrespectful Russian nickname for Ukrainians. "Khokhol" is the Ukrainian word for the long lock of hair Ukrainian Cossacks left on their otherwise clean-shaven heads.

6. seasonable weather . . . earth: Words of the Great Litany in the liturgy of St. John Chrysostom.

7. Shchedrin: Mikhail Yevgrafovich Saltykov (1826–89), who wrote under the pseudonym of Nikolai Shchedrin, was a major satirical novelist and journalist.

8. a Tolstoyan: A member of the movement that adopted the principles of Tolstoy's later social, philosophical, and religious teachings, including manual labor, vegetarianism, and non-resistance to evil.

9. Proudhon . . . property is theft: Pierre-Joseph Proudhon (1809–65), French anarchist, coined the phrase "property is theft" in his book *What Is Property?* (1840).

10. Buckles . . . Schopenhauers . . . : Henry Thomas Buckle (1821–65) was the author of a two-volume *History of Civilization in England* (vol. 1, 1857; vol. 2, 1861), conceived on a scientific basis and a belief in universal laws of history. Arthur Schopenhauer (1788–1860) was an extremely influential German philosopher, known especially for his work *The World as Will and Representation* (1818; expanded in 1844), in which he developed an atheistic metaphysical and ethical system.

11. the day of Elijah the prophet: See note 1 to "The Shepherd's Pipe."

12. *Penderaklia*: The name of a bay in the Black Sea, place of Turkish shipbuilding and scene of battles during the Russo-Turkish War of 1810–11. The name was also given to a refurbished Turkish ship which in 1877 became part of the Russian navy.

13. zemstvo activists: A zemstvo was a local government assembly, instituted by the tsar Alexander II as part of his reforms after the abolition of serfdom in 1861.

14. Butlerov's beehives: Alexander Mikhailovich Butlerov (1828–86) was a distinguished Russian chemist who was also interested in agriculture, horticulture, and beekeeping. His book, *The Bee, Its Life, and the Main Rules of Sensible Beekeeping*, went through more than ten editions before the revolution. However, there was also an English writer, Charles Butler (1571–1647), author of a book on beekeeping (1609), which includes a chapter on how to construct beehives. The Russian spelling of the name could refer to either man, though the former is more likely.

15. property qualifications: The requirement of owning a certain amount of property in order to stand for election or hold government office.

16. the Royal Doors: See note 3 to "The Nightmare."

A BREAKDOWN

1. the image and likeness of God: See note 10 to "The Letter."

2. Saint Mary of Egypt: A sixth-century saint who began life as a prostitute in Alexandria but, after making her way to Jerusalem and undergoing a mystical conversion, retired to the desert for many years. She is commemorated on the fifth Sunday of the Great Lent, and her life written by St. Sophronius of Jerusalem is read on Thursday of the following week.

3. Without my will . . . doth draw me: Lines from Pushkin's dramatic poem *Rusalka* ("The Water Nymph," 1832), which was made into an opera (1848–55) by Alexander Dargomyzhsky (1813–69).

4. *The Leaflet*: i.e., *The Moscow Leaflet*, a cultural and political paper of the time.

5. Marshal Bazaine: François Achille Bazaine (1811–88) served under Louis-Philippe and Napoleon III, rose to the rank of maréchal, the highest rank in the French military, was accused of treason under the Third Republic in 1873, but escaped and died in exile.

6. Aïda: Heroine of the opera of the same name (1871), by Giuseppi Verdi (1813–1901), set in ancient Egypt, which tells the love story of a captured Ethiopian princess and an Egyptian general and is usually staged with elaborate costumes.

7. *Niva*: a popular illustrated magazine.
8. **Wednesday:** Orthodox Christians abstain from eating meat on Wednesday and Friday.

THE PRINCESS

1. **Archimandrite:** In the Russian Orthodox Church, the title given to the abbot of a large and important monastery.
2. **lose the image and likeness:** See note 10 to "The Letter."
3. **thirty-five thousand messengers:** A borrowing from a fantastical speech by Khlestakov, central character of *The Inspector* (1836), a comedy by Nikolai Gogol (1809–52).
4. **"How glorious is our Lord in Zion . . .":** A hymn composed at the end of the eighteenth century by Dmitri Bortniansky (1751–1825) to words by the poet Mikhail Kheraskov (1733–1807).
5. **What is Hecuba to you . . . :** See *Hamlet*, Act II, scene 2, ll. 562–3: "What's Hecuba to him or he to Hecuba / That he should weep for her?"

AFTER THE THEATER

1. **the sort of letter Tatiana wrote:** In Book III of Pushkin's novel in verse, *Evgeny Onegin* (1825–1832), Tatiana, the heroine of the novel, makes a desperate confession of her love in a letter to Onegin. Pushkin's poem-novel was made into an opera by Tchaikovsky.

HISTORY OF A BUSINESS ENTERPRISE

1. **Mikhailovsky:** Nikolai Konstantinovich Mikhailovsky (1842–1904) was a social and literary critic and one of the founders of the Narodniki, a movement that favored "going to the people [*narod*]." He was an early supporter of the revolutionary "People's Will" movement.
2. **Pisarev:** Dmitri Ivanovich Pisarev (1840–68), writer and critic, was an extreme proponent of utilitarianism, the cause of "the hungry and naked people."
3. *The Messenger of Europe*: See note 3 to "The Kiss."

NEIGHBORS

1. **If you ever need my life, come and take it:** Chekhov later used this same line in act 3 of *The Seagull* (1896).
2. **humiliated and insulted:** The title of a novel by Dostoevsky published in 1861.
3. **Pisarev . . . Dobrolyubov:** For Pisarev, see note 2 above to "History of a Business Enterprise." Nikolai Alexandrovich Dobrolyubov (1836–61) was a radical utilitarian journalist, critic, and poet.
4. **in Dostoevsky's taste:** There are many mismatched marriages in Dostoevsky's novels.
5. **Khoma Brut:** The naïve "philosopher" and seminary student who is suddenly confronted with otherworldly horror in Gogol's story "Viy" (1835).

FEAR

1. **visions . . . in that sleep of death:** See *Hamlet*, Act II, scene 1, ll. 66–68: "For in that sleep of death what dreams may come, / When we have shuffled off this mortal coil, / Must give us pause."

2. **Shakespeare's . . . bench:** cf. *The Merchant of Venice*, Act V, scene 1, l. 54: "How sweet the moonlight sleeps upon this bank!"

BIG VOLODYA AND LITTLE VOLODYA

1. *par dépit:* "out of spite" (French).

2. *Pardon, je ne suis pas seul:* "Excuse me, I'm not alone" (French).

3. **as Derzhavin had Pushkin:** Gavrila Romanovich Derzhavin (1743–1816) was a statesman and the major poet of his generation. During a public examination at the imperial lycée in Tsarskoe Selo on January 8, 1815, the fifteen-year-old student Pushkin recited one of his own poems before the old master, who was greatly impressed.

THE TEACHER OF LITERATURE

1. **Count Nulin:** The horse is named after the hero of Pushkin's poem *Count Nulin* (1825), a comic take-off on Shakespeare's narrative poem *The Rape of Lucrece* (1594).

2. **Maria Godefroi:** Marie Godefroy was a circus equestrienne whom Chekhov had once seen perform and found disappointing.

3. **the Third Department:** The imperial secret police, created by the tsar Nicholas I in 1825.

4. **Shchedrin:** See note 7 to "The Name-Day Party."

5. **Onegin . . . Boris Godunov:** For *Onegin* see note 1 to "After the Theater." *Boris Godunov* (1831) is Pushkin's drama about the man who ruled Russia as regent (1585–1598) and then tsar (1598–1605).

6. **Lermontov:** See note 1 to "On the Road."

7. **Of his kingdom there shall be no end:** The angel Gabriel's words to the Virgin Mary in Luke 1:33.

8. **"The Sinful Woman":** A very popular narrative poem (ca. 1857) by Alexei Konstantinovich Tolstoy (1817–75), poet, novelist, playwright, and satirist.

9. **Lessing's *Hamburg Dramaturgy*:** Gotthold Ephraim Lessing (1729–81), writer, dramatist, and thinker, was a major figure of the Enlightenment in Germany. *Hamburg Dramaturgy* (1767–69) is a collection of essays written during the years when he served as dramaturg for the Hamburg National Theater.

10. **Oh, not in vain . . . doth remain:** Nikitin plays on lines from a poem by Lermontov (see note 1 to "On the Road").

11. **Kalka . . . Chukotsky Noses:** The battle between invading Mongols and a coalition of Russian forces on the Kalka River in southern Ukraine took place in 1223. Chukotka, a peninsula on the far northeastern coast of Siberia, is said to look on the map like a nose cut off from a face.

12. *The Messenger of Europe:* See note 3 to "The Kiss."

13. after the Dormition: See note 3 to "The Witch."

14. sang "Holy God" all the way to the cemetery: The chant is called the Trisagion (the "thrice holy"): "Holy God, Holy Mighty, Holy Immortal, have mercy on us."

15. Theophany: The Orthodox feast of the Theophany, celebrated on January 6, commemorates the baptism of Christ in the Jordan by John the Baptist, at which the Trinity was made manifest.

16. the Great Lent: See note 3 to "Reading."

IN A COUNTRY HOUSE

1. a bad Sobakevich: Mikhailo Semyonovich Sobakevich, a solid, bear-like landowner, is one of the main characters in Nikolai Gogol's novel *Dead Souls* (1842).

2. Goncharov: The writer Ivan Alexandrovich Goncharov (1812–91), best known for his novel *Oblomov* (1859), was indeed from a wealthy merchant family in Simbirsk, on the Volga, some 400 miles east of Moscow.

3. Flammarion: Nicolas Camille Flammarion (1842–1925) was an astronomer and writer, author of many books, including early science fiction novels, and interested also in psychic research, spiritism, and reincarnation.

THE PECHENEG

1. Pecheneg . . . Zhmukhin: The Pechenegs were a semi-nomadic Turkic people from Central Asia, considered cruel and uncultivated, who migrated westwards during the Middle Ages and in the tenth century laid siege to Kiev. Zhmukhin, the central character of the story, is dubbed a "Pecheneg" by his neighbors. The name Zhmukhin is a plausible Russian name, but has suggestions of pushing, squeezing, oppression.

2. the Donetsk line: The railway line to Donetsk, a major industrial city in the Ukraine, was opened in 1870.

3. Novocherkassk: A new city founded by the leader of the Don Cossacks in 1804 as an administrative center in the Rostov region, bordering the Ukraine, and developed with the help of a French engineer, who nicknamed the city "little Paris."

4. passports: Russians were required to carry "internal passports" when traveling within Russia.

IN THE CART

1. the zemstvo office: See note 13 to "The Name-Day Party."

ABOUT LOVE

1. This story is the third in what is known as the "little trilogy." The first two are "The Man in a Case" and "Gooseberries."

2. this is a great mystery: See Paul's letter to the Ephesians 5:31–32: "For this cause shall a man leave his father and mother, and shall be joined unto his wife, and they two will be one flesh. / This is a great mystery; but I speak concerning Christ and the church."

3. *The Messenger of Europe*: See note 3 to "The Kiss."

IONYCH

1. zemstvo doctor: A doctor officially appointed to work under the auspices of the local government assembly (zemstvo).

2. Ascension: The feast celebrating Christ's ascent to His Father forty days after Easter.

3. When I'd not yet drunk tears: Words from an elegy by the poet Anton Antonovich Delvig (1798–1831), a fellow student of Pushkin's at the lycée in Tsarskoe Selo, set to music by Mikhail Lukyanovich Yakovlev (1798–1868), also a student at the lycée.

4. *Jeanchik . . . dites . . . du thé*: "Jeanchik ['Jean,' French version of 'Ivan,' with Russian diminutive ending], tell them to serve us tea."

5. Luchinushka: A popular Russian folk song, set to music by several composers.

6. Die now, Denis . . . : A comment supposedly made to the playwright Denis Ivanovich Fonvizin (1745–92) by Prince Grigory Alexandrovich Potemkin (1739–91), general, statesman, and favorite of the empress Catherine the Great, after the premiere of his play *The Dunce* (or *The Minor*) in 1782, the first "classic" of Russian theater.

7. Thy voice . . . languid . . . : The first line of Pushkin's poem "Night" (1823).

8. Pisemsky . . . *A Thousand Souls*: Alexei Feofilaktovich Pisemsky (1821–81) was a prominent playwright and novelist, contemporary of Dostoevsky, Turgenev, Tolstoy. His novel *A Thousand Souls*, considered his best, was published in 1858. "Feofilaktych" is a familiar form of his patronymic.

THE NEW DACHA

1. on the stove: See note 2 to "Anguish."

2. rapping on boards: Night watchmen carried special boards which they rapped on with hammers as they made their rounds.

3. The Elevation: The feast of the Elevation of the Cross, a major Orthodox feast, takes place on September 14.

4. a mere collegiate secretary: See note 1 to "Joy" and note 1 to "The Exclamation Point."